T0028678

# Praise for
## *The Books of Jacob*

"Sophisticated and ribald and brimming with folk wit . . . The comedy in this novel blends, as it does in life, with genuine tragedy." —*The New York Times*

"Just as awe-inspiring as the Nobel judges claimed . . . Miraculously entertaining and consistently fascinating. Despite his best efforts, Frank never mastered alchemy, but Tokarczuk certainly has. . . . Haunting and irresistible."
—*The Washington Post*

"Monumental . . . Could help the Swedish Academy restore its rather tattered reputation as an arbiter of serious literature . . . Tokarczuk is as comfortable rendering the world of the Jewish peasantry as that of the Polish royal court. . . . Incalculably rich in learning and driven by a faith in the numinous properties of knowledge."
—*The Wall Street Journal*

"Yes, there's a miracle in these pages. It's not about the Virgin Mary or the false Messiah Jacob Frank, however, but the way Tokarczuk can make a period so distant from us in every way feel so completely alive." —*Los Angeles Times*

"Tokarczuk aims high, spinning a layered, majestic, polyphonic novel based on a real-life figure. . . . A golden age of historical fiction is upon us: Tokarczuk links arms with Hilary Mantel and Colson Whitehead, connecting our own perilous moment with the past." —*Oprah Daily*

"A colossal work—an epic, a fable, a history, sometimes a satire, always a magnum opus." —NPR

"Funny, tragic, comprehensive, and at times hilariously graphic . . . both earthy and ethereal." —*The Boston Globe*

"You can practically smell the damp earth, the household fires, the dry paper of Nobel laureate Tokarczuk's epic set across the villages of eighteenth-century Poland. Everything about *The Books of Jacob*, including Tokarczuk's generous, comfortable style, is vast but meticulously detailed." —*Vulture*

"Could well be a decade-defining book akin to Bolaño's *2666*."
—*The A.V. Club*

"Contains an entire overflowing, sensual world to get lost in . . . Bewitching account of untold fissures in history, minor religions, little lives, and splinterings-off. It is rich, strange, astonishing in scope, and delightfully enigmatic. . . . Tokarczuk's magnum opus shows us a world on the precipice of a great change, one hand clinging to certainty while the other reaches for transcendence."
—*World Literature Today*

"Truly an epic historical novel." —*Hey Alma*

"Deeply researched [and] fascinating . . . [It] has the power to both enlighten and unnerve, especially in its eerie reflection of the rampant prejudices and inequalities that roil our world today." —*Hadassah Magazine*

"As crowded as a Bruegel painting . . . visionary . . . Tokarczuk is wrestling with the biggest philosophical themes: the purpose of life on earth, the nature of religion, the possibility of redemption, the fraught and terrible history of eastern European Jewry. . . . A landmark." —*The Guardian*

"A kind of literary miracle." —*The Times* (London)

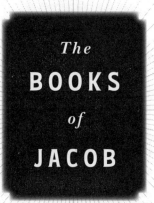

*The*

# BOOKS

*of*

# JACOB

*OR:*

## A FANTASTIC JOURNEY
### ACROSS SEVEN BORDERS,
*five languages,*
### AND THREE MAJOR RELIGIONS,
*not counting the minor sects.*

Told by the **DEAD**,
supplemented by the **AUTHOR**,
drawing from a range of **BOOKS**,
and aided by **IMAGINATION**, the which
being the greatest natural **GIFT** of any person.
That the **WISE** might have it for
a record, that my compatriots **REFLECT**,
laypersons gain some **UNDERSTANDING**,
AND MELANCHOLY SOULS
OBTAIN SOME SLIGHT ENJOYMENT

# Olga Tokarczuk

*Translated by*

# JENNIFER CROFT

★

RIVERHEAD BOOKS | NEW YORK

RIVERHEAD BOOKS
An imprint of Penguin Random House LLC
penguinrandomhouse.com

Copyright © 2014 by Olga Tokarczuk
English translation copyright © 2021 by Jennifer Croft
Originally published in Poland as *Księgi Jakubowe* by
Wydawnictwo Literackie, Kraków, in 2014
English-language edition first published in Great Britain by
Fitzcarraldo Editions, London, in 2021
First American edition published by Riverhead Books, 2022

Penguin Random House supports copyright. Copyright fuels creativity, encourages diverse
voices, promotes free speech, and creates a vibrant culture. Thank you for buying an authorized
edition of this book and for complying with copyright laws by not reproducing, scanning, or
distributing any part of it in any form without permission. You are supporting writers and
allowing Penguin Random House to continue to publish books for every reader.

Riverhead and the R colophon are registered trademarks of
Penguin Random House LLC.

This book has been published with the support of the
©POLAND Translation Program.

The Library of Congress has catalogued the Riverhead hardcover edition as follows:

Names: Tokarczuk, Olga, 1962– , author. | Croft, Jennifer (Translator), translator.
Title: The books of Jacob : or: A fantastic journey across seven borders, five languages, and
three major religions, not counting the minor sects. Told by the dead, supplemented by the
author, drawing from a range of books, and aided by imagination, the which being the
greatest natural gift of any person. That the wise might have it for a record, that my
compatriots reflect, laypersons gain some understanding, and melancholy souls
obtain some slight enjoyment /
Olga Tokarczuk ; translated by Jennifer Croft.
Other titles: Księgi Jakubowe. English
Description: First American edition. | New York :
Riverhead Books, 2022. | Includes bibliographical references.
Identifiers: LCCN 2021020020 (print) | LCCN 2021020021 (ebook) |
ISBN 9780593087480 (hardcover) | ISBN 9780593087497 (ebook)
Subjects: LCSH: Frank, Jacob, approximately 1726–1791—Fiction. | Jewish messianic
movements—Europe—History—18th century—Fiction. | Poland—History—
18th century—Fiction. | GSAFD: Biographical fiction. |
Historical fiction. | LCGFT: Biographical fiction. | Historical fiction.
Classification: LCC PG7179.O37 K7513 2022 (print) |
LCC PG7179.O37 (ebook) | DDC 891.8/537—dc23
LC record available at https://lccn.loc.gov/2021020020
LC ebook record available at https://lccn.loc.gov/2021020021

First Riverhead hardcover edition: February 2022
First Riverhead trade paperback edition: January 2023
Riverhead trade paperback ISBN: 9780593087503

Printed in Canada
3rd Printing

*Book design by Amanda Dewey*
*Map by Meighan Cavanaugh*

This is a work of fiction. Names, characters, places, and incidents either
are the product of the author's imagination or are used fictitiously,
and any resemblance to actual persons, living or dead, businesses,
companies, events, or locales is entirely coincidental.

*For my parents*

# CONTENTS

Prologue  *965*

## I. THE BOOK OF FOG

# 4.

# II. THE BOOK OF SAND

## 5.

## 6.

## 7.

## 8.

## 9.

## 10.

## 11.

**12.**

# III. THE BOOK OF THE ROAD

**13.**

**14.**

## 15.

## 16.

# IV. THE BOOK OF THE COMET

## 21.

## 22.

# V. THE BOOK OF
# METAL AND SULFUR

# VI. THE BOOK OF
# THE DISTANT COUNTRY

## 26.

# VII. THE BOOK OF NAMES

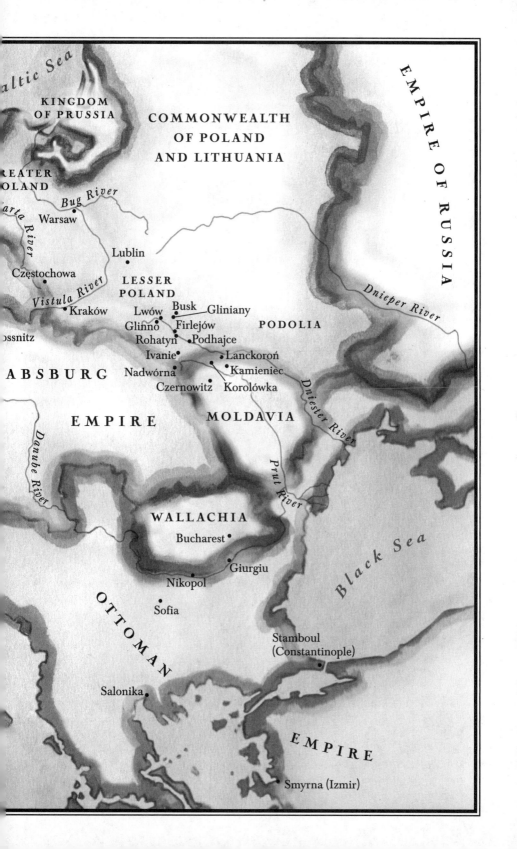

# THE BOOKS OF JACOB

# Prologue

---

Once swallowed, the piece of paper lodges in her esophagus, near her heart. Saliva-soaked. The specially prepared black ink dissolves slowly now, the letters losing their shapes. Within the human body, the word splits in two: substance and essence. When the former goes, the latter, formlessly abiding, may be absorbed into the body's tissues, since essences always seek carriers in matter—even if this is to be the cause of many misfortunes.

Yente wakes up. But she was just almost dead! She feels this distinctly now, like a pain, like the river's current—a tremor, a clamor, a rush.

With a delicate vibration, her heart resumes its weak but regular beating, capable. Warmth is restored to her bony, withered chest. Yente blinks and just barely lifts her eyelids again. She sees the agonized face of Elisha Shorr, who leans in over her. She tries to smile, but that much power over her face she can't quite summon. Elisha Shorr's brow is furrowed, his gaze brimming with resentment. His lips move, but no sound reaches Yente. Old Shorr's big hands appear from somewhere, reaching for her neck, then move beneath her threadbare blanket. Clumsily he rolls her body onto the side, so he can check the bedding. Yente can't feel his exertions, no—she senses only warmth, and the presence of a sweaty, bearded man.

Then suddenly, as though from some unexpected impact, Yente sees everything from above: herself, the balding top of Old Shorr's head—in his struggle with her body, he has lost his cap.

And this is how it is now, how it will be: Yente sees all.

# I.

## *The Book of*

# FOG

| Ex aqua | Z wody | |
| ascendit | wstępuie | ascéndere, n. 3. wstępo- |
| *vapor.* 1 m. 3. | pára, 1 | wać. |
| Inde fit | ztąd się ftawa | |
| *nubes;* 2 f. 3. | obłok, 2 | |
| & prope terram | a bliſka źiemie | |
| *nebula* 3 f. 1. | mgła. 3 | |
| E nube | Z obłoku | |
| ftillat ( defluit gut- | kropi (kapie kropla- | ftillare, n. 1. kropić. |
| (tatim | (mi | defluere, n. 3. kapać. |
| *pluvia* 4 f. 1. | deſzcz, 4 | |
| & *imber.* m. 3. | i deſzcz gwałtowny, | |

Quæ

# *1.*

## 1752, Rohatyn

It's early morning, near the close of October. The vicar forane is standing on the porch of the presbytery, waiting for his carriage. He's used to getting up at dawn, but today he feels just half awake and has no idea how he even ended up here, alone in an ocean of fog. He can't remember rising, or getting dressed, or whether he's had breakfast. He stares perplexed at the sturdy boots sticking out from underneath his cassock, at the tattered front of his faded woolen overcoat, at the gloves he's holding in his hands. He slips on the left one; it's warm and fits him perfectly, as though hand and glove have known each other many years. He breathes a sigh of relief. He feels for the bag slung over his shoulder, mechanically runs his fingers over the hard edges of the rectangle it contains, thickened like scars under the skin, and he remembers, slowly, what's inside—that heavy, friendly form. A good thing, the thing that's brought him here—those words, those signs, each with a profound connection to his life. Indeed, now he knows what's there, and this awareness slowly starts to warm him up, and as his body comes back, he starts to be able to see through the fog. Behind him, the dark aperture of the doors, one side shut. The cold must have already set in, perhaps even a light frost already, spoiling the plums in the orchard. Above the doors, there is a rough inscription, which he sees without looking, already knowing what it says—he commissioned it, after all. Those two craftsmen from Podhajce took an entire week to carve the letters into the wood. He had, of course, requested they be done ornately:

## HERE TODAY AND GONE TOMORROW.
## ИO USE TO MILK IS YOUR SORROW

Somehow, in the second line, they wrote the very first letter backward, like a mirror image. Aggravated by this for the umpteenth time, the priest spins his head around, and the sight is enough to make him fully awake. That backward И . . . How could they be so negligent? You really have to watch them constantly, supervise their each and every step. And since these craftsmen are Jewish, they probably used some sort of Jewish style for the inscription, the letters looking ready to collapse under their frills. One of them had even tried to argue that this preposterous excuse for an *N* was acceptable—nay, even preferable!—since its bar went from bottom to top, and from left to right, in the Christian way, and that Jewish would have been the opposite. The petty irritation of it has brought him to his senses, and now Father Benedykt Chmielowski, dean of Rohatyn, understands why he felt as if he was still asleep—he's surrounded by fog the same grayish color as his bedsheets; an off-white already tainted by dirt, by those enormous stores of gray that are the lining of the world. The fog is motionless, covering the whole of the courtyard completely; through it loom the familiar shapes of the big pear tree, the solid stone fence, and, farther still, the wicker cart. He knows it's just an ordinary cloud, tumbled from the sky and landed with its belly on the ground. He was reading about this yesterday in Comenius.

Now he hears the familiar clatter that on every journey whisks him into a state of creative meditation. Only after the sound does Roshko appear out of the fog, leading a horse by the bridle; after him comes the vicar's britchka. At the sight of the carriage, Father Chmielowski feels a surge of energy, slaps his glove against his hand, and leaps up into his seat. Roshko, silent as usual, adjusts the harness and glances at the priest. The fog turns Roshko's face gray, and suddenly he looks older to the priest, as though he's aged overnight, although in reality he's a young man yet.

Finally, they set off, but it's as if they're standing still, since the only evidence of motion is the rocking of the carriage and the soothing creaks it makes. They've traveled this road so many times, over so many years, that there's no need to take in the view any longer, nor will landmarks be necessary for them to get their bearings. Father Chmielowski knows they've now gone down the road that passes along the edge of the forest, and they'll stay on it all the way to the chapel at the crossroads. The chapel was erected there by Father Chmielowski himself some years earlier, when he had just been entrusted with the presbytery of Firlejów. For a long time he had wondered to whom to dedicate the little chapel, and he had thought of Benedict, his patron saint, or Onuphrius, the hermit who had, in the desert, miraculously received dates to eat from a palm tree, while every eighth day angels brought down for him from heaven the Body of Christ. For Father Chmielowski, Firlejów was to be a kind of desert, too, after his years tutoring His Lordship Jabłonowski's son Dymitr. On reflection, he had come to the conclusion that the chapel was to be built not for him and the satisfaction of his vanity, but rather for ordinary persons, that they might have a place to rest at that crossroads, whence to raise their thoughts to heaven. Standing, then, on that brick pedestal, coated in white lime, is the Blessed Mother, Queen of the World, wearing a crown on her head, a serpent squirming under her slipper.

She, too, disappears into the fog today, along with the chapel and the crossroads. Only the treetops are visible, a sign that the fog is beginning to dissipate.

"Kaśka won't go, good sir," Roshko grumbles when the carriage comes to a stop. He gets out of his seat and vigorously crosses himself—once, twice, and then again.

He leans forward and peers into the fog as he would into water. His shirt pokes out from underneath his faded red Sunday doublet.

"I don't know where to go," he says.

"What do you mean, you don't know? We're on the Rohatyn road now," the priest says in astonishment.

And yet! He gets out of the britchka to join his servant. Helplessly they circle the carriage, straining their eyes into the pale gray. For a moment they think they see something, but it's only that their eyes, unable to latch on to anything, have begun to play tricks on them. But how can they not know where to go? It's like getting lost in one's own pocket.

"Quiet!" the priest says suddenly, and raises his finger, straining to hear. And indeed, from somewhere off to the left, through the billows of fog, the faint murmur of water reaches their ears.

"Let's follow that sound," the priest says with determination. "That's water flowing."

Now they'll slowly creep along the river people call the Rotten Linden. The water will be their guide.

Soon Father Chmielowski relaxes back inside his carriage, stretching his legs out before him, allowing his eyes to drift within this mass of fog. Right away he slips into his musings—for man thinks best in motion. Slowly, reluctantly, the mechanism of his mind awakens, wheels and pinions starting up, the whole getting going just like the clock that stands in the vestibule of the presbytery, which he purchased in Lwów for an exorbitant sum. It'll be just about to chime. Did not the world emerge from such a fog? he starts to wonder. After all, the Jewish historian Josephus maintains the world was created in the autumn, at the autumn equinox. A reasonable notion, since of course there were fruits in paradise; given the apple hanging from the tree, it must indeed have been autumn . . . There is a logic to it. But right away another thought occurs to him: What kind of reasoning is this? Could not Almighty God create such paltry fruits at any time of year?

When they come to the main road leading to Rohatyn, they join the stream of persons on foot and horseback and in every variety of vehicle who appear out of the fog like Christmas figurines sculpted from bread. It is Wednesday, market day in Rohatyn, and the peasants' carts are loaded with grain sacks, cages with poultry fowl—all sorts of agricultural bounty. As the carts roll slowly by, merchants skip between them, carrying every imaginable commodity—their stalls, cleverly collapsed, can be thrown over their shoulders like carrying poles; then, in a flash, unfolded, they are tables strewn with bright materials or wooden toys, eggs bought up from the villages for a quarter of what they cost here, now. Peasants lead goats and cows to be sold; the animals, frightened by the tumult, stop among the puddles and refuse to budge. Now a wagon flies by them, its cover a tarpaulin riddled with holes; it carries a load of the exuberant Jews who converge upon the Rohatyn market from all over. Next a very ornate carriage wedges its way through, though in the fog and the crowd it has trouble preserving its dignity—its vibrant little lacquered doors are caked with mud, and the cerulean-cloaked coachman's countenance is wan, as he must not have been expecting such a commotion and is now desperately seeking any opportunity to get off this terrible road.

Roshko is persistent and will not be forced onto the field; he keeps to the right side with one wheel in the grass, one on the road, and moves steadily forward. His long, gloomy face gets flushed, then taken over by a hideous grimace; the priest glances at him and remembers the etching he studied yesterday, featuring spitfires in hell with faces very like Roshko's right now.

"Let the Very Reverend through! Nu, poshli! Out of the way!" shouts Roshko. "Out!"

Suddenly, without warning, the first buildings appear in front of them. Evidently the fog changes all perception of distance, as even Kaśka seems confused. She lurches, yanking the drawbar, and were it not for Roshko's firm hand and whip, she would have overturned the britchka. In front of them is a blacksmith's; maybe Kaśka got spooked by the sparks spewing from that furnace, or else by the anxiety of the horses waiting their turn to be shod . . .

Farther on is the inn, in a state of partial ruin, reminiscent of a rural cottage. A well-pole juts out over it like a gallows, piercing the fog, then disappears somewhere higher up. The priest sees that the filthy fancy carriage has come to a stop here, the exhausted coachman's head fallen to his knees; he doesn't leave his seat, nor does anyone emerge from inside. Already a tall, skinny Jew and a little girl with tousled hair are standing before it. But the vicar forane sees no more—the fog subsumes every passing view, each scene as fleeting as a flake of dissolving snow.

This is Rohatyn.

It starts with huts, tiny houses made of clay with straw thatch that seems to be pressing the structures down into the ground. The closer you get to the market square, the shapelier these little houses become, and the finer the thatching, until thatch disappears altogether into the wooden shingles of the smaller town houses, made of unfired bricks. Now there is the parish church, now the Dominican monastery, now the Church of Saint Barbara on the market square. Continuing on, two synagogues and five Orthodox churches. Little houses all around the market square like mushrooms; each of these contains a business. The tailor, the ropemaker, the furrier in close proximity, all of them Jews; then there's the baker whose last name is Loaf, which always delights the vicar forane because it suggests a sort of hidden order that—were it more visible and consistent— might lead people to live more virtuous lives. Then there's Luba the swordsmith, the facade of his workshop more lavish than anything nearby, its walls newly painted sky blue. A great rusted sword hangs over the entrance to show that Luba is an excellent craftsman, and that his customers have deep pockets. Then there's the saddler, who has set out a wooden sawhorse in front of his door, and on it a beautiful saddle with stirrups that must be plated in silver, so they gleam.

In every place there is the cloying smell of malt that gets into all that is up for sale and gluts a person just as bread can. On the outskirts of Rohatyn, in Babińce, are several small breweries that give the whole region this satiating scent. Many stalls here sell beer, and the better shops also keep vodka, and mead—mostly trójniak. The Jewish merchant Wachshul, meanwhile, sells wine, real Hungarian and Rhineland wine, as well as some sourer stuff they bring in from Wallachia.

The priest moves among stands made out of every imaginable material—boards, pieces of thickly woven canvas, wicker baskets, even leaves. This good woman with the white kerchief on her head is selling pumpkins out of a cart; their bright orange color draws in the children. Next, another woman offers up lumps of cheese on horseradish leaves. There are many women merchants besides, those who have suffered the misfortune of widowhood or who are married to drunks; they trade in oil, salt, linen. The priest generally purchases something from this lady pasztet-maker; now he gives her a kind smile. After her are two stands that feature evergreen branches—a sign they're selling freshly brewed beer. Here is a rich stall that is operated by Armenian merchants, with light, beautiful materials, knives in ornamental scabbards. Next to it is the dried sturgeon stand, with a sickening scent that gets into the wool of the Turkish tapestries. Farther along, a man in a dusty smock sells eggs by the dozen in little baskets woven out of blades of grass, which he keeps in a box that hangs from his skinny shoulders. Another sells his eggs sixty at a time, in large baskets, at a competitive, almost wholesale price. A baker's stall is completely covered in bagels—someone must have dropped one into the mud because a little dog is now rapturously scarfing it up off the ground.

People sell whatever they can here. Floral materials, kerchiefs, and scarves straight from the bazaar in Stamboul, and children's shoes, and nuts, and that man over by the fence is offering a plow and all different sizes of nails, as thin as pins or as thick as fingers, to build houses. Nearby, a handsome woman in a starched bonnet has set out little clappers for night watchmen, the kind that sound more like crickets' nocturnes than a summons from sleep, alongside bigger ones, loud enough to wake the dead.

How many times have the Jews been told not to sell things having to do with the Church. They've been forbidden by priests and rabbis alike, to no avail. There are lovely prayer books, a ribbon between their pages, letters so marvelously embossed in silver on the cover that when you run your fingertip along their surface they seem warm and alive. A smart, almost lavishly dapper man in a yarmulke holds them like they're relics, wrapped in thin paper—a creamy tissue to keep the foggy day from sullying their innocent Christian pages, fragrant with printing ink. He also has wax candles and even pictures of the saints with their halos.

Father Chmielowski goes up to one of the traveling booksellers, hoping he might find something in Latin, but all the books are Jewish; beside them lie yarmulkes and other things of which the priest does not know the nature.

The farther you look down the little side streets, the more obvious the poverty becomes, like a dirty toe sticking out of a torn shoe; a plain old poverty, quiet, low to the ground. There are no more shops now, no more stalls—instead, hovels like doghouses, thrown together out of flimsy boards picked from around the trash heaps. In one of them, a cobbler fixes shoes that have been mended again and again, patched up and re-soled repeatedly. In another, a tinker has set up shop, surrounded by hanging iron pots. His face is thin and sunken. His cap is drawn down over his forehead, which is covered in brown lesions; the vicar forane would be afraid to have his pots mended here, lest this wretch pass along some terrible disease through his touch. Next, an old man sharpens knives along with all types of sickles and scythes. His workstation consists of a stone wheel tied around his neck. When given a thing to sharpen, he sets up a primitive wooden rack that several leather straps make into a simple machine, the wheel of which, set in motion by his hand, hones the metal blade. Sometimes sparks fly and then careen into the mud, which provides particular pleasure to the filthy, mangy children around here. From his profession, this man will earn groszy: a pittance. Someday, this wheel may help him drown himself—an occupational advantage of sorts.

On the street, women in tattered rags gather dung and wood shavings for fuel. It would be hard to say, based on their rags, whether this is a Jewish poverty, or Eastern Orthodox, or Catholic. Poverty is nondenominational and has no national identity.

"Si est, ubi est?" the priest wonders of heaven. It certainly is not here in Rohatyn, nor is it—or so he thinks—anywhere in the Podolian lands. It would be a grave mistake to think things are better in the big cities. True, Father Chmielowski has never made it to Warsaw or Kraków, but he knows a thing or two from the Bernardine Pikulski, who is more worldly, and from what he's heard around nobles' estates.

God situated paradise, or the Garden of Eden, in a delightful unknown place. According to the *Arca Noë*, paradise is somewhere in the land of the Armenians, high up in the mountains, though Brunus insists it's sub polo antarctico: below the South Pole. The signs of proximity to paradise are the four rivers: Gihon, Pishon, Euphrates, and Tigris. There are authors who, unable to locate paradise on earth, put it in the air, fifteen cubits higher than the highest mountain. But this strikes the priest as extremely silly—for how could that be? Wouldn't those living on Earth be able to glimpse heaven from below? Could they not make out the soles of the saints' feet?

On the other hand, one cannot agree with those who try to spread false claims, such as the notion that the Scripture on paradise has mystical meaning only—in other words, that it ought to be understood in some metaphysical or allegorical sense. The priest believes—not only because he's a priest, but also from his deep conviction—that everything in the Scriptures must be taken literally.

He knows everything about paradise, having just last week completed that chapter of his book. It's an ambitious chapter, drawing on all the books he has in Firlejów—and he has a hundred thirty of them. Some he went to Lwów for; others, all the way to Lublin.

Here is a corner house, modest—this is where he's going, as instructed by Father Pikulski. The low doors are wide open, letting out an unusual smell of spices amidst the surrounding stench of horse shit and autumn damp. There is another irksome scent, with which the priest is already familiar: Cophee. Father Chmielowski does not drink Cophee, but he knows he will have to acquaint himself with it at some point.

He glances back, looking for Roshko, who is examining sheepskins with grim attention; farther back, he sees the whole market absorbed in itself—no one returns his gaze, for the market is all-consuming. Hustle and din.

Above the entrance hangs a crude handmade sign:

### SHORR GENERAL STORE

This followed by Hebrew letters. There is a metal plaque on the door, with some symbols next to it, and the priest recalls that according to Athanasius Kircher, the Jews write the words *Adam hava, hutz Lilith* on the walls when a woman is due to give birth, to ward off witches: "Adam and Eve may enter here, but you, Lilith, you evil sorceress, must leave." That's what those symbols must mean, he thinks. A child must have been born here not long ago.

He takes a big step over the high threshold and is entirely submerged in the warm fragrance of spices. It takes a moment for his eyes to adjust to the darkness, since the only light inside is admitted through a single little window, cluttered with flowerpots.

An adolescent boy stands behind the counter, with a barely sprouted mustache and full lips that tremble slightly at the sight of the priest, before attempting to arrange themselves into some word or other. The priest can see he is unnerved.

"What is your name, son?" the priest asks, to show how comfortable he feels in this dark little low-ceilinged shop, and to encourage the boy to talk, but he does not respond. So the priest repeats, more officially now, "Quod tibi nomen est?" But the Latin, intended as an aid to communication, winds up sounding too formal, as if the priest has come to perform an exorcism, like Christ in the Gospel of Saint Luke when he poses the same question to a man possessed. The boy's eyes bulge, and still all he manages is a "buh, buh" sound before he bolts back behind the shelves, bumping into a braid of garlic bulbs hanging from a nail, and then vanishes.

The priest has acted foolishly. He ought not to have expected Latin to be spoken here. He takes a bitter look at himself, notices the black horsehair buttons of his cassock poking out from underneath his coat. That must be what has scared the boy off, thinks the priest: the cassock. He smiles to himself as he recollects Jeremiah, who in a near-frenzy stammered, "A, a, a, Domine Deus ecce, nescio loqui!"—"Lord God, for I cannot speak!"

From now on, the priest will call the boy Jeremiah in his head. He doesn't know what to do, with Jeremiah having disappeared. He looks around the store, buttoning his coat. Father Pikulski talked him into coming here. Now it doesn't really seem like such a good idea.

No one comes in from outside, for which the priest thanks the Lord. It would hardly be your ordinary scene: a Catholic priest—the dean of Rohatyn—standing in a Jewish shop, waiting to be helped like some housewife. At first Father Pikulski had advised him to go and see Rabbi Dubs in Lwów; he used to go there himself, and had learned a lot from him. And so he went, but Old Dubs seemed to have had enough by then of Catholic priests pestering him with questions about books. The rabbi had seemed unpleasantly surprised by the priest's request, and what

Father Chmielowski wanted most he didn't even have, or at least pretended not to have. He made a polite face and shook his head, tut-tutting. When the priest asked who might be able to help him, Dubs just threw up his hands and looked over his shoulder like someone was standing behind him, giving the priest to understand that he didn't know, and that even if he did, he wouldn't tell. Father Pikulski explained to the dean later that this was a question of heresies, and that while the Jews generally liked to pretend they didn't suffer from that problem, it did seem that for this one particular heresy they made an exception, hating it head-on.

Finally Father Pikulski suggested he go and visit Shorr. The big house with the shop on the market square. As he said this, he gave Chmielowski a wry, almost derisive look—unless Chmielowski was imagining it, of course. Perhaps he should have arranged to get his Jewish books through Pikulski, despite not liking him very much. Had he done so, he wouldn't be standing here, sweating and embarrassed. But Father Chmielowski has a bit of a rebellious streak, so here he is. And there is something else a little irrational in it, too, an element of wordplay. Who would have believed that such things had any impact on the world? The priest has been working diligently on one particular passage in Kircher, on the great ox Shorobor. Perhaps the similarity between the two names—Shorr and Shorobor—is what brought him here. Bewildering are the determinations of the Lord.

Where are the famous books, where is this figure inspiring such fear and respect? The shop looks like it belongs to an ordinary merchant, though its owner is supposedly descended from a renowned rabbi and sage, the venerable Zalman Naftali Shorr. They sell garlic, herbs, pots full of spices, canisters and jars containing so many seasonings, crushed, ground, or in their original form, like these vanilla pods and nutmegs and cloves. On the shelves, there are bolts of cloth arranged over hay—these look like silk and satin, very bold and alluring, and the priest wonders if he might not need something, but now his attention is drawn to the clumsy label on a hefty dark green canister: *Thea*. He knows what he will ask for now when someone finally comes back—some of this herb, which lifts his spirits, which helps him to continue working without getting tired. And it assists with his digestion. He might buy a few cloves, too, to use in his evening mulled wine. The last few nights were so cold that his freezing feet prevented him from focusing on his writing. He casts around for some sort of bench.

Then everything happens all at once: from behind the shelves appears a stocky man with a beard, wearing a long woolen garment and Turkish shoes with pointed toes. A thin dark blue coat is draped over his shoulders. He squints as if he's just emerged from deep inside a well. Jeremiah peeks out from behind him, along with two other faces that resemble Jeremiah's, rosy and curious. And meanwhile, at the door that leads to the market square, there is now a scrawny boy, out of breath, perhaps even a young man—his facial hair is abundant, a light-colored goatee. He leans against the doorframe and pants—he must have run here as fast as he could. He looks the priest up and down and smiles a big, impish smile, revealing healthy, widely spaced teeth. The priest can't quite tell if it's a mocking smile or not. He prefers the distinguished figure in the coat, and it is to him that he says, with exceptional politeness:

"My dear sir, please forgive this intrusion . . ."

The man in the coat regards him tensely at first, but the expression on his face slowly changes, revealing something like a smile. All of a sudden the dean realizes that the other man can't understand him, so he tries again, this time in Latin, blissfully certain he has now found his counterpart.

The man in the coat slowly shifts his gaze to the breathless boy in the doorway, who steps right into the room then, pulling at his dark jacket.

"I'll translate," the boy declares in an unexpectedly deep voice that has a bit of a Ruthenian lilt to it. Pointing a stubby finger at the dean, he says something in great excitement to the man in the coat.

It had not occurred to the priest that he might need an interpreter—he simply hadn't thought of it. Now he feels uncomfortable but has no idea how to get out of this delicate situation—before you know it the whole marketplace could hear of it. He would certainly prefer to get out of here, out into the chilly fog that smells of manure. He is beginning to feel trapped in this low-ceilinged room, in this air that is thick with the smell of spices, and to top it all off, here's somebody off the street poking his head in, trying to see what's going on.

"I'd like to have a word with the venerable Elisha Shorr, if I may be permitted," says the dean. "In private."

The Jews are stunned. They exchange a few words. Jeremiah vanishes and only after the longest and most intolerable silence does he reemerge. But evidently the priest is to be admitted, because now they lead him back behind the shelves. He is followed by whispers, the soft patter of children's feet, and stifled giggling—and now it seems that behind these thin walls there are veritable crowds of other people peeking in through the cracks in the wood, trying to catch a glimpse of Rohatyn's vicar forane wandering the interior of a Jewish home. It turns out, too, that the little store on the square is no more than a single enclave of a much vaster structure, a kind of beehive with many rooms, hallways, stairs. The house turns out to be extensive, built up around an inner courtyard, which the priest glimpses out of the corner of his eye through a window when they briefly pause.

"I am Hryćko," pipes up the young man with the narrow beard. Father Chmielowski realizes that even if he did wish to retreat now, he could not possibly find his way back out of the beehive. This realization makes him perspire, and just then a door creaks open, and in the doorway stands a trim man in his prime, his face bright, smooth, impenetrable, with a gray beard, a garment that goes down to his knees, and on his feet woolen socks and black pantofles.

"That's the Rabbi Elisha Shorr," Hryćko whispers, thrilled.

The room is small and sparsely furnished. In its center, there is a broad table with a book open atop it, and next to it, in several piles, some others—the priest's eyes prowl their spines, trying to make out their titles. He doesn't know much about Jews in general; he only knows these Rohatyn Jews by sight.

Father Chmielowski thinks suddenly how nice it is that both of them are of moderate height. With tall men, he always feels a little ill at ease. As they stand facing one another, it seems to the priest that the rabbi must also be pleased that they have this in common. Then the rabbi sits down, smiles, and gestures for the priest to do the same.

"With your permission and under these unlikely circumstances I come to Your Excellency altogether incognito, having heard such wonders of your wisdom and great erudition . . ."

Hryćko pauses in the middle of the sentence and asks the priest:

"In-cog-neat?"

"And how! Which means that I implore discretion."

"But what is that? Imp-lore? Disc . . . ration?"

Appalled, the priest falls silent. What an interpreter he's wound up with—one who understands nothing he says. So how are they supposed to talk? In Chinese? He will have to attempt to speak simply:

"I ask that this be kept a secret, for I do not conceal that I am the vicar forane of Rohatyn, a Catholic priest. But more importantly, I am an author." Chmielowski emphasizes the word "author" by raising his finger. "And I would rather talk here today not as a member of the clergy, but as an author, who has been hard at work on a certain *opuscule* . . ."

"Opus . . . ?" ventures the hesitant voice of Hryćko.

". . . a minor work."

"Oh. Please forgive me, Father, I'm unskilled in the Polish language, all I know is the normal words, the kind people use. I only know whatever I've heard around the horses."

"From the horses?" snaps the priest, a bit excessively perhaps, but he is angry with this terrible interpreter.

"Well, because it's horses I handle. By trade."

Hryćko speaks, making use of gestures. The other man looks at him with his dark, impenetrable eyes, and it occurs to Father Chmielowski that he might be dealing with a blind man.

"Having read several hundred authors cover to cover," the priest goes on, "borrowing some, purchasing others, I still feel that I have missed many volumes, and that it is not possible for me to access them, in any case."

Here he stops to wait for a response, but Shorr merely nods with an ingratiating smile that tells Chmielowski nothing at all.

"And since I heard that Your Excellency is in possession of a fully realized library," says the priest, adding hurriedly, reluctantly, "without wishing to cause any trouble, of course, or any inconvenience, I gathered up the courage, contrary to custom, but for the benefit of many, to come here and—"

He breaks off because suddenly the door flies open and with no warning a woman enters the low-ceilinged room. Now faces peer in from the hallway, half visible in the low light, whispering. A little child whimpers and then stops, as if all must focus on this woman: bareheaded, wreathed in lush curls, she doesn't look at the men at all, but rather gazes fixedly, brazenly, at something straight ahead of her as she brings in a tray with a pitcher and some dried fruits. She is wearing a wide floral dress, and over it an embroidered apron. Her pointy-toed shoes clack. She is petite, but she is shapely—her figure is attractive. Behind her pads a little girl carrying two glasses. She looks at the priest in such terror that she inadvertently crashes into the woman in front of her and falls over, still clasping the glasses in her little hands. It's a good thing they are sturdily made. The woman pays no attention to the child, though she does glance once—rapidly, impudently—at the priest. Her dark eyes shine, large and seemingly bottomless, and her overwhelmingly white skin is instantly covered in a flush. The vicar forane, who very rarely has any contact with young women, is terribly surprised by this barging in; he gulps. The woman sets the pitcher and the plate on the table with a clatter and, still looking straight ahead, leaves the room. The door slams. Hryćko, the interpreter, also looks perplexed. Meanwhile, Elisha Shorr leaps up, lifts the child, and sits down with her in his lap. The little girl wriggles loose and runs after her mother.

The priest would wager anything that this whole scene with the woman and the child coming in here was staged solely for the purpose of everyone getting a look at him. It is something, a priest in a Jewish home! Exotic as a salamander. But so what? Isn't he seen by a Jewish doctor? And are not his medicaments ground by another Jew? The matter of the books is a health issue, too, in its way.

"The volumes," says the priest, pointing to the spines of the folios and the smaller Elzevir editions lying on the table. Each contains two symbols in gold, which the priest assumes are the initials of their owner, as he can recognize the Hebrew letters:

ש"ע

He reaches for what he thinks will be his ticket into the fold of Israel and carefully sets the book he's brought before Shorr. He smiles triumphantly: this is Athanasius Kircher's *Turris Babel*, a great work in terms of both content and format; the priest took a big risk in dragging it all the way here. What if it fell into the fetid Rohatyn mud? Or what if some ruffian snatched it from him in the marketplace? Without it, the vicar forane would not be what he is today—he'd just be some ordinary rector, a Jesuit teacher on some estate, a useless clerk of the Church, bejeweled and begrudging.

He slides the book toward Shorr as if presenting his own beloved wife. He delicately raps its wooden cover.

"I have others," he comments. "But Kircher is the best." He opens the book at random, landing on a drawing of the Earth represented as a globe, and on it, the long, slender cone of the Tower of Babel.

"Kircher demonstrates that the Tower of Babel, the description of which is contained within the Bible, could not have been as tall as is commonly thought. A tower that reaches all the way to the moon would disrupt the whole order of the cosmos. Its base, founded upon the Earth, would have had to be enormous. It would have obscured the sun, which would have had catastrophic consequences for all of creation. People would have needed to use up the entire earthly supply of wood and clay . . ."

The priest feels as if he is espousing heresies, and the truth is he doesn't even really know why he is saying all this to the taciturn Jew. He wants to be regarded as a friend, not as an enemy. But is that even possible? Perhaps they can come to understand each other, despite being unfamiliar with each other's languages or customs, unfamiliar with each other in general, their objects and instruments, their smiles, the gestures of their hands that carry meaning—everything, really; but maybe they can reach some understanding by way of books? Is this not in fact the only possible route? If people could read the same books, they would inhabit the same world. Now they live in different worlds, like the Chinese described by Kircher. And then there are those—and their numbers are vast—who cannot read at all, whose minds are dormant, thoughts simple, animal, like the peasants with their empty eyes. If he, the priest, were king, he would decree that there be one day each week reserved for the peasants to read; by urging all peasants to engage with literature, he could instantly change the Commonwealth. Perhaps it also has to do with the alphabet—that there isn't only one, that there are lots of them; each produces its own type of thinking. Like bricks: some, fired and smooth, yield cathedrals, while others, of rough clay, become the peasants' shacks. And while Latin is clearly the most perfect, it appears that Shorr does not know Latin. Father Chmielowski points out an illustration, and then another, and another, and he notices his interlocutor begin to lean in with rising interest, until finally he pulls out a pair of spectacles, elegantly set in wire—Chmielowski wouldn't mind having a pair like that himself, he'll have to inquire how he might order them. The interpreter is curious, too, and the three of them lean in over the illustration.

The priest glances at them, pleased to have hooked them both. He sees strands of gold and auburn hair in the Jew's dark beard.

"We could exchange books," suggests the priest.

He goes on to say that in his library in Firlejów he has two more titles by the great Kircher, *Arca Noë* and *Mundus subterraneus*, kept under lock and key, too valuable to consult on a daily basis. He knows there are other titles, too, but with these he is familiar only through the mentions he has seen here and there. And he has built up a collection of numerous old-world thinkers, including, he says, hoping to win Shorr over, "by the Jewish historiographer Josephus."

They pour him kompot from a pitcher and offer him a plate of dried figs and dates. The priest places them in his mouth with great reverence—it's been a long time since he had any, and their unearthly sweetness immediately restores his strength. He thinks he needs to state his business, that it's high time, so he swallows the sweetness and cuts to the chase; yet before he has finished, he understands that he's been hasty, and that he won't get what he wants.

Perhaps it is the sudden change in Hryćko's manner that tips him off. He would bet, as well, that the boy is inserting his own words as he

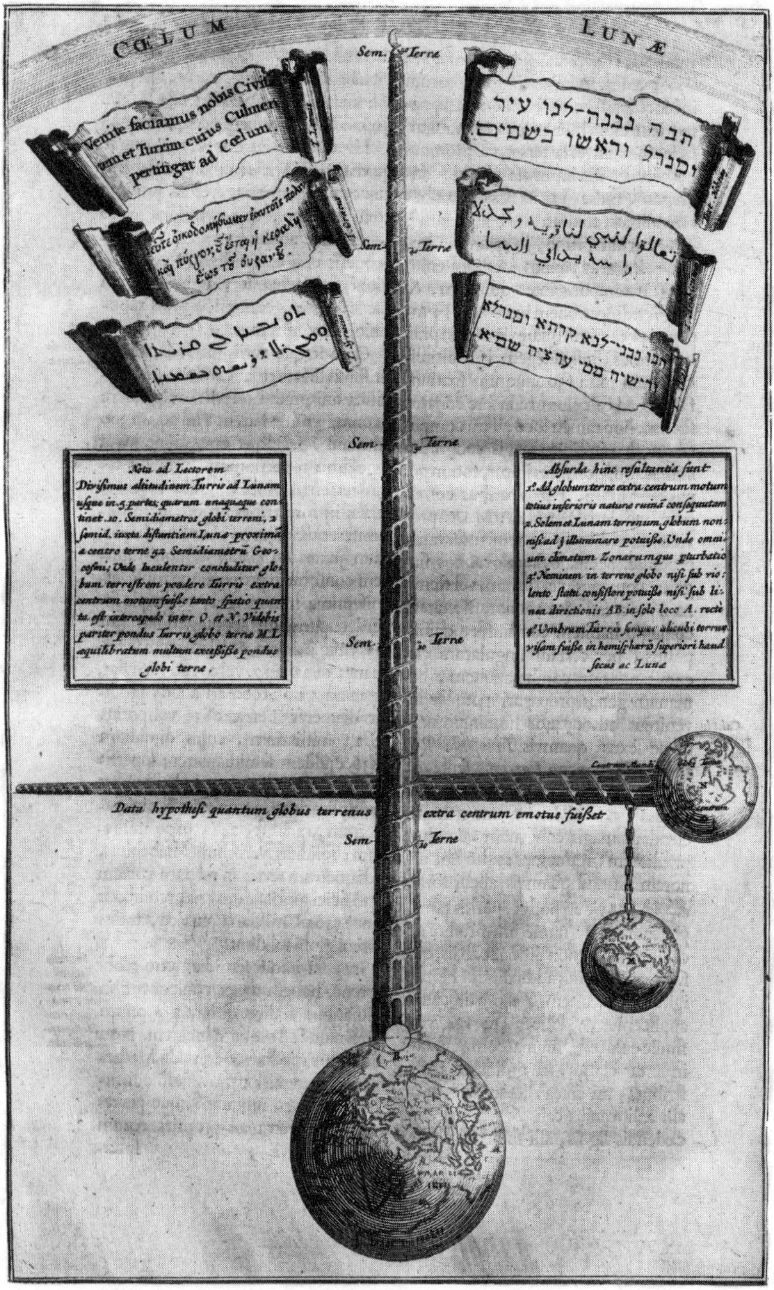
CŒLUM LUNÆ
Venite faciamus nobis Civitatem et Turrim cuius Culmen pertingat ad Cœlum.
Nota ad Lectorem
Divisimus altitudinem Turris ad Lunam usque in 5 partes; quarum unaquaque continet 10. Semidiametros globi terreni, 2 semid. iuxta distantiam Lunæ proximā a centro terre 52 Semidiametrū Geocosmi; Unde luculenter concluditur globum terrestrem pondere Turris extra centrum motum fuisse tanto spatio quantu est interspacio inter O. et N. Videbis pariter pondus Turris globo terre M.L. æquilibratum multum excessisse pondus globi terre.
Absurda hinc resultantia sunt
1º. Ad globum terre extra centrum motum totius inferioris nature ruinā consequutam
2. Solem et Lunam terrenum globum non nisi ad ½ illuminare potuisse. Unde omnium climatum Zonarumque perturbatio
3º. Neminem in terreno globo nisi sub violento statu consistere potuisse nisi sub lineæ directionis AB. in solo loco A. recte
4º. Umbram Turris semper alicubi terris visam fuisse in hemisphærio superiori haud secus ac Luna
Data hypothesi quantum globus terrenus extra centrum emotus fuisset

translates, be they warnings or the contrary, ad libs intended to help the priest's case. Elisha Shorr edges into his chair and leans his head back, closing his eyes, seemingly endeavoring to consult his inner depths.

This continues until the priest, without intending to, exchanges a significant glance with the young interpreter.

"The rabbi is listening to the voices of his elders," whispers the interpreter, and the priest nods knowingly, although in fact he still does not know what is going on. Perhaps this Jew really is in some sort of magic contact with assorted demons—he knows they have quite a few of them amongst the Jews, all those lamias and Liliths. Shorr's hesitation, and his shut eyes, make the priest think it really would have been better not to have come at all, the situation being such a delicate and unusual one. He hopes he has not exposed himself to infamy.

Shorr gets up and turns toward the wall, bows his head, and remains thus for a moment. The priest grows impatient—is this a sign that he should leave? Hryćko shuts his eyes, too. Have they fallen asleep? The priest clears his throat discreetly. This silence of theirs has robbed him of whatever remained of his confidence. Now he really is sorry he came.

Suddenly Shorr, as if nothing had happened, starts toward the cabinets and opens one. Solemnly he extracts a thick folio bearing the same symbols as all the other books, and he sets it on the table in front of the priest. He opens the book backward, and the priest sees the beautifully made title page . . .

"*Sefer ha-Zohar*," Shorr says piously, and then he puts the book back inside the cabinet.

"Who could read it for you, anyway, Father . . . ," Hryćko says, to cheer him up.

The priest leaves two volumes of his *New Athens* on Shorr's table as an enticement to exchange in the future. He taps them with his index finger and then points to himself, aiming right in the middle of his chest: "I wrote this. They ought to read it—if only they knew the language. They'd learn a lot about the world." He awaits a reaction, but Shorr only raises his eyebrows a little.

---

Father Chmielowski and Hryćko walk out into the chilly and unpleasant air together. Hryćko is still babbling on about something; the priest, meanwhile, is sizing him up: his youthful face covered in the light-colored down of what will become a beard, his long, curled eyelashes, which lend him something of the aspect of a child, his peasant clothing.

"Are you Jewish?"

"Oh, no . . . ," says Hryćko, shrugging. "I'm from here, from Rohatyn, from that house just over there. Orthodox, in theory."

"Then how'd you learn their language?"

Hryćko moves closer to the priest, and they walk almost shoulder to shoulder—evidently he feels he has been encouraged to adopt this sort of familiarity. He says his mother and father were taken by the plague of 1746. They had done business with the Shorrs—his father was a tanner— and when he died, Shorr took Hryćko, his grandmother, and his younger brother under his protection, paying off the Father's debts and generally providing for this trio of neighbors. And besides, living in the neighborhood, you interact more with Jews than you do with your own, and you talk their language—Hryćko himself doesn't even really know when he learned it, but now he uses it as fluently as if it were his own, which comes in pretty handy for trade and such, since the Jews, especially the older ones, are wary of Polish and Ruthenian. The Jews are not what people say they are—especially not the Shorrs. There are a lot of them, and their home is nice and warm and welcoming, always something to eat and a little glass of vodka when it's cold. Now Hryćko is learning his father's trade: the world will always need leather.

"But don't you have any Christian kin?"

"I do, I do, but a long way away, and they don't seem to mind us too much. Oh, there you go—my brother, Oleś." A little boy who looks like he's about eight, covered in freckles, comes running up to them then. "No reason for you to concern yourself, good Father," says Hryćko cheerfully. "God created man with eyes in the front, not the back of the head, and that means we've got to think about what's to come, not what has been."

The priest does indeed consider this evidence of God's ingenuity, although he can't quite recall where in the Scripture it is actually written.

"Learn their language well enough with them, and you'll translate those books."

"Not me, Your Excellency, no, sir, I'm not one for reading. I find it boring! I'd rather trade, I like that. Horses best. Or like the Shorrs—vodka, beer."

"Oh, dear, so they've corrupted you already . . . ," says the priest.

"What do you mean? You think alcohol is worse than other wares? People need to drink, life is hard!"

He rambles on about something or other, trailing after the priest, although Father Chmielowski would happily be rid of him at this point. He stands facing the marketplace, looking around for Roshko, first among the sheepskin coats and then over the whole of the square, but more people have arrived, and there's no chance of finding his driver. So he decides to go on alone to his carriage. Meanwhile, his interpreter has entered so fully into his role that he continues to explain things, clearly delighted that he can. He says that there is to be a great wedding in the Shorrs' home, since Elisha's son (the very one the priest saw in the shop, the one he was calling Jeremiah, whose real name turns out to be Isaac) is marrying the daughter of some Moravian Jews. Soon the whole family will be here, and all the relatives from around these parts—Busk, Podhajce, Jezierzany, Kopyczyńce, but also Lwów and maybe even Kraków, though it's late in the year, and to his mind—to Hryćko's mind—it would be better to wed in the summer. And Hryćko, ever loquacious, goes on, saying it would be great if the Father could come to a wedding like that, too, and then he evidently pictures it, because he bursts out laughing, the same laugh that the priest initially mistook for mockery. Father Chmielowski gives Hryćko a grosz.

Hryćko looks at the grosz and in a moment is gone. The priest stands there but will soon take the plunge into the marketplace as though into choppy waters, drowning in it as he pursues the delicious smell of those terrines that were available somewhere around here.

# 2.

## Of calamitous leaf springs and Katarzyna Kossakowska's feminine complaint

At the same time, Katarzyna Kossakowska (née Potocka), the wife of the castellan of Kamieniec, has just entered Rohatyn with her somewhat older lady companion; they are on their way from Lublin to Kamieniec, and they have already been traveling for several days. An hour behind them are carriages with trunks, and in them clothing, bedding, and table settings, so that when it is time to stay the night somewhere, they will have their own porcelain and cutlery, at least. Although messengers are dispatched to alert family and friends on nearby estates to the women's approach, sometimes safe and comfortable lodgings fail to materialize. Then they are left with wayside inns and public houses, where the food can be quite poor. Elżbieta Drużbacka, being a woman of a certain age, scarcely tolerates this. She complains of indigestion, no doubt because every meal gets jolted around in her stomach by the motion of their carriage, like cream in a butter churn. But heartburn is not such a serious ailment. Worse off is Kossakowska—her belly has hurt since yesterday, and now she sits in the corner of the carriage, weak and cold and damp, and so unbelievably pale that Drużbacka has started to fear for her friend's life. This is why they stop to seek help here, in Rohatyn, where Szymon Łabęcki is the starosta; Łabęcki, like just about every person of significance in Podolia, is connected with the family of the castellan's wife.

It is market day, and the pale orange-pink carriage bedecked in golden ornament with a coachman out front and an entourage of men in vivid uniforms has caused something of a sensation since passing the first toll-house. Now it has to stop at every moment because the road is obstructed by pedestrians and animals. Cracking the whip over their heads doesn't help. The two women concealed inside this vehicle on leaf springs with the Potocki coat of arms painted across its doors are borne across the choppy waters of the multilingual, business-frenzied crowd as if protected by a priceless seashell.

In the end, the carriage, as might have been predicted in such a crowd, runs over some sort of drawbar and breaks one if its springs, that latest amenity that only complicates the journey now. Kossakowska falls from her seat onto the floor, her whole face a grimace of pain. Drużbacka, cursing, leaps straight out into the mud and is off in search of help herself. First she tries some women holding baskets, but they giggle and run away, speaking Ruthenian, so then she tugs at the sleeve of a Jew in a hat and coat—he tries to understand her and even responds with something in his language, pointing farther down toward the river. Then, having lost the last of her patience, Drużbacka sees two well-heeled merchants who have just gotten out of their coach and entered the fray; she blocks their path, but they turn out to be Armenian—at least she thinks so—merely passing through. All they do is shake their heads. Then some Turks smirk at Drużbacka—at least that's how it feels.

"Does anyone here speak Polish?" she finally screams, furious with this crowd all around her and furious that this place is where she is. They say it's one kingdom, a united Commonwealth, but here everything is completely different from how it is in Greater Poland, where she comes from. It is wild here, and the faces are foreign, exotic, and the outfits almost comical, their sukmanas disintegrating into rags, strange fur hats and turbans, bare feet. Tiny, buckling houses made out of clay, even here, on the market square. The smell of malt and dung, the odor of damp, decaying leaves.

At last she sees, right in front of her, a frail old white-haired priest, his outer garments not in great condition, a bag slung over his shoulder, gaping at her in surprise. She seizes him by his coat and shakes him, hissing through her teeth:

"For the love of God, help me find Starosta Łabęcki! And not a word of this to anyone! You must keep it absolutely quiet!"

The priest squints at her. He's frightened—he doesn't understand if he's supposed to answer or not breathe a word. Maybe point toward Łabęcki's home? This woman tugging at his coat so mercilessly is short, with a somewhat rounded figure, prominent eyes, and a sizable nose; a curly lock of silvering hair pokes out from under her hat.

"It's a very important person, incognito," she tells the priest, nodding at the carriage.

"Incognito, incognito!" the priest murmurs excitedly. He fishes some young boy out of the crowd and tells him to lead the vehicle to the starosta's house. The child, much defter than might have been expected, helps to unharness the horses so that the carriage can be turned around.

Inside the vehicle with its curtained windows, Kossakowska moans. After every moan comes an emphatic curse.

## Of bloodstained silks

Szymon Łabęcki, married to Pelagia, of the Potocki family, is a cousin—a distant one, but a cousin all the same—of Katarzyna Kossakowska. His wife isn't there, she's visiting her family's estate in the next village over. Overwhelmed by their unexpected arrival, he hurriedly buttons up his French-cut jacket and pulls down his lace cuffs.

"Bienvenue, bienvenue," he repeats mechanically, as Drużbacka and the servants take Kossakowska upstairs, where their host has given his cousin the finest rooms in the house. Then, muttering something to himself, he sends for Rubin, the medic of Rohatyn. "Quelque chose de féminin, quelque chose de féminin," he says.

He is not altogether pleased about this visit—or rather, he isn't pleased at all. He was just getting ready to head to a certain somewhere, a place where cards may, on a regular basis, be played. The very thought of it raises his blood pressure in an agreeable way, as if the best liqueur were taking effect. Yet how much nervous energy does he squander upon this addiction! His only consolation is that more important people, and richer people, and people commanding much greater respect, also sit down to a game of cards from time to time. Lately he's been playing with Bishop Sołtyk, hence this better outfit. He was just about to head out, his vehicle was already harnessed. But of course now he can't go. Someone else will win. He takes a deep breath and rubs his hands together, as if trying to reassure himself that it's okay, he'll get to play some other evening.

Kossakowska's fever rages all night long; Drużbacka fears her friend may be delirious. She and Agnieszka, the lady-in-waiting, apply cold compresses to her head, and then the hurriedly summoned medic arranges herbs about; now their aroma, which seems to contain anise and licorice, hovers in a sweet cloud over the bedclothes, and Kossakowska falls asleep. The doctor tells them to put cold compresses on her belly and on her forehead. The whole house gets calmer, and the candles dim.

Of course, it's not the first time Kossakowska is so troubled by her monthly ailment, and it will certainly not be the last. There is no one to blame for it—the reason is most likely the way young girls are brought up on these nobles' estates, in musty manors, without any physical exercise. The girls sit hunched over their embroidery hoops, embellishing their priestly stoles. The diet in such places is heavy, meaty. Muscles get weak. And on top of all that, Kossakowska likes to travel, whole days spent in a carriage, relentless noise and jostling. Nerves and endless intrigues. Politics. For what is Katarzyna if not the emissary of Klemens Branicki—it is his interests she is pursuing now, after all. She does a good job of it because she has the soul of a man. That's what people say about her, anyway, and she is treated in accordance with this view. Drużbacka doesn't see that supposed masculinity. All she sees is a woman who likes to be in charge. She's tall and sure of herself, and she has a booming voice. People also say that Kossakowska's husband, who is not exactly blessed by nature—he is shrimpy and misshapen—is impotent. When he was trying for her hand, they say he stood atop a sack of money to compensate for his small stature.

Even if children are not in God's plan for her, Kossakowska does not appear at all unhappy. The gossip is that when she argues with her husband, when she gets really angry, she seizes him by the waist and sets him on the mantel, and because he's afraid to get down, he is forced to hear her out. But why would such an attractive woman choose a runt like him? Very likely in order to fortify the family finances, as finances are best fortified by such political stratagems as these.

The two women undressed Kossakowska together, and with every article of clothing the castellan's wife shed, the being by the name of Katarzyna emerged a bit more from within, and then there was Kasia, moaning and crying as she sank through their fingers, depleted utterly. The doctor told them to place dressings of clean linen between her legs and give her lots of fluids, to force her to drink, particularly his decoctions of some bark or other. How thin this woman seems to Drużbacka, and because she is so thin, how young, though in fact she is already thirty.

When Kossakowska fell asleep, Agnieszka and Drużbacka got to work on the bloodied clothing with its vast crimson patches, starting with her underwear, her petticoats and her skirt, finishing with her navy-blue coat. How many such bloodstains does a woman see over the course of her lifetime, wonders Drużbacka.

Kossakowska's beautiful dress is made of thick, cream-colored satin, covered here and there with little red flowers, bellflowers, and one little green leaf on the left side and another on the right. It's a light, cheerful pattern, which suits Kossakowska's slightly darker skin and dark hair. Now bloodstains have flooded these joyful little flowers, their ominous, irregular contours completely swallowing up any ordered pattern. As if malicious forces had escaped from somewhere, surfacing here.

There is a particular kind of science that exists on these sorts of estates—the science of coaxing out bloodstains. For centuries it has been taught to future wives and mothers. If a university for women ever came about, it would be the most important subject. Childbirth, menstruation, war, fights, forays, pogroms, raids—all of it sheds blood, ever at the ready just beneath the skin. What to do with that internal substance that has the gall to make its way out, what kind of lye to wash it out, what vinegar to rinse it with? Perhaps try dampening a rag with a couple of tears and then rubbing carefully. Or soak in saliva. It befalls sheets and bedclothes, underwear, petticoats, shirts, aprons, bonnets and kerchiefs, lace cuffs and frills, corsets, and sukmanas. Carpets, floorboards, bandages, and uniforms.

When the doctor leaves, both women, Drużbacka and Agnieszka, sleep. They've fallen asleep on either side of the bed—one kneeling, with her head resting on her own hand on the bed, leaving a mark on her cheek that will remain for the duration of the evening, the other in an armchair, with her head dropping onto her chest; her breathing sets the delicate lace around her throat in motion, like anemones in a temperate sea.

## The white end of the table at Starosta Łabęcki's

The starosta's house looks like a castle. Moss-covered stone standing on ancient foundations, hence the damp. In the yard, a massive chestnut that is already releasing its glistening fruits, sending yellow leaves, too, in their wake. This makes it look like the whole outdoors is covered in a lovely orange-gold carpet. From the great hall, the visitor enters a series of drawing rooms that are sparsely furnished but brightly painted, with splendid ornaments. The floor, an oak parquet, has been polished so that it shines. Preparations for winter are under way—in the vestibule stand baskets of apples that will be taken around the winter bedrooms, to which they will lend their fragrance as they await the Christmas holiday. Outside there is much hustle and bustle, the peasants have carted in wood and are busy making piles. Women bring in baskets of nuts; Drużbacka can't get over their size. She has cracked one of them, and now she relishes its soft, flavorful meat as her tongue investigates the lightly bitter taste of its skin. The smell of plums simmering for jam comes to her from the kitchen.

The medic passes her downstairs, mutters something under his breath, and goes back upstairs. She has already gleaned that this "saturnine"

Jew, as Łabęcki called him, a doctor trained in Italy who keeps quiet and who is never fully present here, nonetheless commands the full respect of the starosta, who's spent enough time in France to abandon certain prejudices.

By the following afternoon, Kossakowska has ingested a little broth, after which time she asked that pillows be placed behind her, to prop her up, and paper and ink be given to her.

Katarzyna Kossakowska, née Potocka, wife of the castellan of Kamieniec, whose dominion extends over numerous villages and towns, mansions and estates, is by nature a predator. Predators, even after falling into dire straits, such as into the grips of a poacher's trap, lick their wounds and go back into battle. Kossakowska has animal instincts, like a she-wolf in a pack of males. She will always be fine. Drużbacka ought rather to worry about herself. Drużbacka ought instead to consider: What kind of animal is she? She survives thanks to the predators, keeping them company, entertaining them with light verse. She is a tamed wagtail—a little bird with a lovely warble—but she will be blown away by any gust of wind, the draft from a window knocked open by a storm.

By afternoon, the priest has come—a little too soon, still wearing the same coat and that bag of his that would suit a traveling salesman more than it does a priest. Drużbacka spots him the second he enters the house.

"I beg the vicar forane's forgiveness for my impetuousness earlier. I fear I may have even dislodged some of your buttons," Drużbacka says to him, and leads him by the elbow into a drawing room, although she doesn't quite know what she'll do with him there. They won't be called to table for another two hours.

"Oh, that was a specialem statum . . . Nolens volens I was of some use to the honorable castellan's wife, and her health."

Drużbacka has grown accustomed by now to hearing somewhat different types of Polish around the different Polish estates, so these Latin interjections merely amuse her. She spent half her life as a lady-in-waiting and a secretary. Then she got married, had children, and now, after her husband's death and the birth of her grandchildren, she tries to go it alone, or to be with her daughters, or maybe Mrs. Kossakowska, even if it's as a lady-in-waiting. She is pleased, now, to be back on landed property, where there's so much going on, and where poetry may be read in the evenings. She has several volumes in her luggage, although she is too shy to take them out. She doesn't talk. Instead, she listens as the priest chatters away, gradually coming to a common language with him, despite all the Latin, for it turns out that the priest has just visited the palace in Cecołowce, belonging to the Dzieduszyckis, and that he is hatching a plan to replicate where he lives, in his presbytery, the things he has learned from being there. Delighted and animated by the liqueur he's now had three glasses of, happy that someone will listen to him, he speaks.

Yesterday Kossakowski, the castellan, was sent for in Kamieniec, and he is expected at any moment. He will no doubt arrive by morning, perhaps even in the middle of the night.

Around the table sit residents and guests of the house, permanent and temporary. The less important ones have been seated at the boring end, where the white of the tablecloths does not quite reach. Among the residents is the host's uncle, an older gentleman, somewhat heavyset, who wheezes and calls everyone "illustrious sir" or "illustrious madam." There is also the manager of the Łabęckis' properties, a shy, mustachioed man with excellent posture, as well as the former religious instructor to the Łabęckis' children, the highly educated Bernardine priest Gaudenty Pikulski. He is immediately caught up by Father Chmielowski, who takes him over to the corner of the room to show him his Jewish book.

"We did an exchange, I gave him a copy of my *Athens*, and he gave me a Zohar," Father Chmielowski says proudly, and takes the tome out of his bag. "I would love for you to . . . ," he starts, then continues in the impersonal: "If just a little bit of time could be found, to give me just a little taste of what's inside this book . . ."

Pikulski looks at the volume, opening it from the back and reading it, his lips moving along.

"This is no Zohar," he says.

"What do you mean?"

"Old Shorr stuck you with some ordinary Jewish fairy tales." He runs his finger from right to left along the incomprehensible symbols. "'Jacob's Eye.' That's what it's called. Some kind of little folk story."

Shorr-changed, the priest thinks, but he just sighs. He shakes his head. "He must have gotten mixed up. Well, anyway, I'm sure I'll find some wisdom here. If I can get someone to translate it for me . . ."

Starosta Łabęcki gives a sign with his hand, and two servants bring in trays with liqueur and tiny glasses, as well as a serving dish with thinly sliced crusts of bread. Whoever wishes may in this way whet their appetite, since the lunch to be served is heavy and abundant. First soup, and then boiled beef cut up into irregular pieces, brought in along with other meats— roast beef, game like venison and boar, and some chickens, served with boiled carrots, cabbage with bacon, and bowls of kasha glistening with fat.

Father Pikulski leans over the table toward Father Chmielowski and says in a low voice:

"Stop by my place sometime, I have Jewish books in Latin, too, and I can help you with Hebrew. Whatever gave you the idea of going to the Jews?"

"You advised me to do so, my son," answers Father Chmielowski, who finds this slightly vexing.

"I said that as a joke! I didn't think you'd go."

Drużbacka proceeds cautiously with her meal; beef is tough on her teeth, and she sees no toothpicks here. She picks at some chicken and rice and glances furtively at two young servants clearly not yet entirely familiar with their new employment, since they continue making faces at one another across the table and generally clowning around, thinking that the guests, absorbed in their meal, will notice nothing.

Though presumably still weak, Kossakowska has ordered for her ample sickbed in the corner of the room to be supplied with candles and now asks to be served rice and chicken meat. Soon she requests Tokay.

"Well, I guess the worst is behind you, madam, if you are ready for some wine," says Łabęcki with almost imperceptible irony. He's still a little irritated he didn't get to go play cards. "Vous permettez?" He stands, and with an exaggerated bow, he fills Kossakowska's glass. "To your health."

"I ought to be drinking to the health of that medic, who managed to get me back on my feet again with that tincture," says Kossakowska, and takes a big gulp.

"C'est un homme rare," says Łabęcki. "An educated Jew, though he has been unable to cure me of my gout. He studied in Italy. Apparently, he can take a cataract out of your eye with a needle, and just like that, your vision is restored—at least that was what happened with one of the noblewomen from around here. Now she can embroider even the tiniest stitches."

Kossakowska pipes up again from her corner. She has finished eating and is lying back against the pillows, pale. Her face keeps changing in the candlelight, like she's grimacing again.

"Everywhere is full of Jews now, just you wait, they'll gobble us up with dumplings soon," she says. "Our gentlemen don't want to work, and they won't take care of their own property, so they rent it out to the Jews, and they go off and live in the capital. So now I look, and I see it's a Jew in the bridge house, a Jew managing the land on the estate, a Jew cobbling, a Jew sewing the clothes. They've taken every industry."

As the lunch goes on, the conversation turns to the economy, which, here in Podolia, is always floundering, though the riches of Podolia are so great. It could make a flourishing country. The potash, the saltpeter, the honey. Wax, tallow, canvas. Tobacco, cattle, horses—there's so much, and yet it can't be sold. But why? inquires Łabęcki. Because the Dniester is shallow, and broken up by rapids, and the roads are terrible, impassable in the spring thaw. And how can trade proceed when Turkish marauders cross borders with impunity and, in packs, prey upon travelers—one must travel with armed guards, hire security.

"But who can afford it?" Łabęcki laments. His dream is for things to be as they are in other countries, for trade to flourish and for the wealth of the people to increase. So it is in France, although of course the land is hardly better there, nor the rivers.

Kossakowska thinks all this is owing to the noblemen who pay the peasants in vodka, rather than money.

"Did you know that on the Potockis' estates the peasants already have so many days of mandatory labor that they can only do their own work on Saturdays and Sundays?"

"We give them Fridays off, too," snaps Kossakowska. "In any case, what matters is that their work is rotten. Half our crops go to them in exchange for the harvest of the other half, yet even those generous gifts from heaven cannot be turned to our advantage. To this day, my brother has an enormous heap of grain being feasted on by worms—there is no way to sell any of it."

"Whoever hit upon the idea of fermenting cereals for vodka ought to be given a huge gold medal," says Łabęcki, and taking the napkin out from under his chin, he gives the sign to retire to the library, where they will smoke their pipes, according to time-honored custom. "Vodka goes by the gallon now in carriages that take it over to the other side of the Dniester. True, the Koran prohibits drinking wine, but it says nothing about vodka. And anyway, the land of the Moldavian hospodar is close enough, and there the Christians can drink liquor to their heart's content . . ." He laughs, showing his teeth, which have yellowed from tobacco.

Starosta Łabęcki is an accomplished man. In the library, the place of honor is taken by *Instruccions for young Gentlemen by the Marquis de La Chétardie a Knight of the Army and highly distinguish'd at the Royal Court of France, here briefely assembled, in which a young Gentleman asks and receives answers, at the last Lwów academies, a Vale and farewel from His Lordship the Magnanimous Szymon Łabęcki, Starosta of Rohatyn, this memento for his Friends duly submitted to print.*

When Drużbacka politely inquires what the subject matter of this book is, it turns out that it's a chronology of significant battles and that—this becomes clear after a longer speech by Łabęcki—it is more of a translation than an original book written by him.

Which, it is true, is not entirely evident from the title.

Then everyone has to listen in the smoking room—the ladies, too, as both are passionate smokers—to the story of Starosta Łabęcki giving the dedication speech at the inauguration of the Załuski Library.

When the starosta is summoned because the doctor has arrived to perform his treatments, the conversation turns to Drużbacka, and Kossakowska reminds them that she is a poet, which takes the vicar forane by surprise, politely suppressed. When she produces a small tome, he greedily reaches out for it, since printed pages inspire in him an instinct that is difficult to master: the need to seize and not let go before getting a good look—if only a fleeting one—at the whole. And so it is now; he opens it, brings it to the light in order to get a better look at the title page:

"It's a rhyming book," he says, disappointed, though he quickly corrects himself and nods in apparent appreciation. *A collection of spiritual, panegyric, moral, and worldly rhymes* . . . He doesn't like that they're poems, he doesn't understand poetry, but the volume rises in his esteem when he sees that it has been published by the Załuski brothers.

From outside the not-quite-closed door comes the starosta's voice, suddenly somewhat meek:

"Oh, wonderful Asher, this ailment makes my life so vile, my toes hurt, please do something, my dear man."

Another voice follows immediately, this one deep and with a Yiddish accent:

"I'm going to give up trying to treat you. You were supposed to not drink wine and not eat meat, especially red meat, but you refuse to heed the advice of your medic, so it hurts, and it's going to hurt. I do not intend to treat you by force."

"Come, now, don't take offense, they're not your toes, they're mine! You really are the devil's medic . . ." The voice fades into the distance as the two men retreat deeper into the manor.

## 3.

## Of Asher Rubin and his gloomy thoughts

Asher Rubin walks out of the starosta's home and heads toward the market square. With evening, the sky has cleared, and now a million stars are shining, but their light is cold and brings down a frost upon the earth, upon Rohatyn. The first of this autumn. Rubin pulls his black wool coat tighter around him; tall and thin, he looks like a vertical line. The town is quiet and cold. Candlelight glimmers weakly from some windows, but, barely visible, it looks more like a mirage, and could easily be conflated with the trail left by the sun on your iris from a sunnier day, and Rubin's memory goes back, lingering on objects it's encountered before. He is interested in what we see when our eyes are closed, and where that thing we see comes from. Whether from impurities on the eyeball, or because the eye is configured more like the lanterna magica he saw in Italy.

The idea that everything he sees now—the darkness punctuated by the sharp points of the stars above Rohatyn, the outlines of homes, small, tilted, the lump of the castle, and not too far away the sharply pointed church tower, like apparitions, the well-pole shooting askew into the sky, as if in protest, and maybe even the rumble of the water from somewhere farther down, and the very light scraping of the leaves the frost has taken—the idea that all of that arises out of his own mind is both terrifying and alluring in equal measure. What if we're imagining all of it? What if each of us sees everything differently? Does everyone see the color green the same? Or is "green" maybe just a name we use as if it were a paint to coat completely distinct experiences in order to communicate, when in reality every one of us is viewing something different? Is there not some way this can be verified? And what would happen if we were to really *open* our eyes? If we were to *see* by some miracle the reality that surrounds us? What might that be like?

Asher has these kinds of thoughts fairly frequently, and then he starts to be afraid.

Dogs begin to bark, and men's voices rise, and shouts break out—that must be coming from the inn on the market square. He goes in among the Jewish homes, passing to the right of the big, dark mass that is the synagogue; from down where the river is comes the smell of water. The market square separates two groups of Jews who are in conflict with one another, mutually hostile.

Who are they waiting for? he thinks. Who is it that's supposed to come and save the world?

What do the two factions hope for? There are those in Rohatyn who are faithful to the Talmud, squeezed into just a few homes that make up something like a fortress under siege, and there are the heretics, the rene-gades, toward whom, deep down, Asher feels an even greater aversion, for they are primitive, superstitious, with their muddy, mystical prattle, clanging their amulets, smiling their secret cunning smiles, like Old Shorr. These people believe in a miserable Messiah, the kind who's fallen as low as anyone can go, for it is only from the lowest place, they say, that you can rise to the highest. They believe in a tatterdemalion Messiah who has already arrived. The world has been saved already, although you might not see it at first glance, but those in the know cite Isaiah. They skip the Shabbat, they commit adultery—sins incomprehensible to some, to oth-ers so banal there is no sense in giving them much thought. Their houses on the upper part of the market square stand so close together it looks like their facades have been joined, creating one row, strong and solid like a military cordon.

That's where Asher is going now.

This Rohatyn rabbi, a greedy despot eternally agonizing over petty absurdities, often summons him, too, to the other side of the square. He does not particularly esteem Asher Rubin, who rarely goes to synagogue and doesn't dress in the Jewish or the Christian fashion, but rather in between, in black, in a modest frock coat and an old Italian hat by which the townspeople recognize him. In the rabbi's house, there is a sick young boy for whom Asher can do nothing. In truth, he wishes him death, so that his undeserved young suffering might end soon. It is only on account of this boy with the twisted legs that he feels any sympathy for the rabbi; otherwise he considers him merely a vain and mean-spirited lout.

He is certain the rabbi would like for the Messiah to be a king on a white horse, riding into Jerusalem wearing gold armor, perhaps with an army, too, with warriors who would seize power alongside him and bring about the final order of the world. That he'd want him to be like some famous general. He would strip the masters of this world of their power, and they would give him every nation without a fight, kings would pay him tributes, and at the River Sambation he would find the ten lost tribes of Israel. The Temple in Jerusalem would be released fully formed from heaven, and that same day, those who had been buried in the Land of Israel would rise from the dead. Asher smiles to himself when he remembers that those who died outside the Land of Israel would not be resurrected for another four hundred years. He believed that as a child, even though it struck him as cruelly unfair.

Both sides accuse each other of the worst sins, both engage in a war of intelligence. Each is as pathetic as the other, thinks Asher. Asher Rubin is a misanthrope, after all—it's strange he became a doctor. People always irritate and disappoint him.

As for sins, well, he knows more about them than anyone. Sins get written on the human body like on parchment. The parchment differs little from person to person. Their sins are surprisingly similar, too.

## The beehive, or:
## The home of the Shorr family in Rohatyn

In the Shorrs' house on the market square as well as in several others—for the Shorr family is big and has many branches—preparations for the wedding are ongoing. One of the sons is getting married.

Elisha has five of them, and one daughter, the eldest of the children. The first son is Solomon, now thirty, who takes after his father and is cautious and quiet. He is reliable and enjoys widespread respect. His wife, Haikele, thus nicknamed to differentiate her from Solomon's sister, Hayah, is expecting another child. She comes from Wallachia, and her beauty draws attention even now, when she is pregnant. She makes up funny little songs she sings herself. She also jots down little stories for the women. Nathan, who is twenty-eight, with a sincere, gentle face, is proficient in conducting business with the Turks; he is always on the road, making good deals, though no one really knows what kind of deals they are. At this point he rarely comes back to Rohatyn, but he came for the wedding. His wife, a lady, is dressed in elegant, lavish clothing; she comes from Lithuania and looks down on the Rohatyn clan. She has lush hair that she wears high on her head, and her dress is tight. The carriage in the courtyard belongs to them. Then there is Yehuda, lively and lots of fun. They tend to have trouble with him, however, because it's hard to keep his violent nature in check. He dresses in the Polish fashion and carries a saber. His brothers call him "the Cossack." Right now his business is in Kamieniec, where he is the main supplier for the fortress, which earns him a pretty good living. His wife died not long ago in childbirth; the child could not be saved, either. He has two little ones from that marriage, but he has made it clear he's already looking for another partner; the wedding will be a good occasion for it. He likes the oldest daughter of Moshe from Podhajce, who is fourteen now, old enough to marry. And Moshe is an honorable man, very learned; he studies Kabbalah, knows the whole Zohar by heart, and can "grasp the mystery," whatever that might mean to Yehuda. For him, truth be told, that is less important than the beauty and intelligence of the girl whose Kabbalist father named her

Malka, or Queen. Elisha's youngest son, Wolf, is seven. His freckled and joyful face is most often seen next to his father.

The groom is the boy Father Chmielowski called Jeremiah, whose real name is Isaac. He is sixteen years of age now, and apart from the fact that he is tall and ungainly, he does not have too many characteristics of his own just yet. His bride, Freyna, comes from Lanckoroń and is a relative of Hirsh, the rabbi of Lanckoroń, who is the husband of Hayah, daughter of Elisha Shorr. Everyone here in this low-ceilinged but extensive home is in some way family, has some connection—blood, marriage, trade, loans cosigned, carts borrowed.

Asher Rubin comes here fairly often. He is called not only for the children, but also for Hayah. She is always coming down with mystery ailments, which he can treat only by talking with her. In fact, he likes these visits to Hayah. They are perhaps the only thing he does like. And it is usually Hayah who insists on having him brought in, since no one in this home believes in any kind of medicine. They converse, and the ailment passes. Sometimes he thinks that she is like that newt that can summon up all different colors at will in order to better hide from a predator or look like something else. And so one day Hayah has a rash, the next day she can't really breathe, the next she has a bloody nose. Everyone believes it is because of spirits, dybbukim, demons, or maybe ba'aley kabin—bałakaben, as they're known around here—the limping underground creatures that guard treasures. Every illness she has is significant, and every one leads to a prophecy. Then they send him away. Then he is no longer necessary.

It amuses Asher to note that among the Shorrs it's the men who do business and the women who prophesy. Every other female in the family is a prophet. And to think that in his Berlin newspaper today he was reading that in far-off America it was demonstrated that lightning is an electrical phenomenon and that by means of a simple rod you could defend against "God's wrath."

But such information does not reach this far, not all the way to Rohatyn.

Now, since their wedding, Hayah has moved in with her husband, but she comes here often. They married her off to the rabbi of Lanckoroń, one of theirs, a true believer, and a friend of her father's, significantly older than Hayah. They already have two children. Father and son-in-law are like two drops of water: bearded, gray-haired, with sunken cheeks that hold the shadow of the rooms where they station themselves most often. It's a shadow they wear on their faces wherever they go.

When telling the future, Hayah goes into a trance, and during her trances, she plays with little figures made of bread or clay, which she sets out on a board she has painted herself. And then she prophesies. For this she needs her father, who puts his ear to her lips, so close it looks like she is licking it, and he closes his eyes and listens. Then he translates what he has heard from the language of the spirits into human language. A lot of it turns out to be true, although a lot of it also doesn't, Asher Rubin doesn't know how to explain it, and he doesn't know what kind of disease it is. Because he doesn't know, he finds it unpleasant, and he tries not to think about it much. They call this prophesizing "ibbur," which means she is inhabited by a good and sacred spirit that gives her information that would ordinarily be unavailable to humans. Sometimes all Asher does is let her blood; he tries, when he does this, not to look her in the eye. He believes this procedure purifies her, weakens the pressure in her veins so that the blood doesn't overwhelm her brain. The family listens to Hayah just as much as they listen to Elisha Shorr.

But now they have called Asher Rubin to see a dying old woman who came to their home as a wedding guest. She got so weak on the way they had to put her straight to bed; they are afraid she'll die during the wedding itself. So Asher probably won't see Hayah today.

He goes in through a dark, muddy courtyard, where just-slaughtered geese, fattened all summer long, hang upside down. He walks through a narrow entryway and smells the fried cutlets and onions, hears someone somewhere grinding pepper in a mortar. The women are noisy in the kitchen; the cold air is burst by the steam that comes out from there, from the dishes they're preparing. There are the smells of vinegar, nutmeg, bay leaves; there is the aroma of fresh meat, sweet and sickening. These scents make the autumn air seem even colder and more unpleasant.

Men behind the wooden partition speak aggressively, as if they're arguing; you can hear their voices and also smell the wax and damp that has permeated their clothing. The house is full to bursting.

Asher passes children; the little ones pay him no attention, too excited about the impending festivities. He passes through a second courtyard, weakly lit by a single torch; here there is a horse and cart. Someone Rubin can't quite see is unloading this cart in the dark, carrying sacks inside the chamber. In a moment Asher catches a glimpse of his face and balks involuntarily—that's the runaway, the boy Shorr pulled out of the snow half dead last winter, his face all frostbitten.

At the doorstep, he runs into a tipsy Yehuda, whom the whole family calls Leyb. As a matter of fact, Rubin's name isn't Rubin, either, but Asher ben Levi. Now, in the semidarkness and the throng of guests, all names seem somehow fluid, interchangeable, secondary. After all, no mortal holds on to his name for very long. Without a word, Yehuda leads him deep into the house and opens the door to a small room where young women are working, and in the bed by the stove lies an old woman, supported by pillows, her face dried out and pale. The women who were working greet him effusively and position themselves around the bed, curious to watch him examining Yente.

She is little and thin, like an old chicken, and her body is limp. Her chicken's rib cage rises and falls at a rapid rate. Her half-open mouth, covered by extremely thin lips, caves inward. But her dark eyes follow the medic's movements. After he has chased all the onlookers from the room, he lifts her covers and sees her whole figure, the size of a child's, sees her bony hands clutching strings and little leather strips. They have wrapped her up in wolf hides up to her neck. They believe that wolf hides restore heat and strength.

How could they have brought along this old woman with so little life left in her, thinks Asher. She looks like a shriveled-up old mushroom, with her wrinkled brown face, and the candlelight further and more cruelly carves it up, until gradually the woman ceases to appear human; Asher has the sense that soon she will be indistinguishable from nature— from tree bark, gnarled wood, a rough stone.

She is obviously well taken care of here. After all, as Elisha Shorr explained to Asher, Yente's father and Elisha Shorr's grandfather, Zalman Naftali Shorr—the same man who wrote the famous *Tevu'at Shorr*—were brothers. So there was nothing surprising in her wanting to attend her relative's wedding, since there would be cousins from Moravia and from distant Lublin here, as well. Asher crouches beside the low bed and immediately smells the saltiness of human sweat and—he thinks for a moment, looking for the right association—childhood. At her age, people start to smell like children again. He knows there is nothing wrong with this woman—she's simply dying. He examines her carefully and finds nothing other than old age. Her heart is beating unevenly and weakly, as if out of exhaustion. Her skin is clear, but thin and dry like parchment. Her eyes are glassy, sunken. Her temples are sinking, too, and that's a sure sign of impending death. From under the slightly unbuttoned shirt at her throat he can see some strings and knots. He touches one of the old woman's clenched fists, and for a moment she resists, but then, as if ashamed, her fist blossoms open like a dry desert rose. In her palm lies a piece of silk cloth, completely covered in thickly made letters: ע״ש.

It almost seems to him that Yente is smiling at him with her toothless mouth, and her deep, dark eyes reflect the candles' burning; Asher feels as if that reflection were reaching him from very far away, from the unfathomable depths that all human beings hold within them.

"What's wrong with her? What's wrong with her?" Elisha asks him, suddenly bursting into that cramped little space.

Asher rises slowly and looks into his anxious face.

"What do you think? She's dying. She won't last the wedding."

Asher Rubin makes a face that speaks for itself: Why would they have brought her here in such a state?

Elisha grabs him by the elbow and takes him aside.

"You have your methods, don't you, that we don't know. Help us, Asher, please. The meat has already been chopped, the carrots peeled. The raisins are soaking in their bowls, the women are cleaning the carp. Did you see how many guests there are?"

"Her heart is barely beating," says Rubin. "There's nothing I can do. She should never have been brought on such a journey."

He delicately frees his elbow from the grasp of Elisha Shorr and heads for the door.

Asher Rubin thinks that most people are truly idiots, and that it is human stupidity that is ultimately responsible for introducing sadness into the world. It isn't a sin or a trait with which human beings are born, but a false view of the world, a mistaken evaluation of what is seen by our eyes. Which is why people perceive every thing in isolation, each object separate from the rest. Real wisdom lies in linking everything together—that's when the true shape of all of it emerges.

He is thirty-five, but he looks a lot older. The last few years have hunched him over and made him go completely gray—before, his hair was jet-black. He's also having trouble with his teeth. Sometimes, too, when it's wet out, the joints in his fingers swell; he is delicate, he has to take care of himself. He has managed to avoid marriage. His fiancée died while he was studying. He barely knew her, so her death did not sadden him. Since then he has been left in peace.

He comes from Lithuania. Because he did well in school, his family collected funds in order for him to continue his education abroad. So he went to study in Italy, though he did not finish. He developed a sort of generalized incapacity. He barely had enough strength, as he was returning, to make it to Rohatyn, where his uncle Anczel Lindner sewed vestments for Orthodox popes and was well-off enough to take him in under his roof. Here Rubin started to feel a little like himself again. Despite the fact that he had a few years of medical studies behind him by then, he had no idea what was wrong with him. An incapacity, an inability. His hand would be lying before him on the table, and he would not have the strength to raise it. He didn't have the strength to open his eyes. His aunt smeared sheep's fat with herbs on his eyelids several times a day, and this brought him slowly back to life. The knowledge imparted to him by his Italian university came back to him bit by bit, and eventually he started treating people himself. This is going well for him now, although he feels trapped in Rohatyn, as if he were an insect slipped into resin and frozen for all time.

## In the beth midrash

Elisha Shorr, whose long beard gives him the look of a patriarch, is holding his granddaughter up in the air, tickling her stomach with his nose. The little girl giggles, showing her still-toothless gums. She leans her head back, and her laughter fills the whole room. It sounds like doves cooing. Then droplets start to fall onto the floor from her diaper, and her grandfather rushes to pass her to her mother, Hayah. Hayah passes her along again to the other women, and the little one vanishes into the depths of the house, a trickle of urine marking her path along the worn floorboards.

Shorr must step out of the house and into the chilly October afternoon in order to cross over to the next building, where the beth midrash is located, and from which come, as usual, many male voices, sometimes raised and impatient, so that one might be excused for mistaking this reading and studying area for some sort of bazaar. He goes to the children, to the room where they are being taught to read. The family has many children—Elisha alone has nine grandchildren already. He believes that children should be kept on a tight leash. Studying, reading, and prayer until noon. Then they work in the store, help around the house, and learn to do practical things, like bills and commercial correspondence. But also working with the horses, chopping wood for the stove and making even stacks of it, performing little household repairs. They have to know how to do everything, because any and all of it could come in handy. A man has to be independent, self-sufficient, and ought to know a little bit about a lot. He also has to have one real skill that will allow him to make a living when he needs to—this is to be determined according to talent. You have to pay careful attention to whatever the child becomes really attached to and fond of—this is a method that can't lead astray. Elisha lets the girls study, too, but not all of them, and not together with the boys. His eagle eye gets straight to the heart of things, and he can see clearly which of the girls will make a clever pupil. On those with less aptitude, those more frivolous, there is no sense in wasting time, as they will still make good wives and will bear many children.

There are eleven children in the beth midrash, almost all of them his grandchildren.

Elisha himself is nearing sixty. He is small, wiry, quick-tempered. The boys, who are already there waiting for their teacher, know their grandfather is coming to check on their progress. Old Shorr does this every day, so long as he is in Rohatyn and not on one of his frequent business trips.

Now he races in, his face slivered by two vertical wrinkles, which makes him look even more severe. But he doesn't want to scare the children. So he makes sure to smile at them. Elisha looks at each one of them individually first, and he is filled with a tenderness he tries to conceal. He addresses them in a muffled voice, somewhat hoarse, like he's trying to rein himself in, and he takes several large nuts out of his pocket; they are genuinely enormous, almost the size of peaches. He holds them in his open palms and offers them up to the children. They watch with interest, thinking he will give them these nuts now, not expecting to be tricked. But the old man takes one of them and cracks it open in the iron grip of his bony hand. Then he holds it up to the first boy, Leybko, Nathan's son.

"What is this?"

"A nut," Leybko pronounces with satisfaction.

"What's it made of?" says Shorr, moving on to the next boy, Shlomo. Shlomo is less certain. He looks up at his grandfather and squints:

"A shell and a kernel."

Elisha Shorr is pleased. Now he has them watch as, slowly and theatrically, he takes out the nut's kernel and eats it, closing his eyes in rapture, smacking his lips. It's odd. Little Israel on the last bench starts to laugh at his grandfather—it's so funny how he rolls his eyes.

"Ah, but that's too simple," Elisha says to Shlomo, growing serious all of a sudden. "Look, there's another kind of little shield here on the inside of the shell, and a coat that covers the kernel."

He sweeps up the nuts and holds them out for the boys to peer over his hands.

"Come and see," he says.

All this is to teach the children that the Torah's structure is the same. The shell is the simplest meaning of the Torah, its description of what happened. Then we start to get down into its depths. Now the boys write four letters on their little tablets, *peh, resh, dalet, shin,* and when they have managed this, Elisha Shorr asks them to read aloud what they have written—all the letters together and each on its own.

Shlomo recites it like a little poem, but as if he doesn't understand:

"*P, pshat,* that's the literal meaning, *R, remez,* that's the figurative meaning, *D, drash,* that's what the learned say, and *S, sod,* that's the mystical meaning."

At the word "mystical," he starts to stammer, just like his mother. He is so similar to Hayah, Elisha thinks, moved by it. This discovery puts him in a good mood. All these children are of his blood, there is a part of him in each of them, as if he were a chopped log sending out splinters.

"What are the names of the four rivers that flow from Eden?" he asks another boy, one with big ears that stick out from his diminutive face. That's Hillel, his sister's grandson. He responds at once: Pishon, Gihon, Hiddekel, and Phrath.

In walks Berek Smetankes, the teacher, who observes this sweet scene through the eyes of the others. Elisha Shorr is sitting among the children, telling stories. The teacher assumes a blissful expression to please the old man, rolls his eyes in pleasure. He has very light skin and almost white hair, hence his sobriquet, Smetankes, which sounds like the Yiddish word for sour cream. Deep down, he is terrified of this little old man, and he doesn't know of anyone who isn't. Maybe only the two Hayahs, the little one and the big one—daughter and daughter-in-law. Both of them behave however they wish with him.

"There were once four great sages, whose names were Ben Asai, Ben Soma, Elisha ben Abuyah, and Rabbi Akiba. One after the other they went to paradise," begins the old man. "Ben Asai, well, he saw it, and he died."

Elisha Shorr breaks off, pauses dramatically, and with raised brow tries to gauge the effects of what he has just said. Little Hillel's jaw drops in astonishment.

"What does that mean?" Shorr asks the boys, but of course no one responds, so he raises a finger to the ceiling and finishes: "Well, it means that he got into the River Pishon, a name that can be translated as: lips that learn the strict sense."

He straightens out his second finger and says:

"Ben Soma, well, he saw it, and he lost his mind." He contorts his face into a grimace, and the children laugh. "And what does that mean? That means he got into the River Gihon, a name that tells us that the person is only seeing the allegorical meaning."

He knows the children won't understand much of what he's saying. That's okay. They don't need to understand it, all that matters is that they learn it all by heart. That will enable them to come to understand eventually.

"Elisha ben Abuyah," he goes on, "looked and became a heretic. That means that he got into the River Hiddekel, and he got lost in the great many possible meanings."

He points three fingers at little Isaac, who starts to squirm.

"Only Rabbi Akiba went into paradise and came back out unscathed, which means that having plunged into the River Phrath, he got the deepest meaning, the mystical one.

"And those are the four paths to reading and understanding."

The children gaze covetously at the nuts that lie before them on the table. Their grandfather cracks them open in his hands and passes them around. He watches them as they gobble the last crumbs. Then he walks out, his face crinkles up, his smile disappearing, and through the labyrinths of his house, which resembles a beehive, he goes to Yente.

## Yente, or: Not a good time to die

Yente was brought from Korolówka by her grandson Israel and his wife, Sobla, who were also invited to the wedding. They are true believers, like everyone here. They live far away, but the family sticks together.

Now they really regret doing what they did, and no one remembers whose idea it was. It doesn't matter that Grandma wanted to come. They had always been afraid of her, because she had always been the ruler of their home. There was no saying no to her. Now it makes them shake with fear that she is going to die in the Shorrs' home, and during a wedding at that, which will cast a dark shadow over the lives and futures of the newlyweds. When in Korolówka they got into the carriage, covered in tarpaulin, which they and some other guests had rented out, Yente was in perfect health and even clambered up onto her seat by herself. Then she asked for some snuff, and off they went, singing, until, tired, they tried to go to sleep.

Through the canvas, dirty and torn, she watched the world they were leaving behind them folding itself up into winding lines of road, balks, trees, and horizon.

They traveled for two days, the carriage shaking mercilessly, but Old Yente bore it well. They stayed with relatives in Buczacz, and at dawn the next day they set off again. Along the way, they got swept up in a dense fog, and when that happened, all of a sudden, all of the wedding guests began to feel uncomfortable, and that was precisely when Yente started to groan like she needed the others to pay her some attention. Fog is turbid water, and all sorts of evil spirits travel in it, spirits that cloud the minds of animal and man. Wouldn't their horse run off the road and take them all up to the steepest riverbank? And from there they would crash into the chasm. Or would they not all be overtaken by evil creatures, cruel and terrible, or would the entrance to the cave where the dwarves hide their treasures underground not yawn open in the middle of the road, those dwarves as hideous as they are rich? Perhaps so much fear had weakened Grandma.

In the afternoon, the fog subsided, and they saw, not too far ahead of them, the astonishing mass of the castle of Podhajce, uninhabited and fallen into ruin. Over it circled great flocks of crows that time and time again burst up off the half-collapsed roof. The fog retreated from their frightful cawing, which bounced off the castle walls and came back as echoes. Israel and his wife, Sobla, the eldest in the carriage besides Yente, determined to stop. They spread out by the side of the road, to rest; they took out bread and fruit and water—but Grandma wasn't eating anymore. Of the water she drank only a few drops.

When, late at night, they finally arrived in Rohatyn, she could not stand on her own, and they had to assemble some men to carry her into the house. The assembly turned out to be unnecessary—one would have been enough. How much could Old Yente weigh? Nothing. As much as a skinny goat.

Elisha Shorr received his aunt with some uneasiness, but he gave her a nice place to sleep in her own little chamber and brought in some women to take care of her. In the afternoon, he went to see her, and they whispered together, as they always had. They'd known each other his whole life.

Elisha gave her a worried look. But Yente knew exactly what was worrying him:

"It's not a very good time, is it?" she asked.

Elisha didn't answer. Yente gently narrowed her eyes.

"Is there ever really a good time to die?" Elisha said, philosophically, at last.

Yente said she would wait until the crowd of guests had passed; now their exhalations steamed the windowpanes and weighed down the air. She would wait until the wedding guests went home, after the dancing and the drinking, once the sullied, trampled sawdust had been swept from the floors, once the dishes had been washed. Elisha looked at her as if concerned for her, but in reality, in his mind he was already elsewhere.

Yente has never liked Elisha Shorr. He is someone whose insides are like a home with all sorts of different rooms—part of him is one way, other parts of him are another. From the outside, it looks like one building, but on the inside you can see that it is many. You can never know what he'll do next. And there's something else, too—Elisha Shorr is always unhappy. There is always something he is missing, something he misses—he wants what others have, or the opposite, he has something others don't, and he considers it useless. This makes him a bitter and dissatisfied man.

Since Yente is the eldest, everyone who comes for the wedding immediately goes to pay her a visit. Guests stream into her little room at the end of the labyrinth, in the second house, which you have to pass through the courtyard to reach, and which is just across the street from the cemetery. Children peer in to see her through the cracks in the walls—high time to seal them before winter sets in. Hayah sits with her a long while. Yente puts Hayah's hands on her face, touches her eyes, her lips, and her cheeks—the children see this. She pats her head. Hayah brings her treats, gives her chicken broth to drink, adding a spoonful of goose fat, and Old Yente smacks her lips for a long time when she's finished, licking her thin, dry lips, although even the fat doesn't give her enough strength that she might get up.

As soon as they arrive, the Moravians Solomon Zalman and his extremely young wife, Sheyndel, go to visit their old cousin. It took them three weeks to get here from Brünn through Zlin and Preschau, and then Drohobycz, but they will not go back the same way. In the mountains some escaped serfs attacked them, and Zalman had to pay them a considerable ransom—they were lucky they didn't take everything they had. Now they'll go back through Kraków, before snow falls. Sheyndel is already pregnant with her first child, she's just informed her husband of it. She is often nauseated. She is not at all helped by the smell of coffee and spices that greets you when you enter the vast Shorr household, and when you go into the little shop. She also doesn't like how Old Yente smells. She fears this woman as she would a wild animal, with her bizarre dresses and hair on her chin. In Moravia old women look a lot tidier—they wear starched bonnets and neat aprons. Sheyndel is convinced that Yente is a witch. She's afraid to sit down on the edge of the bed, although everyone keeps telling her to do so. She's afraid the old woman will pass something on to the child in her belly, some dark madness, indomitable. She tries not to touch anything in that little room. The smell never stops making her sick. Her Podolian relatives all seem wild to her. Finally, however, they push Sheyndel toward the old woman, so she perches on the very edge of the bed, ready to flee at any time.

She does, however, like the smell of wax—she secretly sniffs every candle—and of mud mixed with horse droppings and—now she knows—of vodka. Solomon, significantly older than she is, with a solid build and a belly, a middle-aged man with a beard, proud of his lovely little wife, brings her a shot of vodka every once in a while. Sheyndel tastes the drink but cannot swallow it. She spits it out on the floor.

When the young wife sits down at Yente's bedside, Yente's hand shoots out from underneath the wolfskins and lands on Sheyndel's belly, although Sheyndel isn't showing yet. But Yente can see that a separate soul has taken up residence in Sheyndel's belly, a soul still indistinct, hard to describe because many; these free souls are everywhere, just waiting for the opportunity to grab some unclaimed bit of matter. And now they lick this little lump, which looks a bit like a tadpole, inspecting it, though there is still nothing concrete in it, just shreds, shadows. They probe it, testing. The souls consist of streaks: of images, and recollections, memories of acts, fragments of sentences, letters. Never before has Yente seen this so clearly. Truth be told, Sheyndel, too, gets uncomfortable sometimes, for she, too, can feel their presence—as if dozens of strangers' hands were pressing on her, as if she were being touched by hundreds of fingers. She doesn't want to confide in her husband about it—and anyway, she wouldn't be able to find the words.

While the men sit in one chamber, the women gather in Yente's room, where they scarcely fit. Every now and then one of them brings in a little bit of vodka from the kitchen, wedding vodka, in semi-secret, like a smuggler, but of course this, too, is part of the fun. Crowded together and excited about the impending festivities, they forget themselves and start to clown around. But it doesn't seem to bother the ailing Yente—she may even be pleased that she's become the center of this merriment. Sometimes they glance at her, uneasy, feeling a little guilty as she suddenly dozes off, then a moment later awakes with a childlike smile. Sheyndel gives Hayah a significant look as Hayah straightens the wolfskins on the old woman, wraps her own scarf around Yente's neck, and sees all the amulets she wears there—little pouches on strings, little pieces of wood with symbols written out on them, figures made of bone. Hayah doesn't dare to touch them.

The women tell terrible stories—about ghosts, lost souls, people buried alive, ill omens.

"If you only knew how many evil spirits were lurking in a single droplet of your beloved blood, you would all turn over your bodies and your souls at once to the Creator of this world," says Tzipa, a woman considered learned, wife of Old Notka.

"Where are the spirits?" asks one of the women in a tremulous whisper, and Tzipa picks up a stick off the dirt floor and points at its tip:

"Here! Here they all are, take a good look."

The women stare at the tip of the stick, their eyes squinting in a funny way; one of the women starts to giggle, and in the light of just a few candles now, they see double or triple, but they don't see any spirits.

## What we read in the Zohar

Elisha, with his eldest son, his cousin Zalman Dobrushka of Moravia, and Israel of Korolówka, who's pressed his forehead into his forearms so hard that all can see how very guilty he feels, are stewing over an important question: What to do in a home about to host both a wedding and a funeral? The four of them sit huddled together. After a little while the door opens and Rabbi Moshko walks in, shuffling his feet. Rabbi Moshko is particularly knowledgeable about Kabbalah. Israel leaps up to help him over to where they are. There is no need to explain things to the elderly rabbi—everyone knows, it's all anyone's been talking about.

They whisper among themselves, until finally Rabbi Moshko begins:

"We read in the Zohar that the two dissolute women who stood before King Solomon with one living child were named Mahalath and Lilith, yes?" The rabbi breaks off inquiringly, as if giving them time to summon up the corresponding passage in their minds.

"The letters of the name Mahalath have a numerical value of 478. Lilith, meanwhile, 480, yes?"

They nod. They know now what he's going to say.

"When a person takes part in a wedding celebration, he rejects the witch Mahalath with her 478 demon companions, while when a person mourns someone close, he overcomes the witch Lilith with her 480 demon companions. This is why we find in Kohelet 7:2 that 'it is better to go to a house of mourning than to go to a house of feasting, for death is the destiny of every man; the living should take this to heart.'"

Which means: They should call off the wedding and wait for the funeral instead.

Dobrushka gives a knowing look to his cousin Elisha and then gazes up at the ceiling emphatically, disappointed by the verdict. He cannot simply sit around here forever. He has his tobacco business in Prossnitz, in Moravia, which he really has to keep on top of. And delivery of traditionally prepared wine for all the local Jews there, on which he enjoys a monopoly. These relatives of his wife's here are nice people, but simple folk, a little backward, superstitious. His Turkish concerns are doing well with them, so he decided to come and visit. But he cannot simply sit around for all eternity. What if it snows? As a matter of fact, no one is pleased by this outcome. Everyone wants the wedding, and they want it now. They can't wait, everything is ready.

Elisha Shorr is certainly not happy with the verdict. The wedding must take place.

Once he is alone, he summons Hayah, she will advise him, and as he waits for her, he flips through the pages of that priest's book, of which he cannot understand a single word.

## Of the swallowed amulet

In the night, when everyone has gone to sleep, Elisha Shorr, writing by candlelight, scratches out the following letters on a tiny piece of paper:

המתנה, המתנה, המתנה

Hey-mem-tav-nun-hey. Hamtana: waiting.

Hayah stands in the middle of the room wearing a white nightgown, tracing an invisible circle around herself in the air. Now she lifts the little piece of paper over her head. She stands this way for a long while. Her mouth is moving. She blows on it a few times, then she rolls up the tiny piece of paper very carefully and slips it inside a wooden carrier the size of a thumbnail. She stays there for a long time, in silence, head bowed, till suddenly she licks her fingers and sticks the strap through the hole in the amulet, which she hands to her father. Elisha, candle in hand, glides through the sleeping, rustling, intermittently snoring household, through the narrow hallways, to the room where Yente lies. He pauses at the door and listens. Evidently untroubled by anything he hears there, he softly opens the door, which humbly submits to him without a sound, revealing cramped quarters faintly lit by an oil lamp. Yente's sharp nose is pointed straight up at the ceiling, casting a defiant shadow on the wall. Elisha has to pass through it in order to lay the amulet on the dying woman's neck. When he leans over her, her eyelids start to flutter a little, and Elisha freezes mid-motion—but it's nothing, she's clearly just having a dream: her breathing is so light as to be almost imperceptible. Elisha ties the ends of the strap and slides the amulet under the old woman's nightgown. Then he turns on his toes and vanishes without a sound.

When the candlelight disappears under the door and gets faint in the cracks between the wood, Yente opens her eyes and, with a weakening hand, feels for the amulet. She knows what's written on it. She breaks the strap, opens the carrier, and swallows the amulet like a little pill.

Yente lies in a small, cramped room, where the servants keep coming in with the guests' coats and laying them at the foot of the bed. By the time the music starts from all the way inside the house, you can barely see Yente beneath the pile of garments; only when Hayah drops by is order restored, the coats winding up on the floor. Hayah bends down over her elderly aunt and listens for her breathing, which is barely perceptible, so weak it seems a butterfly would stir up more of a breeze by fluttering. But her heart is beating. Hayah, slightly flushed from the vodka, presses her ear to Yente's breast, to the cluster of amulets, strings, and straps, and she hears a delicate boom, boom, very slow, the beats as distant from each other as Yente's long breaths.

"Grandma Yente," Hayah calls her quietly, and she has the impression that the old woman's half-closed eyes have trembled, and her pupils have moved, and that something like a smile has appeared on her lips. It's a stray smile—it undulates, sometimes the corners of her mouth rise, sometimes they fall, and then Yente looks dead. Her hands are tepid, not cold, and her skin is soft and pale. Hayah fixes her hair, which has come out from under her kerchief, and she leans in to her ear: "Are you still with us?"

And again that smile comes from somewhere to the old woman's face, lasting just a moment and then vanishing. Hayah is being called from afar by the stomping of feet and the loud sounds of the music, so she kisses the old woman on her lukewarm cheek and runs to dance.

The rhythmic stomps reach Yente's chamber—the wedding guests are dancing, although here you can't quite hear the music, which gets stuck in the wood walls, the winding corridors breaking it down into individual murmurs. All you can hear is the boom, boom of dance steps and, from time to time, a high-pitched squeal. There was an older woman watching over Yente, but roused by the wedding, she went off. Yente is curious, too, about what's going on out there. She is surprised to discover that she can easily slide out of her body and be suspended over it; she looks right at her own face, fallen and pale, a strange feeling, but soon she floats away, gliding along on the drafts of air, on the vibrations of sound, passing without difficulty through wooden walls and doors.

Now Yente sees everything from above, and then her gaze goes back to under her closed eyelids. That's how it goes the whole night. Soaring and renewed descent. Back and forth over the border. It tires her, she's never worked as hard as she is working now, not cleaning, nor in the garden. And yet both the falling and the rising are pleasant. The only nasty thing is that movement, whistling and rough, that tries to push her out to somewhere far away, past the horizons, that force, external and brutal, that it would be impossible to face were the body not protected by the amulet, from the inside, irreversibly.

Strange—her thoughts blow over the whole region. "Wind," says some voice in her head, which must be her own. Wind is the vision of the dead as they gaze upon the world from where they are. Haven't you ever noticed the fields of grass, she wants to say to Hayah, how the blades bow down and are parted? That has to be because there is a dead person watching. Because if you counted all the dead you'd find that there are many more of them than there are of the living. Their souls have been cleansed already over their meanderings through lots of lives, and now they await the Messiah, who will come to finish the task. And they look upon everything. That's why wind blows on earth. Wind is their watchful gaze.

After a moment of startled hesitation she, too, joins in with this wind that flies over the houses of Rohatyn and the impoverished little settlements, over the carts clustered together on the market square in the hope that some customer might happen by, over the three cemeteries, over the Catholic churches, the synagogue, the Orthodox church, over Rohatyn's public house—and it dashes onward, rustling the yellowed grass on the hills, at first chaotic, in disarray, but then, like it's learning dance steps, it speeds along the riverbeds all the way to the Dniester. There it stops, for Yente is astonished by the mastery of the winding line of the river, its filigrees, like the outlines of the letters *gimel* and *resh*. And then it turns around, though not because of the border that has colluded with the river and that divides two great countries from each other. For Yente's vision knows no such borders, after all.

## 4.

## Pharo and Mariage

Bishop Kajetan Sołtyk has a serious problem. Even prayer, deep and sincere prayer, can't wash away his thoughts. His hands sweat, he wakes up too early, as the birds are just beginning their songs, and he goes to bed late, for obvious reasons. So his nerves never get a good rest.

Twenty-four cards. Each player receives six, and then a thirteenth is turned up to indicate the trump suit, meaning the one that will beat every other. The bishop can only calm down once he has been seated at the table, or perhaps once the trump card is lying there, exposed. Then a feeling like a blessing comes over him. His mind finds its proper balance, a wondrous equilibrium, his eyes focus on the table and on the aspect of the cards, taking everything in with just a glance. His breathing evens out, the sweat releases its hold over his forehead, his hands become dry, certain, quick, his fingers shuffle the cards smoothly, revealing one after the next. This is his moment of real delectation—yes, the bishop would prefer never to eat again, and to give up all other corporeal pleasures, rather than relinquish this instant.

The bishop plays Mariage with equals. Not long ago, while the canon of Przemyśl was staying here, they would play till morning. He also plays with Jabłonowski, Łabęcki, and Kossakowski—but it's not enough. Which is why recently something else has started happening, though he hates to even think of it.

He pulls his vestments up over his head, changes into ordinary clothes, and puts on his cap. Only his valet, Antoni, knows about what happens, and Antoni is almost like family and gives no indication that he is taken aback by it in any way. One ought not to be taken aback by a bishop, a bishop is a bishop, he knows what he's doing when he asks you to take him to a tavern on the outskirts of town, to a place he must know people will be playing Pharo for money. The table will be occupied by traveling merchants, noblemen in the middle of a journey, foreign guests, clerks carrying letters, and all variety of adventurers. In taverns not overly clean, and smoky, it feels like everyone is playing, the whole world, and like cards unite people better than faith or language. You sit down at the table, you fan out your cards, and there follows an order that is understandable to anyone. And one must simply adapt to that order, if one wishes to win. The bishop thinks it's like a kind of new language that unites them in a brotherhood for that one night. When he is short on cash, he has them summon some Jew, but that one only lends small sums. For larger amounts, he gets promissory notes from the Jews in Żytomierz, guaranteeing them eventual repayment with his signature.

Anyone who sits at the table can play. Of course the bishop would prefer a better class of people, would prefer to play with peers, but they only rarely have enough money, most of which seems to be in the possession of traveling merchants or Turks, or officers, or others, people from unknown climes. When the banker pours the money out onto the table and shuffles the cards, those who wish to play against him, the punters, come and occupy their seats, each with his own deck. A player takes from this a single card or more and places it before him, and on it, he lays his stake. Having shuffled, the banker reveals all of his cards in turn, laying the first down by his right hand, the second by his left, the third again by his right, the fourth by his left—and so on till the whole pack is dealt out. The cards to the right are what the house takes, while those to the left go to the punters. Therefore, if a person placed before him a seven of spades, and on it a ducat, and in the banker's deck the seven of spades falls to the right, then the player loses his ducat; if it falls to the left, then the banker pays out a ducat to the punter. This rule also has exceptions: the last card but one, though placed to the left, goes to the bank. When a punter has won, he may end the game, or he may play anew starting with a different card, or he may also parole. That's what Bishop Sołtyk always does. He leaves the money he wins atop his card, bending up the corner of the card. If he loses then, he has still lost only the sum with which he started.

It is a more honest game—all in the hands of the Lord. How could anyone possibly cheat?

As the bishop's card debts grow, he calls upon God to shield him from a scandal when it all comes out. He demands divine cooperation—after all, he and God are on the same side of this battle. But God acts somewhat sluggishly, and sometimes it seems like He wants to make another Job out of Bishop Sołtyk. It sometimes happens that the bishop curses Him; then of course he repents and begs forgiveness—as everyone knows, he is hotheaded. He gives himself a fast by way of penance and sleeps in a hair shirt.

No one knows yet that he has put his bishop's insignia in hock in order to pay off some of his debts. With those Żytomierz Jews. They didn't want to take it, he had to talk them into it. When they saw what was in the bishop's chest, which he had covered in sackcloth for disguise, they jumped back and started wailing and lamenting, waving their hands like they had seen some ungodly thing in it.

"I can't accept this," the eldest of them said. "To you, this is worth more than silver and gold, but to me it's just metal for the scales. If we were found with these, they'd beat us within an inch of our lives."

So they grumbled, but the bishop insisted, raised his voice, frightened them. They took the insignia, and they paid him for it in cold, hard cash.

The bishop, who has not managed to get the money back by playing cards, now desires to take the insignia back by force, even if he has to send in some armed men. Apparently they keep it in a little room under the floorboards. If anyone found out, the bishop's life would not be spared.

So he is prepared to do whatever it takes to ensure that the insignia is restored to his residence.

Meanwhile he tries to win it back at Pharo, trusting blindly in divine intervention on his behalf. And it's true: he starts out doing well. The room is very smoky, there are four of them at the table: the bishop himself; a traveler dressed in the German style, but who speaks good Polish; a local nobleman who speaks Ruthenian and curses in the same, with a young girl, almost a child, who sits on his lap, whom the nobleman pushes away when the cards aren't going in his favor but sometimes also pulls close to caress her almost fully naked chest, drawing reproachful looks from Bishop Sołtyk; and finally, some merchant who looks to the bishop like a converted Jew, who is the one who has been winning so far. Before every deal, the bishop feels sure his cards will appear in the proper column, and during every deal he watches in disbelief as they go down on the other side. He genuinely can't believe it.

## Polonia est paradisus Judaeorum . . .

Bishop Kajetan Sołtyk, coadjutor of Kiev, who hasn't slept and is exhausted, has just dismissed his secretary and is now writing a letter to the Bishop of Kamieniec, Mikołaj Dembowski.

> Hurriedly and in my own hand I must inform you, my
> friend, that though I am in good physical health, I am
> tormented by troubles that here press in from all sides so that I
> sometimes feel as cornered as an animal. You have come to my
> aid many times, and so this time, too, I turn to you as to a
> brother, in the name of our long-standing friendship, which it
> would be in vain to seek among others.
> Interim . . .

Meanwhile . . . Meanwhile . . . Now he doesn't know what to write. How, after all, can he explain himself? Dembowski doesn't play cards himself, how could he understand Bishop Sołtyk's situation? Suddenly he's overwhelmed by a feeling of great injustice, he feels in his breast a gentle, warm pressure that seems to be dissolving his heart and turning it into a trickling pulp. He recalls taking up the bishopric in Żytomierz, his first arrival in the dirty, muddy town, enclosed on all sides by forest. His thoughts rush out to his pen now, quick and easy, and his heart is fortified, and his energy returns. He writes:

> You must remember well that when I took up the bishopric in Żytomierz, the place was rife with every type of sin. Whether bigamy or polygamy, vice was universal. Husbands would sell off their wives when they committed bad deeds and exchange them for new women. Neither concubinage nor debauchery was considered wicked, and apparently, upon marriage, both parties promised each other mutual freedom in that respect. Moreover, there was no observance of religious dictates, none of the commandments, everywhere just sin and depravity, moreover misery with poverty.
>
> I must scrupulously remind you, too, of how the diocese had been divided into 3 deaneries: Żytomierz with 7 parishes, including 277 villages and towns, Chwast with 5 parishes, or 100 villages and towns, and Owruck with 8 parishes, 220 villages and towns. Altogether the Catholic population is a mere 25,000. And my income from the humble episcopal estates has totaled 70,000 Polish zlotys; with expenditures for the consistory, and the diocesan school, that amount was nothing. You are aware of how little comes in from such poor properties. My own income as bishop was exclusively any revenue from the villages of Skryhylówka, Wepryk, and Wolica.
>
> The moment I arrived here, I occupied myself first thing with getting the finances in order. It turned out the cathedral had in its possession in capital from offerings by the pious a total amount of 48,000 Polish zlotys. This capital was invested in private land, and a certain sum was borrowed from the Dubno kahal, upon which the annual interest amounted to 3,337 Polish zlotys. Meanwhile, my expenses were great: church maintenance, four vicars' salaries, the organist, the cantor, et caetera.

The chapter, meanwhile, was modestly funded, with a variety of donations in the amount of 10,300 bringing in an annual income of 721 Polish zlotys. In addition, from the village donated by Prince Sanguszko, there was an additional income of 700 Polish zlotys, but the proprietor of the village, Zwiniacz, did not, for a period of three years, pay any interest on the 4,000 zlotys he had borrowed. The amount donated by a certain officer by the name of Piotr remained in the hands of Canon Zawadzki, who neither invested it, nor gave any tithe of it, and the same was the case with the sum of 2,000 Polish zlotys that remained in the hands of Canon Rabczewski. In sum, the chaos was great, though I made haste to organize it all.

You are in the best position to appreciate how much I have accomplished, my dear friend. You have visited us, and you have seen it with your own eyes. I'm now completing the construction of the chapel, and these drastic expenses have exhausted my purse for the time being, but things are moving in the right direction, which is why I am asking you, my trusted confidant, for support, for some 15,000 zlotys, which I would pay back immediately after Easter. I have worked to encourage the generosity of the faithful, which at Eastertime will no doubt yield its fruits. For instance, Jan Olszański, the chamberlain of Słuck, put 20,000 zlotys into his property at Brusiłow, allotting half the interest of it to the cathedral, and the other half to the increase of the quantity of missionaries. Głębocki, the cup-bearer of Bracław, donated 10,000 zlotys to the establishment of a new canonry and to an altar for the cathedral and gave 2,000 zlotys for the seminary.

I'm including all this information because I'm doing a good business here and want to assure you that your loan will be repaid. In the meantime, I have entered into some unfortunate dealings with the Żytomierz Jews, and in their impudence, they truly know no limits, thus I would require the loan as soon as possible. It is astonishing that within our Commonwealth these Jews may so flagrantly break with law and good custom. Not for nothing did Popes Clement VIII, Innocent III, Gregory XIII, and Alexander III

keep on ordering the burning of their Talmuds, and yet
when we wanted to do the same thing here, not only
had we no support, but the secular authorities even
opposed us.

It's an odd thing that the Tatars, the Aryans, and the
Hussites were all expelled, and yet somehow no one thinks to
get rid of the Jews, although they are the ones bleeding us dry.
Abroad they even have a saying about us: Polonia est paradisus
Judaeorum . . .


## Of the presbytery in Firlejów
## and the sinful pastor living in it

This autumn is like a piece of embroidery done by invisible needles,
thinks Elżbieta Drużbacka, riding in a large britchka on loan from the
starosta. Deep bronzes in plowed furrows and a brighter streak of dried
earth in the fields, and pitch-black branches, to which the most stubborn
leaves are still clinging, pied splotches. And there remain blades of grass
that are succulent and green, as if they have forgotten it's the end of
October, and that it freezes at night.

The road is straight as an arrow and runs along the river. On the left
side, a sandy ravine, the ground ragged from some long-ago catastrophe.
You can see peasants' carts going down over that yellow sand. Restless
clouds float across the sky; one minute it's gray and gloomy, the next a
piqued sun bursts out from behind the clouds, everything on the ground
suddenly becoming alarmingly distinct, sharp.

Drużbacka misses her daughter, who is currently expecting her fifth
child, and she thinks that in reality she ought to be with her now, not on
some new peregrination in some foreign country with an eccentric castellan's wife, and certainly not going off to see some jack-of-all-trades priest.
But on the other hand, Drużbacka lives to be transported. You might
think—but you'd be wrong—that being a poet is a sedentary profession,
nearer to a garden than a public house, suitable for a homebody.

The priest is awaiting her at the gate. He grabs the horse's harness as if he's been unable to think of anything other than this visit, and immediately taking his visitor's arm, he guides her to the garden by the house.

"After you, my good lady."

The presbytery stands just off the dilapidated road. It's a small wooden manor house, whitewashed nicely and well cared for. You can see that in the summer it was encircled by clusters of flowers, which now lie slumped and yellow, low to the ground. Already someone's hand has gone about putting things in order, placing a portion of the stalks in a pile that is only smoldering—the fire evidently feels unsure of itself in such damp air. Among the stalks roam two proud peacocks, one of them old and resigned, with not much of his tail left. The other is confident, even aggressive, he runs up to Drużbacka and butts into her dress again and again until the frightened woman steps aside.

She looks around the garden—it's beautiful, every flower bed delimited with clean, straight lines, round stones placed along the path, and everything planned out according to the finest botanical art: by the fence are roses for vodka and no doubt for church wreaths, too; farther down, angelica, anise, plants for incense. Over the stones creep thyme, mallow, hazelwort, and chamomile. Not many of the herbs are left at this time of year, but their presence can be gathered from the little wooden tablets placed before them, containing their names.

From the presbytery, a meticulously raked path leads into the heart of a small park, and on either side of the path, there is a somewhat primitive bust with a caption carved underneath it. Over the entrance to the garden, there is a clumsy inscription on a slat, which the priest very obviously attempted himself:

**To preserve the body from foul stench,**
**Here is this garden's healthy fragrance.**

Such verses make Drużbacka wince.

The grounds are rather small; at some stage, the embankment slopes sharply down toward the river, but there, too, the priest has readied a surprise: stone steps, a little bridge over a tiny stream, past which point stands the church: high, imposing, and gloomy. It towers over cottages with thatched roofs.

Going down the steps, you can see the lapidarium on either side. You are supposed to stop at each stone and read its caption.

Ex nihilo orta sunt omnia, et in nihilum omnia revolvuntur: From nothing came everything, and to nothing will everything return, reads Drużbacka, and suddenly a shudder passes through her, both from the cold and from that caption, somewhat awkwardly engraved into the stone. So what was the point of it all? she wonders. Of all this effort? These paths and little bridges, little gardens, wells, steps—these inscriptions?

The priest now leads her to the road along the rocky path, and in this way, they complete their orbit around the modest property. Poor Drużbacka—she seems not to have expected such a turn of events. She does have good shoes, leather shoes, but she nearly froze in the carriage and felt more like warming her old back at a stove than scampering about in the wilderness. At last, after this forced promenade, her host invites her inside; at the door to the presbytery, another inscription, engraved on a large plaque:

> *Benedykt Chmielowski, the priest*
> *Firlejów's sinner now deceased*
> *Just a parson in Podkamień*
> *Vicar forane of Rohatyn*
> *Not worthy, and gone in a flash*
> *Not canon now, but dust and ash*
> *For his sins he begs for prayers*
> *That they not gore him there like mares*
> *Almighty Father, who art sublime,*
> *You have fulfilled him for all time.*

She looks at him in astonishment.

"What can this be? Are you already preparing for death?"

"Better to have it all ready in advance, so as not to unnecessarily burden bereaved relatives later on. I want to know what will be on my tombstone. Otherwise it would be some foolishness, no doubt—not what I would write myself. At least this way I know."

Drużbacka, too tired, takes a seat and starts to look around for something to drink, but the table in the room is empty, not counting papers. The house smells of damp mixed with smoke. The chimneys have probably not been cleaned in some time. And the draft is cold. In the corner stands a stove lined with white tiles, and next to it a basket filled with wood, so much that she can tell the stove was only just lit—no wonder the room hasn't heated up yet.

"I really froze out there," says Drużbacka.

The priest, wincing like he's just swallowed a piece of rotten food, quickly opens a cupboard and takes out a cut-crystal carafe and two glasses.

"Mrs. Kossakowska looked very familiar to me . . . ," he begins uncertainly, pouring the liqueur. "At one time, I knew her eldest sister . . ."

"Mrs. Jabłonowska, you mean," Drużbacka says, distracted, flooding her mouth with the sweet drink.

A jaunty, rotund woman enters the room—she must be the priest's housekeeper—carrying two bowls of steaming soup on a tray.

"Whoever saw a guest flitting around in the cold so," she chides the priest, and he evidently feels uncomfortable under her reproachful gaze. Drużbacka, meanwhile, is slowly coming back to life. Blessed be that stout lady savior. The soup is thick, vegetable, with potatoes and noodles swimming in it. It is only now that the vicar forane notices Drużbacka's muddied shoes and her hunched back; now he realizes she's shivering all over, and out of instinct he makes a gesture as if to embrace her, although of course he doesn't follow through with it.

A dog trots into the room after the housekeeper. It's medium-sized, shaggy, with floppy ears and wavy chestnut fur. Very gravely, it sniffs around Drużbacka's dress. And when Drużbacka bends down to pet it, she glimpses puppies, four of them, each of them different. The housekeeper wants to kick them out of the room right away, and she reproaches the priest for yet again failing to close the door. But Drużbacka asks if they can let the dogs stay for now. So they accompany them into the evening, delighted to sit near the stove, which finally heats up the room enough for the guest to be able to remove her fur-lined vest.

Drużbacka looks at Father Chmielowski and suddenly understands how very lonely this aging, neglected man is, bustling all around her, wanting to impress her as a little boy might. He sets the cut-crystal carafe on the table and examines the glasses under the light, making sure they're clean. His ragged, threadbare cassock of camlet wool has worn thin at his stomach, and here a lighter patch shines bright. She doesn't know why, but Drużbacka finds it exceptionally touching to see all this, and she has to look away. She picks up a puppy and puts it on her lap—it's a female, the one that most resembles the mother; she rolls right over onto her back, revealing her delicate little belly. Drużbacka starts to tell the priest about her grandchildren, all of them girls—though who knows, perhaps this only makes him feel worse? Chmielowski listens inattentively to her, his eyes flitting around the room as he tries to think what else this woman might like. The priest's liqueurs are delicious, and Drużbacka nods appreciatively. Then it is finally time for the main dish. Pushing aside the glasses and the carafe, Chmielowski proudly lays before her on the table his great work. Drużbacka reads the title out loud:

*"New Athens, or the Academy of Every Science, divided into different titles as into classes, issued that the Wise might have it as a Record, that Idiots might learn, that Politicians might practice and that melancholy Souls obtain some slight Enjoyment from it . . ."*

The priest, leaning back comfortably in his chair, downs his liqueur in one gulp. Drużbacka exclaims with unrestrained admiration:

"Beautiful title. It's so hard to give a work a good title."

The priest answers modestly that what he would like is to create a compendium of knowledge of the sort that could be found in every home. And in it a little about everything, so that a person might reach for such a book whenever there is something he does not know, and there he might find it. Geography, medicine, human languages, customs, but also flora and fauna and curiosities of all kinds.

"Just imagine, madam—everything at hand, in every library, nobleman's and peasant's. All of mankind's knowledge collected in one place."

He has already amassed a lot of it, which he published in two volumes a few years ago. But now he would like to also have, aside from Latin, a knowledge of Hebrew, and from Hebrew to draw more tasty tidbits. But obtaining Jewish books is difficult, you have to ask their Jewish owners, and few among the Christians can read in that language. Father Pikulski has volunteered for now to translate this and that for him, but Benedykt, not having the language himself, cannot really gain access to that wisdom.

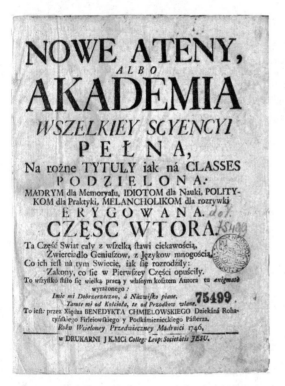

"The first volume came out in Lwów at the printery of one Golczewski . . ."

Drużbacka is playing with the dog.

"I am now writing a supplement to both books, which is to say volumes three and four, and that is where I am thinking of concluding my description of the world," Father Chmielowski adds.

What is Drużbacka to say? She puts down the puppy, replacing it in her lap with the book. Yes, she knows this book, she once read it in the home of the Jabłonowskis, who owned the first edition. Now she opens to a chapter on animals and finds something there about dogs. She reads in a powerful voice:

"'In Piotrków we had a dog so delightful that at the command of its master it would take a knife into the kitchen, and there it would clean it with its paws, rinse it in water, and deliver it back.'"

"That was her mother that did that." The priest smiles, pointing at his dog.

"But why is there so much Latin in this, Father?" Drużbacka says, skimming the next section. "Not everybody understands it."

The priest shifts uneasily.

"But what do you mean? Every Pole speaks in Latin as if it were his mother tongue. The Polish nation is a gens culta, polita, capax of every type of wisdom, justifiably relishing Latin and pronouncing it the best of all the nationalities. We do not say, like the Italians, Redzina, but Regina, not tridzinta, quadradzinta, but triginta, quadraginta. We don't ruin Latin like the Germans and the French, who in the place of Jesus Christus say *Jedzus* Kristus, instead of Michael, Mikael, instead of charus, karus . . ."

"But which Poles, dear Father? Women, for example, rarely speak Latin, for they have frequently not been taught it. And the middle classes don't really know Latin at all, and after all, you do want them and even classes lower than them to read this . . . Even the starosta prefers French over Latin. It strikes me that in the next edition you might as well weed out all your Latin, in the same way that you weed your garden."

The priest is shocked by this critique.

It would appear that this lady he is hosting is more interested in his dogs than she is in his books.

The sun is nearly setting by the time she gets into the britchka and the priest hands her a basket with two puppies in it. It will be dark by the time she gets back to Rohatyn.

"You could spend the night in my humble priestly quarters," offers the priest, though he is angry with himself for offering.

Once the carriage has gone, the priest doesn't know what to do with himself. He expended more than just the strength required for two hours' time—he expended the energy of a whole day, of a week. The fence's slats have slumped over by the hollyhock, leaving a distasteful gap, so the priest, not thinking overmuch what he is doing, gets right down to work. But then he freezes and can feel a kind of stillness trickling into him from every side, along with doubt, and past that there's a collapse of all the things that haven't yet been named, and chaos is created, and everything starts to rot with the leaves, to tumefy before his eyes. He still forces himself to fasten the slats to the fence, but then suddenly it seems too hard to him, and the slats slide out of his hands and fall onto the damp ground. The priest goes inside, kicks his shoes off in the dark vestibule, and then goes into his library—the low-ceilinged room with beams exposed along the ceiling now seems suffocating to him. He sits down in his armchair. The stove is as hot as it can get, and the white tiles that cover the copper enamel are slowly warming up. He looks at the old woman's little book, picks it up, smells it. It still smells of printing ink. He reads:

> . . . true, shriveled, there is the horror she inspires
> Junctures fastened with veins like lots of thin wires;
> She never sleeps, eats, or drinks, cannot deserve,
> Her entrails can be seen just past her ribs' curve,
> Where her eyes had been, deep crevices are scored,
> Where her brain resided, as if pitch were poured.

"Protect us, Lord God, from all that is evil," whispers the priest, and sets aside the book. She seemed like such a nice lady.

And suddenly he knows that he has to summon back up that old, childlike enthusiasm that causes him to write. Since otherwise he will perish—he'll decay in the autumnal damp like a leaf.

He sits down at the table, stuffs his feet into a pair of wolfskin boots sewn for him by his housekeeper so that he doesn't freeze as he sits still for hours to write. He puts out his paper, sharpens his quill, rubs his icy hands together. At this time of year, he always feels like he will not survive the winter.

---

Father Chmielowski knows the world only through books. Whenever he sits down in his Firlejów library and reaches for a book, whether for a handsome folio edition or just a little Elzevir, it always feels if he is setting off on a journey to some unknown country. This metaphor appeals to him, he smiles to himself and starts trying to set it in a graceful sentence . . . Yet it is easier for him to write about the wide world than it is to write about himself. Always focusing on something or other, he is never focused on himself, and since he's never written down the things that have happened to him, now it seems to him that he has no biography. If that woman who writes such gloomy verses were to ask him who he is, how he's spent his years, what would he say? And if he wanted to write it down, there wouldn't be more of it than just a few pages, so not even a booklet, not even one of those diminutive Elzevirs, barely even a brochure, just a scrap of paper, the little life of a non-saint. Neither a peregrinator nor a surveyor of foreign lands.

He dips his pen in its ink and holds it for a moment over the sheet of paper. Then, with fervor, he begins:

> The story of the life of Father Joachim Benedykt Chmielowski, of the Nałęcz coat of arms, pastor of Firlejów, Podkamień, and Janczyn, vicar forane of Rohatyn, canon of Kiev and poor shepherd of a paltry flock, written in his own hand and not imposing of high-level Polish, so as not to obscure the meanings, dedicated ad usum to the Reader.

The title takes up half the page, so the priest reaches for the next sheet of paper, but his hand seems to have numbed up—it doesn't want to or can't write anything more. When he wrote "to the Reader," Drużbacka appeared before his eyes, that little older lady with her hale complexion and her bright, shiny eyes. The priest promises himself that he will read those verses of hers, though he doesn't expect anything much of them. Folly. It must just be folly and impossible platoons of Greek gods.

It is a shame she had to leave.

He takes another sheet of paper and dips his pen in the ink. But what is he to write? he wonders. The story of the priest's life is the story of the books he read and wrote. A true writer has no biography. What of interest, then, can there be? His mother, seeing little Benedykt's love of books, sent him to the Jesuits of Lwów at the age of fifteen. That decision considerably improved his relationship with his stepfather, who never cared for him. From then on, they almost never saw each other. Immediately after that, he went to seminary and was soon ordained. His first employment was with the Jabłonowskis at their estate, as the preceptor to young—though only five years younger than himself—Dymitr. There he learned how to seem older than he really was and how to speak in a tone of perpetual instruction, which to this day some people take ill. He was also permitted to avail himself of his employer's library, which was quite ample, and there he discovered Kircher as well as Comenius's *Orbis pictus*. In addition, his hand, that recalcitrant servant, took to writing on its own, particularly during that first spring he spent there, humid and stuffy, especially when Lady Joanna Maria Jabłonowska happened to be nearby—she was Dymitr's mother and his employer's wife (which the priest tried not to think about). Head over heels in love, dazed by the strength of his feeling, absentminded, weak, he waged a terrible battle with himself in his efforts to reveal nothing, dedicating himself entirely to his work and writing a book of devotions for his beloved. This maneuver enabled him to distance himself from her, to defuse, to sanctify, to sublimate, and when he presented her with the manuscript (before it got published in Lwów, upon which time it attained considerable popularity, going through several more editions), he felt as if he had married her, entered into a union with her, and that he was now giving her the child of that union. *The course of one whole year*—a prayer book. In this way, he discovered that writing saves.

Joanna was at that age, so dangerous for so many men, between the age of the mother and the mistress. This made the erotic allure of motherhood less obvious and made it therefore possible to luxuriate in it at leisure. To imagine your own face pressed into the softness of that lace, the

faint scent of rosewater and powder, the delicacy of skin covered in peach
fuzz, no longer so firm or so taut, but warm, gentle, soft as suede. Through
her intercession, he received from King Augustus II the presbytery in
Firlejów, and as a twenty-five-year-old with a broken heart, he took up
that small parish. He had his collection of books brought in, and he built
for it beautiful carved cases. Of his own books, there were forty-seven;
others he would borrow from monastic libraries, from the bishopric, from
magnates' palaces, where they often languished uncut, mere souvenirs
from excursions abroad. The first two years were hard. Especially the
winters. He strained his eyes because darkness would fall fast, and yet
he could not stop working. He wrote two strange little books, *Flight of the
Saints to God* and *Journey to That Other World*, which he wasn't brave
enough to publish under his own name. Unlike the prayer book, they did
not do particularly well and went missing amidst the shuffle of this world.
The priest has a couple of copies of them here, in Firlejów, in a special
trunk he had covered in sheet metal and equipped with good locks in case
of fire, theft, or any other cataclysm, to which mere mortals' libraries are,
after all, not immune. He remembers exactly the shape of the prayer book
and the smell of its cover—made of dark, plain leather. It's strange, he
also remembers the touch of Joanna Jabłonowska's hand, she had a habit
of covering his hand with hers in order to pacify him. And something
else: he remembers the delicate softness of her cool cheek when—out of
his mind with love—he dared to kiss her once.

And that's it for his life, it likely wouldn't take up any more space than
the title itself. His beloved died before *New Athens* was published, though
that, too, was written out of love.

But he has met with this strange decree of Providence of late, likely so
that he will begin to reflect upon his life. In Kossakowska's features he recognized her elder sister, and Drużbacka had served her for years, including
at Princess Jabłonowska's, until the bitter end. She had told him that
she'd been with Joanna when she'd died. This had disconcerted him
considerably—that Drużbacka turned out to be a messenger from the past.
Her touch, her cheek, her hand had passed somehow into the poetess. Now
nothing is so clear or colorful as it was—it's all sort of blurry, without any
definite contours. Like a dream that vanishes on waking, that flies out of

your memory like fog from over a field. The priest doesn't fully understand it, but he also doesn't really want to understand. People who write books, he thinks, don't want to have their own stories. What would be the point? In comparison with what is written, life will always be boring and bland. The priest sits with his pen, which has already dried up, until the candle burns out and with a quick hiss is extinguished. He is flooded with darkness.

## Father Chmielowski tries to write a letter to Mrs. Drużbacka

Father Chmielowski feels unsatisfied with what he managed to say during Drużbacka's visit. Because in fact he did not manage to say much, probably because of his natural shyness. All he did was boast, drag the poor lady around on a rocky path, in the winter, in the damp. The very idea that the intelligent and educated Drużbacka might take him for an ignoramus and an idiot now torments him. It torments him until he finally decides to write her a letter and lay out his rationale.

He begins with a beautiful turn of phrase:

Conductress of the Muses, Favorite of Apollo . . .

But here he gets stuck for the whole day. He finds the phrase pleasing until sometime around lunch. By dinner, it strikes him as pompous and pathetic. Only in the evening, when mulled wine has warmed up his mind and body, does he sit down boldly to a fresh sheet of paper and write his thanks to her for coming to visit his "Firlejów Hermitage" and for bringing a little light into his monotonous gray life. He feels sure she'll understand the word "light" broadly and poetically.

He also asks after the puppies and confides in her all his troubles, like that a fox got all his hens, and that now if he wants eggs he has to send for a peasant. But he's afraid to get new hens, for he would only be sentencing them to death by fox's maw. And so on.

He does not wish to admit it, but after he sends his letter, he waits for her answer. He waits and waits. He tries to estimate how long the post might take to get to Busk, where Drużbacka is. But it isn't far, after all. The letter should have arrived by now.

It comes at last. Roshko searches for its recipient all over the presbytery, holding the letter stiffly in his outstretched hand. He finds the priest in the cellar, decanting some wine.

"Goodness, you gave me such a scare," starts the priest. He wipes his hands on the apron he always puts on when performing his domestic tasks, and then he takes the letter carefully, between two fingers. He does not open it. He examines the seal and his own name calligraphed in beautiful, self-assured penmanship, the flourishes fluttering over the paper like battle flags.

It is only later, after an hour or so, when the library has been heated by the stove, when he has warmed himself with some mulled wine and covered his feet with a fur, that—taking very great care indeed—he opens the letter and reads.

## Elżbieta Drużbacka writes to Father Chmielowski

*Christmas 1752, Busk*

My dear wise and generous Father,
  What wonderful luck that I am able, during this time so near the birth of Our Lord and Savior, to wish you every good fortune, and in addition, the safekeeping of your health and your well-being—for after all, we are so brittle we risk being knocked over by anything at any time. Yet may everything turn out for you just as you wish it, and may the grace of the Divine Infant Jesus endlessly favor you.
  I remain deeply impressed by my visit to Firlejów, and I must confess that I had imagined you, a priest of such renown, quite differently: that you would have a large library,

and that in it rows of secretaries would sit at the ready,
writing, rewriting. And yet instead you live as humbly as
a Franciscan.

I admire in you your botanical arts, your ingenuity in all
things, and your enormous erudition. As soon as I got home I
had the great pleasure of dedicating my evenings to a rereading
of your *New Athens*, which of course I know well, having
devoured its every page when it was first published. When my
eyes would allow it, I read your book for hours on end. Now
I enjoy the special circumstance of knowing the Author
personally, and it even happens that I can hear his voice—
as if you were here to read it aloud to me—but it is also the
case that the book possesses a strange magic: it can be read
without pause, here, there, and something interesting always
remains in one's mind, giving one fantastic pretexts for
thinking of how very great and complex this world is, so
much so that one cannot possibly comprehend it in thought—
no doubt only in fragments, the bits and pieces of small
understandings.

Now night arrives so quickly, and darkness daily swallows
up the moments of our lives, and candlelight is but a poor
imitation of light, which our eyes cannot bear for too long.

I know, however, that your *New Athens* project is the work of
a true genius with enormous courage, and it is of enormous
value to all of us who live in Poland, for it is a true compendium
of all that we know.

There is, however, one thing that troubles my reading of
your wonderful work, my dear Father, and it is the very thing
we spoke of while sitting in your home in Firlejów—I refer to
Latin, and not only to it, but to its overwhelming abundance
in your work, everywhere interjected, like salt poured too
enthusiastically upon a meal, which, instead of elevating its
taste, makes it difficult to swallow.

I understand, my dear Father, that Latin is a worldly
language, versed in all things, and that it contains more useful
words than Polish, but whoever does not know it will not be
able to read your book—will get lost in it completely! Have you
not thought about those who would love to read you but who

do not know Latin—the merchants, the petite bourgeoisie who have a somewhat reduced level of education, or even those more intelligent tradespersons? They are the ones who could really benefit from the information you so scrupulously collect, as opposed to your confrères, priests, and academics, who already have access to books. If they wish it, of course, which they do not always. And I shan't even mention the women who often know how to read quite well, but who, since they weren't sent to school, will sink into Latin as if it were quicksand, right away.

## Bishop Kajetan Sołtyk writes a letter to the papal nuncio

He saved this letter to write yesterday evening, but in the end, exhaustion overcame him, and so he must begin his day with this unpleasant task. His secretary is still half asleep; he stifles a yawn. He's toying with the quill, testing out different thicknesses of lines when the bishop begins his dictation:

> Bishop Kajetan Sołtyk, coadjutor of Kiev, to papal nuncio Niccolò Serra, Archbishop of Mitylene

Then the boy tasked with the stoves enters the room and starts raking out ash. The scraping of the dustpan is unbearable to the bishop, and all the thoughts in his head go flying into thin air like a cloud of that same ash. And of ash smacks the matter at hand.

"Come back and do this later, son," he says to him, softly, and then he takes a moment to regather his scattered thoughts. Then the pen goes on the attack against the innocent paper:

> Once more I congratulate Your Excellency upon this new station in Poland, in the hopes that it will be an occasion for the comprehensive fortification of faith in Jesus Christ in lands so

particularly cherished by Him, for here in the Commonwealth
we are the most faithful of His stable, the most devoted to Him
in our hearts . . .

But Bishop Sołtyk has no idea how to get to the point. First, he wanted
to deal with the matter more generally—he didn't expect an explicit
request for a report, even less from the nuncio. He is surprised by this
because the nuncio has spies everywhere, and though he himself does
not poke his Italian nose in others' affairs, he does take advantage of
other, zealous people's noses.

The secretary waits with
raised pen, its end having
already collected a sizable
drop. But that man, very experienced, knows perfectly
the habits of a drop of ink,
and he waits until the very
last moment before he shakes
it back into the inkwell.

How to describe it, thinks
Bishop Sołtyk, and what
comes to mind are fine sentences like: "The world is
quite a perilous pilgrimage
for those who sigh after eternity," which would show the bishop's uncomfortable and exhausting situation as he is now called upon to explain
his actions, his righteous but unfortunate actions, when he ought to be
dedicating his thoughts to prayer and the spiritual needs of his flock.
Where to begin? Perhaps when the child was found, which happened just
outside Żytomierz, in the village of Markowa Wolica, this very year, not
long ago?

"Studziński, right?"

The secretary nods and adds the boy's first name: Stefan. He was
eventually found, but as a corpse, bruised and covered in wounds, seemingly from pricking. In the bushes by the road.

Now the bishop brings his focus to within himself. He starts his dictation:

> . . . some peasants, having found the child, carried him
> to their Orthodox church, passing near that inn where
> he must have been tortured and where the blood from the
> very first wound on his left side must have been let,
> and due to this suspicion, and others, too, two inn-keeping
> Jews were taken in that village, along with their wives,
> and they confessed to everything and informed on others.
> Thus the matter resolved itself, thanks to divine
> justice.
>      I was immediately alerted to the whole business and
> did not neglect to enter into it with all that was in my power,
> and right away in crastinum I ordered the heads of the
> neighboring properties and the lords to give up other guilty
> parties, and whenever they appeared sluggish on that account,
> I undertook myself to go around the properties and persuade
> their lordships to arrest. So were thirty-one men and two
> women arrested, and brought in shackles to Żytomierz, they
> were placed in pits dug especially for this purpose. After holding
> an inquisitio I sent the accused to the municipal court. For
> these most vile murderers unworthy of further investigation, the
> court determined to proceed to the strictissime examination of
> the Jews appearing then before them, all the more so since some
> of them changed the testimonies they had given to the
> consistory court and had been utterly destroyed by damning
> evidence given against them by Christians. Then the accused
> were taken to be tortured and were burnt three times by the
> minister of holy justice. From these corporal confessions it soon
> became apparent that Yankiel and Ela, the innkeepers at
> Markowa Wolica, talked into it by Shmayer, the rabbi of
> Pawłocz, somehow kidnapped this child, took him into the inn,
> made him drink vodka, and then the rabbi cut into his left side
> with a pair of shears, and then they read their prayers from their
> books as others among the Jews stuck him with pins and big
> needles, and from all his veins they squeezed out all his

innocent blood into a bowl, the which blood the rabbi then
distributed amongst those present, pouring it into vials
for them.

The bishop takes a little break in his dictation and has some Tokay
brought to him, which always does him good—good for the blood. It is fine
that it is on an empty stomach. He can also tell that breakfasting time is
about to turn into lunching time, and he is starting to get hungry. And
therefore angry. But what can he do. The letter has to go out today. So he
goes on:

*Diverses Manieres dont le S.ᵗ OFICE fait donner la QUESTION.*

So when the accuser in the matter of young Stefan,
describing his dolenda fata, according to procedure made his
oath with seven witnesses that the aforementioned Jews were
the cause of the bloodletting and death of the child, the court
sentenced them to a cruel death.

The seven engines of this crime and ringleaders of this Pagan cruelty were to be tied together with hemp rope, both hands covered in pitch, and this having been lit, taken by the master of the pillory from the market square in the town of Żytomierz through the town up to the gallows. There they were to be flayed alive, then quartered, their heads stuck on stakes, the quarters hung up. Six were sentenced to quartering, while one—since he joined the holy Catholic faith along with his wife and children at the last moment—was given a lighter sentence, to merely be beheaded. The remainder were acquitted. The successors of those sentenced to death were required to pay a fine to the victim's father of 1,000 Polish zlotys under penalty of eternal banishment.

Of the initial seven, one managed to escape, and a second accepted conversion and was, along with the one sentenced to beheading, removed by me from death.

As for the rest, their sentence was executed justly. Three of the guilty, hardened in their evil, were quartered, while three who had converted had their punishment commuted to beheading, and their bodies I myself took with many of the clergy to the Catholic cemetery.

On the second day I performed the baptism of thirteen Jews and Jewesses, while for the tortured child I had an epitupticum prepared, and the sacred body of that innocent martyr I had buried on church grounds with great solemnity.

Ista scienda satis, terrible, yet in all respects absolutely necessary in order to punish the perpetrators of such a shameful act. I trust Your Excellency will find in these clarifications everything he wished to know, and that it will allay the unease expressed in his letter that we have done something here that would go against the Church, Our Holy Mother.

## Zelik

The one who escaped simply jumped off the cart that was taking those under arrest, all tied up, to be tortured. It turned out to be easy, since they were not securely tied. The fate of the fourteen prisoners, including two women, was already sealed, since they were considered essentially dead already, and it occurred to no one that one might try to escape. The cart, convoyed by a troop of men on horseback, went into the woods just outside Żytomierz for a mile. And it was there that Zelik ran. Somehow he worked his hands out of their tether, waited for the right moment, and when they got closest to the thicket, in one jump he was out of the cart and gone into the woods. The other prisoners just sat quietly with their heads bowed, as if celebrating their own impending deaths, and the guards did not immediately realize what had happened.

Zelik's father, the man who loaned money to Sołtyk, shut his eyes and started praying. Zelik, when his feet had touched the undergrowth, looked back and made sure to remember what he saw: an old man hunched over, an old married couple huddled together, their shoulders touching, a young girl, his father's two neighbors with their white beards contrasting with the black of their overcoats, the black-and-white splotch of a tallit. Only his father gazed back at him, calmly, as if he had known everything all along.

Now Zelik travels. He does so only by night. By day he sleeps; he lies down at dawn, when the birds make the most noise, and he gets up at dusk. He walks and walks, never on a road, but always next to one, in the thicket, trying to bypass open tracts of land. And if he must pass through an exposed area, he tries to make it at least one where crops are growing, for not everything has been harvested just yet. On his journey he scarcely eats—once in a while an apple, a bitter wild pear—but he does not experience hunger. He is still shaking, as much from terror as from anger or outrage; his hands keep shaking, and his stomach convulses, and his intestines seize up, and sometimes he vomits bile, spitting afterward for a long time in disgust. He's had a couple of very bright nights on account of a full moon that shone, seemingly pleased with itself. Then he saw in the distance a pack of wolves, heard their howling. A herd of roe deer watched him—surprised, they followed him calmly with their eyes. He was also spotted by some old man who was wandering, blind in one eye, shaggy and filthy; the old man was deeply afraid of him, kept crossing himself and vanished fast into some bushes. From afar, Zelik observed a small group of escaped serfs who were trying to cross the river into Turkey—he watched as men on horseback rode up, caught them, and tied them up like cattle.

The next night it begins to rain, and the clouds cover the moon. Zelik manages to cross the river. The whole next day he tries to dry out his clothes. Frozen, weak, he thinks constantly about one thing. How could it be that the gentleman for whom he managed the forest's accounts—a decent man, as far as he could tell—turned out to be evil? Why would he testify to a lie before the court? How was it possible that he lied under oath, and not about money or business, but on this, when people's lives were at stake? Zelik cannot understand it; the same images replay over and over before his eyes: arrested, dragged out of their houses along with others, with his old, deaf father, who didn't understand at first what was happening. And then that horrific pain that governs the body and rules the mind; pain, the emperor of this world. And then the tumbrel, taking them from the cells to the torture chamber, through the town, where people spit on them—spit on the wounded and destroyed.

After a month or so, Zelik makes it to Jassy, where he seeks out some friends of his mother's. They take him in, knowing what has happened; he spends some time there recovering. He has trouble sleeping, is afraid to shut his eyes; in sleep, when he does finally fall—as if slipping down the clay shores of a morass, charging into water—he sees his father's body, covered in sludge, unburied, terrible. By night he is gnawed by the fear that death is lying in wait for him in the darkness and might snatch him up again—there, in the darkness, is death's beat; there are the barracks of its armies. Since he escaped in such a banal way, since it didn't even notice him gone from the heap of people it already owned, it will have designs on him forever.

That is why Zelik can't be stopped now. Now he's heading south, on foot, like a pilgrim. Along the way he knocks on the doors of Jewish households where he spends night after night. Over dinners he tells his story, and people pass him along from home to home, from town to town, like brittle, fragile goods. Soon the news precedes him—they know his story and know where he is going; he is enveloped in a kind of reverence and care. Each helps him as he can. He rests on the Shabbat. One day each week he writes letters—to his family, to the Jewish councils, to the rabbis, to the Council of Four Lands. To Jews and Christians. To the Polish king. To the pope. He goes through many pairs of shoes and uses up about a quart of ink before he makes it to Rome. And by some miracle, as though greater forces really are looking out for him, the day after he arrives in Rome, he finds himself standing face-to-face with the pope.

RUSSIA RUBRA,
PODOLIA,
VOLHYNIA ET
UKRAINA.

P. 113.

# II.

## *The Book of*
# SAND

| Super *terra* funt | Na ziemi fą | terra, f. 1. ziemia. |
|---|---|---|
| alti *montes*, 1 | wyfokie gory, 1 | altus, a, um, wyfoki, a, e. mons, m. 3. gora. |
| profundæ *valles*, 2 | głębokie doliny, 2 | profundus, a, um, głębo- ki, a, e. vallis, f. 3. dolina. |
| elevati *colles*, 3 | wyniosłe pagorki, 3 | elevatus, a. um, wyniosły, a, e. collis, m. 3. pagorek. |
| cavæ *fpeluncæ*, 4 | wklęsłe iafkinie, 4 | cavus, a, um, wklęsły, a,e. fpelunca, f. 1. iafkinia. |
| plani *campi*, 5 | rowne pola, 5 | planus, a, um, rowny, a. e. campus, m. 2. pole. |
| opácæ *fylvæ* 6 | ciemne lafy. 6 | opacus, a,um, ciemny,a,e. fylva, f. 1. las. |

IX.

## 5.

# Of how the world was born of God's exhaustion

Every now and then, God wearies of his own luminous silence, and infinity starts to make him a little bit sick. Then, like an enormous, omnisensitive oyster, his body—so naked and delicate—feels the slightest tremble in the particles of light, scrunches up inside itself, leaving just enough space for the emergence—at once and out of nowhere—of a world. The world comes quick, though at first it resembles mold, delicate and pale, but soon it grows, and individual fibers connect, creating a powerful surrounding tissue. Then it hardens; then it starts to take on colors. This is accompanied by a low, barely audible sound, a gloomy vibration that makes the anxious atoms quake. And it is from this motion that particles come into being, and then grains of sand and drops of water, which divide the world in two.

We find ourselves now on the side of sand.

We see, through Yente's eyes, a low horizon and an enormous sky, gold and orange. Great bulbous cumulus clouds flow westward, unaware that soon they'll drop into the abyss. The desert is red, and even the most diminutive pebbles cast long and desperate shadows, with which they try to dig into solid matter and cling on.

Horse and donkey hooves barely leave traces, gliding over the stones, kicking up just a little dust that immediately settles, covering whatever little furrows arise. The animals go slowly, heads bowed, exhausted from long days of journeying, as if in a trance. Their backs have grown accustomed to the weights placed on them every morning, after an overnight stop. Only the donkeys raise a ruckus, shattering the dawn with their squall of suffering and unbearable confusion, waking people up. But now even those born rebels have gone silent, hoping to stop for the night somewhere soon.

People move among them, slender against the backdrop of the animals' shapes, which are rounded, deformed by their loads. Like clock hands that have freed themselves from faces, independently now they mark a stray, chaotic time no clockmaker will ever be able to quell. Their shadows, long and sharp, jab the desert, vex the falling night.

Many of them are dressed in long, light-colored coats, wearing turbans on their heads that were once green, but which the sun has faded. Others are hidden under the big brims of their hats; their countenances differ little from the shadows cast by stones.

This is a caravan that set out a few days ago from Smyrna, heading north through Constantinople, and then through Bucharest. Along the way, it will splinter, and others will join in. Some of the merchants will break off in just a few days, in Stamboul; they will be traveling through Salonika and Sofia to Greece and Macedonia, while others will continue all the way to Bucharest, some even to the very end, along the Prut to the Polish border, which they'll cross, besting the shallow Dniester.

Every time this caravan stops for the night, they must remove the goods they are transporting from the backs of the animals and check those that lie carefully packed inside carts. Some of them are fragile, like the batch of chibouks, long-stemmed Turkish pipes, each individually wrapped in tow and also tightly bound in linen. There is also some Turkish weaponry and a parade harness; there are ornate woven carpets and the woven belts with which the noblemen of Poland tie their long żupans.

Then there are dried fruits and other delicacies in wooden boxes, protected from the sun, assorted spices, and even lemons and oranges, packed unripe so that they might last the journey.

There is an Armenian among them, a certain Jakubowicz, who joined the caravan at the last minute, transporting luxury goods in a separate carriage: the finest carpets, Turkish kilims. Now he frets over these wares, flies into a rage at the drop of a hat. He had been on the verge of getting on a ship to take everything from Smyrna to Salonika in just two days, but sea trade is dangerous now—one could be taken into slavery, the stories go around whenever the caravan stops to rest around a fire.

Nahman Samuel ben Levi of Busk has just sat down with a slender box placed on his knees. Nahman is transporting tobacco tightly packed in hard packets. Not a lot of it, but he's still expecting to make a sizable profit, since he bought the tobacco cheap, and it's of good quality. He also has on him, in specially sewn pockets, other small but valuable things: beautiful stones, mostly turquoise, as well as several sticks of highly compressed resin that resembles tar. This can be added to a pipe and smoked— Mordechai's favorite.

They spent many days readying the caravan, while at the same time going around to all the different offices to get, for a sizable baksheesh, a firman—an order to the Turkish authorities to allow the caravan to pass.

That's why Nahman is so tired, and why it's so hard for him to shake off his exhaustion. The thing that helps him most is the sight of the stony desert. Now he goes out beyond the camp and sits there, at some remove from all the chatter. The sun has gotten so low that the long dark shadows cast ahead by the stones look like earthly comets, the opposites of those on high, these made of shade instead of light. Nahman, who sees signs wherever he looks, wonders what kind of future is portended by these lowly bodies, what fortune they are trying to tell. And as the desert is the only place on earth where time spins around, loops back then leaps ahead like some fat locust, select pairs of eyes might be able to get a glimpse into the future here. This is in fact how Yente sees Nahman now, at a time when he has aged, is frail and hobbled. He sits before a little window that doesn't let in much light, as cold flows from the thick stone walls. The hand that holds his pen visibly trembles. In the little hourglass that stands next to his inkwell, the last few grains of sand trickle down: his end is near now, but Nahman is still writing.

The truth is, he can't stop himself. It's like an itch that goes away only when he begins to scratch out the chaos of his thoughts into sentences. The pen's noise soothes him. The trace it leaves on a piece of paper brings him pleasure, like eating nothing but sweet dates, like holding lokum on his tongue. And soon everything falls into place. Because Nahman has always had the sense that he's a part of something bigger, something unprecedented and unique. That not only has nothing like this ever happened before, but also that it never will—never can—again. And that he is the one who must write it all down for all those who've not been born yet, because they're going to want to know.

He always has his writing gear on hand: that shallow wooden case, rather ordinary to look at, but it holds quality paper, a bottle of ink, a box of sand with a lid, a supply of quills, and a knife to sharpen them. Nahman doesn't need much: he sits on the ground, opens up his case to turn it into a low Turkish table, and just like that he's ready to start writing.

Ever since he started keeping company with Jacob, however, he has met with displeased, reproachful looks. Jacob doesn't like the scratching of the pen. Once he glanced over Nahman's shoulder. It's a good thing Nahman happened to be just balancing accounts at the time, since Jacob has insisted that his words not be recorded. Nahman had to assure him he would not do that. Yet the issue still weighs on him. Why not?

"I don't get it," he said to Jacob once. "Don't we sing: 'Give me speech, give me a tongue and the words to tell the truth about You'? And that's in *Hemdat Yamim*."

But Jacob scolded him:

"Don't be such a fool. If a person wants to storm a fortress, he won't get in by talking. Words come and go. A person's got to have an army. We, too, must act, and not just speak. Did our forefathers not chatter, not pore over written words enough? What did all that talking do for them? What came of it? It's better to see with your eyes than write down a bunch of words. What do we want some sage for? If I catch you writing, I'll have to knock some sense into you with my fist."

But Nahman knows what he's doing. His primary task is *The Life of His Holiness Sabbatai Tzvi* (of blessed memory). But this he's drawing up for order's sake, that's all, just laying out the facts, both the well-known ones and the lesser-known ones; a few he embellishes a bit, but of course that's not a sin—rather a service, as they'll be easier to remember this way. Underneath, however, at the very bottom of the case, he also has another little bundle—sheets of paper hand-bound with thick twine. Scraps. These he writes in secret. From time to time he breaks off, burdened by the notion that whoever reads this work will still need to know the identity of the person who wrote it. There is always a hand behind the letters, always a face that emerges from the sentences on the page. After all, even reading the Torah, one immediately feels some other pres-

ence, a great presence whose true name cannot be contained in any—even gilded, even weighted—letter. And yet the Torah and the world entire are composed of God's names. Every word is his name, every thing. The Torah is woven from God's names like a fabric, like a great arigah, although as is written in the Book of Job: "No mortal knows its order." No one knows which is the thread and which the warp, nor can anyone discern the pattern on the right or its relation to the pattern on the left.

The sage Kabbalist Rabbi Eleazar realized long ago that parts of the Torah had been given to us out of order. For if they had been in their proper order, everyone would have instantly become immortal, would have been able to revive the dead, work miracles. Which was why—to maintain the order of this world—the pieces had been put in disarray. Do not ask by whom. The time for that has not yet arrived. Only the Holy One will be able to put them in order.

Nahman knows that behind his *Life of His Holiness Sabbatai Tzvi*, in the bundle of those other pages sewn up with twine, he himself, Nahman Samuel ben Levi of Busk, can be seen. And he pictures his own image:

small in stature, ordinary. Always on the road. He documents himself.
He calls those notes "scraps," for they are what remains after other, more
important work. Crumbs—such is the stuff of life. His writing on the lid
of the case set up on his lap, in the dust and discomfort of travel, is in
essence tikkun, the repair of the world, mending the holes in its fabric so
filled with overlapping patterns, squiggles, tangles, trails. This is how to
view this strange pursuit of Nahman's. Some people heal others, some
build homes, others study books and rearrange the words in them to find
the proper meaning. Nahman writes.

### Scraps, or: A story born of travel's exhaustion, by Nahman Samuel ben Levi, Rabbi of Busk. Where I come from

I know I am no prophet, and I know there is no Holy Spirit in me.
I hold no sway over voices, nor can I see into the future. My origins
are lowly, and there is nothing that elevates me from the dust. I am
like so many others, and I belong to those whom the matzevot will
crush first. And yet, I also see my own advantages: I am suited
to business and to travel, I count quickly and have a gift for
languages. I am a born messenger.

When I was a child, my speech was like the patter of rain on the
wooden roofs of shoddy sukkoth, a dull drumming in which words
became indistinguishable. Furthermore, some force deep down
inside me was unable to complete a phrase or sentence started and
instead had to repeat it several times, hurriedly, rendering it almost
into gibberish. I was a stutterer. In despair, I realized my parents
and siblings could not understand me. Then my father boxed my
ears and hissed: "Speak slowly!" And so I had to try. I learned how
to go outside myself, in a sense, and take myself by the throat, so as
to restrain the rattle that would otherwise be found there. I finally
managed to break down the words into syllables, to water them
down like soup, like my mother would do with our barszcz on the
second day, so that there might be enough for everyone. But I was
also clever. Out of politeness, I would wait for others to finish
speaking, even though I often knew after just a few words what it
was they wished to say, and the way they would say it.

My father was the rabbi of Busk, just as I was to become later on, though I would not hold that position for long. He and my mother operated a tavern on the edge of the swamps, not much frequented, which meant we lived in poverty. Our family, both my mother's and my father's sides, had come to Podolia from the west, from Lublin, and before that from the Germanic lands, whence they were expelled, narrowly escaping with their lives. Of those times not many stories have survived, perhaps just the one that was the second thing to terrify me as a child, namely the story of the fire that consumed all of the books.

Of my childhood, however, I do not remember much. Mostly just my mother, whose side I never left, always clinging to her skirt, causing my father to be perennially angry with me, predicting I would become a mama's boy, a feygele, an effeminate weakling. I remember the plague of mosquitoes when I was just a few years old, when all the apertures of our home were stuffed with rags and clay, and our bodies, hands, and faces turned red from all the bites, as if we'd all come down with smallpox. My wounds were salved with fresh sage, but the traveling merchants who made the rounds of the villages also sold a foul-smelling miracle cure they had extracted from the earth somewhere in the vicinity of Drohobycz . . .

So begins Nahman's somewhat free-form manuscript. He likes to reread these opening pages. They make him feel the ground beneath him is more solid, or as if his feet have suddenly grown. Now he goes back to the camp, because he's gotten hungry, and joins in with the rest of the company. The Turkish guides and porters have just returned from their prayers and are horsing around, getting ready for dinner. Prior to eating, the Armenians shut their eyes and ceremoniously make the seal of the cross over their bodies. Nahman and the other Jews pray in a hurried way. They are all hungry. They will wait to pray for real until they get home. They sit in loose packs, every man with his wares, with his mule, but all can see each other well enough. As they start to sate their hunger, they begin to converse, and eventually to relax and make jokes. Darkness falls all of a sudden—in a moment it is night, and they have to light the oil lamps.

Once, one of the visitors who had come to hunt at Lord Jabłonowski's stopped in at the tavern, where it was mainly my mother who ran the operation. This guest was known to be a drunk and a brute. Since it was hot and stuffy, swamp gas hovering just above the ground, his daughter, a princess, desired to rest at once. Thus was our family thrown outside, to accommodate her, but I hid behind a stove and observed in a state of heightened emotion this scene: a beautiful lady, with footmen, ladies-in-waiting, and valets, entered the room. The pomp, the colors, the fashions, the beauty of these people made such a great impression upon me that my cheeks burned crimson, and soon my mother grew worried for my health. When those powerful people left, my mother whispered into my ear: "My little fool, in the world to come, the duksel will stoke the pezure for us," meaning that in the next life the princess would add fuel to our stoves.

On the one hand, it was a source of great delight to me that somewhere up there, where the plans for the world were drawn up day by day, there was a strictly enforced system of justice. On the other hand, I felt pity for us all, and in particular for that proud lady, so lovely and so out of reach. Did she know about this? Had someone told her? Did they explain to people in their church that this was how things were going to be? That everything would be reversed, and the servants would become the lords, and the lords the servants? But would this in fact be just and good?

Before they departed, the gentleman dragged my father out of the room by the beard, his guests guffawing at the joke. And as they were leaving, he told his soldiers to drink up all the Jewish vodka, a task they eagerly undertook, and plundering the tavern, they destroyed the whole property without so much as a thought.

Nahman has to get up. As soon as the sun sets, it gets terribly cold, not like it does in the city, where the heat lasts longer, held by the warmed walls, and where, by this time, your shirt would be sticking to your back. He picks up a lamp and puts on a fustian coat. The porters are playing dice; the game soon leads to argument. The sky is strewn with stars, and Nahman reflexively orients himself by them. To the south, he can see Smyrna—or Izmir, as Reb Mordke prefers to say—which they left the day before. It is a city characterized by the chaos of uneven buildings that look like stacks of blocks, by a seemingly infinite quantity of roofs interwoven with minarets' slim silhouettes and—every now and then—the domes of temples. And he can almost hear, from beyond the horizon, the muezzin's voice, insistent, plaintive in the darkness, and he is almost sure another voice will answer now, from within the caravan, and in an instant the air will be filled with Muslim prayer, which is supposed to be a hymn and an encomium, but which sounds more like complaint.

Nahman looks north and sees far, far away, in the folds of the swirling obscurity, a little village that extends over the swamps, under the low sky that reaches all the way down to the church tower. It seems completely devoid of color, as if made out of peat coated in a fine layer of ash.

When I was born, in 5481–1721 according to the Christian system—my father, a new rabbi, was just taking up his position, not yet realizing the nature of where he had chosen to settle down.

In Busk, the river Bug connects with the Pełtew. The city has always belonged to the king, not to the gentry, which is why life was easy enough for us there, though no doubt also why it was always being destroyed, now by the Cossacks, now by the Turks. If the sky is a mirror that reflects time, then an image of burning homes is ever o'erhanging Busk. The town would be totally destroyed and then rebuilt chaotically, in all directions, upon that swampy ground, water reigning supreme in Busk, so that whenever the spring thaws came, mud would creep onto the roads and cut off the town from the rest of the world, and the town's inhabitants, like all inhabitants of swamps and peat bogs, would simply sit in their damp shacks, gloomy, stagnant, almost as if they'd been covered in mold.

The Jews lived in little groups around a number of different neighborhoods, but the highest concentration of them was in the Old Town and in Lipiboki. They were often in the horse trade, taking the animals from town to town, to different fairs and marketplaces, and some had small tobacco shops, although most of these were truly the size of a doghouse. Some of them farmed, and there were a few craftsmen. For the most part people lived in squalor, miserable and superstitious, wishful for some salvation to come.

We watched the Ruthenian and Polish peasants around us, and we saw that they were always bent over the land, straightening up only come evening, when they would sit out on the little benches in front of their houses with a certain superiority about them. But it was better to be a Jew than a peasant. They would take stock of us as well, wondering where those Jewish women might be going on those Jewish carts, and why were they so noisy! Their women squinted, having been blinded by the sun all day as they gathered the ears of corn left behind by the harvest.

In the spring, when the riverside pastures turned green, hundreds or maybe even thousands of storks flew into Busk, strutting about regally, extending their necks with great dignity, so proud. This must have been the reason such a quantity of children followed: the peasants believed the storks brought them.

There is a stork on Busk's coat of arms, standing on one leg. So did we, the people of Busk, always stand on one leg, ready to set forth into the world, yet tethered to a lifelong lease, a single tenancy. All around us it was swampy and wet. We had the right to leave, officially, yet that right was unstable, murky as the dirty water.

Busk, like many little Podolian towns and much of the countryside, was inhabited almost entirely by us, by people who called each other "one of ours" and themselves "the true believers." We believed with a pure heart and very deeply that the Messiah had already come to Turkey and that when he'd gone, he'd left us a successor, and above all a path down which we were enjoined to go.

The more my father would read and discuss at the beth midrash, the more he, too, would incline toward such views. Within a year of coming to this place, having read all the texts pertaining to the teachings of Sabbatai Tzvi, he became fully convinced by them, his innate sensitivity and feeling for religion conducive to such a shift.

"Because how can it be?" he would say. "Why, if God so cherishes us, is there so much suffering in the world? You have only to go so far as the market square in Busk, and your legs will buckle under the weight of all that pain. If He cherishes us so, then why are we not healthy, why are we not preserved from hunger, and not only us—why not others, as well, so that we don't have to gaze upon illness and death?" He would hunch over as if wanting to demonstrate the weight of this hardship. And then he would fall back into his usual diatribe against rabbis and their rules, and he would start to lose his temper and gesticulate.

As a child, I would often see him on the little market square, in front of Shila's shop, standing around with others, boisterously gabbing. His small, plain figure appeared larger as he talked, for he spoke with fervor and conviction.

"From a single rule in the Torah, the Mishnah came up with dozens, and the Gemara many dozens more; meanwhile, in the later commentaries, there are as many rules as there are grains of sand. So tell me: How is it we're supposed to live?" he would say, so dramatically that passersby would pause.

Shila, who wasn't too concerned about business, being more interested in the company of gregarious men, would nod his head sadly, offering them his pipe: "Pretty soon nothing will be kosher any longer."

"It's hard to follow the requirements when you're starving," the others agreed, and sighed. Sighing, too, was a part of conversing. Most of them were simple merchants, but sometimes teachers from the yeshiva would come and add their insights to this daily market square lament. And then there were complaints about the hierarchies of the gentry and the hostility of the peasants, which could truly poison life, not to mention the price of flour, the weather, a bridge destroyed by a flood, fruit rotting on the trees from excess moisture.

And so, from childhood on, I, too, absorbed this eternal grudge against creation. Something is not right; there is some untruth afoot. Something must have been left out from what we learned in our yeshivas. Certain facts have been concealed from us, no doubt, and this is why we cannot assemble the world as we know it into a single whole. There has to be a secret somewhere to explain it all.

Since the time of my father's youth, everyone in Busk spoke in this way, and the name Sabbatai Tzvi came up often—and not in a whisper, either. It sounded to my child's ears like the gallop of horses bearing riders who were racing to our defense. These days, it would be wiser not to pronounce that name too loud.

## My youth

From the beginning, I wished to study the Scriptures, like many boys my age, but as an only child, I was also much attached to my mother and father. It was only when I turned sixteen that I realized I wanted to be in the service of some good cause and that I was also the kind of person who would never be satisfied with what was, always wanting what was not yet.

Which is why when I first started to hear talk of the great master the Baal Shem Tov, and of the fact that he was accepting students, I decided to join one of those little cohorts, and it was in this way that I left behind my native Busk. To the despair of my mother, I set out on my own for the east, to Międzybóż, a journey of some two hundred miles. On the first day I encountered a boy just a little bit older than myself who was setting out with the same purpose from Glinno and had already been on the road for three days. Leybko, as he was called, had just been married, though he could scarcely even grow a mustache, and he was so terrified of his own marriage that he convinced his wife and parents-in-law that before he began to earn a living, he needed first to commune with true holiness and have his fill of it, so that it might keep him through the years to come. Leybko came from a respected family of Glinno rabbis, and the fact that he wound up falling in with the Hassidim was a great misfortune as far as his family was concerned. Twice his father had come after him and begged him to return home.

Soon he and I were inseparable. We slept under a single tattered blanket and shared every bite of bread. I liked talking with him, he was a very sensitive person and thought differently from everyone else. We continued our conversations into the night under that ragged blanket, dissecting all the greatest mysteries.

And it was he, as a man already married, who introduced me to that other mystery that exists, between a woman and a man, which seemed to me then just as fascinating as all the questions of the tzimtzum.

The house was big and made of wood, with low ceilings. We slept side by side in a bed that was as wide as the whole room, cuddled together, skinny boys under filthy blankets amongst which we often found lice; we would cover our calves in mint leaves after we had been bitten. We ate little—bread, olives, a bit of turnip. Sometimes women brought in special treats for us, like raisins, but there were so many of us boys that we would get only a couple each, just enough that we did not forget the taste. On the other hand, we read voraciously, without pause, which left our eyes always bloodshot— this was how people came to recognize us. We looked like white rabbits. And in the evenings, when the Besht was able to dedicate some of his sacred time to us, we would hear him and his conversations with the other tzaddikim. Then I began to be interested in problems that my father had not been able to resolve for me in a convincing way. Like how could the world exist, since God is everywhere? Since God is everything in everything, then how could there be things other than God? And how could God have created the world out of nothing?

We know that every generation has thirty-six holy persons, and that it is thanks to them that God is able to maintain the existence of the world. Without a doubt, the Baal Shem Tov was one of them. Although the majority of holy men remain unrecognized, just living their ordinary lives as poor tavern keepers or cobblers, the Besht's virtues were so great it would have been impossible to keep them secret. He did not suffer from pride, and yet whenever he appeared, everyone somehow felt intimidated, which wearied him greatly. He carried his holiness like so much heavy luggage. He did not in any way resemble my father, who was always sad and angry. The Besht shone one color after the other. One minute he looked like an old sage, and he spoke in a serious tone with his eyes half closed; the next something came over him, and he would throw caution to the wind, let himself be at ease with us, joking and eliciting roars of laughter. He was always ready to do something unexpected, something shocking. In this way, he attracted attention to himself, and there he invariably kept it. To all of us, he was the center of the world.

No one here was drawn to lifeless, empty rabbinism. In that respect we were all alike, and my father would have approved of it. There were daily readings of the Zohar, eagerly anticipated, and many of the older men were Kabbalists with clouded eyes, who were incessantly discussing with one another the divine mysteries in the same way they might have talked about household practicalities such as how much they fed the chickens or how much hay they had left for the winter . . .

Once a Kabbalist asked the Besht if he believed the world to be an emanation of God. "Oh, yes," he said, "the whole world is God." Everyone wholeheartedly seconded this enthusiastic response. "And evil?" asked the Kabbalist, tricky and malicious. "Evil, too, is God," calmly retorted the Besht, and he was placid, but now a murmur passed through all those present, and soon the voices of other learned tzaddikim and various holy and distinguished men piped up. All conversations in this place provoked violent reactions—the overturning of chairs, sobs, cries, men pulling out their hair. Many times did I watch them debate this very question. And my blood boiled then, too, for indeed, how could it be? All this that surrounded us—how to account for it? Under what rubric were we to place hunger and bodily injury, and the slaughter of animals, and children felled by the plague and laid row upon row in the earth? In such instances, I was never able to shake the impression that ultimately, and irrefutably, God must not give a damn about us.

It sufficed for someone to point out that evil was not evil in itself, but rather only in the eyes of man, and a skirmish would break out at table; water would spill out from a broken jug and soak into the sawdust on the floor; one man would run out of the room in anger; another would have to be prevented from dealing a blow. Such was the power of the spoken word.

This was why the Besht always said to us: "The secret of evil is the only one God doesn't ask us to take on faith, but rather has us consider." And so I considered this all day and all night, for sometimes my lanky body that ceaselessly demanded food did not let me sleep, out of hunger. I considered that perhaps it was true that God recognized the mistake he had made, expecting the impossible from humankind. For he had wanted a person without sin. Therefore God had to make a choice. He could punish for sins, punish incessantly and become a kind of eternal oeconomist of our world, the manager who whips the peasants when they do not work as they are supposed to in their master's fields. Yet God might also, in his infinite wisdom, have been ready to bear human sinfulness, to leave a space for the weakness of man. God might have said to himself: I cannot have a person who is simultaneously free and fully subject to me. I cannot have a creature free from sin who would be at the same time a person. Better sinful humanity than a world without men.

Oh, we all agreed with that! We skinny boys in our ripped kapotas with sleeves that had always been too short, sitting on one side of the table, with the teachers on the other.

I spent several months with the Besht's holy men, and though it was hard and cold, I did feel that it was only now that my soul was catching up with my body, which had not only been growing but was becoming more manly. My legs were covered with black hair just as both my chest and my stomach got harder. And now my soul, too, chased after my body, becoming stronger. In addition to this, I had the impression that I was developing a new sense, the existence of which had stayed a secret to me until now.

Some people have a sense of unearthly things, just as others have an excellent sense of smell or hearing or taste. They can feel the subtle shifts in the great and complicated body of the world. And some of these have so honed that inner sight that they can even tell where a holy spark has fallen, notice its glow in the very place you would least expect it. The worse the place, the more fervently the spark gleams, flickers—and the warmer and purer is its light.

But there are also those who do not have this sense, who must simply trust the remaining five and entrust the world to them. And just as a man born blind knows not what light might be, or a deaf man music, or a man without a sense of smell the plenitude of flowers, so, too, can those without the sixth sense be merely bewildered by mystical souls, take them for madmen, for fanatics, for people who make up such things for reasons unknown.

That year, we disciples of the Besht (of blessed memory) began to be tormented by a strange ailment, as he himself called it with sadness and disquiet, though I did not know what he was thinking of.

Once during prayer one of the older boys burst into tears and could not be calmed. He was taken to see the holy one, and there the miserable wretch, sobbing, admitted that as he was praying the Shema he had pictured Jesus Christ and had thus directed the words of his prayer to him. As soon as that young man uttered those terrible words, everyone covered their ears with their hands and closed their eyes, so as not to give their senses access to such sacrilege. But the Besht merely shook his head sadly, and then he gave a simple explanation that brought us great relief: the boy had to pass near some sort of Christian shrine every day, and there he would see Christ. And when one looks at something a long time, or sees it often, that image gets inside the eyes and the mind, eating into them like lye. A person's mind needs sanctity, so it seeks it everywhere, like a plant shoot growing in a cave that rises toward any, even the slightest, light. That was a good explanation.

Leybko and I had a hidden passion: we would endeavor to listen to the words that surfaced in the murmur of prayers spoken on the other side of a partition, attuned to how the phrases ran together as the recitations picked up speed, mixing their meanings. The stranger the results of these games, the greater our enjoyment.

In Międzybóż all were as attentive to words as we were; thus the town itself seemed wayward, will I, nill I, insubstantial, as if in that contact with the word, matter hid its tail between its legs and cowered, ashamed. The muddy, cart-trod road appeared to go nowhere, while the little cottages set along it and the house of learning—the only one with a wide wooden porch of rotted, blackened wood, into which we bored holes with our fingers—seemed to belong to a dream.

I could also say that we bored holes into words, glimpsing thus their cavernous interiors. My first revelation concerned the similarity between two words.

Now, to create the world, God had to withdraw from Himself, leave within His body a blank space in which the world could take up residence. God vanished from this space. The word *disappear* comes from the root word *elem*, and the site of that disappearance is known as *olam: world*. Thus even the name for the world contains within it the story of God's departure. The world was able to arise solely because God was not in it. First there was something, and then that something was gone. That is the world. The world then, in its entirety, is lack.

## *Of the caravan, and how I met Reb Mordke*

When I returned home, in order to retain me, my family married me to sixteen-year-old Leah, an intelligent, trusting, sympathetic girl who would give me support until the day she died. Yet the marriage did not serve its purpose, for, having found a pretext in the form of a job working for Elisha Shorr, I set off on a business trip to Prague and Brünn.

It was on this journey that I met Mordechai ben Elias Margalit, known to everyone as Reb Mordke, may the memory of this righteous one be a blessing. He was another Besht to me, but he was also the only one, for I had him all to myself, while he, evidently feeling the same thing that I did, took me on as his student. I do not know what so attracted me to him—those who say that certain souls recognize each other instantly and cling to one another inexplicably are right. The truth is that I disconnected from the Shorrs and decided to remain with him, forgetting the family I had left in Podolia.

He was a disciple of the famous rabbi Jonatan Eibeschütz, who was in turn heir to the oldest teachings.

At first, Reb Mordke's theories seemed muddled to me. I had the impression that he was in a state of perpetual elation, which caused him to breathe shallowly, as if he feared taking in too much earthly air; only once filtered through a pipe did it allow him to live.

But the mind of the sage is unfathomable. Throughout our journey I was completely dependent upon him; he always knew when to set out and what road to take so that we would be transported in comfort and by good people, fed by some pilgrims or others. His ideas, at first glance, would appear preposterous, but when we gave in to them, it always turned out well for us.

We studied together by night, and by day I would work. Often enough, dawn would catch me at my books, and my eyes started to suppurate from the constant effort. The things Mordechai gave me to read were so incredible that my practical young Podolian mind bucked like an old workhorse someone suddenly decided to turn into a courser.

"My son, why do you reject that which you have not yet tried?" Mordechai asked, just when I had decided to go back to Busk to take care of my family.

So I said to myself then, very reasonably: He is right. Here I can only gain, not lose. So I will wait patiently until I find something good for myself in all this.

I gave in to him, renting out a little room behind a wooden partition, living modestly, spending my mornings working in trade and dedicating my evenings and my nights to my studies.

He taught me the permutations and combinations of letters, and also the mysticism of numbers and other "roads of the Sefer Yetzirah." I traveled down each of these roads for two weeks, until the form of each had been etched into my heart. In this way, he guided me through four whole months, at the end of which, suddenly, he told me to "erase" it all.

That evening, he packed my pipe with abundant herbs and gave me a very old prayer, the author of which cannot now be known, and which soon became the expression of my own voice. It went like this:

> My soul
> will not let itself be locked in any prison,
> iron cage or cage made out of air.
> My soul wants to be like a ship in the sky,
> and the body's boundaries cannot hold it back.
> And no walls will ever imprison it:
> not those that have been built by human hands,
> nor the walls of politeness,
> nor the walls of civility
> or good manners.
> It will not be entrapped by pompous speeches,
> by kingdoms' borders,
> good breeding—anything.
> My soul flies over all of that
> with the greatest ease,
> it is above what is contained in words,
> and beyond what cannot even be contained in words.
> It is beyond pleasure and beyond fear.
> It exceeds what is lovely and lofty
> just as it does what is terrible and vile.
>
> Help me, merciful God, and keep life from wounding me.
> Give me the ability to speak, give me language and words,
> so that I might speak the truth
> of You.

## My return to Podolia, and a strange vision

Some time later I returned to Podolia, where, after my father's sudden death, I took up the position of rabbi of Busk. Leah was willing to receive me, and I felt a great deal of tenderness toward her for this. She knew how to orchestrate a plentiful and peaceful life. My little son grew and matured. Busy with my work and tending to my family, I put some distance between myself and the chaos of my journey, along with any notion of Kabbalah. The community was sizable and divided into "ours" and "those," and as a young and inexperienced rabbi, I had many activities and duties.

One winter night, however, I could not fall asleep and suddenly felt very strange. I had the overwhelming impression that everything around me was false, that it was artificial, as if the world had been painted by some skilled artist on canvases hung up all around. Or, to put it another way: as if everything around me had been made up, and by some miracle had taken the shape of reality.

Several times already, when I was working with Reb Mordke, I had had this impression—tormenting, fear-inspiring—but this time it was so acute that I began to be as afraid as I had been when I was a child. Suddenly I felt imprisoned, like someone cast into a dungeon where the air was just on the verge of running out.

I got up trembling, added fuel to the stove, and went to the table, where I laid out the books given to me by Reb Mordke. Harking back to what he had been teaching me, I undertook to link the letters I beheld and to meditate upon them in the philosophical method of my master. I thought this might occupy my mind, and that in this way, the fear would pass. And I spent the time thus until morning, when I set about performing my usual tasks. The next night I did the same thing, until three in the morning. Leah, worried about my strange behavior, got up with me, carefully freeing herself from the little hands of our slumbering son and coming to look over my shoulder to see what I was doing. I could see the disapproval in her face, but it did not dissuade me. As a very pious woman, she did not recognize any Kabbalist teachings, and was suspicious, too, about our righteous Sabbatian rituals.

By the third weird night, I was so tired that at around midnight I dozed off a little, pen and paper in my lap. When I came to, I saw that the candle was spluttering out, so I got up to take another. But I saw that the light did not dim even when the candle was extinguished! In astonishment, I realized that it was *me* shining, that the glow that filled the room was coming from within me. I said out loud to myself: "Is this possible?" But of course I heard no response. I slapped my own face, pinched my cheek, but it altered nothing. So I sat like that until morning, my hands down, my head empty—and I was shining! Until at dawn the light waned, then finally disappeared.

That night I saw the world in a completely different way than I had ever seen it before, illuminated by a pale gray sun, small, miserable, and crippled. Darkness was emerging out of every nook and cranny. Wars and plagues were raging the whole world over, rivers overflowing their banks as the earth quaked. Each and every human seemed like such a brittle being, like the merest eyelash or speck of pollen. I understood then that human life is made of suffering, that suffering is the true substance of the world. Every single thing was screaming in pain. And then I saw further into the future, when the world had changed, the forests had vanished and in their places cities grew, and all sorts of other things were happening I could not understand, could not even conceive of, for they exceeded my capacity. This overwhelmed me to such a degree that I fell with a great clatter to the ground, and—at least so it seemed to me—I glimpsed then the essence of salvation. Here my wife came in and cried for help.

### On an expedition with Mordechai to Smyrna, due to a dream of goat droppings

It was as if my master Mordechai already knew about everything. A few days later he appeared out of the blue in Busk because he had had a strange dream. He had dreamed that in front of the synagogue in Lwów he saw the Jacob of the Bible handing out goat droppings to passersby. Most of those who received these gifts were offended or burst into raucous laughter, but those who accepted the gift and swallowed it respectfully began to shine from within like lanterns. Thus in this vision, Mordechai, too, held out his hand to receive the gift.

When, delighted by his arrival, I told him about my own incredible experience with the light, he listened to me attentively, and in his eyes I detected pride and tenderness. "You are just at the beginning of the road now. If you were to travel farther down it, you would see the world around us now is already ending, and that is why you see it as if it were untrue, and you detect not the light from the outside, which is false and illusory, but rather the light that is internal, that comes from God's own scattered sparks, which the Messiah is to regather."

Mordechai decided I had been chosen for his mission.

"The Messiah is coming now," he said to me, leaning in to my ear until his lips touched my auricle. "He is in Smyrna."

At the time, I didn't understand what he meant, but I knew that Sabbatai (of blessed memory) was born in Smyrna, so it was of him that I thought, even though he had long since passed. Mordechai suggested we go south together, uniting business and our search for the truth.

In Lwów, Grzegorz Nikorowicz, an Armenian, operated a Turkish trade—he mostly imported belts from Turkey, but he also dealt in carpets and rugs, Turkish balsam and weaponry. He had settled in Stamboul, to keep an eye on his business from there, and every so often his caravans with their valuable goods would set out for the north, then head back to the south. Anybody could join in with them, not only Christians—anyone who demonstrated goodwill and had enough money to chip in to pay the caravan's leader and the armed guards. You could carry goods from Poland—wax, tallow, honey, sometimes amber, although that did not sell as well as it once did—and you had to have in addition enough to sustain you on the road, and once you got there, to invest in goods to take back with you, in order to earn something off the whole expedition.

I borrowed a modest sum, to which Mordechai added some of his savings. We had, therefore, a little capital, and we set out gladly on our journey. That was the spring of 1749.

Mordechai ben Elias Margalit, Reb Mordke, was already a mature man by then. Infinitely patient, he was never in a hurry, and I had never met anyone with as much kindness and understanding toward the world. I often served as a pair of eyes for him for reading, since he could no longer see the smaller letters. He listened to everything attentively, and his memory was so good that he could repeat it all without error. He was still a very able man and quite strong, and I grumbled from fatigue on the road far more frequently than he.

Our caravan was joined by all and sundry, anybody at all who
wanted to make it to Turkey and back in one piece—Armenians and
Poles, Wallachians and Turks going home from Poland, often even
Jews from Germany. All of them would eventually scatter along the
way, to be replaced by others.

The trail led from Lwów to Czernowitz, then to Jassy along the
Prut and finally to Bucharest, where we made a longer stop. We
determined to break off from the caravan, and from there we
unhurriedly went where God would lead us.

During our stops, Mordechai would add to the tobacco we
smoked in our pipes a tiny lump of resin, and this made our
thoughts rise high and reach far, made everything appear filled with
some hidden sense, with deep meanings. I would become
motionless, my hand slightly raised, and remain like that for hours
in ecstasy. Even the most minimal movement of my head revealed
great mysteries. Every blade of grass belonged to this deep system of
meanings, an indispensable aspect of the vastness of this world,
built intelligently and perfectly, the tiniest thing connected with the
greatest.

By day we went around the little streets of the towns we passed
through, going up and down steps, viewing the goods on display.
We looked closely at young girls and boys—not for our own pleasure,
but rather because we also worked as matchmakers for such youths.
In Nikopol, for example, we would say that in Ruse there was a
young man, kind and well-educated, by the name of—let's say—
Shlomo, whose parents were seeking for him a nice wife with a
dowry. In Craiova we would say that in Bucharest there was a nice
girl, a good girl, without much of a dowry, but so pretty you had to
squint to even look at her, and that girl was Sara, daughter of the
cattle merchant Abraham. We carried such information as ants
transport their bits of leaves and sticks until an anthill arises from
the earth. If it came to a wedding, we would be invited, and for our
matchmaking we would earn a grosz or two as well as being able to
eat and drink our fill. We would always immerse ourselves in the
mikvah seventy-two times, as many as there are letters in God's
name. Afterward we could afford the juice of pomegranates
squeezed before our very eyes, lamb shashliks and good wine. We
had bigger business planned that would ensure the comfort of our
families and allow us to dedicate ourselves to studying our books.

We slept with the horses in stables, on the ground, in the straw,
but once the warm and fragrant air of the south had enveloped us,

we slept on riverbanks, beneath the trees, in the pleasant company
of pack animals, holding on tightly to the sides of our coats, for we
kept what was most valuable to us stitched inside. The odor of dirty
water, silt, and rotting fish would somehow become enjoyable after
a while as Mordechai discoursed upon it in ever greater depth,
hoping to convince me that that mixture was the true smell of the
world. In the evenings, we would talk in hushed voices, so in tune
with one another that no sooner had either of us started than the
other already grasped his point. While he would tell me about
Sabbatai and the complex pathways along which salvation makes its
way to us, I would tell him about the Besht, trusting that it would
be possible to unite the wisdom of those two good men, though this
did not turn out to be the case. Again and again we argued the
merits of each. I said that the Besht felt that Sabbatai had the spark
of holiness, but that Samael had quickly captured it, and in so
doing, had taken Sabbatai as well. Reb Mordke would wave his
hands then, as if he wanted to drive those terrible words away. I
also told him what I had heard at the Besht's from someone's lips—
that apparently Sabbatai had gone once to the Besht and asked if he
would repair him, for he felt himself to be a deeply unworthy
sinner. Such a rectification, or tikkun, consisted in the holy man
joining with the sinner's soul, step by step, passing through all
three of the soul's different forms. First the nefesh of the holy
one—his animal spirit—connected with the sinner's nefesh, and
then, when it became possible, ruah—the feelings and will of the
holy one—joined with the sinner's ruah, so that in the end, the holy
one's neshama—that divine aspect we all carry within ourselves—
could join with the sinner's neshama. And when this happened, the
Besht could feel how much sin and darkness was in this man called
Sabbatai, and he pushed him of necessity away from himself, so that
Sabbatai fell down all the way to the bottom of She'ol.

Reb Mordke didn't like that story. "This Besht of yours
understood nothing. The key is in Isaiah," he said, and I nodded,
for I, too, knew that famous verse from the Book of Isaiah, 53:9,
that the Messiah's grave was placed amongst the wicked. That the
Messiah must come from the lowest spheres, that he must be sinful
and mortal. And one more definition soon came to Reb Mordke's
mind, and that was the sixtieth tikkun in the Tikkunei haZohar:
"The Messiah will be internally good, but he will be clothed in
evil." He explained that these words applied to Sabbatai Tzvi, who,
under pressure from the sultan, gave up the Jewish faith and

converted to Islam. And so, smoking, observing the people we met and having conversations, we made it all the way to Smyrna, and there, during the hot Smyrna nights, I took in that strange knowledge, kept in secret, that prayer and meditation alone cannot save the world, much though it may have been attempted. The Messiah's task is terrible—the Messiah is a sheep for the slaughter. He must enter into the very heart of the kingdom of shells, into darkness, and he must carry out the liberation of the holy sparks from that darkness. The Messiah must descend into the abyss of every type of evil and destroy it from within. And he must go in as if he belonged, a sinner among others who will not arouse the suspicions of the forces of evil around him, so as to become the powder that will blow up the fortress from inside.

I was young then, and although I had an awareness of suffering and pain from what I had already glimpsed of life, I still trusted the world to be good and humane. I enjoyed the cool, fresh early mornings and all the things I had to do. I enjoyed the bright colors of the bazaars where we sold our silly wares. I relished the beauty of women, their cavernous black eyes and their lids lined in black, and the delicacy of boys, their nimble, slender bodies—yes, that could make my head spin. I enjoyed dates laid out to dry, their sweetness, and the veins in turquoise, which I found touching, and all the colors of the rainbow in the spices at the bazaar.

"Do not be fooled by all that gilding. Scratch it with your fingernail, and you will see what's underneath," said Reb Mordke, and he dragged me into filthy courtyards, where he began to show me a completely different world. Ulcerous, ill women begging outside the bazaar, male prostitutes dressed as women, ruined by hashish and sick and poor, crumbling mud huts on the city's edges, packs of mangy dogs scrounging through the trash, in between the bodies of their companions, starved to death. It was a world of unthinkable cruelty and evil, in which everything raced toward its own destruction, toward death and decay.

"The world doesn't come from a kind or caring God," Reb Mordke told me, when he decided I had seen enough. "God created all of this by accident, and then he was gone. That is the great mystery. The Messiah will come quietly when the world is submerged in the greatest darkness and the greatest misery, in evil and in suffering. He will be treated like a criminal. So the prophets have foretold."

That evening, at the edge of the enormous trash heap just outside the town, Reb Mordke took out of his bag a tome covered in thick broadcloth to conceal its true identity, to make it inconspicuous so that no one would covet and steal it. I knew what book it was, but Mordechai had never offered to let me read it with him, and I hadn't had the courage to ask, although I was dying of curiosity. I figured the time would come when he would offer it to me of his own accord. And that is what happened. I felt the weight of that moment, a chill ran through me, and my hair stood on end as I took the book and stepped inside the circle of light. Overwhelmed, I began to read out loud.

It was the treatise *VaAvo haYom el haAyin,* or *And I Came this Day unto the Fountain,* written by Eibeschütz, my Reb Mordke's master. And I felt then that I had become the next link in a long chain of the initiated that extends across the generations, that begins further back even than Sabbatai, than Abulafia, than Simon bar Yochai, than, than . . . and on, all the way to the dawn of time, and that this chain, though it sometimes gets lost in the mire, though it gets grown over with grass and covered up in the rubble strewn by wars, nonetheless persists and grows into the future.

*6.*

## Of a strange wedding guest
## in white stockings and sandals

The stranger who enters the room must bow his head to do so, so that the first thing everyone notices about him isn't his face but his clothing. He is wearing a light-colored coat of a sort that isn't common in Poland, sullied, and on his feet are muddy white stockings and sandals. A bag made of colorful leather strips hangs from his arm. At the sight of him, the conversation dies down; only when he raises his head and the lamplight creeps over his face does the general cry come:

"Nahman! It's our Nahman!"

Not everyone knows him, so there are whispers:

"What Nahman, who's Nahman? From where? The rabbi of Busk?"

They immediately lead him to Elisha, to where the elders are sitting— Rabbi Hirsh from Lanckoroń, Rabbi Moshe from Podhajce, the great Kabbalist, as well as Solomon Dobrushka from Prossnitz, and there the door shuts behind them.

The women spring into action. Hayah and her assistants prepare vodka, hot barszcz, and bread with goose lard. Hayah's younger sister readies a bowl of water for the traveler to be able to wash up. Only Hayah is permitted to enter the room where the men are. Now she watches Nahman as he carefully cleanses his hands. She sees a small, slender man accustomed to being hunched over, his face affable, the corners of his eyes tilting downward, as though he were eternally sad. He has long, silky chestnut hair and a flaxen-russet beard. His elongated face is still young, though wrinkles have settled in around the eyes—Nahman is always squinting. The lamplight turns his cheeks orange and red. Once he has sat down at the table, Nahman takes off his sandals, completely inadequate at this time of year with these Podolian spurts of foul weather, and now Hayah studies his big, bony feet in their light-colored, dirty socks. It strikes Hayah that these feet have traveled all the way from Salonika, Smyrna, and Stamboul, still in their coating of Macedonian and Wallachian dust, in order for good news to reach this place. Or perhaps it is bad news? It is not yet clear what to make of Nahman's arrival.

She glances furtively at her father, Elisha Shorr, curious as to what he might be about to say. But he has turned away, toward the wall, and is swaying slightly back and forth. Whatever news Nahman has brought to them is of such great weight that the elders have determined together that he must share it with everyone.

Hayah watches her father. She feels acutely the absence of her mother, who died last year. Old Shorr had wanted to remarry, but Hayah wouldn't allow it, and she never will. She doesn't want a stepmother. She holds her little daughter in her lap. She has crossed her legs, creating something like a little pony for the child. From under her ruffled skirts, beautiful red lace-up boots reach halfway up her calves. Their polished toes, neither pointed nor round, are eye-catching.

First Nahman hands Shorr the letter from Reb Mordke and from Isohar of Podhajce, which Shorr takes a long time to read in silence. They wait until he's done. The air gets thick, as if it's taking on a burden.

"And everything tells you that this is really the one?" Elisha Shorr asks Nahman, after what feels like an eternity.

Nahman assents. His head is spinning from exhaustion, and from the vodka he has drunk. He feels Hayah's gaze on him, sticky, wet—like a dog's tongue, you could say.

"Let him rest, all of you," says Old Shorr. He stands and gives Nahman a friendly pat on the shoulder.

Others come up, too, and touch the newcomer's shoulder, or his back.

A circle is formed as they place their hands on their companions' shoulders on either side. For a moment this circle closes, and in the middle of it, something seems to appear, a kind of presence—something odd. They stand this way, leaning in to the circle's center, their heads lowered, almost touching. Then someone takes the first step back. It is Elisha, and soon the rest of them move aside, exhilarated, with flushed faces; finally, someone gives Nahman tall boots with sheepskin uppers to warm his legs.

## Nahman's Tale: Jacob's first mention

The murmurs and the clamor slowly die down, but Nahman waits awhile, aware that he now has their full attention. He starts by taking a deep breath. This is followed by an absolute silence. The air he takes in and then releases from his lungs is from a different world—Nahman's breath rises like challah dough, golden, and the room begins to smell of almonds, to shimmer with the warmth of the sun at noon, to carry the aroma of a far-flung river—because this is the air of Nikopol, a Wallachian town in a distant country, and the river is the Danube, on the bank of which lies Nikopol.

The Danube is so wide that sometimes on foggy days you can't even see the other side. Over it looms a fortress with twenty-six towers and two great gates. The castle is replete with guards, their commander residing above the prison, where the debtors and the thieves are kept. At night, the guards beat drums and cry: "Allahu Akbar!" The area is rocky, dry in the summer, but in the shadows of people's homes grow figs and mulberries, and there are grapevines on the hills. The town lies on the southern bank of the river, and has some three thousand beautiful houses covered in tiled roofs or shingles. Most neighborhoods are Turkish, interspersed with a few Jewish and Christian quarters. Nikopol's market is always crowded, for it has as many as a thousand dazzling stalls. The craftsmen have their workshops in the well-built halls next door. Especially numerous are the tailors, who are famous for sewing every vesture, every żupan or shirt, though their finest works are their Circassian prayer robes. And how many nations are represented at this bazaar! Wallachians, Turks, Moldovans and Bulgarians, Jews and Armenians, and sometimes even merchants from Gdańsk.

The crowd gleams with its different colors, chatting in different languages, arraying astonishing goods for sale: fragrant spices, vivid carpets, brightly colored rugs, Turkish delicacies so sweet you'll grow dizzy with pleasure, dried dates and raisins of every sort, beautifully dyed leather slippers stitched with silver thread.

"Our people often have stalls there, or keep trading agents—a number of us are in fact quite familiar with that hallowed place." Nahman repositions himself in his seat and looks at Old Man Shorr, but Elisha's face is inscrutable, betraying not so much as a trace of a blink.

Nahman sighs again and is quiet, reining in everyone's impatience. All eyes appear to exhort him, to say, Go on, go on, man, because of course they know that the real story—the one they're all here for—hasn't gotten under way yet.

First Nahman tells them of the bride. When he speaks of her—of Hana, daughter of the great Tovah—he makes, without realizing it, several gentle gestures that lend a velvet softness to his words. Old Man Shorr's eyes fall halfway shut now, as if in a smile of satisfaction—for this is precisely how one ought to speak of young brides. Nahman's audience nods contentedly. The beauty, gentleness, and thoughtfulness of young women are what give humanity hope. Once more, too, at the mention of Hana's father's name there is a burst of happy smacking, so Nahman is quiet for another moment, to give his listeners time to take their full pleasure in all this. In how the world is filling out, coming together again. The tikkun has begun.

The wedding took place in Nikopol a few months earlier, in June. With Hana we are already familiar. Her father is Yehuda Tovah ha-Levi, the great hakham, whose writings have made it all the way here, to Rohatyn, and Elisha Shorr has them in his cabinet; he was studying them not long ago. Hana was Tovah's only daughter among many sons.

What this Jacob Leybowicz might have done to deserve her, however, remains unclear. Who is this person of whom Nahman speaks so glow-ingly? And why him? Jacob Leybowicz from Korolówka? No, Czerno-witz. So is he one of us? What are you talking about, he must be one of us, if Nahman's telling us of him. He's someone from here—someone remembers now he knew this Jacob's father, so wouldn't he be the grand-son of the same Yente who is in the process of dying in this very house? Everyone looks over at Israel from Korolówka and his wife, Sobla, but they're not sure what's about to be said yet, so for now they just sit tight—though Sobla's face does flush bright red.

"Yehuda Leyb from Czernowitz, that's this Jacob's father," says Elisha Shorr.

"He was the rabbi of Czernowitz!" blurts Moshe from Podhajce.

"Rabbi, shmabbi," grunts Yeruhim, who does business with the Shorrs. "He taught children how to write in yeshiva. Buchbinder, they called him."

"He's the brother of Moses Meir Kamenker," Shorr says gravely, and there is a hush, because this Moses Meir Kamenker is a hero—he smug-gled holy books into Germany for our brothers and sisters in faith, suffer-ing a curse in punishment.

Now it all comes back to them. They begin to talk over each other, saying how this Yehuda was a tenant first in Bereżanka and Czernowitz, in the service of the local lord, collecting taxes from the peasants. It seems the peasants even beat him once. And when he went and told on them, the lord ordered for them to be beaten to the point that one of them died from the blows. Then this Buchbinder had to depart the region, for the peasants would never have left him alone after that. The Jews turned against him, too, since he would openly read from the writings of Nathan of Gaza.

He was a strange fellow, unpredictable. Somebody remembers that after the curse was put on his brother, the rabbis turned on Leyb, ulti-mately forcing him to resign and move to Czernowitz in Wallachia, where under Turkish rule you could live in peace.

Malka, Shorr's sister, pitches in: "They were always drawn to the Turks, anyway, with their fear of the Cossacks."

Nahman realizes that the figure of the father is an unpopular one. The more they find out about him, the worse it will be for the son. So he determines to move on.

This makes sense: prophets never come from within. All prophets must come from elsewhere, must suddenly appear, seem strange, out of the ordinary. Be shrouded in mystery, like the one the goyim have, even, of the virgin birth. A prophet has to walk differently, talk differently. Ideally he hails from some unimaginable locale, source of exotic words and untasted dishes and unsmelled smells—myrrh, oranges, bananas.

And yet a prophet must also be one of our own. Let him have at least a drop of our blood, let him be a distant relative of somebody we know, even if perhaps we've forgotten what they look like. God never speaks through our neighbor, through the guy we're in a fight with about the well, or the one whose wife attracts us with her charms.

Nahman waits for them to finish.

"I, Nahman of Busk, was a groomsman at that wedding. The other groomsman was Reb Mordke of Lwów."

Into the minds of those assembled in those cramped quarters, in that low-ceilinged room, comes a thought that reassures them. Everyone is connected to everyone else. The world is simply the multiplication of this room in the Shorrs' Rohatyn home above the market square. Through the slits in the curtains and the haphazardly nailed door starlight seeps in, which means that even the stars are close acquaintances, that some forebear or cousin must certainly have had some close contact with them. Say one word in a room in Rohatyn, and soon it will be carried all around the world, on the paths and roads taken by commercial expeditions, with the help of the messengers who roam the earth incessantly, bearing letters and repeating gossip. Like Nahman ben Levi of Busk.

Nahman knows what to talk about now, giving every detail of the bride's garments, of the beauty of her twin brother, Hayim, the two as alike as drops of water. He describes the dishes served at table, and the musicians and their exotic instruments, never before seen here in the north. He describes the figs ripening on the trees, the stone house situated so that you can see the great Danube from it, and the vineyards, where clusters of grapes have already formed; soon the grapes will look like Lilith's nipples as she nursed.

The groom, Jacob Leybowicz, is muscular and tall, says Nahman; dressed after the Turkish fashion, he looks like a pasha. He's already spoken of as "wise Jacob" even though he's only thirty. He studied in Smyrna with Isohar of Podhajce (here once more the admiring smacks of the lips of his listeners). In spite of his youth he has already amassed a considerable fortune, trading silk and precious stones. His bride is fourteen years old. They make a handsome couple. During the wedding, the wind stops blowing.

"Then," says Nahman, and he pauses again, though he is in a hurry for this story to be told, "then Jacob's father-in-law went under the huppah and whispered something into Jacob's ear. Even if everyone had been perfectly silent, if the birds had stopped singing and the dogs had stopped barking, if all the carriages had come to a halt—even so, no one would have overheard the secret Tovah told to Jacob. Because it was the Raza deMehemenuta, the secret of our faith, although few are the men who are wise enough to hear it told. The secret is so powerful that they say your body starts to shake all over if you learn it. It can only be whispered into the ear of the person closest to you, and on top of that only so that no one can see, so that no one guesses either by reading the lips of the teller or by the changes in the listener's awestruck face. It can only be whispered into the ear of the chosen, who have sworn they will never repeat it to anyone lest a curse bringing illness or sudden death befall them.

"How can this great secret be contained in a single sentence?" Nahman anticipates the question. "Is it a simple assertion, or perhaps the opposite—a negation? Or perhaps it is a question?"

Whatever it is, he who learns this secret will forever be at peace and certain of his actions. From this point forward, the most complicated thing will seem simple. Perhaps it's something complex, because complexity is always closest to the truth, a sentence that acts as a cork that closes off the mind to thought while opening it to truth. Maybe the secret is a curse, a dozen syllables that seem to be without meaning, or a string of numbers, the numerical values of corresponding letters that reveal a completely different meaning: gematric perfection.

"It was in search of this secret that Hayim Malach was sent from Poland to Turkey many years ago," says Shorr.

"Did he bring it back?" asks Yeruhim skeptically.

A murmur goes around the room. Nahman's story is enticing, but it's hard for people to believe that what he's describing has to do with someone from around here. Holiness? From here? "Jacob Leybowicz" sounds like the name of every butcher. There's a furrier from Rohatyn with exactly the same name.

Late in the evening, when everyone's gone home, Old Man Shorr takes Nahman by the arm, and together they walk out in front of the store.

"We've got to get out of here," he says, gesturing toward the muddy Rohatyn market square and the dark, hurtling clouds, so low you can almost hear them tearing as they catch on the church tower. "We're not allowed to buy land, settle down permanently. They chase us off in all directions, and in every generation there's some disaster, some gezerah. Who are we, and what awaits us?"

They take a few steps away from each other, and in the darkness there is the sound of streams of urine striking the boards of the fence.

Nahman sees a little cottage, stooped beneath a cap of straw thatch, with tiny little windows, rotted boards; beyond it loom others with the same stoop, stuck together like the cells of a honeycomb. And he knows that there is a whole network of passages and walkways and nooks and crannies where carts of wood sit, waiting to be unloaded. And there are courtyards bordered by low fences, atop which during the day clay pots heat up in the sun. Beyond that lie passages that lead to other courtyards so small you can barely turn around in them, each faced with three doors that lead to three different homes. Higher up are attics linking the tops of these little homes, full of pigeons that mark out time with layers of droppings— living clocks. In gardens the size of an overcoat spread out on the ground cabbage leaves struggle to coil, potatoes swell, carrots cling to their beds. It would be wasteful to devote space to flowers other than hollyhocks, which grow straight up. Now, in December, their naked stalks seem to support the houses. Along the little streets the trash heap extends to the fences, guarded by cats and feral dogs. And so it goes through the whole village, along the streets, through the orchards and the bounds of the fields to the river, where the women busily rinse out all the filth of the settlement.

"We need someone who will support us in everything, someone who will sustain us. Not a rabbi, not a hakham, not a rich man, not a warrior. We need a strong man who looks like a weak man, someone with no fear. That man will be the one to get us out of here," says Elisha Shorr, smoothing down his heavy coat. "Do you know anybody like that?"

"Where?" says Nahman. "Where would we go? To the Land of Israel?"

Elisha turns around and starts back. Nahman catches a whiff of his scent for a second, tobacco not completely dried.

"Into the world." Elisha Shorr makes a gesture with his hand as if to indicate some area above them, out over the roofs of Rohatyn.

When they are back inside, Elisha Shorr says:

"Nahman, bring him here. This Jacob."


## Isohar's School, and who God really is: The next installment in the story of Nahman ben Levi of Busk

Smyrna knows it sins, deceives, cheats. In the narrow little streets, by day and by night, trade takes place; someone always has something to sell, someone always wants to buy something. Goods pass from hand to hand, fingers extending for coins that disappear into deep coat pockets, into the folds of wide trousers. Little bags, handbags, purses, boxes—everywhere coins sound, everyone hoping to make money on every transaction. On the stairs of the mosques sit people known as sarafs, who keep on their laps little tables with a groove along the side that serves to slide away coins already counted. Next to them stand sacks of silver and gold or the currency for which the client wishes to exchange their money. They must have every type of money that exists in the whole world, and they know the exchange rates by heart; no wise book, not even the best map, portrays the world so clearly as the profiles of rulers with their names minted into copper, silver, and gold. It is from here that they really rule, gazing sternly out at their subjects like pagan gods.

Here the little streets create a circuitous tangle in which a person not paying close attention to where they are going will easily get lost. The better-off have their stalls and shops on these streets, their storerooms extending deep into the buildings and even crossing into the apartments where the merchants keep their families and most valuable goods. The narrow streets are often roofed, which makes the city resemble a real labyrinth, in which many visitors have gone astray before finding themselves back in territory they have already explored. Almost nothing grows here; in places without a house or a temple, the earth is dry and rocky, covered in trash, rotting waste that dogs and birds dig through, battling each other over every bite.

Smyrna is filled with Jews from Poland who have come for charity—since they have known only poverty where they come from—or for business deals, whether smaller ones that can be counted in a couple of pieces of gold or big ones there aren't enough sacks for. They roam, they make inquiries, they strike their deals, and it does not occur to some of them to go back home. The Smyrna Jews look down on them, don't understand their language and communicate with them instead in Hebrew (if they can) or in Turkish. The new arrivals can be recognized by their warmer clothing, which is dirty, frayed at the hem, often in poor condition that reflects their having crossed a sizable swath of the world. Now this clothing is disheveled and undone in places—it's too hot for it.

Some of the wealthy Podolian merchants maintain agents here—to turn around the merchants' wares, lend and borrow money, issue guarantees of travel, and maintain the entire business in the proprietors' absence.

Many of them, most of them, are followers of Sabbatai Tzvi. They don't even hide it, and openly proclaim their Messiah without fear of persecution here in Turkey, since the sultan tolerates different religions as long as they do not get too intrusive. These Jews are already somewhat acclimated to their new home; they have even grown slightly Turkish in their aspects, and their demeanor is free. Some, less sure of themselves, still dress in the old Jewish way, and yet from their homespun Podolian

garments something foreign, something colorful, now protrudes—an ornate bag or a fashionably trimmed beard, or maybe Turkish shoes made
of kid leather. And just like that, faith manifests itself in clothing. But it
is also well known that many of those who still look like the truest Jews
are in the sway of Sabbatian ideas.

Nahman and Reb Mordke are friendly with all of them, because it's
easy to talk to them, and they see this great vibrant world in similar ways.
Recently they came across Nussen, who, like them, comes from Podolia,
and who navigates Smyrna better than any native.

One-eyed Nussen, the son of the saddler and harness-maker Aron of
Lwów, buys up delicate dyed kidskin with patterns embossed in it; he
packs up this leather and organizes its transport to the north. Some of it
he leaves in Bucharest, Vidin, Giurgiu, some of it he sends onward to
Poland. To Lwów he sends exactly enough to keep his sons' workshop in
business—they will turn the kidskin into book covers, wallets, purses.
Nussen is fidgety, agitated, and he speaks quickly, mixing several languages at once. In the rare moments when he smiles, he reveals even,
snow-white teeth—it is a very special sight, and his face becomes beautiful then. He knows everyone here. He deftly moves between stalls, down
the narrow streets, avoiding the carts and the donkeys. His one weakness
is women. He can't resist a single one, which means he's always getting
into trouble and is unable to save the money to ever go back home.

Thanks to Nussen, Reb Mordke and Nahman find Isohar of Podhajce. Nussen takes them both to him, proud to know the wise man
personally.

Isohar's school is a two-story building in a Turkish district, narrow
and tall. Inside the cool courtyard, a little orange tree grows, and past
that is a grove of old olive trees, in the shade of which vagrant dogs often
come to sit. They get chased out, stones thrown at them. They're all yellow, as if they all come from the same family, born of a single canine Eve.
They leave the shade reluctantly, regarding humans as eternal sources of
distress.

Inside, it's cool and gloomy. Isohar greets Reb Mordke heartily, his
chin trembling with emotion. The two old men, slightly hunched over,

hold on to each other's arms and circle, as if celebrating the dance of the white clouds that hang from their lips in the guise of beards. They step around each other, similar in appearance, though Isohar is smaller and paler—you can tell he rarely ventures into the sun.

The newcomers receive a room to sleep in, just big enough for two. Reb Mordke's renown gets conferred upon Nahman, and he is treated with great respect. At last he can get a full night's sleep on clean and comfortable linens.

The neophytes sleep on the ground downstairs, in a row, more or less like at the Besht's in Międzybóż. The kitchen is in the courtyard. Water is retrieved by means of giant jugs dipped into the Jewish well in the other courtyard.

In the study room, there is always such a clamor that it resembles a bazaar—except that here the business at hand is of another sort. It's never clear who is a teacher and who is a student. Learn from the young, the inexperienced, those who remain untarnished by books—that is Reb Mordke's counsel. Isohar takes it a step further—though he remains the axis of this sanctuary, and it is around him that everything turns, this beth midrash nonetheless works more like an anthill or a beehive, and if it is overseen by a queen, she can only be Wisdom. A young person has many freedoms here. He has the right and the obligation to ask questions; there are no stupid questions, and each must be considered properly.

The same discussions take place here as in Lwów or in Lublin, just the circumstances and the surroundings have changed—here it happens not in a damp hut filled with smoke, not in the beth midrash room on the floor covered in sawdust that smells of pine trees, but rather under the open sky, on warmed stones. In the evenings, the men get drowned out by cicadas, so that you have to raise your voice to speak clearly and be understood.

Isohar teaches that there are three paths toward spiritualization. The first is the broadest and the simplest. This path is followed, for example, by Muhammadan ascetics. They'll seize any possible ploy to kick out all natural forms—meaning all the images of the earthly world—from their souls. This is because such images interfere with the forms that are

properly spiritual—when such a form appears in the soul, it must be kept
separate and thus nurtured in the imagination until it occupies the entire
soul; in this way, we become capable of prophecy. For example, they will
ceaselessly repeat the name Allah, Allah, Allah, and so on, endlessly,
until that word occupies the whole of their minds—they call this "extinguishing."

The second is the philosophical path, and it has a sweet scent to our
reason. It consists in the student's acquiring knowledge in some field, for
example in mathematics, and then in others, until finally he reaches theology. Any subject he has penetrated and that his human reason has mastered will come to dominate him, while to him it will seem that he is an
expert in each of these disciplines. He'll begin to understand complicated
connections and be convinced that this is the result of a broadening and
deepening of his human knowledge. But he will not realize that it is the
letters grasped by his mind and imagination that are acting upon him in
this way, ordering his mind with their movements, opening the door to
inexpressible spiritualization.

The third path consists in Kabbalist shuffling, pronouncing and
counting of letters, which leads to true spirituality. This path is the
best, and besides, it also gives great pleasure, since by traveling it one can
commune with the very essence of creation and get to know who God
really is.

It isn't easy to calm down after these kinds of conversations, and once
he has smoked one last pipe with Reb Mordke, Nahman sees, just before
he falls asleep, strange images of hives of luminous bees or of shadowy
figures from which other figures emerge. Illusions. He can't sleep, and his
sleeplessness intensifies this heat he's never known before, to which people from the north, like him, have trouble growing accustomed. Nahman
sits many times by himself at night on the edge of the trash heap and
looks at the starry sky. The first thing every neophyte must understand is
that God, whatever he is, has nothing in common with humankind, and
that he remains so far away as to be completely inaccessible to the human
senses. The same is true of his intentions. At no point will people ever
learn what he is up to.

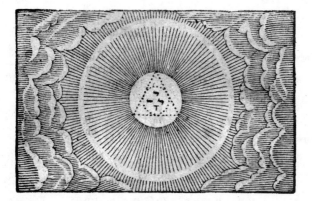

## Of Jacob the simpleton and taxes

Already as they were on their way here they heard of Jacob from fellow travelers, that he was a student of Isohar's who was famous amongst the Jews, though it was not yet clear exactly why. Was it his cleverness and his strange behavior, which broke every rule known to man? Or perhaps his wisdom, uncommon in such a young person? Apparently he considered himself to be a simpleton, and he had people call him that—am ha'aretz, simpleton, or, in his version, amuritz. There were rumors he was a freak. It was said that when he was around fifteen years old, back in Romania, he dropped by the inn where duty was collected from the sale of goods, and, sitting down at a table, ordered wine and food, took out some sort of paperwork, and demanded that both goods and duty be brought straight to him. He listed these meticulously and took the money for himself. He would have gone to jail had some wealthy woman not interceded on his behalf, putting the stunt down to youthful folly; under her protection, he was dealt with very mildly.

Everyone listens to this story and smiles approvingly, patting one another on the back. Reb Mordke likes it, too, but Nahman sees the man's behavior as improper, and to tell the truth, he is surprised that not only Reb Mordke, but also the others are chuckling contentedly.

"Why does this delight you all so much?" he asks, annoyed.

Reb Mordke stops laughing and glares at him.

"Why don't you think about what's good about that story," he says, and reaches calmly for his pipe.

To Nahman it is clear that this Jacob deceived people and took money from them that did not belong to him.

"Why are you on their side?" asks Reb Mordke.

"Because I also have to pay a head tax, although I've done nothing wrong. So I feel sorry for those people who lost what rightfully belonged to them. When the real collector comes, they'll have to pay all over again."

"And what is it you suppose they're paying for?"

"What do you mean?" Nahman is surprised by what his master is saying. "What do you mean, what for?" He has no words, so obvious is the answer to him.

"You pay for being Jewish. You live by the grace of the lords, the king. You pay your taxes, but when an injustice befalls you, no lord and no king is going to intercede on your behalf. Is it written somewhere that your life must cost money? That your year or your month has a price, and that every day of yours can be converted into gold?" says Reb Mordke, methodically filling his pipe.

This gives Nahman much more food for thought than the theological disputations. How did it happen that some have to pay while others collect? Where did it come from that certain people have such an amount of land they can't even traverse it all, while others have only a little plot, paying so much in rent they can't even afford a loaf of bread?

"It was given to them by their mothers and fathers," he says without conviction when, on the following day, they return to the conversation. He already knows where Reb Mordke's argumentation will head.

"And where did their parents get it?" asks the old man.

"From their parents?" says Nahman, but then he breaks off. He is starting to see how this whole conceptual machinery operates, so he goes on, becoming his own interlocutor. "Or they did favors for the king and got land in exchange for them. Or they purchased the land and now pass it down to their descendants—"

An ardent Nussen interrupts him mid-phrase:

"Seems to me land oughtn't to be sold or purchased. Just like water and air. Nor do people deal in fire. Those are things given to us by God, not to each of us individually, but to all of us together. Like the sky and the sun. Does the sun belong to anyone? Do the stars?"

"No, they don't, because they have no use value. Whatever a person can profit from must be someone's property . . . ," Nahman tries.

"You're telling us the sun has no use!" cries Yeruhim. "If the hands of the greedy could only reach it, they would slice it into pieces, lock it in a vault, and sell it off when the right time rolled around."

"And yet the earth is carved up like the corpse of an animal, taken over, watched, guarded," Reb Mordke mutters to himself, but his attention is increasingly consumed by the pipe, and everyone knows that he is about to float away into that gentle ecstasy in which "tax" becomes an incomprehensible word.

The subject of taxes in Nahman's tale has stirred up a lot of emotions among his Rohatyn audience, and now Nahman must wait to continue, since they have begun to talk amongst themselves.

They offer each other all sorts of warnings, for example not to do business with "those other Jews," for no good can come of it. Everyone knows what happened with Rabbi Isaac Babad of Brody, who misappropriated municipal money. And how can anyone afford the taxes here? They're too high, and they're applied to everything, so that it stops making sense to ever do anything at all. It would be better to lie down and sleep from morning to night, watch the clouds float over the sky and listen to the chatter of the birds. Christian merchants don't have such troubles, the taxes they pay are reasonable enough, and the Armenians have it a lot easier since they, too, are Christians. That's why the Poles and the Ruthenians consider Armenians their own kind, although those gathered in the Shorrs' home would disagree. The mind of an Armenian is impenetrable, wily, and deceitful. An Armenian can even talk a Jew into voluntarily doing something that is against his own interests. Everyone goes along with them because they seem so nice, but in reality, they're slippery as snakes. Meanwhile, the Jewish community has to pay higher and higher tributes, and the kahal has gone into debt from paying the head tax for

Jews who couldn't pay it themselves. And so the richest rule, and their sons and grandsons follow suit. They give their daughters in marriage to other men in the clan, and in this way, their capital remains intact.

Is it possible to avoid paying taxes somehow? To escape the entire construct? If you try to be honest and respect the order of things, the rules will betray you right away. Was it not just resolved in Kamieniec to throw all of the Jews out of town over the course of a single day? And now they cannot settle within six miles of it. What can you do with something like that?

"Our house had just been painted," says the wife of Yeruhim, whose business is vodka, "and I had a lovely little garden."

The woman starts to cry, mostly for the lost parsley and cabbage, which had been flourishing. The parsley was as thick as a hardy man's thumb, the cabbage the size of an infant's head. She wasn't even allowed to take that with her. The comparison to an infant's head effects a mysterious result—other women start to cry as well, so they pour themselves a dash of vodka, and, still sniffling, they are soothed, and then they go back to their work, to darning or plucking goose down, since their hands ought never to be idle.

## Of Nahman's appearance to Nahman, or: The pit of darkness and the seed of light

Nahman sighs, which silences the animated crowd. The most important part is coming now—everyone can tell. They freeze mid-motion, as though before a revelation.

The modest business interests of Nahman and Mordechai are not going particularly well in Smyrna. Too much of their time is taken up by the business of God; investing time in formulating questions, in thinking— these are expenses. And since every answer raises new questions, the expenses relentlessly increase, and their interests founder. There is always a shortfall when they do the accounts, more on the "owed" side than on the "received." One thing's for sure: If there were a trade in questions, Nahman and Mordechai would earn a fortune in it.

Sometimes his young disciples send Nahman out to battle someone in a disputation. He's the best at this and can beat anyone. Many of the Jews and Greeks, eager to debate, provoke the neophytes. It's a form of street-fighting—the opponents sit opposite one another, and around them gathers a crowd. The challenger chooses the topic—it actually doesn't matter what he picks, the point is to see who can present his arguments in such a way as to make his opponent bend in the face of them, render him unable to counter. The loser of these competitions pays up, or buys dinner and wine. That turns into the occasion for the next disputation, and that's how things keep going. Nahman always wins, which means they never go to bed hungry.

"One afternoon, when Nussen and I were looking for someone for me to battle, I stayed out in the street, as I preferred to watch the knife sharpeners, the fruit sellers, the pomegranate-juice squeezers, the street musicians, and the swirling and omnipresent crowd. I squatted down by the donkeys, in their shade, as the heat was severe. At some point, I noticed that out of the crowd some person or other had emerged and was heading toward the door of the home where Jacob lived. It took a moment, several heartbeats, for me to comprehend who it was I was seeing, although almost immediately he had struck me as familiar somehow. I looked up at him from where I squatted as he went to Jacob's door dressed in his fustian kapota, the same kind I had back in Podolia. I saw his profile, the straggly stubble on his cheeks, his skin mottled with freckles, his red hair . . . Suddenly he turned to me, and that's when I recognized him. He was me!" Nahman falls silent for a moment, just to be able to hear the astonished or suspicious cries:

"What do you mean? What does that mean?"

"That's a bad omen."

"That is an omen of death, Nahman."

Not paying attention to this, he continues:

"It was hot, and the heat made the air sharp as knives. I felt weak, and my heart seemed to be hanging from the thinnest of threads. I wanted to get up, but I had no power over my own legs. Feeling I was dying, all I could do was cling to the donkey, who—I remember this—looked at me in surprise at this sudden surge of tenderness."

Somewhere in the room a child starts laughing loudly and is upbraided by its mother, then stops.

"I saw him like I might a shadow. The light was blinding, afternoon sun. He stood over me—I was only half conscious now—and leaned over to touch my burning forehead. Instantly the clarity of my thoughts was restored, and I stood up . . ."

His listeners breathe a sigh of relief. There are murmurs and whispers from all corners. It's a good story, people like it.

But Nahman is making it up. In reality, he fainted by the donkeys, and no one came to save him. His companions picked him up from there later. And it was only in the evening, as he was lying in a dark room with no windows, cool and quiet, that Jacob came to him. He hesitated at the threshold, leaned his arm against the door, and peered into the room from there—Nahman saw only his outline, a dark silhouette in the rectangle of the doorway against the backdrop of the stairs. Jacob had to lower his head to come into the room. He paused before taking this step, which of course he didn't yet know would change his life. In the end, he made up his mind and went in, to Nahman on his sickbed and Reb Mordke sitting next to him, on top of the sheet. Jacob's hair flowed in waves from the fez he was wearing to his shoulders. The light played over his abundant dark beard for a moment, eliciting ruby gleams. He looked a bit like a big kid.

When Nahman, having recovered, went out into the streets of Smyrna, passing hundreds of people hurrying about their business, he couldn't shake the thought that among them might be the Messiah, but that no one was able to recognize him. And the worst of it was that the Messiah himself might not be aware of it.

When he heard this, Reb Mordke nodded his head a long time before saying:

"You, Nahman, are a sensitive instrument. Sensitive, delicate. You might even be this Messiah's prophet, just as Nathan of Gaza was the prophet of Sabbatai Tzvi (of blessed memory)."

And after the long pause it took him to crush the bits of resin and mix them with his tobacco, he added mysteriously:

"Every place has two characters—every place is double. What is sublime is also fallen. What is clement is at the same time base. In the deepest darkness lies the spark of the most powerful light, and vice versa: where omnipresent clarity reigns, a pit of darkness lurks inside the seed of light. The Messiah is our doppelgänger, a more perfect version of ourselves—he is what we would be, had it not been for the fall."


## Of stones and the runaway with the horrible face

Suddenly, as everyone is talking over one another, and Nahman is rinsing his throat with wine, there's a thudding against the roof and the walls, and there's a cry, then a commotion. Through a broken windowpane, a stone has flown into the room, knocking over some candles; lustfully, fire starts to lick the sawdust sprinkled over the floor. An older woman rushes to the rescue, putting out the flames with her heavy skirts. Others have already raced outside, crying and screaming, and in the darkness, those on the inside can hear men shouting to one another, although the hail of stones has stopped. After a long while, people begin to trickle back inside, their faces flushed with anger and excitement, but then shouts sound again from outside, and soon several men burst in great agitation into the main room, where people were dancing until moments ago. Among them are two of the Shorr brothers—Shlomo and Isaac, the bridegroom—as well as Moshek Abramowicz of Lanckoroń, Hayah's brother-in-law, a strong, sturdy man who has in his grip some skinny wretch who kicks and spits furiously all around him.

"Haskiel!" Hayah shouts at him, and goes to look him in the face. Covered in snot and crying with rage, he turns away so that he doesn't have to look her in the eye. "Who was with you? How could you?"

"You bad seeds, you traitors, you heretics!" he cries, till Moshek punches him in the face so hard that Haskiel staggers and falls.

"Leave him alone!" cries Hayah.

So they let him go, and he struggles to get up off his knees, searching for the exit as blood from his nose stains his light-colored linen shirt.

Then the eldest of the Shorr brothers, Nathan, goes up to him and says calmly:

"Nu, Haskiel, tell Aron not to try any more of that. We don't want to shed your blood. But Rohatyn is ours."

Haskiel bolts, tripping over the edges of his coat. By the gate, his gaze falls on a figure standing calmly by. Its face is horrible, deformed, and at the sight of it, Haskiel begins to yelp in fear.

"A golem. A golem!"

Dobrushka from Prossnitz is shaken and holds his wife to him. He complains the people here are all savages, that in Moravia everyone does whatever they want in their own homes, and no one interferes in it. Just imagine, throwing stones!

A displeased Nathan Shorr gestures to the "golem" to go back to the shed where he lives. Now they'll have to get rid of him, lest Haskiel rat them out.

The runaway—that's what they call this big, silent fugitive peasant with the frostbitten face and red hands. His features have been blurred by the scars that remained after he thawed. His great red hands are bulblike, beaten up and swollen. They inspire respect. He is strong as an ox, and gentle. He sleeps in the cowshed, in an annex that shares one warm wall with the house. He is enterprising and hardworking, and he does his work earnestly and well, slow but steady. His dedication is strange, for who are the Jews to him? As a peasant, he surely holds them in contempt, hates them as the reason for many of his own misfortunes—they lease out the nobles' holdings, they collect the taxes, they intoxicate the peasants in their taverns, and as soon as one of them starts to feel a little more confident, he takes to acting like a serf-owner.

Yet there is no sign of resentment in this golem. It may be that there is something wrong with his head, that in addition to his face and hands some part of his mind was affected by the frostbite—that would be why he is so slow, as if perpetually ensconced in ice.

The Shorrs found him in the snow one harsh winter, as they were going home from market. They had only stopped because Elisha needed to answer nature's call. There was another fugitive with him, dressed like him in a peasant's sukmana, in shoes stuffed with straw, with a bundle in which only crumbs of bread and socks remained, but that one was dead.

The bodies were already dusted with snow, and Elisha thought at first they were dead animals. The corpse the Shorrs left in the woods.

It took a long time for the runaway to thaw. Slowly he came back to life, day by day, as if his whole soul had been frozen and were now melting back to its normal temperature, just like his body. His frostbite didn't heal fully; his skin festered, and kept falling off in sheets. Hayah washed his face; it is she who knows him best, is intimate with his robust and lovely body. He slept indoors all winter, up until April, while they debated what to do with him. They were supposed to report him to the authorities, who would have seized him and punished him severely. They were disappointed he didn't talk; since he wasn't talking, he had no history or language, and it felt as though he had no home and no country. Shorr took an inexplicable liking to him, and whatever Shorr did, so did Hayah. The sons reproached the father: Why would they keep someone who needed so much food and was in addition foreign to them, a spy in the hive, a bumblebee amongst the honeybees? If the authorities found out, it would bring no end of trouble.

Shorr decided not to mention it to anyone, and if anyone asked, to simply say he was a cousin from Moravia, a bit slow in the head, which was why he wasn't speaking. The good thing about the runaway was that he never went out on his own, and he knew how to patch up the cart, hoop wheels, till the garden, thresh what he found in it, whitewash the walls—plus he did all sorts of little tasks around the yard in exchange for food and board, never asking for more.

Shorr sometimes observes him, his simple movements, the way he works—efficient, swift, mechanical. He avoids looking him in the eye; he is afraid of what he might see there. Hayah told him once that she had seen the golem crying.

Shlomo, his son, told him off for this display of pity, and for taking the runaway in.

"What if he's a murderer?" he asked, raising his voice.

"Who knows what he is," said Shorr. "Maybe he's a messenger."

"He is a goy," Shlomo said.

That was true—he was a goy. Keeping such an interloper was a terrible transgression. If the wrong person found out, Shorr would really be in trouble. But the peasant doesn't react when they pantomime for him to leave. He ignores Shorr and everyone else, turns around, and simply returns to his pallet near the horses.

Shorr thinks that it is bad to be a Jew, that Jews have it hard in life, but that being a peasant is harder. There really is no fate worse than theirs. In that respect, Jews and peasants are equals, in the sense that they share the lowest rung in the hierarchy of creation. Only vermin might be ranked beneath them. Even cows and horses, and especially dogs, get better care.

### Of how Nahman winds up with Yente and falls asleep on the floor by her bed

Nahman is drunk. A couple of glasses sufficed, since he hasn't had anything to drink for a long time, and he's exhausted from his journey. The strong local vodka knocked him right off his feet. He wants to go out for some fresh air, but he wanders around in the labyrinth of corridors, searching for the courtyard. His hands grope along the rough wooden walls and finally find a handle. He opens this door and sees a tiny room, with just enough space for a bed. At the foot of the bed towers a pile of coats and furs. Someone with a pale, freckled, exhausted face emerges and looks at Nahman in a wary, unfriendly way, then passes him in the doorway and disappears. That must be the medic. Nahman staggers, places his hand on the wooden wall. The vodka they have plied him with and all that goose lard are really hitting him now. The only light here comes from a small oil lamp—a tiny flame that would need to be turned up to show any of the room at all. When Nahman's eyes have grown accustomed to the darkness, he sees on the bed a very old woman in a crooked bonnet. For a moment, he isn't sure who he is looking at. It's almost like a joke— a woman on her deathbed in a home hosting a wedding. The woman's chin is lifted, her breathing heavy. She rests against some pillows, her small, shriveled fists clenched atop the embroidered linen bedspread.

Is that Yankiele Leybowicz's—Jacob's—grandmother? Nahman is

horrified and simultaneously cheered by the sight of this strange old woman; behind him, his hands feel for the hasp of the door. He waits for a sign from her, but Yente seems to be unconscious, or at least, she isn't moving; beneath her lashes gleams a section of her eye, reflecting the lamplight. Drunk Nahman thinks she might be summoning him in some way, so he tries to master his fear and his disgust, and he squats beside the bed. But nothing happens. From up close, the old woman looks a little better, almost as if she were simply sleeping. Only now does Nahman notice how exhausted he feels. The tension falls away from him; his back hunches, and his lids grow heavy. He has to shake himself a few times so as not to fall asleep, and now he rises to leave the room but is sickened and frightened by the thought of the crowd of guests with their inquisitive looks and their endless rounds of questions. And so, certain no one will come in here, he lies down on a sheepskin rug by the bed and, like a dog, curls into a ball, dead tired now, for they have sucked all the life out of him here. "Just for a little while," he says to himself. When he closes his eyes, he sees Hayah's face—her intrigued, admiring gaze. He begins to feel blissful. He can smell the damp floorboards and the odor of rags, unwashed clothing and the smoke that is in everything here and that reminds him of his childhood, and he knows he is home.

If she could, Yente would burst out laughing. She sees the sleeping man as if from above, but definitely not with her closed eyes. Her new vision hovers over the sleeping man, and the strangest part is that from here, Yente can detect his thoughts.

In the sleeper's mind, she sees another man. She can also see that, like her, the sleeper loves this man. To her, the man is still a child—a newborn, still covered in the dark fuzz found on children expelled into the world too early.

As he was being born, wicked sorceresses explored the perimeter of the house, but they couldn't get inside because Yente was standing guard, along with a dog whose father was a real wolf, one of those that roamed on its own and claimed its prey out of the chicken coops. Yente's dog's name was Vilga. When the child of Yente's youngest son was being born, Vilga ran around the house all day and all night, exhausting herself to the point of unconsciousness, but managing to keep the sorceresses and Lilith at bay. Later, they took the dog with them when they went to Czernowitz.

There are few who do not know that Lilith was Adam's first wife, but that since she didn't want to be obedient to Adam, or to lie beneath him as God decreed, she fled to the Red Sea. There she turned red as though flayed. God sent three fearsome angels after her, Senoy, Sansenoy, and Semangelof, to drag her back by force. They accosted her in her hiding place, tormented her, and threatened to drown her. But she didn't want to go back. Even if she had wanted to, she would no longer have been able; Adam would have been forbidden to accept her, for according to the Torah, a woman who has lain with another must not resume relations with her husband. And who was Lilith's lover? Samael himself.

So God had to create a second, more obedient woman for Adam. This one was gentle, if rather stupid. The unfortunate creature ate the forbidden fruit, resulting in the Fall. That was how the rule of law came to be, as a punishment.

But Lilith and all beings similar to Lilith belong to a world from before the Fall, which means that human laws do not apply to them, that they're not bound by human rules or human regulations, and that they don't have human consciences or human hearts, and never shed human tears. For Lilith, there's no such thing as sin. Their world is different. To human eyes, it might seem strange, as if drawn in a very fine line, since everything it contains is more luminous and lightweight, and beings belonging to that world may pass through walls and objects, and each other, back and forth—between them, there are no differences as there are between people, who are closed in on themselves as though in tin cans. Things are different there. And between man and animal there isn't such a great gap, either—maybe only on the outside, for in their world you can converse soundlessly with animals, and they will understand you, and you them. It's the same with angels—here they're visible. They fly around the sky like birds, sometimes huddling on the roofs of houses where their own houses are, like storks.

Nahman wakes up, his head spinning with images. He gets up unsteadily and looks at Yente; after a brief moment of hesitation, he touches her cheek, which is barely lukewarm. Suddenly he is afraid. She has seen his thoughts. She's watched him dream.

Yente is awakened by the creaking of the door, and she's back inside herself. Where did she just go? In her scattered state, it seems to her she won't be able to return to the hardwood floor of this world. So be it. It's better here—times intermingle, overlap. How could she ever have believed in the flow of time? She had thought time flowed! Now she finds it funny. It's obvious that time spins around like skirts whirling in a dance. Like a linden top twirled onto a table and sustained in motion there by the reverential eyes of children.

She sees those children, their faces reddened from the heat, snot running from their noses, their mouths half open. There is little Moshe, and next to him is Tzifka, who will die of whooping cough not long from now. And there is Yankiele, as little Jacob is then known, and his older brother Isaac. Yankiele can't resist and with a sudden movement takes a jab at the top, which sways like a drunk man and falls over. His older brother wheels around in a rage and Tzifka starts to cry. At the noise, their father appears, Leyb Buchbinder, angry to be torn away from work, and he seizes Yankiele by the ear so hard he almost lifts him up into the air. Then he points his finger at him, hissing through his teeth that Jacob is about to finally get what's coming to him, and then he locks him in the storage shed. For a moment, there is a silence, but then from behind the door Jacob begins to scream, and he screams for so long that no one can bear to listen to it or do anything else, so Leyb, red with anger, drags the child out of the shed and hits him several times in the face, until his nose starts bleeding. Only then does his father release his grasp on the boy and allow him to race out of the house.

When the child has not come back by nightfall, the search begins. First the women look for him, and then the men join in, and soon the whole family and their neighbors are walking around the village, asking if anyone has seen the little boy. They make it all the way to the hovels where the Christians live, and they ask there, too, but no one has seen the child with the bashed-up nose.

The village is called Korolówka. From above, it resembles a three-pointed star. This is where little Jacob was born, right there, on the outskirts of the village, in the house where his father's brother Yaakiev still lives today. Yehuda Leyb Buchbinder and his family are visiting now from Czernowitz, have come for the bar mitzvah of the youngest son of his brother, taking the opportunity to spend some time with the family; they hadn't planned to stay for long—in a few days they were to return to Czernowitz, where they had moved several years before. The family home where they are staying is small—it's hard to fit everyone in—and it sits next to the cemetery, so they assume that little Yankiele might have run there and hidden amongst the matzevot, but how will they be able to spot him? He's such a slip of a thing, even if their search is now aided by the rising moon and the silver glow that floods the village. The boy's mother, Rachel, gets weak from crying. She's always known it would end up like this eventually, that if her brutal husband didn't restrain himself from beating Jacob it would all turn out exactly like this.

"Yankiele!" cries Rachel, hysteria audible in her voice. "The child is gone, and why is that? You killed him! You killed your own son!" she shrieks to her husband. She grabs a fence picket and shakes it until she has ripped it out of the ground.

The men have run down to the river, spooking the flocks of geese grazing on the pastures; little white feathers float after them and come to rest in their hair. Others have rushed to the Orthodox cemetery, where it is known the boy goes sometimes, at the very edge of the village.

"Some demon has gotten into that child, some dybbuk, there are lots of them here, right near the cemetery. One of them must have gotten into him," repeats his father, who is also frightened now. "I'll show him when he comes back," he adds immediately, to hide his fear.

"What did he do?" Yehuda Leyb Buchbinder's brother asks a shaken Rachel.

"What did he do? What did he do?" she mocks him, gathering strength for a final burst. "What could he have done? He's a child!"

At dawn, the whole village comes out.

"The Jews have lost a child! The Jews have lost a child!" the goyim call in both Polish and Ukrainian.

They take up clubs and sticks and pitchforks, and they set out as if mobilizing against some werewolf army, against the underground kobold kidnappers, against the cemetery's devils. Someone has the idea of going into the forest, outside the village—that's where Priest's Hill is, he could have run there.

By noon, a small search party is standing at the entrance to a cavern. Narrow and terrifying, it is shaped like a woman's private parts; going inside is akin to climbing back into the womb. No one wants to go.

"He wouldn't have gone in there, either," they try to tell themselves. Finally a boy with washed-out eyes—they call him Bereś—screws up his courage; two others follow him. At first you can hear their voices from inside, but then there is quiet, as if they've been swallowed up by the earth. After a quarter of an hour, Bereś reemerges with the child in his arms. Little Jacob's eyes are open wide in terror, and his relentless sobs have given him hiccups.

The whole village keeps talking about this event for several days, and a group of adolescents united by a common goal begins an exploration of Jacob's cave, shrouding it in the great secrecy to which children that age are prone.

Hayah walks into the room where Yente is lying. She leans over her, checking carefully whether her eyelids are trembling, whether some vein on her sunken temples might be pulsing to the rhythm of her very weak heart. She takes the old woman's little head in her hands.

"Yente?" she asks quietly. "You alive?"

But what is Yente supposed to say to that? Is that even the right question? Hayah ought instead to ask: Do you see, do you feel? How does it work, you moving rapidly as thought across the rippling ruffles of time? Hayah should know how to ask. Yente, who doesn't have the strength to give any answer at all, goes back to where she was a moment ago, or maybe not exactly there, because now it's a little later on, but that doesn't really matter.

Yehuda Leyb Buchbinder, Yente's son, little Jacob's father, is impulsive, unpredictable. He always feels like he's being persecuted by someone for his heresies. He doesn't like people. Isn't it possible to live, think, and do what you like, but in such a way that no one finds out? Yente wonders. For that is what they have been taught: we will quietly lead a double life, following in the footsteps of the Messiah. We just have to master absolute silence, looking away, living in secret. Is that so hard, Yehuda? Not to give away your feelings, not to betray your thoughts? The inhabitants of this world, abyss-dwellers, understand nothing anyway, the great truth is as far away from them as Africa might feel. They are subject to laws we must reject.

Buchbinder is simply a contrarian, always in disagreement with everyone. And his son takes after him, he's exactly the same way, which is of course the reason they don't get along. Yente's gaze travels up under the damp bellies of the clouds and easily finds her son, asleep with his head resting on top of a big book. His oil lamp is burning out. His black beard has covered the writing on the page, shadows have carved little nests into his thin, sunken cheeks, and his eyelids tremble. Yehuda sleeps.

Yente's vision hesitates. Should she go inside his dream? Why does she see everything at once, all times swirled together, and on top of that, people's thoughts? Yente can see thoughts. She orbits her son's head; along the wooden table ants are marching, one after the other, in perfect single file. When Yehuda wakes up, he will wipe them off the table's surface in a single motion, not even realizing.

## Of Yente's onward wanderings through time

Yente remembers how a few years later Yehuda came to visit her in Korolówka on his way to Kamieniec. He was traveling with Jacob, who was fourteen years old at the time. The father was hoping to teach his son a little bit about his business so that he could start to get involved.

Jacob is thin, ungainly, a black mustache just starting to sprout under his nose. His face is covered with red pimples. Some of them have white, pus-filled tips, and his skin is ugly, reddened, shiny; Jacob is very ashamed of all this. He's grown out his hair, and he wears it in such a way that it falls over his face. This annoys his father, who often grabs that "mop," as he calls it, and throws it back over his son's shoulders. They're the same height now, and from behind they could be brothers. Brothers always in an argument. Whenever the younger one tries to talk back, the older one smacks him over the head.

In the village, only four homes remain with the true faith. In the evenings, they close the door, close the curtains over the windows, light the candles. The younger members of these families take part only in the readings of the Zohar and the singing of the psalms. After that, an adult takes them to another cottage. It is better that their impressionable eyes don't witness and that their ears don't hear what happens when the candles start to be put out.

Now even during the day the grown-ups sit behind closed shutters, waiting for news of the Messiah, who will have to show up at some point, after all. But that news from the world arrives with a delay, belated, for here someone has already dreamed of the Messiah—that he'll be coming from the west, the fields and forests, villages and towns curling up behind him like patterns on a carpet. What remains of the world is a tight roll, a scroll covered with tiny symbols that are not quite legible. In the new world, there will be a different alphabet, different symbols, other rules. Maybe it will go bottom to top, instead of top to bottom. Maybe people will move from old age into youth, and not the other way around. Maybe people will arise out of the earth and eventually vanish into the bellies of their mothers.

The coming Messiah is a suffering, aching Messiah, trodden down by the evil of the world and the misery of people. He might even resemble Jesus, whose mangled body hangs in Korolówka from crosses placed at almost every crossroads. The conventional Jews look away from this hideous figure, but the true believers look upon it. For was not Sabbatai Tzvi, too, a suffering savior? Was he not locked away in prison, and was he not tormented and oppressed?

While the parents whisper amongst themselves, the heat ignites in the children's minds all sorts of ideas for games. Then Jacob appears, neither an adult nor a child. His father has just chased him out of the house. His father's face was flushed, his gaze absent; no doubt he had been crying over the Zohar, something that has been happening more and more.

Jacob, whom everyone here still calls Yankiele, has banded the children together, from the eldest to the youngest, Christian and Jewish, and this harmonious band has set out for the cemetery. From his uncle's house toward the village, they set off down a sandy road bordered with silverweed, until they reach the inn and pass the tavern of Solomon the Jew, also known as Black Shlomo. Now they're walking uphill, toward the Catholic church and the wooden presbytery, then farther, past the church cemetery, until they get to the last homes in the village.

From the top of the little hill, the village looks like a garden surrounded by fields of grain. Jacob has brought several boys and two little girls out of that garden and led them through the fields. They have climbed above the village, which extends beneath them like a string of beads; the sky is clear, and the nearing sunset gilds the cerulean firmament. They enter a little forest. The trees that grow here are unusual ones that none of the children have ever seen before. Suddenly everything becomes strange, different. They can no longer hear the songs from down below, and voices vanish into the softness of the leaves, so very green it almost hurts to look at them. Are these the trees from the fairy stories? one of the younger boys asks, and Jacob begins to laugh and says that here it is always spring, and the leaves never get yellow and never fall down. Here is the cavern where Abraham rests, says Jacob, miraculously brought here from the Land of Israel, brought just for him so that he might show it off. And next to Abraham lies Sara, his wife and sister. And wherever Abraham is, time does not flow, so if you go into that cave and sit there a little, and then go out again after an hour, it would likely turn out that on the earth, on the outside, a hundred years had passed.

"I was born in this cave," he proclaims.

"That's a lie," one of the girls says resolutely. "Don't you listen to him. He's always making things up."

Jacob gives her an ironic look. The girl takes her revenge for it:

"Pimple face," she snaps.

Now Yente flies back into the past, where Yankiele is still little and has barely calmed down from his crying. She is trying to get him to sleep, and she looks at the other children, who are lying in a row on the bed. All of them are sleeping, except Yankiele. The little boy has to say good night to everyone around him. He whispers, neither to himself nor to her, quieter and quieter, but with intensity: "Good night, Grandma Yente, good night, Brother Isaac and Sister Hana and Cousin Tzifka, good night, Mama Rachel," and he names all of their neighbors and remembers everyone he came into contact with that day and says good night to them as well, until Yente starts to be afraid that if he keeps going like this, he'll never finish, because the world is so enormous, and even reflected back by such a tiny little mind, it is still endless, and Yankiele will keep talking this way until morning. And then the boy says good night to the neighborhood dogs and cats and heifers, to the goats, and finally to objects. A bowl, the ceiling, a pitcher, some buckets, pots, plates, spoons, the eiderdown, the big pillows, flowers in pots, the curtains, the nails.

Everyone in the room has already gone to sleep, the fire in the stove has dimmed, becoming just a lazy red glow, someone is snoring, and here this child is, talking and talking, softer and softer, but into his words now creep strange mistakes and slips, and there is no one left awake to correct him, so slowly this litany contorts bizarrely, becomes a magic spell, incomprehensible, spoken in an old, forgotten tongue. Finally, the child's voice softens fully, and then he goes to sleep. Then Yente stands up carefully and looks tenderly at this strange boy, who ought not to be called Jacob, but rather Trouble, and she notices his eyelids trembling, which means he has already moved on, into a dream where he'll embark upon new antics.

## Of the terrible consequences of the amulet's disappearance

In the morning, when everyone is sleeping off the wedding in every corner of the house, when the sawdust in the big room is so trampled that it looks like dust, Elisha Shorr enters Yente's bedroom. He is tired; his eyes are bloodshot. He sits on the bed beside her, sways back and forth and whispers:

"It's all over now, Yente. You can go. Don't be angry I kept you this long. I had no alternative."

Gently, he pulls out from under her neckline a handful of strings and leather straps, looking for one in particular, and slides them one by one through his fingers. He assumes his tired eyes have overlooked it. He does it several times—he counts the tiny teraphim, the cases, pouches, bone tablets with spells scored into them. Everyone wears them, but old women like Yente always wear the most. There must be dozens of angels hovering around Yente, guardian spirits and other beings, nameless ones. But his amulet is not there. He finds only the string it was attached to, untied, with nothing on it. The spell has vanished. But how?

Elisha Shorr sobers up, his movements growing nervous. He starts to palpate the old woman. Yente lies there like a log, not moving, with that smile slowly spreading over her face, the same smile his daughter Hayah glimpsed before. He lifts her inert body and searches under her back, under her hips, uncovers poor Yente's skinny extremities, her big, bony feet that stick out stiff from under her skirt, he digs in the folds of her shirt, checks the insides of her palms, and finally, more and more terrified, searches in the pillows, in the sheets, the blankets and the quilts, under the bed and around the bed. How is this possible?

It's a funny sight, this eminent, mature man rummaging around in the bedding of an ancient woman, as if mistaking her for a young one, trying clumsily to clamber in with her.

"Yente, are you going to tell me what's happened?" he says to her in a fierce whisper, as to a child who has committed some monstrous offense, but she, of course, does not respond, only her eyelids tremble, and for a moment her eyeballs move to one side, and then the other, and her smile quivers slightly, almost imperceptibly, but doesn't fade.

"What did you write on it?" Hayah asks her father in an urgent whisper. Sleepy, in a nightshirt with a kerchief on her head, she's run in here at his summons. Elisha is distressed, the wrinkles on his forehead settling into soft rolling waves, their pattern drawing Hayah's gaze. This is how her father always looks when he feels guilty.

"You know what I wrote," he says. "I held her back."

"Did you hang it around her neck?"

Her father nods.

"Father, you were supposed to put it in a box and lock it."

Her father shrugs helplessly.

"You're like a child," says Hayah, at once tender and enraged. "How could you? You just put it right around her neck? Well, where is it?"

"It's nowhere, it's gone."

"Nothing disappears just like that!"

Hayah sets about searching, but she quickly sees there is no point.

"It's gone. I've looked," he says.

"She ate it," says Hayah. "She swallowed it."

Shaken, her father is silent; then, helplessly, he asks:

"What can we do?"

"I don't know," she says. There is a pause. "Who else knows about this?" she asks.

Elisha Shorr thinks. He has taken his fur cap off his head and is rubbing his forehead. His hair is long, thin, sweaty.

"Now she won't die," he says to his daughter, despair rising into his voice.

A strange expression of shock and suspicion appears on Hayah's face, then slowly it turns into one of amusement. She laughs, quietly at first, then louder and louder, until a deep roar fills the small room and explodes through the wooden walls. Her father covers her mouth with his hands.

## What the Zohar says

Yente is dying and not dying. That's right: "Dying and not dying." That's how the learned Hayah explains it.

"This is exactly the way it is in the Zohar," she says, trying to temper her irritation, since everyone is making a very big deal out of it. People from Rohatyn are starting to come up to their home and look in through their windows. "There are many phrases like this in the Zohar that seem contradictory at first glance, but when you look more carefully, it becomes clear that there are things that are impenetrable to reason and that do not work according to our systems. Doesn't the Old Man from the Zohar begin his peroration exactly in this way?"

Hayah says this, standing in the vestibule, to several tired but trusted guests who have come here because they got a whiff of some sort of miracle. They could use a miracle right now. Among them is Israel of Korolówka, Yente's grandson, who brought her here. Of all of them, he seems to be the most anxious and concerned.

Hayah recites: "For who are the beings who, when they rise, go down, and when they go down, climb up; and two being one, the one who is three."

Her listeners nod as if this were exactly what they had expected, and Hayah's words have calmed them down. Only Israel does not seem to be satisfied with this response, because he genuinely doesn't know whether Yente is alive or not. He immediately begins with his question:

"But—"

Hayah, tying a thick wool scarf under her chin, for it has gotten cold, responds impatiently:

"People always want things to be simple. This or that. Black or white. People are idiots. Was not the world made out of countless shades of gray? You can take her home," she concludes, speaking to Israel.

Then she quickly crosses the courtyard and vanishes into the annex where Yente lies.

In the afternoon, the medic Asher Rubin comes back and conducts a careful examination of the patient. He asks her age. Old, is the answer. At last, Rubin pronounces this to be something like a coma, and says they mustn't for God's sake treat her as if she were dead—rather as if she were sleeping. But they can see from his face that he does not really believe what he is saying.

"Most likely she'll die on her own, in her sleep," he adds, by way of consolation.

After the wedding, as the guests are heading out, the wooden wheels of their carriages carving deep ruts into the road before the Shorr home,

Elisha Shorr goes up to the cart where Yente has been laid. When no one is watching, he says quietly to her:

"Don't be angry with me."

She doesn't answer him, of course. Israel, Yente's grandson, comes over. He is angry with Shorr. Shorr could have kept his grandmother and let her die here. He and Sobla have argued about this, because she didn't want to leave Yente behind. Now he whispers to her: "Grandmother, Grandmother." But no answer comes, and no reaction. Yente's hands are cold; they have rubbed them in theirs, but that didn't heat them up. Even so she breathes evenly, slowly. Asher Rubin has taken her pulse several times and cannot believe it is so slow.

## Pesel's tale of the Podhajce goat and the strange grass

Elisha gives them an additional cart lined with hay. The whole family from Korolówka now sits in the two carriages. It drizzles, and the boards with which they have covered Yente are soaked, so the men build her a makeshift roof. She really looks like a corpse now, and so on the road the people they encounter say a prayer, and the goyim bid her farewell with the sign of the cross.

When they stop in Podhajce, her great-granddaughter, Pesel, Israel's daughter, remembers that they stopped in the same spot for a rest three weeks ago, and that her great-grandmother, still healthy and conscious at the time, told them the story of the Podhajce goat. Now Pesel, weeping intermittently, tries to tell the story the same way her great-grandmother did. The others listen to her in silence, realizing—and this draws tears to everyone's eyes—that this was the last story Yente ever told. Did she hope to send them some sort of message through this story? To reveal some sort of mystery? At the time, the story was funny—now it seems to them odd, incomprehensible.

"Not far from here, in Podhajce, right by the castle, there lives a goat,"

Pesel says in a weak voice. The women hush one another in turn. "You won't see him now, because he doesn't care for people and lives like a hermit. He is a highly educated goat, a wise animal that has seen many things, both good and terrible. He is three hundred years of age."

Instinctively, everyone looks around for the goat. All they see is the dried brown grass, goose droppings, and the great clump of the ruins of the Podhajce castle. The goat must have some relevance to all of this. Pesel uses the toe of one of her leather travel shoes to pull down the hem of her skirt.

"In ruins like these, a strange grass grows, a divine grass, perhaps, since no one sows it and no one harvests it. And a grass left to its own devices also acquires a wisdom of its own. So it is only this grass the goat eats, no other. There is a certain Nazirite who took a vow not to cut his hair or touch dead bodies; he knows all about the grass. The goat has never ingested any other grass than this kind that grows in front of the castle of Podhajce, the wise grass. That is why the goat's wisdom grew along with his horns. But they were not the ordinary horns that ordinary animals possess. These ones were soft, they would wriggle around, then twist. The wise goat concealed his horns. By day, he wore them twisted to look perfectly normal. But by night, he would go out, right over there, up to that wide level of the castle, into that once-great courtyard, now collapsed, and from there he would reach out his horns to the sky. He would stretch taller and taller, standing on his hind legs to get as close as he could, until at last, he'd hook the tips of his horns over the edge of the moon, which was young and horned just like him, and he would ask, 'What's up, moon? Isn't it high time for the coming of the Messiah?' The moon looked around among the stars then, and they paused for a moment in their journeys. 'The Messiah has come already, in Smyrna—didn't you know, wise goat?' 'I know, good moon. I just wanted to make certain.' And so they chatted all through the night, and in the morning, when the sun came up, the goat twisted its horns back to how they were supposed to be and went on grazing on that wise grass."

Pesel falls silent. Her mother and her aunts weep.

# Father Chmielowski writes a letter to Mrs. Drużbacka, whom he holds in such high esteem, in January 1753, from Firlejów

Since Your Departure, my Head has been filled with Questions and whole Sentences I did not have the Opportunity to utter at our Meeting, and since You have given me License to write, I shall take Advantage of the Opportunity to defend myself against certain of Your Charges, as well. And since we are in the Depths of Winter in Firlejów now, all I do is tend the Stove and sit over my Papers all Day long, though it spoils the Eyesight, as does the Smoke.

You ask: Why Latin? And You, like other Members of the fairer Sex, advocate for Polish to be more widely employed in written Forms. I have Nothing against the Polish Language—but how are we to speak in it, since there aren't enough Words?

Is it not better to say "Rhetoric" than "Way with Words"? Or "Philosophy" instead of "Love of Knowledge"? "Astronomy" as opposed to "Learning about Heavenly Bodies"? You save Time, and it's easier on the Tongue, too. You can't manage without Latin in Music, either—as it happens, Tone, Texture, and Melody are all from Latin. And if Poles—as is now invaluit Usus—were to give up Latin and the Borrowings from Latin made into Polish by Way of Calques, to begin only speaking and writing in natively Polish Terms, then we would need to return to the long-lost and now incomprehensible Slavic we find in that Song of Saint Wojciech:

The Time hath come, Hour of Bede and God's right Rede.

But what does this mean? What is an Hour of Bede? What Rede is right? Would Your Ladyship wish to say "Tir" instead of "Glory"? I doubt it! "Lyft" rather than "Air," "Lac" instead of "Sacrifice"? How foolish such Words sound; what a Lac it would be. Meanwhile, anywhere in the World You can communicate with the Aid of Latin. Only Pagans and Barbarians avoid it.

The Polish Language is clumsy in so many Ways and sounds like a mere Peasant's Tongue. It is suitable for the Description of the Landscape, of Agriculture at the most, but it would be difficult to express complex Matters in it, or higher Themes, or spiritual ones. Whatever Language a Person speaks is the Language in which he thinks. And Polish is neither clear nor tangible. It is more suited to a Traveler's Descriptions of the Weather, but not to Discourses, where one must exert one's Mind and express oneself clearly. Well, it does lend itself to Poetry, my dear Madam, our Sarmatian Muse, for Poetry is indistinct and intangible. Though it really does give some Pleasure in the Reading, which cannot be expressed directly here. I know of what I speak, for I have ordered from Your Publisher Your little Rhymes and found in them great Pleasure, though not Everything seems to me clear and obvious in them, on which Subject I shall write to You again at a later Date.

I opt for a shared Language, held in Common; let it even be a little simplified, but such a Tongue that Everyone in the whole World might understand it. This is the only Way that People will have Access to Knowledge, for Literature is a Form of Knowledge—it teaches us. For Example, Your Verses might teach the attentive Reader what grows in the Forest, what Type of wild Flora and Fauna there are, and a Person might pick up various gardening Skills, and learn about various domestic Cultivars. One can, by Means of Poetry, train in all Sorts of useful Arcana, and perhaps the most useful Thing is that one can also learn of others' Ways of Thinking, which is very valuable indeed, for without this one might conclude that Everyone thinks alike, and after all, this is not true. Every one of us thinks differently, and imagines Something altogether singular when he is reading. Sometimes it unsettles me greatly to think that what I write with mine own Hand may be understood in a completely different Way from how I had intended.

And so, if You'll allow, it seems to me that Print was invented and Black put on White so as to make a good Use of it, so as to record the Knowledge of our Ancestors and collect it so that every one of us might gain Access to it, even the smallest, so long as he learns how to read. Knowledge ought to be like clean Water—for free and for Everyone.

I thought for a long While about how I, Your humble
Servant, might bring You some Pleasure with my Letters, given
all that is occurring around You, our native Sappho. Ergo I have
taken up the Idea of sending You in every Letter the various
Miranda I have devised within my Books, that You might boast
of them in the good Society in which You—unlike myself—
appear.

And so today I shall begin with Devil's Mountain, which is
near Rohatyn, about eight Miles from Lwów. On the very Day
of Easter, in the Year of 1650, on April 8, before the War by
Beresteczko with the Cossacks, this Mountain was transferred
from Place to Place, i.e., Terrae Motu (earthquake), i.e., ex
Mandato (by the Will of) Our Great Lord. The Rabble, not
knowing of Geology, believe that Devils wished to knock down
Rohatyn with this Mountain, except that the Rooster crowing
robbed them of their Power. Hence the Name. I read this in
Krasuski and Rzączyński, both of the Soc. Jesu, thus I have it
from a trustworthy Source.

# 7.

## Yente's story

Yente's father, Mayer of Kalisz, was one of those righteous few to be granted a glimpse of the Messiah.

This was before her birth, in dismal, wretched times, when everyone was urgently clinging to the hope of a savior, for people's misery was so great it seemed impossible the world could go on any longer. Such pain can't be relieved by any world. It certainly can't be explained or understood, and no one would believe it corresponds to God's designs. And anyway, those with a sensitive eye, most often older women who had seen a great deal during their lifetimes, had noticed that the machinery of the world is breaking down. For instance, one night in the mill where Yente's father delivered grain, the milling wheels came apart, every last one. And then the sow thistles, with their yellow flowers, arranged themselves one morning into the letter *alef.* In the evening, the sun set bloody, a deep, dark orange, so that everything on earth turned brown as though coated in dried blood. The reeds along the river grew so sharp they'd cut human calves. The wormwood got so toxic that its scent could topple a grown man. Not to mention Khmelnytsky's massacres. How were those supposed to fit into God's plan? As early as 1648, terrible rumors of slaughters began to spread from country to country, and with them came the refugees, the widows and the agunot, the orphaned children, the crippled—all irrefutable proof that the end was on its way and the world would soon give birth to the Messiah, that the birthing pains had already begun and, as had been written, the old law would soon be null and void.

Yente's father had traveled to Poland from Regensburg, whence his whole family was expelled for the same eternal Jewish sins. Settling in Greater Poland, they traded in grain, like many of their kin and co-religionists, sending that lovely golden stuff to Gdańsk and on into the world. It was a good business, and they lacked for nothing.

The enterprise was really just getting under way when, in 1654, a plague broke out; many souls were taken by the pestilential winds. Winter put a stop to the spread of the disease, but then the cold did not let up for months and months on end, and those whom the plague had spared now began to freeze to death in their own beds. The seas turned to ice, so that you could cross on foot to Sweden; the ports ceased their operations, the roads were all impassable, the livestock perished en masse. When spring finally came, so, too, did accusations that all of these misfortunes had been caused by the Jews. Trials began all over the country, and the Jews, in order to defend themselves, sent for help from the pope, but before their messenger managed to return to Poland, the Swedes arrived, laying waste to cities and towns. And once again the Jews were ripped to shreds, for being unbelievers.

And so Yente's father moved with his family from Greater Poland to the east, to relatives in Lwów, where he hoped to find a peaceful haven. Here, they were far from the world—all things arrived with some delay, while the earth revealed itself to be more fertile than any they'd encountered. And as in those colonies to which the people of the west were so eager to immigrate, there was plenty of space for everyone. But it lasted only a moment. After the expulsion of the Swedes, amidst the ruins of the towns, on ruthlessly looted market squares, people started asking all over again who could be responsible for the Commonwealth's misfortunes, and more often than not, they came up with the same old answer: It was infidels and Jews, plotting with the invaders. At first they went after the Polish Brethren, but soon the pogroms began.

Yente's maternal grandfather came from Kazimierz, near Kraków. He had a small business there that produced felt caps. In the summer of the Christian year of 1664—5425 by the Jewish calendar—one hundred twenty-nine people died in riots. It started when one Jew was accused of stealing the sacramental bread. Yente's grandfather's shop was pillaged and destroyed. Having traded the rest of his possessions for their safety, he put his whole family in their wagon and headed southeast, to Lwów, where their kin lived. It was a good idea: the Cossack element in this part of the world had already had its fun under Khmelnytsky in 1648. Gezerah—the Great Catastrophe—could not occur again. It's just like what they say about lightning: It's safest to stand where it's already struck.

They settled in a village not far from Lwów. Here, too, the earth was rich, with thick soil, dense forests, and rivers filled with fish. The great nobleman Potocki kept it all in perfect order, never permitting any deviation from the rules. By that point, Yente's family must have thought that there was nowhere on earth they could hide—that it would be better to simply submit to God's will. And yet, things were good for them here. They brought in wool for felt from Wallachia, and other goods as well, so that soon their business really prospered, and they were back on their feet—they had a home with an orchard and a little workshop, a yard that geese and chickens roamed, fat yellow melons in the grass, plums they used to make slivovitz as soon as frost set in.

Then, in the autumn of 1665, along with their goods from Smyrna came the news that soon shook all the Jews of Poland: *The Messiah has arrived.* Everyone who heard this instantly fell silent and tried to make sense of this short sentence: *The Messiah has arrived.* For it is not a common phrase. And it is a final answer. Anyone who pronounces it will watch the scales fall from his eyes, will see the world completely differently from that day forward.

In truth, had there not already been sufficient signs of end times? Those monstrous yellow nettle roots that tangled insidiously underground around the roots of other plants, along with the extraordinarily rampant bindweed that year, its shoots thick as ropes. All sorts of greenery climbing the walls of houses, trees seeming ready to reach for people's throats. Apples with several seeded cores, eggs with two yolks, hop that grew so savagely it suffocated a heifer.

The Messiah was known as Sabbatai Tzvi. He already had thousands of people from all over the world in his retinue, preparing to travel with him to Stamboul, where he was to tear the sultan's crown from his head and proclaim himself king. With him, too, went his prophet, Nathan of Gaza, a great scholar who wrote down the Messiah's words and sent them out into the world for all the Jews to read.

Right away a letter came to the Lwów kahal from Rabbi Baruch Peysach of Kraków, saying there was no more time to wait—they needed to get to Turkey as quickly as they could, to bear witness to these final days. To be among the first who would see.

Mayer, Yente's father, did not easily succumb to such visions.

He said: If it were as you all say, then a Messiah would come in every generation, he'd be here this month, and there the next. He'd be born again after every riot and after every war. He'd intervene after every misfortune. And how many of those have we had? Countless.

Yes, yes, his listeners would nod. He was right. But everyone could sense that this time was also different. And once again the game of signs began—the clouds, the reflections on the water, the shapes of the snowflakes. Mayer finally made up his mind to go because of some ants he'd seen as he was giving the matter serious thought: they were moving up the table leg, in a row, obediently, calmly, and when they got to the tabletop, one after another they scooped up a tiny morsel of cheese and went back down just as calmly and contritely. Pleased, he decided to take this as a sign. He already had money and goods set aside, and being a highly esteemed man, considered reasonable and wise, he had no trouble finding a place in that great caravan that was to travel all the way to Sabbatai.

Yente was born years after all this happened, so she isn't sure whether she'd have any share in the holiness of her father's eyes as he beholds the face of the Messiah. His companions were Moshe Halevi, his son and stepson from Lwów, and Baruch Peysach of Kraków.

From Kraków to Lwów, from Lwów past Czernowitz, to the south, to Wallachia. The closer they got, the warmer it got, the less snow there was, and the more fragrant and gentler the air became, as her father would later recall. They would spend their evenings contemplating the Messiah's arrival. They came to the conclusion that the misfortunes of the preceding years had been blessings in disguise, for they made a kind of sense, foretelling the coming of the savior, just as painful contractions foretell the birth of a new person. As the world gives birth to the Messiah, it must suffer, and all laws must break, conventions be eradicated, oaths and promises crumble. Brothers must lunge at one another's throats, neighbors hate each other; people who once lived next door must now slit one another's throats in the night and drink down the blood that rushes up to greet them.

The Lwów delegation found the Messiah in jail, in Gallipoli. As they were traveling south from Poland, the sultan, disquieted by the Jewish turmoil and by Sabbatai Tzvi's plans, seized him and locked him up in the fortress.

The Messiah imprisoned! Inconceivable! How could such a thing occur? A great anxiety now took hold among all those who had come at that time to Stamboul, and not only from Poland. Prison! The Messiah in prison, could that be? Did that fit with the prophecies? What about Isaiah?

But wait, what kind of prison was it? And was it really prison? And

COSTANTINOPOLI, SUE VEDVTE, E LUOGI VICINI.

what was "prison," anyway? After all, Sabbatai Tzvi, amply provided for by the faithful, could scarcely have told the difference between this incarceration in the Gallipoli fortress and a stay in a palace. The Messiah did not eat meat or fish; people said he subsisted on fruit alone—and the freshest of these were picked for him from the surrounding territories and brought in by ship. He loved pomegranates, loved digging his long slender fingers into their granular insides, fishing out the ruby seeds and popping them into his holy mouth. He didn't eat much—just a few seeds; people said his body derived life-giving strength directly from the sun. They also said in great secret—which nonetheless traveled faster than it would have had it been a slightly lesser secret—that the Messiah was a woman. Those who had been close to him had glimpsed his feminine breasts. His skin, soft and rosy, smelled like a woman's skin. In Gallipoli, he had at his disposal a great courtyard and salons outfitted in carpets, where he would give his audiences. Was that really prison?

This was how the delegation found him. First, they waited a day and a half, so numerous were those eager for an audience with the captive. They watched the thrilled crowd pass before them, effervescent in their many tongues. Speculation circulated: What was going to happen next? Jews from the south, darker-skinned, wearing dark turbans, crossed paths with Jews from Africa, colorfully clad like dragonflies. The Jews of Europe looked funny, dressed in black, wearing stiff collars that collected dust like sponges.

Mayer and the others had to fast for a day, and then bathe in a bath-house. At last, they were given white robes and allowed to see His Majesty the Messiah. This happened on a holy day, according to the newly designed messianic calendar. For Sabbatai Tzvi had abolished all traditional Jewish holidays, having invalidated the old Law of Moses, which he would replace with some other, still-to-be-articulated law, according to which no one knew how to behave or what to say just yet.

They found him sitting on a richly carved stool, in scarlet robes, in the company of pious sages who asked them why they were there and what it was they hoped for from their savior.

It was decided that Baruch Peysach would speak for them, and he started by describing the many misfortunes of the Polish lands, and with them the misfortunes of Polish Jews, and as evidence he submitted the chronicle of misfortunes of Meir ben Samuel of Szczebrzeszyn, titled in Hebrew *Tzok haIttim*, meaning *Distress of the Times*, published several years before. But as Baruch was carrying on in a tearful voice about wars and diseases, pogroms and human injustice, Sabbatai suddenly interrupted him and, indicating his scarlet robes, shouted in a booming voice: "Can you not see the color of revenge? I am clothed in scarlet, as the prophet Isaiah says: It is for me the day of vengeance; the year for me to redeem has come." Everyone cowered at the sound of that voice, so strong and unexpected. Then Sabbatai ripped off his shirt and gave it to Isaiah, David Halevi's son, and to the others he handed out lumps of sugar and told them to put them in their mouths, "that a youthful strength might awake in them." Mayer tried to say that they didn't need youthful strength, that what they needed was to be left to live in peace, but the Messiah cried, "Silence!" Mayer, as only Mayer could, managed to glance surreptitiously at the savior and to see his gentle, beautiful face, its delicate features and the extraordinary beauty of his eyes, bordered by those lashes, damp and dark. And he saw the Messiah's dark and generous lips, still trembling in outrage, and his silky-smooth cheeks, which quivered almost imperceptibly, and he thought how soft they must be to the touch, like the finest suede. And it surprised him that the Messiah's breasts were indeed like a woman's, generous, with brown nipples. Someone rushed to cover him in a shawl then, but the sight of the Messiah's naked breasts remained in Mayer's memory to the very end of his life, and then—as happens with remembered images—got divided up into words and then reconstituted from these words inside the minds of his children.

Mayer the Skeptic felt something then like a sting in his chest, a tug of emotion, and that must have deeply wounded his soul, because he passed that wound along to his children and, later, his grandchildren. Yente's father, Mayer, was Elisha Shorr's granduncle.

And? That's it. They wrote it all down, every movement and every word. The first night they sat in silence, not understanding what had just happened to them. Was this some kind of sign? Would they be saved? With the end times drawing near, would anyone be able to grasp with reason what was going on? After all, *everything would be different, opposite to how it was before.*

In the end, after settling up all their business, they returned home to Poland in a strange and solemn mood.

The news of Sabbatai's apostasy left them thunderstruck. It happened on the 16th day of the month of Elul of 5426, or the 16th of September, 1666, but they only found out about it once they were home. That day an unexpected early snow fell, covering the crops that had not yet been collected from the gardens: pumpkins, carrots, and beets that were still living out their ripeness in the earth.

The news was delivered by messengers in robes ripped in woe at their chests, their faces dirtied from their ceaseless travels. They walked through village after village without respite, wailing. The evil sultan of the infidels had threatened Sabbatai with death if he did not convert to Islam. He had threatened to behead him. And so the Messiah had agreed.

At first, their homes were taken over by sobbing, and disbelief reigned. Then a silence fell. For a day, or two, or three, no one really wanted to talk. What was there to say? That once more we were the weakest, having been deceived—that God had abandoned us? Our Messiah, crushed? How could that be, when we expected him to dethrone the sultan, take power over the whole world, and exalt the humiliated? Once more over the poor Podolian villages great gray fustian clouds gathered; the sky looked like the roof of a ruined tent. To Mayer, it seemed the world had begun to rot, that gangrene had set in. Sitting at their heavy wooden table with his youngest daughter, tiny as a pea, poised on his lap, he wrote out, like everyone, gematrical columns. It was only when the cold set in that letters and explanations began to circulate, and not a week went by that some traveling merchant did not bring them some new tidbit. Even the milk-man, who delivered milk and butter around the neighboring villages, be-came during that period a wise man, drawing systems of salvation with his finger on whatever surface he could find.

From these shaky, broken reports and tales it was necessary to assem-ble a whole, reach for the books, consult with the wisest of men. And gradually that winter a new knowledge began germinating, which come spring was strong and powerful like the new shoot of a plant. How could we have been so wrong? The sadness had blinded us, sunk us in despair unworthy of good men. Yes, he had converted to the faith of Muhammad— but not really, only on the surface, only his image, his goal, meaning his shadow, donned the green turban, while the Messiah concealed himself to wait for the better time that was about to come, that was a matter of days away, that was very nearly here already.

Yente can still see the finger that drew the sefirotic tree in the flour strewn across the table, while at the same time she finds herself in the countryside, near Brzeżany, eighteen years before. It is the very day she was conceived. Only now can she see it.

In this strange state in which she finds herself, is Yente able to launch some little changes? Influence the course of events? Can she? If she could, she would change this one day.

She sees a young woman walking through the fields with a basket in her hand, and in it, two geese. Their necks move to the rhythm of her steps, their beady eyes look around with the trust common to domesti-cated animals. A mounted Cossack patrol comes galloping out of the forest, getting bigger as she watches in approach. It is too late to run away, the woman stands astonished, covers her face with the geese. The horses surround her, closing in. As if on command, the men dismount, and now everything happens very fast and in silence. They push her down softly onto the grass, the basket falls, the geese get out of it, but they stay close, hissing a little, quietly, threatening, warning, bearing witness to what's going on. Two of the men hold the horses, while one of them unfastens the belt of his broad, wrinkled trousers and lies down on top of the woman. Then they trade, the next one faster than the first, as though they have to perform these few movements in haste—there is no sign of their enjoying it, in fact. Their seed pours into the woman and then drips out onto the grass. The last one presses down hard upon her neck, and the woman starts to resign herself to the fact that she will die, but the others hand him his reins, and the man gets back on his horse. He looks at her for a moment longer, as if wanting to remember his victim. Then they quickly ride away. It all takes just a few minutes.

The woman sits with her legs akimbo, the indignant geese looking at her, honking their disapproval. With a bit of her petticoat she wipes between her legs, then rips up some leaves and grass. She runs to the stream and raises her skirts high and sits down in the water, pushing out all the semen from inside her. The geese think this is an encouragement to them, and they scamper up to the water's edge. But before they can quite make up their minds to get in, overcoming their usual anserine reserve, the woman stuffs both of them back in the basket and returns to the path. She slows as she comes to the village, going slower and slower, until finally she stops, as if she has reached an invisible border.

This is Yente's mother.

And this must be the reason that she always watched her daughter so closely; eventually, Yente grew accustomed to the looks, to the suspicious gaze cast from where her mother sat working on something at the table, stood cutting vegetables, peeling hard-boiled eggs, scrubbing pots. Her mother watched her all the time. Like a wolf, like a dog getting ready to sink its teeth into your shin. With time, a slight grimace began to appear in connection with this watching: a light rise in the upper lip, pulling it up toward her nose—not an expression of animosity or revulsion, just barely visible, insignificant.

She remembers how, as her mother was braiding her hair one day, she found a dark mole over little Yente's ear and rejoiced in it. "Look," she said to Yente's father, "she has a mole in the same spot as you, but on the other side, like a reflection in the mirror." Her father listened only absentmindedly. He never suspected a thing, for his whole life. Yente's mother died with the secret clenched in her fist. She died in a kind of convulsion, in a fury. She'll no doubt come back as a wild animal.

She was the eleventh-born. Her father named her Yente, which means: she who spreads the news, and she who teaches others. Her mother didn't have the strength to take care of her by then—she was fragile of both mind and body. Yente was dealt with by the other women who were always bustling around the house—cousins, an aunt, and, for some time, her grandmother. She remembered her mother sliding off her cap in the evenings—then Yente would see from up close her wretched hair, cut short and sloppily, growing over her unhealthy, flaking skin.

Yente had six older brothers who went to yeshiva and, at home, quoted passages from the Scriptures under their breath while she hung around the table at which they sat, too little to be assigned real women's work. She also had four older sisters, one of whom was already married; significant efforts were being made to match up another.

Her father, detecting her interest and zeal, showed her the letters of the alphabet, thinking they would be like little pictures for her, like jewels and stars—lovely *alef*, like the reflection of a cat's paw, *shin* like a little boat with a mast made out of bark and let out onto the water. But—who knew how or when—Yente learned the letters in a different way, in such a way as to be able to make words of them soon. Her mother slapped her hands for this with an unexpected ferocity, as if Yente was reaching for too much. Her mother didn't know how to read. She would listen happily, however, as Yente's father, on rare occasions, or more often as their old relation, Abramek the Cripple, told the women and children stories from the books in Yiddish. Abramek always did this in a plaintive voice, as if the written words were by nature akin to a lament. He would start at dusk, by the dim light of the candles, and so, along with reading, there would appear in the house in the evenings the unbearable sadness of the village Kabbalists, of whom there were many in those days. You could develop a taste for this sorrow in the same way that some grow fond of vodka. They would all be overcome by such melancholy that someone would begin to cry and keen. Then they would want to touch with their hands everything of which Abramek had told, and they would reach out for something tangible—but there was nothing there. That lack was terrible. There began true despair. All around them darkness, cold, and damp. In the summer dust, dry grass, and stones. Where is all that, that world, that life? Where's paradise, and how can we get there?

To little Yente it seemed that every such evening of stories would grow dense, darker, impenetrable, especially when Abramek the Cripple would say:

"And it is known that the space of the world is filled with ghosts and evil spirits, born of human sin. These float in that space, as is written clearly in the Zohar. We have to guard against them attaching to us on the way to the synagogue, and this is why we must know what is written in the Zohar, namely that the damage-doer lies in wait for you on the left side, for the mezuzah may be placed only on the right side, and on the mezuzah is written God's name: Shaddai, which will defeat the damage-doer, which explains the mezuzah's inscription: 'And Shaddai will be on your doorframe.'"

They nodded their heads in agreement. This we know. The left side.

Yente knew this. "The air is full of eyes," her mother would whisper to her, jerking her around like a rag doll every time she got her dressed. "They are watching you. Just put out a question before you, and the spirits will instantly answer. You just have to be able to ask. And to find those answers you receive: in the milk that has spilled into the shape of the letter *samech*, in the imprint of a horse's hoof in the shape of the letter *shin*. Gather, gather these signs, and soon you will read a whole sentence. What is the art of reading from books written by man when the whole world is a book written by God, even the clay path that leads up to the river. Look at it. The goose feathers, too, the dried rings of the wood of the fence boards, the cracks in the clay of the houses' walls—that is exactly like the letter *shin*. You know how to read, so read, Yente."

She feared her mother, and how. The tiny little girl stands before the thin, small woman, who is perpetually muttering something, always with spite. Shrew, that's what everyone in the village called her. Her moods changed so frequently that Yente never knew whether her mother, setting her down on her lap, would kiss her and hug her or squeeze her shoulders painfully and shake her like a rag doll. So she preferred to just keep out of her way. She would watch her mother's skinny hands putting the last of her dowry back in the chest—she had come from wealthy Silesian Jews, but little of that wealth remained. Yente heard her parents moaning in bed, and she knew that this was her father chasing the dybbuk out of her mother, something he kept secret from the rest of the family. Her mother would at first try faintly to escape him, but then she would take a deep breath, like someone submerging herself in cold water, in the icy water of the mikvah, where she could hide out from evil.

Once, in a time of great poverty, Yente watched in secret as her mother ate the rations intended for everyone—her back hunched, her face lanky, her eyes empty. They were so black you couldn't see her pupils in them.

When Yente was seven years old, her mother died in childbirth along with the child who didn't have the strength to make its way out from inside her. To Yente's mind, it had obviously been a dybbuk, which she had eaten when she stole the provisions intended for everyone, and which her father had not managed to banish during those nocturnal struggles. That dybbuk had set up shop in her mother's stomach and not wanted to leave. Death—that was the punishment. A few days before the fatal childbirth, fat and swollen, with pale eyes, she'd woken her sleeping daughter at dawn, pulling her by the braids, and said:

"Get up. The Messiah has come. He is already in Sambor."

After the death of his wife, Mayer, guided by some hazy sense of guilt, took over the care of his little daughter himself. He didn't really know what to do with her while he was studying, so she just sat with him and looked at what he was reading.

"So what will salvation look like?" she asked him once.

Mayer, brought back to reality, stood up and leaned back against the stove.

"It's simple," he said. "When the last little spark of divine light returns to its source, the Messiah will appear to us. All laws will be invalidated. The division between kosher and non-kosher will disappear, like the division between holy and cursed. Night will cease to be distinguishable from day, and the differences between men and women will disappear. The letters in the Torah will rearrange themselves so that a new Torah will come to be, and everything in it will be opposite. Human bodies will be light as spirits, and new souls will come down into them, straight from the throne of the good God Himself. Then the need to eat and drink will vanish, sleep will become superfluous, and every desire will dissipate like smoke. Corporeal reproduction will give way to the union of holy names. The Talmud will become covered in dust, completely forgotten and unnecessary. Everywhere will be bright from the glow of the Shekhinah."

Then, however, Mayer thought it fitting to remind her of the most important thing:

"Between the heart and the tongue lies an abyss," he said. "Remember that. Thoughts must be concealed, particularly since you were born, to your great misfortune, a woman. Think so that they think you are not thinking. Behave in such a way that you mislead others. We all must do this, but women more so. Talmudists know about the strength of women, but they fear it, which is why they pierce girls' ears, to weaken them. But we don't. We don't do that because we ourselves are like women. We survive by hiding. We play the fools, pretend to be people we are not. We come home, and then we take off our masks. But we bear the burden of silence: masa duma."

And now, as Yente lies covered up to her neck in a Korolówka woodshed, she knows she has deceived them all.

*8.*

**Honey, and not eating too much of it, or:**
**Isohar's school in Smyrna, in the Turkish land**

In Isohar's school, Nahman has perfected gematria, notarikon, and temurah. You can wake him up in the middle of the night and have him shuffle letters around and produce words. He has already considered and calculated the numbers of words in the prayers and blessings, to uncover the secret principles according to which they were written. He's compared them with others, transformed the words, rearranged the letters. Many times, when he was unable to sleep during those sweltering Smyrna nights, when Mordechai had drifted off into silence, smoking his pipe, and in order not to give longing and anxiety access to his heart, he would relish this play until dawn with his eyes closed, creating out of words and letters completely new, unlikely meanings and connections. When the gray dawn would light up the little square with its few miserable olive trees, under which dogs slept amidst the trash, it would strike him that the world of words was much more real than the one his eyes could see.

Nahman is happy. He always sits behind Jacob. He loves to look over his shoulder. That is why he can relate to the Scriptures, it being written in the Book of Proverbs 25:16: "If you find honey, eat just enough—too much of it, and you will vomit."

Meanwhile, aside from hakkarat panim (knowledge of physiognomy) and sirtutim (knowledge of chiromancy), selected students—now including Nahman and Jacob—are instructed in yet another secret thing under the guidance of Isohar and Reb Mordke. In the evenings, just two candles are left in the small room, and the students sit along the wall on the floor. Their heads are to be placed between their knees. In this way, the human body resumes the position it was in inside the mother's belly, and therefore, when it stayed in close proximity to God. When you sit like this for a few hours, when your breath returns to your lungs and you can hear the beating of your own heart, that's when your mind launches its journeys.

Jacob, tall and strong, always has the garland of an audience around him. He tells them tales of his youth in Bucharest, while Nahman mostly eavesdrops. Jacob tells how he stood up for a Jew when suddenly two janissaries sent by the agha attacked. Fighting with a rolling pin, he routed the Turkish guard. And when he was brought to court, not having done anyone any real physical harm, the agha so appreciated his bravery that he not only released him, but also presented him with gifts. Nahman obviously doesn't believe him. Yesterday he told of a miraculous drill that, when coated in some magical herbs, could reveal treasure buried underground.

Seeing Nahman's gaze intently focused upon him—ordinarily Nahman instantly glances away when Jacob looks at him—Jacob provokes him in Turkish:

"What's your problem, feygele, looking at me like that?"

He says it with the intention of offending Nahman, who squints with surprise. Even more so for the fact that Jacob has used the Yiddish word *feygele*—little bird—but also a man who likes men more than women.

Jacob is pleased, for he has caused Nahman confusion, and he grins.

For some time they seek a common language. Jacob starts with what the Jews of Smyrna speak, Ladino, and Nahman, not understanding, responds in Hebrew. Neither of them feels right chatting in the street in the holy language, so they break off, and Nahman switches to Yiddish. But here again Jacob has a rather strange accent, so instead he responds in

Turkish, fluently, joyfully, as though finding himself suddenly on home
turf, though Nahman doesn't feel completely at home here. In the end
they speak a mixture, not worrying about the provenance of words; words
are not nobility that want their genealogical trees retraced. Words are
merchants, swift and useful, now here, now there.

What is the name of the place where people go to drink kahve? It's a
kahvehane, right? And a dark, stocky Turk from the south who goes home
wearing goods bought at the bazaar is a hamal. And the stone market,
where Jacob always goes during the day, that's the bezestan, isn't it? Jacob
laughs. He has nice teeth.

### Scraps: What we were doing in Smyrna in the Jewish year 5511 and how we met Moliwda, and also, how the spirit is like a needle that pokes a hole in the world

I took to heart what Isohar had taught us. He said that there are
four types of readers. There is the reading sponge, the reading
funnel, the reading colander, and the reading sieve. The sponge
absorbs everything it comes into contact with; and it is evident he
remembers much of it later, too. But he is not able to filter out what
is most important. The funnel takes in what he reads at one end,
while at the other, everything he's read pours out of him. The
strainer lets through the wine and keeps the sediment; he ought not
to read at all—it would be infinitely better if he simply dedicated
himself to some manual trade. The sieve, on the other hand,
separates out the chaff to give a result of only the finest grains.

"I want you to be like sieves, and to discard all that is not good
or interesting," Isohar would say to us.

Thanks still to his Prague acquaintances and a widespread high
opinion of Reb Mordke, we both found employment—to our great
fortune—helping out the Trinitarians, who were buying Christian
war prisoners out of Turkish slavery. We earned good money for
this, too. We took over for a Jew who died suddenly from some fever
and who needed replacing quickly. Our task was to supply them
during the time of their stay in Smyrna; since I was now fluent in

Turkish, and, as I have said already, my knowledge of Polish was fairly good, they engaged me also for the purposes of translation, thanks to which I soon became, as the Turks say, a dragoman, or an interpreter.

The purchases took place at the port. The Trinitarians went down to the temporary cells where the prisoners were kept and conversed with them, to learn where they were from and whether they had families that could underwrite their ransom, repaying the Trinitarian brothers the money they'd put up.

There were sometimes amusing stories, like that of the peasant woman from near Lwów. Her name was Zaborowska, and her little son, born in captivity, was called Ismail. This woman nearly ruined the transaction by insisting that she would not give up the Muhammadan faith and that she would not baptize her son, which, for the Trinitarian brothers, was a difficult potion to swallow.

There was another translator who worked for the Trinitarians, a man who intrigued me immediately, for I heard him conversing with someone in Polish, though he was dressed according to the Turkish style. He had hair lightened by the sun and a close-cropped reddish beard. He was of a stout and sturdy stature—it seemed safe to assume he'd be enduring and hale. I watched him out of the corner of my eye, but I did not wish to bother him until the proper occasion arose. At some point, he noticed that I was trying to explain something in Polish to newcomers from Lesser Poland who had come all the way here in order to buy back their relative, and he came up to me and, patting me on the back, embraced me as one of his own. "Where are you from?" he asked without ceremony, which moved me to my core, as no nobleman had ever treated me with such sincerity before. And then he addressed me in good Hebrew, as well as in Yiddish, our native tongue. He had a deep voice; he could orate. I must have made a stupid face, for he burst out laughing—loud, tipping his head back, so that I could practically peer down his throat.

Some mysterious business dealings, about which he did not wish to speak, had brought him to Smyrna, though he did claim to be the prince of an island in the Greek sea, which was named the same as he: Moliwda. But he told us this as if casting us a fishing line—would we believe him, would we allow ourselves to be caught? He spoke as if he did not fully believe himself, as if he had in his possession several other versions, equally true. In spite of this, we stuck together somehow. He assumed a sort of fatherly role with

respect to me, though he was but a few years older. He asked us all
about Poland—I had to tell him of completely ordinary things,
which visibly cheered him: how the nobility and the bourgeois get
along in Lwów, what the shops are like, whether you can find good
kahve there, what the Jews do to earn their living, and what about
the Armenians, what people eat, what type of alcohol they drink. To
tell the truth, I was not much acquainted with Polish affairs. I told
him of Kraków and Lwów, described Rohatyn in detail, as well as
Kamieniec and my hometown, Busk. I must admit that neither of us
was able to avoid those sudden waves of homesickness that strike
travelers when they find themselves distant from their native lands.
But it seemed to me that he had not seen his home in a very long
time, as he asked after such trivial and mundane things. Instead, he
told of his adventures at sea with pirates, and he so described the
marine battles that even the Trinitarians in their white habits and
crosses squatted down beside us in order to hear. With the brothers
he switched to Polish, and from the way they spoke together (I did
not yet understand everything then), it was evident they valued him
very much and treated him in an exceptional manner, as a true
nobleman. They called him "Count Kossakowski," which in some
strange fashion took my breath away, since I had never looked upon
a count from such proximity, even though he was quite a bizarre
sort of man.

The longer we knew Moliwda, the more he surprised us. As
though it weren't enough that he read and spoke fluent Hebrew, he
also knew the foundations of gematria! He quickly demonstrated
knowledge that far surpassed the horizons of any ordinary goy. He
spoke Greek, and could write in Turkish so well that he could issue
quittances in it.

One day Tovah from Nikopol showed up at Isohar's. We had not yet
met him, but we had heard only the highest praise of him, and had
even studied his book and his poetry. He was a modest and reserved
man. Everywhere he went, he took his thirteen-year-old son with
him, a beautiful boy; together they gave the impression of an angel
looking after a sage.

The disputations that began with his arrival led us into
completely uncharted territories.

Isohar said:

"There is no sense in awaiting major events anymore—solar
eclipses, floods. The odd process of salvation is going on right

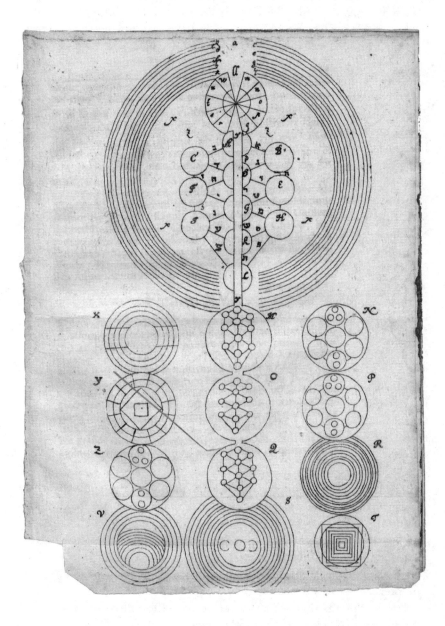

here," and he beat his breast so that it thundered. "We are rising from the deepest depths, just as he has risen and has fallen in that unrelenting battle with the forces of evil, with the demons of darkness. We will free ourselves, we will be free on the inside, even if we are to be slaves here, in the world . . . Only when we are free will we raise up the Shekhinah out of the dust, we the ma'aminim, the true believers."

I wrote down these words with a joyous sense of satisfaction. That was how to understand Sabbatai's actions. He chose freedom in his heart, rather than freedom in the world. He had converted to Islam in order to be faithful to his mission of salvation. And we fools expected him to show up before the sultan's palace with a thousand armies bearing shields of gold. We were like children wanting wonderful toys, ahaya aynayim, illusions, magic for those with limited minds.

Those of us who think God addresses us by means of external events are wrong, as naive as children. For he whispers directly into our innermost souls.

"It is a great mystery and an extraordinary one that he who is most beaten down shall become our redeemer—he who has reached the bottom of the abyss of the most horrendous darkness. Now we await his return; he will come back in various guises, until the mystery is fulfilled in one—when God incarnates as a man, when the Devekut occurs, and the Trinity prevails." Isohar pronounced the word "trinity" more quietly, so as not to rile those who believed that such a weak Messiah would be too Christian. But does not every religion have some truth to it? All of them, even the most barbaric, have been permeated by the holy sparks.

Then, from within his haze of smoke, Reb Mordke spoke:

"Or maybe the Messiah gave us an example, that we, too, would follow him into that darkness? Many in Spain converted to the faith of Edom."

"God forbid," said Tovah. "It is not for us insignificant persons to imitate the Messiah. Only he is capable of venturing into mud and filth, submerging himself fully in it, and coming back out in one piece, completely clean, unsullied."

Tovah thought that it would not do to get too close to Christianity. When later, excited, we discussed the Trinity with others, he claimed that the Christian teachings on the Trinity are a distorted version of an older understanding of the divine mystery, which no one can remember anymore. It is but a pale shadow, riddled with mistakes.

"Keep your distance from the Trinity," he warned.

This image got etched into my memory: three grown men, bearded, enveloped in the quivering light of an oil lamp, whole evenings spent talking aimlessly of the Messiah. Every letter that arrived from brothers in Altona or Salonika or Moravia or Lwów or Kraków or Stamboul or Sofia was cause for another sleepless night, and in Smyrna at that time our thinking gradually got more harmonious. Isohar seemed the most restrained, while Tovah could be sarcastic, and I must confess that I avoided his furious gaze.

Yes, we know that since he, Sabbatai Tzvi, had come, the world had had a different, deadened countenance, and though it appeared the same, it was in fact a completely different world from the one before. The old rules no longer applied; the commandments we had once followed to the letter, trusting as children, had lost their logic. The Torah seems the same, and nothing in it has literally changed, no one has transformed the letters, but it can no longer be read in the old way. In those old words, a completely new meaning appears, and we see and understand it.

Whoever in this redeemed world keeps to the old Torah simply honors the dead world and the dead law. This man is the sinner.

The Messiah will complete his painful journey, destroying empty worlds from within, reducing dead laws to rubble. We must thus annihilate the old order, so that the new one may prevail.

Do not the teachings and the Scriptures show us clearly that this was precisely why Israel was scattered over the face of the earth, so that every spark of holiness could be collected, even at the farthest reaches of the world, and from its deepest depths? Has not Nathan of Gaza also taught us that at times those sparks have lodged deeply and shamefully inside matter, like jewels that have become lodged in shit? At the most difficult moments of tikkun there was no one able to extract them again, except for that one person—it was for him alone to enter into sin and evil in order to retrieve the sparks of holiness inside. This is why Sabbatai Tzvi had to accept Islam, had to betray on behalf of all of us, so that we would not have to do the same. Many are unable to understand this. But we know from Isaiah—the Messiah must be rejected by his own as well as by outsiders. So goes the prophecy.

By now Tovah was preparing to leave. He had bought silk brought here by ship from China, and Chinese porcelain, carefully packed in paper and sawdust. He had bought Indian oils. He went to the bazaar himself to get presents for his wife and his beloved daughter, Hana, about whom I heard for the first time then, without yet knowing how things would turn out later. He perused embroidered slippers and scarves shot through with gold thread. Reb Mordke and I went to him as he was resting, having sent his aides to the customs offices for firmans, since in a few days they were to set off again for home. Thus everyone who had family in the north was now writing letters and packing up small parcels so that they might accompany Tovah's caravan over the Danube—to Nikopol and Giurgiu, and from there onward to Poland.

We sat beside him, and Mordechai brought out a bottle of the finest wine. As a man unaccustomed to drinking, Tovah was affected quickly. After two glasses, his face softened into an expression of childlike surprise, his eyebrows rising, his forehead wrinkling, and I became aware that now I was seeing the true face of this wise man, that Tovah had always been on guard until now. Reb Mordke started to poke fun at him: "How can you not drink, when you own your own vineyard?" But the purpose of our visit was something else entirely. I felt just as I had when, in the past, we had made matches for young people. Now, the youth to be matched was Jacob. We pointed out that he was often in the society of the Salonika Jews, who were supporters of Konio, the son of Baruchiah, which Tovah liked very much, as he, too, had allied with them. But both Reb Mordke and myself kept on obstinately returning to something else, and our obstinacy—the obstinacy of "those two from Poland," as Tovah called us—was like a spiral that at first seemed to be abating, but that soon returned to the same place as before, except in slightly different form. The place to which every conversation returned, after the furthest-reaching digressions and the widest-ranging associations, was Jacob. What did we want? We wanted to marry Jacob to Tovah's daughter, and in that way, to make Jacob a respectable man. An unwed Jew is no one, and he will be taken seriously by no one. And what else? What idea came into our heads as if by miracle? It was a bold thought, maybe dangerous, but I suddenly saw it in its totality, and it struck me as absolutely perfect. As if I had understood at last what all of this had been for—my travels with Reb Mordke, all of our studying. And maybe it was the wine that relaxed my mind, for suddenly everything became so clear to me. Then Reb Mordke said on my behalf:

"We will arrange his marriage with your daughter, and he will go to Poland as a messenger."

That was what we wanted. And surprisingly, Tovah did not say even one word against it, for he had heard, of course, of Jacob, as everyone had.

So we sent for Jacob, and he came after a while, and with him came a whole pack of boys his age, and some Turks. They remained on the other side of the square, while Jacob stood respectfully before us. I remember that I got goose bumps at the sight of him, I felt my body tremble, and I experienced a love greater than I had ever felt for anyone before. Jacob's eyes were shining with excitement, and he struggled to repress that ironic smile of his.

"If you, Mordechai, you, Tovah, and you, Nahman, are the sages of our age," he said with exaggerated deference, "then surely you will be able to transform ordinary metal into gold. That way I will know for certain that you are messengers from on high."

I didn't know if he was just playing around or being serious.

"Sit," Reb Mordke snapped. "That kind of miracle only the Messiah himself can work. You know that. We've talked about it before."

"And where is he, this Messiah?"

"What, you don't know?" Reb Mordke glared at him. "You're always hanging around with his followers."

"The Messiah is in Salonika," said Tovah calmly. The wine seemed to stretch out his words. "After Sabbatai Tzvi's death, the Holy Spirit passed from him into Baruchiah (of blessed memory)." For a moment he was silent, and then he added, as if hoping to provoke a certain reaction: "And now they say the spirit has found itself a home in Baruchiah's son, Konio. They say it's him—that he is the Messiah."

At this, Jacob ceased to be able to keep a straight face. He smiled broadly, and we were all relieved, for we hadn't known where this conversation was headed.

"If you say so, then I'll go to him right away," Jacob said after a moment. "I want to do whatever I can for him. If he wants me to chop wood, I'll chop wood for him. If he tells me to carry the water, I'll carry it. If he's in need of someone to go into battle, I'll be first among the troops. Just say the word."

It is said in the tractate Hagigah 12: "Woe to them, the creations, who see and know not what they see." Somehow, this happened that same night. First, Jacob stood before Reb Mordke, and Reb Mordke, praying and invoking the most powerful words, touched Jacob's lips over and over, and his eyes, and his eyebrows, and then he spread a kind of herbal unction over his forehead, so that Jacob's eyes got glassy and he grew quiet, docile. We took off his clothes and left only one lamp burning. Then, with a trembling voice, I began to sing that song that we all knew, but that has now taken on a completely different meaning, for we were no longer asking for the spirit to descend, as everyone does on a daily basis, in a general way, for the sake of the improvement of the world, for our salvation—now we were asking for a truly tangible descent of the spirit into the naked body we had right here before us, the body of a man, of a brother, whom we knew well, but whom we also did not know. We were putting him to a trial by the spirit, trying to determine whether he could endure such an onslaught. And we weren't asking for any ordinary sign, as before, for the comfort of our hearts. We were asking for action, for an arrival in our world, our filth, our gloom. We set out Jacob like bait, like a dazed lamb before a wolf. Our combined voice rose, then finally turned shrill, as though we'd become women. Tovah rocked back and forth; I felt nauseated, as though I had eaten something spoiled, and I felt I would faint. Only Reb Mordke simply stood there, at ease, his eyes raised high toward the ceiling, where there was a little window. Maybe he thought the spirit would come in through that small window.

"The spirit circles around us like a wolf around those trapped in a cave," I said. "It seeks the smallest hole to get through to those weak figures living in the shadow world. It sniffs, it checks each crack, each sliver, smelling us inside. It moves like a lover consumed by desire, in order to fill with light those delicate creatures, like underground mushrooms. And people—little, fragile, lost—leave him signs, marking stones with olive oil, and tree bark, and doorframes; people make signs on their foreheads in oil, so that the spirit might enter."

"Why does the spirit like olive oil so much? Why all that anointing? Is it to make it slippery, so it will be easier for it to go inside of matter?" Jacob asked once, and all the students burst out laughing. And I did, too, because it was so bold it could not be unwise.

Everything happened so quickly. Jacob suddenly got an erection, and his skin became covered in sweat. He had strangely bulging, unseeing eyes, and he was sort of buzzing. Then he was thrown down on the ground, and there he remained, in a strange, contorted position, shaking all over. In a natural impulse, I took a step toward him to help him, but the unexpectedly strong hand of Reb Mordke stopped me. It lasted but a moment. Then from underneath Jacob there began to slowly flow a stream of urine. It is difficult for me to write of this.

I will never forget what I saw there, and I have never seen anything so real that might testify to how foreign we are to the spirit in our earthly, corporeal, material forms.

## Of the wedding in Nikopol, the mystery under the huppah, and the advantages of being foreign

A mid-eighteenth-century map of Ottoman territory displays a vast terrain marked only intermittently with cities. Most of these settlements were located along rivers, especially the Danube; on the map, they look like ticks latching on to bloodstreams. The element of water dominates here—it seems to be everywhere. The empire begins with the Dniester to the north, grazes the shores of the Black Sea to the east, and reaches south across Turkey and the Land of Israel, continuing farther around the Mediterranean Sea. Not much is missing for it to come full circle.

And if the movements of people might be indicated on a map like this, it would show them leaving chaotic trails, unpleasant to the eye. Zigzags, twisting spirals, lopsided ellipses—the record of travel for commerce, pilgrimage, merchants' expeditions, visits to families, homesickness, and flights.

There are many bad people around, some of them really very cruel. They might spread out a kilim on the highway and drive spears into the ground around it—this is a sign that they must be paid a fee, without the traveler ever even glimpsing the villain's cunning face. If the traveler opts not to pay, spears will rain down on him from the surrounding thickets, and then the highwaymen will follow and chop the traveler into bits with their swords. Some travelers, however, are not daunted by such dangers. And so the caravans move onward, bales of cotton on their carts. Whole families in carriages, on the way to relatives. Holy fools, exiles, and eccentrics who have already survived so much that nothing fazes them, including murderers' forced tributes. Members of the sultan's government who, at a leisurely pace, luxuriating, collect taxes, taking a rich cut for themselves and their confidants; the carriages of pashas' harems, which leave in their wake the fragrance of oils and incense; herders driving their cattle south.

Nikopol is a small city, and from its position on the southern bank of the Danube it sends ferries across to Turnu, the Wallachian town also called Greater Nikopol, on the other side of the wide river. Anyone who travels from south to north must stop here, to sell some of the goods he is carrying or exchange them for others. This is why there is so much happening in this city, why business is booming. Here, in Nikopol, Jews speak Ladino, a language they brought with them from Spain when they were exiled, picking up new words along the way, its pronunciation changing until it became what the Sephardic Jews speak in the Balkans. Some spitefully refer to it as broken Spanish. But why should it be broken? It's a beautiful language, after all. Everybody here speaks it. Sometimes they switch to Turkish. Jacob was raised in Wallachia, so he knows Ladino well, although the witnesses to his wedding, Mordechai of Prague and Nahman of Busk, do not even try to use the few Ladino words they know, preferring to continue speaking Hebrew and Turkish.

The wedding lasted seven days, from the 24th day of the month of Sivan, 5512 (in other words, June 6, 1752). The father of the bride, Tovah, borrowed money to make this happen and is already worrying that he will fall into financial ruin, since even aside from the burden of this event, things haven't been going particularly well for him lately. The dowry was rotten, but the girl is lovely and couldn't stop staring at the groom. This was no cause for surprise—Jacob was in fine spirits and funny, graceful as a red deer. The relationship was consummated on the very first night, or so the groom boasts—and consummated several times, at that. No one asked the bride. Surprised by the intrusion of her husband—sixteen years older than she—into the drowsy flower beds of her body, she gazed inquisitively into the eyes of her mother and her sisters on the following day. So this is how things are?

As a married woman, Hana received a new outfit, worn in the Turkish fashion—soft sirwal, and over them a Turkish tunic embroidered in roses and decorated with precious stones, and also a beautiful cashmere scarf, now tossed onto a balustrade, since it is very hot.

The necklace she received from her husband was so valuable that it was taken from her right away and locked up in a chest. But Hana did have a different kind of dowry—the prestige of her family, the resourcefulness of her brothers, the books written by her father, the ancestry of her mother, who descends from Portuguese Jews, and her own sleepy beauty, and her gentleness, which has delighted Jacob thus far, since he is accustomed to slim, proud, impertinent women with strong wills like the Jewish women of Podolia, his grandmother, his sisters and female cousins, or the mature widows he permitted to spoil him in Smyrna. But Hana is as gentle as a doe. She gives herself to him with love, taking nothing for herself—for pleasure he has yet to teach her. She gives herself to him with surprise in her eyes, and this excites Jacob. She observes him carefully, like he's a horse she might have been given as a gift. Jacob dozes, and she examines his fingers, the skin on his back, the pockmarks on his face, wrapping his beard around her finger, until finally, when she has worked up the courage, she gazes in utter astonishment at his genitalia.

A trampled garden, an overturned fence, dancers who've gone out to cool down and come back in scattering sand—a sign that the desert is nearby—across floors covered with kilims and cushions. Dirty dishes not yet cleared away, though there have been women bustling around since early morning, the smell of urine in the orchard, scraps of food thrown out for the cats and the birds, bones picked clean—this is all that is left of the feast, which lasted several days. Nahman's head hurts; he may have overdone it with the Nikopolian wine. He is lying in the shade of a fig tree, watching Hana poking at the house with a stick, trying to get at a wasps' nest. She'll be sorry shortly, and they'll all have to run away. She's upset that so soon after the wedding the men want to leave. She's barely even glimpsed her husband, and already he is moving on.

Nahman pretends to be sleeping, but he takes secret peeks at Hana. He doesn't really like her—she seems a little bland to him. Who is this girl who has been given to Jacob? He wouldn't be able to describe her if he were to return to his Scraps. He doesn't know whether she's intelligent or stupid, cheerful or melancholic, whether she's short-tempered or the opposite, good-natured. He doesn't understand how this girl with the round face and the greenish eyes can be a wife. They don't cut married women's hair in Nikopol, so he can see how wild and beautiful hers is, dark brown, like coffee. She has lovely hands with long, thin fingers and fecund hips. She doesn't look fourteen. She looks like she might be twenty, like a woman. Pretty and curvy—that's how she should be described. That's enough. And to think that a few days ago he regarded her as he would a child.

He also takes a look at Hana's twin brother, Hayim. There is such a likeness between them it gives him chills. Hayim is shorter, slimmer, livelier, with an oval face, his hair in boyish disarray, down to his shoulders. Because his body is trimmer, he also looks younger. He is quick and always laughing boisterously. His father has chosen him as his successor, and now the siblings must be separated, which won't be easy. Hayim wants to go to Craiova, too, but his father needs him here, or maybe merely fears for him. Daughters are destined to be given away, and everyone knows from the start they'll leave the nest, like money neatly put away that must later be paid back to the world. When Hana stops scowling and forgets she's gotten married, she goes up to her brother and whispers something or other into his ear, their dark heads leaning in together. It is a beautiful sight to behold, and not only for Nahman; he can see that everyone enjoys the double image—only united are the siblings complete. Should man in fact not be like this, double? What would it be like if we all had twins, boys for girls, girls for boys? We could all talk without words.

Nahman also watches Jacob. It seems to him that Jacob's eyes have been covered by a film of some sort since the wedding. Perhaps it's exhaustion, perhaps the result of all the toasts—but where is his bird's gaze, the ironic look that makes everyone else glance down or away? Now he's put his hands behind his head—there are no strangers here, he feels relaxed; his wide sleeve has slid all the way down to his shoulder and bared the concavity of his armpit, lushly overgrown with dark hair.

His father-in-law, Tovah, murmurs something into Jacob's ear, his hand resting on Jacob's back, so that you might wonder—Nahman thinks spitefully—whether it was Tovah who married Jacob, and not Hana. Hayim, meanwhile, spars with everyone, but Jacob he avoids. When Jacob tries to grab his attention, Hayim falls silent and scurries off. For some reason this amuses the adults.

As for Reb Mordke, he doesn't leave his house, he does not care for the sun. He sits alone in his chamber, leaning up against some cushions, and he smokes his pipe—slowly, lazily, savoring each particle of smoke, thinking things over, closely examining every moment of the world under the watchful gaze of all the letters of the alphabet. Nahman knows he's waiting, that he's standing guard, keeping watch so that everything he sees—even when he's not looking at anything—will come to pass.

Under the huppah Tovah said something to Jacob, one short sentence, a few words, its beginning and end getting tangled in his ample beard. Jacob had to lean in to his father-in-law for a moment, and then serious surprise, even astonishment appeared on his face. Then Jacob's face set, as though he were trying to master a grimace.

The guests ask after the groom, they want to hear once more those stories that Mordechai, Reb Mordke, who now sits with them at the table, is glad to tell. He is always either filling up his pipe or emerging at regular intervals from within a cloud of smoke, to say how he and Nahman ben Levi brought Jacob to Tovah. He tells the story in his croaking voice:

"'This is the husband for your daughter,' we said. 'Only him.' 'But why him?' asked Tovah. 'He is exceptional,' I said, 'and she, thanks to him, will attain the highest honors. Look at him. Don't you see? He is great.'" Reb Mordke breathes in the smoke from his pipe, which smells of Smyrna, Stamboul. "But Tovah hesitated. 'Who is he, this boy with the pitted face, and where are his parents from?' he asked. Then I, Reb Mordke, and Nahman of Busk here—we patiently explained that his father is a famous rabbi, Yehuda Leyb Buchbinder, while his mother, Rachel of Rzeszów, comes from the finest home, that she is a relative of

Hayim Malach, whose cousin was given in marriage to Dobrushka in Moravia, the great-grandson of Leybele Prossnitz. And there are no madmen in his family, nor sick people, nor cripples. The spirit only goes into the chosen. Oh, if only Tovah had a wife he could go to for advice, but he doesn't, since she died."

Reb Mordke doesn't say anything for a moment, reminded of Tovah's hesitation, how it annoyed them, seeming like the hesitation of a merchant fretting over wares. This was Jacob they were talking about!

Nahman listens to Reb Mordke, but how does he know that Jacob is *Jacob*? He watches him now, sitting across from his father-in-law in silence. Jacob has lowered his head and is gazing at his shoes. The heat makes it so that words can't reach pronouncement, grown heavy and slow. Jacob won't take off his Turkish costume now—the new, brightly colored turban on his head, the same one he wore at the wedding, the color of fig leaves. He looks nice in it. Nahman sees his soft Turkish leather shoes with the toes curled up. Then the hands of both men rise in the same moment as they take sips of coffee from their little cups.

Nahman knows that Jacob is Jacob because when he looks at him as he is doing now, from afar, without Jacob being aware, Nahman feels a pressure in the vicinity of his heart, as though some invisible hand were holding him by it, hot and wet. This sense of being squeezed makes him feel good, calm. His eyes fill up with tears. He could just look and look and look in this way. What further proof could he want? It's the heart that knows such things.

Jacob has begun to introduce himself not as before, not as Yankiele Leybowicz, but as Jacob Frank. Frank is what Jews from the west are called in Nikopol; that's what they call his father-in-law and his wife, Hana. Frank, or Frenk, means foreign. Nahman knows Jacob likes this—being foreign is a quality of those who have frequently changed their place of residence. He's told Nahman that he feels best in new places, because it is as if the world begins afresh every time. To be foreign is to be free. To have a great expanse stretch out before you—the desert, the steppe. To have the shape of the moon behind you like a cradle, the deafening symphony of the cicadas, the air's fragrance of melon peel, the rustle of the scarab beetle when, come evening, the sky turns red, and it ventures out onto the sand to hunt. To have your own history, not for everyone, just your own history written in the tracks you leave behind.

To feel like a guest everywhere you go, occupying homes just for a while, not bothering about the garden, enjoying the wine without forming any attachment to the vineyard. Not to understand the language, and therefore to register gestures and faces better, the expressions in people's eyes, the emotions that appear on faces like the shadows of clouds. To learn a foreign language from scratch, a little bit in every place, comparing words and finding orders of similarity.

This state of foreignness must be carefully guarded, for it gives enormous power.

Jacob had told him one thing, as if in jest, Jacob being Jacob, as if for laughs, an unclear thing that instantly made a permanent home in Nahman's memory, for it was Jacob's first teaching, though perhaps he did not know that yet. The thing was that you have to practice saying no, every single day. What does that mean? Nahman promises himself he will ask, but when? There isn't any time left now. He has grown sad and irritable—maybe there was something wrong with the wine. He couldn't say when he began to turn from a master to a friend, and then, imperceptibly, into a student. He let it happen, somehow.

Jacob never talks like the tzaddikim do, in long, complicated sentences brimming with rare and precious words, always harking back to quotes from the Scriptures. He speaks concisely and clearly, like someone who earns his living at the market or drives a cart. He's always joking, but you can't tell if he's actually joking in what he says or being serious. He looks you straight in the eye, says a sentence like he's firing a shot, and then waits for a reaction. Usually his persistent gaze, like that of a bird—eagle, falcon, vulture—flusters his interlocutors. They look away, they falter. Sometimes he'll start laughing, apropos of nothing, to everyone's relief. He can be rude; he can be outrageous. He often mocks. If you get on his bad side, he'll grimace, and his eyes will become like knives. He says wise and stupid things. No man should trust him too much, for he will make fun of anyone—Nahman has seen him do so, though Jacob has not yet turned his vulture's gaze on him. Because of all of this, Jacob seems at first glance like someone familiar, a peer, but soon, after a little conversation, people realize that there is nothing familiar about him—that he is peerless.

The groom is getting ready to go now. Yehuda Levi ben Tovah, Jacob's father-in-law, has found him a good job in Craiova. It is a sizable city situated on the Danube, a gate between the north and the south. Tovah has a brother-in-law there who is a successful merchant, and he needs help with his warehouse—dispatching things, invoicing. The whole commercial network is run by a macher named Osman of Czernowitz; people say that whatever he touches turns to gold. Gold flows from Poland, from Moravia, they pay him for Turkish goods and the things that they don't have up north. Why do they not produce hats made of wool felt in Poland? Why do they not weave carpets? And craft faience, and glass? They don't make much there, importing everything, which is why someone like Osman must exist at the border, the salt of the earth, helping to channel the impulses of the world. The turban that wreathes his suntanned face makes him look like a Turk.

Reb Mordke thinks he will remain in Nikopol; he is old, tired. He needs soft pillows, clean sheets; his mission seems to have come to an end, the mystery revealed, Jacob matched and married and now a fully grown man. One broken gear in the machine of the world has been fixed. Now, perhaps, Reb Mordke can retreat into the shadows, into the smoke of his pipe.

Come tomorrow, everyone will part. Jacob and Hershel ben Zebu, Hana's young cousin, will set out for Craiova, and at least for now, Nahman will go back to Poland. He will carry the good news to the brothers in Podolia, Rohatyn, Glinno, and Busk, and after all of that, he will be free to go back to his own home. He thinks about this with a mixture of happiness and aversion. As everyone knows, it isn't easy to go home.

It takes them until midnight to say goodbye. The women have been sent off to sleep; the men have closed the doors. Now they're drinking that Nikopolian wine and concocting schemes for the future, playing with little crumbs of bread on the table, sprinkling them into little hills, twirling the little balls. Nussen is already asleep on a cotton bale, he has closed his one eye and doesn't see Jacob, gaze blurry, stroking Nahman's face, or Nahman, drunk, resting his head on Jacob's chest.

At dawn, not yet fully conscious, Nahman sits down in a cart that will carry travelers to Bucharest; he has gold sewn into his light-colored kapota, everything he has earned from this expedition—not bad. And he will carry some dozen bottles of aloe oil that he will sell in Poland for a considerably higher price. Deep in the pocket of his white wool overcoat that he bought at the bazaar in Nikopol, he has a clump of fragrant resin. There is also a bag of letters and a whole pack of gifts for the women in the cart. His freckled, chapped face is wet with tears, but as soon as they get past the town's outskirts, he is overcome by such elation he feels as if he were flying over the stony tract toward the sun, which is just coming up and completely blinds him.

He is lucky: in Bucharest, he joins the caravan of the Kamieniec company of Wereszczyński, David and Muradowicz—so say the cases on the carts. The load smells of coffee and tobacco. The caravan is heading north.

After almost three weeks, Nahman reaches Rohatyn in good stead and dirty stockings, and in his dusty, light-colored overcoat he stands at dusk in front of the Shorr house, where they are just preparing for a wedding of their own.

## In Craiova: Of trade on holy days and of Hershel, faced with the dilemma of the cherries

The workshop of Abraham, Tovah's brother-in-law, is a veritable treasure trove; he trades all over Europe the things the Orient does best, which flow through Stamboul to the north in a colorful stream of all kinds of bright and shining merchandise, much vaunted at the courts of Budapest and Vienna, Kraków and Lwów. The Stamboul fabrics, which come in all different colors, interwoven with gold, in amaranth, red, green, in cerulean stripes or embossed with floral patterns, lie rolled up in bales and covered in canvas to protect them from dust and sun. Next to these, soft Algerian carpets made of wool so delicate it feels like damask, fringed or trimmed with galloon. And camlet, also in bales and of various colors, from which European men's fancy jackets are fashioned, and lined with silk, which is also present here in great abundance.

There are also little kilims, tassels, fringes, mother-of-pearl and lacquer buttons, small decorative weapons, lacquer snuffboxes—a gift for the refined gentleman—and fans painted with scenes—for European ladies—pipes, expensive stones. There are even sweets: halva and Turkish delight. To the warehouse come Bosnians, known here as "Greeks," bringing leather goods, sponges, fluffy towels, brocade, delightful Khorasan and Kerman scarves with lions and peacocks embroidered on them. And it all smells different—some exotic, foreign scent emanates from the pile of kilims, the fragrance of unfathomable gardens, blooming trees, fruits.

"Subhanallah"—"Praise Allah"—say the clients when they enter this place. "As-salamu alaykum."

They have to bow their heads because the entrance is low. Jacob never sits in the office, but rather at a little table having tea, dressed lavishly, like a Turk, in a blue-green Turkish caftan and a dark red Turkish cap. Before they get down to business, they always have to have two or three little glasses of tea. The local merchants also want to get to know Tovah's son-in-law, so Jacob gives audiences of sorts, which angers Abraham. But on the other hand, Abraham's small warehouse is always full of people now. Precious stones and ready-made jewelry in semi-wholesale quantities are traded here. Strung beads and malachite of every possible size hang from hooks and cover the stone walls with a colorful pattern of undulating lines. The most valuable goods, including an exceptionally expensive pearl, can be found in the glass display cabinet.

Jacob stands and greets each guest with a bow. After just a few days of his working in Abraham's warehouse, it has become the most popular place in all of Craiova.

Several days after the arrival of Jacob and his entourage, the fast of Tisha BeAv begins. It commemorates the destruction of the Temple—a dark and difficult time, a day of sadness; the world also slows down then, as though grown sad, and having started to stagger out of that sadness. The Jews, some dozen households in Craiova, close their stores, don't work, sit in darkness, and read Jeremiah's Lamentations, recollecting their misfortune.

This is good for Abraham, since as a true believer, and as a follower of

Sabbatai Tzvi and his successor, Baruchiah, he celebrates the holiday in a different way, aware that in the end times, everything is done in reverse. For Abraham, then, this is a joyful holiday.

Baruchiah was born exactly nine months after the death of Sabbatai Tzvi, on the ninth day of the month of Av—exactly as predicted! And on a day of mourning, the day of the destruction of the Temple. AMIRAH, as Sabbatai's name has been written, or Adoneinu Malkeinu Yarum Hodo—Our Lord and King, His Majesty, will be exalted—returned and lived for those years as Baruchiah in Salonika. In 5476, the Christian year 1726, he was recognized as God incarnate, for the Shekhinah, which had previously gone into Sabbatai, had now descended into him. This is why all those who believe in Baruchiah's mission have converted the day of mourning into a day of joy, to the outrage of other Jews. Women wash their hair and dry it in the August sun outside, clean their homes, adorning them with flowers, sweeping the floors so that the Messiah may arrive to a neat and tidy world. This world is terrible, it is true, but perhaps it can be spruced up a little here and there.

For on this worst and darkest of days, light is born. Sadness would be nothing without some knowledge of joy. At the very bottom of that sadness, that mourning, there is a dash of joy and holiness—and vice versa. Isaiah 61:3 says: "Bestow on them a crown of beauty instead of ashes, the oil of joy instead of mourning, and a garment of praise instead of a spirit of despair." And of course, clients of all kinds, of every dress and language, continue to come to Abraham. Jacob and Hershel are already in the office. Who will ring up the bags of tobacco, and how many of them will fit onto the cart? Lots. Who will provide goods to the merchant from Wrocław who is paying in cash and placing large orders?

Clients, even those who are sworn enemies of the followers of Sabbatai Tzvi, cannot restrain their curiosity and also take a peek inside. They refuse the little glass of vodka offered by the hand of an apostate. Nay, nay, nay, they cry in alarm. Jacob plays little tricks to scare them further. His best one is when he asks them what they have in their pockets.

"Nothing," they answer in surprise.

"Well, what about those eggs? Stole them, eh? Which of the stalls did you swipe them from?"

"What eggs?" the clients say. "What are you talking about?"

Then in a bold swoop Jacob reaches into their pocket and pulls out an egg. The little crowd bursts out laughing, the delinquent's face turns red, and he doesn't know what to say, which only cracks people up even more. Jacob pretends he is angry, and looks serious—he frowns, examines them with his bird's gaze: "Tell me why you didn't pay for this! You are a thief! An egg thief!" And quickly everyone starts to repeat the charge, until even the accused begins to struggle with the idea that he might have stolen something, even if he didn't mean to. But then he sees on Jacob's face a slightly raised eyebrow, an amused look, so he, too, smiles, then soon guffaws, and it's clear that the best thing he can do under the circumstances is reconcile himself to being the butt of the joke, offer himself up as a laughingstock, and walk away.

None of this amuses Hershel. If it were to happen to him, if an egg came out of his pocket, he would die of shame. He isn't yet thirteen and was sent here by his family, after the death of his parents. Until then he lived in Czernowitz; now he will probably stay with Abraham, a distant relation.

He doesn't know how things are supposed to go with the fast on Tisha BeAv, no one has told him the secret, no one has initiated him into why he is to be joyful here over the course of this day, while elsewhere others are grave. In his family home, solemnity always presided on this holiday. It is only here that his experience is different, but no one has bothered to teach him the religious nuances. He understands now that Sabbatai is the Messiah—but why did he not save the world, not change anything? And how exactly would a saved world differ from an unsaved world? For his parents, simple folk, it was obvious—the Messiah would appear as a warrior, wipe the sultans off the face of the earth, along with kings and emperors, and then take over the world. The Temple of Jerusalem would rebuild itself, or God would drop it down from heaven, cast in gold. All the Jews would go back to the Land of Israel. First those who were buried there would be resurrected, followed by those who were buried elsewhere in the world, outside the Holy Land.

Here, people thought otherwise. Hershel asked about it, but Jacob said nothing.

Strange is a salvation that can't be seen. It takes place not here, in the visible world, but somewhere—this Hershel can't quite understand—in some other world, right nearby or maybe underneath the visible world. The Messiah has already come and inverted the lever of the world, which is a lever like that on a well pump, without anybody even noticing. Now everything is reversed: river water goes back to its source, rain to clouds, blood into wounds. It turns out that Mosaic law was temporary, that it was created just for the world before salvation, and that it is no longer in effect. In other words: now one should relate to it the other way around. While the Jews are fasting, one ought to eat and drink, and while they mourn, one must make merry.

Nobody particularly looks after him; they treat him like an idiot of sorts. Sometimes Jacob looks at him in such a way as to turn Hershel beet red. He is Jacob's helper, he cleans his clothes, sweeps the office, brews the coffee. In the evening, as they tally the day's take, he writes the numbers in the columns.

He isn't sure of anything and he's ashamed to ask, there is some sort of mystery around all of this. Since he hasn't yet had his bar mitzvah, they don't let him in when they gather for their prayers. They close the door. Is he supposed to fast or not fast?

So on the fasting day of Tisha BeAv, Hershel cleans the cellars, sweeps out the cotton dust and mouse droppings. He hasn't eaten since morning, recalling this day as a fast. That was how it was before. He didn't want to look while they were eating upstairs. Now hunger has seized him by the stomach, making his innards lament. In the cellar they keep wine and carrots. Pots of compote sit here in the cool. He could just try it. But Hershel can't make up his mind to do it, he can't convince himself to eat, after all, his whole life until now he wasn't permitted to eat on fasting days, so now instead he takes just a teeny-tiny cherry out of the compote and eats half. If Sabbatai Tzvi is the Messiah, then he is fulfilling the command and breaking the law in keeping with the new law, although if he is not the Messiah, then he's still fasting—for what is one little cherry for a whole day?

The next morning he asks Jacob. He has brought the Tractate Yoma, which reads:

"One who eats a large date-bulk of food, equivalent to a date and its pit, or who drinks a cheekful of liquid is liable to receive the punishment of karet. All foods that one eats join together to constitute a date-bulk; and all liquids that one drinks join together to constitute a cheekful. However, if one eats and drinks, the food and beverage do not join together to constitute a measure that determines liability, as each is measured separately."

Jacob looks at the text and at Hershel, who is fairly panic-stricken, with mock seriousness. Then he bursts out laughing. Jacob laughs as he is wont to do, that deep, sonorous laughter, from the belly itself, infectiously, and he can probably be heard all over Craiova, until Hershel starts to join in with him in spite of himself; at first he only smiles, but then he starts to giggle. Then Jacob pulls him in by the hand and, shocking him, kisses him on the lips.

Hershel wonders if the young husband might not miss his wife, whom he left with her father; she sends him love letters, entreating him to come home or asking him incessantly when he'll take her with him. Hershel knows because he reads these letters in secret, while Jacob isn't watching. Sometimes he imagines the white hand that wrote those letters. This brings him pleasure. Jacob doesn't file the letters away, his documents are in a jumble, orders lie scattered over the table; Hershel tries to pick them up and organize them somehow. He accompanies Jacob when he goes to see clients, mostly women clients, wealthy townswomen whose husbands have left, captains' wives and widows who send for Jacob, asking for him in particular, so he can show them what he's selling. They arrange it so that when Jacob drops his purse, as if accidentally, Hershel takes it as the signal to make his excuses and leave. Then he waits for Jacob on the street, not taking his eyes off the door to the woman's home.

When Jacob steps out, he does so at a vigorous pace. He always walks like this, splaying his legs a little, straightening his galligaskins, his Turkish pantaloons. He looks at Hershel in triumph and claps his hand over his own crotch in Turkish fashion. Hershel wonders what attracts women to this man. There is something women can always discern, a thing they always recognize a man by, even Hershel understands this. Jacob is beautiful, and wherever he shows up, everything takes on a meaning, comes together like it has been tidied up.

Jacob promised Tovah that he would study, but Hershel sees that read-ing tires him, that the period of fervor into which Reb Mordke and Nah-man once thrust him has passed. The books lie fallow. Sometimes he doesn't open the long letters Nahman sends him from Poland for several days. Hershel collects these letters, reads them, and puts them in a pile. Jacob is much more interested in money right now. He has deposited with Abraham's cousin all that he has earned this year. He would like to have a home and vineyards in Nikopol or Giurgiu. The kind where you can see the Danube from the window, and the vines could climb up a set of wooden supports and make green walls and a green roof. Then he'll bring Hana. For the time being he frolics with the clients, or he leaves midway through the day and disappears somewhere. He must be running a side operation, which Abraham does not much care for. He asks Hershel about it, and the boy, whether he likes it or not, must cover for Jacob. He wants to cover for Jacob. So he comes up with unbelievable stories. Says that Jacob goes and prays over the river, that he borrows books, that he is mak-ing sales, that he is checking on a shipment that is being unloaded right now. The first time Jacob invites Hershel to his bed, Hershel does not protest. He gives himself to Jacob completely, blazing like a torch; were it possible, Hershel would give him more—his life, even. Jacob calls this Massa Zar, or the Stranger's Journey—an act of reversal, the opposite of the written law, which in the face of the purifying fire of the Messiah has spluttered out like an old wet rag.

## Of a pearl and Hana

Jacob is determined to give Hana the most precious pearl. For a few days, he and Hershel have wandered jewelers' shops. With great pomp Jacob has extracted the pearl from the little box where it rests on a piece of silk; whoever takes it in his fingers squints in ecstasy, smacking his lips. It's a miracle, not a pearl. It's worth a fortune. Jacob relishes their ecstasy. But then what tends to happen is that the jeweler returns the pearl as if it were a shred of light that's caught between his fingers—no, no, he would not dare drill into it; the miracle might break, and the loss incurred would be enormous. Please try somewhere else, maybe someone else will do it for you. Jacob is angry. At home, he sets this pearl on the table and stares at it in silence. Hershel gives him a bowl of the olives Jacob so adores. Later he'll have to pick up the pits strewn all over the floor.

"There's no one left. These cowards who are frightened of a pearl," says Jacob.

When Jacob is angry, he moves faster than he usually does, and more stiffly. He furrows his brow, drawing his eyebrows down. Hershel fears him then, although Jacob has never done him any harm. Hershel knows that Jacob loves him.

In the end, he tells the boy to get ready, and they put on their oldest clothes, the most worn ones, and they go to the port and take the ferry across the river. There, on the other side, they go up to the first decent-looking stand they find that does polishing. With firm conviction in his voice and gestures, Jacob tells the man to take this fake trinket, which is worth almost nothing, he says, and just make a hole through it. "I've got a girl I want to give it to."

Now the pearl is produced directly from Jacob's pocket; he tosses it onto the scale pan, making small talk; the man takes the pearl boldly, without any ecstasy or sighs, puts it in his vise, and, still chatting with Jacob, drills a hole through it; the gimlet goes through the pearl like it's passing through butter. The man takes a modest fee and goes back to his interrupted tasks.

Back on the street, Jacob says to an astonished Hershel:

"That's how you've got to do things. Don't ever make a fuss about them. Make a note of that."

These words make an enormous impression upon Hershel. From that moment forward, he wants to be like Jacob. And being close to Jacob evokes in him some incomprehensible excitement, produces a warmth that flows all through his small body, so that the boy feels safe and powerful.

Over Hanukkah they go to get Hana in Nikopol. The young wife runs out to meet them, before Jacob has even scrambled out of the cart with presents for the whole family. They greet each other in an official way, a little stiffly. Everyone here treats Jacob like someone more significant than an ordinary merchant, and he in turn takes on a gravity of tone Hershel has never heard from him before. He kisses Hana on the forehead, like a father. He greets Tovah as though they are both kings. He's given his own room, but he quickly disappears into Hana's in the women's part of the home. Hershel still leaves him the made bed, while he sleeps on the floor by the stove.

By day they eat and drink, and they pray without putting on tefillin. Besides, the boy sees that they do not keep the kitchen kosher here, they eat ordinary Turkish bread, dipping it in olive oil and herbs, crumbling cheese with their hands. They sit on the floor like Turks. The women wear wide-legged pants made from lightweight material.

Hana comes up with the idea of visiting her sister in Vidin. First she proposes it to her father, but he merely scowls at her, and Hana quickly understands that she is supposed to ask her husband now. She plays with the pearl hanging on its gold chain, Jacob's gift to her. Hana has clearly had enough of her parents, must want to show off her wedded status, wants Jacob to herself, wants travel, wants a change. Hershel sees she's still a child, just like him, that she's pretending to be a grown woman. He spies on her one time as she's bathing in the back part of the garden. She is plump, with wide hips, big buttocks.

During their three days of travel along the Danube from Nikopol to Vidin, Hershel falls in love with Hana. Now he loves both of them, Jacob and Hana, with a single feeling. It is a strange state to be in. He obsessively desires to be near Hana. He still remembers her buttocks, big and soft and innocent—he wants to storm them.

Just before they come to Vidin, they ask Hershel to drive up into the surrounding rocky hills outside the city. Out of the corner of his eye, Hershel can see where Jacob's hand is heading, and he tightens his fingers around the reins. They tell him to wait with the horses like a servant, while they disappear in between rocks that resemble petrified monsters. Hershel knows that it will be a while, so he lights up a pipe and adds to it a dash of the resin he has been given by Jacob. He takes a drag like old Reb Mordke, and the horizon softens. He leans against a rock and looks down at the huge brown grasshoppers, all angles. And when he lifts his gaze to the rocks above, he sees a white stone city outstretched past the horizon, and—how strange—it is a city that looks at people, and not the other way around. He doesn't know how to explain it, the fact that the rocks are watching. In fact it doesn't surprise him at all. He's watching, too. He sees a naked Hana bracing her arms wide against the rock wall, and, pressing into her backside, a half-naked Jacob, moving slowly, rhythmically. Jacob suddenly turns to look at Hershel where he sits behind the horses, and although he looks at him from far away, his look, so hot and powerful, gives Hershel an erection. Soon the brown grasshoppers meet a wet impediment in their path. It must surprise them to encounter this potent splotch of organic matter, this abrupt incursion into their insect world.

## 10.

### Who the person is who gathers herbs
### on Mount Athos

On his small boat from the port in Develiki, Count Antoni Kossakowski reaches the harbor at the base of the mountain. He feels profoundly
grateful, deeply emotional, and the pain that was only just recently
squeezing his chest now passes completely, though it isn't clear whether
it's because of the sea air and the wind, which, bouncing back off the
steep bank, takes on an inimitable smell of resin and herbs, or because
of his proximity to a holy place.

   He ponders this sudden change in his own mood and sense of well-
being. A radical and unexpected change. When he left cold Russia a few
years earlier for the Greek and Turkish countries, he became another
man, someone "luminous and airy," as he might say. Is it that simple—is
it just about light and heat? Oh, the sun—its abundance renders colors all
the more intense, and because it heats the land, fragrances dazzle. And
because of all that sky, the world appears to be subject to mechanisms
other than the ones that apply in the north. Here Destiny is still in effect,
the Greek version of Fatum that sets people in motion, marking out their
paths like little strings of sand that flow along a dune from top to bottom,
creating arabesques and other figures of which the finest artist would
hardly be ashamed, twisting, chimerical, exquisite.

Here in the south, all this exists quite tangibly. It grows in the sun, lurks in the heat. And the awareness of its existence brings Antoni Kossakowski relief, so that he becomes lighter, softer, more tender toward himself. At times he feels like crying, that's how free he feels.

He considers that the farther south he goes, the weaker Christianity becomes, the stronger the sun, the sweeter the wine, the more Fatum there is—and the better his life gets. His decisions are not decisions, arriving instead from outside, having their proper place in the order of the world. And since it is this way, there is less responsibility, and therefore less of that internal shame, that unbearable feeling of guilt for everything he has done. Here every action can be corrected, you can have a chat with the gods, make them a sacrifice. That is why people are able to look at their reflections in the water with respect. And look upon others with love. No one is bad, no murderer can be condemned, because it is all part of a larger plan. That is why you can feel the same love for the executioner as you can for the condemned. People are gentle and good. The evil that happens comes not from them, but rather from the world. The world can be evil—and how!

The farther north you go, the more people concentrate on themselves, and in some sort of northern madness (no doubt due to the lack of sun) they ascribe to themselves too much. They make themselves responsible for their actions. Fatum is punctured by raindrops, then farther on, snowflakes making a final incursion, and soon it disappears altogether. What remains is the conviction that destroys every person, supported by the Ruler of the North, the Church, and its ubiquitous functionaries, that all evil is in man yet can't be fixed by man. It can only be forgiven. But can it be forgiven? Hence comes that tiring, destructive feeling that one is always guilty, from birth, that one is stuck in sin and that everything is sin—doing something, not doing it, love, hate, words, and even thoughts. Knowledge is a sin, and ignorance is a sin.

He lodges at an inn for pilgrims run by a woman everyone calls Irena or simply Mother. She is a petite person with dark skin, always dressed in black; sometimes the wind whips her hair, which has gone completely gray, from under her black kerchief. Even though she is an innkeeper, they all address her with great respect, as if she were a nun, though it is known that she has grown children somewhere in the world, and that she is a widow. Irena oversees the prayers every evening and every morning and chants in a voice so pure it opens pilgrims' hearts. She has what seem to be two serving-maids in her employ—at least Kossakowski thought they were serving-maids at first, only noticing after a few days that they were in fact castrates, but with breasts. He has to be careful not to stare at them, for if he does, they stick out their tongues at him. Someone tells him that there has always been an Irena here at the inn, for hundreds of years, and that that's how it must be. This Irena comes from the north and does not speak flawless Greek, instead mixing in words Antoni often knows, so he thinks she is probably Wallachian or Serbian.

There are only men around, not a single woman (aside from Irena, but is she a woman?), not even a single animal that is female. It would distract the monks. Kossakowski tries to focus on a greenish-winged beetle traipsing down the path. He wonders whether it is also male . . .

Along with the other pilgrims, Kossakowski climbs to the top of the hill, but they cannot be admitted to the monastery. People like him are assigned to a special place in the stone house under the holy wall, where he sleeps and eats. In the early mornings and in the evenings they dedicate themselves to prayer according to the holy monk Gregory Palamas. This consists of repeating, "Lord Christ, Son of God, have mercy upon me" a thousand times a day. Those praying sit on the ground, their heads curled into their stomachs, as if they are fetuses; as they do this, they hold their breath as long as possible.

In the morning and the evening a high male voice summons them to communal prayer—across the whole place you can hear it call, "Molidbaaa, Molidbaaa." All the pilgrims drop whatever they are doing and race up to the monastery. Kossakowski associates this with the behavior of birds alerted to a predator by other birds.

By day, at the port, Kossakowski tends to his garden.

He has also reported to the port as a longshoreman, helping to unload the ships that come in once or twice a day. It's not about the meager income he earns from this work, but rather about the opportunity to be with people, and to go up to the monastery and even enter the outer courtyard. There, the caretaker, a robust monk in his prime, receives food and other goods, gives them cold, almost icy water to drink, and offers them olives. These deliveries do not happen often, however, since the monks are largely self-sufficient.

At first, Kossakowski is resistant, viewing with some disdain the pilgrims possessed by that religious mania of theirs. Instead, he devotes himself to his walks along the stony paths that surround the monastery, along the heated earth, incessantly disrupted by the cicadas' little bows, the land that from the mixture of herbs and resin smells like something to eat, like a dried herb-encrusted cake. On these walks Kossakowski imagines the Greek gods living here once, the very same ones he learned of at his uncle's house. Now they return. They wear glimmering gold robes, have very light skin, are taller than people. Sometimes he almost thinks he's walking in their footsteps, that if he hurries he might still be able to catch up with the goddess Aphrodite, glimpse her magnificent nakedness; the scent of hyssop becomes for a moment the half-animal smell of a perspiring Lord. He exerts his imagination; through it he wants to see them, he needs them. The gods. God. Their presence in this resiny fragrance, and especially the secret presence of some force that is sticky and slightly sweet, pulsing in every creature, makes it so that the world seems full, filled to the brim. He makes every effort to imagine it—this presence. His member swells and, like it or not, Kossakowski has to relieve himself on the holy mount.

One day, just when he seems happiest, he falls asleep at noon in the shade of a shrub. Suddenly the rumble of the sea wakes him up—it sounds ominous, even though it has been with him the whole time. Kossakowski leaps up, looks around. The high, strong sun separates everything into light and shadow. Everything has paused, he sees from afar the waves of the sea stuck in stillness, above them hangs an isolated seagull that looks like it's affixed to the sky. His heart rises to his throat, he leans forward to try to stand, but the grass beneath his hands dissolves into dust. Everything turns to dust. There is nothing to breathe, the horizon has come dangerously close, and in a moment its gentle line becomes a noose. In this moment, Antoni Kossakowski realizes that the plaintive rumble of the sea is a lament, and that all of nature is taking part in this process of mourning those gods of whom the world has been in such desperate need. There is no one here. God created the world, and the effort of doing so killed him. Kossakowski had to come all the way here to understand this.

This is why he starts to pray.

Yet prayer fails. In vain he brings his head into his stomach, curling his body up into a ball, similar to how it was before his birth—that's how they taught him to do it. Peace, however, does not come, his breathing won't even out, and the words "Lord Jesus Christ," repeated mechanically, bring him no relief. Kossakowski can only smell his own scent—the stink of a sweating, middle-aged man. Nothing more.

The next day, early in the morning, unswayed by Irena's objections and unmoved by the responsibilities he's casting off, he gets on the first decent sailboat and doesn't even ask where it's heading. He can still hear the call of "Molidbaaa, Molidbaaa" from the shore, and it feels as if the island is calling to him directly. Only out at sea does he learn that he is sailing to Smyrna.

In Smyrna things turn out very well for him indeed. He finds a job with the Trinitarians, and for the first time in a long while he manages to earn some decent money. He spares himself no expense: he buys himself a fine set of Turkish clothing. He orders wine. Drinking brings him enormous pleasure, so long as he has good company. He notes that whenever, in conversing with Christians, he mentions that he has been on Mount Athos, it arouses great interest, so every evening he adds some new detail to his story, until it has become a never-ending array of adventures. He says he is Moliwda. He's happy with this new designation—which of course is not a name. Moliwda is more than a name, it's a new coat of arms, a proclamation. His previous denomination—first name, last name—fits a little tight now, a little worn and insubstantial, as if it's made of straw, so he gets rid of it almost completely. He uses it only with the Trinitarian brothers. Antoni Kossakowski—what's left of him?

Moliwda would like to examine his life now with a certain distance, like these Jews from Poland he's met here. By day they do what they're supposed to, focused and always in good moods. In the evenings, they converse without pause. At first, he eavesdrops—they assume he cannot understand. They're Jews and yet Moliwda feels so close to them. He even wonders, quite seriously, if it might be that the air, the light, the water— nature—just sort of settle into a person, so that those raised in the same country must bear similarities to one another, even when everything divides them.

He likes Nahman best. Clever and talkative, he knows how to twist things around in a debate to prove any assertion, even the most absurd. He also knows how to ask questions that astonish Moliwda-Kossakowski. Nonetheless, he sees that the vast knowledge and intelligence of these people gets used up in bizarre word games, of which he has only the most general idea. One time he buys a basket of olives and a large jug of wine and goes to visit them. They eat the olives, spitting the pits under the feet of passersby who are running late, for dusk is coming; the heat of Smyrna, sticky, moist, is loosening its grip somewhat. Then the oldest of the men, Reb Mordke, begins to lecture on the soul. It is in effect in three parts, he says. The lowest part—the hungering part, the desiring part, the part that gets cold—that is nefesh. That part animals have, too.

"Soma," says Moliwda.

"The higher part, that's the spirit, ruah. That part animates our thoughts, makes us become good people."

"Psyche," throws in Moliwda.

"While the third part, the very highest part—that's neshama."

"Pneuma!" Moliwda exclaims. "What a fine discovery for me!"

Reb Mordke, unruffled, goes on:

"This is the truly holy soul, which only a good holy husband and Kabbalist can obtain; and one gets it only by delving into the mystery of Torah. Thanks to that we can view the hidden nature of the world and of God, for it is a spark that chipped off Binah, the divine intellect. Only nefesh is capable of sin. Ruah and neshama are impeccable."

"Since neshama is God's spark in man, how can God punish us for our sins with hell? If he did, wouldn't he be punishing himself as well, in particle form?" asks Moliwda, a little overexcited by the wine. With this question he gets the attention of both of his companions. All three of them know the answer to this question. Wherever there is God—the great God, the greatest God—there is neither sin nor any feeling of guilt. Only the little gods produce sin, similar to how dishonest craftsmen counterfeit coins.

After their work for the Trinitarians, they sit down in the kahvehane; Moliwda has learned to take pleasure in drinking bitter coffee and smoking long Turkish pipes.

Moliwda takes part in the payment of 600 zlotys by way of ransom for Piotr Andruszewicz of Buczacz, and another of 450 zlotys for Anna of Popielawy, who spent a few years at the court of Hussein Bayraktar of Smyrna. He remembers their names because he wrote up the purchasing agreements, in Turkish and in Polish. He knows the prices paid for people here in Smyrna: for one Tomasz Cybulski, a forty-six-year-old nobleman, quartermaster of the Jabłonowski regiment, in captivity for ten years, they paid the great sum of 2,700 zlotys and sent him straight to Poland, under escort. For some children they paid 618 zlotys each; for Jan, an old man, the price was just 18 zlotys. Jan comes from Opatów and weighs about as much as a goat; he spent his whole life in Turkish captivity, and now, it seems, he doesn't have anyone left in Poland to go back to; still, he's overjoyed. Moliwda watches the old man's tears flow down his face, made swarthy by the sun, wrinkled. Moliwda also pays careful attention to Anna, who is a mature woman now. He likes the imperiousness and pride with which she treats the Trinitarians and himself, the translator. He can't understand why a rich Turk would get rid of this beautiful woman. Judging by what she has told Moliwda, he promised her her freedom out of love, because she was homesick. In a few days she is to board a ship to Salonika, and then travel over land to Poland. Moliwda, possessed by some incomprehensible passion, tempted by her white, abundant body, once more throws all caution to the wind and agrees to the insane escape plan she proposes instead. Anna Popielawska does not intend to return to Poland at all, not to some boring estate somewhere in Polesia. Moliwda doesn't even have time to say goodbye to his friends. They flee on horseback to a small port city north of Smyrna, and there, with Moliwda's money, they rent a home from a Christian woman, the wife of a Greek merchant, where for two weeks they give themselves over to every form of delight. They spend their afternoons on the expansive balcony that looks out over the waterfront, where every day at around this time the Turkish agha passes by with his janissaries. The janissaries have white feathers in their caps, and their commander wears a purple coat lined with a thin silver fabric that shines in the sun like the belly of a fish just tossed up onto the shore.

In the heat, on the balconies, Anna Popielawska and Moliwda lie out on ottomans, catching the eyes of the young men who strain and flex before them. They are a previously unimaginable sight for the Turks. This is how the blond Anna Popielawska catches the eye of that agha. A short conversation starts up between the two of them one afternoon while Moliwda is reading inside the house, in the shade. The next day she vanishes along with all of the money Moliwda had saved from his work with the Trinitarians.

Moliwda goes back to Smyrna, but the Trinitarians already have another dragoman, and the two endlessly conversing Jews have gone. He signs on to a ship's crew and goes back to Greece.

Looking out at the marine horizon, hearing the splash of waves hitting the sides of the hull, he becomes amenable to recollection. Thoughts and images come together in long ribbons; he could look at them closely and see what comes out. He remembers his childhood. Those years seem stiff to him, like the starched dress shirts his aunt prepared for him and his brothers on Easter, the roughness that took days to surrender to the warmth of the body and its sweat.

Moliwda always reflects on his childhood when he finds himself at sea—he doesn't know why. Evidently the water's limitlessness makes him feel a little dizzy; he has to grasp at something.

His uncle, whose hand they had to kiss, kneeling, by way of greeting, had a second wife, dangerously young—she created around herself an atmosphere completely incomprehensible to young Antoni, an atmosphere of theater, of pretense. She came from very poor, disreputable nobility, and so had to strive for some better version of herself. She was ridiculous in her efforts. When guests came to their estate, she would stroke her nephews' faces with ostentatious tenderness, gently grabbing them by the ears and boasting, "Oh, yes, little Antoni, life will smile on this one." After the guests left, she would stow the boys' elegant garments in the wardrobe in the hallway, as if one day other orphans left by other dead relatives might show up, this time of superior provenance.

The flight of his lover, the sea, and this memory from his childhood make Moliwda feel frighteningly lonely. His only relief will come, not too long from now, from the Wallachian Bogomils, whom many stubbornly, and erroneously, maintain are Filippians. They will give him some respite from the torment of having a self broken in two (what a strange ailment— no one seems to suffer from it anymore, and there is no way to speak of it, and no one to tell). And all this has happened because Moliwda is fully convinced by now that his life has reached its natural conclusion, and that there won't be any other world.

## 11.

**How in the town of Craiova
Moliwda-Kossakowski runs into Jacob**

Two years later, in the spring of 1753, Moliwda is thirty-five years old and a little thinner due to the diet of the Bogomils. He has pale, watery eyes that are hard to read. His beard is sparse, reddish gray, the color of a jute sack, and his face is tanned from the sun. On his head is a very dirty white Turkish turban.

Moliwda is about to go and see this madman, this holy fool all the Jews keep talking about, saying how the soul of the Messiah has entered him, which is why he doesn't act like a normal person. He's seen many like this already, as if the soul of the Messiah enjoyed incarnating in someone new every couple of days.

He doesn't get too close. He stays on the other side of the street, leaning against the wall, filling his pipe with the relaxed, languorous movements of a Turk. Smoking, he watches all of the commotion. It's mostly young men milling around, Jews and Turks. Something's going on inside the building, and now a cluster of the young whippersnappers are pushing their way through the door, you can hear bursts of laughter.

When he's finished smoking, Moliwda decides to go inside, too. He has to bend down to pass through the dark hallway until he reaches the courtyard, where a small well has been converted into something like a fountain. It's cool here, and some men are lying under a tree with broad leaves, almost all of them in Turkish clothing, but there are a few, too, in Jewish gabardines, who don't sit on the ground, but rather on stools. There are also some dressed in the Wallachian style, and clean-shaven burghers, and two Greeks, recognizable by their characteristic wool coats. For a moment those gathered look at Moliwda with suspicion, and finally a thin man with a pockmarked face comes up to him and demands to know what it is he's come for. Moliwda responds in perfect Turkish: "To listen." The man backs off, but the mistrust in his eyes remains. He glances over at Moliwda every so often. They must think he's a spy. Let them think so.

In the center of a loose semicircle stands a tall, well-built man, dressed like a Turk. He speaks carelessly, in a voice that carries and vibrates so that it would be difficult to interrupt him. He speaks Turkish, slowly, with a strange foreign accent. It's not the accent of a learned man—more like a merchant's accent, or even a vagabond's. He uses words that sound straight out of the horse trade, but Greek and Hebrew words creep in, no doubt ones he has been taught. Moliwda grimaces, as the clash is too great and makes an unpleasant impression. This can't be anything, really, he thinks, but then suddenly it dawns on him that this is the language of all these people around him, this mix of people who are always on the road, instead of some language carefully assembled in a single place for the benefit of a few. This is why it's hard to figure out what sort of accent it is. Moliwda doesn't know yet that in every language Jacob speaks you can detect a foreign accent.

Jacob Frank's face is oblong, and he's fairly light-skinned for a Turkish Jew; his skin is rough, especially his cheeks, which are covered in tiny pits that must be scars, like an attestation of some calamity, as if a flame had harmed his face at some point in the distant past. There is something unsettling about that face, thinks Moliwda, and it also arouses an involuntary respect—Jacob's gaze is completely impenetrable.

In great astonishment, Kossakowski recognizes the old man sitting closest to this supposed prophet, smoking a pipe, closing his eyes each time he takes a drag. His beard is thick, gray, yellowed from the tobacco;

the old man is not wearing a turban, but rather a simple Turkish cap, from beneath which sticks out hair that is as wild as it is gray. He gives himself a little time to remember where he has seen him before.

"What a small world," he says to the old man in Turkish, trying to sound nonchalant. The old man turns to him and after a moment a hearty smile bursts forth out of his thick gray beard.

"Well, well, look at that, our great lord, the aristocrat," Reb Mordke says ironically, indicating Moliwda with his finger and addressing a one-eyed man who is dark as an Arab. "So you managed to break free, I see." He laughs loudly, delighted by the twist of finding not only Moliwda but himself back in Jacob's company again. They embrace and clap each other's shoulders. They greet each other more enthusiastically than they might have had they been old friends.

Moliwda stays with them until evening, observing the constant movement at this place—men come and go, drop in for a moment, then return to their tasks, their caravans, their stalls. In private conversations they give each other addresses and names of Turkish clerks who can be bought off. They have little notebooks especially for this purpose; you can buy them at the stalls here. Then they rejoin the general conversation as if they had never left. The disputation is ongoing. Someone asks a question, a stupid one or a provocative one, and the race begins: everyone wants to answer at the same time, they all shout over one another. Sometimes they can't understand one another—some of them have caught an accent somewhere, like a disease, so that they must repeat everything twice. There are also translators, and then Moliwda recognizes the Jewish language from Poland, that strange blend of German, Polish, and Hebrew. When he hears it, he is overwhelmed by sudden emotion, especially when he sees that one of the speakers is Nahman, who has resurfaced here as well. Nahman speaks the way Malka and her sisters spoke, and suddenly Moliwda is covered with a warm coat of images from those times. For instance: crops, grain all along the horizon, light yellow, and interspersed in them the dark blue points of cornflowers; fresh milk and a just-cut loaf of bread that is lying on the table; a beekeeper in a halo of bees, extracting sheets sticky with honey.

But who cares, there is honey in Turkey, too, and bread. Moliwda feels deeply ashamed of himself. He banishes the suddenly blooming bouquet of images to the back of his mind and is present again, just as the discussion is winding down and the prophet is telling little tales, a spiteful smile lurking on his face. He tells of how he fought a hundred highwaymen, how he slashed his way through them like through nettles. Someone interrupts him, shouts out something over the heads of those assembled. Others leave or just move away, into the shadows of the olive trees, and there, smoking their pipes, they murmur commentaries on all that they have heard. At some point, Nahman's voice takes over. He speaks in a learned, elegant manner. He invokes Isaiah. It would be hard to outtalk him. He has evidence for everything. When he cites the appropriate passage from the Scripture, he looks up, as though somewhere in the air a library hangs, invisible to others' eyes. Jacob does not react to Nahman's lectures, gives no indications that he's heard. When Nahman finishes, Jacob doesn't even nod to him. What a strange school.

It is getting dark by the time the audience thins out, and a raucous group of young men forms around this Frank. Then they head into town. They meander noisily down its narrow streets, looking to get into fights. They intercept passersby, comment on the street performers, drink wine, make trouble. Moliwda and Reb Mordke follow at a distance of several steps, so as to avoid becoming embroiled in a brawl should one erupt. This little group with Jacob at its head has some sort of strange power; they're like young bucks looking for a chance to prove their mettle. Moliwda likes this. It would be nice to be in their midst, shoulder to shoulder with them, to clap them on the back, move in the cloud of their scent— the tart sweat of young men, wind, dust. Jacob has a rakish smile on his face, which makes him look like an amused little boy. Moliwda catches his eye for a moment and wants to lift his hand and wave, but already Jacob is turning away. Women selling fruit and men selling pancakes dart out of the way of this retinue. Suddenly the whole procession stops for a moment. Moliwda can't see what's going on up there ahead, but he waits patiently, buys himself a piece of cake with sweet syrup poured on top and eats it with great pleasure. Up ahead there is some sort of commotion, voices raised, an outburst of laughter. Yet another incident with Jacob. What happened this time, he isn't sure.

## The story of His Lordship Moliwda, or Antoni Kossakowski, of the Ślepowron coat of arms, which is also known as Korwin

He comes from Żmudź, his father was a Hussar in the Crown Army. He has five brothers: one of them is a military man, two are priests, and of the other two he knows nothing. Of the priests, one lives in Warsaw, and they exchange letters once a year.

He hasn't been in Poland for over twenty years. At this point, it is a strain for him to put together any even remotely eloquent sentence in his native tongue, but by some miracle, he still thinks in Polish. And yet for many things he lacks the Polish words. He has had so many experiences in life that he lacks the Polish words to describe them all. He does this with the aid of a mixture of Greek and Turkish. Now, working for the Jews, Hebrew words enter the mix. Described in these languages, Moliwda is a hybrid, a strange creature from the antipodes.

In Polish, he can tell of his childhood in the home of the Kowno stolnik Dominik, Kossakowski's uncle, who—after the sudden death of both his parents—took him in along with his five brothers. But the uncle was demanding, and ruled his home with an iron fist. When he caught one of his nephews in a lie, or some prevarication, he would backhand him hard. In cases of more severe transgressions (when, for instance, Antoni ate a little honey out of the pot and then, hoping to cover up his crime, added a little water, which spoiled the remainder), he would take out a leather scourge—probably intended for self-flagellation, as the family was very pious—that would slice through the boy's naked back and buttocks. The most robust of the brothers the uncle prepared for a military career, and the two calmer and more trustworthy ones he sent off to the priesthood, but Antoni wasn't suited for either. Several times he ran away from home, and the servants would search for him around the village or dig him out of peasants' barns, where he had cried himself to sleep in the hay. Uncle Dominik's methods were hard and painful, but at last there came a hope that Antoni might find his place in good society. His influential uncle had, after all, educated him well, and soon he arranged for the fifteen-year-old to take up a position in King Stanisław Leszczyński's chancellery. He got him the appropriate clothing, bought him a travel case and shoes, sets of undergarments, and a handkerchief, and, so equipped, the boy set off for Warsaw. Once he got there, it turned out no one knew what to do with such a youngster, so he was made to write out copies of documents in his fine hand and to trim the wicks of candles. He told the chancellors that his uncle had found him in the forests of Żmudź, where a she-wolf had raised him for several years, so that he was fluent in the languages of dogs and wolves, and that he was the son of the sultan, begotten when the sultan was traveling incognito to the Radziwiłłs'. When he had had enough of copying out boring reports, he hid a whole folder of them behind a heavy piece of furniture under a window, where, since the panes weren't fully sealed, they were ruined by damp. There were other offenses, too—schoolboy stuff, like when some older kids got him drunk and left him in a brothel in Powiśle, and he only narrowly escaped with his life, taking three full days to recover. In the end, he took the money he had so unwisely been entrusted with and used it to reign over Powiśle, until what he had left was stolen, and he was beaten up.

Moliwda has thought a lot lately about what would have happened if he had stayed in the chancellery, what he might have become by now—maybe a lord, a royal officer in the capital, under the new king, who is so rarely in Warsaw, residing instead by the border with Saxony, in order to be close to Dresden. What has become of Moliwda instead?

He was told in the chancellery never to show his face around there again; his uncle had been informed. He had come after his nephew, but he hadn't dared beat him now as he had done in the past—after all, young Antoni was, in spite of everything, in the employ of the king.

By way of punishment, his uncle sent him instead to the ancestral estate of Antoni's dearly departed mother, which was being run by a local steward. Antoni was informed that he would now learn the techniques of agronomy—tillage, harvest, birthing sheep, keeping chickens. The estate was called Bielewicze.

Antoni, still a teenager, a young lord, arrived at Bielewicze toward the end of winter, when the ground was still frozen. For the first few weeks he was so consumed by guilt and a sense of squandered opportunity that he barely left the house, praying fervently and rummaging around in the empty rooms for traces of the mother he had lost. In April, for the very first time, he made it to the mill.

The mill at Bielewicze was leased to Mendel Kozowicz, who had only daughters, one of whom was Malka. Malka was already betrothed to some good-for-nothing; their wedding was coming up. Antoni started visiting the mill daily, on the pretense of bringing in grain and checking on its grinding—all of a sudden he became a great landlord, returning to look in on the progress of that grain, checking the flour. He would take a pinch of it between his fingers and raise it to his nostrils to see whether the rye was stale, and he would emerge from the mill dusted in flour, looking like a white-haired old man. But he never cared as much about the flour as he did about Malka. She told him her name meant Queen, but she didn't look like a queen, more like a princess—small, quick, with black eyes and uncommonly dry, warm skin, like a little lizard, so that when they brushed arms once, Antoni heard a rustle.

No one noticed the love affair. Maybe it was all those clouds of flour in the air, or maybe it was because the romance was a rather odd one. Two children who had fallen in love. She was just a little bit older than he was, but it was enough that she could show him which stones hid crawfish and where the agaric grew in the grove as they took their walks together. It was really more like two orphans joining forces.

During the summer harvest, Antoni was never seen in the fields, and he was rarely

seen at home. By the Jewish New Year, in September, it was clear that Malka was pregnant, and someone—some madman—advised him to abduct her, christen her, and marry her, so that both families, presented with a fait accompli, would find their fury defused.

And so Antoni kidnapped Malka, and he took her to the city and there, having bribed a priest to quickly baptize her, Antoni married his princess. He and the sacristan were the witnesses at the christening. She was given the Christian name Małgorzata, the Polish version of Margaret.

But this was not enough. But this was nothing. As they stood side by side before the altar, anyone—the best example being Yente, who sees all— would have said this was a couple, a couple composed of a boy and a girl of around the same age. But in reality, there was a chasm between them that could never be filled, a chasm so deep that it reached clear to the center of the earth, maybe even farther. It would be hard to explain it in words. To say she was a Jew, and he a Christian? That wasn't it. That meant very little. At its heart it was that they represented two types of people, which at first glance no one could see, two human beings similar to one another but diametrically opposed: for she would not be saved, while he would live eternally. While still in her earthly guise, she was in fact already ash and phantom. From the perspective of the miller Kozowicz, who rented the mill from Dominik, their differences were even bigger: Malka was a real person, whereas Antoni was a creature who merely resembled a person, false, not even worth paying attention to in the real world.

Unaware of these differences, the couple showed up just once at the mill at Bielewicze, but it was obvious that there would never be a place for them there. Malka's father was so devastated by what had happened that he grew weak and fell ill. The family tried to lock Malka in their cellar, but she escaped.

Antoni and his young wife moved, then, to the Bielewicze estate, but it turned out to be just for a few months.

The servants greeted them with some reserve. Malka's sisters started coming to see her right away; increasingly intrepid, they would peer under the tablecloths, rummage around in drawers, caress the bedcovers.

They would sit down at the table together, five girls and one boy with barely any hair on his face yet. The young couple would make the sign of the cross, and Malka's sisters would pray in their language. A republic of Jewish children. As the girls chirped in Yiddish, Antoni quickly grasped the tone, and the words came to his tongue as though of their own accord. It certainly seemed like they were a good family, a perfect family—just the children, without any prime mover.

After several months, disturbed by such a course of events, the steward sent letters to Uncle Dominik, who arrived as dark and stormy as a hail cloud. When young Antoni realized that he was about to receive a thrashing in the presence of his wife, now very much with child, the young couple packed up and went to the mill. Kozowicz, however, fearing his master, upon whom his livelihood depended, dispatched the two under cover of night to relatives in Lithuania. At this point their trail was lost.

## Of what draws persons together, and certain clarifications regarding the transmigration of souls

Moliwda spends more and more time in the warehouse where Jacob works. Business takes place here during the morning hours, when the heat isn't too bad yet, or late in the evening. For the couple of hours after the sun sets, there is wine instead of tea for long-standing clients.

Moliwda knows Osman of Czernowitz well. He knows him thanks to certain Turks—he won't say from where, he's vowed to keep it a secret. Mystery, concealment, masks. If one were to view these mysteries through Yente's all-seeing eyes, one would soon understand that they met during the secret gatherings of the Bektashi.

This is how Moliwda introduces himself—as a long-standing client. What makes the greatest impression about him is that he is—as he himself is eager to emphasize—a Polish count. On the faces of his Jewish interlocutors this evokes an expression of disbelief and a sort of childlike respect. He says a few words in Turkish and in Hebrew. His laugh is deep, infectious. Throughout September, Moliwda goes to see Jacob every day. Up till now he has only actually purchased a turquoise clip, and even that Jacob sold to him at a scandalously low price, to Nahman's outrage. Reb Mordke likes to sit around with them, talking over different things. The stranger the subject, the better.

Some traders from the north come in, speaking a foreign language. Nussen focuses his attention on them, turns from scholar into salesman. They turn out to be Jewish merchants from Silesia, interested in malachite, opals, and turquoise. Jacob also shows them pearls; whenever he's trying to make a sale, he raises his voice. Seeing the transaction through takes hours; the tea flows, young Hershel brings sweets and whispers into Jacob's ear that Abraham says to also show them some carpets. The merchants fuss and grumble in their language, consulting one another in murmurs, certain no one understands them. They ought not to be so confident. Nussen listens with his one eye closed, and then, behind the curtain, where Nahman sits, he relates the latest:

"They only care about the pearls, they have the rest already, and they paid more for it. They're regretting not coming here before."

Jacob sends Hershel to get pearls from Abraham and from other stalls. And when in the late evening they wrap up the deal, and the day is acknowledged to have been exceptionally good, this motley family spreads out rugs and pillows in the largest room of the house and has a late supper that rapidly becomes a feast.

"Yes, the people of Israel will devour Leviathan!" Jacob exclaims, as if making a toast, and he pushes a piece of meat into his mouth; grease runs down his chin. "The great, enormous hulk of the monster, delicious and soft as quail meat, or like the flesh of the most delicate fishes. Folks will be feasting on Leviathan for so long they'll satisfy their centuries-old hunger."

All of them eating, they laugh and joke.

"The wind will flutter the white tablecloths, and we'll throw the bones under the table for the dogs," Moliwda adds.

Nahman, relaxed by the good wine from Jacob's cellar, says to Moliwda:

"When you look at the world as good, then evil becomes the exception, something missed, something mistaken—and nothing suits you. But if you were to switch it around—say that the world is evil, while good is the exception, then everything works out elegantly, understandably. Why don't we want to see what is obvious?"

Moliwda picks it up from here.

"Where I come from, they think of the world as being divided into halves. Two ruling forces, one good, one evil . . ."

"Where is it you come from?" Nahman inquires, his mouth still full.

Moliwda dismisses him with an impatient gesture and goes on:

"There is no man who would not wish ill upon another, no country that would not rejoice in the fall of another country, no merchant who doesn't want his competitors bankrupt . . . Give me the creator of all that. The one who botched the job!"

"Moliwda, give it a rest," says Nahman. "Have some food. You're not eating, you're only drinking."

They all talk over one another; Moliwda has stirred up a hornet's nest. He breaks off a piece of flatbread and dips it into some seasoned olive oil.

"What's it like where you come from?" Nahman pipes up. "You might tell us how your people live."

"Oh, I don't know." Moliwda tries to evade their curiosity; his eyes are slightly hazy from an excess of wine. "You would have to swear never to reveal the secret."

Nahman nods without hesitation. This seems obvious to him. Moliwda refills their glasses; the wine is so dark it leaves a purple stain on their lips.

"This is how it is, I'll tell it to you straight," Moliwda starts, his tongue getting all tangled. "It's all very ordinary. There's light, and there's dark. Dark attacks the light, and God creates men to try and defend it."

Nahman slides away his plate and raises his eyes to Moliwda. Moliwda looks into the dark, deep eyes of Nahman of Busk, and the sounds of feasting float away somewhere beyond them both. In a quiet voice, Nahman tells of the four great paradoxes that must be contemplated by anyone who considers himself a thinking person.

"First, in order to create a finite world, God had to limit himself, but there still remains an infinite part of God completely unengaged in creation.

"Isn't that so?" Nahman asks Moliwda, to make sure he's following.

Moliwda assents, so Nahman goes on: "If one accepts that the idea of the created world is one of an infinite number of ideas in the infinite mind of God, then it is, without any doubt, marginal and insignificant. It is possible that God didn't even notice he had created something." Nahman monitors Moliwda's reactions closely. Moliwda takes a deep breath.

"Second," Nahman continues, "creation as an infinitesimal part of God's mind strikes Him as insignificant, and He is only barely involved in this creation; from the human perspective, this indifference may be perceived as cruelty."

Moliwda downs his wine in one gulp, slamming the cup against the table.

"Third," Nahman continues in a quiet voice, "the Absolute, as infinitely perfect, had no reason to create the world. So that part of the Absolute that did lead to creation must have outsmarted the rest, and must go on outsmarting it now, and we take part in those machinations. Do you get me? We are taking part in a war. And fourth—since the Absolute had to limit Himself, in order for the finite world to arise, our world is for Him a kind of exile. Do you understand? In order to create the world, the all-powerful God had to make himself as weak and passive as a woman."

They sit in silence, spent. The sounds of the feasting return; they can hear Jacob telling bawdy jokes. Then Moliwda, very drunk by now, claps Nahman on the back, for such a long time that it becomes the subject of indecent jokes, until finally he lays his head on Nahman's shoulder and says into his shirt:

"I know all this."

Moliwda disappears for a few days, then comes back for a day or two. He spends those nights at Jacob's.

When they sit until evening, Hershel adds hot ash to the tandir, the clay oven that sits on the ground. They rest their feet on it; a pleasant, gentle warmth travels higher with the blood and heats up the whole body.

"Is he çubuklu?" Moliwda asks Nahman, looking at Hershel. That's what the Turks call epicenes, those equipped by God in such a way that they can pass as a woman or a man.

Nahman shrugs.

"He's a good boy. Very dedicated. Jacob loves him."

After a moment, feeling that honesty on his part will oblige Moliwda to similar sincerity, Nahman says:

"Is it true what they say about you, that you are a Bektashi?"

"That's what people say?"

"And that you were in the service of the sultan . . ." Nahman hesitates for a moment. "As a spy."

Moliwda looks at his interlaced hands.

"You know, Nahman, that it's a good thing to keep company with them. And I do." A moment later he adds: "There's also nothing wrong with being a spy, so long as you serve some good purpose with it. You know this, too."

"I do. What do you want from us, Moliwda?"

"I don't want anything. I like you, and I admire Jacob."

"You, Moliwda, are a high-minded man tangled up in mundane things."

"Then we're alike."

But Nahman doesn't seem convinced.

A few days before Nahman sets out for Poland, Moliwda invites them to visit. He comes on horseback and has with him, too, a strange carriage, which is where Nussen, Nahman, and the rest wind up. Jacob and Moliwda ride up ahead. It takes about four hours, because the road is tricky and narrow, and winds uphill.

On the road Jacob is in a good mood and sings in his beautiful, powerful voice. He starts with the holiday songs, in the old language, and he finishes with the Yiddish ditties the badchan performs at weddings to entertain the guests:

*What is life, after all,*
*if not dancing on graves?*

When he finishes, he turns to filthy songs of wedding nights. Jacob's powerful voice echoes off the rocks. Moliwda rides half a step behind him and suddenly realizes why this strange man so easily attracts people to him. In everything he does, Jacob is absolutely authentic. He is like that well from the folktale. No matter what a person shouts into it, it will always answer the same.

## Jacob's story about the ring

They rest along the way, in the shade of some olive trees, with a view of Craiova before them. How small this city seems now—like a little handkerchief. Nahman sits next to Jacob and locks his head in the crook of his arm, seemingly in play, and Jacob gives in to it, and for a moment they tussle like puppies. It strikes Moliwda that they're just big kids. On such stops, someone always has to tell a story, even if it's one everybody already knows. Hershel asks, a little grumpily, for the one about the ring. Jacob, who never needs to be asked twice, launches into it right away.

"Once upon a time there was a man," he opens, "who had an extraordinary ring, passed down from generation to generation. Whoever wore that ring was a happy man, things went well for him. Yet despite his good fortune, he did not lose his sympathy for others and did not shy away from helping them. And so the ring belonged to good people, and whoever wore it would pass it down to his child.

"It so happened that one set of parents gave birth to three sons at once. They grew up healthy and in brotherly love, sharing everything and supporting one another in all pursuits. Their parents thought and thought about what would happen when the boys grew up, and they would have to give one of them the ring. They discussed it well into the night, until at last the children's mother proposed the following solution: they would take the ring to the best goldsmith and have him make two more exactly like it. The goldsmith would have to make sure the rings were identical, so that no one could tell which was the original. For a long time they searched, and at last they found one, an extraordinarily talented man, whom with great effort and great pains they were able to convince to carry out the task. When the parents came to pick up the rings, the goldsmith mixed up all three in front of them, and they couldn't tell which was which. Even the goldsmith was astonished to find that he could not tell them apart.

"When the sons reached adulthood, a grand ceremony took place at which the parents handed the boys their rings. The boys weren't entirely satisfied, although they tried not to betray their emotions in order not to hurt their parents' feelings. Each of them, in his heart of hearts, believed that it was he who had received the real ring, and so the brothers began to look upon one another in suspicion and mistrust. After the deaths of their parents, they immediately went to a judge so that he might once and for all resolve their doubts. Yet even the wise judge was unable to do this, and instead of issuing a determination, he told them: 'Apparently, this treasure has the property of making its wearer good to God and to man. As this does not seem to apply to any of you, it may be that the real ring has been lost. Live, then, as if your ring were the real one, and your life will show whether or not you were right.'

"And just like those three rings, there are three religions. And he who was born into one of them ought to take the other two like a pair of pantofles and walk in them toward salvation." Moliwda knows this story. Most recently he heard it from a Muslim with whom he was doing business. For his part, he has been very much taken with the prayer he heard Nahman recite in lilting Hebrew. He doesn't know if he's got the whole thing, but what he did manage to memorize he's put into Polish, recomposing the whole, so that now, when he says it over in his head, relishing the rhythm, his mouth floods with waves of pleasure, as though he were eating something good and sweet.

> Beating its wings, seeking the aether,
> But neither crane nor raven,
> My soul, which knows no conqueror,
> Soars up into the heavens.
>
> It can't be trapped in sulfur, iron,
> Get tangled in the heart,

Will never die of plague in prison,
Be subject to man's court.

Breaking down walls, it freely flits
Over rumors and smooth words,
For it wants not your narrow streets,
Your alleys, boulevards.

Knowing no limits, it roams free,
Mocks what you all deem wise,
Calls beauty ugly secretly,
Dispels illusions, lies.

It shakes its plumes and sees a light
That can't be put in words,
It cares not who and what sort might
Hold places in this world.

O Father, help me wield my tongue
So that I voice my pain
And add truth to man's talk—o let
My soul glimpse the divine.

After a while, this sweetness turns into an almost unbearable longing.

### Scraps: *What we saw among Moliwda's Bogomils*

Although I would very much like to, I am unable to make a record
of everything, for after all, things are so inextricably bound
together that should I merely tap the tip of my pen against one,
then it nudges another, and soon a great sea has unfurled itself
before me. What kind of dam are the edges of my paper, is the trail
of ink I leave? How, then, would I be able to express all that my
soul has received in this life, and in a single book, at that?

Abulafia, whom I studied with great zeal, says that the human
soul is part of the great cosmic stream that flows through all
creatures. It is a single force, one motion, but when a person is
born into a physical body, when he comes into the world as an

individual being, that soul has to separate from the rest, otherwise a person would not be able to live—the soul would drown in the One, and the person would go mad in just a few instants. That is why such a soul gets sealed, that is, seals are stamped upon it that will not let it mix with that unity but will allow it to operate in the finite, bounded world of matter.

We need to be able to keep our balance. If the soul is too voracious or too porous, then too many different forms will get inside it and thereby distance it from the stream of the divine.

After all it is said: "He who is full of himself has no space left for God."

Moliwda's village consisted of some dozen small, neat houses made of stone and covered in slate, between which ran paths lined with pebbles; the homes stood at uneven intervals around the trampled little meadow, through which flowed a stream, creating a small pool. Higher up was the water catchment, a construction built of wood, which, like a mill wheel, propelled certain machines, no doubt to grind grain. Behind the homes stretched little gardens and orchards, thick, well-tended, and we could from our very entrance glimpse ripening pumpkins.

On the grass, which was already dry by this time of year, gleamed great canvas rectangles that made it look as though the village had been decorated with white holiday collars. There was something strange about it, for a little village, and I soon realized that there were no fowl here, so that there was none of what leaps out at one in every town: the toddling ducklings, the incessantly honking geese, and the furiously attacking ganders.

Our arrival caused a great deal of commotion, the little child sentries being the first to run out to us, having been the first to detect newcomers. Startled by the presence of outsiders, they clung to Moliwda as though they were his own children, and he spoke tenderly to them, in a croaking language we did not know. Then some men showed up from somewhere, bearded, squat, in shirts made of raw linen, and seemingly gentle, and only after them did the women run up, laughing. And everyone was dressed in white, and all in linen, and we could see that they made the cloth themselves, for across the common lands around the village there shone recently woven pieces of it everywhere, hung out to whiten in the sun.

Moliwda took down the sacks of what he'd bought in the city. He told the peasants to greet the guests, which they gladly did, forming a circle around us and singing a short, joyful song. The gesture of greeting here was a hand placed over the heart, then transferred to the mouth. I was entranced by the appearances and manner of these peasants—though that word seemed to apply rather to some other form of person, for unlike the peasants I had seen before, in Podolia, these people were cheerful and welcoming, and evidently sated.

We were completely astonished—even Jacob, whom nothing is able to surprise in general, seemed amazed by the extent of our welcome, and for a moment, he seemed to almost forget who he was. The fact that we were Jews did not bother them in the least; on the contrary, it was precisely because we were different from them that they showed themselves so well disposed toward us. Only Osman seemed not to be surprised by our reception; he kept on asking Moliwda about their provisions, their division of labor, their income from the vegetables they were cultivating, their weaving. But Moliwda didn't seem comfortable answering all these questions, and to our astonishment, it turned out that the person who had the most to say on such matters was a woman whom they called "Mother," although she wasn't old.

We were led into a large room, where the young people, girls and boys, waited upon us as we ate. The food was simple and delicious—aged honey, dried fruits, olives, and a baked eggplant spread they applied to a crust they baked directly on a hot stone—with spring water to drink.

Moliwda behaved in a dignified and calm manner, but I noticed that although he was treated with respect, he was nonetheless not their master. Everyone called him "brate," and he called them "brate" and "sestro," which meant that they considered one another brothers and sisters, like one great family. When we had had our fill, the woman they called "Mother," also dressed in white from head to toe, came to sit with us. She smiled warmly at us, although she scarcely spoke. It was clear that Moliwda held her in the highest esteem. When she started to gather herself, he stood, and following his example, we all stood and were led into the room where we were to spend the night. Everything was very modest and clean, and I slept splendidly, though I was so tired I had nary the strength to continue taking notes. For example, to record the fact that in my room the bed was merely bedclothes on the floor, and, instead of a wardrobe, I had only a stick suspended from strings on which to hang my clothes.

On the second day, Jacob and I observed how well Moliwda had arranged things there.

He surrounded himself with twelve brothers and twelve sisters—they made up the management of this village, on equal terms, women and men. When the time came to make some determination, they gathered on the little square to vote. When they agreed to something, they raised their hands. All of the huts and all their other holdings, like the well, the carts, the horses—belonged to everyone, to anyone who needed them, and he or she would take it as if on lease, would borrow it, and then, having done with it, give it back. There were few children, since they viewed procreation as a sin, but what young ones there were did not remain with their mothers, but were also communal, with several older women taking care of them, since the younger women worked in the fields or the home. We saw them painting the walls of the homes and adding to the whitewash a dye to make the houses light blue. The children were never told who their father was, and the fathers didn't learn it, either; that could have given rise to injustices, partiality to their descendants. Because the women did know, they played an important role here, equal to that of the men, and it was apparent that for this reason these women were different from women elsewhere—calmer and more reasonable, sensible. The community's accounts were kept by a woman, who could read and write and reckon. She was very learned, and Moliwda addressed her with respect.

We all wondered about Moliwda's role here: Was he in charge, or merely helping, or maybe even in the service of that woman, unless perhaps she was in his? But he just laughed at us and mocked us, saying we were still seeing everything in that old, worst way: insisting on ladders wherever we went, one person standing above another, forcing the lower one to do all kinds of things. This one more important, that one less. Whereas here in this village near Craiova, they had arranged things in a different way. Everyone was equal. Everyone had the right to live, eat, be happy, and work. Anyone could leave at any moment. Did anyone ever leave? Sometimes. Rarely. Where would they go?

And yet, we had the strong impression that Moliwda and that woman with the gentle smile were the ones in charge. At first we all wondered, quietly, whether she was his wife, but he soon corrected our mistake: she was his sister, just like every woman here. "Do you sleep with them?" Jacob asked him straight out. Moliwda just shrugged and showed us the big, carefully tended vegetable gardens, which yielded crops twice a year, and he said that it was off these gardens that the community lived, off the gifts of the sun, because if you looked at it the way he did, it all came from the sun, from the light, which was of course for free and for all.

We took our repast at the long tables where everyone else was sitting, too, first loudly reciting a prayer in a language I could not recognize.

They didn't eat meat, just plant foods, occasionally cheese, when someone had given them some. They were disgusted by eggs just the same as they were by meat. Of the vegetables, they did not eat broad beans, since they believed that souls might reside there before being born, in those little grains laid out in a pod like in some coffer. On this we agreed: Some plants contained more light than others—the most light being held by the cucumber, and also the eggplant and all types of long melons.

They believed in the transmigration of souls, as we did, and in addition Moliwda said he considered that this belief was once universal, until Christianity came along and buried it. The Bogomils valued the planets and considered them their rulers.

What most astonished us, although Jacob and I did not betray it, was the fact that there were so many similarities to what we ourselves believed. The Bogomils believed, for example, in the so-called holy speech to be used during rites of initiation. It was holy because it was the opposite: it was shameless. Everyone who passed through initiation had to hear out a story offensive to common decency, and this came from a very old tradition in their faith, from a time when it was pagan mystery plays in honor of the ancient goddess Baubo or the unbridled Greek god Dionysus. I was hearing the names of these gods for the first time, Moliwda pronounced them quickly and as though ashamed, but I made a note of them right away.

After lunch, we sat down over sweets, traditional Turkish baklava, in Moliwda's little home; a dash of wine was served with it, made here—I had seen the little vineyard behind the gardens.

"How do you pray?" Jacob asked him.

"That is the simplest thing of all," said Moliwda. "It's the heart's prayer: 'Lord Jesus, have mercy on me.' You don't have to do anything special. God hears you."

They told us marriage was sinful, too. That was the real sin of Adam and Eve, since it should be as it is in nature—people should connect with one another through their souls, not through some dead convention. Those who join together in spirit, spiritual brothers and sisters, can physically commingle, and the children of such unions are gifts. Those born of married couples are "children of dead law."

In the evening, they stood in a circle and began to dance around a woman in the center who was a virgin. At first she appeared in white robes, then after the sacred act she changed into a red robe, and in the end, when all were greatly weakened by the frenzied rhythm of their dance around her and fell down from their exhaustion, she donned a black coat.

All of this felt strangely familiar to us, and returning to Craiova, to Jacob's office, we spoke in such excitement that for a long time that night we were unable to fall asleep.

A few days later, Nussen and I set out for Poland with goods and with news. For the whole of the journey our heads were filled with scenes from Moliwda's village. Nussen especially—he dreamed, entranced, as we were crossing the Dniester again, that such villages might be established back home in Podolia. What I liked most about it was that it was not important there whether we were mother or father, daughter or son, woman or man. There was no great difference between us. We were all just forms that took on light whenever it so much as glistened over matter.

## 12.

## Of Jacob's expedition to the grave
## of Nathan of Gaza

*Whoever behaves as irrationally as Jacob en route to the grave of Nathan the prophet must be either a madman or a saint,* Abraham writes his brother Tovah.

My business has suffered from having hired your son-in-law. There were more people and more conversations in my shop than ever before, but the monetary gain from that has been slight. If you ask me, your son-in-law is ill-suited to shop life. I don't say that as a reproach, for I know the expectations you have for him. He is a restless and agitated man, not a sage but a rebel. He abandoned everything, and, having been dissatisfied with the money I'd been providing him in exchange for his work, he gave himself a severance payment when he left by stealing several valuable things. I am including an accounting of it on a separate sheet of paper. I hope you will prevail upon him to pay me back the amount I have tallied. They got it into their heads, him and his followers, to visit the grave of Nathan of Gaza (of blessed memory). And although it was a noble purpose, because of their hot heads they did it too abruptly, forsaking everything in their haste to depart—though they had just time enough to offend any number of people, and to borrow money from those whom they hadn't yet offended. There is no place for him here now, even if he wanted to come back, although I suspect he will not want to return.

I deeply want to believe that you knew what you were doing, giving Hana to someone like him. I believe in your wisdom and your deep prudence, which often ventures far beyond ordinary understanding. I will only tell you that I felt after he left such great relief. Your son-in-law is not suited for this office. I think there are a lot of things he isn't suited for.

## Of how Nahman follows in Jacob's footsteps

Finally, at the beginning of summer, having settled matters in Poland, collected letters and merchandise, Nahman and Nussen set out for the south. Their road leads toward the Dniester, through the fields, a beautiful sun shining, the sky enormous. Nahman has had enough of that Podolian filth, of village smallness, envy and simplemindedness, he yearns for figs on the trees and the smell of coffee. But most of all, for Jacob. To Isohar he carries gifts from Shorr; for Reb Mordke, he has an amber tincture all the way from Gdańsk, a medicine to help him with his aching joints.

The banks of the river are now covered with brown grass, dry as bone, which under human and animal footsteps crumbles into dust. Nahman stands on the bank looking south, toward the other side. Suddenly he hears a rustling in the scrub nearby, and a moment later, a black-and-white dog comes out of it, skinny and dirty, with swollen teats. Puppies scramble after her. The dog passes him, not even noticing the man standing motionless, but one of the puppies spots him and stops, perplexed. For a moment, they size each other up. The puppy looks at him curiously, trusting, but then, as though someone has just informed it that it's standing face-to-face with its greatest enemy, it darts off after its mother. Nahman interprets this as a bad omen.

In the evening, they cross over the Dniester. On the shore, peasants

burn bonfires, and along the water, wreaths float with lit candles. Shrieks
and giggles resound. Near the shore, girls wade into the water up to their
knees, in long white shirts hitched halfway up their thighs. Their hair is
down, and they wear wreaths on their heads. They look at them, these
Jews on horseback, in silence, until Nahman starts to think they're not
really village girls bidding them farewell at all, but rather water spirits
who float up to the surface by night to drown whatever humans they
encounter. Suddenly one of them leans over and starts splashing them,
and the others join in, laughing. The men urge their horses on across the
river.

News of some new holy man comes to them more often and more
colorfully, the deeper they venture into Turkish territory. For a time, they
ignore it. But it is impossible to keep this up for long. At the stops they
make, where Jewish travelers usually swap gossip picked up on the road,
they find out more and more details, for example that this holy man is in
Sofia with some vast company and is working miracles there. Many take
him for a con man and a swindler. In the stories it's an old Jew from Turkey, or sometimes a young man from Bucharest, so that it takes them a
while to realize that all these people, all these travelers, are talking about
Jacob. Once that sinks in, Nahman and Nussen don't sleep the whole
long night, trying to figure out what has happened in their absence. And
instead of feeling happy—for is this not exactly what they'd hoped for?—
they begin to be afraid. The best medicine for fear and anxiety is the
writing box. Nahman takes it out at every stop and writes down what is
being said of Jacob. It goes like this:

In one of the villages, he spent half a day jumping on horseback
over a certain hole, a deep hole into which it would be dangerous to
fall. The horse, tired, began to resist with its hooves, but Jacob kept
insisting. Soon the whole village was standing around him and that
hole, and the Turkish guards came to see what the cause of the
throng was and whether it wasn't by any chance an uprising against
the sultan.

Or:

Jacob went up to one wealthy-looking merchant, reached into the man's pocket, took out of it something like a snake, and waved it around, shouting over people's heads. A terrible tumult arose, and the horrible screech of women spooked the horses of the Turkish guards, while Jacob burst out laughing, and he laughed so hard he lay down and rolled in the sand. Then the crowd, embarrassed, saw that it was no snake, but rather just a string of wooden beads.

Or:

In some great synagogue he went up onto the bimah, and when it was time to read the Law of Moses, he ripped off the top of the pulpit and started to wave it around, threatening to kill everyone, and everyone ran right out of the temple, thinking him a madman, capable of absolutely anything.

Or even:

Once on the road he was attacked by a highwayman. Jacob simply shouted up into the sky, and in the blink of an eye, a storm gathered, with lightning that so frightened the highwayman and his associates that they fled at once.

Now, in smaller letters, Nahman adds:

We rushed to Sofia, but we didn't manage to catch him there. We asked all of our own everything we could about him, and they told us in animated tones of his exploits in that city, saying, too, that when he had done, he and his whole group had set off for Salonika. And now, they said, he rode like a tzaddik in a cart at the head of the caravan, behind him all the other carts and carriages, horses and people on foot, taking up the whole road and sending up a cloud of dust over everyone's heads. Wherever he stopped, people wanted to know who this was, and when it was explained to them, they dropped whatever it was they had been doing and wiped their hands on their kapotas and then joined in with this caravan out of curiosity, if nothing else. So they told us. And they would hold forth further on the handsomeness of the horses and the quality of the carriages, assuring us that there were hundreds of people now involved.

Then I saw this "company" myself—paupers and mendicants, the kind who will never have a place to hang their hats. Sick and broken people desperate for some small miracle, though desirous still of scandal and sensation. Youngsters who had run away from their homes and their heavy-handed fathers; merchants who, out of lack of equilibrium, had lost everything, and now, full of bitterness and spite, were seeking any kind of satisfaction; all types of madmen and those who had simply fled their families, having had their fill of dull obligations. Add to this, too, female beggars and ladies of light virtue, sensing the advantages of being in such a big group. Not to mention the abandoned women, widows no one wants, children in hand, as well as Christian ragamuffins, and vagrants without any sort of occupation. This was the element that began to follow Jacob, and if you were to ask them what was happening and in whose wake they were following, none of them would know how to respond.

In Skopje, I asked our prophet Nathan at his grave—I asked him quietly, not even moving my lips, but in my mind alone, as secretly as possible—whether we couldn't meet Jacob as soon as possible; sometimes thoughts would come into my head that suggested that I lacked humility and a proper assessment of my own person, but I did begin to think that he was going mad without me, and that as soon as I found him, he would calm down and stop stubbornly imitating the First One (of blessed memory). That this hullabaloo on the road was a sign that he needed me.

Nahman and Nussen find themselves in Salonika on the fourth day of the month of Tishrei in 5515, or September 20, 1754, and immediately, though it is already dark and they are ready to drop from exhaustion, they go in search of Jacob. It is a hot night, and the city's walls are warm, the air cooling lazily, in light bursts of breeze from somewhere in the mountains; the wind brings in the scent of live plants, wood, leaves. Everything is bone-dry in the city. It smells of oranges, the kind already swollen with juice, the sweetest and best to eat, that in the blink of an eye become overripe and fetid.

Nahman sees him first, in front of the beth midrash, where the Salonika Jews' disputes always take place. They are already dispersing—it is late—but Jacob still stands there, discussing something heatedly, surrounded by men. Nahman glimpses the Greek-attired young Hershel. He goes up closer, and although he can't hear what they're talking about, he begins to shiver. Hard to explain on a night as hot as this. He writes:

Only then did I understand how much I had missed him; only now did all the hurry of our journey fall away, all that frenzy that hadn't left me for one moment over the past several months.

"What is that man saying?" I asked the man standing next to me.

"He is saying that Sabbatai was not really the Messiah, that his nature was not divine, but rather that he was an ordinary prophet who came to announce his successor."

"He's right," said another man standing near me. "If his nature had been straight from God, he would have changed the world visibly. But as it is, what's changed?"

I didn't venture into these considerations with them.

I saw him among the others. He had gotten very thin. He had deteriorated. His beard had grown. But something new had also appeared in him—a new fervor, a self-assuredness. Who had led him to this, who had helped him get like this while I was gone?

As I looked thus at his movements, as I listened to what he said, I slowly realized that it was good that he was able to give relief to others with what he said. It also seemed to me that in his heart there was a kind of wholeness that already knew what direction to go in and what to do. And looking at him sometimes sufficed; it was the same thing that attracted other people to him.

There is nothing that brings greater relief than the certainty that there is someone who really knows. For we ordinary people never have such certainty.

Many times, when I was in Podolia with my family, I had thought about him. I missed him, especially before I fell asleep, when my thoughts wandered freely, and there was no way to control them anymore. It was sad, because next to me lay my wife, to whom I was unable to dedicate much attention. Our children were born frail and quickly died, and I didn't even think about that then, but it seemed to me that Jacob's face was becoming my face, and I was falling asleep beneath his countenance instead of under my own. And now I was beholding that face once more in life; and now it was before my very eyes.

And so in the evening, when we sat down at last all together, Jacob, Reb Mordke, Isohar, Nussen, young Hershel, and I, I felt happy, and since there was no lack of wine, I got drunk, but it was as if I were a child—I felt defenseless, altogether open, ready for whatever fate would bring, and certain that whatever happened, I would be with Jacob.

## Of how Jacob faces off with the Antichrist

In Salonika there lives the successor and son of the Second, Baruchiah. This man is known as Konio.

He has many followers here, and many treat him as the holy man in whom dwells the soul of Baruchiah. It takes them a long time to get to him. His blessing, and an initiation by him into the teachings of his father, would confirm Jacob's exceptional status. Nahman takes letters from Isohar and Reb Mordke to the tall house without windows, in the middle of the city, which looks like a white tower. Apparently the inside of the compound has a lovely garden with a fountain and peacocks, but the outside looks more like a fortress. The white walls are smooth, as though made of sleek granite. In addition, the house is watched by guards who once tore Nahman's clothing when he was too insistent in his demands for an audience.

Jacob, upset by that injustice—Nahman's caftan was brand-new, he had just bought it at the market for a large sum—tells them to leave him at that inaccessible tower while they hide in a grove nearby. Then he leans up against the wall and begins to sing as loudly as he can, nearly bellowing like an ass, in the old Sephardic tongue. When he finishes his song, he moves to another side of the house and starts it again from the beginning.

"Mahshava se in fue esta . . . ," he bellows, off-key, and he grimaces and contorts his body into strange poses. Of course this draws attention; people can barely restrain their laughter at the sight of him; there is a crowd and then an uproar.

So a little window opens, high up, and Konio himself sticks his head out; he shouts down something in Ladino, and Jacob answers, and for a minute they converse. Nahman glances inquiringly at Isohar, who knows this ancient language of the Jews of Spain.

"He's asking for an audience," Isohar explains.

The window slams shut.

Jacob sings under the tower until evening, until he goes completely hoarse.

There is nothing for it. Konio is unavailable, and uninterested in interlopers come from Poland. Even if Wise Jacob is among them, singing under his window. For that's what he is called now: Wise Jacob.

But Salonika is filled at this time with every sort of mage and miracle-worker, and there is some self-proclaimed Messiah or dark sorcerer offering instruction on every street corner. People are talking a lot about one particular Jew who considers himself the Antichrist Messiah, and they say that whoever exchanges so much as a single word with him will instantly be dragged over to his side.

Jacob wants to test him, wants to face off with someone like that; he talks of this intention for several days, until a whole group has gathered around him—small-time merchants, students, itinerant peddlers, cobblers who have closed their stalls—if only to see something out of the ordinary. They tramp through town and find this man with his retinue in a garden courtyard where he is delivering his teaching. He is a big man, with the build of a peasant and dark skin—another Sephardic Jew— bareheaded and with his hair curled into long matted cords. He's wearing a white robe; against his dark skin, this robe seems to be gleaming. Jacob sits before him with that little smile of his that he gets whenever he starts plotting something, and he asks the man brashly who he thinks he is. The man, although accustomed to greater reverence, answers calmly: he is the Messiah.

"Give some sign of that," Jacob says to him, looking around at the people who will be their witnesses.

The man stands and starts to walk away, but Jacob doesn't give up. He follows him and repeats:

"Give some sign of that. Move that piece of the fountain by the wall. As the Messiah, you ought to be able to do that."

"Get out of here," says the man. "I don't want to talk to you."

Jacob will not let it rest. The man turns away and starts to whisper curses. Then Jacob grabs him by the locks, provoking the man's companions to come to his defense. They push Jacob, and he falls into the dust.

In the evening, he tells everyone who wasn't with him during the day that just as the biblical Jacob wrestled with the angel, so, too, has he now wrestled with the Antichrist.

Nahman, who had so missed Jacob after not seeing him for a while, now accompanies him everywhere he can, which means he neglects both business and study. All matters connected with earning money lie fallow. The goods brought from Poland still have not been sold. Some of Jacob's adventures really embarrass Nahman, some he genuinely can't accept. Jacob wanders the city, looking for any opportunity to fight. He finds himself, for example, some learned Jew, asks him some intelligent question, and so arranges things that the other man, feeling obligated to respond, finds himself drawn into Jacob's disquisitions, and before he knows it, both of them are sitting in a shop drinking Turkish coffee, and Jacob is offering a pipe, and the man dares not refuse, but it's the Shabbat, after all! And then when it comes time to pay up, the religious Jew obviously doesn't have any money on him—it being the Shabbat—so Jacob pulls the turban off the poor man's head and puts it down as a guarantee, which means that the man, made a laughingstock, must now go home with a bare head. He gets up to so many things like this that people start to fear him. Even his own.

It would be difficult for Nahman to bear the humiliation of anyone in this way, even if it were his greatest enemy. Jacob, meanwhile, is extremely pleased with himself.

"Whoever fears, respects. That's just the way it is."

Soon everyone in Salonika recognizes Jacob, and Reb Mordke and Isohar decide they should release him from the obligations of trade. And that they, too, ought to dedicate themselves exclusively to study.

"Take care of whatever you have to, but don't try and make any new contacts," says Reb Mordke to a shocked Nahman.

"What do you mean?" asks Nahman. "How will we live? How will we eat?"

"Alms," answers Reb Mordke matter-of-factly.

"But work has never been an impediment to studying before," says Nahman.

"Now it is."

## The appearance of ruah haKodesh, when the spirit descends into man

In the month of Kislev of the year 5515 (or November 1754), Jacob announces by way of Nahman and Nahman's writings that he is opening his own beth midrash, his own school, and immediately many students enroll. Especially since—an absolutely extraordinary thing—the first student is Rabbi Mordechai, Reb Mordke. Making a ceremonious entrance, his dignified figure attracts much attention; people trust and admire him a great deal. Since he in turn trusts this Jacob, then Jacob must be someone truly special. Several days later, Jacob brings Nahman and Nussen into his school. Nahman is embarrassed by his new Greek clothing, which he's bought to replace what was destroyed, using the money from the sale of the wax imported from Podolia.

Some days later, they receive the news that, in Nikopol, Hana, Jacob's wife, has given birth to a daughter, and that, according to a decision she and Jacob made long ago, this daughter has been named Eva, nicknamed Avacha. They had a portent of this—Nussen's she-donkey gave birth to twins: gray herself, one of her babies was a female, completely white, while the other was a male, dark, an unusual coffee color. Jacob is delighted, and for several days he acts more serious and tells everyone that a daughter was born to him on the same day he himself gave birth to a school.

Then something strange happens, something that was long awaited, or at least it has been known that it had to happen, that it was inevitable. It is hard to describe, even though it's one event, in which everything happens in a certain order, even though for every movement, for every image, there exists a corresponding word, but maybe it will be best if told by a witness, especially since he is writing everything down anyway.

Shortly after that, Nussen tore me from my slumber, saying that
something strange was going on with Jacob. Nussen tended to sit up
and read into the night, and everyone always went to sleep before
him. Nussen woke up several of the others who were then with us in
the midrash, and they, sleepy and scared, went down into Jacob's
room, where several lamps were burning and where Rabbi
Mordechai had already gone. Jacob was standing in the middle of
the room amidst overturned furniture, half naked, his breeches
barely remaining on his skinny hips, his skin gleaming with sweat,
and his face pale, his eyes strange somehow, unseeing, trembling all
over, as though seized by fever. This went on for some time, with us
standing before him, watching him and waiting to see what would
happen; no one had the boldness to lay so much as a finger upon
him. Mordechai undertook to say a prayer in a mournful,
overwhelmed voice, so that I was shaken, too, and the others also
were worried by the sight of what was happening right here before
us. For we understood that the Spirit had descended amongst us.
The curtains between this and that world had been rent, time had
lost its purity, the spirit was forcing its way into us like a battering
ram. The small stuffy room became thick with the smell of our
sweat and there was also the smell of something like raw meat, like
blood. I became nauseated, and then I felt all the hairs on my body
rear up; I saw, too, that Jacob's manhood was bulging against the
material of his breeches, until at last, he moaned and fell onto his
knees with his head down. A moment later he spoke softly, hoarsely,
words not everybody understood: "Mostro Signor abascharo," which
Reb Mordke repeated in our language: "Our Lord descends."

And so Jacob knelt in that unnatural position, shrunken, sweat
beaded on his back and shoulders, his wet hair matted to his face.
His body quaked, stopped, quaked again, and again, as though gusts
of cold air were shooting through it. Then, after a long while, he
collapsed insensate onto the floor.

Such is the ruah haKodesh, when the spirit descends into man. It resembles illness, sticky and incurable, like a sudden weakening. A beholder
of it might well feel disappointed. What the majority assume will be a
solemn, noble moment turns out to be more like a flogging, or a birth.

When Jacob knelt, shrunken as though in a painful spasm, Nahman
saw above him a luminescence and pointed it out to someone—clearer
air, as though heated to glowing by cold light, an irregular halo. Only

then, at the sight of that light, did the rest of them drop to their knees, and over them, slowly, as though they were submerged in water, circled something that resembled gleaming iron filings.

News of all of this quickly made its way around the city, and people began to camp outside the home where Jacob lived. He also began to have visions.

Nahman scrupulously recorded them all:

Led from room to room, he floated through the air, on either side of him a beautiful maiden. In the rooms he saw many women and men, and in some of the rooms he noticed religious study groups, and from above he heard what they were saying and understood everything perfectly from the very first word. There were so many of these rooms, and in the last one he glimpsed the First, Sabbatai (of blessed memory)—he was dressed in Frankish clothing, like our own, and around him were gathered many students. The First said to Jacob: "So you are the Wise Jacob? I have heard that you are powerful and brave of heart. That makes me happy, because I have made it all the way here and have no strength to go farther. Many have taken on this weight before, but they have collapsed beneath it. Are you not afraid?"

And the First showed Jacob the abyss that looks like a black sea. On the other, distant shore, a mountain rose. Then Jacob cried: "Let it happen! I am going!"

The news of this vision travels around Salonika, passing from ear to ear, often with some new detail. It spreads around the city like news of arriving ships carrying extraordinary wares. Even more people come to listen to Jacob out of curiosity, his school is bursting at the seams. People clear the way for him with reverence and respect. Some, bolder, extend their hand to touch his robes. They have already begun to call him hakham, or wise man, though this makes him angry, and he tells everyone he is a simpleton. Even the older ones, who knew the old Kabbalah well, now recognize his greatness. They crouch in the shade and discuss him, and these sages discern the secret signs told by the ancient prophets.

Jacob also dreams of divine palaces. He has been where the First is. He has seen that same door. He has gone after him. He has walked the same path.

They begin every day by listening to Jacob's dreams. They wait for him to wake up, are there at his first movement. He is not to rise or touch anything, instead he must speak right away, straight out of sleep, as though bringing news from those worlds, greater, more distant, closer to the light.

Students of Baruchiah's son Konio—the one who wouldn't receive them—come, too, and they also listen to Jacob, which pleases Reb Mordke most of all. Most of them, however, listen to Jacob with some suspicion, coming in with their opinions formed. They treat him as the competition, like someone who brazenly set up a salvation stall right next to theirs, that is just like theirs but with better prices. They ask, loudly and theatrically: Who is this stray?

But the ones who most adhere to Jacob are the Jews from Poland, those who do business in Salonika or who got stuck here and can't go back to their families, having squandered all their money. They are easy enough to recognize. Nahman, for instance, can immediately sniff them out in a crowd, even if they are wearing Greek or Turkish clothing and striding quickly down the cramped little streets. He sees himself in them—they make the same gestures, have the same bearing and the same slightly uncertain, slightly impudent step. The poorer ones tend to wear nondescript, dully colored clothing, and even if one of them has gotten himself a scarf or a better coat, Rohatyn still leers out from under it, or Dawidów, or Czernowitz. Even when, to protect against the sun, he wraps his head in a turban, Podhajce and Buczacz still jut out from under his pant legs, Lwów from his pockets, and his slippers, seemingly Greek, still clap as though stepping straight out of Busk.

## Of why Salonika does not care for Jacob

Then the situation changes. One day, when Jacob is teaching, some bruisers armed with sticks come into the classroom. They go after those standing nearest the door. They strike blindly. Nussen gets hit, he's bleeding, his nose is broken. On the floor, streaks of blood, and shouts—a clamor that can be heard from everywhere. The students flee outside, and soon they are afraid to return—for this all happens again the next day. Everyone knows it's followers of Konio, Baruchiah's son, who are trying to chase off Jacob, insisting that only they can offer instruction in Salonika. Some of them have familiar faces, the faces of friends—they are, after all, also true believers, but now those old friendships don't count. There isn't room in Salonika for two contenders for Messiah. Nussen places guards outside the midrash, to stand there all day and all night. Even so, someone sets fire to it twice. Several times Jacob is attacked on the street, but he is strong, able to defend himself. Nussen, as he is doing the shopping, nearly loses his only eye in an attack. And—this is the strangest one—the Salonika Jewesses have conspired against Jacob; angry women, young and old, attack him as he is going to the baths and throw stones at him. After that, he limps for several days, but he is ashamed to admit it was women who did it.

From one day to the next, the local merchants stop doing business with them as well. Now, when Jacob's men enter their stalls, they treat them like strangers, turning away and vanishing among their wares. This makes their situation very uncomfortable very quickly. In order to sell or to buy anything, they have to go to the bazaars on the city's outskirts, where no one knows them. Konio's followers have declared war on Jacob and his entourage. They conspire against him with the Greeks, meaning the Christian merchants, and they, too, turn away at the sight of them. Nussen's guards at the beth midrash are no help when Konio's people post theirs as well, who beat up anyone who attempts to enter Wise Jacob's school. The money runs out very quickly, and unfortunately, the school has to be closed.

In addition, an unexpectedly severe winter set in—

Nahman writes later. They do not have money for even the worst fuel. They sit shut inside their rented home, fearing for their lives. Jacob coughs.

I have often thought about how success and good fortune can
suddenly transform into misery and humiliation.

There wasn't any money, which is why I will remember that
Salonika winter as being ravenous and thin. In order to fill our
stomachs, we would often go begging for alms, as many of the
learned have done here before. I always tried to ask people calmly
and politely for spare change, but Jacob would use very different
methods. Once, just before Passover, we stopped by to see a certain
Jew who kept funds for the poor. I spoke to him first, for in such
situations it worked to our advantage that I spoke well and could
make the types of arguments that would make a good impression, as
a learned man, and trustworthy. So I said that we were from a
cursed land, where Jews have suffered the greatest misfortunes as a
result of terrible persecutions and where the direst poverty prevails,
where the climate is hostile, though for all this the people there are
honest and wholly dedicated to the faith . . . And so I spoke, trying
to awaken pity in him, but he didn't even look at me.

"We've got enough domestic alms-collectors here, we can't be
maintaining foreign ones on top of this."

So I replied:

"In our country, even a foreigner can find support."

This treasurer gave me a spiteful smile and looked me in the eye
for the first time:

"So what did you come wandering in here for, leaving behind
that magnificent country, since things were going so well for you
there?"

I was about to come back with a clever retort when Jacob, who
until that moment had been standing calmly behind me, shoved me
aside and shrieked at him:

"How dare you ask why we left our country, you little scumbag?!"

The other man took a step backward, frightened by Jacob's tone,
but he didn't answer, and in any case he would have been unable to,
for Jacob was already leaning in to him and shouting:

"Why did Jacob the Patriarch leave his country and go to Egypt?
Isn't that where Passover comes from? If he had stayed in his
country, you would have no holiday now, you scoundrel, and we
would have no need for holiday meals!"

The man was so frightened he instantly gave us a few levs and,
apologizing profusely, showed us to the door.

Perhaps it was all for the best, since our deprivation that winter
ultimately focused us and sharpened our senses. There was no force

capable of extinguishing Jacob's flame. He—as was shown in a variety of situations—was able to shine like a precious stone even in the worst of conditions. Even in rags, as we begged for alms, there was a kind of majesty that emanated from him, and everyone who met with him knew that he was encountering an extraordinary being. And was afraid. It's strange, but in that poverty, instead of perishing, we began to understand. It was as if we had only disguised ourselves in that cold, that pain, and that destitution. Jacob in particular—freezing and tattered, he inspired even greater compassion, but also greater respect than any self-satisfied, wealthy hakham.

And then another miracle occurred: Jacob's fame so increased across Salonika that in the end, Konio's true believers showed up, for now they wished to buy him off. They offered him a considerable sum of money to either join with them or leave the city.

"Now you come?!" he cried bitterly. "Now you can kiss my ass! You're too late."

In the end, hostility toward him became so severe that Jacob stopped sleeping at home. He had a Greek gentleman sleep in his bed, a man hoping to get into the stone trade with us. Jacob went to sleep in the kitchen, or so he told us all. I knew very well that he went to see a widow who often provided him with financial support as well as with the comforts of her body. One night, someone broke into the house and stabbed the Greek under his blanket. The murderer vanished like a shadow.

This event alarmed Jacob to such an extent that for some time he left Salonika for Larissa, while we pretended he'd remained. On the very first night of his return, they prepared an ambush for him.

From then on, Jacob spent every night in some new place, and we began to fear for our lives and for our health, so—there was no alternative—we determined to leave Salonika to the mercy of its evil and go back to Smyrna. The worst thing was that it was our own people who so desired Jacob's demise. Now even he had nothing good to say about them. He spoke of them with contempt, calling them effeminate and saying that of everything Baruchiah had taught them, all that had stayed with them was a fondness for sodomy.

### *Scraps: Of the curse of Salonika and Jacob's molting*

As soon as we had made the decision to flee Salonika and started to
ready ourselves for the road, Jacob fell ill. One day his body became
covered in abscesses, and his skin came off in bloody sheets as he
howled in pain. What sort of illness comes on so suddenly, so
unexpectedly, and takes on such symptoms as these? The first thing
that came to everyone's mind was that this must be a curse. Jacob
believed it, too. Those Koniosos must have hired some sort of
sorcerer, although among their own they had several who might well
have the skill to cast such a curse upon their rival.

At first, Reb Mordke applied the bandages himself, swathing
Jacob in amulets he had prepared, mumbling spells, while he filled
the pipe with dark resin for the patient, since smoking it alleviated
his pain. But helpless in the face of his beloved Jacob's continued
suffering, he called up a certain woman, old and trembling, reputed
to be the finest healer. They said she was a witch, and extremely
famous, one of those Thessalonians who have lived just outside the
city for centuries and know how to disappear. She coated his
wounds in a foul-smelling liquid that stung and burned, and Jacob's
howling could be heard all over town. As he moaned in pain, she
chanted some kind of spells over him, in a language no one could
recognize, so bizarre it was. She patted him on the buttocks like she
might a child, and when it was over, she wouldn't accept any
payment, saying it hadn't been an illness at all, that Jacob had
merely been molting. Like a snake.

We looked at one another in disbelief, and Reb Mordke burst
into tears like a little boy.

"Molting like a snake!" Overcome, he raised his hands to heaven
and cried, "Our Lord, to the ends of the earth—thank you!" And
then he pulled on everyone's sleeves and repeated, thrilled, "The
serpent is the savior, nahash. Is this not evidence of Jacob's
messianic mission?" His dark, teary eyes shone, reflecting the little
flames of the lamps. I soaked the bandages in a warm herbal
decoction, as the old woman had instructed, in order to be able to
lay them upon the crusted-over wounds. It wasn't that the wounds
themselves were terrible, though the pain they caused was real and
acute—but it was mainly the fact that they were there. Who did this?
Who cast this curse? I thought at first with anger and bitterness.
But now I knew that no one would be able to do anything bad to

Jacob. When the spirit enters a human being, everything must change in his body, start up afresh. A man leaves his old skin aside and covers himself in a new one. Yes, this is what we talked about through the night before we left.

Nussen and I were squatting down beneath the trees. We were waiting for a miracle. The sky in the east got pink, the birds began to sing, and then the call of the muezzin joined in with theirs. When the sun began to make its way out from under the horizon, the little homes with their flat roofs covered themselves in long, damp shadows and all the smells of the world awoke: orange flowers, smoke, ash, and yesterday's rotting remains tossed out onto the streets. And incense, and donkey excrement. I felt unimaginable happiness overflowing in me—it was a miracle, and a sign that every day the world arises anew and gives us a new chance for tikkun. It gives itself over into our hands trustfully, like an enormous and uncertain animal, crippled and dependent on our will. And we must harness it to our work.

"Will we find Jacob's shed skin on the floor?" Hershel asked in excitement, as I stood and in the light of the rising sun, to the accompaniment of the muezzin's wailing, I danced.

That day, Jacob woke angry and suffering. He told us to pack our paltry goods, and since we had no money for a ship, we set out on donkeys along the shore to the east.

En route to Adrianople, we camped by the seaside. Jacob was hissing in pain, and the dressings I made for him didn't help at all. Then a woman passing through on a donkey, no doubt also a witch, like all Thessalonian women, advised him to enter into the salty seawater and to stand there as long as he could take it. Jacob did as she said, but the water did not wish to take Jacob. He staggered in it, got knocked over, and the sea ejected him, weak, onto the shore. He tried to throw himself upon the waves, but it looked as if they were fleeing from him, and he was left in the wet sand. Then—I saw this myself and record it here as an eyewitness—Jacob raised his hands to the sky and gave a series of horrific shouts. He shouted so that all the nearby travelers paused, uneasy, and the fishermen, who were readying their nets, stopped mid-motion, and the women who were selling fish straight out of the basket, and even the sailors who were just coming into port looked up and over. Nussen and I couldn't bear to hear it. It was as if they were skinning him alive.

I covered my ears, and then a strange thing happened—suddenly the sea let him in, a wave came up, and Jacob plunged into it up to his neck, and in the end, for a moment, all of him disappeared under the water, his hands and feet flashing, and the water turned him over like a little scrap of wood. At last he emerged onto the shore and lay in the sand like a dead man. Nussen and I ran up to him and, getting our robes wet, dragged him farther onto the shore. To tell the truth—I thought that he had drowned.

But after this bath the skin fell off him in sheets all day, and underneath appeared new and healthy skin, pink like a child's.

In two days Jacob was healthy and when we got to Smyrna he was young again, and so handsome and full of light, like himself again. And this was how he presented himself to his wife.

Nahman is very happy with what he's written. He hesitates over whether or not to mention the adventures at sea that came next. He could describe it—the trip was certainly dramatic enough to be described. He dips his pen, then instantly flicks the drops of ink onto the sand. No, he won't write about that. He won't write that for a small sum a little trade ship agreed to carry them to Smyrna. The passage was cheap, but the conditions were very bad. They had barely settled in belowdecks, and the ship had sailed out to sea, when it turned out that its proprietor, a man who was neither a Greek nor an Italian, but some Christian, was not a merchant at all, but rather a pirate. When they demanded to be taken straight to Smyrna, this man abused them and threatened to have his thugs throw them all overboard.

Nahman remembers the date well—it was July 25, 1755, the day of the patron saint of this horrible man, a saint to whom he prayed incessantly, confessing all his crimes (which they had to hear, and which made the blood in their veins run cold). A terrible squall descended on the water. It was Nahman's first time experiencing something so abominable, and he became convinced that he was going to die that day. Terrified, he tethered himself to the mast, in order that the frenzied waves not wash him away, and he lamented loudly. Then, in a panic, he clutched at Jacob's coat, trying to hide under it. Jacob, who had no fear in him, tried at first to calm him, but when nothing helped, he began to ridicule poor Nahman, making fun of the whole situation. They held on to the flimsy masts, and when those broke under the beating of the waves, they grabbed hold of

anything they could. The water was worse than a robber—it washed out all the loot from below the deck and also took one deckhand who was drunk and barely able to stay on his feet. The loss of this man to the depths caused Nahman to completely lose control of himself. He jabbered incoherent words of prayer, tears as salty as the seawater blinding his eyes.

Amused by Nahman's state, Jacob had him make confession as well, and—worse still—had him make an assortment of promises to God. In his terror and his tears, he bound himself never again to touch wine or any spirits, or to smoke a pipe.

"I swear, I swear!" he shouted with his eyes closed, too terrified to think clearly, which brought Jacob great joy, so that in the midst of the storm he guffawed like a demon.

"And you'll clean up after me when I shit!" Jacob shouted over the storm.

And Nahman answered:

"I swear, I swear."

"And wipe my ass!" shouted Jacob.

"And wipe Jacob's ass. I swear, I swear I'll do it all!" answered Nahman, until the others, who were all listening, also started to collapse with laughter and mock the rabbi, and this ended up engaging them more than the storm, which passed like a bad dream.

Even now Nahman can't shake his sense of shame and humiliation. He doesn't speak a word to Jacob all the way to Smyrna, although Jacob often puts his arm around his shoulder and pats him on the back. It is hard to forgive someone for having fun at your misfortune. But—strangely— Nahman also finds an odd pleasure in it, a pale shadow of unspeakable delectation, a slight pain, when Jacob's arm squeezes the nape of his neck.

Among all the oaths that Jacob laughingly forced Nahman to take, there was the promise he had made that he would never leave him.

## Scraps: Of triangles and crosses

In Smyrna everything seemed familiar to us, as if we had been gone for just one week.

Jacob and Hana, and that tiny little girl who had recently been born to them, rented a small house on a side street. Hana, with the dowry given by her father, even arranged it so that it was pleasant to go there and sit for a bit, while she, in the Turkish fashion, would disappear with the child into the women's part of the home, although I often felt from somewhere her gaze on my back.

Isohar, having heard about the entrance of the Holy Spirit into Jacob, had begun to behave completely differently from before. He began to seek out my company, as a direct witness of Jacob and as his voice. We would gather daily for long sittings, and Isohar ever more fervently would urge on us the study of the teachings of the Trinity.

This forbidden idea we found so thrilling, so illicit, that we wondered whether it was so for every Jew, whether it had, as it did for us, the same force as those four Hebrew letters that create the name of God.

In the sand strewn over the table that served as our slate, Isohar drew triangles and marked their corners according to what was in the Zohar, and then according to the teachings of Sabbatai Tzvi, blessed be his name. Someone stopping by might have thought that we were children playing at drawing.

There is the God of truth in the spiritual world and the Shekhinah imprisoned in matter, and as if "underneath them," in the lower corner of the triangle, there is God the Creator, the cause of Divine sparks. When the Messiah comes, he eliminates the First

Reason, and then the triangle stands on its head, now the God of
Truth is on top, and beneath him is the Shekhinah and the
Shekhinah's vessel, the Messiah.

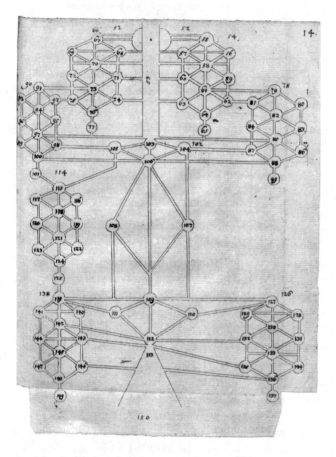

Much of this I did not understand.

"Yes, yes, yes," was all Isohar would say, time and again. He had
aged a great deal of late, as though he were traveling faster than the
rest of us, alone out in front. He would also show us two lines
crossing each other, giving rise to the cross, the quadruplicity that
is the world's stamp. He drew two intersecting lines and skewed
them slightly.

"What does this remind you of?" he asked.

And Jacob instantly glimpsed the mystery of the cross.

"That's the *alef*. The cross is the *alef*."

In secret, once I remained alone, I raised my hand to my
forehead and touched my skin, saying, "God of Abraham, Isaac, and

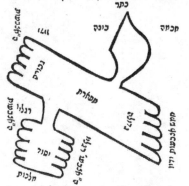

Jacob," for I was only beginning to grow accustomed to this thought.

One Smyrna night, stuffy from the fragrance of the orange blossoms, for it was already spring, Isohar revealed to us the following secret:

There is one God in three figures, and the fourth is the holy Mother.

Some time later, urged on by my letters, there came to Smyrna a merchant's caravan from Podolia, and with it, Elisha Shorr and his sons, Nathan and Solomon. With Jacob, Isohar, and Reb Mordke, I maintained that it was divine will guiding us, placing us in front of people and having us meet with precisely the ones we most needed to see, but the truth was otherwise. I had been writing to Reb Shorr even from Salonika, describing to him Jacob's ruah haKodesh, and other details of what had happened with us there. However, truth be told, I had not believed that this would cause that older man to saddle his horses, take out the carts, and head off on such far-flung travels. But the Shorrs were always able to unite matters of the spirit with business dealings of various kinds, and so while the brothers took up the sale and purchase of goods, Old Man Shorr conversed with us, and slowly out of those evenings emerged a vision of the days that were supposed to come and that we were supposed to be guided by. He found great support in the person of Reb Mordke, who had long been muttering about this subject, citing his own strange dreams. But the Shorrs cared not for dreams.

Did Jacob know what we had in store for him? He got very sick then and almost died, but when he awoke from his fever, he said he'd had a dream. That he had dreamed of a man with a white beard, who had said to him: "You will go north, and many are the persons you will draw there to the new faith."

Wise Jacob objected: "How am I to go to Poland, when I don't understand the Polish language and have all of my affairs here, in the Turkish country. And I have a very young wife, with a newborn daughter—she won't want to go with me." So Jacob defended himself before us and before his own dream as we sat there, a ceremonial committee of four: Isohar, Elisha Shorr, Reb Mordke, and myself.

"That man with the beard, whom you saw in your sleep, that is Elijah—didn't you realize?" said Reb Mordke to him. "When things are hard for you, he will go ahead of you. You will go first, and then Hana will come to you. In Poland you will be the king and the savior."

"I will be with you," added I, Nahman of Busk.

## Scraps: Of meeting Jacob's father in Roman, and also of the starosta and the thief

At the start of October 1755, we headed north in two wagons pulled by several horses. We certainly did not resemble what we were—messengers of some significant matter—but had rather the appearance of ordinary merchants circling around and around like ants. On the road to Czernowitz we went to Roman to visit Jacob's father, who after his wife's death lived there on his own. We paused at the city's tollhouse so that Jacob could put on his best costume, for what purpose I know not.

Yehuda Leyb Buchbinder lived in a very little house with just one room, cramped and smoky. There was no place even for the horses, so they stood outside all night. There were just the three of us, Jacob, Nussen, and I, as the Shorrs' caravan had set forth for Poland long before.

Yehuda Leyb was of tall stature, but skinny and wrinkled. His face at the sight of us took on an expression of dissatisfaction and disappointment. His thick, bushy eyebrows almost concealed his eyes, particularly since he had a habit of tilting his head forward and glowering. Jacob had been very excited at the prospect of seeing his father, but they greeted each other almost indifferently. His father seemed happier about the arrival of Nussen, whom he knew well, than about seeing his own son. We brought good food: a wealth of cheese, carboys of wine, a full pot of olives, all of the finest quality, purchased along the way. Jacob had spent most of what he had on these treats. But the sight of them did not cheer Yehuda in the slightest. The old man's eyes remained sad and avoided meeting other people's.

Jacob, too, who had previously so rejoiced, now slumped and was silent. So it is: our parents remind us of what we like least about ourselves, and in their growing old we see our many sins, I thought, but perhaps this was something more—sometimes it happens that the souls of parents and children are fundamentally hostile to one another, and they meet in life in order to remedy this hostility. But it doesn't always work.

"Everyone around here has the same dream," said Yehuda Leyb at the very start. "Everyone has dreams about the Messiah already being in some town, somewhere nearby, except that no one ever remembers the name of that town or the name of that Messiah. I had the same dream, and I sort of recognized the name of the town. Others say the same and always fast for days on end to try and have a second dream that will tell them what the city's name might be."

We drank wine and snacked on olives, and finding myself the most garrulous, I told of everything that had happened with us. I told it in the same way I am telling it here, but it was evident that old Buchbinder was not listening. He was silent and kept looking around his own room where there wasn't anything that might have drawn his gaze. At last Nussen spoke up.

"I don't understand you at all, Leyb. We came here from the world and are telling you all these things, and getting nothing back from you. You listen with one ear and ask no questions. Are you well?"

"But what do I get out of your telling me stories about some heavenly fair?" Leyb responded. "What do I care for this wisdom of yours, when I'm just curious how it's supposed to be benefiting me? How much longer will I have to live like this, alone, in pain, in sorrow? What is God prepared to do for us, tell me of that."

Then he added:

"I no longer believe that anything will change. No one knows the name of that little town. I had thought it was something like Sambor, Sampol . . ."

We went out with Jacob in front of the little house, where a river flowed downhill. Jacob said that all of their homes had looked like that: they stood on a river and every evening the geese would come out of the water, one after the other, that's how he recalled it from his childhood. By some miracle, the family had always settled on a river just like this one—flowing between the hills, shallow, sunny, swift. They would race into it and splash water all around; in places by the shore where the whirlpools had washed away the sand, you could learn to doggy-paddle from one side to the other. Suddenly Jacob remembered that once, when he and the other children were engaged in their usual games, he had decided to play the starosta, and since he had to exercise his authority, there also had to be a thief. So they cast a little boy in that role, tied him to a tree, and burned him with a metal bar heated in their campfire, wanting to get him to confess where he'd hid the horses. The little boy begged them to stop, reminding them they were just playing, that there were no horses. But then the pain became too great, and the boy nearly passed out, and then he screamed out that he had hidden the horses here, and there. Then Jacob let him go.

I had no idea what to say to such a story. When it had come out, his father had beat him with birch switches, said Jacob after a moment's silence. As he spoke, he was pissing on his father's nearly collapsing fence.

"He was right to do so," I answered, for that cruel story had astonished me. The wine was hitting me now, and I wanted to go back inside, but he grabbed me by the sleeve and pulled me to him.

He told me always to listen to him, and that when he told me I was the thief, then I was to be the thief. And when he told me I was the starosta, then I was to become the starosta. He said this straight to my face, and I could smell the fruity wine on his breath. I was frightened of his eyes, darkened with anger, and I dared not oppose him. When we went back inside, both of the older men were crying. Tears ran down their cheeks and soaked into their beards.

"What would you say, Yehuda, if your son were to go to Poland on a mission and teach there?" I asked him as we were leaving.

"God forbid."

"Why do you say that?"

He shrugged.

"They'll kill him. There are lots of folks that could kill him there. They're just waiting for someone like him."

Two days later, in Czernowitz, Jacob got the ruah haKodesh again in the presence of many of the faithful. Again he was thrown to the ground, and for the whole rest of the day he said nothing other than something like "ze-ze-ze," which as we listened we realized was "Ma'ase Zar, Ma'ase Zar," or "Strange Deed." He was shaking all over, and his teeth were chattering. Then people went up to him, and he laid his hands on them, and many went away healed. Some of ours from Podolia were there, men who crossed

borders openly or illegally to work small trades. They sat around in
front of the shack like dogs, despite the cold, waiting for Jacob to
come out, wanting to just touch his coat. I recognized several
among them, including Shyle from Lanckoroń, and talking with
them I got homesick, with my home being so nearby.

One thing was for sure—our people from Czernowitz supported
us, and it was clear that the legend of Jacob had a wide range already,
and knew no borders. And it was as though everyone had been
waiting for him, as though there were no longer any way of saying no.

At the end we spent another night with Jacob's father, and I told
him that story about the starosta and the thief.

Then Leyb said:

"Watch out for Jacob. He really is a thief."


## Of Jacob's dance

People gather in a village on the Turkish side, since the guards won't let
them into Poland. They have reports of a plague there. Some musicians
returning from a wedding have sat down, exhausted, on the logs ready
to be floated across the river. They have drums, flutes, and bağlamas,
little instruments with strings they pick with cherrywood bark.

Jacob comes up to them and removes his overcoat, and his tall figure
begins to move rhythmically. At first he stomps his foot, but in such a way
as to speed up the player, who reluctantly accepts this rhythm, faster than
he'd wanted. Now Jacob rocks from side to side and, stepping faster and
faster, he shouts at the rest of the players, and they understand that this
strange man is demanding that they start playing, too. An older man arrives
from somewhere with a santur, a Turkish zither, and when he joins in with
the players, the music becomes complete, perfect for dancing. Then Jacob
puts his hands on the shoulders of two onlookers jerking from side to side,
and they begin to take little steps. The drums beat out a clear rhythm,
which carries over the water to the other side and down the river. Soon
others join in—Turkish cattle herders, merchants, Podolian peasants all toss
aside their traveling bags, discard their sheepskin coats. A row of dancers
forms, and its ends curl in until eventually a circle is made, which instantly
begins to spin. And those whom the ruckus and hoopla draw in also begin

to sway, and then, as if in desperation, as if they've had enough of waiting, as if they've decided to go for broke right here and now, they join the circle. Jacob leads the dance around carts and surprised horses, set apart from the rest by his tall hat, but when the hat falls off, it isn't clear anymore that he is the one who is the leader. Behind him goes Nahman, ecstatically, like a saint, with his hands raised up, his eyes closed, a blissful smile on his face. Some beggar, despite his limp, transforms into a dancer, grinning, wide-eyed. Women laugh at the sight of him, but he just makes faces back. After a moment's hesitation young Shlomo Shorr joins in; he has come with his father to wait for Jacob, to safely convey him over the border. The flaps of his wool overcoat fluttering around his thin figure, Nussen behind him with the scar on his face, and then a somewhat stiff Hershel. Children and servants link up with this procession and a dog barks at them, running up to their stomping feet and jumping back. Some girls set down the carrying poles they've brought to get water, and lifting up their skirts, tentatively step with their bare feet, so petite they don't even reach Jacob's breast. A fat peasant woman in wood-soled shoes stuffed with straw is also starting to move now, and the Turkish vodka smugglers begin to dance, playing inno-cent. The drum goes faster and faster, and the dancers' feet move faster and faster. Jacob starts to whirl like a dervish, the dance circle breaks off, people fall down on the ground in heaps of laughter, sweaty, red with effort.

That's how it ends.

After it's over, a Turkish guard with a big mustache approaches Jacob.

"Who are you?" he asks him in Turkish, in a threatening tone. "Jew? Muslim? Rus?"

"Can't you see, stupid? I'm a dancer." Jacob pants. He leans over, rest-ing his hands on his own knees, and then he turns away from his inquis-itor as if wanting to show him his bottom. The guard grabs for his saber, offended by that "halfwit," but Old Shorr, who until now has been sitting in the cart, calms him down. He takes his hand.

"What kind of idiot is this?" asks the guard, furious.

Reb Elisha Shorr says that he's a holy fool. But this means nothing to the Turk.

"Well, if you ask me, he's a crackpot," he says. Then he shrugs and walks away.

SVECIÆ PARS.

Stockholm
Telie
DANIÆ PARS
o. Hafnia
Schonen
Elsterbo
Bornholm
Haro
Völbergia
Certholma
Gosse
Sando Faro
Weshy
Bode
Oelandia
Gotlandia
Asborg
BALTICUM
MARE

Sinus Finn.
Revel
ESTHO
Dago I.
LIVO
Oesel inf.
Sinus Livoni
cus
Pal.
Riga
Kokonhaus
Semigal.
Curlandia
Goldingen
Liba
Sevenbergen

Vulgo. De Oost Zee.

Rugia
Wolgast
Vssen Colberg
DUCATUS
POMERANIÆ
Stetin
Garth
Dresen
Kustrin
Brancfurt
Crossen
Glogaw
POMEREL
Cassubia
Dantzig
Palat.
Marienburg
Schwetz
Bromberg
New marckt
Posnanien
Inowlacz
sis Palatinas
Poma
sien
Elbing
Libst.
Gradentz
Culm Pal.
Thorn
Brestuw
Ploczt
Brescie
rabou
Szachsouue
Lencecia
Sirad
Breslaw
Brisk
Oppelen
BOHE
MIÆ
PARS
Praga
Oppelen
Ducatus
Rastbor
Iegerndorf
Troppa
Olmuntz
MORA
VIA
Domubius flu.
Brin
Wein
Presburg
HUNGARIÆ
AUSTRIÆ
PARS
PARS

Memel
SAMOGITIÆ
Krozi
Rosiene
Koningsberg
DUCA
Rosenberg
Heilsberg
PRUS.
Custtin
Bartenst.
Neueburg
Angerburg
Troki
Vilna
Tros
et Cass. Merica
Sie
Kara
Bielsk
MAZO
VIA
War
cauia
Luthuen
Pal.
Sendomir
Cra
co
Sandec
Caso Mer
Raua
Pal.
POLO
NIA
Sas
MINOR
Palat.
Cracovia
Cra
co.
vien
sis
Pal.
Chelmen
sis
RUS
SIA
RUBRA
Sohaut
Cast.
Iaroslaw
P.Prz
Przemisl
Leopolis
Glinany
Thorow
Habics

Trokensis
Vilna
LI
sis
ais
Bresticen
sis
PALAT,
Vol hy
nie
Woldomirra
Olyka
Dubr
Swt al.
Kucko
Ostrog
Sokal
terio.
Ostra
Zborou
sis
Pal
Pinsk
Nougr
len
sis
Pal.
Castellan
Wilhensis

MA

LI
Pa
Mohylow
WALACHIA

MOLDA

Seret flu.

Brahilo

Nova totius
REGNI POLONIÆ,
Magniq, Ducatus
LITHUANIÆ,
cum suis
PALATINATIBUS
ac Confiniis.
Ægidium Valkenier Excu.

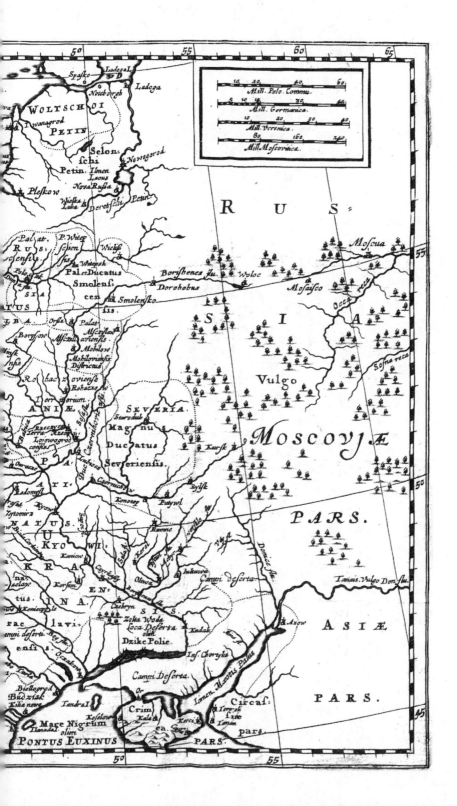

# III.

# *The Book of*
# THE ROAD

| *Viator* 1 m. 3. | Podroźny, 1 | humerus, m. 2. ramie. |
| portat *humeris* | nieśie na ramieniu, | bulga, f. 1. (torba taiſtra) |
| in *bulga*, 2 | w torbie (taiſtrze) | |
| quæ capere nequit | co nie może zabrać | |
| | (ogarnąć,) | |
| *funda*, 3 f. 1. | w kieſzen; 3 | |
| vel *marſupium*; 4 | | |
| (n. 2. | | |
| tegitur | okrywa się | |
| *lacerna*; 5 | opończą; 5 | lacerna, f. 1. opończa. |
| tenet *manu* | w ręku trzyma | manus, m. 2. ręka. |
| *baculum*, 6 | laſkę; 6 | baculus, m. 2. &, um, n. 2. |
| quo ſe fulciat; | ktorą się podpiera; | laſka. |
| opus habet | potrzebuię | viaticum, n. 2. ſtrawa |
| *viatico*, | ſtrawnego, | podroźna. |
| | | ut & |

Fo
grim
Bo
drzw
L
hors
au p

Le

Le
met, p
dans u
ee qui

dans ſe
ni dans

Il e
d'une
le b
à la m
pour s
il d
être fo
(qu

## 13.

### Of the warm December of 1755, otherwise known as the month of Tevet 5516, of the country of Polin, and pestilence in Mielnica

The travelers stand grouped together on the shore of the Dniester, on its low-lying southern bank. The frail winter sun casts red shadows over all that it can reach. December is warm—strangely, abnormally so. The air is an interleaving of warm gusts with freezing, and smells of newly dug-up earth.

Before them is the high, steep bank on the other side, now vanishing into shadow, the sun having dipped below the dark face they must now scale.

"Polin," says Old Shorr.

"Poland, Poland," everyone repeats joyfully, and their eyes are made narrow as slits by their smiles. Shlomo, Shorr's son, begins to pray, to thank the Lord that they have made it in one piece, all together. Quietly he speaks the words of his prayer; the others all join in, mumbling, careless, their minds on other things, loosening the saddles, removing their sweaty hats. Now they will eat, drink. They need to rest before the crossing.

They don't wait long. Night has barely started to fall when the Turkish smuggler arrives. They know him, it's Saakadze, they've worked with him many times. When it is completely dark they ford the river on horseback and in their carriages. The only sound is the splash of the water beneath the horses' hooves.

On the other side, they separate. The steep wall seems dangerous only when seen from the other bank. Saakadze leads them along a path that slopes up gently. Both Shorrs, with their Polish papers, ride ahead to the guardhouse, while Nahman and a few of the others wait a bit in perfect silence, then go down some side paths.

Polish sentries guard the village, not admitting travelers from Turkey due to the plague. Old Shorr and his son, whose papers and permits are in order, argue with them for a while to divert their attention, then bribe them, for it gets quiet, and the travelers continue on their way.

Jacob has Turkish papers that say he is the sultan's subject. That's how he looks, too, in his tall hat and his fur-lined Turkish coat. Only his beard sets him apart from a real Turk. He appears fully at ease, with just the tip of his nose sticking out above his collar. Perhaps he's even sleeping?

They reach the village, quiet and pitch-black at this time of night. No one stops them; there are no sentries. The Turk bids them farewell, stuffing the coins they give him under his belt; he is proud of the job he's done. He smiles, baring a set of white teeth. He has deposited them before a little inn, where a slumbering innkeeper evinces great surprise at these late arrivals, at their having been admitted into town.

Jacob falls asleep immediately, but Nahman spends the whole night tossing and turning in his not particularly comfortable bed, burning candles and examining the sheets for bedbugs. The tiny windows are filthy, with desiccated stalks upon the sills; perhaps they were once flowers. In the morning, their host, a middle-aged Jew, thin and ill at ease, serves them heated water with some matzah crumbled in. The inn looks quite luxurious, but their host explains that as the plague has racked up victims, people have grown more and more afraid to leave their homes, terrified to purchase things from those who have been stricken. They have already eaten their own stores here at the inn, so he begs their forgiveness and urges them to arrange for their meals on their own. As he says all this, he keeps his distance, avoiding their breath and their touch.

This strange, warm December has reinvigorated those minuscule creatures that ordinarily, fearing frost, spend this season hibernating underground; spurred by this unseasonable warmth, they have surfaced to destroy and kill. They lurk in the dense, ineffable fog, in the stuffy, toxic cloud that hangs over the villages and towns, in the fetid vapors given off by infected bodies that people everywhere refer to as "pestilential air." As soon as they make their way into a person's lungs, they enter the bloodstream, igniting it, and then they squeeze into the heart—and at that point, the person dies.

When in the morning the newcomers go out onto the streets of this village, which is called Mielnica, they see a big, almost completely empty market square with low homes around its edges and three streets that issue from it. There is a terrible damp chill—apparently the warm days are over now, or else here, on this high embankment, the climate is completely different. In the puddles in the mud they marvel at the low-racing clouds. All the shops are closed. Only one empty stall still stands on the square; a hemp rope flutters before it, the kind a hangman might employ. Somewhere a door creaks open, and a bundled-up figure flits past the houses. This is what the world will look like after the Final Judgment, emptied of people. How hostile, how nefarious it is, thinks Nahman, as he counts the money in his pocket.

"They don't take money from people with the plague," Jacob said when he saw Nahman about to go shopping. He was washing up in the icy water, the southern sun still preserved in the skin of his naked torso. "Don't pay them," he added, splashing cold water all around him.

Nahman has ventured confidently into a little Jewish shop, having seen someone emerge from it. Behind the counter stands a little old man, as though his family has required this of him, to make contact with the world so that its younger members will not have to.

"I would like wine, cheese, and bread," says Nahman. "Several loaves."

The old man gives Nahman the loaves of bread, not taking his eyes off him, as if surprised by his foreign-looking costume, though here at the border he shouldn't be surprised by much of anything anymore.

When Nahman, having paid, starts to leave, he sees that the old man is staggering strangely, unsteady on his feet.

---

Nahman's stories are not always to be believed—even less so when he writes them down. He has a propensity for exaggeration. He detects signs in everything; in everything, he seeks and finds connections. What happens is never quite enough for Nahman—he wants what happens also to have some heavenly, definitive meaning. He wants it to be meaningful, to have consequences for the future—wants even minor causes to provoke great effects. This is why he slumps so often into melancholy—has he not mentioned that himself?

When he gets back to Jacob, he tells him the old man fell down dead as soon as he handed over Nahman's purchases, before he even had a chance to take his money. Jacob laughs at this, pleased. Nahman likes to bring him pleasure in this way. He likes his deep, hoarse laughter.

## What is gleaned by the sharp gaze of every variety of spy

Since crossing the Dniester, Jacob has been followed by spies, although Yente sees them better than they see Jacob. She watches them scribble inept reports on dirty roadhouse tabletops, entrusting them to messengers who will carry them to Kamieniec and Lwów. There they are transformed in chancelleries, taking on a more refined character, becoming disquisitions, rubrics of events; they wind up on better paper and earn seals—and so, as official dispatches, they go by post to Warsaw, to the tired clerks of that collapsing state, to the papal nuncio's palace that drips with so much luxury, and also, via the secretaries of the kahalim, to Wilno, Kraków, and even Altona and Amsterdam. They are read by Bishop Dembowski, who is freezing in his dilapidated mansion in Kamieniec, and by the rabbis of the Lwów and Satanów kahalim, Hayim haKohen Rapaport and David ben Abraham, who send each other frequent messages riddled with insinuations and vague hints, as this whole shameful matter is difficult to express in straightforward holy Hebrew words. Finally, they're read by officials in Turkey, who need to know what's happening in this neighboring country, especially since they're in business with its noblemen. The hunger for information is great all around.

The spies, whether royal, ecclesiastic, or Jewish, report that Jacob has proceeded to Korolówka, where he was born and where a portion of his family still lives, in particular his uncle, Yankiel, the rabbi of Korolówka, with his son, Israel, and his wife, Sobla.

Here—according to the spies' reports—some twenty people have come to join him; most of them are relatives, all have ceremoniously written down their names, in so doing vowing to keep their faith in spite of any threats of persecution and without fear. And if it becomes necessary to convert to another religion, they will follow Jacob in this. They are like soldiers, one of the spies writes in a flight of poetic fancy—ready for anything.

The spies also know about Yente in the woodshed by the house. They describe her as "one holy old lady," "an elderly woman who doesn't want to die," and "a witch who is three hundred years old."

It is to her Jacob goes first.

Sobla leads him to the woodshed, opens the wooden door, and shows him what he asked to see as soon as he arrived. Jacob stands transfixed. The woodshed has been transformed into an elegant room, kilims woven by the local peasants hanging on the walls, striped and colorful, the floor covered in the same. In the center of the room stands a wide bed with beautiful bedding, embroidered, now a little dusty—Sobla sweeps the blades of grass and cobwebs away with her hand. A human face, meanwhile, peeks out from under the covers; above them lie her arms and her pale, bony hands, so that Jacob, who has remained irreverent, who is still quick to make a joke, now finds his knees going weak. This is his grandmother, after all. Others, too—Nahman and Nussen, Reb Mordke and Old Moshe from Podhajce, who is also here to say hello to Jacob—come peer down at Yente. At first, Jacob just stands there petrified, but then he starts to sob, theatrically; the others follow. Sobla stands in the doorway, keeping out the curious; men have crowded into their small yard, pale and bearded under their fur hats, stamping their feet in the fresh snow to stay warm.

This is Sobla's big moment, and she is proud that Yente looks so lovely.

She shuts the door and comes inside so she can show them how Yente's eyelids tremble slightly, how her eyeballs move beneath them, traveling through unimaginable worlds.

"She's alive," Sobla reassures them. "Touch her, she's even a little bit warm."

Obediently, without hesitation, Jacob touches his finger to Yente's hand. Then he jerks it back. Sobla giggles.

What, Wise Jacob, do you have to say about this?

It is known, of course, that Israel's wife is opposed to these true believers, which is what they call themselves, twisting things around, since they are not true to the traditional faith at all. Like many women, she doesn't like Jacob. Especially when she sees him praying without phylacteries! And when he contorts his body in strange ways, gritting his teeth. Up to his old tricks, thinks Sobla. Jacob tells her to go to the gentiles' shop—higher up there is a village of goyim—to get some Christian bread. Sobla declines. Someone else fetches the bread, and Jacob starts to pass out pieces of it, and some are so in awe of him that they receive it, committing sacrilege. His behavior is bizarre, too; he suddenly stops to listen as though hearing voices only he can hear. He says nonsensical things in some strange language, repeating, for instance, "ze-ze-ze," and trembling all over. What that is supposed to mean, Sobla has no idea—no one knows, but his disciples take it seriously. Moshe from Podhajce explains to Israel that what Jacob's chanting is just "Ma'asim Zarim, Ma'asim Zarim," that he's talking about the "Strange Deeds"—in other words, that from which it would be necessary to begin. Foreign deeds, bizarre, strange things, incomprehensible at first glance, that would seem very odd indeed to the uninitiated—though the initiated, those closest to Jacob, would understand. They now have to do everything that was once prohibited. Hence that Christian bread, formerly impure.

Israel thinks about this all afternoon. Since the long-awaited, much-anticipated messianic times have dawned, Jacob is right: the laws of this world—the laws of the Torah—cannot be in effect anymore. Now everything is the other way around. But this idea fills Israel with fear. He sits on a bench and watches with his mouth open as the world is utterly transformed. His head is spinning. In the yard, Jacob promises there will be more of them, these "Strange Deeds," and that they must be performed concertedly, with zeal. Breaking the old laws is necessary, is the only thing that will hasten the arrival of salvation. In the evening, Israel asks for some of that gentile bread, and he chews it slowly, laboriously, thoroughly.

Meanwhile, Sobla is an exceptionally practical person and not at all interested in such things. Were it not for her sound reasoning, they would have starved to death a long time ago, given that Israel's only pursuits are things like tikkun, Devekut, salvation, and the like. Besides, he has an ailment in his lungs that means he can't even chop wood properly. So Sobla gets the water heated so she can cook some chickens, oversees the preparation of a thick broth. She goes about her business. She's helped by Pesel, who is eight and resolute—the two of them are peas in a pod. Sobla is breastfeeding yet another child—Freyna. Freyna is voracious, which is why Sobla is so thin. The rest of the children run around the house.

Sobla would be quite curious to see the wife of this off-putting cousin she has to host in her home—they say she's given him a daughter. Is she ever going to come to Poland to join her husband? What's she like? And what sort of family is it that they have out there in Nikopol? Is it true that Jacob is rich there, and that he has his own vineyard? And if so, what could he be after here?

On the first day, there isn't time for anything, since people are always clustering around him, touching him, tugging at his sleeves. Jacob gives a lengthy talk to those assembled, full of parables. He proclaims a new religion, one accessible exclusively through Esau, meaning Christianity, just as Sabbatai crossed over to Ishmael, meaning the Turkish faith. The progress of salvation depends upon extracting from those religions the seeds of revelation and sowing them in one great divine revelation, the Torah of Atzilut: Torah of the World of Emanations. In this religion of the end of days, all three religions will be braided into one. On hearing this, some people spit into the snow and leave.

Then there is a feast, which leaves Jacob so tired or drunk that he goes to bed immediately—not alone, of course, for in Sabbatian homes a particular type of hospitality is practiced. To keep Jacob warm, Moshe from Podhajce sends his youngest daughter for the night.

Right after breakfast, Jacob asks to be taken up to the hill where the caves are. There his companions are to wait for him, while he vanishes into the forest. More shuffling of feet in snow. A substantial little crowd gathers, including village goyim, too, asking what is going on. They'll later tell the curious authorities: "A learned Jew came from Turkey, Your Honor. Big, with a Turkish hat on and pockmarks all over his face." More villagers join them, waiting for him to come back from the forest, sensing something significant is happening, certain Jacob is conversing with underground spirits. By the time he does return, it's starting to get dark, and with the dusk falls snow. The whole company heads back to the village, cheerful though cold, happy they will find vodka and warm broth on their return. In the morning they'll head out again, this time going farther, to Jezierzany, for Hanukkah.

The spies know exactly what happens next: This prophet, Jacob, spends two weeks with Simha ben Hayim and starts to see a light over the heads of certain of the faithful. It is a halo, greenish, or maybe cerulean. Simha and his brother have this light over their heads, and it means they have been chosen. Everyone would like to have a halo, some people can even feel it, a slight tingling sensation along their scalps, warm, as though they were without kippot. Someone says that such a halo comes from an invisible little aperture in the head through which an internal light pours forth into the world. It's that little hole that tingles. Everyone should get rid of whatever mats of hair they have there that might interfere with the light's passage.

**"Three things are too wondrous for me;
the fourth I can't understand."
—Book of Proverbs 30:18**

When Jacob walks through villages or towns, the local traditional Jews run after him, shouting, "Trinity! Trinity!" as though it were a slur. Sometimes they pick up stones and throw them at his followers. Others, those under the sway of Sabbatai Tzvi, the forbidden prophet, look on in curiosity, and it is primarily from them that Jacob draws ever more followers.

People are poor here, and because they're poor, they've grown suspicious. The poor can't afford to place too much confidence in anyone. Before the fat man gets skinny, the skinny man will croak, as the saying goes around these parts. They want miracles, signs, shooting stars, water become blood. They don't completely understand what Yankiele Leybowicz, called Jacob Frank, is saying. But because he's tall, handsome, and dressed like a Turk, he seems exceptional, and he makes a big impression. In the evening, as they talk around the fire, Jacob complains to Nahman that he feels like a merchant with the most beautiful pearl for sale, and yet here they treat him like some rag-and-bone man and can't appreciate the value of the pearl, taking it for a fake.

He tells people what Isohar has taught him, what Reb Mordke tells him to say in the evenings, and what he has learned from Nahman. Nahman is well-versed in every disputation, but lacks Jacob's good looks and powers of persuasion. But when Jacob puts these ideas forward, he adds quite a bit of his own. He especially loves striking comparisons and never balks at profanity. He talks like a simple Jew, like the milkman from Czernowitz, like the harness-maker from Kamieniec, except that he throws in lots of Turkish words, blending them into his Yiddish phrases, the result something like challah with raisins.

At the Christian New Year, they head for Kopyczyńce, encountering on the road many richly bedecked sleighs going in the opposite direction, local magnates traveling solemnly and in high style to church. The horses slow to pass, and the members of each procession turn to look at one another in stunned silence. Jacob is wearing an open fur-lined overcoat with a broad collar and a dyed, fur-lined kalpak, and he looks like a king. The noblemen, meanwhile, shrouded in their own furs, look heavyset, squat, their hats adorned with feathers at the forehead, fastened by ornate, expensive brooches. The women, pale but for their cold red noses, look as though they're drowning in their fur-lined robes.

In Kopyczyńce, the tables have already been set, and all the true believers from the village are waiting outside the home of Shlomo and his wife,

Zytla, shuffling from foot to foot, stamping to keep the cold at bay, talking amongst themselves. The sky reddens as the sleighs pull up. The crowd quiets down and in rigid silence watches Jacob go inside. Just before he makes it to the door, he pauses, comes back, goes up to Rivka and her little daughter, and her husband, Shyle, and looks just above their heads, as if he has seen something there. This causes a stir, and even the chosen ones feel ill at ease. When he goes inside, Rivka starts to snivel, and so does her little girl, who is maybe three years old, and a lot of people suddenly start to cry, whether from stress or cold or exhaustion it isn't clear. Some traveled all night. Some of them were also in Jezierzany before, and even Korolówka.

Inside, Jacob is ceremoniously received by Hayim from Warsaw, whom everyone respects because he runs a business in the capital. There, too, Jacob's fame has spread, and people would like to know what's going to happen now that the world is nearing its end. Jacob patiently explains all afternoon, so that the panes of the tiny little windows get white with steam, which the frost instantly transforms into filigreed palm trees.

That evening, those who peer in through the tiny windows can't see much. The candle flames flicker and keep going out. The Holy Spirit descends into Jacob again: ruah haKodesh. Not much of it can be seen— just a bit of shadow on the wall from the candle flames, flickering, uncertain. A woman's cry is interrupted.

When it's over, Shlomo, in accordance with the ancient law, dispatches Zytla to Jacob's bed. But Jacob is so tired that Zytla, wearing her good nightgown, clean and scented, feeling angry and rejected, has no choice but to go back to her husband.

In Hayim's parents' house, Jacob converts three people. Jacob likes Hayim very much because he has a zeal for organization, and the very next day, he gets to work. Now, from village to village, they are followed by a proper retinue, some dozen carts, people on horseback, and others on foot who can't keep up with the rest of the caravan and don't reach their destination until evening, tired and hungry; they sleep anywhere they can, in the barn, on the floor of the inn. Jacob is passed from one village to the next like a bizarre and holy wonder. Whenever they stop to rest, new people come and look in through the windows, listening to whatever he is saying. They don't entirely understand him, but still they get tears in their eyes. They are moved not only by Jacob, whose gestures have gotten more brusque now, decisive, like he's here for the moment but already elsewhere in his mind, with Abraham, with Sarah, with Sabbatai, with the great sages who have broken down the world into just the letters of which it is composed. There's also a comet that has appeared in the sky and is getting bigger and bigger every day; it follows Jacob every evening, as if he were the comet's son, a spark of light fallen from the sky. The procession goes through Trembowla, Sokołów, Kozowa, Płaucza, Zborów, Złoczów, Hanaczówka, and Busk. They all lift their heads to the sky. Jacob heals people by placing his hands on their heads, and lost things are found, abscesses diminish, women achieve long-awaited pregnancies, and the love between husbands and wives is restored. Cows give birth to twins with strange colorations, while chickens lay unusual eggs with two or even three yolks. Polish noblemen come to watch this Frank, this Turkish or Wallachian Jew, work miracles like no one's ever seen before and talk about the end of the world. Will Christians be saved, too, or is this only the Jewish end of the world? It isn't clear. They want to talk with him. In conversation via a translator—either Nahman or Hayim from Warsaw— the noblemen try to maintain their superiority, first calling him over to their carriages; Jacob goes up and answers politely. He starts by saying he's a simple man, a simpleton, but just the way he looks at them makes them lose their self-assurance. Soon they are standing in the crowds with the others, differentiated only by their thick furs and the feathers in their hats.

In Busk, the whole town has spilled from its houses, burning torches; a severe frost has taken hold, and the snow creaks underfoot. Jacob spends an enjoyable week in the home of Nahman's brother, Hayim, and his wife. The little boys follow Jacob around like a king's pages. Here, Jacob sees a cerulean halo over almost everybody's head. Just about the whole town is converted to the faith of the Holy Trinity, as Jacob himself calls it. By day, they bring him suffering children, that he might lay his hands on them. Then they send for him from Dawidów, and then they want him in Lwów. In Lwów, he gets to speak in a great hall, and a massive crowd comes to see him, but when he broaches the necessity of turning to the faith of Esau, that is, the Catholic faith, to bring about the Final Days, people start to leave, grumbling. The Jews of Lwów are wealthy, hostile, spoiled. Lwów is not as receptive to Jacob as the poor villages and towns. The rich and the satisfied are in no hurry for the Messiah; the Messiah is, after all, the one on whom the world must wait forever. The one who arrives is a false Messiah. The Messiah is the one who never arrives. That's the whole point. When Jacob starts to speak in a Lwów synagogue, his audience drowns him out. So Jacob smashes the pulpit and throws it into the crowd, and then he has to run away because the crowd starts to close in on him in fury.

Even at the inn, he is not treated very well, although Hayim is paying a pretty price. The woman who keeps the inn snaps at Jacob rudely. He tells her to make sure to check her pockets, since she has a silver tymf there. She stops, astonished.

"How would I have that?"

He insists she reach into her pockets—all this takes place in the presence of witnesses. And she does pull out a coin, not as valuable since they started being counterfeited, but still, money. She looks at it, a bit embarrassed, then looks away and would like to leave, except that Jacob grabs her by the arm.

"You know exactly how you have that, don't you?" asks Jacob without looking at her, because he is looking over the heads of the curious little crowd that has already gathered.

"Don't say anything, mister, please," begs the innkeeper, wresting her arm free.

But he has no intention of listening to her and is already shouting, raising his head high so that everyone can hear:

"She got it from a nobleman she sinned with last night."

People burst out laughing, thinking he has made this up, but to their surprise, the innkeeper acknowledges it to be true! She says that he is right, to the astonishment of their spectators, and then, beet red, she disappears.

Now Jacob's message becomes as clear and distinct as the footprints stomped in the snow for warmth by those who didn't make it inside and will have to find out about all of this secondhand. It is a question of uniting the three religions: Judaism, Islam, and Christianity. Sabbatai was the First, and he opened the door to Islam, while Baruchiah paved the way to Christianity. What appalls everyone and makes them stomp and shout? It's the fact they have to ford the Nazarene faith as they would a river, and that Jesus was a shell and a shield for the true Messiah.

At around noon, the idea seems shameful. By the afternoon, it's up for discussion. By evening it's been assimilated, and late at night it's perfectly obvious that everything's exactly as Jacob says.

Late at night, yet another aspect of the idea, which they hadn't really taken into consideration before, occurs to them—that once they are baptized, they will cease to be Jews, at least as far as anyone can tell. They will become people—Christians. They will be able to purchase land, open shops in town, send their children to any schools they wish . . . Their heads spin with possibilities, for it is as though they have suddenly been given a strange, almost inconceivable gift.


## The Lord's female guardians

The spies have been aware that as early as Jezierzany, Jacob has been accompanied by a young lady, later joined by a second. Both are purportedly there to guard him; the first one, a beautiful Busk girl, has light hair and pink cheeks and is invariably smiling, and she always walks one step behind him. The second one, Gitla, from Lwów, is tall and as proud as Queen Saba, and barely speaks. They say she is the daughter of one Pinkas, the secretary of the Lwów kahal, but she insists she is of royal blood, descended from the Polish princess her great-grandfather abducted one day. They sit on either side of Jacob like guardian angels, wearing beautiful furs on their shoulders, hats on their heads like noblewomen wear, decorated with precious stones and peacock feathers. At their sides sit small Turkish swords in turquoise-lined sheaths. Jacob positions himself between them like he might between the pillars of a temple. Soon the darker one, Gitla, becomes his true bodyguard, pushing ahead in crowds and barring access to him with her person, using a walking stick to protect his flanks. She keeps a warning hand on her sword. The fur only gets in her way, and soon she switches it for a red military doublet decorated with white silk cords. Her lush, unruly curls pop out from under her fur-lined military cap.

Jacob won't go anywhere without her, and, as if she were his wife, he spends every night with her as well. He says God has sent her to protect him. She will accompany him on through Poland, she will keep him safe. For Jacob is afraid—he's not blind, after all, and behind the backs of his followers he can see the quiet mob that spits at his mention, that mutters curses. Nahman sees that, too, which is why he has guards placed around whatever house they're sleeping in that night. Only a jug of wine and the beautiful Gitla can calm Jacob's nerves. The other guards can hear their giggles and amorous moans through the thin wooden walls of each humble home. Nahman doesn't like it. Moses, the rabbi of Podhajce—the one who advised the Shorrs to call off the wedding—also warns that such a display is egregious, and that it will cause some to speak ill of Jacob—even though he himself, a recent widower, can't help but look at Gitla with interest from time to time. Gitla gets on everyone's nerves, puts on airs, looks down at the other women. Hayim from Warsaw and his wife, Wittel, cannot stand her. Although Jacob gives up the light-haired girl in Lwów, Gitla he keeps. In any case, the light-haired one is soon replaced.

The whole tour takes a solid month. Every night it's different lodgings, different people. In Dawidów, Jacob greets Elisha Shorr like a father—Shorr in a floor-length overcoat and a fur-lined hat, his sons on either side of him. With a trembling hand, Shorr points out a strange glow over Frank's head, and the longer they look at it, the bigger it gets, until all those present kneel down in the snow.

When he stays with the Shorrs again in Rohatyn, Old Shorr says, in front of everyone:

"Jacob, show us your strength. We know you have received it."

Jacob refuses, saying he's tired, saying it's time to get some sleep after all those long disputations, and he heads upstairs to his rooms. But his feet on the oak steps leave tracks that look almost burned into the wood, permanently imprinted for all to see. From that night on, people come to behold those divine tracks in pious silence, and there in Rohatyn they also keep one of his embroidered Turkish pantofles.

The spies sent from the Lwów kahal take detailed notes on everything, from the contents of the new prayer Jacob Leybowicz Frank has brought with him to the fact that he adores kaymak and Turkish sweets with sesame seeds and honey. His companions always carry them in their baggage. In the prayer, Hebrew words intermingle with Spanish, Aramaic, and Portuguese, so that no one can understand exactly what is being said, which makes it sound all the more mysterious. They pray to someone they call Señor Santo, sing "Dio mio Baruchiah." From the snippets they have heard, the spies try to reproduce the contents of the prayer, coming up with this:

"Let us know your greatness, Señor Santo, for you are the true God and Lord of the world, and king of the world who was incarnate and who destroyed once and for all the order of creation, raised yourself up to your proper place to cast aside all other created worlds, and apart from you there is no other God, neither high nor low. And do not lead us into temptation or shame, so we kneel and praise your name, great and mighty king. For He is holy."

### Scraps by Nahman of Busk kept secret from Jacob

When God had Jews set forth into the world, He already had in mind the end point of such a journey, though they did not know of it yet; He wanted them to go toward their destiny. The end point and the point of departure are divine; impatience is human, as is believing in chance and hoping for adventure. And so when it came time for the Jews to settle somewhere for some longer stay, they showed—like children—discontent. Joy, on the other hand, when once more they were called upon to leave. And so it is now. God is thus the frame of every journey. Man provides its contents.

"Are we already in the worst possible place? Is this Busk?" Jacob asked me, and burst out laughing as we came up to Busk.

In Busk, we received Jacob in the home of my brother, Hayim ben Levi, as my wife did not wish to host him. Because she was heavily pregnant, I acquiesced. She, like many women, was disinclined to the new teachings. My one son who had survived his infancy was named Aronek, and Jacob took a particular liking to him. He would hold him on his lap, which gladdened me to my very soul, and he would often say that the little boy would grow into a great sage whom no one would be able to defeat with words. This gave me pleasure, though I knew that Jacob was familiar with my situation, aware that none of my other children had ever survived a year. Little Aronek became very flushed that evening, and Leah scolded me for taking a weak child outside and carrying him about in the cold.

She went with me once to Hayim's, but that was enough for her. She asked if it was true what they said about us.

"What is it they say?" I asked her.

"You promised to bring us a truly learned rabbi, but because of him"—and she nodded toward the window—"God has punished us. He has us bear children who die."

"Why because of him?" I asked.

"Because you've been going with him for several years now. Wherever he is, there you are."

What could I say? She may have been right. On the other hand, maybe God was taking away my children so as to bring me closer to Jacob.

Every evening came together in a similar way: First, a communal dinner—kasha, cheeses, baked meat, bread, olive oil, potatoes. Everyone sat down together at those long tables—women, children, and young people, those who contributed something to the meal as well as those who had nothing to contribute, who were provided for and did not go away hungry. Then Jacob told his tales of the Turkish countries, often humorous and entertaining, so that the majority of the women, enchanted by his beautiful speech and humor, let go of their negative opinions of him, while the children agreed he was the best storyteller they had ever heard. Then there was a communal prayer that he had taught us, and after the women had cleaned off the table and put the children to sleep, we who were ready to participate in the nocturnal studies remained.

He always began with the burden of silence. He would raise his index finger and move it, pointing upward, back and forth in front of his face, and our eyes would all follow that finger, behind which his face would melt and vanish. Then he would begin with the words "Shloisho seforim niftuchem," which meant "The three books are opening." At this a thrilling quiet fell, and you could almost hear the rustle of the pages of the holy books. Then Jacob would break that silence and remind us: "Whatever you hear here must fall into you as it would into a grave. And going forward, this will be our religion: silence."

He said:

"If a person wanted to claim a fortress, he would never be able to get there by just talking about it—for words are fleeting. He'd have to go in with an army. That's what we have to do: walk, not talk. Did our grandfathers not have enough discussion, did they not strain their eyes over the Scriptures? What good did any of it do them? What purpose did it serve? It's better to see than to speak. We have no use for know-it-alls here."

It always seemed to me that whenever he mentioned know-it-alls, he would look directly at me. For it was I who was striving to preserve his every word, though he had forbidden me from writing down those words. And so I would write them in secret. I feared that all of them, now so intent upon him, would forget every single thing the very second they went out the door. I did not understand the prohibition. When the next morning I sat down as though to do our accounts, to write letters, or determine schedules, underneath what I was doing I had placed another sheet of paper, and there I wrote, like I was translating for myself, the words spoken by Jacob:

"You have to go over to Catholicism," he told the simple people. "Make peace with Esau. You have to go into the darkness, that's as clear as day! For salvation awaits us only in darkness. Only in the worst place can the Messianic mission begin. The whole world is the enemy of the true God, don't you know that?

"This is the burden of silence. Masa duma. Words are such a weighty burden that it is as though they carried half the world inside themselves. You must listen to me and follow me. You must cast aside your language, and with each nation speak its proper tongue."

It is virtuous not to allow anything ugly to leave one's lips. It is virtuous to keep quiet, to keep everything one sees and hears inside. To be constant. Just as the First, Sabbatai, invited guests to his wedding and stood the Torah under the huppah as his bride, so, too, have we now replaced the Torah with a woman. Since then she has come naked every evening, with no concealment, here among us. Women are the greatest mystery, and here, in the lower world, they are the Holy Torah's counterpart. We will join with her, gently at first, with just our lips, with a movement of the mouth that pronounces the word that is read and in so doing re-creates the world from nothing every day. For I acknowledge—I, Nahman Samuel ben Levi of Busk—that there is a Trinity with one God, and that the Fourth Person is the Holy Mother.


## Of secret acts in Lanckoroń and an unfavorable eye

Nahman won't describe it—yes, words do add weight. When he does sit down to write, Nahman divides things into what can be written and what cannot. He must be careful to remember this. Especially since Jacob always says: No traces, keep everything a perfect secret, no one can find out who we are and what we do. Even though he actually makes quite the ruckus, with his strange gestures and the odd things that come out of his mouth. He speaks so enigmatically that it's hard to figure out what he means. That's why people stay together for a long time after he leaves, trying to interpret for themselves and one another the words of this Frank, this foreigner. What did he say? In some sense, each can only understand it all as best he can, in his own way.

When they reach Lanckoroń, on January 26, guided by Leybko Abramowicz and his brother Moshek, both on horseback, they head straight for Leybko's home. It's already very dark.

The village lies on a steep slope that goes down to a river. The road, rocky and uncomfortable, leads up. The night is thick and cold; light gets bogged down in it a short way from its source. It smells of smoke from damp wood, and the outlines of houses loom in the near-blackness; here and there, a dingy yellow glow makes its way out of a little window.

Shlomo Shorr and his brother Nathan are meeting with their sister. Hayah the prophet has lived in Lanckoroń since her wedding with the local rabbi, Hirsh, who runs a tobacco business here and enjoys great respect among the true believers. Nahman feels slightly dazed at the sight of her, as though he's just had vodka.

She comes with her husband, and as they stand there in the doorway, Nahman first thinks it is her father, so much does Hirsh resemble Old Shorr. Which isn't that surprising, given they are cousins. Hayah has grown more beautiful since having children, she's very thin and tall. She wears a bloodred dress and a light blue scarf, like a young maiden. Her hair is tied back with a colorful schmatte, and it cascades down her back. From her ears hang Turkish earrings.

The dusty little windows always let in too little light, so all day they burn wicks submerged in oil inside a clay shell, hence the stench of soot and burnt fat. Both rooms are crammed with furniture, and there is a scuttling sound, a rustling from somewhere that never lets up. Since it's winter, the mice have sought shelter from the frosts beneath the roof; they are creating vertical cities in the walls and horizontal ones under the floors, cities more complex than Lwów and Lublin combined.

In the front room above the hearth there is a recess to allow the air to reach the fire, but it's always getting clogged, and the stove smokes. So everything is permeated by the mixed scent of smoke and mice.

They close the door carefully and cover the windows. It could seem as if they've gone to sleep—they've been traveling all day, they're tired, just like the spies. There is already an uproar in the village, that this Sabbatian plague has reached all the way here. But there are also two curious people, Gershon Nahmanowicz and his cousin Naftali, the one who leases the land from the local lord and thinks very highly of himself because of it. He creeps up and manages to peek in through a window (someone must have left a bit of it exposed). The blood rushes from his head, and he stands there like someone's cast a spell on him, and he can't tear his eyes away, and although he can peer through only a vertical strip, by moving his head around he can nonetheless take in the whole scene. And so he sees—barely, by the light of a single candle—a circle of seated men, and in the middle of the circle, a half-naked woman. Her large, firm breasts seem to be glowing in the dark. This Jacob Frank walks around her in circles, seemingly babbling to himself.

Against the backdrop of all the clumsy objects in Leybko's home, Hayah's body is perfect, miraculous, as though she were come from another world. Her eyes are half closed, and her mouth is half open, so that you can see the tips of her teeth. Droplets of sweat glisten on her shoulders and her chest, and her breasts look so heavy as to make the viewer want desperately to hold them up. Hayah is standing on a stool, the only woman amidst the many men.

Jacob is the first to approach her. He has to stand ever so slightly on tiptoe to reach her breasts with his lips. It looks as though he even holds her nipple for a moment in his mouth, as though he might be swallowing a couple of drops of milk. And then the second breast. Next goes Reb Schayes, an old man with a sparse beard that comes down to his waist. His lips, moving like a horse's, seek Hayah's nipple, blindly—Reb Schayes doesn't open his eyes. Then Shlomo Shorr, Hayah's brother, comes up, and after a moment's hesitation does the same, though hurriedly, and then everyone's doing it—an emboldened Leybko Aronowicz, their host, and right behind him his brother, Moshko, and then another Shorr, this time Yehuda, and then Isaac of Korolówka, and each of them, even those who have been standing back, hiding in the shadows, now coming forth, knows that he has been admitted into the great mystery of this faith, and in this way he's become a true believer, and these people are his brothers, and so it will be until the savior destroys the old world and reveals the new. Because the Torah itself has entered Hirsh's wife, Hayah; that is what beams out now through her skin.

You have to close your eyes, and you have to go into the darkness, because it's only out of the darkness that you see clearly, Nahman thinks to himself, taking Hayah's breast into his mouth.

## How Gershon caught the heretics

Later they will say it was Jacob himself who ordered the windows to be covered so carelessly—so that people might see. Now the onlookers run quietly back to the village, to the rabbi, and in a flash a group has gathered, armed with sticks.

Gershon is right—he first has them glance through the crack between the curtains, and then when they break down the door, for a moment they see a naked woman trying to cover herself with some piece of clothing, and people fleeing along the edges of the room. Gershon roars. Someone jumps through a window, but is caught by those outside. Someone else successfully escapes. The remainder are tied up, still a little tipsy, with the exception of Hayah, and Gershon orders they be taken to the rabbi. Acting on his own authority, he requisitions their carriages, horses, books, and fur-lined overcoats, after which he goes to the local magnate's estate. But Gershon doesn't know that it's Carnival, and that the lord has guests. Furthermore, the lord does not wish to wade into Jewish problems—he owes them money—and cannot determine exactly what the situation is, which of them are mixed up in it and which aren't. So he calls his steward, Romanowski, being far too engaged with the delectation of his cornelian cherry liqueur to go himself. The courtyard is lit, and the smell of roast meat seeps out, along with the sound of music and ladies' laughter. Curious flushed faces peek out from behind the lord. The steward Romanowski puts on his long boots and pulls down a rifle from the wall, calls some farmhands, and together they go through the snow. Their righteous indignation, Jewish and Christian, brings to their minds unquiet images of some great sacrilege, a pervasive, extra-denominational blasphemy. When they get there all they see are freezing men, tied up two by two, with no coats, shivering. Romanowski shrugs. He doesn't understand what's going on. But just in case, he puts them all in jail in Kopyczyńce.

The Turkish authorities soon learn about what's happened, and by the third day, a small Turkish division comes to demand that Romanowski release the prisoner Jacob Frank, subject of the High Porte, a demand with which Romanowski is happy to comply. Let the Jews or the Turks deal with their own heretics for once.

People say that over the course of the three days he spent in jail in Kopyczyńce, before the Turks came to get him, Jacob once more received the Holy Spirit, the ruah haKodesh, and shouted strange things, like that he would convert to the Christian faith and take twelve of his brothers with him, as confirmed later by Reb Schayes and another man from Korolówka who was confined to the same cell. When the Turks did liberate him, they gave him a horse at once, which he mounted, heading straight for Chocim, on the other side of the Turkish border. The spies reported to Rabbi Rapaport in Lwów that, as he left, he said in Hebrew, clear as a bell: "We will be taking the royal road!"

## Of the Polish princess Gitla Pinkasówna

Lovely Gitla is the only daughter of Pinkas, secretary to Rapaport, rabbi of Lwów. There's something wrong with her—her mind is not altogether sound—and she's caused her father no end of trouble, which is why he sent her to be raised by his sister in Busk, so that she might take in the healthy country air there and cease making scenes back in Lwów.

Her beauty is a concern, though it's a trait that often pleases parents. She is tall, slender, with a dark, oval face, prominent lips, and dark eyes. She walks around in an unfaltering state of disarray, always wearing eccentric clothing. All summer she traversed the damp meadows outside town, reciting poems, going to the cemetery by herself, always with a book in hand. Her aunt thinks that's what happens when you teach a girl to read. Gitla's careless father did as much, and this is the result. An educated woman is the cause of many misfortunes. And in a way, here is proof of this. What normal person spends her time in a cemetery? The girl is nineteen, she should have been married long ago, and while boys and men are attracted to her, no one wants to get married to somebody like that. They say she let some boys feel her up. They did that just past the cemetery, where the road enters the forest. Who knows whether it led to anything more?

Gitla's mother died when the girl was just a few years old. For a long time, Pinkas was a widower, but a few years back he took a new wife who could not stand her stepdaughter. The feeling was mutual. When the stepmother gave birth to twins, Gitla ran away from home for the first time. Her father found her in a tavern on the outskirts of Lwów. Young as she was, she was sitting and kibitzing with the card players. Yet they did not take her for a traveling whore. She spoke good Polish and was obviously well-educated and well-mannered. She said she wanted to go to Kraków. She was attired nicely, too—in the finest dresses—and she behaved as if she were waiting for someone. The tavern keeper thought she was some great lady who had found herself in a dire situation. She told everyone she was the great-granddaughter of the king of Poland, and that her father had found her in a basket lined with swan's down, and that a swan had even nursed her with its milk. Her listeners laughed more at the swan's milk than at the basket. When her father burst into the tavern, he slapped her hard, in front of everyone. Then he dragged her to his cart, forced her into it, and drove off in the direction of Lwów. Poor Pinkas still hears the echoes of the guffaws and bawdy jokes he heard in the tavern that day. That's why he decided to find his daughter a husband as soon as possible, to marry her to the first man who might want her, while—so he hoped—she was still a virgin. He hired the best matchmakers, and soon there were willing candidates from Jezierzany and Czortków. Then she started going into the hay with the boys, so that everyone could see. She did it on purpose so that there wouldn't be a wedding. And there was no wedding. Both suitors retracted their proposals, the one from Jezierzany and the one from Czortków—news traveled fast. Gitla moved into a room in an annex to the main house, like a leper.

In the winter of that disastrous year, however, Gitla got lucky, or maybe unlucky, who knows. A caravan of sleighs appeared at the inn, and the newcomers dispersed across the town. Gitla's aunt, who was also hosting Gitla's stepmother with the twins, two boys, voracious and hirsute as Esau, locked the whole family inside, closed the shutters, and told them all to pray so that the voices of the heathen might not reach their innocent ears.

Gitla, ignoring her stepmother's admonitions, threw on the little Hutsul sheepskin coat her father had given her and went out into the snow. She stomped through the village to the redheaded Nahman's home, where the Lord had stopped in for a bit. She waited by the door with the rest of them, their faces covered by the clouds of vapor from their breath, shifting from one foot to the other to keep warm, until the Lord known as Jacob finally exited with his entourage. Then she grabbed his hand and kissed it. He tried to wrest it from her grasp, but Gitla had already uncovered her thick, beautiful hair, and now she said what she always said: "I am a Polish princess, the granddaughter of the Polish king."

The others burst out laughing, but it made an impression on Jacob. He looked her up and down and then stared straight into her eyes. What he saw there no one ever learned. But since then, Gitla has never left his side, not for a moment. People say the Lord has been exceedingly pleased with her. They say that his strength has increased on account of her, and that she, too, has been granted great power from heaven, has felt it in herself. When once some tatterdemalion came to attack the Lord, she used that power to take the rogue down, throwing him into the snow so forcefully that he couldn't get up for a long while. By Jacob's side, she has been like a she-wolf, right up until that calamitous night in Lanckoroń.

## Of Pinkas and his shameful despair

As Pinkas toils for Rapaport, he tries not to stand out, flitting sideways, huddling over his writings; now, as he copies out documents, he can barely be seen. But the rabbi with the eternally narrowed eyes can see better than even most young people. He seems just to be passing by, but Pinkas can feel his gaze on him as though he were being stung by nettles. Finally the moment comes—Rapaport calls for him when he's alone. He inquires about Pinkas's health, his wife, the twins, politely, mildly, as is his wont. Finally, he asks, not looking at his secretary:

"Is it true that . . ."

He doesn't finish, but nonetheless Pinkas feels flushed, as if a thousand infernal white-hot needles pierced his skin.

"I've met with some misfortune."

Rabbi Rapaport simply nods his head sadly.

"Do you understand, Pinkas, that she is no longer a Jewish woman?" he asks mildly. "Do you understand that?"

Rapaport says that Pinkas should have done something a long time ago, back when she started saying she was a Polish princess, or even earlier, when everyone could see something was going wrong with her, that some dybbuk had possessed her and turned her dissolute and mouthy and vulgar.

"When did she start behaving strangely?" asks the rabbi.

Pinkas thinks for a long time. Since the death of her mother, he says. Her mother was a long time in dying, in agony, from a tumor in her breast that spread throughout her body.

"It's very understandable that it would have happened then," says the rabbi. "Around dying souls gather many free dark spirits. They seek a vulnerable place they might break into. Despair weakens people."

Pinkas listens, his heart tightening. He knows the rabbi's right, for the rabbi is wise, and he, Pinkas, understands this logic and would say the same to someone else—when one piece of fruit has started to rot, it must be thrown out before it spreads to the rest of the basket. But when he looks at Rapaport, so self-assured, albeit sympathetic, closing his eyes as he speaks, Pinkas thinks of blindness—that maybe there is something that even this great, wise man might not see. Maybe there are some truths that elude the capacity of reason, maybe not everything can be contained within the Scriptures, maybe a new entry needs to be created for his Gitla, something about people like her. Maybe she actually is a Polish princess, in her soul . . .

Rapaport opens his eyes. Seeing Pinkas bent over like a broken stick, he says to him:

"Cry, brother, cry. Your tears will cleanse the wound, and it will heal quickly."

But Pinkas knows that wounds like these will not heal, ever.

## 14.

## Of the Bishop of Kamieniec Mikołaj Dembowski, who doesn't realize he is merely passing through this whole affair

Bishop Dembowski is convinced he's an important man. He also thinks he'll live for eternity, for he considers himself righteous and just, perfectly in tune with the teachings of Christ.

Looking at him through Yente's eyes, it would seem that in some sense, he is right. He hasn't killed, betrayed, or raped anyone, and, every Sunday, he gives alms to the poor. Sometimes he gives in to corporeal desire, but it must be acknowledged that he puts up a valiant struggle, and, whenever it gets the better of him, he quickly leaves the incident behind and never returns to it in his mind. Sins get stronger when you think about them, when you fret about them and revisit their unfolding—when you give in to despair. And the instructions are clear: Do your penance and move on.

The bishop has a bit of a penchant for luxury, but he justifies this to himself by remembering his fragile health. He would like to be of great service to the world; he is therefore grateful to God that he was able to become a bishop—that was a lucky break.

He sits at the table and writes. He has a round, fleshy face and big lips that might be called sensual were it not for the fact that they belong to a bishop. He has fair skin and fair hair. Sometimes, when he gets over-heated, he turns beet red, looks cooked. He has put on a warm woolen mozzetta over his rochet, and his feet are warming in fur slippers the women have sewn for him, since his feet get so cold. His Kamieniec home is never quite heated enough; all warmth escapes from it, and there are drafts though the windows are small; it is always dark inside. The windows of his office overlook the little street outside the church. Now, as he looks out, he sees some elderly beggars arguing, and after a moment one of them attacks the other with a stick. The injured man shrieks and whimpers, and the other beggars rush into the fight, and soon the din has grown into a full-blown assault upon the bishop's ears.

The bishop tries to write:

Sabbaticians
Saspatians
Sabbsciples
Sabbitists
Sabbadabbas

In the end, he turns to Father Pikulski, that slight man in his forties with gray hair that looks as if it's been glued to his head, sent here especially by Bishop Sołtyk as an expert in this very matter, currently working just outside the cracked door, the light of his candle making his big head cast a long shadow on the wall.

"How was it written, once more?"

Father Pikulski comes over to his colleague's desk. His features have sharpened over the last couple of years, since we last saw him having lunch in Rohatyn; he's just been shaved, and there are cuts on his prominent chin. What barbarian did that to him? the bishop thinks.

"It would be better, Your Excellency, to write 'Contra-Talmudists,' since they speak out against their Talmud—that's the one thing we really know. It's safer that way for us, not to get into all their theologies. But people call them Shabbitarians."

"What do you think of all this, Father?" asks the bishop, pointing to the letter lying before him on the table. It's a request from the elders of the

kahal of Lanckoroń and Satanów for some intervention in the matter of a certain dissent from Mosaic law, the besmirching of the most venerated traditions.

"I think they are out of their depth."

"Is it about the iniquities those people were performing in some tavern? Is that the reason?"

Pikulski waits for a moment, looking like he's making calculations in his head—and perhaps that is what he's doing. Then he puts his hands together and says, without looking at the bishop:

"I think they want to show us that they do not want anything to do with those heretics."

The bishop clears his throat, impatiently wiggling a slippered foot, and Father Pikulski understands that he is supposed to keep speaking.

"Just as we have the catechism, so, too, do they have the Talmud. It is, to put it succinctly, a commentary on the Bible, but a specific one that has to do with how to observe the Mosaic laws and commands." Father Pikulski becomes more animated, pleased to be able to show off the information he's been collecting so scrupulously all these years; he looks down at a nearby chair and raises an eyebrow. The bishop gives a barely visible nod, and Father Pikulski pulls the chair up close to the bishop and sits down. He has a musty smell—the poor man has his rooms on the ground floor—as well as the lingering scent of lye from the barber who made such a horrendous mess of his morning shave.

"It was written by their rabbis many hundreds of years ago, and in it they explained all things—what to eat and when, what is allowed and what is not. Without it, their entire complicated structure would collapse."

"But you told me all the laws were in the Torah," the bishop interrupts him gruffly.

"But after the destruction of the Temple in Jerusalem, once they were in exile, it was hard for them to obey the Torah—in a foreign country, in a different climate. Besides, those laws are very specific, relating to their old, pastoral lifestyle, and the world had changed, and thus there was the Talmud. Just remember, Your Excellency, the fourth book of the Torah, what it says about trumpets and armies, tribal heads, tents . . ."

"I suppose . . . ," sighs the bishop.

"And this Frank has been saying it is all a lie."

"That's quite a serious accusation. Does he say this of the whole Torah?"

"The Torah does not bother him, but his holy book is the Zohar."

"I am aware of that. So what is it exactly that these others want?"

"They want Frank to be punished. The Talmudists of the village of Lanckoroń drove out these heretics, brought a suit against them that centers on the so-called sin of the Adamites, and put a curse on them. What else can they do? That's why they've turned to us."

The bishop looks up.

"Sin of the Adamites?"

"Oh, you know . . . ," says Pikulski, suddenly flushing and repeatedly clearing his throat, but the bishop, in some spontaneous act of mercy, allows him to not finish the sentence. Nonetheless Father Pikulski soon resumes: "They had to let this Frank out of jail, but now he's operating out of Turkey. During the Jewish fast he was riding around in his carriage proclaiming to his followers that since theirs was the true God, and they believed in him completely, why would they hide? He said: 'Come, let us reveal ourselves and show them all. Let them see who we are.' Then, in the midst of the fast—this strict Jewish fast—he poured everyone vodka and served them pork and pastries."

"Where did they come from, so suddenly, and in such a quantity?" the bishop wonders, wiggling his toes inside their furred slippers. He had already heard about how some Jewish heretics have been defying the Torah's rules, convinced they'd been invalidated by the arrival of the Messiah. But what does that have to do with us? thinks the bishop. They are foreigners, and their religion is bizarre and convoluted. It's an internal dispute—let them go after each other. But now he's hearing other things as well: that apparently they've been availing themselves of curses and spells, that they've been trying to coax wine out of walls, using the mysterious powers described in the Book of Creation. Apparently they meet at out-of-the-way bazaars and recognize one another by means of a range of secret signs—for instance, by inscribing the initials of their prophet, *S.T.*, on books, stalls, and even on their wares. And furthermore—this the bishop made sure to make note of—they do business with each other and support one another in closed societies. He had heard that when one of them is accused of shady dealings of some sort, the others all testify to his integrity, putting the blame on someone outside the group.

"I still haven't finished writing the report for Your Excellency," Pikulski blurts. "The Zohar is also a commentary, another kind of commentary, I would say, mystical, not having to do with the law, but rather with questions of how the world came into being, of God Himself . . ."

"Blasphemies," says the bishop. "Let's get back to work."

But Father Pikulski is still standing there. He's some ten years younger than the bishop, maybe more, but he looks quite aged. It must be because he's so thin, thinks the bishop.

"It's a good thing Your Excellency sent to Lwów for me," Father Pikulski says. "I am at Your Excellency's disposition, and I don't think Your Excellency would find another soul better versed in Jews than I am, or in this Jewish heresy."

Having said this, Father Pikulski flushes, clears his throat, and lowers his head. He worries he may have gone too far, and thereby committed the sin of pride.

The bishop doesn't notice Father Pikulski's embarrassment. He is wondering why he is so cold, as though his blood were not reaching his body's extremities, as though it were flowing too slowly—but why would his blood have become so reluctant?

The bishop has had enough problems with the local Jews. What an infernal tribe, insidious and insistent—whenever you throw them out, they come slinking back around the edges, so there's nothing you can do about them short of something decisive, irreversible. Nothing else helps.

Had the bishop himself not brought about the royal decree against the Jews in the eighth year of performing his office, that is, Anno Domini 1748? He had so pestered the king about it, sending letters and filing petition after petition until at last the king had issued his edict: All the Jews of Kamieniec would have to leave within twenty-four hours. Their homes would go to the town, and their school would be razed. The Armenian merchants played their part in it, for the Jews had raised their ire by undercutting them on prices and trading in an unofficial, even illicit manner. The Armenians repaid the bishop handsomely. But the problem did not go away. Thrown out of Kamieniec, the Jews moved to Karvasary and Zinkowcy, immediately violating the restriction on them settling closer than three miles from town, and yet no one seemed to care to do a thing about it, and the authorities turned a blind eye. They would still come into town each day, so as to do at least a little bit of business. They'd send their women. Worse, their customers began to follow them out past Smotrycz to Zinkowcy, where they created an illegal market that diminished the size of the Kamieniec market. More complaints were lodged against them, not least that Jewesses from Karvasary were brought in to make those bagels of theirs, although this, too, was prohibited. Why do I have to be the one to handle all of this? the bishop thinks.

"They say the laws of the Torah no longer apply to them," Father Pikulski goes on. "And that the form of Judaism based on the Talmud is a religion of deception. There can be no more talk of a Messiah to come— the Jews have been waiting in vain for the Messiah . . . They also say that God exists in three parts, and that this God lived on earth in human form."

"Well, of course. That they're right about." The bishop perks up. "The Messiah won't come now because he already came. But you're not going to tell me, my good man, that they believe in Jesus Christ." The bishop crosses himself. "Now give me that letter from those crazy people."

He looks over the document as though expecting something special: seals, watermarks . . .

"Do they know Latin?" says the bishop suspiciously, reading the letter these Contra-Talmudists have submitted to him, which is unquestionably written in a learned hand. "Who writes for them?"

"They say it is a man named Kossakowski, but from which Kossakowskis he comes, I know not. I do have it on good authority that they are paying him quite well."

## Of Father Chmielowski's defense of his good name before the bishop

Father Chmielowski rushes up to the bishop, delicately kisses his hand; the bishop, meanwhile, raises his eyes to the heavens—whether in a blessing for this new arrival or a gesture of boredom, it would be difficult to say. Pikulski also greets the priest—effusively, for him—by bowing low and extending his hand to shake Father Chmielowski's briefly. The old priest—ill-shaven, white-haired, wearing a ragged cassock (appallingly, some of the buttons are missing), and carrying an old bag that has lost its strap so he has to hold it under his arm—smiles broadly.

"I hear you're staying with His Excellency for good," he says congenially, but evidently Pikulski detects some reproof in this, for his face turns red again.

The vicar forane launches into his supplication right away. He does so boldly since he knows the bishop well, from when the bishop was just an ordinary priest.

"Your Excellency, I did not come here to pester. I came to ask for your brotherly counsel. What is to be done?" he opens dramatically.

From his bag, he pulls out a package of sorts, wrapped in a grubby linen cloth, and sets it down in front of him, keeping his hands on it as he explains his business.

The issue goes back many years, to when the vicar forane was still preceptor for the magnate's son on the estate of Joseph Jabłonowski. In his free moments, he had been given license to make use of the castle's library. He would go there often, whenever his charge was otherwise occupied, and he spent every spare instant he had reading in that font of good knowledge. Even back then he was starting to take notes and copy out whole passages from books, and what with his terrific memory, he also managed to retain a lot.

Now, as yet another edition of his book has been printed—Father Chmielowski jabs at the package with his forefinger—this ancient case has reared its ugly head again: he is accused of having stolen both the idea and a number of the facts and interpretations from a manuscript by Prince Jabłonowski, which supposedly had lain for all to see on the table in the library, where the priest could easily have cribbed from it at will.

The priest falls silent for a moment, unable to catch his breath, while the bishop, alarmed by his fervor, leans toward him over the desk and glances uneasily at the package, trying to remember "this ancient case."

"How could I have cribbed?" exclaims the vicar forane. "What does 'cribbed' even mean? My entire project is a thesaurus stultitiae—a collection of foolish little things! I gathered all of the knowledge of mankind in my volumes—so how would I not have borrowed from other sources? How would I not have perused? Aristotle's wisdom or Sigebert's chronicles or Saint Augustine's holy works cannot belong to any one person! Even if he is a magnate, and his holdings include vast treasures, still, knowledge does not belong to him, and it cannot be stamped or imprinted or staked off like a field! As though he doesn't have enough already, he has to ruin the one thing I do have—my good name and the reader's esteem. When, omni modo crescendi neglecto, with great effort I brought the work to completion, now he wants to destroy its reception with such libel? Dicit: Fur es! That I would have stolen his idea! How innovative of an idea is it to write down a few interesting things? Whatever curiosis I have found wherever, I have sine invidia, with no jealousy whatsoever, brought it out onto the stage of my *Athens*. And what is wrong with that? Anyone could have had the same idea. Just show me where!"

Here the vicar forane in a single movement liberates the tome from its packaging and holds this fresh edition of *New Athens* up to the bishop's eyes. The pungent smell of printer's ink assaults their nostrils.

"This is the fourth edition, is it not?" Bishop Dembowski says, trying to calm him down.

"Well, exactly! People read this more frequently than you might think, My Dearest Excellency. In many noble houses, and amongst certain of the townspeople, this book sits in the living room, and persons young and old alike will reach for it, and bit by bit, nolens volens, they soak up information on the world."

At this Bishop Dembowski falls deep into thought; wisdom, after all, is merely the ability to mete out judgments.

"Perhaps the allegations are unwarranted, but the person making them is a highly respectable man," he says, though a moment later he adds, "Although he is quarrelsome and embittered. What am I to do?"

Father Chmielowski would like the Church's support for his book. Especially since he is, after all, one of its officers. He stands bravely in the ranks of the faithful and works for the good of the Church, not caring for his own advantage. He reminds the bishop that the Commonwealth is a destitute country when it comes to books. Apparently there are as many as six hundred thousand nobles in it, while a paltry three hundred titles are published every year, leaving the elites to enrich their minds how, exactly? Peasants cannot read, by definition, such is their lot that books are irrelevant to them. The Jews have their own—most of them don't know Latin. For a moment he is silent, and then, staring at the threads on his cassock that once held buttons, he says:

"Your Excellency, you promised two years ago that you would make a contribution to this publication. My *Athens* is a treasure trove of information that everyone must have."

The priest does not want to say it, lest the bishop suspect him of pride, but he would be delighted to see the book in every landed estate, read by everyone, for that is how he has been writing it: for everyone. Why could women not sit down with it? Some of its pages would even be suitable for children . . . although not just any pages, he mentally notes.

The bishop clears his throat and leans back a bit, so Father Chmielowski adds, in a quieter, slightly less fervent voice:

"But nothing came of that. I paid for everything myself, giving the Jesuit printers all of the money I had set aside for my old age."

The bishop thinks that he must somehow extricate himself from the absurd demands of this old acquaintance. No money—where would he get it?—and no public backing. The bishop hasn't even read this book, and he doesn't particularly like Chmielowski. He is too disorganized to be a good writer, and he certainly doesn't strike the bishop as a wise man. And if they are talking of aid, it ought to be to the Church, not from it.

"Father, you live by your pen, so use it to defend yourself," he says. "Write your explication, put your arguments down in some sort of manifesto." He sees that the priest's face is growing longer and sadder, and, pitying the old man, he quickly adds in a softer tone, "I'll support you among the Jesuits, but don't advertise it publicly."

The priest obviously did not expect this sort of reception, but before he can say more, a secretary who looks like an overgrown rodent appears in the doorway, and so Chmielowski just picks up his package and leaves. He tries to exit slowly and with dignity so no one can tell how deeply disappointed he is.

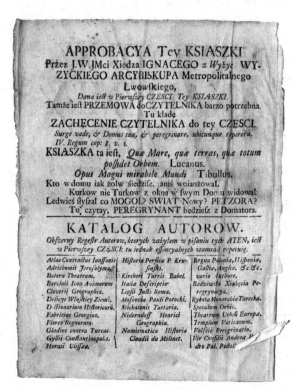

Roshko takes him home, shrouded in furs. The snow is up to the roofs of the thatched cottages, and the sleigh glides lightly, as though they were flying. The sun reflects off every snowflake, blinding the priest. Just before they reach Rohatyn a cavalcade of sleighs and sleds emerges from that brightness, bearing many Jews, then noisily vanishes into the blinding white. The priest does not yet know that a long-awaited letter has arrived for him at home.

## What Elżbieta Drużbacka writes to Father Chmielowski in February of 1756 from Rzemień on the Wisłoka

I would like to write to you, my dear friend, with greater frequency, but with my daughter in childbed, all the administration of the estate has fallen onto little old me, my son-in-law being on the road at present, a journey that has lengthened in duration by more than a month on account of the terrible snows, which have made a portion of the great highway completely impassable, while the rivers have all overflowed, isolating a good many settlements completely.

From early morning on I am up and running around—cowsheds, pigsties, henhouses, making preserves out of whatever the servants have brought in; from dawn, all the effort it takes to obtain any dairy, lumps of cheese for soup, cheese pancakes and quark, smoked meat, fattened poultry, lard, flour, kasha, bread, mushrooms, dried fruits, confections fried in honey, wax and tallow for candles, oils for the lamps and for fasting days, wool, yarn, leather for shoes, sheepskins for coats. In order for bread to make it to the breakfast table, a million things must happen first, and I must personally ensure they happen, often in cooperation with many other people, most of them women. Women are the ones who operate the querns, the spinning wheels, the looms. It is on their watch that the smokehouses smoke, that dough rises in the kneading troughs, bread bakes in the ovens, candles are pressed into shape, herbs are dried for home pharmacies, lard is salted, vodka is distilled and spiced, beer is brewed, meads fermented, stores placed in the larders and the granaries. For three of any home's quoins rest upon the woman of the house, and the fourth upon God.

I have not written a single line in months, and I would be glad at this point, to tell you the truth, to take a little rest from this old mill. I have two daughters, as you know, and one of them has so taken to giving birth that she has now produced a fourth little girl. Things are going well for her, she has a good husband with a good career, and it is obvious that they are very close. What more could a person want than such human closeness?

I try to look upon everything with good humor, tho' there are many things awry. Why is it, for instance, that some have such an excess in life, while others such a lack? And not only of material goods, but also of activities, time, luck, or health. If only everything could be divided evenly . . .

I have already asked Countess Denhoff once to help me sell my wine, for I make good wine, tho' not from grapes, but rather out of berries, or, perhaps most of all, wild rose. It is strong, and the fragrance and flavor of my wine are widely praised. I will send you, too, dear friend, some bottles.

As I write, the doors have crashed open, and the little girls are racing in, chasing Firlejka, who came inside with muddied paws that need to be wiped off, but the dog keeps escaping between the legs of the tables and chairs and everywhere leaves filthy tracks, mud seals, as it were. Whenever I look at her, at this crumb of God's creation, I think of you, my dear friend. How are you, how is your health, and—above all—how is your great work going? The girls squeal and holler, the dog doesn't understand what all the fuss is about, and when the youngest falls down on the floor, the dog, thinking it's a game, eagerly begins to grab her and shake her by the dress. Oh, there is a great laundering in store.

Kindly include, in your letter to me, some interesting little tales, that I might shine in society when at last I return to it.

In May I will be going to the Jabłonowskis' again, at their invitation . . .

## Father Chmielowski to Elżbieta Drużbacka

It was so generous of You to send Your Wine, and I truly love the Taste of it. I drink it in the Evenings, when my Eyes have tired and are no longer capable of working, but what I can do, and with great Pleasure, is look into the Fire and sip Your Wine. I thank You for it from the very Bottom of my Heart, just as I do for Your Books of Poetry.

Of all of Your Poems I like best the one that praises the Forests and a Life of Solitude, on which Point I completely agree. I leave aside the Poems on Love, for such Things I neither understand nor have the Time for, and in any Event, it would hardly be befitting of my spiritual Station to attend to Vanities of this Kind. All this mortal Loving is valued too highly, and it sometimes seems to me that when People do attend to it, what they really mean is Something else, that this "Love" of which they speak is some Kind of Metaphor, the which I simply cannot grasp. Perhaps only Women have Access to it, or maybe Men with more feminine Traits. Is the Meaning Caritas, or rather Agape?

I admire the Spontaneity of Your Poetry, which seems to flow like Beer from a Tap. Where does all that fit within You? And how are You able to just invent all of those beautiful Sentences and Notions? I see, dear Friend, that my Work is of an altogether different Nature. I invent Nothing, offering instead the quinta Essentia of several hundred Authors whom I have read from Cover to Cover.

You, my Friend, are completely free in what You write, while I must stand on the Foundations of that which has already been written. You draw from the Imagination and the Heart, scrupulously reach into Your Feelings and Your Fantasies as tho' into a Purse, and scatter gold Coins all around You, where they gleam, luring the Masses. I contribute Nothing of my own, merely citing and compiling. I mark my Sources very carefully, which is why I place throughout a sort of "Teste," which advises the Reader to go and see for himself in the Mother Book, to note how Information weaves together, gathering across the Centuries. In this Manner, when we quote and cite our Sources, we build an Edifice of Knowledge, and we enable that Knowledge to proliferate as I do my Vegetables or Apple Trees. Quoting is like grafting a Tree; citing, indicating a grafted Quote's Source, like sowing Seeds. Consequently we need not fear Fires in Libraries, a Swedish Deluge, or the Uprisings of a Khmelnytsky. Every Book is a Graft of new Information. Knowledge should be useful and readily available. Everyone should have at least the Rudiments of every indispensable Subject—Medicine, Geography, Natural Magic—and they ought to know a Smattering of Facts about foreign Religions and Nations. One must obtain the guiding Principles and have them settled in one's Head, for et quo Modo possum intelligere, si non aliquis ostenderit mihi? And instead of having to pore over Volume after Volume, having to purchase whole Libraries, the Reader, thanks to my Work, has it all without multa Scienda.

I often stop to wonder how to encapsulate it, how to handle such Vastness? Whether to just choose a few Passages and translate as faithfully as possible or to summarize the Authors' Arguments and simply indicate where they have been taken

from, so that the more curious Reader might track them down, if he is able to locate the Volume in Question in some Collection.

I worry that simply summarizing someone's Views cannot convey a full Sense of their Spirit—the linguistic Habits of the Author get lost, his Style, too, and Humor and Anecdotes cannot simply be summarized. Such Compilations are therefore mere Approximations, and if someone else then summarizes the Summaries, only the very Dregs will be left, out of which all of the Information has been squeezed. I know not whether what remains is like the Pulp of those Fruits in the Wine, from which all that is essential has already been extracted, or whether, a Contrario, it would be the Opposite, Aqua Vitae, when something that is more diluted, weaker, is distilled into Spirits—is fortified.

What I wanted was to achieve this Type of Distillation. In order that the Reader might not have to trouble himself with all these Books that I have here on my Shelves—and there are a hundred and twenty of them—nor with the ones from which I read and made extensive Notes on Visits to Houses and Convents and Estates.

Do not think, dear Friend, that I value my own Efforts over Your Poems and Romances. Yours are written to amuse, and mine are in the Service of Study.

My great Dream is someday to set out on a distant Peregrination, but I am not thinking of Rome or other exotic Locales, but rather of Warsaw. There I would strike out straightaway for one particular Location: the Daniłowicz Palace, where the Załuski Brothers—Your venerable Publishers—have amassed a Library of Thousands of Volumes and made it available to anyone who wishes and is able to read . . .

Please give Firlejka's Ear a little Pet from me. I am so very pleased that You named her that. Her Mother has had another Litter. I have not the Heart to drown them, so I hand them out around the neighboring Cottages, and coming as they do from a Priest, even the Peasants are happy to accept them . . .

## What Pinkas records, and what goes unrecorded

It would be wrong to think that only bishops have spies; the letters have also been piling up on Rabbi Rapaport's table in Lwów. Pinkas is his most distinguished secretary, his external memory, his archive, his address book. Always half a step behind the rabbi, small but standing very straight, a bit like a rodent, he takes every letter in his long, slender fingers, delicately turns it over in his hands, paying attention to every detail, splotch, stain, and then carefully he opens it—if there is a seal, then he tries to break it in such a way as to crumble it as little as possible, so that the seal preserves the mark of its sender. Then he carries the letters to the rabbi and waits for him to tell him what to do with them—set them aside for later, copy, or answer straightaway. In the latter case, Pinkas sits down to write.

But since he lost his daughter, it is hard for him to focus on the letters. Rabbi Rapaport, understanding this (or maybe fearing that in his state of internal commotion he might make some error—that he isn't fit to serve as secretary anymore) now has him merely read or at most bring him the letters. For the writing, he has employed someone else, easing Pinkas's workload. This is unpleasant for Pinkas, but he tries to stifle his somewhat wounded pride. Yes, he must admit, he has met with misfortune.

He remains nonetheless avidly interested in what is happening in connection with the cursed followers of this Frank, those vile creatures who do not hesitate to defile their nests. That is Rabbi Rapaport's expression. Rapaport has been reminding everyone what must be done under such circumstances:

"The tradition of our fathers has been to say nothing on matters connected with Sabbatai Tzvi—nothing good, and nothing bad; to neither censure nor condone. And were someone to insist on asking questions, were someone to be curious about the way things were, then he must be threatened with herem."

But things cannot be ignored into infinity. That is how they wound up in the shop of one Naftuła in Lanckoroń—he, Rapaport, and some

other rabbis, forming a rabbinical court. They deliberate, having interrogated their prisoners not long ago. They had to protect them from the
angry mob gathered outside the shop, grabbing at them in a frenzy, shouting, "Trinity! Trinity!"

"It's like this," says Rapaport. "As Jews, we are sitting in the same boat,
and we're sailing over a stormy sea, and all around us there are sea
monsters—every day, at every hour, some great danger lies in wait for us.
And any day, and at any hour, the massive storm that will drown us out
of existence could arise."

He raises his voice here, a thing he almost never does:

"But sitting in the boat with us are also miscreants, Jews from the
selfsame stock. Yet it is only at first glance that they seem to be our brothers, for in reality, they are rogues, the devil's seed that has gotten into our
midst. They are worse than the Pharaoh, than Goliath, the Philistines,
Nebuchadnezzar, Haman, Titus . . . For lo! they are worse than the serpent in Eden, since they curse the God of Israel, and that not even the
serpent dared to do."

All the eldest, most respected rabbis from around these parts are seated
at the table. With their beards, in the weak light of the oil lamps, they
resemble one another, and together they lower their eyes in despair. Pinkas
and another secretary at a side table have been charged with taking minutes. Pinkas stops writing to watch the rabbi of Czortków, who has arrived late, drip damp snow from his coat onto the waxed wooden floor,
creating small puddles that reflect the lamplight.

Rabbi Rapaport raises his voice again, and the shadow of his finger
pokes at the low ceiling:

"But they don't take into consideration the common good of the Jews,
and they go on drilling a hole in our boat, not even realizing that we will
all drown!"

Not all of them agree, however, that Gershon of Lanckoroń did the
right thing by reporting on those disgusting rites in one of the houses of
that town.

"Although the shiniest thing is what attracts attention in this matter,
that thing is not at all the most important or the most dangerous," Rapaport continues. He signals to Pinkas that what comes next is not to be

recorded. "The real danger is elsewhere and has mostly gone unnoticed, because it has been overshadowed by the breasts of Hayah, Shorr's daughter. Everyone has been focusing on female nudity and wallowing in that sensational little tidbit, but in the meantime, the important thing, the most important thing is what Melech Naftuła, who was there, saw with his own eyes and testified officially to having seen: *the cross!*"

A silence ensues, in which only the wheezy exhalation of Moshko of Satanów can be heard.

"And with that cross they tried working all sorts of different miracles, burning candles on it and brandishing it over their heads. That cross is the nail in our coffin!" The rabbi has raised his voice again. "Isn't that right?" he asks Naftuła, who seems frightened by the thing he has revealed to them.

Naftuła nods.

"What will the goyim think now?" Moshko from Satanów asks. "To them we're all the same. A Jew is a Jew, and it's going to look to them like all Jews are like those. That all Jews treat the cross in such a sacrilegious way. That they abuse it so. We know what will happen, it's happened before—before we can explain ourselves, they will have ushered us into the torture chamber."

"Perhaps the matter should have been kept within the fold?" asks the dripping rabbi. "It could have been talked over quietly and handled prudently then."

But there is no more "fold." It is impossible to resolve anything with them, because they, too, insist with all their might. And they have the protection of such powerful persons as Bishop Dembowski (at the mention of this name there is an uneasy shuffling) as well as Bishop Sołtyk (at this the majority of the rabbis stare down at the dark floor, and one of them sighs plaintively).

"So maybe it would in fact be better," wise Rapaport goes on, "if we washed our hands of this filth altogether, let the royal courts roll around in the mud with them—from now on, we will maintain that we have nothing to do with those renegades. For are they even still Jews?" he asks dramatically.

There is a moment of tense silence.

"They are no longer Jews, since they are adherents of Sabbatai, may his name be erased for all eternity," he concludes, and it sounds like a curse.

Yes, after those words, Pinkas feels relieved. He's let out all the rotten air and is now taking in a big fresh breath. The discussion lasts until midnight. Pinkas, taking the minutes, listens closely to all the things that come between the phrases worth his writing down.

The herem is issued the next day. Now Pinkas has his hands full. The letter about the herem has to be copied out many times and sent as quickly as possible to all the kahalim. In the evening, he delivers it to the little Jewish printshop near the market square in Lwów. Late at night he returns home, where his young wife greets him with reproaches, being irritable as usual on account of the twins, who, she says, are sucking the life out of her.

## Of the Seder HaHerem, or the order of the curse

The curse boils down to a few words pronounced in a certain order and at a certain time, all to the sound of the shofar. This occurs in a synagogue in Lwów, by the light of black wax candles, by an open holy ark. Readings from the Torah include Leviticus 26:14–46 as well as Deuteronomy 28:15–68, and then the candles are extinguished, and everything gets frightening, just as divine light has ceased to shine onto the cursed ones from this point forward. The voice of one of the three judges conducting the ceremony carries across the whole of the synagogue, disperses over the great crowd of the faithful:

"We hereby proclaim to all who are gathered here that we have long since been informed of the hideous views and acts of Yankiele Leybowicz of Korolówka, and we have made repeated attempts to bring him back from the path of evil. Being unable, however, to reach his hardened heart, and receiving every day some new bit of information on his heresies and activities, having witnesses to hand, the rabbinical council has determined that Yankiele Leybowicz of Korolówka must be cursed and cast out of Israel."

Pinkas, who stands in the very center of those gathered and can almost feel the warmth of the bodies of the other men, shuffles uneasily. Why are they calling the cursed man Yankiele Leybowicz instead of Jacob Frank, negating, in a way, everything that has happened lately? Suddenly Pinkas has the worrying suspicion that in cursing Yankiele Leybowicz, they are leaving Jacob Frank unscathed. Doesn't the curse go after the name, like a trained hunting dog told to fetch? What if the curse, addressed wrongly, doesn't make it to the right man? Perhaps a person could, by changing his name, his residence, country, and language, escape the herem, that weightiest of condemnations? Whom are they cursing? The wayward troublemaker? Or the kid who seduced and pulled off petty schemes?

Pinkas knows that according to the Scriptures a person upon whom herem has been placed should die.

He sticks out his shoulders and pushes his way to the front, whispering all around: "Jacob Frank, not Yankiele Leybowicz." Or the one and the other. At last, those standing nearest understand what Pinkas means. There is a slight commotion, and in the end the rabbi goes on with the herem, his voice growing more plaintive and more terrible, until the men who are listening hunch over, and the women in the women's courtyard cry in alarm in the face of this horrifying mechanism called forth as though from the darkest cellar, a kind of soulless giant made of clay that now will be in force forever, impossible to revoke.

"We curse and condemn and cast off Yankiele Leybowicz, also known as Jacob Frank, with the same words with which Joshua cursed Jericho, with which Elisha cursed his children, as well as with the words of all the curses written in the Book of Second Law," says the rabbi.

A murmur rises up all around, and it's not clear if it is of regret or if it is of pleasure, but it is as though it has come not from people's lips, but rather from within their robes, from the bottoms of their pockets, from their wide sleeves, from the cracks in the floor.

"Let him be cursed by day and cursed by night. Cursed when he goes to bed and when he gets up, when he enters his home and when he leaves it. May you never forgive him, Lord, and may you never recognize him!

May your anger burn from here on out against this man, may you weigh him down with all your curses, and may his name be erased from the Book of Life. We warn all never to exchange a word with him, in conversation or in writing, never to grant him any favors, never to be under one roof with him, not to be within four cubits of him, and not to read any document dictated by him or written in his hand."

The words die down, transforming into something almost solid, a creature made of air, an indefinable and enduring being. The synagogue is closed, and they all head home in silence. Meanwhile, far away, in another place, Jacob sits surrounded by his people; he is a little tipsy, and he doesn't notice a thing; nothing around him has changed, nothing has happened, except, perhaps, an abrupt swoon of the candlelight.

## Of Yente, who is always present and sees all

Yente, always present, sees the curse like something blurred, like those strange monsters that float before our eyes, twisted scraps, tiny, translucent organisms. And the curse will now hold on to Jacob as the white clings to the yolk.

But in fact, there is nothing about this that is concerning or even surprising. Look—there are many such curses all around, lesser, weaker, perhaps, more insignificant. Many are hounded by these, as they orbit the human heart like slimy moons—all those to whom someone has ever said, "I hope you croak," when their cart went off the road into the cabbage fields, its wheels crushing fully grown heads, and the girls cursed by their own fathers because they went into the bushes with a farmhand, and the man in the beautifully embroidered żupan cursed by his own serf over yet another day of serfdom, and then that same serf, who's been cursed by his wife when he allowed their money to be stolen or drank it away at the tavern. To him, too, the words "May you keel over and die" have been said.

Those able to see the way Yente sees things would realize that in fact the world is made of words that, once uttered, lay claim to every order, so that all things seem to occur at their behest. All things belong to them.

Every curse, even the slightest, has an effect. Every single word that's said.

When Jacob finds out about the herem a few days later, he is sitting with his back to the light, so no one sees the expression on his face. The candles cast a sharp light onto his rough, uneven cheek. Is he going to get sick again, like he did back in Salonika? He has Nahman summoned, and together they pray, standing up, until morning. They pray to protect themselves. The candles burn, and the room becomes stuffy and hot. Just before dawn, as their legs are getting almost too weak to hold them, Jacob carries out a secret ritual, and then Mordechai pronounces words just as powerful as the curse and points them in the direction of Lwów.

In Lwów, Bishop Dembowski wakes up one morning and feels as though his movements have grown slower, as though they now require of him a greater effort. He doesn't know what this could mean. But when a possible explanation for this strange, unexpected indisposition comes to him, he begins to feel afraid.

Yente lies in the shed and neither dies nor awakens. Her grandson Israel, meanwhile, goes around the village telling of this marvel with a degree of terror and distress that only vodka is capable of assuaging. He presents himself as the good grandson who dedicates whole days to his grandmother and has no time left for work. Sometimes the contemplation of it brings him to tears, and sometimes to fury, and then he gets into fights. But in reality, the ones who take care of Old Yente are Pesel and Freyna, his daughters.

Pesel gets up at dawn and goes to the shed, which is after all an annex to their cottage, and there she checks that everything is still all right. It is always all right. Only once did she see a cat sitting on the old woman's body, a strange cat. She chased it off, and now she always makes sure the door is very tightly closed. Sometimes Yente is covered in something like dew, drops of water on her skin and on her clothing, but it's strange water that doesn't evaporate, that can only be dispersed with a feather duster.

Then she gently wipes Yente's face. Her hand always hesitates before touching the skin, which is cool, delicate and soft, but supple. Sometimes it seems to Pesel that it crackles slightly, or, perhaps more precisely, that it creaks, like a new leather shoe, like a harness bought at market. Once Pesel, intrigued, asked her mother, Sobla, to help her, and very carefully they lifted up the body to check if there were any bedsores. They pulled aside the dress, but there was nothing.

"Her blood no longer flows," Pesel says to her mother, and it sends chills down both of their spines.

But she isn't a dead body, either. When she is touched, the slow motion of her eyeballs under their lids quickens. There can be no doubt.

To satisfy her curiosity, Pesel tried one other thing, but this she did alone, without witnesses. She took a sharp little knife and nicked a bit of skin at Yente's wrist. She was right: no blood emerged, but Yente's eyelids quivered uneasily, and something like a long-held breath escaped her lips. Was that possible?

Pesel, carefully observing the life of this one laid to rest, if she could be described as such, does see certain changes occur, very subtle ones. She repeatedly tells her father that Yente is shrinking, for instance.

Meanwhile, outside, a tired crowd is waiting. Some of them have been walking the whole day to get here, while others have rented a room with someone in the village, having come from farther away.

The sun rises over the river and travels quickly up into the sky, casting long, wet shadows. Those waiting warm themselves in its sharp rays. Then Pesel lets them inside, where she allows them to remain for some time. At first, they stand shyly, not daring to go up to this thing that's like a bier. She does not permit them to pray out loud—have they not troubles enough already? So they stand and pray in silence, conveying to Yente their pleas. She seems to fulfill those requests that have to do with fertility and infertility, as the case may be—the ones that have to do with women's bodies. But men come, too; they say that Yente helps with hopeless causes, after a person has lost everything.

That summer, as Jacob Frank flits from town to town with his havurah, teaching and inspiring so many good and evil thoughts, the biggest crowds come here, to Korolówka, to see his grandmother.

Israel's yard is in a state of disarray. Horses are tied to the fence, it smells of their dung, and there are flies all around. Pesel admits the pilgrims in small batches. Some of them are God-fearing Jews, poor people from around here, and some are travelers who deal in buttons or sell wine by the mug. Others come guided by their curiosity. They arrive in carriages and leave Sobla cheese, a chicken, or a bark basket filled with eggs. Good: that will go to the family. When the guests have gone, the girls have to spend their evening cleaning, clearing the yard of trash, sweeping the shed, and raking the trodden ground. When it is rainy, Sobla brings sawdust and covers the floor of the shed with it, to absorb the moisture.

Now, in the evening, Pesel has lit a candle and covered the body of the departed with handknitted socks, children's shoes, little caps, embroidered kerchiefs. She mutters under her breath. At the sound of the door creaking, she starts. It's just Sobla. She breathes a sigh of relief.

"Mama, you scared me."

Sobla stares in astonishment.

"What are you doing? What is this?"

Pesel is undeterred; she doesn't stop taking socks and kerchiefs out of the basket and laying them on the body. She just shrugs.

"*What? What?*" she repeats in a mocking tone. "The Mayorkowiczes had a child with an ailment of the ears who was healed by wearing a little hat like this. The socks are for aching feet and bones. The kerchiefs can be used for anything."

Freyna is standing against the wall, wrapping the socks in clean pieces of linen, which she finishes with a ribbon. Tomorrow these items will be sold to the pilgrims.

Ever since she heard about the curse, Sobla has known that this will all end badly. Does the curse also apply to the family of the condemned? It must, of course. Her breasts have been sore for some time now. She has urged Israel not to get involved in these religious disputes anymore. To get rid of Yente. Sometimes she stands by the window that looks out onto the cemetery and the hills that slope clear down to the river, and she wonders what direction they will go in when they have to run away.

What frightened her the most was the story of Joseph of Rohatyn, whom she knew—he was here, with Jacob, in the winter. That man went to synagogue and divulged his error, admitting to each and every one of his sins. He told them about breaking the Shabbat, not keeping the fast, forbidden corporeal relations, and the fact that he prayed to Sabbatai Tzvi and Baruchiah, that he carried out kabbalist rituals, that he ate forbidden foods—everything that happened in Korolówka while Jacob was around. Thinking about it makes Sobla's head spin—she almost vomits out of fear. Israel, her husband, might well admit to all the same things. Joseph was sentenced to thirty-nine lashes—and that was nothing, compared with the rest of his sentence. He was forced to divorce his wife and to declare his children bastards. He was banished from the Rohatyn kahal and forbidden further contact with any Jews. He is to rove the earth until his death.

Sobla rushes to Yente's bier and furiously removes the socks and hats and throws them to the ground. Pesel looks at her in shock and anger.

"Oh, Mama," she says. "You really just don't get it."


### The Bishop of Kamieniec Mikołaj Dembowski writes a letter to the papal nuncio Serra, while his secretary adds a little something from himself

The letter is from the bishop, but it was written from start to finish by Father Pikulski. He is now reading it to the bishop, who is more interested in the renovations to his summer residence in Czarnokozińce, eager to go and check on their progress himself.

The nuncio, meanwhile, would like to know what's going on in the strange matter of the Jewish heretics. It has already come to light, thanks to the Jews themselves and their rabbinical court, that the network of Sabbatian kahalim—the heretics—extends far and wide. It exists in Galicia, in Bukovina, in Hungary, Moravia, and Podolia. All of these kahalim are secret; the heretics feign traditional Jewish beliefs; at home, however, they engage in diabolical rituals, committing among other sins that of the Adamites. The rabbis are shocked and frightened by this. They have sent a respectful letter about it to the nuncio.

The bishop's letter, in Pikulski's hand, relates before the rabbinical court in Satanów the details of the trial of the Jewish heretics who were captured:

> The hearings took place in the chambers of the kahal. The estate's guards, and, on the Jewish side, the guard of the mikvah, a certain Naftali, led in the accused with tethers around their necks and their hands tied, so that they had no way to shield themselves from the blows they received from the crowd, which also spat on them. Some of them were so frightened that they confessed to everything before they were even questioned, immediately begging to be pardoned, swearing that they would never again resort to similar misdeeds. Such was the case of one Joseph of Rohatyn. Others denied everything, insisting that their presence at the trial must have been the result of some mistake, as they had nothing to do with the heretics.
>
> After just one day of hearings, it was possible to paint a picture on the basis of the testimonies that would strike fear into the heart of any onlooker. Not only did they profane their Shabbat and other holy days, and eat foods forbidden to the Jews, but also they lay with persons unwedded to them, the men and the women committing such adulteries with the full knowledge and blessing of their spouses. The epicenter of this heresy is thought to be the Shorr family and its head, Elisha Shorr, who was furthermore accused of maintaining intimate relations with his daughter-in-law. It seems accusations such as these provoked a great deal of tumult, so much so that the wives of the accused left their husbands en masse, initiating divorce proceedings.
>
> The rabbis realize that they must put a stop to this sect and its disgusting practices, which could paint God-fearing Jews such as themselves in a very bad light, which is why they decided on a very severe next step, namely, to curse Jacob Frank, condemning him with herem. The sect is to be systematically persecuted, and studying the Zohar and Kabbalah, so dangerous to malleable minds, has been forbidden to persons younger than forty years of age. Anyone who believes in Sabbatai Tzvi and his successors, Baruchiah or Nathan of Gaza, is now cursed. These will never be permitted any public role or

function; their wives and daughters are to be regarded as concubines, and their sons as bastards. They will not be admitted into their own homes, nor will their horses be given fodder. And all Jews must immediately report such cursed persons upon sight.

The Council of Four Lands in Konstantynów has confirmed the above.

The determination to curse these people spread quickly through the country, and we have now had reports that these Shabbitarians, as they are popularly known, are indeed being persecuted. They are being attacked in their homes, beaten, their sacred books taken from them and destroyed.

It is said that the men who have been apprehended are half shaved, their partial beards a sign that they are neither Jews nor Christians, but rather straddling the two religions. This universal persecution, however, is such a blow to the Jewish apostasy that it will undoubtedly prove fatal to it. Besides, the leader of these renegades has traveled to Turkey, and, fearing for his life, will likely not return again.

"What a shame," the bishop exclaims. "There might have been a chance for us to actually convert them."

Pikulski rushes through the niceties at the end of the letter and then passes it to the bishop to sign. He sprinkles sand over the ink and begins composing a letter of his own in his head. Perhaps he'll seem presumptuous, but he, too, is concerned for the good of the Church. He returns to his chambers and writes his own missive to the nuncio, which he will send to Warsaw with the same messenger. It includes, among other passages:

The Bishop, in his goodness, would wish to see them as precious lambs nuzzling up to our Holy Mother Church, but I would be so bold as to warn against such a naive understanding of the situation. It is necessary to take careful stock of what lies underneath the declarations of these sect members who call themselves Contra-Talmudists. Not wishing to cast aspersions on His Excellency the Bishop, I would nevertheless read in such an inclination a desire to gain personal recognition through the enlistment of throngs of new Christians.

Based on what I have understood about this matter, while Frank does talk about the Holy Trinity, he does not have in mind the Christian Trinity, but rather a Trinity of theirs that purportedly includes a female named Shekhinah. This has nothing in common with Christianity, as Your Excellency will no doubt agree. As for baptism, Jacob mentions it only vaguely and as it suits him. It seems, as well, that he says something very different to people in the villages—where he passes himself off as a teacher, a traveling rabbi—than behind closed doors, to his closest circle of disciples. He has many supporters, especially Contra-Talmudist Jews from Nadwórna, Rohatyn, and Busk. To what extent, however, this is out of deep religious desire, and to what extent a desire to enter into our Christian fold for reasons beyond religion, no one can guess just yet. Therefore, guided by my great preoccupation, I make so bold as to entreat the authority of our Church to urgently and carefully investigate this matter prior to taking any steps . . .

Father Pikulski finishes and stares at a single point on the wall across from him. He would be glad to handle this matter himself, to serve the Church. He knows Hebrew well and has penetrated the mysteries of the Jewish religion. It generates in him something along the lines of quivering disgust. Something along the lines of dirty fascination. Those who have not glimpsed it close up—and most haven't—have no idea of the enormity of the institution that is this Mosaic faith. Brick after brick, plus vast, squat vaults that fortify each other—it is almost impossible to imagine how anyone could have come up with such an architecture ever. Father Pikulski believes that God did in fact make a covenant with the Jews, did love them and hold them close to him, but that he cast them off. He withdrew and gave the world over to a nice, clean, fair-haired Christ, in a simple robe, focused and determined.

Father Pikulski would like to be able to ask the nuncio to appoint him, on account of his linguistic talents and the vastness of his knowledge, as adviser on this case. How to put that in writing? He leans over the page of crossed-out sentences and tries to cobble together a few more.

## Bishop Dembowski writes to Bishop Sołtyk

At that same time, Bishop Dembowski, his imagination also on fire, takes a sheet of paper from a drawer and smooths it with his hand, to remove all the invisible specks of dust. He begins with the date, February 20, 1756, and soon his hand is gliding over the paper with panache, creating big, bold letters; he draws visible pleasure from the flourishes with which he embellishes especially the letters *J* and *S*.

> They want a big public Disputation, they want to sit down opposite the Rabbis they're against & show them that the Talmud is bad. In Exchange, they would agree to be baptized, & that would be, or so they say, some several Thousand People. If this were to come to Fruition, the Feat of it would gain Poland Renown all around the World—that in the Holy Commonwealth we managed to convert the Pagans without going all the Way to India, instead converting our very own local Savages. Secondly, setting aside their good Intentions, these Shabbitarians also profoundly hate their Jewish Talmudic Brothers . . .
>
> As soon as they were arrested, because of some Iniquities conducted in a Home in Lanckoroń, they were turned in to us by some of those other Jews, with whom I maintain good Relations & have many Dealings of my own. They accused these Heretics of the Sin of the Adamites, which would not in itself reach the Consistory Court, but for the Heresy that underlies the Accusation. But whose Heresy? Not ours! How are we to handle a Jewish Heresy, knowing nothing whatsoever of the Matter, & very little of Judaism itself? Thank God I can rely on someone else in these Questions, the Jesuit Father Pikulski, who is fairly well acquainted with them.
>
> The whole Affair is delicate, & this is how I see it: It is better for us to live alongside the Rabbis harmoniously & keep them in their current Place, as they have often given Evidence of their Loyalty. On the other Hand, this new Fervor might also

be useful to us, were we ever to wish to exert any type of Pressure on the Jewish Congregations & the Rabbis. They have put a Curse on the Anti-Talmudists, & most of the cursed have been arrested by royal Authority. Some of them are at Large because they did not attend the Gathering in Lanckoroń. I sent a Delegation for those just as soon as I learned of all this. They came to see me in Czarnokozińce, but without their Leader this time. Him I have seen only once, & even then, briefly & in Secret. This leader, Jacob, being a Turkish Subject, had to be freed immediately, & no sooner had he been freed than he set out for Turkey.

This time a certain Krysa took the Lead, a coarse Man, a sort of pettifogging Character, though he does speak decent Polish, the which made him seem more intelligent to me than that Frank. Being himself impetuous & violent, he relied on the Charm & Eloquence of his Brother, & so together they laid out for me how they were being persecuted by the Rabbis & have had no Peace from them, being threatened with Death, attacked along the Roads & divested of all their Property. Nor do the Rabbis let them live or carry on any Business, & so those who are against the Talmud & who adhere in many matters to our most holy Faith would nonetheless prefer to maintain their Independence & settle down somewhere outside the others' Control & found their own Towns from scratch or take over existing ones, such as Busk or Podhajce, whence in fact they come.

As for Frank himself, these Krysas did not have the highest Opinion of him, least of all since he ran off after causing all these Problems & is no doubt now safely ensconced in Chocim or Czernowitz & biding his Time there to see what happens here. They say he immediately converted to Islam. If this is true, it certainly does not bode well for Someone who only recently declared such fervent religious Feelings for our holy Church. It would in fact suggest that they are like Atheists & take Pleasure in this sort of religious Anarchy, wandering into & out of other people's Faiths.

To my Mind, this elder Krysa would be a better Leader to those Shabbitarians if he weren't so ugly & impetuous.

Leadership needs the right Attitude, the right Height, the right
Type of Charm, even if it's of the most ordinary Variety, which,
when properly deployed, inspires both warm Feelings &
Attention.

I must say I am well-disposed toward them. Though I feel
no great Sympathy with them, for they are foreign to us, quite
different from us, & seemingly somewhat perverse, I would still
like to see all of them end up as Children of God here with me
in the Church. I suspect that You agree with me completely &
fully support the matter of their Baptism. Meanwhile I am
writing them a safeguard so that the Talmudists do not bother
them any further, for all sorts of terrible things have been
occurring here. As if it were not enough to have placed this
Jewish Curse on Jacob Frank, they've also been burning the
Heretics' Books, the Nature of which I have only the foggiest
Idea.

I must point Your Attention to these few People who have
been accused & targeted by the Talmudist Rabbis. If ever they
were to require Help of any sort from You, I would ask You to
take their Request into Consideration. They are as follows:

Leyzor & Yeruhim of Jezierzany
Leyb Krysa of Nadwórna
Leybka Shaynowicz Rabinowicz & Moshko Dawidowicz of
   Brzeżany
Hershko Shmulewicz & Itzek Motylowicz of Busk
Nutka Falek Meyerowicz, known as Old Falek
Moshek Leybka Abramowicz & his Son Yankiel of Lanckoroń
Elisha Shorr of Rohatyn with his large Family
Leybka Hershko of Satanów
Moshko Izraelowicz with his Son Yosek of Nadwórna
Moses Aronowicz of Lwów
Zelik with his Son Leybko & Leybko Shmulewicz

The bishop is so tired that his head droops down toward the piece of
paper, eventually falling just under the name "Shmulewicz." The ink
from "Zelik" smears his pale and pious temple.

## Meanwhile . . .

All those mentioned by the bishop, every last one, are now sitting in the home of a man named Berek, in Kamieniec. It's the end of February, and a piercing chill steals into the room through every crack in the walls—and there are many.

"He did the right thing by going to Turkey, with all the mayhem he created here," says Leybko Shmulewicz to Krysa, referring, of course, to Jacob.

Says Krysa:

"It seems to me that he ought to be here with us. Seems to me he may have fled for good—that's what some people say."

"Who cares about that, let them talk. The important thing is that the letters reach him; he's right over the river, in Chocim. Poland, Turkey— what kind of border is that? The important thing is for him not to waste away over there with the Turks, but to let us know what to say and do here, and how."

"As if we didn't know ourselves," mutters Krysa.

Now, as the voices die down, Shlomo Shorr, who has just arrived, stands up again; his towering figure inspires respect.

"Look, the bishop is favorably inclined toward us. He examined the three of us, my brother, Nahman, and me. All of us were released from jail and allowed to go home. That's an end to our misery. There will be a disputation between us and them. That's what we were able to obtain."

There is a clamor, which Shorr hushes, gesturing toward Moshe from Podhajce in his fur-lined coat. Now Moshe rises with some effort and says:

"For everything to go according to our plan, we must definitively hold to two true things: that we believe in the Trinity, which is the one God in three persons—but not get into any discussions on topics like who is in the Trinity and so on—and that we reject the Talmud once and for all as a source of errors and blasphemies. And that's it. Just that."

They disperse in silence, shuffling through the sawdust on the floor.

## How Gitla's stepmother's pessimistic predictions come true

When the turmoil erupted in Lanckoroń, and they arrested all the men, Gitla didn't suffer overmuch. Hayah's husband came to get her right away, and she took in both "guardians" for that night. Making their beds for them, serving them soured milk, Hayah, whose breasts were so recently being ceremonially kissed, looked more like an ordinary housewife.

"There's nothing here for you, dear child," she said to Gitla, sitting on her bed and caressing her cheek. "You must leave, go back to Lwów, and apologize to your father. He'll take you in."

The next day she gave them each a couple of groszy and sent them on their way. They immediately set off in opposite directions without a word, Gitla leaving behind her a trail of blood in the snow. She paused to turn her fur-lined coat inside out and headed for the road. She was hoping to get a lift from a passing sleigh and make it to Lwów, although not on account of her father, but rather because she had reason to believe that Jacob, the Lord, would likely end up there.

Come February, Gitla has reached Lwów, but she does not dare let her father see her. She spots him once as he walks to the kahal, keeping close to the city wall, old and hunched over; he takes little steps and is talking to himself. Gitla feels sorry for him, but she doesn't move from where she's standing. She goes to her dead mother's sister, who lives near the synagogue, but her aunt has already heard about everything that's happened and shuts the door in her face. Gitla listens through the closed door as they lament the fate of her father. Then she stands on the corner of the street where the Jewish homes begin. The wind flutters her skirt, and bits of snow melt into her flimsy stockings. Soon she will put her hand out for alms or start selling herself for bread, and everything will be as her stepmother predicted—she will hit rock bottom. Which is why for now she stands in the freezing cold with dignity, or so she hopes. And yet some young Jew in a shtreimel presses a grosz into her hand without even looking at her, and Gitla uses it to buy herself a warm obwarzanek. Slowly she reconciles herself to the thought that she looks like a harlot—dirty, with matted hair, and hungry. And suddenly she feels absolutely free. She goes into the first decent courtyard she comes across and up to the first decent building, and then she climbs the stairs to the first floor and knocks on the first decent-looking door she encounters.

The person who opens the door is a tall, stooping man in a nightcap and a dressing gown thinly lined with dark fur. He has spectacles over his nose. He is holding a candle before him that lights up his face and sharp features.

"What do you want?" he asks in a hoarse, low voice, and reflexively starts searching for groszy to give her alms.

"I am the great-granddaughter of the Polish king," says Gitla. "I am looking for a decent place where I can spend the night."

## 15

## How the old minaret in Kamieniec turns into a column with the Holy Mother on top

In the summer of 1756, Nahman, Jacob, and Shlomo Shorr show up in Kamieniec as ordinary Jews from just outside Smotrycz who came to sell garlic. Nahman has a carrying pole over his shoulders with baskets of garlic attached on either end. Although Jacob is now wearing a shabby kapota, he would not agree to bast shoes and is instead wearing good leather boots that stick out from beneath his wide-leg trousers. Dressed in an outfit that is half Turkish, half Armenian, he resembles a vagabond who doesn't belong anywhere, the kind the borderlands are full of, the kind no one pays any special mind. Shlomo Shorr, tall and thin, has such dignity in his face that he's harder to make look like a vagabond. In his long dark coat and peasant's shoes, he looks more like a cleric of some undetermined religion, and he arouses people's automatic respect.

The three of them now stand before Kamieniec's Peter and Paul Cathedral among a sizable crowd that is observing with great excitement the placement of a statue atop a tall column. This event has attracted all those from the little neighboring villages and the nearby alleyways, and customers from the stalls at the market. Even the priests have come out to watch the wooden crane raise this gold figure. A moment earlier they had been talking in an animated, noisy way, but now, looking at the sculpture, which has suddenly begun to sway, threatening to snap the cords and send everything careening onto the onlookers, they have quieted down. The crowd moves back a bit. Some of the workers are foreign; people are whispering they're from Gdańsk, that the whole statue was even cast in Gdańsk, completely covered in thick gold, and that it took a full month for it to be brought here in carts the authorities commissioned that made their way from post house to post house. The column itself, meanwhile, was built by the Turks, and for years that crescent of theirs was atop it, those heathens having made it part of a minaret. But now the Holy Virgin has returned and will tower over the town and the heads of its inhabitants.

At last, the statue is in place. The crowd sighs, and someone starts singing. Now the whole figure can be seen. The Holy Mother, the Mother of Mercy, the Virgin Mary, Queen of the World, is portrayed here as a young woman, running with the carefree grace of a dancer, her arms outspread and raised as though in greeting. As though she were about to pick you up and squeeze you tight. Nahman raises his head and covers his eyes as the white sky blinds him, and it seems to him that she is saying, "Come, dance with me," or "Play with me," or "Give me your hand." Jacob raises his hand into the sky and points at the statue, unnecessarily, since it is what everyone has come to see. Nahman knows, though, what Jacob is trying to indicate—that this Virgin is the holy Shekhinah, God's presence in the dark world. Then the sun jolts out from behind the clouds, completely unexpectedly, since the sky has been cloudy since morning, and one of its rays hits the statue, and all that Gdańsk gold starts to gleam like a kind of second sun, and suddenly the square in front of the cathedral in Kamieniec shines with a fresh and joyful light, and the Virgin, who is running in the sky, is pure goodness, like someone who alights among people to give them hope—that everything will be good. Everyone sighs ecstatically at this powerful show of pure light. The Holy Virgin. People squint and kneel before this obvious evidence of her miracle. It's a sign, it's a sign, they all repeat, and the crowd is kneeling, and they are, too. Nahman's eyes fill with tears, and his feelings are shared by the others. A miracle is a miracle, regardless of the creed.

To them, it seems that the Shekhinah is descending into this statue

gilded in Gdańsk, and that in this glimmering guise she will guide them
to the bishop's residence like a mother, like a sister, like the most tender
lover who would give up everything just to gaze upon her beloved for even
a moment, even if he's dressed in the shabbiest kapota. But before they go
in for their secret audience with Bishop Dembowski, Jacob, being Jacob,
unable to endure any solemnity, breaks away from the crowd and, in a fit
of childish mischief, starts to wail along the city wall like an old Jewish
beggar, hunched and lame.

"Insolent Jewry," hisses some heavy townswoman about him. "No
respect for what's sacred."

That same day, late in the evening, they present the bishop with a manifesto of nine theses they plan to defend at the disputation. They also
request some protection, since the Talmudists are still persecuting them.
And then there's the curse. That's what angers the bishop the most. Curse!
What is this Jewish curse of theirs?

He has them sit while he reads:

"One: We believe in everything the God of the Old Testament commanded mankind to believe in. We believe in everything He taught.

"Two: The Scriptures cannot be effectively comprehended by human
reason without God's Grace.

"Three: The Talmud, filled with unprecedented blasphemies toward
God, ought and needs to be rejected.

"Four: God is One, and He is the creator of all things.

"Five: This very God is in three Persons, indivisible in nature.

"Six: God may take the form of human flesh upon Himself and be
subject to every passion apart from sin.

"Seven: In accordance with the prophecy, the city of Jerusalem will
not be rebuilt.

"Eight: The Messiah promised in the Scriptures will not come again.

"Nine: God Himself will bear within Himself the curse of the first
parents and of the whole nation, and the one who is the true Messiah is
God Incarnate."

"Is it good like that?" asks Nahman, placing a small Turkish purse of delicate goatskin—it looks like it's embroidered with crystals and turquoise, beautiful handiwork—discreetly on the small table by the door. The bishop can guess what is inside—they wouldn't have come with just anything. It will contain expensive stones, enough of them to set a whole monstrance. Imagining this makes his head spin. But the bishop has to focus. It's not easy, for this seemingly small matter has suddenly taken on enormous dimensions: the opponents of these ragamuffins have gotten to Baruch Yavan, aide to Chief Minister Brühl—on the bishop's table lie letters from Warsaw, relating in detail all the palace intrigues—and now wield this powerful man at court, the Polish king's most important adviser. Who would have thought that kissing a naked woman in some village in the middle of nowhere would ever attain such proportions?

The bishop takes the purse, and in so doing, he takes Frank's side, though the brazenness of this Jew annoys him. The Jew demands a disputation. Demands protection. Demands land, to settle down "quietly," he says. And furthermore: the Jew demands ennoblement. The bishop must thoroughly protect them, and then they'll get baptized. He also wishes for those most eminent among them (here the bishop struggles to imagine their "eminence," for they are after all only leaseholders, furriers, shopkeepers) to be able to try for ennoblement according to the law of the Commonwealth. And that they might gain the right to settle down on church lands.

The other one, the redhead who translates for Jacob, explains that the tradition since back when they lived in Spain was to organize such disputations when some thorny question arose. The time has come to do so. He translates Frank's words:

"Take even a few hundred rabbis and intelligent bishops, and lords, and the best scholars. Let them debate me and my people. I'll answer every question they ask, because the truth is on my side."

They are like merchants come to make a profit: their asking price is high.

But they also have a lot to offer in return, the bishop considers.

## What Bishop Dembowski ponders
## as his face is being shaved

It really is strange how very cold and damp the bishop's mansion is in Kamieniec Podolski. Even now, in summer, when in the early morning the barber comes, the bishop as he sits must warm his feet with a hot stone wrapped in thick linen.

He has had his chair moved to the window, and before the barber sharpens the knife, wiping the blade on the leather strop with great pomp and circumstance, before he prepares the lather and carefully—so as not to sully His Holiness in any way, God forbid—covers up his shoulders with embroidered linen towels, the bishop has time to look over the latest missives from Kamieniec, Lwów, and Warsaw.

The day before, the bishop met with a man called Krysa, who is apparently working in the name of Jacob Frank, but also seems to be playing his own hand. With great determination, the bishop has been summoning the so-called Talmudists, learned rabbis from all over Podolia, asking them to participate in the disputation, but the rabbis have been dodging his summons. Once, twice, he has ordered them to appear before him, but they haven't done so, evidently holding the office of the bishop in contempt. When he fines them, they just send Hershko Shmulewicz, a very clever Jew, apparently a representative, who comes up with every conceivable excuse on their behalf. Meanwhile, the contents of their purse are very concrete, if decidedly less elaborate: gold coins. The bishop attempts not to betray that he has already taken a stand, and that it is with the other ones.

If only he could understand these Jews the same way he can more or less comprehend the intentions of a peasant! Yet here you have their tassels, their hats, their bizarre speech (which is why he is so favorably disposed toward Pikulski's efforts in this regard, to master their language), their suspicious religion. Why suspicious? Because it's too close. Their books are the same, Moses, Abraham, Isaac on the stone under his father's knife, Noah and his ark—all of it's the same, and yet, with them it appears in some strange new context. Even Noah doesn't look the same, exactly—he's disfigured, somehow, and his ark is not the same, but rather Jewish, more ornamental, Eastern, bursting at the seams. Even Isaac, who was always a blond little stripling with rosy skin, has now transformed into a wild child, sturdier, not quite so defenseless. With us, everything is somehow lighter, as though more conventional, sketched in an elegant hand, thinks the bishop—delicate, meaningful. Their faith is dark and concrete, almost uncomfortably literal. Their Moses is an old pauper with bony feet; ours a dignified elder with a flowing beard. It strikes Bishop Dembowski that it is Christ's light that illuminates in such a way the Christian side of the Old Testament—the one we share with the Jews— hence these differences.

The worst is when a foreign thing is disguised as something that belongs. As though they were mocking us. As though they were making a joke out of the Holy Scriptures. And there is one more thing: their stubbornness! After all, the Jews have been around for longer, and yet they persist in their error. It is certainly not unreasonable to suspect that they must be up to something. If only they were as open in their behavior as the Armenians. When the Armenians are up to something, you know it's only ever over gains that can be measured in gold.

What are all these Jews discussing? wonders Bishop Dembowski, observing them from the window as they gather in small groups of three or four and debate in their halting, singsong language, accompanying their words with movements of the body, too, and gestures: they stretch their heads forward, they shake their beards, they hop like someone burned when they don't agree with the reasoning of one of the others. Is it true what Sołtyk, a friend the bishop trusts, always says about them? That, urged to do so by some commandment, by some dark beliefs they hold, they permit in their squat, damp little houses such practices as require Christian blood? God forbid. It can't be, and the Holy Father in Rome has stated clearly that they must not believe in such things, must snuff out the rumor that Jews make use of Christian blood. Oh, but just look at them. Out of the window, the bishop watches the small square in front of his mansion where a seller of paintings, a young boy still, shows a holy picture to a girl dressed in the Ruthenian style in an embroidered shirt and a colorful skirt. The girl cautiously touches with the tip of her pinkie the little depictions of the saints—this Jewish salesman has both Catholic and Orthodox likenesses for sale—while he pulls from his breast pocket a cheap little medallion and places it in her hand; their heads lean in to almost meet over the medallion of the Virgin. The bishop knows the girl will buy it.

The barber puts the lather on his face and starts to shave him. The razor scrapes him quietly, slicing away his hair. Suddenly the bishop's imagination makes the leap beneath their frayed kapotas, and he is tormented by the image of their members. They are circumcised. This both fascinates and shocks him, and also makes him angry in some way he can't quite understand. He clenches his jaw.

If this peddler of holy pictures—which is against the law; they really have absolutely no respect for the rules!—were to be stripped of this tallit of his and dressed in a cassock, would he look any different from the clerics walking just over there? And if he, the Bishop of Kamieniec, Dembowski of the Dąb coat of arms, who is patiently waiting to be named archbishop of Lwów—if he were to be stripped of his rich robes and dressed in those tattered Jewish kapotas and set out with those pictures before a mansion in Kamieniec . . . The bishop winces at this absurd idea, though for a moment he can see himself, fat and pink, as a Jew selling pictures. No. No.

If it were as people said, if they were so powerful, then they would be wealthy, and not poor like these Jews just outside. Are they strong or weak? Do they pose a threat to the bishop's mansion? Is it true that they hate the gentiles and find them filthy? And that they have tiny dark hairs all over their bodies?

God would not allow them to have such power as Sołtyk thinks—after all, they rejected Christ's act of salvation, and therefore no longer have any relation with the true God; cast off the path to salvation, they have wandered out into the wilderness somewhere.

The girl doesn't want the medallion—she unbuttons her shirt just below her neck and pulls out her own, which she shows to the boy, who eagerly moves in closer to her neck.

The girl does buy the picture, however, and the salesman wraps it up in thin, stained paper.

What are these other people like when they take off their robes? the bishop wonders. What changes in them when they are alone, he thinks, dismissing the deeply bowing barber, and realizes that it is time for him to go and change for mass. He goes to his bedroom, happy to get rid of the heavy cassock he wears at home. For a moment, he stands naked, wondering whether he is committing some sort of terrible sin; already he has started to beg God to forgive him for it—whether it is the sin of shamelessness or maybe just of human piteousness. He feels the lightest cool breeze rustle ever so gently the tiny hairs on his stocky, hairy body.

## Of Hayah's two natures

Jacob has brought with him several horsemen, richly dressed after the Turkish fashion—men who have been given a special room. Their leader is Hayim, Hana's brother. They speak only Turkish to each other. Jacob Frank is now known as Ahmed Frenk, and he has a Turkish passport. He is untouchable. Every day a messenger delivers news to him from the disputation in Kamieniec.

At word that Jacob Frank has secretly stationed himself for the duration of the Kamieniec disputation at her father's house in Rohatyn, Hayah takes her youngest child, packs a trunk, and sets off from Lanckoroń to Rohatyn. It is hot, the harvest will begin soon; slowly, gently, waves make their way across the golden fields of crops that stretch out past the horizon, and it looks as though the whole earth, soft and gold, were sighing. Hayah is wearing a light-colored dress and a cerulean veil. Her baby daughter sits in her lap. Hayah sits up straight and calm in the carriage, breastfeeding the little one. A couple of dapple-gray horses draw a light coach covered in a linen tarpaulin. To all appearances, it is transporting a wealthy Jewish woman on her way somewhere. The peasant women stop and bring their hands up to their eyes in order to see the woman better. Hayah, as soon as she meets their gaze, gives a little smile. One of the women reflexively crosses herself; Hayah cannot tell if it is at the sight of a Jewish woman or of a woman with a child wearing a blue veil.

Hayah passes her daughter to a servant and runs straight to her father, who stands up from his accounts as soon as he sees her and starts to hem and haw with happiness. She leans into his beard and breathes in its familiar fragrance—coffee and tobacco, the safest smell in the world, or so it seems to Hayah. Soon the whole house has come running—her brother Yehuda and his wife, petite as a little girl, with pretty green eyes, and their children, and the servants, and Hryćko, who is now called Hayim and who lives next door, and also the neighbors. It gets noisy, and Hayah sets out her traveling baskets, takes out the gifts she's brought. Only once she has fulfilled this pleasant duty and eaten the chicken broth that is daily fed to Jacob—chicken feathers float through the kitchen—can she look in on the guest.

Hayah goes up to Jacob and takes a good look at his sun-darkened face, where after a moment's seriousness the ironic smile she knows so well appears.

"You've aged, but you're still beautiful."

"And you've gotten all the more handsome because you've lost weight. Your wife must not be giving you anything to eat."

They embrace like brother and sister, but Jacob's hand gently slides over Hayah's lean back, as though caressing her.

"I had no choice," says Jacob, and takes a step back. He fixes his shirt, which has slipped out from under his galligaskins.

"You did the right thing by running. Once we've made our deal with the bishops, you'll return like a king," says Hayah, taking his hands.

"They wanted to kill me in Salonika, and they want to kill me here."

"Because they're afraid of you. But that is your great strength."

"I won't come back here again. I have a house and a vineyard. I'll study the Scriptures . . ."

Hayah bursts out laughing, and she laughs sincerely, joyfully, with her whole body.

"I can see it already . . . studying the Scriptures . . . ," she says, catching her breath and unpacking the books and teraphim from her small trunk. Among the statuettes there is one that is special; it is ayelet ahuvim, the favorite doe—a deer figurine carved out of ivory. Jacob takes it in his hand and looks it over, rather inattentively, and then he reads the titles of the books Hayah has set out on the table.

"You figured it would be some techinot, some sort of women's supplications, no?" Hayah says, flicking her skirt, setting the white feathers swirling across the floor.

Yente, who is never far, watches Hayah.

Who is Hayah? And are there two Hayahs? When she goes through the kitchen in the morning carrying a little bowl of onion, when she wipes the sweat from her brow with her hand, furrowing her forehead, where a vertical wrinkle appears—then she is a matriarch, an eldest daughter who has taken on the obligations of a mother. As she goes she stomps her boots, and you can hear her throughout the whole house, and then she is the daytime Hayah, sunny and bright. During prayers she becomes a zogerke, a reciter who helps women who can't read, or can't read well, to orient themselves during the service, to figure out which prayer to say when. She can be overbearing. The menace of her furrowed brow tamps down all disobedience. Everyone, even her father, fears her quick steps, her shouting when she disciplines the children, when she fights with the man with the cart who brought two sacks of flour from the mill with holes in them, or her rage when she throws plates, to the despair of the servants. How did it come about that Hayah was granted so much license?

It is said in the Zohar that all females on earth dwell within the mystery of the Shekhinah.

This is the only possible way to understand Hayah's becoming this gloomy woman with disheveled hair, sloppy clothing, an absent gaze. Her face ages in the blink of an eye, as wrinkles break over her face, as she furrows her brow and tightens her lips. It is dusk already, and the house has fallen into splotches of light cast by the lamps and candles. Hayah's face loses its features, those angry eyes are covered now by heavy lids, and her face swells and droops and becomes ugly, like the face of a sick old woman. Hayah is barefoot, and her steps are heavy as she makes her way through the hall to the room where they await her. She touches the walls with her fingers as though she were really the Virgin without Eyes. The assembled have filled the room with incense, burning sage and Turkish herbs; the air gets thick, and Hayah starts to speak. Whoever has seen this happen once will forever feel strange about seeing her again by day, shredding the cabbage.

Why did Shorr give his beloved daughter the name Hayah? And how did he know that this baby, born early in the morning in a stuffy room where water was steaming in huge pots on the stove, in an attempt to heat the house in the cold January winter, would become his beloved daughter, the most brilliant of children? Was it because she was conceived first, of his best seed, at the pinnacle of his strength? When their bodies were smooth, elastic and clean, unstained, and their minds were full of good faith, not yet broken by anything? And yet the girl had been born lifeless, not breathing, and the silence that followed the drama of labor was like that of the grave. He had been afraid the tiny thing would die. He was terrified of the death he had no doubt was already encircling their home. Only after the midwife had availed herself of some whispered spells did the child start to cough and then cry. And so the first word that had come to Elisha's mind in connection with this child was *hai*—"to live." Hayim is life, but not vegetable life, not mere physical life, but rather the kind that permits prayer, thought, and feeling.

"VaYitzer haShem Elohim et haAdam Afar min haAdama, vaYipah beApav Nishmat Hayim, baYehi haAdam leNefesh Hayah," Elisha recited as he saw the child. Then God made man from the dust of the earth and breathed into his nostrils the breath of life (nishmat hayim), making man a living being (nefesh hayah).

And then Shorr felt like God.

## The shapes of the new letters

The leather in which the book is bound is new and of good quality—smooth, and fragrant. Jacob takes pleasure in touching its spine, and he realizes that it is rare to see a new book, as if it were only the older ones that could be trusted and consulted. He has such a book, with which he's never parted—everyone should have one like that. But his is a man-uscript, a much-read copy of *And I Came this Day unto the Fountain*, which he always has in his luggage. It is a little haggard now, if a stack of pages sewn together can be described like an old man. The title page has been damaged in several places, the paper yellowed from the sun when he left it out on a windowsill. What negligence! His father always hit him on the hands for such slips and negligence.

This new volume is a thick book. The bookbinder has pressed the pages in tight, so that when it's opened, they crack like bones stretched too violently, resisting. Jacob opens it at random and holds it forcefully so that the strange book does not shut in his face while his eyes wander along the string of letters from right to left, but then he recollects that here you have to go in reverse, from left to right, and his eyes struggle to perform this circus trick. Before long—although he does not understand a word—he is finding pleasure in this movement from left to right, as though against the current, in spite of the world. He thinks perhaps this other direction of movement is the fundamental thing, that this is what he ought to study and to practice: this gesture initiated by the left hand but completed by the right; a revolution in which the right arm retreats before the left, and day begins with sunrise, with light, in order to sub-merge itself at last in darkness.

He examines the shapes of the letters and worries he will not be able to remember them. There is one that looks a little bit like *tzadi*, and an-other that seems close to *samech*, and here is one that is kind of like *qof*, but not exactly—it's close, but not quite, and maybe the meanings, too, are close but not quite, edging just near enough to those he knows to let him make out a blurry world.

"This is their collected Geschichte," Shorr says to Jacob in his rumpled shirt. "Something like our 'Jacob's Eye,' with a little bit about everything, about animals, places, it has different stories, some about spirits. It was written by a priest from right here in Rohatyn, can you believe that?"

Now Jacob takes a closer look at the book.

"I'll hire a teacher for you," Elisha Shorr says, and stuffs his pipe for him. "Now listen. We certainly didn't go all the way to Smyrna to collect you just to let you go now. All those people over there in Kamieniec are going out to fight in your stead for what we want to accomplish. You are leading them, even though you can't go there yourself. But you cannot pull out now."

Every evening Hayah kneels before her father and rubs his legs with a mixture of foul-smelling onion juice and something else that fills the house with the smell of herbs all night. But that's not all: Hayah passes her child off to the women and shuts herself in with the men in her father's room, and there they confer. Jacob is surprised by this at first. It isn't a sight he's used to. In Turkey and Wallachia women know their place, and religious scholars keep their distance from them, for women's inherent connection with the lowest world of matter introduces chaos into the world of the spirit. But it doesn't work that way among true believers. Since they are always on the road, they all would perish were it not for their women.

"Ah," says Elisha, as if reading Jacob's mind, "if she were a man, she would be my wisest son."

That first night, according to the old custom, Hayah comes to Jacob's bed. Her body is delicate, if a little bony, with its long thighs and rough mound. Custom dictates they have sexual intercourse without any unnecessary caresses and without words. But Jacob rubs her slightly convex belly for a long time, each time running his hand over her navel, which seems very warm to him. She takes his member boldly in her hand and gently, almost inattentively, strokes it. Hayah wants to know how the acceptance of the Turkish religion occurs, what they do instead of baptism, if you have to prepare for it somehow, how much it cost them, whether Jacob's wife also converted to Islam and whether women have it better there than here. Did his decision to convert really protect him? Did he think he was out of reach of the Polish authorities? And did he know that for Jews—and for her, too—such a conversion would be extremely difficult? And that she believes him, that all the Shorrs would follow him if he would like to lead them. And also: Has he heard all the stories people are telling about him and that she herself has been spreading among the women? Finally Jacob, tired of responding, lies down on top of her and enters her with force, then quickly slides off her, spent.

In the morning, Jacob smiles at her as they are eating. He notices that Hayah is always squinting, which has brought about a web of little wrinkles around her eyes. Elisha is planning to send her to Lwów, to Asher, who has moved there, and who is the best at matching eyes with reading glasses.

Hayah dresses modestly—only once has Jacob seen her in formal attire, on the first day of his studies here, when lots of people from the neighboring areas came to the Rohatyn beth midrash. For that she wore a light blue shawl over her gray dress and put earrings in her ears. She is serious and imperturbable.

Then he sees an unexpected scene of tenderness: her father raises his hand to stroke her face, and Hayah, in a calm, slow movement, lays her head against his chest, in the undulations of his lush, gray beard. Not even really knowing why, Jacob looks away in shame.

## Of Krysa and his plans for the future

Krysa, son of Nussen, has a scar on his face. One cheek is sliced from top to bottom by a straight line, which gives the impression of some sort of hidden symmetry, an impression so disturbing that anyone who sees him for the first time finds himself unable to take his eyes off him, until, seeking but not finding any order, he turns away in a disgust of which he may not even be entirely aware. Yet Krysa is the most intelligent person in Podolia, highly educated and prescient. At first glance you can't see that. And that is good for him.

He has learned that he cannot expect sympathy from others. He must specify exactly what he wants—ask, demand, negotiate. If it weren't for that scar on his face, it would be him in Jacob's place right now, this he knows for sure.

Krysa feels they ought to be independent within Christianity. That is his position now, before the disputation, and that is what he's aiming for as he carries on his misunderstanding-filled conversations with Bishop Dembowski behind his brothers' backs. Because Krysa is convinced he knows better.

"We have to keep our distance from everyone, be right on the edge and do our own thing," he says.

Not too Jewish, not too Christian, that would be the place for them, where they would be free from the control and greed of priests and rabbis alike. And furthermore: he believes that despite being persecuted by their own kind, by Jews, they nonetheless do not cease to be Jewish, even as they draw closer to Christians. They appeal, Krysa and the Jewish heretics, for support, protection, and care; they reach out with the gesture of a child, putting out an innocent hand to bring about an accord. The Christians accept them sympathetically.

Yet the most important thing for Krysa is not this, for as is written in Yevamot 63—and even though he is against the Talmud, he cannot keep from reading it—"Any man who does not have his own land is not a man." And so to receive from the lords a piece of land, to settle down and cultivate the land in relative tranquility—that would be the best thing for everyone. The Jews would no longer persecute them, the true believers would work their land every day, could engage peasants to work it, too. They wouldn't even have to be baptized. This vision unfurls over the table in the smoke-filled room, for as the wind blows it forces the air back down the chimney. Its howling echoes their discussion.

"Never under any lord," someone interjects, and Krysa recognizes Leyb Hershkowicz of Satanów in the darkness.

"Mrs. Kossakowska would take us in on her properties . . . ," Moshe from Podhajce starts.

Krysa lunges forward, his face contorted in anger.

"You want to tie the nooses around your own necks? The nobility will do with us whatever they please, and no laws can touch them. Two generations, and we'll be just like those peasants."

Some voice their agreement.

"With the bishop, too, we'll be like peasants," says Moshe.

Then Shorr's eldest son, Shlomo, who has until now sat motionless, staring at the tips of his boots, says:

"The only option is to go to the king, to take none but royal land, that's what Jacob says, and I agree with him. Under the king we'll be safe."

Krysa's face contorts again. He says:

"You're so stupid. A person extends a hand to folks like you, and you would yank them right down, wanting everything all at once. You have to bargain slowly."

"And create more problems than you bargained for," somebody snarls.

"You'll see, all of you. The bishop and I have an understanding."

# 16.

**Of the year 1757 and of the establishment
of certain age-old truths over the summer
at the Kamieniec Podolski disputation**

In Moliwda's settlement, near Craiova in Wallachia, people believe that
this year, 1757, is the year of the Last Judgment. The names of new angels
are invoked daily so that they will appear as witnesses. It has not occurred
to anyone that if they go on like this it may take many thousands of
years—an eternity—since the number of angels is infinite. Those who
pray believe the world can no longer be saved, that they must simply
prepare for the end, which is imminent. The Last Judgment is like childbirth: once it's under way, it can't be called off or put on hold. But the
brothers and sisters whom Moliwda has left behind for good also believe
that this judgment isn't as we might expect—it is not earthly, with angels'
trumpets, a great scale to weigh the deeds of men, and the archangel's
sword. Instead, it occurs almost unnoticeably, without extravagance. In
a sense it happens behind our backs and in our absence. We have been
judged in that strange year of 1757, in absentia and—this is certain—
without any possibility of appeal. Our human ignorance is no excuse.

Evidently the world has become unbearable not only on the vast, open
plains of Podolia, but here, too, in Wallachia, where it is warmer, where
there is the possibility of vineyards. It needed some sort of ending, some

resolution. Besides, war broke out last year. Yente, who sees everything, knows that this war will last for seven years and will tip the scales that measure human life. The shift is not yet noticeable, but the angels have begun their cleaning: they take the rug of the world in both hands and shake it out, letting the dust fly. Soon they'll roll it up again.

The rabbis are losing the debate in Kamieniec, badly, and this is because no one wants to listen to their convoluted explanations when the accusations are so simple and precise. Reb Krysa of Nadwórna becomes a hero when he manages to make a laughingstock of the Talmud. He stands and lifts a finger in the air.

"Why does the ox have a tail?" he asks.

The room falls silent, intrigued by the posing of such a stupid question.

"What kind of holy book is it that puts such questions to its readers?" Krysa goes on with that finger, which slowly turns toward the rabbis. "The Talmud!" he exclaims after a moment.

The room bursts out laughing. The sound rises to the ceiling of the courtroom, a space unaccustomed to such merry outbursts.

"And what might the Talmudic answer be?" asks Krysa, whose scarred face has flushed. After a pause, he answers his own question triumphantly: "Because it has to chase away the flies!"

There is more laughter.

The rabbis' demands—that the Contra-Talmudists be expelled from synagogue, that they be mandated some dress other than Jewish, and that they no longer be allowed to call themselves Jewish—also seem laughable now. The consistory court, with the gravity that is proper to it, dismisses their supplication, arguing that it simply is not competent to determine who can and who cannot call themselves Jewish.

When the matter of the Lanckoroń accusations is raised, the court avoids taking a stand. There was already an investigation, after all, and it discovered nothing sinful in singing and frolicking behind closed doors. Everyone has the right to pray as he wishes. And to dance with a woman, even if that woman bares her breasts. Besides, the investigation did not conclusively establish that there were any naked women there.

Then everyone's attention turns to the matter of the trial against the

Jewish forgers. One Leyb Gdalowicz and his journeyman Hashko Shlo-mowicz had been striking false coins. The journeyman is acquitted, but his boss is sentenced to be beheaded and quartered. The die that made the coins has already been ceremoniously burned and crumbled prior to the execution. In accordance with the sentence, the guilty man has his head cut off, and his body is quartered and nailed to the gallows. His head is nailed to a stake.

This trial did not help the rabbis. During the final days of the dispu-tation, they had to keep a low profile, stealing along pressed against the walls of houses, so universally had public favor turned against them.

The consistory court, too, had turned to secondary matters, one of them appalling to the Kamieniec Christians. Henshiya of Lanckoroń, a Jew who did business with peasants, had responded to a charge of having dealings with the Shabbitarians by telling his accuser, one Bazyl Knesh, that he could take the cross and stick it up his nethers. For this blas-phemy, Henshiya was sentenced to one hundred lashes, to be meted out in four different parts of the city, so that as many people as possible could view the punishment.

Gershon got the same punishment for having created such turmoil in Lanckoroń and starting all of this in the first place.

The consistory court and Bishop Dembowski also recommended that the holders of the properties where the Contra-Talmudists now found themselves extend their protection to the same.

This opinion was read out and instantly approved.

The court found the Contra-Talmudists innocent of all the calumnies against them and ordered the rabbis to pay 5,000 zlotys to cover the costs of the trial and to compensate those Contra-Talmudists who were beaten and robbed in skirmishes, and to be fined an additional 152 red zlotys for the repair of the church tower in Kamieniec. And the Talmud, that men-dacious and pernicious book, was to be burned throughout Podolia.

After the sentencing a silence fell, as though the Church side were aghast at its own severity, but when a translator conveyed the words of the sentence to the rabbis, cries and laments rose from their bench. They were ordered to calm down, for now they inspired only embarrassment, not sympathy. They had only themselves to blame. They left the court in righteous silence, muttering under their breath.

Moliwda, elated to have returned to his country, also feels that everything has changed. Sometimes it amuses him that he can foresee a certain thing, and then he looks into the sky; there seems to be more of it on these lowlands, and it works like a mirror lens, gathering up image after image into itself, reflecting the earth as a fresco, where everything happens simultaneously and the tracks of future events can be followed. Any person who knows how to look can simply raise his eyes to the sky. There he will see all.

When Jacob and Nahman came to talk him into going back to Poland, he wasn't even surprised. Out of politeness, he feigned hesitation. But the truth is, the sight of Jacob jumping off his horse with panache, in his typically Turkish way, awoke in Moliwda some sudden, boyish joy at the thought of the perilous new adventure to come.

## Of burning books

The Talmuds begin to burn that very same day, October 14, in the evening. Those carrying out the sentences find they don't have to exert themselves too much. Only the first pile, the one in Kamieniec, is formally ignited by the local hangman after a reading of the order signed by Bishop Dembowski. From then on, things run their course.

In most cases, a small crowd breaks into a Jewish home and gets its hands on some book. All of these "talmutes," with their impure pages, written in that twisted alphabet that goes from right to left, are instantly tossed out onto the street, where they get kicked into a heap, which then gets set on fire. The Sabbatians themselves, the Jewish heretics, are exceptionally eager to help the officials, who, being thus relieved of their duties, may go home and have their dinners. And then the goyim and the young men always looking for trouble join in with the Sabbatians. Books burn throughout Lwów, where every square of any significance has its own book burning, whether Talmudic or not. These fires are still smoldering the next day, and then in the evening they blaze back up again with the addition of new books. Now, all printed matter seems sinister, and even Lwów's Christians begin to hide their books and barricade their printing presses, just in case. Over the course of only a few days, all this burning so emboldens everyone that the Kamieniec Jews, who have made this town home, irrespective of the law, have once more begun to move on with all of their belongings, this time to Karvasary, fearing for their lives. The sight of the burning books, their pages fluttering in the flames, draws people in, arrays them in a circle, like a magician at a fair who has ordered chickens to do as he says. People gaze into the flames and find they like this theater of destruction, and a free-floating anger mounts within them, although they don't know whom to turn it on—but their outrage more or less automatically makes them hostile to the owners of these ruined books. Now one whoop would suffice to send the frenzied crowd into the nearest Jewish residence that the Contra-Talmudist guards, hoping to prevent the plunder of their own homes, might direct them toward.

Those who were only recently considered wretched, sinful, and accursed have now become legislators and enforcers. And vice versa, those who formerly judged and instructed now find themselves judged and instructed. The rabbi's place is no longer the home of a rabbi, but a public house that all can enter, opening the door with the force of their feet. Inside, you pay no mind to shrieks of protest and instead proceed directly to the place you know books are usually kept, often in a glass case, and you pull them out one by one and then eviscerate them, holding them by their covers like chickens before they are boiled.

Some woman, often the oldest one in the house, throws herself in front of the books in desperation as though defending a weird, disabled grandchild who has been reduced to these paper dimensions, but the rest of the household is afraid to oppose the violence, evidently knowing already that the capricious forces of the world have switched sides, for who knows how long. Sometimes the women make their way to one of the ringleaders, and sometimes he's a cousin misguided by the Sabbatian idea, and they take his hand and try desperately to catch his eye: "Itzele, what are you doing? Your mother and I used to play together down by the river!" The elders mutter from the corner: "Your hand will wither and drop off for this sacrilege."

In Busk there aren't so many Talmuds to burn, given how few Talmudists are left here. Most people are followers of Sabbatai. A little fire burns behind the synagogue, but it burns badly, smoking, since the books fell into a puddle and now don't seem to want to catch fire. They don't have the same determination here. Those doing the burning act as if they're carrying out a sentence; a bottle of vodka makes its way around the fire. Young goyim try to get in on the auto-da-fé—throwing anything on flames always appeals to them, even if they don't really know what's happening. But they have already heard that this is some internal matter of the Jews', so now they stand around with their hands in the pockets of their linen trousers and just gaze into the blaze.

The worst of it occurs in Kamieniec, Rohatyn, and Lwów. In these places, blood is spilled. In Lwów a madding crowd burns the whole of a Jewish library collected in a house of prayer. The windows are shattered, the pews wrecked.

The following day the riots worsen—come afternoon, the unconstrained crowd, no longer only Jewish but mixed, colorful, wild, cannot distinguish between the Talmud and other books. All that matters is that a book be filled with those bizarre letters, inherently hostile since illegible. This crowd, which has gathered for the next day's market in Rohatyn, feels empowered to enact violence against books, and unleashes a boisterous, delighted frenzy, setting out on a hunt. People stand at the entrances of homes and demand that books be handed over, like hostages. If a homeowner is deemed to be hiding something, they strike. Blood is shed, hands and arms are broken, teeth are bashed out of mouths.

Meanwhile, outraged by the lost disputation, the rabbis have called for prayer and strict fasting, the kind of fast that has mothers refraining from breastfeeding their babies. In Lwów, Rapaport has a room for writing letters, and work there buzzes by candlelight until morning. Rabbi Rapaport himself is lying down; he was beaten in front of the synagogue, and it's hard for him to breathe; some fear that he has broken ribs. Pinkas cries while writing out copies of letters. It certainly seems as if the end of the world is approaching, with this latest catastrophe under way, and this one is the most painful, for now people are inflicting pain on their own kind. How is it possible, how could God be putting us through such a horrendously painful trial—how can it not be a Cossack, not some wild Tatar lying in wait for our lives, but our own, our neighbors, a person with whose father or grandfather we used to play as children? They speak our language, live in our towns, and force their way into our temples, though we don't want them there. When a people turns against itself, it means the sin of Israel is great, and God is very angry.

After a few days, when Rabbi Rapaport has more or less recovered, the representatives of the kahalim assemble and mount another fundraising campaign. The money must be conveyed to Warsaw, to the great Yavan, Brühl's confidant, though evidently this is a bad time to bother the king with book burning—there is a war on, after all—since no answer is forthcoming.

## Of Father Pikulski's explanation to the nobles of the rules of gematria

Jerzy Marcin Lubomirski is the commander of a garrison in Kamieniec Podolski, quite a tiresome little town, far removed from the rest of the world—this is his first command post. He is twenty, tall, handsome, and—even apart from any of these happy physical traits—he has yet another advantage: he is heir to an enormous fortune. This lends him great distinction—everyone recognizes him right away, and then can't take their eyes off him. Kamieniec is situated within his vast landholdings. Ever since such extraordinary things have started happening here, ever since this crowd has come out onto the previously empty streets, the prince has felt excited and satisfied at last. He is in constant need of new impressions, just as he needs refreshment. To the farewell dinner for Mikołaj Dembowski, on his advancement to archbishop, he brings half a dozen crates of the finest Rhine wine.

Once the first of these has been consumed, they begin to talk about the latest happenings, and Prince Lubomirski's attention turns to the inconspicuous Father Pikulski, the archbishop's right hand, whose task is to enlighten the nobility on Jewish questions, which are by nature murky and convoluted. Everyone wants to understand what this Jewish fuss is all about.

"There is some consolation in the Jew," Bishop Kajetan Sołtyk pipes up, after barely managing to swallow a big bite of black pudding. He has gained weight recently. Everything about him seems exaggerated. The color of his vestments is too garish, his cuffs too starched, the chain on his chest too shiny. Pleased to have redirected everyone's attention to himself, he continues: "The Jew looks after money and puts in his own as necessary. He is clever and eager to make his own gains, which makes him greedy on behalf of his master, as well. When I want to buy or sell something, I always summon a Jew. He'll have his arrangements with all the merchants in this country. A Jew always knows how to do business. It's in his interest for me to be his client, and that means he will always treat me in such a way that I feel quite sure he's not cheating me and will render me the best service possible. There's no serious lord and landholder around here without Israelites in his service. Is it not so, Castellan Kossakowski?"

Mrs. Kossakowska responds on behalf of her husband:

"Everyone knows Your Excellency was not created to handle matters of agriculture or business. This is precisely why we have administrators. The risk is that when they aren't honest, they may steal. It is simply staggering to think of it."

The topic of theft so moves everyone—and the wine really is quite excellent—that the discussion now fragments into many smaller ones, and everyone begins to converse with everyone else, across the table; the peasants serving them refill their wine, and at a discreet sign from Archbishop Dembowski, they imperceptibly switch the cases and begin to pour a wine of lesser quality, though no one seems to notice.

"What is this Kabbalah everyone is talking about?" Katarzyna Kossakowska inquires of Father Pikulski. "Even my husband has taken some interest."

"They believe the world was created from the word," responds the priest, swallowing loudly and setting down on his plate the sizable forkful of beef that had just been traveling to his mouth.

"Well, yes, everyone believes that: In the beginning was the Word. We believe that, too. So where's the heresy?"

"Yes, Your Ladyship, but we leave it at that sentence, whereas they apply it to even the smallest thing."

The priest responds with evident reluctance. It isn't clear why—he, too, is surprised by it. Could it simply be that in his opinion it is not worthwhile to discuss with a woman such complex matters, which she will no doubt be unable to understand, even being relatively educated? Or perhaps because such questions tend to require he simplify things, regardless of his interlocutors. The bishop is a bishop, but even he requires slow and careful teaching, for he is hardly the cleverest of men. He is undoubtedly a holy man and it is not for me to judge, Pikulski mentally upbraids himself—but sometimes it is hard to talk with him.

He asks for a piece of paper and a pen so he can explain it to them visually, and then he lays it all out between the plates. The bishop encourages him by pushing away the platter with the roast goose and sliding his chair back, turning things over to Pikulski, and giving a significant glance to Kossakowska, for he knows that this unremarkable little priest has hidden strengths, reserves into which he's now reaching, but as though with a little teaspoon, not wishing to betray himself by revealing the huge vats he has at his disposal.

"Every letter has its numerical equivalent. *Aleph* is one, *bet* two, *gimel* three, and so on. That means that every word made up of letters also renders a number." He looks at them inquiringly, to check whether they are following. "Words with the same numerical values are tied to one another by some deep meaning, even if on the surface it seems there is no connection between them. You can count with words, perform arithmetic with them, and all kinds of interesting things can happen."

Father Pikulski does not know if he should end on this, if this might be sufficient, but he can't help himself: "Let us take the following example," he says. "'Father' in Hebrew is 'av.' We write that this way: *alef, bet,* from right to left. 'Mother' is 'em,' or *alef, mem.* But the word 'mother'—'em'—can also be read as 'im.' 'Av,' 'father,' has a numerical value of three, because *alef* is one, and *bet* is two. 'Mother' has a value of forty-one, because *alef* is one, and *mem* is forty. Now: if we add the two words up, 'mother' and 'father,' then we get forty-four—the same value as 'yeled,' which means 'child'!"

Kossakowska, who has been leaning over the priest's hands, jumps back in her chair, clapping.

"How wonderful!" she declares.

*Yod, lamed, dalet,* writes Father Pikulski on the bishop's paper, and gazes down at it in triumph.

Bishop Sołtyk doesn't really follow, and these numbers are already confusing him. He is wheezing. He needs to lose weight. Archbishop Dembowski, meanwhile, raises his eyebrows, a sign that this might be of interest to him in the future.

"According to the Kabbalah, when a man has carnal relations with a woman, their alphabets meet, and it is these alphabets, in intermingling, that occasion the conception of a child."

Archbishop Dembowski coughs delicately once, twice, and then goes back to eating.

"Kabbalah or no," Katarzyna Kossakowska says, her cheeks pink from the wine, "something unprecedented in the world is happening among us now. Thousands of Jews are wanting to convert to the Catholic faith. They are cozying up to us like chicks to a mother hen, poor and exhausted by their own Jewishness—"

"You are mistaken," Father Pikulski interrupts her, clearing his throat out of embarrassment; Kossakowska looks at him, startled by this intrusion into her train of thought. "They have much to gain from it. They have long looked at our country as a shiny new promised land . . ."

"You really have to watch their hands at all times," adds Bishop Sołtyk.

". . . they're now executing a sentence to do with their Talmud, but the sentence ought to be carried out against all their books. The Kabbalah is a certain type of dangerous superstition that really should be banned. It teaches a way of worshipping God that is pure heresy. It allegedly also teaches how to predict the future and promotes the performance of magic. Kabbalah definitely comes not from God, but from Satan."

"You exaggerate, Father." Now Kossakowska is the one to interrupt. "And even if it were to have the stench of sulfur, regardless, soon they will all find another kind of life in the lap of the Church. That's why we're all here, after all, to help these lost souls when they declare their best intentions."

Prince Jerzy Marcin Lubomirski eats his blood pudding; it's the best thing they've served at this dinner. The meat is tough, and the rice is overcooked again. The cabbage gives off a strange, musty smell. His interlocutors are old and boring. He doesn't know anything about Jews, whom he has only ever seen from afar. Only once has he had a more intimate acquaintance with one, one of the girls who is always orbiting the garrison, whores of every stripe and nation, so that the soldiers may pick their type and color.

## Of newly appointed Archbishop Dembowski, who is preparing for a journey

Waiting for his packing trunks, which might arrive at any moment, ready to set off at once for Lwów to assume the archbishopric, the bishop takes another good look at the sets of underwear he has had sewn and then had the women embellish with his monogram: *MD*, Mikołaj Dembowski.

The monograms are embroidered in purple silk thread. And the silk stockings he requested have been sent from abroad, Bishop Dembowski having long since given up on the local linen ones. There are white stockings as well as purple ones that are the same shade as his monogram and that also feature stitching around their delicate cuffs. He has something brand-new, too: long underwear, made of delicate wool, which scratches him a little around the hips but provides him with the warmth of which he has been so desirous.

It would seem that he is pleased. Who knows whether his subtle attempts at the archbishopric might not have been reevaluated in light of recent events—so many poor people, cast out by their own, humiliated, yet feeling the merciful heart of Jesus Christ palpable and near. The bishop will not let the matter rest until this whole Jewish multitude is baptized. It would be a great miracle for all of Europe, perhaps the dawn of a new era. He inspects the books that have been readied for the trunks, and his gaze falls upon a volume just bound in fresh leather. He knows what this is. Smiling, he picks it up, flips through it, and lands on this little ditty:

> *What is wrong with Poland?*
> *Wrong are the roads and the rulers of Poland,*
> *Wrong are the bridges, narrow and broad,*
> *Wrong the countless people who have been spared the rod.*

The bishop smiles to himself, touched by the poem's naiveté. If only Father Chmielowski had as much wisdom as zeal! After a little consideration, he adds this book, with its beautiful binding, to the pile with the rest.

On the last night before his planned departure, Bishop Dembowski goes to bed in his castle in Czarnokozińce quite late, his hand numb from writing letters (all attempting to organize Jewish questions, including a letter to the king that urges him to support this noble campaign). He awakens in the middle of the night drenched in sweat, somehow very stiff, his neck like solid wood, his head aching. He dreamed of something awful, but he can't quite remember what it was. Some sort of trampling, a violence, such sharp edges, the sound of fabric being torn, cracks, a guttural babbling of which he understands not a word. As he lies in the darkness, still trembling with fear, he tries to reach his hand out to ring for a servant, but he feels he cannot move, that the hand that spent the whole day writing letters—his own hand—will not obey him now. That is impossible, he thinks, terrified. This is a dream. An animal panic overwhelms him.

He notices an unusual smell, and with intensifying terror, he realizes he's wet himself. He wants to move but he cannot; this is exactly what he dreamed of—that he could not move. He wants to cry out for a servant, but his lungs will not obey—they don't have the strength to take in any air or to let him make the slightest whimper. He lies motionless until morning, on his back, his breathing fast as a rabbit's. He starts to pray, but since his prayers arise from fear, they break off, and then the bishop doesn't even know what he is saying. He feels as if some invisible figure has come and sat on his breast, some phantom, and if he cannot dislodge it, this phantom will kill him. He tries to calm down and settle back into his body, feel an arm, a leg, sense his stomach, tighten his buttocks, move his finger. But he quickly retreats, for nothing remains there. All that is left is his hand, as though it hangs in an absolute vacuum. The whole time he feels like he is falling, and he has to hold on to the sconce with his eyes; the sconce is high up in the bishop's bedroom in Czarnokozińce, hanging over the trunks he's packed. Thus he remains, in mortal terror.

In the morning a servant finds him, and a big fuss is raised. The medics let his blood; it flows black and thick, and their faces reveal mounting concern.

After his blood is let, the bishop's condition improves somewhat. He starts to move his fingers and his head. Faces bend over him, saying something, asking, looking on in sadness and in sympathy. But they just depress him, they're made up of too many different parts, so that his head spins, and he's dizzy and nauseated—eyes, mouth, nose, wrinkles, ears, moles, warts, there's just too much, it's unbearable, and his eyes flit back up to the sconce. He seems to know that someone's hands are touching him, but all he can feel is the absolute estrangedness of his own body. People stand over him, but he cannot understand their conversations. He catches a word here and there, but he can't hold on to any, as they don't create sentences or meaning. The people leave, and then there is only a candle. In the near-darkness the bishop would very much like for someone to hold his hand; what he wouldn't give for the warm, rough interior of anyone's hand . . .

When the candle goes out, for his caretakers are sleeping, he starts to writhe and scream—or rather, he feels like he is screaming, but in reality he can't get any sound out—so frightened is he of the dark.

The next day his brother comes. Oh yes, he recognizes him: although he does not look upon his face, he hears his voice. He knows that it is he and this brings him relief, so he falls asleep, but there, in his dreams, it is the same as when he is awake. In his dreams he is lying in the same place and has the same terror of darkness. His brother goes away. In the evening his mind begins to generate images. He is in Kamieniec, near his house, near the cathedral, but instead of standing on the ground, he's hanging in midair, at the height of the edge of the roof. He sees that pigeons have nested in the eaves, but their nest is empty save for some broken old eggshells. Then he sees a bright, luminous statue of the Virgin Mary set atop a tall column, the statue he recently blessed, and for a moment the fear subsides, but the instant he looks at the river and beholds the great bulk of the fortress, it returns. He feels on him the indifferent gaze of countless eyes peering from the void, as if millions of people were awaiting him there.

He sees books burning, swelling from the heat and then cracking like potatoes in the flames. But before the flames can lick the white off those pages, the letters, like ants or other speedy little creatures, escape in droves, in strings, and vanish into the darkness. Bishop Dembowski sees them very clearly and is not at all surprised that the letters are alive, some of them scampering on tiny pin-like legs, while others, legless—the simplest letters—either hop or slither. The bishop has no idea what they are called, but this flight of theirs is moving to him, and he leans into them almost tenderly until he sees that none remain, that all that is burning are blank pages.

Then Bishop Dembowski loses consciousness. It does not help to let his blood.

That evening, he dies.

The doctors and those watching over the bishop—his secretary and his closest colleague, Father Pikulski—are utterly dumbfounded by his passing. How can it be? He was in good health. No, he wasn't in good health, he had problems with his blood, which circulated too slowly, was too thick, which is why he died. But he never complained of any ailment. Maybe he just didn't mention it when something was wrong. All he ever said was that he was cold. But that's not a reason for a person to die. And so a decision is made to delay the announcement of his death. For now they just sit there in that big house, not knowing what to do. That same day, the rest of the underwear he ordered arrives, and the trunks for his manuscripts are brought. This happens on November 17, 1757.

## Of the life of dead Yente in the winter of 1757, also known as the year the Talmud was burned, followed by the books of those who burned the Talmud

An event like the archbishop's death is singular and will never be repeated. Every situation and everything that creates it can happen only once. All the individual elements converge for one performance only, just as actors invited to appear will play their roles, although whatever gesture, crossing of the stage, or brief, rushed dialogue will, if taken out of context, instantly slip into the absurd.

And yet it does create a certain chain of events in which we must trust because we have nothing else. If you look at it from very close up, as Yente sees things now, you can see all those bridges, hinges, gears, and bolts, and all the minor instruments that link distinct, singular, and unique events. It is these that form the underpinnings of the world, these that transport this or that word over into events in the vicinity, these that reproduce some gesture or facial expression many times in other contexts, rhythmically, these that bring into contact time after time the same objects or the same people, these that launch the phantom trains of thought between things that are naturally strangers.

All this is clearly visible from where Yente is now; everything can be seen flickering and ceaselessly transforming—how beautifully it pulsates. Nothing can be grasped in its entirety because it has already passed away, disintegrated into particles, and immediately created a completely new and equally fleeting pattern, though the previous one seemed to make sense a second ago, or looked lovely, or was amazing. When you try to follow any human figure, she or he changes, so that it would be hard to be certain, even for a moment, that it is still the same person. This one, for instance, was a grimy child, fragile as a wafer, just a moment ago, but is now a tall, sturdy woman who steps out of a house and in one fell swoop has tossed out the dirty liquid from a bucket. The wash water wrecks the white of the snow and leaves yellow stains across its surface.

Only Yente is unchanging, only Yente can repeat and can keep going back to the same place. She can be trusted.

The news of Bishop Dembowski's death spreads before Hanukkah and Christmas; this news, woeful for some, is a source of joy for others. It is surprising, like someone taking a knife to a patiently woven kilim. So many maneuvers in vain! Another bit of news journeys fast on the heels of that one, reaching Korolówka alongside the snowstorm: as soon as the protector of the true believers died, the rabbis reared their heads again and reinitiated their persecution, so that those whose Talmuds were just being burned are now burning the books of their erstwhile persecutors. As for Jacob Frank, it appears he is under arrest behind the thickest possible walls. Those in Korolówka gaze at one another grimly. By the evening of the day after the news reaches them, they sit together in Israel's shed, and it's hard for them to keep themselves from swapping whispers. Soon their voices grow resounding.

"This is the struggle of greater forces . . ."

"It was the same with Sabbatai. They put him in prison, too . . ."

"That's how it has to be. Imprisonment is part of the plan . . ."

"This had to happen, and now everything will start . . ."

"These are the last days . . ."

"This is the end."

The snow falls on the roads and covers everything around, and even the cemetery and the matzevot disappear beneath an impenetrable whiteness. Wherever you look, there is just snow and more snow. By some miracle, a merchant from Kamieniec manages to make it over these massive tracts of snow all the way to their village. He doesn't even have the strength to unharness his horses. He just squints, his eyes blinded by the frost on his lashes. He says:

"Jacob isn't in prison. He got away from Rohatyn and went straight to

Czernowitz—that's in Turkey. He is with his wife and children in Giurgiu, and he's even—or so people say—setting up some business there."

In a startlingly sad voice, someone says:

"He has abandoned us."

It certainly would seem that way. He has left Poland behind, a dark and gloomy country in spite of the snowy white that covers it. There is no longer a place for him here.

At first they listen to the messenger in disbelief, but soon their disbelief turns to anger, not toward Jacob, who escaped, but rather with themselves, because they should have known how things were going to turn out. The worst is the realization that nothing is ever going to change now. The excrement of the horse standing in front of Israel's home steams in the frost, ruining the clean white sheet of snow, a sad proof of the weakness of all of creation; it rapidly transforms into a frozen lump of matter.

"God has released us from him and from the many temptations he represented," says Sobla, going into the house, where she bursts into tears. She cries all evening. No one knows why she's crying—she didn't even like Jacob, his noisy retinue, those conceited lady guardians, shifty Nahman. She never believed a single word they said, and their teachings made her afraid.

Israel scolds her. But once they are lying under the goose-down duvet, breathing in the damp smell of feathers collected from several generations of geese, he awkwardly tries to hold her to him.

"I feel like I'm in prison . . . My whole life is a prison," Sobla sobs, taking a lot of air into her lungs, but she is unable to say anything more. Israel doesn't say anything, either.

Then an even more astonishing piece of news comes to them—that over there in Turkey, Jacob has converted to the Muslim religion. Now Israel, too, sinks into a chair, overcome. His mother is the one to remind him that it was the same with the First, Sabbatai. Did he not don a turban? Is this not also in the design for salvation? Their speculations go into the night. For some, this is an act of cowardice, an unimaginable act. For others, it is a clever political move. No one believes that Jacob really became a follower of Muhammad.

Even the most bizarre, most frightening thing can start to seem natural, familiar, when it becomes a part of the plan. This is what Israel says. He's now in the lumber trade with Christians. He buys newly hewn trees from the forest from the local lord, then sells them onward. With the donations given to Yente he's been able to purchase a well-built cart and two strong horses—powerful assets. Sometimes, as he is waiting for a load, he squats down with the lumberjacks and they smoke a pipe together. He has especially good talks with the magnate's administrator, who has some idea of the mysteries of religion and other such things, unlike the lumberjacks. It is after one such conversation with the administrator that Israel discovers that the death of Jesus, the Christian Messiah, was also a part of God's plan. Jesus had to be crucified, for otherwise the action of salvation could not have gotten under way. It is strange, but in some twisted way, it does make sense. Israel thinks about it for a long time, struck by the similarity to Sabbatai Tzvi, who had to let himself be imprisoned, had to put on a turban and be willing to go into exile. The Messiah has to fall as low as possible, otherwise he isn't the Messiah. Israel returns with a heavy cart but a light heart.

The flow of pilgrims into Sobla and Israel's yard has stopped completely now. People have begun to fear public miracles; better if they take place concealed somewhere. But Pesel and Freyna do not come to see Yente any less often, although Pesel is preparing for her wedding, the engagement ceremony having just taken place; the boy, like her, is thirteen years old. She saw him twice, and he struck her as pleasant, if a bit immature. She and her sister are embroidering tablecloths now; Freyna will be getting married soon enough, in any case. Sometimes Pesel, when it was still warm, would bring her sewing to her grandmother's, as she calls Yente, and work near her. She would tell her all kinds of stories, confide her plans. That she would like, for example, to live in a big city and be a great lady. Have her own carriage and dresses embellished with lace, and a small silk bag where she would keep a perfumed handkerchief, because she doesn't really know what else a person would keep in such a little bag. Now, however, it is too cold. Her fingers get so frozen they can no longer maneuver the needles. The dewdrops on Yente's body transform into ice crystals, tiny and gorgeous. Pesel discovered this. She would pick them up on her finger, and before they melted, she would take them up to the window, into the sunlight. For a moment, she would behold those miracles. Whole palaces of crystals, whiter than the snow, glittering with glass, chandeliers, cut-glass chalices . . .

"Where did you see all that? In a snowflake?" Freyna wonders. But one day she carefully takes a snowflake onto her fingertip and looks at it under the sun. It is a miracle, exceptionally large, almost the size of a small coin like a grosz. Its crystal beauty disappears in a flash, a beauty not of this world, and thus destroyed by human warmth. But thanks to this one brief instant, it is possible to glimpse that other, higher world, to reassure yourself that it is there.

How is it possible that the frost doesn't get the better of Yente? Israel checks a couple of times, especially in the mornings, when the trees are cracking from the cold. But Yente is barely even cool. Frost settles on her lashes and brows. Sometimes Sobla comes, too, covers herself up with sheepskin and dozes off.

"We can't bury you, Grandma," Pesel says to Yente. "But we can't keep you here. Papa says that the times have gotten very troubled, and no one knows what will happen tomorrow."

"Or if there will even be a tomorrow," adds her sister.

"The end of the world is coming. We are afraid," says Sobla, who is shaken. She thinks Grandma Yente's eyelids are moving—they are, they really are, she can hear them. "What are we to do? Is this one of those hopeless causes you seem to be able to help with? Help us." Sobla holds her breath so that she won't miss even the tiniest sign. But there is nothing.

Sobla is afraid. It would be better not to have the grandmother of that cursed and Turkified Jacob in their barn. It invites disaster. When she found out they had imprisoned him, she had felt a sort of satisfaction—that's where you belong, Jacob, for wanting more than your fair share. You always sat yourself upon the highest branch, you always wanted to be better than everyone. Now you'll end up in a dungeon. Yet when she found out he was safe in Giurgiu, she felt relief. Before, so much had seemed possible, and now the cold and darkness had come back. In October the light retired past the shed and no longer peeked into the yard. The cold would scoot under the stones for the duration of the summer, but it would come back— it would always come back.

Before she falls asleep, Sobla remembers the stories about the cave— how Jacob, back when he was little Yankiele, took such a liking to that place. And how he went missing there when he was a child.

She was a child then, too, and she knew Jacob well, and she was always afraid of him, because he was so rough-and-tumble. They used to play war: some of the children would be Turks, while the others would be Moskals. One time Jacob, as a Moskal or as a Turk, Sobla can't remember, went berserk, fighting with such fury that he couldn't stop, beating another boy within an inch of his life with his wooden sword. Sobla remembers that his father later beat him bloody for it, too.

Now, with her eyes closed, she sees the entrance to the cave—she has never been inside. That place scares her. There is something strange about it: the trees are greener there, and the silence is so frightening, and the ground beneath the birch trees is completely covered in bear's garlic. The bear's garlic is harvested and given to people when they get sick. It always helps. No one knows how big the cave is, but they say it extends for miles underground and is shaped like an enormous *alef*; they say there is a whole city under there. In it live hobgoblins and the limping bałakaben who keep their treasures there . . .

Suddenly Sobla stands, the blanket falling from her shoulders to the ground. She says:

"The cave!"

## Of Asher Rubin's adventures with light, and his grandfather's with a wolf

News of the earthquake in Lisbon reached Lwów last year. News, in general, takes a while to spread. What Asher discovered in a pamphlet illustrated with engravings is horrific. He looks at it over and over, dozens of times, so shaken he cannot look away. What he sees are scenes that might as well be from the Final Judgment. He can't really think about anything else.

The pamphlet tells of piles of corpses, and Asher tries to imagine how many a hundred thousand could be—it's more than the population of Lwów, so you would have to add in the surrounding villages and towns, and summon everyone, Christians and Jews, Ruthenians and Armenians, women and men, the elderly, animals, innocent cows, the dogs around the hovels. How many is a hundred thousand?

Later, however, when he has calmed down a bit, he thinks that after all this is nothing so extraordinary. Maybe no one counted up the victims of Khmelnytsky—those villages, those towns, those nobles' heads cut off and rolling around the grounds of their estates, Jewish women with their stomachs split open. Somewhere he heard that they had hanged a Polish nobleman, a Jew, and a dog together. Nonetheless Asher had never seen engravings such as these, with scenes that defy the human imagination captured in pictures etched meticulously onto metal plates. This particular image takes root in his brain: he sees the depths of the sea storming the city. It looks like a war between the elements: the earth defending itself against water with fire, but the element of water is more powerful; wherever the waves strike, they extinguish all life, destroying and erasing everything. The ships look like duck feathers on a pond, and people are all but

invisible in this Armageddon, what is happening is not happening on a human scale. With one exception—in a boat in the foreground stands a man, no doubt a noble, for he is wearing lovely clothes, holding up his hands, folded in prayer, to the heavens.

Asher gazes with malicious satisfaction at the desperation of this man, noting the absence of the heavens in the picture. A sky reduced to a thin strip over the battlefield. After all, how could heavens be shown here?

Asher has lived for four years in Lwów, practicing medicine, healing eyes. He works with one particular lens grinder to provide glasses to those who cannot see. He learned some of it in Italy, but it is really here that he has been developing his skills and knowledge. He brought along a book that has made a great impression upon him. One passage in particular could be said to be the real foundation of his studies, a guiding principle of sorts: "And I saw," writes its author, one Newton, an Englishman, "that the light, tending to [one] end of the Image, did suffer a Refraction considerably greater than the light tending to the other. And so the true cause of the length of that Image was detected to be no other, than that *Light*

consists of *Rays differently re-frangible*, which, without any respect to a difference in their incidence, were, according to their degrees of refrangibility, transmitted towards divers parts of the wall."

Asher's father was a Kabbalist whose primary area of interest was light, although he was also the leaseholder of two tiny villages on the estates of Prince Radziwiłł in Lithuania. Thus the leases fell to Asher's mother, whose operations were orderly and strict. The village where they lived and kept an inn lay on the Neman River. In addition to several farmsteads, there was also a watermill and a small port with a depot for the ships that sailed in the direction of the Prussian Königsberg. This lease was quite lucrative, and, since his mother had a real gift for administering it, and a strong sense of responsibility, the family earned a good deal of money thanks to hazakah, the traditional Jewish system—far more than they would have under arenda, the traditional Slavic system.

Asher's father was rich in comparison with all the impoverished Jews around them, and thanks to this (as well as help from the kahal) he was in due course able to send his gifted son abroad for his education. He himself lived modestly, however, not trusting innovations, never favoring excess. For him the best-case scenario was that nothing would ever change. Asher remembers how rough his father's hands used to get when he had to do some work around the estate. His skin would crack, and if any dirt made its way inside those cracks, it would give rise to a festering wound. His mother would smear goose fat over those places, and afterward he couldn't touch his books. Asher's father and Asher's uncle were like Jacob and Esau, until finally the uncle moved out to Podolia, where Asher later sought him out, and where he eventually settled down.

Both Poles and Ruthenians lived in the area, and the inn kept by Asher's mother was beloved by all. Their house was very welcoming, and whenever any Jew would come up the road, rich or poor, Asher's mother would greet him with a glass of vodka. The table was always set, and there was always enough food.

A certain Orthodox priest used to come to his mother's inn, a slothful man who could barely read or write, but a drinker of the most dedicated sort. He came within a hair's breadth of bringing about the death of Asher's father, and if he had, the fate of the family might have taken a completely different direction.

This priest would spend whole days at the inn with the peasants, not doing a thing but causing trouble for anyone he could. He would always ask for his tab to be calculated, and yet he would never pay. Eventually, Asher's old man had had enough, and he cut off the priest's vodka. But this so enraged the priest that he decided to get revenge.

Asher's father often illegally purchased wolf pelts from poachers. Among these were some peasants and some petty gentry, along with the occasional brave vagabond. Legally, hunting for forest game was the exclusive privilege of the lord. One night, a hunter from whom Asher's father sometimes purchased the pelts came and knocked on the door of the family's house. He told Asher's father that he had a great specimen, which he took from his cart and deposited on the ground. The old man wanted to take a good look at the dead wolf to appraise its pelt, but it was dark and late, and the poacher was in a hurry, so he just paid him, put the sack aside, and went back to bed.

Not long after this, there was a pounding at the door, and some guards came bursting in. They took an immediate interest in the bag and Asher's father suspected that he was about to be fined for buying poached animals. But you can imagine his horror when it turned out that the body inside the sack was human.

He was shackled immediately and thrown into a dark cell. A trial got under way at once, with the priest accusing Asher's father of having murdered the man himself in order to drain his blood and use it to make matzah, as the Jews were so often accused of doing. Despair took hold of everyone, but Asher's father, a worshipper of sparks of light even in the deepest darkness, did not confess when he was tortured, pleading instead for the hunter to be interrogated. At first the hunter denied everything, but when he was tortured, too, he confessed to having found a drowned man in the water and taken him to the priest to be buried, poor soul. The priest, however, talked him into leaving the body at the Jew's, which was what the hunter did. For this, the court sentenced him to be whipped. Asher's father was set free, but the priest received no punishment.

Asher has learned that people have a powerful need to feel superior to others. It doesn't matter who they are—they have to find someone who's beneath them. Who is better and who is worse depends on a vast array of random traits. Those with light-colored eyes consider themselves to be above those with dark-colored eyes. The dark-eyed, meanwhile, look down on the light-eyed. Those who live near the forest's edge feel superior to those living in the open on the ponds, and vice versa. The peasants feel superior to the Jews, and the Jews feel superior to the peasants. Townspeople think they're better than the inhabitants of villages, and people from villages treat city people as though they were somehow worse.

Isn't this the very glue that holds the human world together? Isn't this why we need other people, to give us the pleasure of knowing we are better than they are? Amazingly, even those who seem to be the worst-off take, in their humiliation, a perverse satisfaction in the fact that no one has it worse than they do. Thus they have still, in some sense, won.

Where does this all come from? Asher wonders. Can man not be repaired? If he were a machine, as some now argue, it would suffice to adjust one little lever slightly, or to tighten some small screw, and people would start to take pleasure in treating one another as equals.

## Of the Polish princess in Asher Rubin's house

A child has been born in Asher's home, and his name is Samuel. In his mind, Asher calls him "my son."

They cohabit without any kind of marriage. Asher pretends that Gitla is his servant—she has barely left the house, in any case, and when she has, she's only gone to market. Asher lives and treats his patients on Ruska Street, in the Christian district, but from his windows he can also see the Turei Zahav Synagogue. On Saturday afternoons, as Shabbat is finishing and the Shemoneh Esreh, the eighteen blessings, are being given, the fervent words reach Asher's ears.

He closes the window. He barely understands that language anymore. He speaks Polish and Italian, and some German. He would like to learn French. When Jewish patients come to him, he speaks to them in Yiddish. He also uses Latin terms.

Lately he's been noticing a real epidemic of cataracts; one in three patients who come to him has them. People don't take care of their eyes, they look directly into the light, and that opacifies their eyeballs, congeals them so they're like the whites of hard-boiled eggs. So Asher has imported from Germany special glasses with tinted lenses, which he himself wears, though they make him look like a blind man.

Gitla, the Polish princess, bustles about in the kitchen. He would rather his patients take her for some relative than a servant, since the servant's role clearly does not suit her, makes her stomp around and slam the doors. Asher hasn't so much as touched her, though it's several months since she gave birth. She cries sometimes in the room he has given her, and rarely does she go out into the yard, even though the sun, like bright thin paper, has now drawn out from every recess all the damp darkness and moldy sadness of wintertime.

When she's in a good mood, which is rare, Gitla looks over his shoulder when he is reading. Then he can smell on her that signature smell of milk, which renders him helpless. He hopes that someday she will develop feelings for him. He was fine on his own, but here he has these two strange creatures who have inserted themselves into his life, one of them unpredictable and the other totally unknowable. Both sit now on the arm of a chair: one is reading, snapping radishes in half with her teeth, while the other is sucking on her large white breast.

Asher can see the girl is melancholy. Perhaps it's because of the pregnancy and delivery that her mood fluctuates so much. When she is in a better mood, she takes his books and newspapers and reads for days on end. She reads well in German, less fluently in Polish, and not at all in Latin. She knows a little Hebrew, though Asher can't tell how much and doesn't ask. They don't converse much, anyway. Asher thought at first that he would put her up until the birth, and once she had delivered the child, he would figure out a place to take them. But now he isn't sure. She doesn't have anywhere else to go, she says she's an orphan, that her father and mother were killed in a Cossack pogrom, although they weren't her real parents anyway. In reality, of course, she is the illegitimate daughter of the Polish king.

"And the child? Whose is that?" Asher finally ventured to inquire.

She shrugged, which gave him some relief; he prefers silence to lies.

It wouldn't be easy to place a young girl with a child. He would have to find out from the kahal where there might be shelters of some sort for such women, he thought back then.

Now things are different. Asher is no longer considering finding them a shelter. Gitla has begun to help around the house and has taken on the cooking. She is finally starting to go out—pulling her cap down over her face and flitting down the streets as though fearing someone might recognize her. She races to the market, buys vegetables and eggs, so many eggs, for she lives off their yolks, which she drizzles with honey. For Asher she cooks good, familiar dishes, like what he remembers from home—tasty kugel, or cholent with mushrooms instead of beef, since Gitla doesn't eat meat. She says Jews do the same thing to animals that Cossacks do to Jews.

But Lwów is not a big city, and it won't be long before the secret is out. The Jewish quarter can be traversed in ten minutes—go out of the Market Square on Ruska Street and turn onto Jewish Street, and then move briskly along down the incredibly boisterous New Jewish Street, where homes are clustered one on top of the other, with endless extensions and stairs and tiny courtyards housing little workshops, laundries, stalls. People know each other well here, and nothing escapes their attention.

## Of the reversal of circumstances: Katarzyna Kossakowska writes to Bishop Kajetan Sołtyk

Your Benevolent Excellency, please hear out your faithful Servant, who is not only the truest Daughter of our Most Holy Church, but also your Friend, in whom you shall always find Succor, even in Moments so terrible as this.

The Bishop's Death shocked us all to such an Extent that for the first few Days in Czarnokozińce, all kept the Silence of the Crypt. Even I did not learn of it at once, as for some Reason it was initially shrouded in the greatest Mystery. It is said to have been an Apoplexy.

The Funeral will not take place until January 29—you have no doubt already received News of it and still have a little bit of Time to make the proper Preparations for the Journey. You must know, Your Excellency, that upon the Death of Bishop Dembowski our Cause has taken a wholly new Turn. The Rabbis swung into Action, as did the King's Advisers, who are quite in their Pocket, and soon it was that nowhere could our Pets find any Backing; without the Bishop, the whole Matter got covered in Ash, with no one to tend to it any longer. Wherever I go, and whatever I say on this Question, I instantly hit a Wall of Indifference. Furthermore, the Frosts are terrible this Year and People have shut themselves up inside their

Houses—no one will so much as poke out their Nose. The Entirety of our Commonwealth seems to be dependent on the Weather. Perhaps this is also why they are putting off the Funeral, so that the Snow might relinquish its Hold enough to make Roads passable. Right now they could hardly dig the Grave.

It worries me, Excellency, that all our Efforts may have been for naught. The Violence previously dealt to the Talmudists has now been turned against our Shabbitarians. The Jewish Communities have been requisitioning their Dwellings—in the best Case, that is, for many have simply been burned, along with Everything inside them. The poor Creatures come to me for Aid, but what can I do for them on my own now that the Bishop has gone? I give them Clothing and a little Money, just enough that they might afford a Carriage over the Dniester. For they are leaving Everything behind and hurtling southward en masse toward Wallachia, where their Leader is to be found. I sometimes envy them this and would myself like to go from here to where it is warm and there is Sunlight. In any Case, I lately saw one of the Shabbitarians' little Villages. It was empty to the last little Shack, and it sent a Chill right down my Spine.

I, too, have somehow lost the Impetus for all Activity. I have been ailing a bit, I must have caught a Cold during my Journey from Rohatyn to Kamieniec, and nothing has been able to restore my internal Warmth since then, even my Husband's much-aged Aqua Vitae. People are saying that Bishop Dembowski was cursed by the Jews, and that this was the Reason he died. An Innkeeper told me that two Curses had been battling for some Time over the Bishop's Head. One was trying to defend him, the other to destroy him. One had been cast by his beloved Shabbitarians, the other by the Talmudist Rabbis. And so the People here all prattle on, although I do not believe in Curses, Jewish or otherwise. But it did sow some Anxiety within me to think that over our Heads some cosmic Wars are being waged by all Kinds of Forces flying around, swirling like Clouds, while we, so fragile and so blithe, are simply unaware.

They're saying the Bishop's Successor is going to be Łubieński, whom I know well and who will, I hope, take up our Cause.

I remain hopeful, Your Excellency and my dear Friend, that
we will meet at the Funeral, which everyone is preparing for as
though for some great Wedding. I myself saw the Herds of
Oxen purchased in Wallachia and chased across the Dniester to
Kamieniec for the Funeral Banquet . . .

## Pompa funebris: January 29, 1758

Archbishop Dembowski's body, carefully groomed, had initially been
transferred from the rumpled bed that witnessed his cruel death to a
special chamber with no windows, where the merciless frosts made the
long wait until the funeral possible. It traveled from there to the sumptuous show chamber, to a four-poster bed, where bouquets of the last
flowers of the season have been placed, along with bundles of spruce and
juniper. Ever since, the unflaggingly praying nuns have kept him constant company.

A whole battery of scribes has been set to writing the notices, and a
makeshift secretariat has popped up—tables arranged like in a monastery's scriptorium, bottles upon bottles of ink, and a special cleric with
curly hair who drowsily sharpens the quills.

The hubbub has done everyone good. They've stopped thinking about
the bishop's contorted body and the horror of his eyes wide open and
bright red, the burst blood vessels testimony to the toll that passing into
the next realm took on him. There was nervous discussion about whether
there would be time to prepare a proper funeral, since it is soon Christmas
and then right away Zapusty, when people eat and drink and visit neighbors and are often away, so they had to take that into account when determining the date of the funeral. It is quite vexing that the bishop died
at such an awkward time.

Now poems are being commissioned to honor the deceased, speeches
written, nuns hired to sew funeral banners and chasubles. Two of the best
painters in Lwów paint coffin portraits. And the living all wonder whether
they have a worthy coat, whether a fur would be more appropriate, and
whether their winter boots are in good condition, since the day of the

*EXTREME ONCTION.*

funeral will no doubt be cold. Should they not order a new fur-lined cloak with a fox fur collar for their wife? They could also do with a Turkish belt, and of course a fur hat, ornamented with a feather and a jewel. The prevailing custom is to come to a funeral richly dressed in the Eastern fashion, in the Sarmatian way—such are the dictates of tradition.

Father Pikulski is not concerned for his own attire—he will be dressed as a priest, in his cassock and his fur-lined black wool coat that reaches down to the ground. Estimates for the funeral have begun to come in, and they contain sums he has never dreamed of. The violet material to cover the walls of the church—they're still discussing how many hundreds of cubits of it, since no one is able to measure the surface area of the cathedral's walls exactly—plus the torches and the wax for candles, that's already almost half of his budget! Organizing the guests' transportation and lodgings is done by one group of people, while another—just as numerous—plans the banquet. Loans from the Jews have already been taken out for the construction of a catafalque in the cathedral, and for the candles.

Archbishop Dembowski's funeral thus becomes an unexpected early high point of this year's Carnival. It is to be a real pompa funebris, with speeches, banners, salvos, and choirs.

There is an issue, since on opening his will and testament they learn that the bishop in fact wanted a quiet funeral, shrouded in modesty. This causes widespread consternation—how can that possibly be? Bishop Sołtyk is right when he says that no Polish bishop may be allowed to pass quietly. It is good that it is icy out, so that the burial can be delayed until everyone learns the news and is able to plan their journey.

Immediately after Christmas, the archbishop's body is ceremoniously and with great pomp brought by sleigh to Kamieniec. Along the way, altars are laid out and masses are conducted, though the cold is nigh unbearable, and clouds of steam rise into the heavens from the mouths of the faithful like prayers. Peasants watch this procession with piety and devotion, kneeling in the snow—the Orthodox ones, too, making the sign of the cross over and over and with fervor. Some assume it is a military march and not a funeral procession.

On the day of the funeral, to the sound of gunshots and salvos, a procession consisting of all three Catholic rites—Latin, Uniate, and Armenian—as well as of szlachta and dignitaries of state, guilds, the military, and the regular population makes its way to the cathedral. Farewell orations are given in different parts of the city, and a Jesuit ordinary gives the final speech. The ceremonies last until eleven at night. Masses are held on the following day, and the body is not placed in its grave until seven in the evening. Torches burn throughout the city.

It is a good thing that the cold had already set in and turned Bishop Dembowski's blackened body into a frozen slab of meat.


## Of spilled blood and hungry leeches

One evening, as Asher stands leaning against the doorframe watching the women bathe little Samuel, someone pounds on the door. Reluctantly, he opens it. He sees a disheveled young man partly covered in blood who splutters half in Polish, half in Yiddish, urging Asher to follow him to save someone, a rabbi.

"Elisha? Which Elisha?" asks Asher, but he is already rolling up his sleeves and pulling his coat from its peg. He grabs his valise from beside the door—it is always there and fully stocked, as a doctor's bag should be.

"Elisha Shorr of Rohatyn was attacked, beaten, broken, Jesus Lord," the man stammers.

"Who are you?" Asher asks him as they are going down the stairs, struck by this use of "Jesus Lord."

"I am Hryćko, Hayim, it doesn't matter, just try not to be frightened, sir, doctor, so much blood, so much blood . . . We had some things to take care of in Lwów and . . ."

He leads Asher around the corner, down a narrow alleyway, and then into a dark courtyard, where they go up some stairs and get into a narrow room lit by an oil lamp. On the bed lies Old Shorr—Asher recognizes him by his high forehead with its receded hairline, though the face is drenched in blood; he recognizes, too, the eldest of his sons, Solomon, Shlomo, and behind him Isaac, and then some others he does not know. All of them are smeared in blood and bruised. Shlomo is holding his ear, blood flowing out between his fingers and then solidifying in dark unmoving streams. Asher would like to ask what happened, but there is a kind of death rattle coming out of the old man's mouth, so instead he rushes to him and carefully props him up a bit, lest, unconscious, he be suffocated by his own blood.

"Give me more light," he says in a calm, controlled voice, and the sons hurry to light more candles. "And water, warm water."

Having carefully removed the wounded man's shirt, he sees on his chest little pouches on a leather cord, with amulets; he wants to take them off, but the other men won't allow it, so he merely moves them over to Shorr's shoulder, to uncover the broken collarbone and the massive bruise on his chest flushed with purple. Shorr's teeth have been bashed out, his nose is broken, and blood is pouring from the cut on his forehead.

"He'll live," he says, perhaps somewhat prematurely, but he wants to reassure them.

Then they start to sing, in a whisper, but Asher doesn't recognize the words—all he knows is that it is the language of the Sephardim, some prayer of theirs.

Asher takes the injured men back to his home, where he has more bandages and other medical supplies. Solomon will need his ear sewn up. Gitla peeks in through the half-open door. Young Shorr looks at her face, but he does not recognize her; she's put on a little weight. Besides, it wouldn't have occurred to him that the medic's woman could have been one of Jacob's lady guardians not so long ago.

When the bandaged men emerge, Gitla, vigorously slicing an onion, sings a Sephardic prayer under her breath. It gets louder and louder.

"Gitla!" says Asher. "Stop mumbling like that."

"In town they're saying the bishop has become a ghost and is pacing around in front of his big house, confessing to all his faults. This is a protective prayer, an ancient one—that's why it works."

"In that case all of us will be ghosts after we die. Stop going on like that, the baby will get scared."

"What kind of Jew are you that doesn't believe in ghosts?" Gitla laughs and wipes her onion tears with her apron.

"You don't believe in them, either."

"These Jews are elated! For them it's a great miracle, greater than the ones that used to happen in the old days. They had been calling the bishop Haman, and now that he's dead, they can beat up the changelings. Old Rapaport already put out an edict, did you hear? Stating that killing a heretic is a mitzvah. Did you hear about that?"

Asher says nothing. He wipes the blood with tows, cleans his tools with a rag, and puts them back in his bag, since he has to go right out to let the blood of Deym the postmaster, who is suffering from apoplexy. He steps into the room where he keeps the leeches in their jars. He takes the smallest one, the hungriest one, since Deym is a man of small stature, so there won't be all that much superfluous blood.

"Lock the door behind me," he says to Gitla. "Both hasps."

It is October again, and that same smell of dried leaves and moisture is in the air. Asher Rubin sees in the darkness small groups of people with lit torches, shouting. They make their way along the city walls, where the poorest of the heretics live. Asher Rubin can hear shrieking. Somewhere toward the city limits a glow is dimly visible—one of their miserable shacks must be burning, one of those places where people live alongside animals. Just like the Talmuds lately burned, so now are the Zohar and the other books forbidden to God-fearing Jews being consumed by flames. Asher sees a cart filled with Jewish youths frenzied and delighted by the burning of heretical books—they are heading out of town, probably to Gliniany and Busk, where the greatest numbers of heretics live. A few people, running with clubs raised over their heads, crash into him. Asher squeezes the jar of leeches tighter and rushes to the sick man's home. When he gets there, he finds that the postmaster has died only moments ago, leaving the leeches to go hungry.

## Mrs. Elżbieta Drużbacka to Father Chmielowski, or: Of the perfection of imprecise forms

... I send these volumes of mine to the venerable Vicar Forane, whose quick eye shall perhaps find something in them beyond mere mundane vanity, for I believe that to express in language the vastness of the world, it is impossible to use words that are too transparent, too unambiguous—that would be like drawing a pen-and-ink sketch, transferring that vastness onto a white surface to be broken up by clean black lines. But words and images must be flexible and contain multitudes, they must flicker, and they must have multiple meanings.

Not that your efforts, dear Father, have gone underappreciated by me—on the contrary, I am deeply impressed by the scale of your work. But it does occur to me that you seek only the counsel of the dead. Your citations and compilations are a way of rummaging around in tombs. Yet facts in isolation soon become unimportant, lose their relevance. Can our lives be described beyond fact? Can there be a description that is based exclusively on what we see and feel, on details, on sentiment?

I try to see the world through my own eyes, and to have my own language, rather than merely repeating someone else's words.

His Excellency Bishop Załuski worried he would, as my publisher, lose money on me, imbuing his correspondence with so much bitterness, and here it turns out that the whole print run has already sold out, and they are getting ready for another. It pains me a bit that now I'm being asked to sell my own poems, published by him. He has sent me a hundred copies, and since the Piarists who run the printing press are troubling him for money, he wants me to move this stock. I informed him that I do not put down my verses out of a hunger for profit, but rather that my readers might reflect and obtain some slight enjoyment. I don't want to make money from them, nor would I know how. How could I? Am I, like some traveling merchant, to take my own poems on a cart around the fairs and press them on people for a penny? Or force them on some nobles and await their benefaction? To be honest with you, my dear friend, I would prefer to deal in wine than in poems.

Did you receive the package I sent via some persons traveling to Lwów? It contained some felt slippers that we made here in the autumn—I myself sewed little, for my eyesight is already quite poor, but my daughter and my granddaughters did—as well as dried fruits from our orchard, plums, pears (which are my favorites), and a little barrel of my signature rose wine; watch out, Father, for it is strong. Most important, the package contained a splendid cashmere scarf for the colder days in your Firlejów seclusion. I permitted myself to include, as well, a little volume you would not have encountered yet. If you were to place your *Athens* and my little handicrafts on a scale, of course they would be incomparable. That's the way it is, I suppose—the selfsame thing comes out very differently in the hands of two different people. Those who are left and those who leave will always draw different conclusions. Likewise the person who possesses and the person possessed, the person who is sated and the one who is hungry—and the wealthy daughter of a nobleman dreams of a little pug from Paris, while the poor daughter of a peasant dreams of a goose to have for meat and feathers. That is why I write:

For my ordinary mind it will suffice,

Unable to count the sky's stars anyhow,
To add up the oaks, and firs and pines precise,
Practice that arithmetic at least for now.

Whereas your vision is quite different. You would like information to be an ocean from which all can draw. And you think that an educated person, on reading every piece of it, will know the whole world without leaving his home. And that human knowledge is like a book, in the sense that it also has its "covers," its bounds, which means it can be summarized and made available to all. It is a glorious goal that motivates you, and for that, as your reader, I am grateful. But I know what I'm talking about, too.

Every person is a little world:
The firmament is where the head is,
The mind's the sun, its rays are words,
And the planets are the senses.

The world errs and takes with it mankind;
Death pursues the day from east to west.
Women keep the world in mind
And on its feet, to stand the test.

You will say: "imprecise, idle chatter." And no doubt you'll be right. Maybe the whole art of writing, my dear friend, is the perfection of imprecise forms . . .

## The Vicar Forane Benedykt Chmielowski writes to Elżbieta Drużbacka

Father Chmielowski is sitting in a strange position; Saba, Firlejka's sister, has just fallen asleep on his lap. He must keep his legs stiff, resting his feet on the crossbar under the table so that the dog doesn't slide off onto the floor. In order to reach the inkwell, he must make an arch over the table, which he manages to do. It is harder with the pens he has on the shelf behind him—he twists around now and tries to reach the box. The quills fall to the floor; the priest sighs. He supposes he will have to wait until Saba wakes up. But since such inactivity is not in his nature, he starts to write with a blunt pen, and it doesn't really look that bad. It's good enough, he thinks.

I send You the very warmest Greetings and Wishes, My Lady, for I myself caught a Cold at the Funeral of Bishop Dembowski, may he rest in Peace, and now, coughing and expectorating, I sit shut in my House and warm my Bones. And I feel old Age coming on at full Speed. The Truth is that the Archbishop's Death has strained my Health, for he was very dear to me, and I had a Kind of Intimacy with him that can only be shared by two Servants of the Church. I think that slowly my own Time is coming, and without having finished my Work, I feel some Anxiety, and the Fear overcomes me that I might never see the Załuski Brothers' Library before I die. I made an Agreement with Bishop Załuski that as soon as Winter abates, I shall travel to Warsaw, which made him very glad, and he has promised me every Hospitality.

Forgive me for conversing with You at such modest Length today, but I am being burned up, I can feel, by Fever, and the sleeping Dog does not permit me to change my Pen. I gave away all of my Saba's Puppies, and now the House is empty and forlorn.

I found Something for You, my dear Friend, and I note it here, hoping to occupy You with Something more interesting than overseeing the Estate, et cetera:

How may a Person sitting in his Room see what is happening outside?

Whosoever might wish to see all the Activities occurring in the Courtyard, not looking with his own Eyes, but lying down, let him make the Room a dark one, shutting out every Shred of Light that might make its Way in from the Outdoors through the Windows. Then let him bore a round Hole, small, directly onto the Courtyard, and in it let him place the Lens from a Perspective or from Spectacles that would represent Things as greater than they are; having done this, have him hang a thin,

white, sturdy
Canvas or a large
Piece of white
Paper in that dark
Room, opposite
that little
Opening. On this
Canvas or Screen
You will see,
kind Friend,
Everything that
occurs in the Courtyard—who goes there, rides there, fights
there, gambols, who removes Something from the Pantry or the
Cellar.

I tried this today and must tell You that it did work, tho' the
Image itself was not particularly clear, and I could recognize
Little from it.

I am also sending You an Item of great Value—the
Calendars of Stanisław Duńczewski. One of them is from last
Year and contains the Suite of Polish Kings to Sigismund
Augustus. The second Calendar, the new one, goes from
Sigismund Augustus to Augustus II. So You will be able to tell
Your Granddaughters of it without having to rely upon Your
Memory o'ermuch, since Memory is always riddled with Holes,
and incomplete . . .

## Of the unexpected guest who comes in the night to Father Chmielowski

The priest stops with his pen poised over the letter in the middle of a
word, for although it is completely dark now, a carriage is approaching
the presbytery of Firlejów. The priest hears the horse hooves in the courtyard, and then impatient nickering. Saba, suddenly awakened, leaps off
his lap and races to the door with a quiet whimper. Sounds spatter in

the damp fog like streams of water poured from a jug. Who could this be at this hour? He goes up to the window, but he can barely see, in the darkness, what's going on out there, and he can hear Roshko's voice, but it's sleepy somehow, reluctant, and a moment later there are other voices that belong to strangers. Fog off the river has enveloped the courtyard once again, and voices barely carry in it, quieting halfway through a word. He waits for Roshko to go to the door, but does not go himself. Where has his housekeeper gone off to? She seems to have dozed off over the big bowl where she was washing her feet before going to bed—in the light of a dying candle, the priest sees her bowed head. He takes the candle and goes to the door himself. He sees some figures standing by the carriage, shrouded from head to toe like specters. Now Roshko comes up, too, with hay in his hair, still half asleep.

"Who goes there?" boldly says the priest. "Who wanders through the night and disturbs the peace of Christian souls?"

Then one of the specters comes closer, the smaller one, and instantly Father Chmielowski recognizes Old Shorr, though he can't yet see his face. He is so surprised it takes his breath away. For a moment, he loses the power of speech. But what are they doing here in the night, these cursed Jews? He does at least have the presence of mind to tell Roshko to go home and get to bed.

The priest also recognizes Hryćko—how he's grown, how manly he's become. Silently, Shorr leads the priest to the cart and then flings the cover off it. Now Father Chmielowski sees an extraordinary thing. The cart is almost completely packed with books. They lie in stacks of three and four, tied up with leather strings.

"Holy Mother of God," says the priest, and with that last syllable, that awestruck "God," he extinguishes the candle flame. Then the three of them silently carry the books into the presbytery, into the chamber where the priest keeps the honey and the wax, and bits of rotten wood used to fumigate bees come summer.

He asks no questions; he simply wants to offer them a glass of mulled wine, which he keeps on the stove, for they seem frozen almost to the bone. Then Shorr throws back his hood, and the priest sees his battered purple face. At this, Father Chmielowski's hands start to tremble as he pours the wine, which has unfortunately already cooled down.

Then they disappear.


## Of the cave in the shape of the *alef*

You have to go through the Christian part of the village, pass the intersection that serves as a little market square where Sobla's brother's tavern is, and where tinctures made of local herbs are sold—as medicine, not alcohol. There is also a warehouse here, as well as a blacksmith's. Next you have to go straight, pass the Christian church and the presbytery, then the Catholic cemetery, a dozen or so whitewashed Masurians' houses (for that's what people from Poland are called here), and farther on, a little Orthodox church, to then leave the village and finally reach the cave. The villagers are afraid to go there—the place is

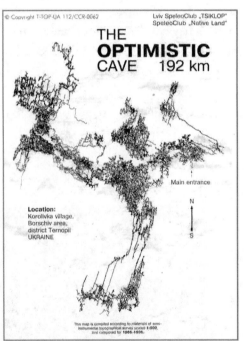

haunted, spring is autumn there, and autumn spring, time flows according to its own rhythm, which is different from down below. Actually, only a few people know how huge this cave is, but somehow everybody knows that it is in the shape of the letter *alef*; it is a great underground *alef*, a seal, the first letter upon which the world rests. Maybe somewhere far away in the world under the earth there are also other letters, a whole alphabet, made out of nothing, out of underground air, darkness, the plash of underground streams. Israel believes that it is a great stroke of luck to live so near the first letter *and* near the Jewish cemetery, with a view of the river. It always takes his breath away to look down from the hill above the village at the world. It is so beautiful and so cruel at the same time. A paradox that seems to be taken straight from the pages of the Zohar.

They take Yente in great secrecy, in the morning. They have placed her in a shroud and covered her in hay as well, in case of prying strangers' eyes. Four men and Pesel. The men go down on ropes through the narrow entrance to the cave, taking the body, which is as light as a bundle of dry leaves. They disappear for a quarter of an hour and return without the body. They have laid it comfortably on skins in a niche in the rock, in the bowels of the earth, as they say. They also say that it was strange to carry a human body in that state, since it is no longer human, more like a bird's. Sobla cries.

It is with relief that they emerge into the sun, which has just come up, and dust off their trousers and return to the village.

Yente's gaze goes along with them for a while, to the road, counting

their hats, but then she gets bored. On her way back, she strokes the tips of the growing grass and shakes the fluff from the dandelions.

The next day, Pesel goes down into the cave. She lights an oil lamp, and after a dozen meters, finds herself in a high chamber. The lamp's flame lights up the strange walls, which look as though they're made of onyx, covered in bulges and hanging icicles. To Pesel, it seems as though she has been transported onto one of those crystals that appeared on Yente's skin. She sees her great-grandmother's body lying on a natural platform, and it looks smaller than it did yesterday. But her skin is pink, and that same smile roves her face.

"Forgive us," says Pesel. "This is just for a little while. We will take you away from here as soon as it is safe." She sits for a spell and talks to Yente about her future husband, who—although he is a year older than Pesel—is really just a child.

# 17.

## *Scraps: My heart's quandary*

It is said in Berachot 54 that there are four who should give thanks to God: he who has emerged unscathed from a voyage at sea; he who has returned from a journey through the desert; the sick man who has been healed; and the prisoner freed from jail. I have lived through all of this, and for this I should thank God—which I do, every day. And as I have gazed upon the bizarre fragility of our lives, I thank God all the more that I am healthy and that I have recovered from the debility I suffered when Shorr and Nussen and I were beaten in the riots following the death of our protector. I have no real tolerance for violence, and I fear pain. I studied to be a rabbi, not to go to war.

As soon as I had regained my health completely (not counting the irreversible loss of two teeth), I began to help my father- and mother-in-law and my Leah to supply the inn with stocks of good vodka, potatoes, lard and cabbage, honey and butter, and warm clothing. Separately, I invested in products—in wax, to be exact— and along with Moshe of Podhajce, Hayim, and Yeruhim Lipmanowicz, with whom I had been keeping my meetings a secret from Leah for weeks, I determined to set off to find Jacob. I would not like to call this a flight, though this may be how Leah thinks of it, shrieking that I always preferred Jacob to her. She has never understood me or my mission.

At the same time, there was a painful split within our group of true believers: the Shorrs seemed to be forgetting about Jacob, or they lost their faith in him, and with it the hope that Jacob would lead them, and so they went, together with Krysa, on a mission to Salonika, to the disciples of Baruchiah, the very same who had so cruelly maltreated Jacob in their day.

I often have the same dream, and Reb Mordke always said to pay attention to dreams that frequently repeat, for they are our link with infinity. I dream that I am wandering around a large house that contains many rooms, doors, passages. I don't know what I'm looking for. Everything is old and moldy, the upholstery on the walls, once lavish, is now faded and torn, and the floors are decayed.

This dream worries me, for I would prefer to dream like the Kabbalists about all the palaces, each containing and concealing the next, with their never-ending corridors that eventually end up at God's throne. In my dream, there are only rotted labyrinths with no exit. When I told Jacob, expressing my concerns, he just laughed: "You're lucky, I dream of cesspools and stables."

In the autumn, I received a letter from Leah asking for a divorce. In the hand of the local rabbi, she accused me of having become a heretic and said that I had betrayed her for all eternity. I cried while writing her the get, or the letter of divorce, but, truth be told, I also experienced relief. There was not much that was keeping us together, and my brief visits home were insufficient for the establishment of a deeper connection. I promised to support my son and take care of her until she was able to arrange things for herself, but she never answered.

When I look at these notes of mine, I see that I rarely speak in them about my wife, whom I married many years ago when I returned from studying with the Besht. I had been allotted a wife from very nearby, the daughter of a relative of my father: Leah. I wrote little about her for the simple reason that I have never been greatly interested in any of the matters that are connected with women, and I always treated my marriage as an obligation to my family and my tribe. As for children, we had one, out of the five Leah gave birth to; the others died not long after arriving in this world. Leah always insisted it was my fault, since I was rarely home, and when I was, I was always occupied with something else. But from my point of view, I fulfilled my obligations in a dutiful way. God was parsimonious when it came to our offspring, giving them to us like bait he would instantly snatch away. Perhaps I could have given her healthy, lovely children who might not have died like the preceding ones. I could have taught Leah to read, I could have built us a home and gone into business so that she would not have to work as a servant, but—this is the truth that burdens me with unrelenting guilt—having taken her for a wife, I neglected her completely.

I asked Moshe of Podhajce for his advice—he is a highly learned man, knowledgeable in matters of magic—and he told me that Leah and I have behind us other painful things arisen from our previous lives which we cannot remember, and that we must separate, so as not to bring any more pain into this world.

There are two people in my life whom I love deeply and constantly—Leah and Jacob. To my misfortune, they are opposites, and they hold one another in mutual disregard. There is no way to bring them to any reconciliation, so that I must maneuver between them.

I do not know how it happened that in the greatest unhappiness, without my wife and without Jacob, I found myself once again with the Besht, in Międzybóż. I made my way as if in a state of delirium, no doubt seeking the same thing that I obtained there in my youth— the wisdom to be able to bear my suffering.

I waited two days for a meeting and during this time did not reveal who I was nor where I had come from. Had I done so, the Besht might not have agreed to see me, for everyone knew he bemoaned our lot, that we were not keeping to the Jewish tenets in the way everyone would have wanted.

Other customs prevailed in the town, which was inhabited almost exclusively by Hasidim. Everywhere there were pilgrims in caftans that went down to their knees, dirty stockings, and shtreimels on their heads. Far from Lwów, from Kraków, all of Międzybóż was concentrated on itself, as though in some wonderful dream. The conversations on the streets were everywhere the same: on God, on names, laying out the meaning of the slightest gesture, the most minor event. They knew nothing there of life in the world, of the war, of the king. Although this way was once so dear to me, it now only deepened my despair, so blind and deaf were they. I envied them that they might ceaselessly immerse themselves in matters of the divine, for such was my nature, as well. On the other hand, I could see that they were becoming defenseless as

children, while on the horizon a new storm was gathering. They
were like dandelions, lovely and light.

I saw a few of our own there, too, who as a result of the sudden
persecutions that came after the death of our protector, Bishop
Dembowski, had also made their way to the Besht, and had been
taken in without any unnecessary questions, though it was
known that the Besht regarded Jacob as a pest. I was particularly
happy to see Yehuda of Glinno, with whom I had made such
close friends years earlier in this same place, and although he has
never been a true believer, he has nonetheless remained close to
my heart.

In Międzybóż it was taught that in every person there is
something good, even in those who strike you as the basest of
villains. I started to understand that everyone has their own
self-interest to protect, and that it is by this that they are guided,
and that self-interest is no failing. There is nothing wrong in
persons desiring the best for themselves. And when I began to think
in this way about what each of us wants, I began to understand
better.

Leah wants a good husband and children, and a basic income, so
that there is a roof over her head and nutritious food to eat. Elisha
Shorr and his sons want to climb higher than they could as Jews.
That is why, as they rise, they desire to join the society of
Christians, for remaining within Judaism they would have to
content themselves with who they are and what they have now.
Krysa is a frustrated ruler who wants control. The bishop, may he
rest in peace, wanted no doubt to serve the king and the Church
and was also no doubt counting on personal glory. The same with
Mrs. Kossakowska, who gave us money for our trip—but for what
purpose? Did she want the credit of helping the poor? Perhaps she,
too, was after glory?

And what does Jacob want? Right away I answered:

Jacob does not need to want anything. Jacob is an
instrument of greater forces, that I know. His task is to destroy this
evil order.

The Besht had advanced in years, but he radiated clarity and
strength, and just the touch of his hand moved me to tears. He
conversed with me for a long time as an equal, and I will be
grateful to him to the end of my days for not sending me away
outright. He finally laid his hand on my head and said: "I forbid

you to despair." He didn't say another word, as though he knew that I had become proficient in disputation and could come up with arguments into infinity on any subject, meaning that lessons were not what I needed. Yet when I left Międzybóż, a young Hasid ran up to me and pressed a tight roll of paper into my hand.

It was written in Hebrew: "Im Ata Ma'amin sheAta Yahol Lekalkel Ta-amin sheGam Ata Yahol Letaken." If you think you are capable of destruction, think how you could build.

It was from the Besht.

### How in Giurgiu we talked Jacob into returning to Poland

In the winter of 1757, the four of us made it to Jacob in Giurgiu, setting off on Hanukkah, carrying the letters of safe conduct that had been obtained for us from the Polish king. We went to find Jacob in order to convince him to return. Without him, and in the hands of others such as Krysa and Elisha Shorr, our cause had come strangely apart at the seams.

There were four of us, like the Evangelists: Moshe ben Israel of Nadwórna, Yeruhim Lipmanowicz of Czortków, my brother Hayim of Busk, and I.

We were tired and half frozen from the journey when he first glimpsed us, for the winter was severe, and along the way we had been attacked and lost our horses, though then when I saw the Danube, I was greatly moved, as if I had reached the very heart of the world, and immediately felt warmth and brightness, although there was much snow.

Jacob had us come close and touch our foreheads to his, and then he held the four of us so tightly to him that it was as if we four and he, at our center, had joined together to create a single man, and we breathed a single breath. We stood for so long that I felt completely united with them, and it came to me that this was not the end, but rather the beginning of our journey, and that he, Jacob, would lead us onward.

Then Moshe, the eldest among us, said: "Jacob, we came here for you. You must return."

Jacob, when he smiled, had the habit of raising one eyebrow. When he answered Moshe, he raised one eyebrow, and I was flooded with an extraordinary warmth—moved by seeing him again, by how beautiful he was, how his presence brought out the best feelings in me.

Jacob said: "We'll see." He took us on a tour of his domain, and his family and neighbors crowded around us, for he enjoyed great respect here, and they did not even know who he truly was.

How well he had arranged things! He had purchased a house and had already begun to move into it, though we were to stay in the old home, which was also nice, Turkish, with painted walls and floors covered in carpets. And since it was winter, there were everywhere small portable stoves, tended by the serving girls, from whom we could scarcely look away, especially Hayim, who liked women above all else. We went to see the new home, with its view of the river; behind the home extended a vineyard, quite sizable. Inside, the home was arrayed with large carpets, filled with beautiful Turkish things. Hana had gained weight since the birth of their little son, Leyb, also called Immanuel, which means "God is with us." She had grown lazy. She spent all day lying around on ottomans, here, there, while the wet nurse attended to the child. She had learned to smoke a pipe, and although she did not speak much, she was with us for almost the whole time, looking at Jacob, following his every move, like our Podolian dogs. Jacob was always carrying around little Avacha, a sweet, calm, obedient child, and it was clear to everyone how attached to her he was. After we had looked around and sat together talking until late at night, I found myself feeling somewhat troubled and confused. I did not understand whether Jacob was trying to show us that he wanted us to leave him alone, or whether he had some other plan about which we knew nothing, and what this would mean. I must confess that when I lay my head against my pillow, before I fell asleep, the image of my wife came back to me, and I was overcome by terrible grief, for my wife was now growing old alone, working hard, ruined, and eternally sad, felled by the hardships of this world. I was reminded of all the people suffering, and all the animals, until an internal sob tugged at my heart, and I began to pray feverishly for the end of this world, in which people merely lie in wait for one another to kill and steal and demean and do harm. And suddenly I realized that I might never go back to Podolia, as there is no place for us there, for us who wish to follow our own path, boldly, freed from all the trappings of custom and faith. And that while the paths we take are never set in stone—I for one have lost my bearings—still we know that the direction is right.

On the third day, after we had already discussed the whole situation, the machinations of Krysa and the silence of the Shorrs, and once we had read him the letters from our fellow true believers, Jacob said that, as the Turks had welcomed our people, offering real aid and not just empty talk, and there being no alternative, we would be obliged to stick with them. We needed to apply for Turkish protection.

"Be smart. We have been talking about this for many years, and yet when it comes to actually doing something about it, you all balk," he said. Then he lowered his voice so that we had to lean in to hear him: "It'll be like getting into cold water: your whole body balks, but then you get used to it, and what seemed to you terribly foreign starts to seem nice and familiar." He told us about a mufti he knew, with whom he did business, who owed much of his wealth to making deals with the Sublime Porte.

Although there was still a great deal of snow, the four of us took sleighs, Hana and little Avacha, as well as Hershel, who was in their service, and farmhands for the sleighs, and, packing gifts, wine, and exquisite Polish vodka, we went to Ruse where the mufti, Jacob's close acquaintance, lived. When we got there, Jacob went out for a word with the agha, who seemed almost like a brother to him, and talked with him a bit, while we, polite guests, relished the sweets that were offered us. They came back happy. And the next day, all of us who were there, along with more of our true-believer brothers and sisters from Ruse, where there were indeed a great number of us, turned up at noon in the mosque. There we all converted to the Islamic religion, putting green turbans on our heads. It all took just a moment; the only thing we had to do was say "Allahu Akbar," and Jacob gave us all new Turkish names: Kara, Osman, Mehmed, and Hasan, and his wife and child would be Fatima and Aisha, like the wives of the prophet. Thanks to this, the faithful reached the number of thirteen, which was necessary if we wanted to found our own camp, as Baruchiah had done.

Suddenly we were safe again. For the second time, Jacob became our hakham, and our Lord. We recognized him as our Lord in everything with complete trust and would have been delighted if he'd said he wanted us all to go to Poland.

As we were returning home from the mosque on our sleighs, we were all in a good mood, and as though it were a kulig, we sang our songs at such a volume that our throats got sore. Then I felt better, and the logic of my thoughts returned. We are progressing toward God through three religions: Jewish, Ishmaelite, and Edomite. So it was written. And long ago I translated into Turkish from Hebrew my favorite prayer, and when I said it in the evening, everyone liked it and even wrote it down for themselves to remember in this new language. This is the prayer:

> Underneath my gray robe I have nothing but my soul,
> Which is there for a moment but will more than console.
>
> It will bounce off every shore, putting up a white sail,
> Nothing can stop it—squalls of the heart are too frail.
>
> And so it will go, drifting in and out of your ports,
> Send your watchmen—nothing will put my soul out of sorts.
>
> Build new walls—my soul will go right through them,
> When intentions are good, it will rightly construe them.
>
> And amidst your borders it will fast get its bearings,
> Counter your words with wiser ones at any hearings.
>
> Pedigree and permanence do not interest my soul,
> Nor courtliness, breeding, or the exercise of control.
>
> If you try to calculate its vastness in a poem,
> It will break free, unable to sit and stay at home.
>
> No one knows if it's lovely or how lofty it is,
> Its bright, expeditious flights rule out analysis.
>
> Help me, O merciful God and everlasting Lord,
> Express that free spirit with my mortal tongue, in words.
>
> Open my calamitous mouth, make my tongue be bright,
> And I will state once and for all: you are good and right.

I was happy. Spring arrived one day not long after that, or one afternoon, really, the sun gathering its strength and beginning to burn our backs. We had already managed to sell all our goods, so we took a break in our bookkeeping. The next morning, singing birds awoke me, and right after that, though I know not how, everything turned green, little blades of grass growing between the stones in the courtyard, and the tamarisk burst into bloom. The horses stood motionless in patches of sun, warming their hides, half closing their eyes.

My window overlooked the vineyard, and that year I witnessed the whole process of life returning after the winter, from beginning to end, from buds to mature grapes. By August it was already time to pluck them, so heavy and full of juice were they. It occurred to me that God was giving me an example: an idea can arrive seemingly out of nowhere. It has its own schedule, advances at its own pace. Nothing can be rushed or bypassed. I crushed the grapes in my fingers and thought how much God had done in this time, letting the vineyards ripen, growing the vegetables in the ground and the fruits on the trees.

Anyone who might think we were listlessly sitting around would be mistaken. By day, we wrote out letters and sent them all over the world to our brothers—this one to Germany, this one to Moravia, this to Salonika, another to Smyrna. Jacob, meanwhile, remaining in intimate relations with the local authorities, met with the Turks often, and I accompanied him. Among the Turks there were also the Bektashi, who considered Jacob one of their own, and sometimes he would go to them, although he didn't want us to accompany him there.

As we had not given up our business while staying with Jacob, several times that summer we set out from Giurgiu to Ruse, on the other shore, and from there we would take our products farther, to Vidin and Nikopol, where Jacob's father-in-law, Tovah, still lived.

I got to know this road along the Danube well—a road along the shore which, though mostly going low, sometimes climbs up high on the escarpment. One can always see from it the massive power of the flowing water, its true potential. When in the spring the Danube overflows its banks widely, as it did that year, one might take it for the sea, so much water is there across the whole of the lowlands. Some riverside settlements face flooding nearly every spring. To protect themselves from deluge, people plant trees of a certain kind along the shore, trees with powerful roots to absorb the water. The villages here appear miserable, their homes made out of clay, with nets hung up to dry alongside. Their inhabitants are small and swarthy, and the women will gladly read one's palms. Farther from the water, among the vineyards, the more prosperous build their houses of stone, and their cozy courtyards are covered with a thick awning of vines that shields them from the heat. It is in these courtyards that family life occurs from spring on, it is here guests are received, here that people work, chat, and drink wine come evening. At sunset, by the river, you often hear a distant song carrying across the water—whence it comes is never clear, nor is it easy to identify what language it is sung in.

Around Lom, the banks climb particularly high, and from there it seems like you can see half the world or more. We always stopped there for supplies. I remember the warmth of the sun's rays on my skin, and I can smell the heated vegetation, a mixture of herbs and the silt in the river. We would buy stores of goat's cheese, as well as pots of zacusca, a well-seasoned paste of eggplants and red peppers roasted over the fire. Now I think that never in my life have I eaten anything as good. The inn was more than just an ordinary rest stop for the horses, the food better than the typical local cuisine. Everything interwove and locked together in that seemingly ordinary moment, and the boundaries of ordinary things dissolved, so that I stopped eating and simply stared, mouth open, into that silvery space, until Jacob or Yeruhim must have bashed me in the back to bring me down to earth again.

Looking at the Danube soothed me. I saw the wind moving the ships' rigging, rocking the boats moored to the shore. I saw that our lives were stretched out between two great rivers, the Dniester and the Danube, which, like two players, set us on the board of Hayah's strange game.

My soul is inseparable from Jacob's. I cannot otherwise explain my attachment. Obviously at some time in the past we were one creature. Reb Mordke must have been there as well, and Isohar, of whose passing we were saddened to learn.

One spring day of Pesach we conducted the old ritual that marked the beginning of the new road. Jacob took a small barrel and attached to it nine candles, while he had a tenth, and he lit that

one and those nine, and then he put them out. He did this three
times. Then he sat down next to his wife, and then the four of us
went up to him individually and joined with him our souls and
bodies, recognizing him as our Lord. And then we did it again, but
all together. Many of our people were waiting behind the door,
wanting to join. It was the ritual Kav haMalkhut, also known as the
Royal Cord.

In the meantime, our brothers fleeing Poland were coming into
Giurgiu en masse, trekking either to Salonika, to our Dönmeh
brothers, lost and determined never to go back to Podolia again, or
here, to Wallachia. Jacob's house was open to them, even to those
who, not knowing who he was, talked about a certain Jacob Frank,
apparently still marauding through Poland and crushing the
Talmudists. This brought Jacob great joy, and he spent a long time
asking them all sorts of questions and dragging the matter out
before he finally revealed to them that he was this very man. It just
meant that his fame was growing, and that more and more people
were hearing of him. Yet Jacob did not seem happy, and Hana and
all of us had to bear the brunt of his bad moods, when he would
curse and summon Israel Osman and have him go off somewhere
with some urgent message, or else go and arrange something or
other with the agha.

The newcomers, hospitably received by Hana, told of how along
the Prut, on the Turkish side, a whole army of true believers waited
to return to their country. They stood out in the cold, hungry and
destitute, watching the Polish shore from afar.

In May, a long and much-anticipated letter arrived from Moliwda,
in which he informed us of his great strivings as well as those of
Mrs. Kossakowska, and various nobles and bishops, with the king
himself, and then we, too, started to think about returning to
Poland. Jacob said nothing, but I saw him stealthily reaching for a
book in Polish in the evenings. I guessed that he was studying the
language in secret, and I learned that I was right when he asked me
one day, as though in passing:

"How can it be that they say one knife, but two knives? It should
be knifes."

I was unable to explain this to him.

We soon received a letter of safe conduct from the king
through the same channel. This was written in a very

elevated style, and I had to put all of my energy into translating it adroitly. I read it so many times that I learned it by heart, and even in the night, waking from a dream, I could have recited any part of it at will:

> Our councils have enjoined us, on behalf of the
> Contra-Talmudists, to take the same under our royal
> protection by means of this iron letter, also known as a
> letter of safe conduct, to defend against the pertinacious
> tentatives of whosoever it may be, including, but not
> limited to, the scurrilous Talmudists alluded to in the
> aforementioned correspondence, not only in the Podolian
> Voivodship, but also in every place in the Kingdom and
> Grand Duchy, where the Contra-Talmudists must be free
> to stay and litigate their uncompleted trial, that its
> outcome should apply to every court, including the
> highest of the Commonwealth, both religious and
> secular, which shall support absolutely all those who have
> sustained injury—that they might exercise the privileges,
> rights, liberties, and freedoms provided the Jews by royal
> writ, safely, freely, and in peace.
>
> The which requests, rightly and fairly addressed to us,
> being granted, thus affirming that the Contra-
> Talmudists, having renounced the Jewish Talmud—as it is
> filled with countless blasphemies, harmful to the general
> good of the True Believers of the Church and Fatherland,
> condemned to burn by the Highest Popes, and already
> burned in some kingdoms, including our own, by just
> decree of the Most Reverend, His Excellency, Bishop
> Mikołaj, in the midst of Our city, Kamieniec Podolski—
> and in this renouncement having come nearer to
> knowing God as He is in Three Persons, yet in Essence
> One, and professing and upholding the teachings of the
> Old Testament . . .
>
> Thus taking the Contra-Talmudists under Our
> protection, in common and individually, this iron letter
> of Godspeed against the pertinacious tentatives of
> the aforementioned and all persons and in
> support of the alleviation of injury to those named in our

writ, we have determined to grant, to extend, and to
distribute . . .

Graced with and supported by this iron letter, the
aforementioned Contra-Talmudists shall stay in the
Kingdom and Grand Duchy without any impediments on
the part of those whose oppression they have feared until
now, trade according to their privileges in every place,
throughout villages, towns, and urban spaces, go to
market, as well as make all purchases decent and
honorable, and shall hold their trial before the courts,
both religious and secular, as well as royal, appearing now
and also further bringing cases or responding to them
later, not only legal transactions, but also others at their
discretion, and they shall act according to the law, to
justice, and to righteousness, and wives, children, and
household servants, too, as effects, shall give reason for
neither problems nor contests, graced with this, our royal
protection, and let it be known that this, our grace, shall
not be used for ill, but rather to the benefit of all of those
who have endured oppression or whatsoever danger
feared, this iron protective letter being submitted to
common knowledge . . .

Augustus Rex
Warsaw, 11th June 1758,
the XXVth year of our reign . . .

As it is not often that the king stands on the side of the
oppressed, our joy was sweeping, as was our excitement, and
everyone began at once to pack, gather, organize, arrange. The little
market squares where in the evenings endless debates would take
place suddenly emptied, as all were occupied with the coming
journey, and news was already reaching us that along the Dniester
and the Prut thousands of our people now camped. We were
returning to Poland.

Learning of the crowds camping along the Dniester, in
Perebekowice, Jacob lavishly provisioned Israel Osman, who was
living in Giurgiu and had long practiced the Muslim religion, and
dispatched him to that poor multitude of Polish exiles who were

sitting there in great sadness, not knowing what to do with themselves. Jacob was very worried about them, most especially since there were more mothers, children, and elderly people among them than men who had set out to make some profit from the situation. They were all living in haphazardly constructed mud huts.

The first to come was Nussen's brother Krysa, known as Smetankes, who received special consideration from Jacob. Arriving from the camp along the Dniester, he made a memorable speech about the sufferings of our brothers and sisters who had been exiled from Poland. Jacob insisted that he and his companions make themselves at home, but as the house was too small, and they did not wish to return immediately, they wound up falling in with us in the vineyards for the duration of the heat. Next, two Kabbalists came to us: Moshe Dawidowicz from Podhajce with Yeruhim Lipmanowicz, which greatly pleased Jacob.

They began every statement with "We ma'aminim," or "We the disciples," as they say in Salonika when wishing to show that they worship Sabbatai. Every day at dawn they would check on the affairs of the world through divination. And Yeruhim would begin every sentence with: "It is time for this . . . It is time for that." In the evenings, Moshe would see a light over Jacob's head—it was slightly bluish, cold, as though frozen: a strange light. We all believed that Jacob needed to return to Poland and lead us. He had to return because our fellow believers, under the leadership of Krysa, who had remained with them, had grown impatient and were beginning to turn to the Sabbatians of Salonika for leadership instead. And apparently the Shorr brothers had already met with Wolf in Hungary, the son of the famous Eibeschütz, to see if he would take over the Polish leadership.

"If you don't go, others will," I repeated to Jacob daily, knowing him well. Whenever it was shown to him that he might be outdone, he would grow angry and gather his forces.

Moshe of Podhajce, when he talked, would lean forward and stretch out his neck, and his piercing, high-pitched voice would immediately attract everyone's attention. When he told stories, he would become so engrossed in them that he would raise his fists over his head, shake his head, raise his eyes to the sky, and roar. He was quite the actor, and there was no one he could not do an impression of. Thus we asked him to do so often.

Sometimes he would imitate me, and I would laugh until I cried, seeing myself in his gestures: impulsive, impatient—he could even

perform my stutter. And he alone, Moshe of Podhajce, was
permitted to mock Jacob: he would stand up very straight, and his
head would come forward a little, his eyes would become round,
avian, penetrating, and he would blink very slowly, and anyone
would swear his nose had grown. Then he would put his hands
behind his back and walk, and just like Jacob, he would drag his
legs slightly, sort of in a dignified way, sort of lazily. At first we
would snicker, and then we would roar with laughter whenever
Moshe did Jacob preaching to people.

Jacob himself laughed with us, and his laughter was deep,
resounding, as if reaching us from the bottom of a well. It
immediately did everyone good when he laughed, for it was as
though he were building a tent over our heads, keeping us safe.
Moshe of Podhajce is a good actor, even though he is a learned
rabbi.

One August day, a breathless Osman of Czernowitz arrived with the
news that the true believers who had been camped out along the
river, armed with the king's letter and encouraged by some
messengers from the new bishop, had crossed over the Dniester
with all of their belongings, a song on their lips, untroubled by
anyone, the border guards merely observing the joyful procession.
Osman said they had scattered over three villages among the
bishop's landholdings in which they had some connections, and
some were now living there—in Uściski, Ivanie, and Harmackie—
and were sending supplications with Osman for Jacob to return.

"They are waiting for you like they are waiting for redemption,"
said Osman, and knelt down. "You don't even know how desperately
they wait for you." And Jacob suddenly started laughing and
repeating with audible relish: "Lustig, unsere Brüder haben einen
Platz erhalten," which I assiduously noted down.

Now almost daily someone appeared from Poland with good
news, their faces flushed, and it became ever clearer that we would
be returning. Hana had already learned of it, for she was often in a
gloomy mood and regarded me with great disgust, not speaking a
word, as though it were my fault that Jacob wished to leave this
lovely home he had with her. And right after the harvest, which was
the best in many years, the grapes so sweet that they stuck to our
fingers, we set off to see our people in Bucharest and obtain their
support. We gathered so many grapes that we were able to buy carts
and horses and make the proper preparations for our journey. In a

letter from Poland we learned from our people that an entire village belonging to the bishop was awaiting us. And for the first time the name was spoken: Ivanie.

There are external and internal things. External things are appearance, and we live amongst external things like people in a dream, and the laws of appearances must be taken for real laws when in fact they are not. When you live in a place and a time in which certain laws are in effect, then you must observe those laws, but never forgetting that they are only partial systems, never absolute. For the truth is something else, and if a person is not prepared to come to know it, then it may seem frightening and terrible, and that person may curse the day he learned of it.

But I do believe that everyone can tell what kind of person he truly is. It is just that deep down, he doesn't want to find out.

## Father Benedykt weeds the oregano

The *Kabbala Denudata* from 1677 by von Rosenroth, written in Latin, was given by Elisha Shorr to Father Chmielowski after he saved his Jewish books. Since the issuing of the royal letter, the books have returned to their owner. Truth be told, this came as a great relief to Father Chmielowski. If anyone had found out what the priest had been keeping in the Firlejów presbytery, there would have been quite

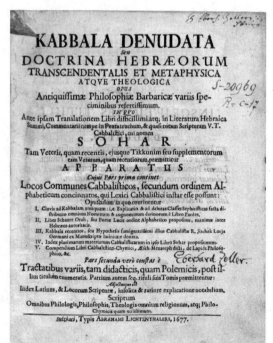

the scandal. For this reason, he also has an ambiguous relationship with his gift. The book was brought by some farmhand, wrapped up in linen, tied with a hemp rope. It must have cost a fortune. The farmhand gave it to Father Chmielowski without a word and disappeared.

Father Chmielowski reads it in the afternoons. The letters are small, so he can only read in broad daylight, by the window. When it gets darker, he opens a bottle of wine and sets aside the book. He holds the wine in his mouth and looks at his garden, and past it, at the ragged meadows across the river. The grass is tall, and a gust of wind will sway it, so that it waves, trembles, as if the meadows were living organisms. Their surface resembles the hide of a horse that balks and shivers when a bumblebee lands on it. With each gust the grass reveals its lighter underbelly, greenish gray like the undercoat of a dog.

To tell the truth, the priest is disappointed; he doesn't understand a thing, even though it is written in Latin, only Latin, but its contents are more like what Mrs. Drużbacka writes. For instance, "My head is filled with dew." What could that mean?

The coming to be of the world is somehow too poetic, he thinks—for us it's snip, snip, in six days God created the world, like a boss who knows how to get something done, instead of thinking about doing it. But here it's all so complicated. And the priest's vision is weakening, and reading tires him out.

It is a strange book. Father Chmielowski had been craving for a long time this kind of general knowledge that explains the beginning and the end, the travels of the planet in the sky and all the miracles and wonders, but this account strikes him as too elusive, and even his favorite Latin scholastics would never have ventured explanations of such miracles— such as that Jesus Christ was Adam Kadmon, pure divine light descended to the earth. Now he thinks about the migration of souls, for instance. To tell the truth, he has heard about this heresy, but he has never given much thought to its logic. The book says that there is nothing wrong in it, that even a good Christian should believe that after death we are reborn in other forms.

Yes, the priest admits quite willingly—for he is above all a practical man—that would be a shot at salvation. Each life in another form would give us more opportunities to perfect ourselves, to redeem our sins. Eternal punishment in hell only rarely makes amends for the whole of the evil that one has inflicted.

But then he feels ashamed of having had such thoughts. Jewish heresies. He kneels at the window beneath the image of Saint Benedict, his patron, and requests his intercession. He also apologizes for his vanity, for letting himself get pulled into such divagations. But what is he to do? The intercession of Saint Benedict doesn't seem to be working, for wild thoughts come once more to his mind . . . The priest has always had a bit of a problem with hell. He could never quite believe in its existence, and the terrifying images he has seen in books—there have been a good number of them—haven't helped. Yet here he reads, for example, that the souls residing in the bodies of pagans who have been cannibals do not proceed directly or always to hell, for that would be merciless. After all, it is not their fault that they were pagans and that they had not seen the light of Christianity. Thanks to their subsequent incarnations, however, they have a shot at improvement, at redeeming the evil they have done. Is that not just?

The priest is so excited and enlivened by this thought that he steps out into the garden to take some fresh air, but as always happens to him in the garden, even though the sun's about to set, he immediately begins to pinch off unnecessary shoots from his plants, and before he knows it, quite to his own surprise, he is on his knees weeding the oregano. But what if the oregano, too, is taking part in this great project of perfection, and in it, too, reside some faint, amorphous souls? What then? And even worse: What if the priest himself is an instrument of eternal justice and at this very moment is punishing the sinful little plants—pulling up the weeds, depriving them of their life?

## The runaway

In the evening, a Jewish cart covered in a hemp horse blanket drives up in front of the presbytery of Firlejów, but it only slows, then turns

around in the priest's courtyard and disappears down the road to Rohatyn. Father Chmielowski looks out from the garden and sees a tall figure
standing motionless alongside the wicker fence. A dark coat flows down
from its shoulders all the way to the ground. A terrible thought
flashes through Father Chmielowski's mind—that this is death, that
death has come for him today. He grabs his wooden rake and lopes over
to meet it.

"Who goes there? Speak at once. I am a priest of the most holy Church
and have no fear of the devil."

"I know that," a man's voice says quietly. It is hoarse, faltering, as
though its owner has not used it in a hundred years. "I am Jan of Okno.
Do not be afraid of me, kind father. I am a good man."

"Then what are you doing here? The sun's gone down."

"The Jews left me here."

The priest goes up and tries to take a look at this newcomer's face, but
he keeps his head down, and his big hood covers everything.

"They've really gone too far this time, those Jews. Who do they take
me for?" mutters the priest, trying to keep his candle going. "What do
you mean, they left you? You keep company with them?"

"Now I keep company with you, Father," answers the stranger. He
speaks in a hazy way, as if carelessly, but he speaks Polish, with just a
slight Ruthenian accent.

"Are you hungry?"

"Not very, they fed me well."

"So what do you want?"

"Shelter."

"You don't have a home of your own?"

"I don't."

The priest hesitates for a moment and then, with resignation, invites
him inside.

"Go on," he says. "There is damp in the air today."

The figure moves uncertainly toward the door, hobbling, and fleetingly his hood shifts and bares a bit of his bright cheek. The man draws
it back over his face, but the priest has already glimpsed something unsettling.

"Look here, at me," he orders.

Then the stranger lifts his head, and the hood falls back onto his shoulders. The priest involuntarily jumps back and cries:

"Jesus of Nazarene, are you a human person?"

"I don't know myself."

"And I am to take you in under my own roof?"

"That's up to you."

"Roshko," the priest quietly calls to his servant, mostly so that this terrible-faced stranger knows he isn't here alone.

"You're afraid of me," the figure laments.

After the briefest moment of hesitation, the priest holds out his arm to encourage the figure to go inside the house. Truth be told, his heart is pounding, and Roshko has disappeared somewhere, as he is wont to do.

"Go on," he says to the stranger, who steps inside ahead of Father Chmielowski. There, in the light of the candle in the holder, he can see more—the lower half of the man's face is completely distorted by scars, as though the skin had been ripped off him. Above that injury, beneath thick black brows, shine big, dark, luminous eyes, young, maybe even beautiful. Or maybe it just seems that way because of the contrast.

"For Christ's sake, what happened to you?" asks Father Chmielowski, shaken to his core.


## The runaway's tale: Jewish purgatory

The priest is surprised by this extraordinary being who calls himself Jan of Okno. Okno—which in Polish means "window"—is a village not far from Toki, many miles from here. The priest doesn't know to whom it belongs, since Jan doesn't want to say. He calls his owner "lord." If it is a lord, it must be Potocki: everything in that area is theirs.

The man eats a little bread and sips some buttermilk. The priest doesn't have any more than that. He offers him vodka, but the man declines. He sits stiffly, without even taking off his cloak, and the smell of horses wafts from him. Saba, her reddish coat bristling, sniffs him all over with great seriousness, as though conscious of his mystery—evidently the newcomer has lots of smells she hasn't encountered before, because it takes her quite a long time until, satisfied, she lies down to sleep by the fireplace.

"I am a corpse," says the man with the terrible face. "You won't denounce a dead body, will you, Father?"

"I commune with the dead," says the priest, showing with his hand the books behind him, lying on the table. "I'm accustomed to their stories. Nothing surprises me. I can even honestly say that I prefer to listen to the dead than to the living."

Then the stranger seems to relax, removing from his shoulders the dark Jewish cloak he's been wearing, showing his strong arms and the long hair that falls onto them. He starts to tell his story in a low voice, in a monotone, as if he had repeated the tale in his head for so long that he'd learned it by heart. Now he gives it to the priest like a handful of coins in exchange for his hospitality.

The father of Jan of Okno came from near Jasło, while his mother was from Masuria. They arrived here as settlers, as colonizers, as they say, since there was little land in their families, and nothing to give to the children. They married and were given a piece of land to cultivate near Tarnopol. The agreement with the lord who owned those lands was that they would work for themselves for fifteen years (which was still good, for other estates offered less—ten, or even five years). Then they were to pay their lease of the lord's land in goods and labor. They also had to commit to performing a number of duties for free, such as helping with the threshing, construction on the estate, shelling peas, even cleaning—there was always something in the house to do, so that there was never enough time for the work their own home needed.

The priest is reminded of the crosses that always fill him with horror and a vague sense of guilt when he sees them. They stand next to the peasants' huts like peasant versions of memento mori. The peasants put pegs into the crosses, one for each year of their release from serfdom.

Then each year they take one out, until one day the cross stands bare—then, in return for those few years of freedom, they have to pay dearly with their own slavery, and that of their entire family as well.

Okno was known for its woven kilims, and his father dreamed of Jan learning that trade.

Jan was born into slavery as the youngest of nine siblings. When he was a child, his parents had to work off their debt to the lord four days a week; by the time he married, it was often seven. That meant that his whole family also had to work on the lord's estate. Often, in order to tend to their own land, they had to dedicate their Sundays to it and couldn't even go to church. Two of Jan's older sisters worked in the house—one as a cook, the other stoking the ovens. When that one got pregnant, the lord had her married off to a man in a neighboring village. That was the first time Jan tried to escape. He had once heard from the freemen and vagabonds who sometimes passed through the village and paused in front of the inn that if he were able to get up to the North Sea, he could join a ship's crew and go to other countries where a person could live better and prosper. Young and inexperienced, he set off on foot, with a little bundle on a stick, happy and sure of himself. He slept in the woods and soon became convinced that the forests were full of fugitives like him. But he got caught by a couple of the lord's farmhands just a few miles away from home. They beat him bloody and dragged him off to jail, which was a kind of dungeon under a cowshed. He spent four months there. After that, he was put in stocks and publicly whipped. He should have been happy the punishment was so mild. To top it all off, the lord ordered him to marry a girl from the house who was visibly with child. That's what was done with flighty men—a family would soon settle them down. But Jan was no less unsettled, and he never came to love the girl. The child died, and his wife ran off somewhere, out of the village. They said she became a whore in the taverns of Zbaraż, and later Lwów. For a while, Jan did his work humbly and learned to weave in someone else's workshop, but when one winter both his parents died, one after the other, he put on his warm clothes and, taking all of their savings, hitched a horse to the sleigh, determined to get to his father's family near Jasło. He knew that

the lord was cruel, but he also knew he was sluggish, and no one would be
in a hurry to chase him in that cold. He made it all the way to Przemyśl,
and there some guards stopped and arrested him when he could neither
provide any documentation nor explain to them who he was or what he
was doing there. After about two months, the lord's people came for him.
They threw him onto a sleigh, tied up like a hog, to take him back. It
would take a few days because the roads were snowed over, and they used
that as an excuse not to rush back to their village. Once they left him tied
up and went into an inn to get drunk. As always happened when they
would leave him on the sleigh at such stops, people would look at him in
silence, with horror in their eyes, though probably what affected them
most was the thought that they might meet a similar fate. A peasant who
escapes for the second time, and who manages to make it that far, is a
dead man. When he begged for something to drink, people were afraid to
help him. In the end, some traders, drunk and more as a joke than out of
any desire to help their fellow man, freed him one night by an inn when
the lord's strongmen had drunk themselves unconscious. But he didn't
have the strength to run far. The lord's drunken myrmidons caught him
again and beat him so badly that he lost consciousness. Fearing the lord's
wrath, they tried to revive him, but feeling certain he was dead, they left
him in an oak grove and covered him in snow so that he didn't give away
their sin. There he lay, facedown, and there, by some miracle, he was
found by some Jews passing by on a couple of carts.

He woke up a few days later in the Shorrs' cowshed, surrounded by
animals and the smell of their bodies, their excrement, engulfed in their
warmth. Around him, people spoke another language, had different faces,
and Jan thought that he had died and found himself in purgatory, and
that for some reason purgatory was Jewish. And that here he would spend
eternity, recollecting the innocent, small sins of his peasant's life and re-
penting them.

## Cousins putting up a unified front
## and launching their campaign

"Now, you are not my uncle, and I am not your aunt. I am, by birth, a Potocka. Of course you may have some connection with my husband, but I do not recognize your line," Mrs. Kossakowska says to him, and gives him leave to sit. His view of her is obstructed by papers, which she gathers and sets aside in a pile, and from there they are taken care of by Agnieszka—inseparable from Katarzyna now—who dries them with sand.

What advantage is she seeking? wonders Moliwda.

"I am the one who attends to our extensive holdings, I oversee all our bills, all the gossip in society, all the correspondence—my husband does not have the inclination for it," she says, as though reading his mind, and Moliwda raises his eyebrows in surprise. "I keep up with the family finances, I make matches, I deliver information, I make agreements, arrangements, I issue reminders . . ."

The castellan, her husband, strolls about the room with a glass of liqueur, walking in a humorous way, like a heron, dragging his feet over the Turkish carpet. He'll soon wear through those soles, thinks Moliwda. He is wearing a pale yellow żupan, tailored so well to fit his rotten figure it actually makes him look elegant.

"Her Ladyship, my wife, is a veritable institution unto herself. The envy of the royal secretariat," he says delightedly. "She is even an expert in my blood relations, making great endeavors on behalf of my kin."

Mrs. Kossakowska shoots him a murderous look. Moliwda knows that despite appearances, it is a happy marriage. Meaning: They each do their own thing.

The castellan lights his pipe and turns to his distant cousin:

"Why is it you are so concerned with these people?"

"Because they've struck a chord with me," answers Moliwda after a moment's consideration. "Right here," he says, and bangs his chest, as though wishing to assure the castellan that he does, in fact, have a heart there. "I feel a real connection with them. They are honest and good, and their intentions are honest and good . . ."

"Jews who are honest and good," says Mrs. Kossakowska with a smirk. "Are they paying you?"

"I'm not doing it for the money."

"There wouldn't be anything wrong with doing it for the money . . ."

"It isn't about money," he repeats. Then he adds: "Although they are paying me."

Katarzyna Kossakowska leans back in her chair and stretches out her legs in front of her.

"Ah, I understand, for fame, to make a name for yourself, like the bishop, may he rest in peace. You're thinking of your career."

"I don't care about my career, you know that already. Had I wanted a career, I would have kept the position I had when I was young, thanks to my uncle, in the royal chancellery. By now I would be a minister."

"Pass me the pipe, please," Mrs. Kossakowska says to her husband, and extends an expectant hand. "You're hotheaded, cousin. So to whom am I to write? And what am I to entreat them to do? Perhaps you could introduce me to this Frank of theirs?"

"He is in the Turkish country now, as they wished to kill him here."

"Who wished to kill him here? We are, after all, known for our national tolerance."

"His own kind. They were persecuted by their own. Their own, meaning the other Jews."

"But normally they stick together," Mrs. Kossakowska says, confused; now she fills the pipe, taking tobacco from an embroidered leather pouch.

"Not this time. These Shabbitarians believe in the necessity of getting out from under the Jewish faith. The greater part of the Jews converted to Islam in Turkey for this reason. While the Jews in the Catholic lands would like to convert to the local faith. For any Orthodox Jew, of course, leaving the faith like this is a fate worse than death."

"But why would they want to join the Church?" asks the castellan, intrigued by this bizarre behavior. "Things have been crystal clear till now. Jews are Jews. They go to synagogue. Catholics are Catholics, who worship in a cathedral, and the Ruthenians have their Orthodox churches—to each his own."

The vision of such upheaval is not to the castellan's liking.

"Their first Messiah says it is necessary to collect what is good from every creed."

"Well, he's right about that," Mrs. Kossakowska jumps in.

"What do you mean, first Messiah? Was there a second? Who's the second?" asks Kossakowski.

Moliwda explains, but reluctantly, as though knowing that no matter what he says, the castellan will immediately forget it anyway.

"Some say there will be three Messiahs. One has already come—that was Sabbatai Tzvi. After him came Baruchiah . . ."

"I haven't heard of any of this . . ."

"And the third will be here soon and will deliver them from all their suffering."

"Why are they suffering so much?" asks the castellan.

"Well, they are hardly prospering. That you can see for yourself. I see it, too—people are living in poverty and humiliation and they are seeking a way out before they are all turned into animals. The religion of the Jews is close to ours, just like the Muslim religion, they're all the same little pieces of the puzzle, you just have to know how to put them all together. They are assiduous in their religion. They seek God with their hearts, they fight for Him, not like us, with our Hail Marys and our prostration."

Mrs. Kossakowska sighs.

"It's our peasants who should be waiting for the Messiah . . . Oh, how we need new manifestations of the Christian spirit! Who still prays assiduously?"

Moliwda hits his poetic stride now; this is an art he has almost perfected.

"It's really more connected with resistance, with rebellion. The butterfly that rises to the sky in the morning is not a reformed, renegade, or renewed chrysalis. It's still the same creation, just raised to the second power of its life. It's a transformed chrysalis. The Christian spirit is flexible, mobile, and omnipresent . . . And it does us a world of good, once we accept it."

"Well, well, you're quite the preacher, cousin," Mrs. Kossakowska says, her words dripping with sarcasm.

Moliwda is toying with the buttons on his żupan, which is brand-new, brown wool, with a red silk lining. He bought it with the money Nahman paid him. But it wasn't enough to cover everything—the buttons are made out of cheap agate, cold to the touch.

"There is an old prophecy that everyone now says comes from the most distant of ancestors, from a long, long time ago."

"I'm always eager to hear a good prophecy." Mrs. Kossakowska breathes in smoke with evident pleasure and turns to face Moliwda. When she smiles, she becomes beautiful. "It shall be so, or it shall not be so. Red sky at night, sailors delight. Red sky in morning, sailors take warning," she says, and laughs. Her husband giggles, too, so they must share a sense of humor—at least they have that in common.

Moliwda smiles and goes on:

"That in Poland shall be born a man of the Jewish nation who will give up his religion and accept the Christian faith and bring along with him many other Jews. It is said that this will be a sign of the approach of Judgment Day in Poland."

Mrs. Kossakowska's face becomes grave.

"And you believe that, Antoni Kossakowski? Judgment Day? Judgment Day is upon us anyway—no one agrees with anyone else, everyone is at war with everyone, the king is in Dresden, caring very little indeed for the problems of his kingdom . . ."

"If you would be so kind as to write to this and that important personage"—Moliwda points to the pile of letters carefully folded and sealed by Agnieszka's slender fingers—"in support of these poor people who are joining with us in this way, we would be the first in Europe. Never has there been such a mass conversion anywhere. They would talk of us at all the royal courts."

"I have no influence over the king—my reach does not extend that far,

I'm afraid!" cries an affronted Mrs. Kossakowska. Then she says calmly: "People say they are approaching the church as they are because they are seeking to gain something from it—that they want to make a profit off it—that they want, as neophytes, to come and live among us. And as neophytes that can immediately get titles, so long as they can put up the cash."

"Does that surprise you, madam? Is there something wrong in wanting a better life? If only you could see these towns of theirs, all mud and poverty and stupefaction . . ."

"Now, that's interesting, because I don't know any Jews like that. The kind I know are all quite cunning indeed, rubbing their hands together in glee, just looking for a way to swindle you out of a grosz, water down your vodka, sell you some rotten seeds . . ."

"How could you know any Jews like that when all you do is sit around palaces and mansions, writing letters and, in the evenings, shining in the pleasant society of . . . ," says her husband.

He was going to say "wastrels," but he stopped himself.

". . . wastrels," she says for him.

"Your network, madam, is vast; you know Branicki well, and even at court you have many trusted acquaintances. No nation can allow such lawlessness to occur, can allow Jews to attack other Jews. The king, in doing nothing, is in essence giving his permission. Meanwhile, they come to us like children. Hundreds, maybe even thousands, of them are stuck along the Dniester, gazing over at the Polish shore, terribly homesick, since as a result of the riots and the lawlessness they have been cast out of their homes, robbed, assaulted. Now they're stuck there, exiled by their own people from their own country. After all, they do belong to this country, but now they're camped out in dugouts all along the river, desperately looking north, hoping to come home, although their homes are now occupied by those other Jews. The land they ought to receive from those of us who have too much of it—"

But Moliwda sees he's gone too far and breaks off his tirade.

"What is it you want?" Mrs. Kossakowska asks, slowly and suspiciously.

Moliwda saves the situation:

"The church should take care of them. You're on good terms with Bishop Sołtyk, they say you are a dear friend of his . . ."

"A dear friend, am I? You know what they say, I wot well how the world wags, he is most loved that has the most bags," Mrs. Kossakowska retorts. "Certainly goes for his affections."

Castellan Kossakowski, bored, sets down his empty glass and rubs his hands together to give himself back a little energy.

"I must make my excuses, for I am off to the kennel. Femka is to whelp. She slutted about with that priest's dog with the long, messy fur, and now we're going to have to drown the pups . . ."

"I'll have them drowned for you. Don't even think about trying to do it yourself, my dear. Soon you'll be saying they take after me in loveliness and are clever and useful as hunting dogs."

"Then you take care of them. I guess I won't," says Kossakowski, angry that his wife would treat him so unceremoniously in front of a stranger.

"I'll take care of them," Agnieszka pipes up suddenly, her face flushing. "If His Lordship would be so kind as to stay their execution . . ."

"Well, if Miss Agnieszka wishes it . . . ," Kossakowski begins gallantly.

"Go already," Mrs. Kossakowska mutters, and her husband disappears from the doorway without finishing his sentence.

"I have already brought this matter to the attention of the new bishop, Łubieński," Moliwda continues. "There are more of them than you all think. In places such as Kopyczyńce, Nadwórna. In Rohatyn, Busk, and Glinno they're the majority now. If we were smart, we would welcome them."

"Sołtyk is the one you need. He can get things done, although only if it's in his own interest. He doesn't like the Jews—he's always running into trouble with them. How much can they pay?"

Moliwda is silent for a moment, considering.

"A lot."

"Is a lot enough to buy back the bishop's pawned insignia?"

"What do you mean?" Moliwda starts.

"He pawned it again. The bishop is perpetually generating new debts at cards."

"Maybe so, I don't know. I'd have to ask. We could all meet together—them, the bishop, Your Ladyship, and me."

"Sołtyk is aiming for the bishopric of Kraków now, as the bishop there is dying."

Katarzyna stands and puts out her hands in front of her, as though stretching. The joints crack. Agnieszka looks at her with concern from over her embroidery hoop.

"You'll have to forgive me, my dear sir, that's the drumbeat of old age in my bones," she says, and smiles from ear to ear. "Tell me, what do they believe in? Is it true that they only favor Catholicism on the surface, that deep down they remain Jews? That's what Pikulski says . . ."

Moliwda sits up straighter in his chair:

"The religion of those traditional Jews consists in fulfilling the orders of the Torah, of living according to the old rituals. They don't believe in any sort of rapture, the prophets came a long time ago, and now it's time to wait for the Messiah. Their God won't reveal Himself again, He has fallen silent. While with the other ones, the Sabbatians, it's all the other way around—they say we live in Messianic times and that all around us we can see signs presaging the arrival of the Messiah. The First Messiah has already come, that was Sabbatai. After him came the Second—Baruchiah—and now comes the Third . . ."

"Pikulski told me that some people say it might be a woman this time."

"I will tell you, Your Ladyship, that I honestly do not care so much about what they believe. What I care about is that they are being treated like lepers. When Jews are wealthy, they can attain the greatest heights, like the one who advises Brühl, but the poor ones live in misery and are abused by all. The Cossacks treat them worse than dogs. Nowhere else in the world is it like that. I was in Turkey, and they have better rights there than they do here with us."

"Well, they did convert to Islam . . . ," Mrs. Kossakowska notes ironically.

"It's different in Poland. Just think, cousin. Poland is a country where freedom of religion and religious hatreds meet on equal terms. On the one hand, Jews can practice their religion as they wish here, they have civil liberties and their own judiciary. On the other, hatred toward them is so great that the very word 'Jew' is derogatory, and good Christians employ it as a curse."

"You're right about that. The one and the other are the results of the laziness and ignorance that predominate in this country, rather than of any innate evil."

"We all want that to be the explanation. It's easier to be stupid and lazy than evil. Someone who never pokes his nose out of his own backwater, who believes to the letter whatever the semi-educated priest tells him to believe, who can barely string two letters together and reads no more than the calendar, readily gives his mind over to every sort of nonsense and prejudice, as I saw recently at Bishop Dembowski's, when he would not stop singing the praises of *New Athens*."

Mrs. Kossakowska looks at him in astonishment.

"You find fault with Father Chmielowski and his *New Athens* now? Everyone is reading it. It is our silva rerum. Do not find fault in books. The books themselves are innocent."

Moliwda, embarrassed, does not speak. So Mrs. Kossakowska continues:

"I'll tell you this much: As far as I can tell, the Jews are probably the only people who can be of any use in this country, since the lords don't know how to do anything and don't care to learn, too busy with their sport. But your Jewish heretics also want land!"

"They are settling on land in Turkey, too. All over Giurgiu, Vidin, and Ruse, half of Bucharest, Greek Salonika. There they buy land and are able to have some peace and quiet . . ."

". . . if they convert to Islam, right?"

"Your Ladyship, they are prepared to be baptized."

Mrs. Kossakowska props herself up on her elbows and leans in toward Moliwda's face, like a man, staring him in the eye.

"Who are you, Moliwda? What is your position here?"

Moliwda answers without blinking:

"I am their translator."

"Is it true you were once with the Old Believers?"

"It is true. I'm not ashamed of it, and I don't deny it. What does it matter?"

"It matters that you are all after money—you heretics."

"There are many roads to God, it isn't ours to judge."

"Of course it's ours. There are roads, and there's the wilderness."

"Then help them, Your Ladyship, to get on the true path."

Mrs. Kossakowska leans back and smiles broadly. She stands, goes up to him, and takes him by the hand.

"And the sin of the Adamites?" She lowers her voice and looks at Agnieszka, but the girl, attentive as a mouse, has already pricked up her ears and extended her neck. "They say their practices are not at all Christian." Katarzyna discreetly fixes the thin fabric over her décolletage. "Anyway, what is the sin of the Adamites? Explain, my enlightened cousin."

"Everything that those who use that term cannot imagine."


## Moliwda sets out and beholds the kingdom of the vagabonds

Since his return to his country, everything has struck Moliwda as foreign and strange. He hasn't been here for many years, and his memory is either short or flawed, or both—he certainly hadn't remembered things being this way. Above all, he is amazed by the grayness of the landscape and the distant horizon. And the light, too—more delicate than in the south, softer. A mournful Polish light that leads to melancholy.

First he travels from Lwów to Lublin in a carriage, but in Lublin he rents a horse—he feels better this way than in some stuffy, clattering box.

He has barely gotten past the tollhouses of Lublin, but already he is entering another country, a different cosmos, in which people are no longer planets that orbit according to established paths, around the market square, the home, the shop, or the field, but are instead errant streaks of fire.

These are the freemen and vagabonds Nahman told Moliwda about, many of whom have come to join the true believers. But Moliwda can see that these untethered people aren't only Jews, as he had thought until now—as a matter of fact, Jews are in the minority here. Moliwda also sees that this is a kind of nation unto itself, different from anything that can be found in cities or towns or rural areas. These are people who do not belong to any lord or to any municipality or other form of government. These are wanderers, frolicsome bandits, fugitives of every sort you can imagine. It seems clear they all share the same distaste for the peaceful, settled life, that they suffer from wanderlust and could not bear to be enclosed by four walls. Or so a person might think at first glance—that they like it this way, that they live like this out of choice. But from the height of his horse's back, Moliwda looks upon them with sympathy and thinks that the majority of these people are in fact the kind who do dream of having their own bed, their own bowl to eat from, and a regular, settled life, but that just isn't how the cards have played out for them, so instead they've had to roam. He knows because his fate has been the same.

Just beyond the city limits, they sit on the side of the road, as if resting after a difficult visit to a human settlement, as if shaking off its foul air, its garbage that sticks to their feet, the filth and noise of the masses. The itinerant merchants count the money they have made. They have laid aside their portable stalls—mostly empty now, the goods they held gone—although they keep an eye out for any scrap enthusiasts who might happen down the road. Oftentimes they're Scots, men who come from their own far-off land to set up a shop they hang over their shoulders: beautifully woven silk ribbons, tortoiseshell combs, holy pictures, remedies for baldness, glass beads, mirrors in wooden frames. Their language is bizarre, and sometimes it is impossible to understand them, but the language of coins is universal.

Nearby rests the picture-maker—an old man with a long beard, wearing a woven hat with a broad brim. He has a wooden rack hung from leather straps, affixed with holy pictures. He has removed from his shoulders this heavy baggage and now feeds on what the peasants have paid him in—dense white cheese and damp rye that transforms into a dumpling in his mouth. A feast! He probably also has bottles of holy water in his leather bag, little pouches of the desert sand Jesus prayed over for forty days, among other wonders, the sight of which will widen his customers' eyes. Moliwda remembers these things from his childhood.

On a daily basis, the picture man pretends to be a saintly person who just happened to become a seller of pictures. Then, as befits a saintly person, he raises his voice a little, so that it will be more like the voice of a priest, and he speaks in a singsong tone, as if reciting the Holy Scriptures, and from time to time he interjects Latin words, regardless of whether they make sense, since it impresses the peasants. The picture man wears a giant wooden cross around his neck, which weighs him down considerably; he has rested it against a tree and is airing out his footwraps on it now. He sells his pictures by first identifying one of the nicer houses in the village, then going there as if in a kind of trance, insisting that the picture itself has chosen this home, and even this particular wall, the one in this chamber—the sacred one. It is hard for a peasant to turn down a holy picture; he will take his hard-earned money out of its hiding place and hand it over.

Just a little farther on is the inn, crooked and small, sloppily whitewashed, but with a porch before its entrance and wooden boards resting on posts that serve as benches. The benches are occupied by old men who are too poor to go inside and order something to eat, so instead they sit and hope for alms from someone who has already satisfied his own hunger and now finds himself in a better mood, with a more sensitive heart than when he turned them down on his way in.

Moliwda gets off his horse, although he hasn't traveled that far yet from Lublin. Immediately two old men rush up to him with laments on their lips. Moliwda gives them some tobacco and stays to smoke himself, and, enchanted, they thank him. He learns from them that they both come from the same village: it is hard for their families to maintain them, so every spring they set out to beg, not returning until winter. They have been joined by a half-blind old woman traveling alone to Częstochowa, she says, but if you take a closer look at her, you'll see all kinds of little pouches of herbs under her apron, some sort of seeds strung on threads, and other medicaments. She must be a woman with considerable know-how—she'd be able to stem blood flow, and help deliver children, but if you paid her enough, she could get rid of a pregnancy, too. She keeps quiet all these things she knows, which is no surprise. They recently burned a woman just like her at the stake in Greater Poland, and last year several were captured in Lublin.

Inside the inn, there are two former Turkish prisoners of war, supplied with Church testimonies that state they have just been released from captivity and order whoever meets them to be charitable toward their bearer, out of Christian sympathy for their ill fate. But the former captives hardly look like they have suffered. They're both fat and jolly, especially now that the first round of vodka has started working on them, and they're just about to order another. Those Turks must have taken pretty good care of them. The innkeeper, a Jewish widow, independent and impertinent, gives them a bowl of potatoes seasoned with onion fried in butter and can't keep from asking questions, curious about what it was like where they were. Everything they say amazes her, sending her hands flying to her cheeks. Moliwda eats the same dish of potatoes, drinks some buttermilk, and purchases a pint of vodka for the road. When he does get back on the road, he sees some commotion right away—it's the bear men, heading to Lublin; they always make a lot of noise so that as many people as possible crowd around them to view the humiliation of the dirty, and probably ill, animal. That sight—who knows why—gives the oglers a strange satisfaction. Now they're poking the bear with a stick. That poor animal, thinks Moliwda, but he understands the joy it brings to the vagabonds: look at that, it's so strong, but it's worse off than I am. Cretinous vermin.

There are always a lot of loose women on such tracts, too, for when a girl is pretty and young, or even just young, men immediately seize on to her, and as soon as they have seized, the girls may as well already be practicing the oldest profession in the world. Some of them are fugitive noblewomen who gave birth to a child out of wedlock, the child of a peasant or farmhand at that, and then the shame for the family is so great that it is better to abandon the child and hope for the mercy of its relatives than to swallow this misfortune. And so the girls leave—their only other option being a convent—with the tacit permission of their offended and indignant family, from the larch manor into the black of night. And if they come to a river, a bridge, a ford, then they fall into the hands of the eternally intoxicated raftsmen, and from then on, every man will demand, for every service—a night at the inn, a lift somewhere—one and the same payment. That's how easy it is to fall.

Moliwda would like to make use of their services, but he fears their diseases and their filth, and the lack of a proper enclosure. He'll wait until he gets to Warsaw.

## How Moliwda is made messenger in the service of a difficult cause

During his first few days in Warsaw, he's stuck in the home of his brother, a priest, who's helped him out a little with equipment and attire, despite the fact that his share of the parish purse is scant. After so many years, Moliwda's brother feels like a stranger, as two-dimensional as a sheet of paper, scarcely even real. For two nights they drink together, trying to break through this unexpected awkwardness that has arisen between them over the course of these twenty-some years. Moliwda's brother tells him stories of Warsaw life, but it is only stolen gossip. Soon he is drunk, and airing a grudge against Moliwda for leaving him behind with their strict uncle, griping that the priesthood isn't really his vocation, that it's no good living on your own like this, that every time he enters the church it seems too big to him. Moliwda claps his brother on the back with the same sympathy he might have for a total stranger he met in some tavern.

Now he tries to arrange to see Branicki, but Branicki is always away, always on some hunting trip. He pleads his way into a meeting with Bishop Załuski, and tries to court the Princess Jabłonowska, who happens to be in the capital. He tries, too, to discover the whereabouts of his friends from twenty-five years ago, but it isn't easy. And so he spends his evenings with his brother; there's not much to talk about with someone you haven't seen in that long; he is a stranger, obsessed with his priestly career, weak, and vain. In fact, everyone in Warsaw strikes Moliwda as self-obsessed and vain. Everyone here pretends to be something they're not. The very city tries to pass itself off as something else, somewhere more populated, more extensive, prettier, when in fact it's just a plain old dump with muddy little roads. Everything is so expensive here that all you can do is window-shop, and it's all imported from elsewhere. Hats from England, French-style frock coats from France, Polish-style fashion from Turkey. And the city itself? Terrible, cold, abysmal, full of empty squares the wind howls down. Magnificent houses are built right in the sand, in the mud, and you see servants transferring ladies from their carriage onto a wooden walkway so that they don't drown in puddles in their thick, fur-lined mantles.

Moliwda feels worn out in Warsaw. He passes his time in the company of not especially demanding people, where the wine flows freely, and where he can tell his implausible tales, especially when he has drunk a lot of alcohol. Tales of calm at sea, or the opposite, of terrible squalls that cast him naked onto a Greek island, where he was found by women, and he doesn't remember what happened next, and when he is asked to repeat a story in different company, he doesn't know what he said before, where his adventures last led him. Of course he never strays too far, just circles around holy Mount Athos and the tiny islets in the Greek sea, along which a giant could step all the way to Stamboul or Rodos.

About the origins of his new name, Moliwda—for he tells people to call him Moliwda now—he tells different stories, but in Warsaw it makes a real impression when he tells people that he's the king of a small island in the Greek sea called Moliwda. The same place where two women discovered him, naked as the day he was born. They were sisters, of noble Turkish lineage. He has even invented names for them: Zhimelda and Edina. They got him drunk and seduced him. He ended up married to them both, for such is the custom there, and after the almost immediate death of their father, he became sole ruler of the island. He reigned for fifteen years and had six sons, and to them he has left that little kingdom, but when the time comes, he will invite them all here, to Warsaw.

The company applauds in delight. The wine flows.

When he finds himself in more educated company, he alters his tale slightly, with it turning out that by chance and by virtue of his otherness, he was recognized as ruler of the island, an advantage that served him well for years, and things were good for him there. Here he starts describing its customs, making them sufficiently exotic as to be interesting to his listeners. He says that his name was given to him by Chinese merchants he met in Smyrna, traders in silk and lacquerware. They called him moli-hua, Jasmine Flower. When he says this, he always sees a smirk appear on his listeners' lips, at least on the lips of the more malicious ones. Nothing resembles jasmine less than Moliwda.

He tells another story when it starts to get late, and a booze-soaked haze of intimacy has set in. In Warsaw, people party until morning, and the women are willing and not at all as shy as might seem at first, when they're all playing the dainty little noblewomen. Sometimes this shocks him—it would be inconceivable amongst the Turks or in Wallachia, where women keep separate and far from men, for ladies to flirt freely in this way, while their husbands do the same in a far corner of the room. Here it's not uncommon to hear—in fact, the higher the orbit, the more often you hear it—that the father of some child is not the one who acts as his father, but rather a friend of the family, some important person, an influential cousin. And no one is surprised by this, no one condemns it—quite the opposite, especially if the actual father is well-connected or holds a high position. That is, for instance, what all of Warsaw is gossiping about with respect to the Czartoryskis' child, that the father is Prince Repnin, a fact about which Mr. Czartoryski appears not even a little bit displeased.

Finally, at the end of November, Moliwda is granted the honor of an audience with Bishop Sołtyk, who is now at court seeking the bishopric of Kraków.

The man he encounters is perfectly empty and conceited. Dark, impenetrable eyes bore into Moliwda, trying to decipher to what extent he might be useful. The bishop's cheeks, which are slightly pendulous, lend him an air of gravity; has anyone ever seen a skinny bishop? Unless he has tapeworm . . .

Moliwda presents the matter of the Sabbatians to him, no longer in a tone of caritas, no longer attempting to evoke concern about their fate or aiming for his listener's heart with beautiful sentiments. For a moment, he searches for the proper approach, and then he says:

"Your Excellency would hold a perfect trump card. Several hundred, maybe even thousands, of Jews, who crossed over to the bosom of the Church, converted to the one true faith. Many of them are also wealthy."

"I thought they were paupers from the street."

"There are wealthier ones among them. They are fighting for titles, and titles are worth mountains of gold. According to the laws of the Republic, a neophyte can apply for a noble title with no great impediment."

"That would be the end of the world . . ."

Moliwda looks at the bishop, who seems restless. His face is impenetrable, but his right hand makes a strange, involuntary gesture, his thumb, index finger, and middle finger rubbing nervously together.

"Who is this Frank, anyway? Some ignoramus, some lout . . . They say that's what he calls himself."

"He does call himself that. He calls himself an amuritz, a simpleton. It's from Hebrew, am ha'aretz . . ."

"You know Hebrew?"

"I know enough. I can understand what he's saying. It isn't true that he's a simpleton. He has been taught quite well by his people, he knows the Zohar, the Bible, and the Mosaic law; he might not be able to say many things well in Polish or in Latin, but he is a well-educated man. And clever. Whatever he sets out to do, he will accomplish. With the help of this person or that . . ."

"So just like you, Mr. Kossakowski," says Bishop Sołtyk, in a flash of perspicacity.

### Of useful truths and useless truths, and the mortar post as a means of communication

Much of that year of 1758 Bishop Kajetan Sołtyk spends in Warsaw. It is a pleasant time, since Warsaw offers abundant diversions. It is autumn, and everyone is coming back into town from their country estates—the social season could now be said to be under way. The bishop has many things on his mind. The first and most important is the expectation— the joyful expectation—that he will be appointed the next bishop of Kraków. The cards have been dealt, he tells himself over and over, and this means that his nomination will take place once the poor, sick Andrzej Załuski—his friend, Bishop of Kraków, and Joseph's brother—has died. In some senses everything has already been settled among these three: Andrzej knows that he will die soon and is reconciled to death, like a good Christian who knows he has lived a holy life, and he has already written to the king recommending the appointment of Sołtyk as his replacement. Although now he has been unconscious for a fortnight, and earthly matters no longer concern him.

But they do concern Bishop Sołtyk. He has already ordered new vestments from the Jewish tailors, and new winter shoes. He spends the evenings with friends, goes to the opera, and to dinners where his presence is requested. Unfortunately, it still happens—he himself laments it extremely—that later he has his carriage take him home so he can change clothes and, according to his own time-honored custom, venture back out to a certain inn on the outskirts of town, where he plays cards. Lately he has managed to wager only small sums, so as not to greatly increase his already massive debt, and this improves his self-esteem somewhat. If only this were the single weakness that plagued mankind!

Another friend of Załuski's appears in Warsaw, Katarzyna Kossakowska, a woman as sly as a fox—Sołtyk does not particularly like her, but he respects her and even fears her a bit. She has real missionary zeal, and she spreads word of her cause to everyone she encounters—she is seeking every kind of support in the capital for those Jewish heretics. She quickly unites those who can help in the matter of convincing the king himself to issue a letter of safe conduct that will protect those miserable souls, who now cling to the Christian faith. It becomes a fashionable topic at the salons, at formal dinners, in the corridors of the opera; everyone speaks of the so-called Jewish Puritans. Some with great excitement, others with a lofty, cool Polish irony. The bishop receives from Kossakowska an unexpected present of a gilded silver chain with a heavy cross on it, also silver, studded with stones. The piece is valuable and rare.

The bishop would have involved himself to a greater degree in this cause of hers had it not been for this business of waiting. He does, in point of fact, have competitors. As soon as Bishop Andrzej Załuski dies in Kraków, he will have to act quickly, be the first to appear before the king and make an impression upon him. It is a good thing the king is in Warsaw, far from his beloved Dresden and Saxony—but with those places now plundered by Frederick Augustus, it is safer for him here.

What a credit it would be in the eyes of God to bring all those Jewish heretics into the bosom of the church. The world has never seen such a thing—and it is only in Catholic Poland that such a thing could ever happen. The entire world would hear of us, thinks Bishop Sołtyk.

While he has been waiting, the bishop has devised a fabulous plan. Namely, he has ordered hired cannoneers with mortars to be positioned all along the road from Kraków to Warsaw, each at a distance of several miles, and just as soon as his man at the bishop's in Kraków learns that Załuski has died, he will let the first cannoneer know to fire in the direction of Warsaw. At that signal, the second cannoneer will fire, and then the third, and so on, in a chain that links them all the way to Warsaw, and in such a way, by this unusual post, Bishop Sołtyk will be the first to know, before any of the official letters sent by the messengers are brought in. The idea was provided to him by Joseph Załuski, who had found it in some book, and who understood his friend's impatience.

Załuski would like to go to Kraków to see his dying brother, but December has been strangely warm—the rivers have flooded, and many roads are impassable, so that he, too, is dependent upon Sołtyk's mortar post.

There is now talk of a papal letter regarding the matter of the ongoing—though lately less frequent—accusations against the Jews of using Christian blood. Rome's stance is clear and irrevocable: such accusations have no basis whatsoever. This embitters Kajetan Sołtyk, as he confides over dinner to his friends Katarzyna Kossakowska and the bishop Joseph Załuski.

"I have heard the testimonies myself. I sat through a whole trial."

"I'd be curious as to what kinds of things Your Excellency would say under torture," Kossakowska says, making a wry face.

Załuski, too, is familiar with the matter, as Sołtyk related to him in great detail the events in Markowa Wolica several years ago.

"I would like to broach this subject in some sort of scholarly work," he says slowly. "And take the time to study all the sources to which I have access in the library. And there are numerous sources on it from all over the world. If the bishop were not taking up so much of my time . . ."

He would like nothing more than to immerse himself completely in his studies and never leave his library. But there is a pained expression on his lively face, which displays every shade of emotion. He says:

"What a shame that everything must be written in French now, rather than in our holy Latin, which, too, discourages me from writing, for my French is not the best. And yet everything is suddenly parlez, parlez . . . ," he says, trying to mock this language he doesn't like.

". . . the words are all so sorry." Kossakowska finishes the popular Polish phrase on his behalf. "As though one's throat were all dried out from speaking it."

A servant instantly appears to refill her glass.

"I can only summarize my views." Bishop Załuski looks attentively at Sołtyk, but the latter is fully absorbed in nibbling meat off rabbit bones and seems not to hear. So he turns to Kossakowska, who has already finished eating and is now fidgeting, wanting to smoke her pipe:

"I have based these views on an in-depth study of sources, but above all on my reflections upon them, as facts recorded and promulgated without rational reflection can be misleading."

He pauses for a moment as though attempting to recall those facts. In the end, he says:

"So I came to the conclusion that the whole misunderstanding arose from a simple mistake with words, or rather, with Hebrew letters. The Hebrew word *d-a-m*"—the bishop now traces the Hebrew signs on the table with his finger—"means at once 'money' and 'blood,' which might lead to any variety of misrepresentation—when we say that the Jews lust after money, it seems that we are saying they lust after blood. And to this was added the popular fantasy that it was Christian blood. That is where the whole fairy tale came from. And there might also be a second reason: during weddings, they give the newlyweds a drink of wine and myrtle known as *h-a-d-a-s*, and they call blood *h-a-d-a-m*, which could have also led to accusations. 'Hadam,' 'hadas'—they're practically the same, do you see, Your Ladyship? Our nuncio is right."

Bishop Sołtyk throws the little bones he hasn't quite finished working on onto the table and roughly pushes his plate away.

"Your Excellency is making a mockery of me and my testimony," he says, surprisingly calmly, but in a formal tone.

Kossakowska leans in to both of them, these corpulent men with the snow-white napkins at their throats, their cheeks red from wine:

"Truth for truth's sake is not worth looking into. The truth in itself is always complicated. What we want to know is what truth we can use, and how."

And not concerning herself with etiquette, she goes ahead and lights her pipe.

In the morning, the mortar post finally delivers the sad news that the Bishop of Kraków Andrzej Załuski has died. In the afternoon, Kajetan Sołtyk appears before the king. It is December 16, 1758.

## Mrs. Kossakowska, wife of the castellan of Kamieniec, writes to Senator Łubieński, Bishop of Lwów

Katarzyna goes nowhere without Agnieszka, and everyone knows that nothing can get done without her there now. Lately the castellan himself makes appointments with his wife through Agnieszka. Agnieszka is serious and silent. A "walking mystery," the castellan calls her, or a "Maid of Orleans." But in her company, his wife softens, and the blade of her malice, which has so often smitten her husband, is blunted. Now the three of them eat dinner together, and—it must be admitted—since Agnieszka took over the kitchen, their meals have started tasting better. The two women even sleep in the same room. Let the girls do as they please, thinks the castellan.

Now Agnieszka unbraids her mistress's and dear friend's hair before the mirror, so as to brush it and rebraid it before she goes to bed.

"I'm losing hair," says Mrs. Kossakowska. "I'm practically bald already."

"What are you talking about? Your hair has always been this way, thin but strong."

"No, I'm practically bald. Don't be silly—don't lie to me . . . Who cares about hair! I am required to wear bonnets, regardless."

Agnieszka patiently brushes her thin hair. Mrs. Kossakowska shuts her eyes.

Suddenly she gives a start, so that Agnieszka's hand freezes where it is over her head.

"One more letter, my dear," she says. "I forgot."

"No, no, my lady. Work is done for the day," answers Agnieszka, going back to her brushing.

Then Mrs. Kossakowska grabs her by the waist and sits her down on her lap. The girl doesn't resist. She is smiling. Mrs. Kossakowska kisses her neck.

"Just one little note to that pompous, sad old bishop."

"Fine, but from bed, and with your broth."

"You're a little shrew, you know that?" says Katarzyna, petting Agnieszka between the shoulder blades, like a dog, and then releasing her from her embrace.

Then, sitting in bed, leaning back against large cushions, almost invisible beneath the flounces of her nightcap, she dictates:

> Having returned to Podolia, I hasten to send Your Excellency my warmest Greetings, heartily congratulating you on the Lwów Bishopric after the terrible Misfortune that befell Your Excellency's Predecessor, Mikołaj Dembowski, may he rest in Peace.
>
> At the same Time, I wish to recommend to you, Father, a distant Relative of my Husband, one Antoni Kossakowski, who after many Years of far-flung Peregrinations has come back into the Arms of the Republic of Nobles and has just now come to me with a Petition, asking for my Intercession as a Relation of his. This Kossakowski has a great Talent in all the Oriental Languages, but especially in Hebrew. I have no Doubt that Your Excellency's keen Attention has already turned to those miserable Jews who, like blind Men, seek the true Faith, feeling

their Way toward the one Light of the Christian Religion, which I heard about here in Kamieniec, as everyone is now discussing it. We were able to get Backing from the King for those pour Souls, and I am wholeheartedly with them, also because I have long since looked at them, these Children of Moses, and seen their difficult Lives here, for which they are responsible so long as they hold on to their Jewish Superstitions. I would be extremely grateful for any little Word from Your Excellency, though of course I have no Wish to fatigue or annoy.

I will soon be traveling to Lwów, I am only waiting for the Weather to improve, and I relish the great Hope that I shall find Your Excellency in good Health. And may Your Excellency never forget that you are always very welcome here, whether in Kamieniec, where my Husband can more often be found, or in Busk, where I am frequently.

## Father Pikulski writes to Senator Łubieński, Bishop of Lwów

I wish to inform Your Excellency that during your absence from Lwów I have managed to discreetly glean some information about Mrs. Kossakowska's protégé. It turns out that Mr. Moliwda (his name apparently comes from an island on the Greek seas that belongs to him, although confirmation of such a thing is impossible) spent a certain portion of his tempestuous life in Wallachia, where he was a superior, or, as they called it, an elder in a community that seems to have been of Bogomils, also known to us as the Khlysts, or Whips. But he is in fact none other than Antoni Kossakowski of the Ślepowron coat of arms, the son of a man named Remigian, a Hussar ensign, while his mother came from the Kamieński family of Żmudź. For twenty-four years, he was considered missing. And only now has he reappeared in his native country under the pseudonym of "Moliwda."

On the subject of this heresy that has been festering for many years amongst the faithful Orthodox, I know only that they believe that the world was not created by a living God, but rather by his evil brother, Satanael. This is why all manner of evil and death prevails upon the earth. This renegade Satanael assembled the world out of matter, but he was unable to breathe life into it, so he asked the good God to do that. God, in turn, gave souls to every creature, which is why they believe that matter is evil, while the soul is good. They also believe that the Messiah will come a second time, and some believe that this Messiah will come in the guise of a woman. The followers of these sects are Wallachian peasants, but there are also some fugitives who have escaped into the Turkish lands, Cossacks and even Ruthenian peasants, runaways and people of the lowest station, the very poorest. Further, I learned that a sizable role is played there by the so-called Mother of God, whom they choose by election; it must always be a woman of impeccable beauty, and a virgin. They do not eat meat, do not drink wine or vodka (which surprises me, since I had information from Warsaw that this Moliwda hardly shies away from alcoholic drinks; this may be a proof that he has broken with the sect), and do not recognize the sacrament of marriage, believing children born of such unions to be cursed. They do believe, meanwhile, in spiritual love between human persons, and when this occurs, corporeal communion is considered holy. Even in a group setting.

Our holy universal Church condemns without exception such terrible heresies, but it is too great and powerful to trouble itself with such aberrations. The most important thing for the Church has always been the salvation of the souls of the faithful. This is why I inform Your Excellency of these suspicions with genuine aggravation. Can a man who has given himself through and through to heretical notions, and who strives to be of service to other heretics, be worthy of our trust? In our beloved Commonwealth, which survives in its greatness only thanks to our collective faith in the universal Catholic Church, there lurks yet the unrelenting danger of schism. The forces of dissenters are still encroaching from east and west, which is why we must all remain highly vigilant. I feel the necessity of this vigilance particularly acutely as a monk.

At the same time, I would pass over in silence certain matters that are of some significance to our joint inquiry. This Kossakowski-Moliwda is fluent in several languages, and his best languages are Turkish and ancient Hebrew, as well as Greek, Russian, and of course Latin and French. He has extensive knowledge of the Orient, is versed in multiple academic fields and also writes poetry. These talents have no doubt kept him afloat over the course of his turbulent life, and they might come in handy to us, if we could be certain of his dedication to the cause . . .

## From Antoni Moliwda-Kossakowski to His Excellency Bishop Łubieński

It makes me very happy indeed that I might at once present my report to Your Excellency, for it is my opinion that my observations may—even if only slightly—illuminate the highly complicated matter of the anti-Talmudists, completely inconceivable to us Christians, as we are unable to penetrate with clear understanding the dark, tangled secrets of the Jewish faith, nor can we penetrate in full the murky Jewish soul. Your Excellency sent me to follow the matter of Jacob Leybowicz Frank and his disciples at close range, but since this famous Jacob Frank is not in our country, and since, as a Turkish citizen, he remains under the protection of the Turks and is no doubt in his home in Giurgiu, I went to Satanów, where a Jewish trial against the anti-Talmudists took place, which I was able to spend a day observing.

It is a nice little town, fairly clean and bright, located on a tall embankment, with an enormous synagogue that towers over the town. Around it is the Jewish district, in total some several dozen houses that reach all the way up to the market square, where the Jewish merchants have taken charge of all the town's

trade. There the Talmudist Jews in their synagogue of such
extravagant dimensions held their trial against the heretics.
There were many interested persons in the audience, not only
Israelites but also curious Christians, and I even saw a few of
the local nobles, who, however, grew bored by the Jewish
language, which is incomprehensible to them, and quickly
departed.

It is with sadness that I must assert and reveal to Your
Excellency that what I glimpsed there did not even remotely
resemble a trial and was instead an attack of rabid rabbis
upon frightened and perfectly innocent small-time merchants,
who, terrified, said whatever came into their minds, and in
this way condemned not only themselves but also their
brothers and sisters. The vitriol that accompanied the charges
was so great that I feared for the lives of the defendants, who
had to bring in people from the manor of the lord of that
region, strong Cossack farmhands, to keep the frenzied crowd
from descending into terrible mob rule. For they were
suspected of practices of adultery according to which wives
would leave their husbands and be subsequently recognized as
whores. Much of their property was taken from them, and they
were released with only what they could carry in their hands.
There is no mercy for them when their own people
attack them, and our system cannot defend them against that.
There has already been a first victim, one Libera of Brzeżany,
tortured to death for wanting to speak on behalf of Jacob
Frank. The news that these Frankists are under the
protection of the king himself has evidently not reached as far
as here.

I understand Your Excellency's agitation at the
excommunico known in Hebrew as "herem," and I share that
agitation. Lest one doubt the mysterious workings of that curse
and its diabolical powers, I had visible evidence of how it plays
out here on earth—it places certain people outside the law,
thereby putting their lives, their possessions, and their bodily
integrity at risk.

In Poland, on the lands inhabited by our Christian
population, the little bits of truth that reach us are gleaned by

the sweat of the brow. But we also have here living with us millions belonging to the oldest people among all civilizations, that is, the Jewish people, who from the depths of their synagogues have never in so many centuries ceased to raise to heaven that plaintive cry, resembling nothing else in this world. It is a cry of abandonment, of being forsaken by God. If there is something that might bring heavenly truth down to earth, is it not those cries, in which these people concentrate and express their entire lives?

It is a paradox that the care these people need now cannot come from their co-religionists, but only from us, their younger brothers in faith. Many of them have begun to approach us with the same kind of trust with which little children approached Jesus Christ, Our Lord.

That is why I am asking you, Your Excellency, to consider another ecclesiastical audience with these same people, and a simultaneous summons to a disputation with their accusers, the Satanów rabbi, the Lwów rabbi, the Brody and Łuck rabbis, as well as all the others who made such serious accusations against them and in consequence of the results cast a curse upon them. We are not afraid of Jewish curses, just as we are not afraid of any other Jewish superstitions, but we do wish to stand in defense of the persecuted and provide them the right to speak for themselves.

Moliwda ends this letter with a great, elegant flourish and sprinkles it with sand. When it has dried, he starts to write another, in Turkish, in tiny script. He begins: "My Jacob."

## Knives and forks

Hana, Jacob's young wife, loves order in her luggage, knowing where everything is packed—her scarves, her shoes, her oils, the ointments for her pimples. In her even, somewhat hulking hand, she loves to make lists of the things she has packed, and then she feels like she reigns over the world, like she's its queen. Nothing worse than disorder and chaos. Hana waits until the ink on her list dries, strokes the end of the feather with the tip of her finger—her fingers are slender, shapely, with nice nails, although Hana can't keep herself from biting them from time to time.

Now she's writing down the things she will take to Poland in two months, when Jacob will have made the arrangements, and when it will have gotten warmer. They will go in two carriages, with seven horses. In one carriage, she will go with Avacha, Immanuel, and the nanny, a young girl named Lisha. In the second carriage will be the servants and the luggage arranged in a pyramid and tied with strings. Her brother, Hayim, will travel on horseback along with his friends, who will help defend this feminine excursion.

Her breasts, swollen with milk, weigh her down. As soon as she thinks of them or of the child, droplets of milk emerge just like that, of their own accord, as though unable to wait for the tiny little lips of the infant, and wet patches form on her light shift. Her stomach hasn't gone down entirely, either—she gained a lot of weight during this second pregnancy, even though the boy was born on the small side. As it turned out, he was born on the same day that Jacob and the whole company crossed via the Dniester into Poland; for this reason, Jacob bade her in a letter to name their son Immanuel.

Hana stands and picks up Immanuel, sits with him, and rests him on her belly. Her breast seems to almost engulf the baby's head. The boy's face is lovely, olive hued, with light blue lids delicate as flower petals. Avacha watches her mother from the corner, furious, pretending to be playing, though in fact she is constantly observing the two of them. She wants to be breastfed as well, but Hana swats her daughter away like a pestering fly: You're too big!

Hana is a trusting person. Trustingly she recites every night before she goes to bed the Kriat Shema al haMita, to protect herself from ill presentiments, nightmares, and the evil spirits that might threaten her and her children, particularly weak as she's been since giving birth. She addresses the four angels as she would friendly neighbors, requesting that they watch over the house while she is sleeping. Her thoughts get away from her, however, and the summoned angels take shape though she tries her hardest not to picture them. Their figures lengthen, tremble like candle flames, and just before she falls into a deep sleep, Hana sees with astonishment that they resemble knives, forks, and spoons, the kind Jacob has told her of, silver and plated in gold. They hover over her, neither guarding her nor ready to slice her into little pieces and consume her.

## 18

## Of how Ivanie, a little village on the Dniester, becomes a republic

Ivanie is not far from the fault that is the bed of the Dniester River. The village is arrayed along the Transnistrian plateau in such a way that it looks like dishes set out on a table, too close to the table's edge. It could all come clattering down with a single careless movement.

Through the middle of the village runs a river, siphoned off every few yards by primitive valves that produce little ponds and pools. Ducks and geese were once kept here. All that's left of them now are a few white feathers: the village was abandoned after the last plague. The true believers have resided here since August, with the Shorrs' financial support and the benevolent bishop's blessing, since the village lies on his landholdings. As soon as the safe conduct was issued by the king, people began to make their way to Ivanie in carts and on foot—from the south, from Turkey, from the north, from the towns of Podolia. They are, by and large, the same people who'd camped out on the border after being expelled from Poland, people who discovered, on finally being permitted to return home, that they no longer had homes. Their jobs had been given to others, and their houses had been looted and occupied, and if they wanted them back, they'd have to come up with some way of asserting their property rights, by law or by force. Some lost everything, especially those who made their living by trade and had left behind market stalls and stock. Those people have nothing now. Shlomo of Nadwórna and his wife, Wittel, belong to this group. Shlomo and Wittel owned workshops in Nadwórna and Kopczyńce that made duvets. All winter, women would come and pluck feathers, overseen by Wittel, who is clever and deft. Then they would sew the warm quilts, the down light and fragrant, the coverings of Turkish damask ornately patterned in pink, all of such high quality that they'd get all kinds of commissions from palaces and estates. But all this was lost in the tumult. Feathers were strewn across Podolia by the wind, the damask trampled or thieved. The roof of the house caught fire. Now it's uninhabitable.

Peeking out from the black and white winter landscape, the little dwellings of Ivanie are overgrown with river reeds. A road winds between them, traveling down the pocked, uneven yards that are strewn with the remnants of abandoned plows and rakes, shards of pots.

The village is run by Osman of Czernowitz, who posts guards at its entrance, to prevent undesirables from straying in. Sometimes the entrance is blocked by carts. The horses stomp cavities into the frozen ground.

Newcomers to the village must first go to Osman and leave all their money and valuables with him. Osman is Ivanie's steward, and he has an iron lockbox where he keeps the common holdings. His wife, Hava, Jacob's sister, manages the donations that come from true believers across Podolia and the Turkish lands—among these are clothing, shoes, tools, pots, glass, and even children's toys. It is Hava who assigns the morning's work to the men of the village. These men will take the cart to get potatoes from a farmer; those will go for cabbage.

The community has its own cows and a hundred chickens. The chickens are a new acquisition—the sounds of coop-building still fill the air, the pounding of the perches being hammered in. Past the little houses lie community gardens. The gardens are pretty, though there isn't much in them yet: the community arrived in August, too late to plant. Vines cover the roofs of the houses, untended, bearing sweet little grapes. There were some pumpkins to harvest. There was an abundance of plums as well— small, dark, and sweet—and trees that bulged with apples. Now that the

cold has set in, everything's turned gray, and the winter theater of putre-
faction has commenced.

People arrived every day throughout the autumn, mainly from Wallachia
and the Turkish lands, but also from Czernowitz, Jassy, even Bucharest.
All thanks to Osman—it is he who brings in their co-religionists, especially those subjects of the sultan who have already converted to Islam.
These differ only slightly from the local Podolian Jews: they're a bit more
tanned, more vibrant, readier to dance. Their songs are a little livelier.
Languages, clothing, and headdress mix. Some wear turbans, like Osman
and his plentiful family, others fur shtreimels. Some sport Turkish fezzes,
and the northerners don four-pointed caps. The children embrace their
new playmates, those from Podolia and those from the east all chasing
each other merrily around the ponds. When winter comes, they chase
each other around the ice. Their quarters are tight. For now, they crowd
inside their little dwellings with their children and all their possessions,
and even so they're very cold, because the one thing they do not have in
Ivanie is wood to burn. In the mornings the little panes of glass in the
windows are covered in frost in patterns that innocently imitate the ad-
vancements of spring—leaves, buds, ferns.

Hayim of Kopczyńce and Osman allocate housing to newcomers.
Hava, who's in charge of provisions, distributes blankets and pots, shows
them where they can cook, where they can wash up—there is even a mikvah at the end of town. She explains that here everyone eats together and
cooks together. All work is communal: the women take care of the sewing, the men tend to the buildings and go in search of fuel. Only children
and the elderly are entitled to milk.

And so the women launder, cook, sew, feed. There has already been
one birth here, of a boy they named Jacob. Meanwhile the men head out
in the mornings on business, seeking trade—earning money. In the evenings they convene. A couple of adolescents make up Ivanie's postal service, delivering packages on horseback, going all the way to Kamieniec if
need be, sneaking across the border to Turkey, to Czernowitz. From there
the post goes on.

Yesterday the other Hayim, the one from Busk, Nahman's brother, brought Ivanie a herd of goats, dispensing them evenly around the various households—there is much rejoicing over this, for there had not been enough milk for the children. The younger women assigned to the kitchen leave their offspring in care of the older women, who have assembled in one of the cottages what they call "kindergarten."

It is the end of November, and everyone in Ivanie is eager for Jacob's arrival. Lookouts have been sent over to the Turkish side. The younger boys stake out the river's high banks, monitor the fords. A solemn silence has descended upon the village, everything ready since yesterday. Jacob's abode glistens. Over the miserable floor of tamped-down clay they've unfurled kilims. Snow-white curtains hang in the windows.

Finally there are whistles and whoops from along the riverbank. He is here.

At the entrance to the village, Osman of Czernowitz awaits, suffused with solemn joy. On seeing them, he starts to sing in a strong and beautiful voice: "Dio mio, Baruchiah . . ." and the melody is taken up by the excited crowd that is there to greet him. The procession that comes around the bend looks like a Turkish formation. In its center is a carriage, and excited eyes seek out Jacob—but Jacob is the man riding ahead on the gray horse, dressed like a Turk in a turban and a fur-lined light blue coat with broad sleeves. His beard is long and black, which ages him. When Jacob dismounts, he touches his forehead to Osman's, and then Hayim's, and finally he lays his hands on their wives' heads. Osman leads him to his house, which is the largest in Ivanie; the yard has been cleared, the entrance lined with spruce. But Jacob points at a little hut nearby, an old shed slapped together out of clay. He says he wants to live alone, anywhere, it doesn't matter where, that hut in the yard there would work fine.

"But you are a hakham," says Hayim. "How could you possibly live alone in a hut?"

Jacob insists.

"I'm a simple man," he says.

Osman doesn't really get it, but he rushes to arrange for the shed to be tidied up for Jacob all the same.

## Of the sleeves of Sabbatai Tzvi's holy shirt

Wittel has thick curls the color of the grass in autumn. She is tall, with a good build. She holds her head high. She has appointed herself to Jacob's service. She glides between Ivanie's houses, graceful, jocular, flushed. She is witty. Since Jacob's hut is in their yard, she has taken on the role of protector, at least until the arrival of his rightful wife, Hana, and their children. For now, Wittel has a monopoly on Jacob. Everybody is always wanting something from him, always pestering him, and Wittel is the one who shoos them away. Sometimes people come down just to look at where the Lord lives, and then Wittel goes and beats carpets on the fence and blocks the entrance with her body.

"The Lord is resting. The Lord is praying. The Lord is delivering his blessing to our people."

By day everyone works, and Jacob can often be seen amongst them, with his shirt unbuttoned—for Jacob never gets cold—as he chops wood in a frenzy or unloads carts and carries bags of flour. Only when the sun sets do they all gather for the teachings. It used to be that the men and women heard the teachings separately, but the Lord has introduced a different custom into Ivanie. Now the teachings are for all adults.

The elders sit on benches while the youth squeeze in along the bundles of grain. The best part of the lessons is the start of them, because Jacob always tells funny stories that make them all burst out laughing. Jacob likes dirty jokes.

"In my youth," he begins, "I went to one village where they had never seen a Jew before. I drove up to the inn where all the farmhands and wenches went. The wenches were weaving, and the farmhands were filling their heads with all sorts of stories. One of them spotted me and launched into insults, and kept on mocking me. He started telling a story about the Jewish God and the Christian God, how the Christian hit the Jew smack-dab in the kisser. This seemed to really crack them up, because they belly-laughed like the guy was a first-class wit. So I told them one about Muhammad and Saint Peter. Muhammad says to Peter, 'I got a good idea to rut you, good and Greek.' Peter didn't want to, but Muhammad was strong, and he tied Peter to a tree and did his thing, Peter howling how his backside was burning, how he'd take him as his saint if he'd only just stop. Well, that little story didn't go over so well, and the farmhands and the wenches cast their eyes down to the ground, but then the more aggressive one said to me, as if to make peace, 'Let's call a truce. We won't say nothing on your God, and you don't say nothing on ours. And let Saint Peter alone.'"

The men chuckle, and the women cast their eyes to the ground, but in fact they all like it that Jacob, a saint and a scholar, is down-to-earth and doesn't put on airs and graces. They like that he lives on his own in that little hut, and that he wears regular clothes. They love him for it. Especially the women. The women of the true faith are confident and gregarious. They like to flirt, and what Jacob teaches pleases them: that they can forget the Turkish customs dictating that they should be shut up inside their homes. He says Ivanie needs women as much as men—for different things, but it needs them all the same.

Jacob also teaches that from now on there is nothing that belongs to just one person; no one has things of his or her own. If anybody needs something, he is to request it of the person who had it last, and his request shall inevitably be granted. Alternatively those in want can go to the steward Osman or to Hava, and whatever their lacks—if their shoes fall apart, or their shirt comes unraveled, or the like—they will be attended to.

"Even without any money?" shouts one of the women, and the other women are quick to respond: "In return for those pretty eyes . . ."

And everyone laughs.

Not everyone is on board with the rule that they must give up their belongings. Yeruhim and Hayim from Warsaw keep saying that it can't last, that people are greedy by nature and will just want more and more and try to turn a profit off the things that they receive. But others, like Nahman and Moshe, say they've seen this kind of community work before, and they stick up for Jacob. Nahman in particular is a big supporter of the idea. He can often be found holding forth on the subject in the households of the village:

"This was exactly how it used to be in the world before there were laws. Everything was held in common, everything belonged to everyone, and everyone had enough, and the commandments 'Thou shalt not steal' and 'Thou shalt not commit adultery' didn't exist because if anybody had said them, nobody else would have understood. 'What is stealing?' they would have asked. 'What is adultery?' We should live in the same way, because the old law no longer applies to us. There have been three: Sabbatai, Baruchiah, and now Jacob. He is the greatest of them, and he is our salvation. We must rejoice that our time is the time of salvation, that the old orders no longer apply."

During Hanukkah, Jacob distributes pieces of Sabbatai Tzvi's shirt as relics. This is a great event for the entire community. It is the shirt that the First One threw to Halabi's son; Shorr recently purchased both its sleeves from Halabi's son's granddaughter—he paid a pretty price for them, too. Now bits of the material—each of them smaller than a fingernail—make their way into amulets, little cherrywood boxes, pockets, and leather pouches worn around the neck. The rest of the shirt is placed in the box at Osman's. It will be given to those who have yet to arrive.

## Of the working of Jacob's touch

Moshe from Podhajce, who knows everything, sits in the warmest spot, among the women weaving. Clouds of fragrant smoke rise toward the wooden ceiling.

"You all know," he says, "the prayer that talks about Eloha encountering the demon of illness, who used to set up shop in people's extremities and so make them sick. But Eloha says to the demon, 'Just as you can't drink down the whole sea, so you will not do any further harm to mankind.' Just like that. And Jacob, our Lord, is like Eloha: he, too, can converse with the demon of illnesses. And all he has to do is give him a dirty look, and off the demon goes."

This makes sense to them. For there is an endless procession of people standing at the door to Jacob's shed, and if Wittel permits them inside, into the presence of the Lord, Jacob will lay his hands on the heads of the suffering, moving his thumb back and forth over their foreheads. Sometimes he blows in their faces. It almost always helps. They say that he has hot hands that can melt away all maladies, any variety of pain.

Jacob's fame quickly spreads through the vicinity, and even local peasants end up coming to Ivanie (to "call on the ne'er-do-wells," as they put it). They're suspicious of these oddballs who are neither Jews nor Gypsies. But Jacob rests his hands on their heads, too. In exchange they leave eggs, chickens, apples, grain. Hava tucks everything away in her chamber and distributes it evenly later on. Every child receives an egg for Shabbat. Hava says "for Shabbat," although Jacob has told them not to keep the Shabbat. All the same, unable to get used to this new edict, they still mark the passage of time from Shabbat to Shabbat.

In February something strange occurs, a real miracle, but of this Moshe knows next to nothing. Jacob has forbidden talk of it. Hayim, on the other hand, witnessed it. A Podolian girl grew very ill—she was dying by the time she was brought in. Her father let out a terrible howl, tearing out his beard in despair: she'd always been his most beloved child. They sent for Jacob. When he arrived, he shouted at them to be quiet. Then he holed up with the girl for a while. When he left, she was cured. He ordered her to be dressed in white.

"What did you do to her?" asked Shlomo, Wittel's husband.

"I had my dealings with her, and she got better," said Jacob. And he refused to say any more on the matter.

Shlomo, a polite and serious man, did not at first understand what he had just been told. He couldn't quite recover from it after. That evening Jacob smiled at him as though perceiving Shlomo's torment, and he reached out and tugged him gently by the nape of the neck, like a girl might do to a boy. He blew into his eyes and told him not to tell anyone. Then he went off and paid him no more mind.

But Shlomo did tell his wife, swearing her to secrecy. And somehow— no one knew how—within a few days all of Ivanie had heard the secret. Words are like lizards, able to elude all containment.

## Of the women's talk while plucking chickens

First, that the face of the biblical Jacob served as the model when God was creating the angels' human faces.

Second, that the moon has Jacob's face.

Third, that you can engage another man to give you children if you can't get pregnant by your husband.

They recall the story of Issachar, son of Jacob and Leah: Leah engaged Jacob to sleep with her and then bore him a son. She compensated Jacob with a mandrake found by Reuben in the desert, much desired by the infertile Rachel. (Then Rachel ate that mandrake and bore Jacob his son Joseph.) All this is in the Scriptures.

Fourth, that you can get pregnant by Jacob without him even brushing up against your pinkie finger.

Fifth, that when God created the angels, right away they opened up their mouths and praised Him. And, too, when God created Adam, the angels piped right up: "Is this the man we are to worship?" "No," replied God. "This is a thief. He will steal fruit from my tree." So when Noah was born, the angels asked excitedly, "Is this the man we are to praise to high heaven?" And God replied in consternation, "No, this is just an ordinary drunk." When Abraham was born, they asked again, but God, who had grown dejected, replied, "No, this one was not born circumcised and will only later convert to my faith." When Isaac was born, the angels asked, still hopeful, "Is it this one?" "No," replied God, terribly displeased. "This one loves his elder son, who hates me." But when Jacob was born, they asked their question once more, and this time, the response was, "Yes, this is he."

Several of the men working on the shed stop doing what they're doing so they can stand in the doorway and eavesdrop on the women. Soon their heads are white with feathers: someone must have snatched up one of the baskets with a little too much zeal.

## Of which of the women will be chosen

"Go to him," Wittel's husband says to her. "He took a liking to you. You will be blessed."

But she resists.

"How could I sleep with him, when I'm your wife? It's a sin."

Shlomo looks at her with tenderness, as at a child.

"You're thinking in the old way—it's almost as though you haven't understood any of what's happened here. There is no sin, and that's that—husband or no husband. The time of salvation is upon us. The notion of sin no longer applies. He is working hard for us, and he wants you. You are the most beautiful."

Wittel frowns.

"I'm not the most beautiful, come on. Even you ogle all the girls here." She pauses. "What would you do?"

"Me? If I were in your place, Wittel, I wouldn't be asking questions. I'd go straightaway."

Truth be told, Wittel receives this permission with relief. She has not been able to think about anything else for days on end. The women who have been intimate with him say that Jacob has two members. More precisely, that whenever he wants to, he has two members, and when he doesn't, he takes his pleasure with one. Soon it will be within Wittel's power to confirm or deny this assertion.

In late February, Jacob sends a carriage for Hana, and Wittel no longer goes to him every night. Hana is called "Highness." A feast is given in honor of Her Highness. For days the women bake, drowning in goose fat, delivering their dinner rolls to Hava's chamber once they're done.

Wittel wishes it were an accident, but unfortunately, it's not: she purposely eavesdrops on Jacob and Hana making love. She feels her stomach get twisted up. She can't understand what they're talking about because they speak in Turkish. It excites her to hear Jacob speaking in Turkish, and she thinks that next time she will ask him to talk Turkish to her, too. She won't have to wait too long for next time: after only a month, Hana, gloomy, disappointed, will return to Turkey.

Already in December, the Lord had ordered all the adults to gather together.

They stood in a circle and remained for a very long time in complete silence, for the Lord had forbidden conversation, and no one had the courage to speak up. Then he had the men move over to stand along the right-hand wall. Of the women, he chose seven, as was done by the First, Sabbatai.

First he took Wittel's hand and named her Eva. Wittel, who had no idea what was going on, immediately flushed all over and shifted her weight from one leg to the other, nervously; she had completely lost all self-confidence. She stood aflame, obedient as a hen. Jacob set her to his right. Then he took Wajgełe, Nahman of Busk's very young new wife, and named her Sarah. She went as though to a beheading, in despair, with her head bowed, glancing at her husband, resigned to her fate. Jacob placed her behind Wittel. And behind her he placed Eva, Jacob Mayor's wife, whom he named Rebecca. Then he spent a long time looking at the women, who lowered their eyes; finally he reached out for lovely Sprynełe, aged thirteen, daughter-in-law of Elisha Shorr, wife of his youngest son, Wolf; her he named Bershava. Now he started to line them up on his left side—the first was Isaac Shorr's wife, whom he named Rachel, and then Hayim of Nadwórna's wife, whom he named Leah. He put Uhla Lanckorońska on the end and named her Afisha Sulamitka.

All the names were the names of the wives of the patriarchs, and the chosen women stood there overwhelmed, in silence. Their husbands also kept quiet. Suddenly Wajgełe, Nahman's new wife, started to cry. This was not the time to cry, although everyone understood why she was doing it.

## Hana's gloomy gaze notes these details of Ivanie

The people in the shacks sleep all in a row on rickety, rotting frames, or on the ground, with simple bundles of hay for bedding. Their beds are not beds, but pallets. Only a few have real beds with linen sheets. The Shorrs have the best beds.

They are dirty and lice-ridden. Even Jacob has lice, which is because he keeps company with the town filth. Or so Hana assumes. Although, in fact, she knows for certain.

This is no community. It's an ordinary rabble, just a muddled crowd. Some can't even communicate, like those who use Turkish or Ladino on a day-to-day basis, like Hana, and don't know the local Jewish tongues.

There are sick and crippled people whom no one is treating. The laying on of hands does not help everyone. On her first day in Ivanie, Hana witnessed the death of yet another child, who died from a cough, simply suffocating.

Many among them are loose women, be they widows, agunot, or whatever else. Some of the women aren't even Jews, that's what Hana thinks. They'll give it up for some morsel of food and because doing so allows them to stay here. She shuts her eyes to the fact that in Ivanie everyone sleeps with everyone, even attaching great meaning to it. Hana does not understand why men place such importance on intercourse. There's nothing so amazing about it. Since her second child, she's lost all interest. She is bothered by the scent of other women on her husband's skin.

Jacob seems completely changed to Hana. At first, he was happy she had come, but then they only slept together twice. Jacob has something else on his mind now, or maybe it's some other woman. That Wittel hangs around him and glares at Hana. Jacob chooses them all over Hana. He barely listens to her; he's more interested in Avacha, whom he carries around with him wherever he goes. He sits her up on his shoulders; their daughter likes to pretend she is riding a camel. Hana stays at home and breastfeeds the baby. She worries about their son, worries he will catch some disease here. Little Immanuel is still ailing, after all. Ivanie's winds haven't helped him, and neither has the extended, seemingly endless winter. The Turkish wet nurse reminds Hana every day that she does not want to be here, either, that she is repulsed by it, and that she'll lose her milk soon as a result.

Back at home in Nikopol it's spring already, while here the first fresh blades of grass have barely forced their way through the old layer of rotted vegetation.

Hana misses her father and his peace and equilibrium. She also misses her mother, who died last year, and when she thinks of her mother, she is beset by premonitions of her own death, and she feels scared.

## Of Moliwda's visit to Ivanie

Moliwda sets out from Warsaw for Lwów when the roads freeze up again, becoming traversable. After his meeting with Archbishop Łubieński, he is taken to Ivanie by a priest named Zwierzchowski, who has now been assigned to the anti-Talmudist question. The priest gives him a whole chest full of catechisms and instructional pamphlets, and rosaries and religious medallions, too. Moliwda feels like one of those street vendors saddled with all kinds of devotional objects. Separately packed in tow is a figurine of the Virgin Mary, carved a little clumsily out of linden and brightly painted, for Mrs. Frank from Mrs. Kossakowska, as a gift and a memento.

He arrives in Ivanie on March 9, 1759, and no sooner has he arrived than he is overcome by emotion, for in Ivanie he sees the image of his own little village close to Craiova, with all the same elements, just colder and so not quite as cozy. The atmosphere is the same, like a never-ending holiday, which the weather even seems to further: there is a slight frost, and way up in the sky the cold sun casts down bright, freezing beams. The world looks cleansed. People make tracks upon the white snow, so you can follow them wherever they go. Moliwda thinks how snow keeps life more honest: everything is somehow more distinct, and every rule applies more absolutely. The people who meet him in Ivanie look radiant and happy despite the brevity of the days. Children with puppies in their arms come running up to his carriage, along with women flushed from work, men flashing big grins. Smoke rises in straight vertical lines from the chimneys, as though a sacrifice made in that spot were being met with unconditional acceptance.

Jacob greets Moliwda ceremoniously, but once they are inside his little shack, and once they are alone, he fishes Moliwda's stocky figure from inside his wolf fur and holds him for a long while, patting him on the back and repeating, in Polish, "You came back, you came back."

Then they're all here: the Shorr brothers—though not the father, who hasn't quite recovered from that beating—as well as Yehuda Krysa and his brother and brother-in-law. Nahman is here, newly remarried to some young girl (marrying them off at that age is barbaric, Moliwda thinks), Moshe surrounded by smoke, the other Moshe, the Kabbalist, with his whole family—everyone is here. Now they crowd into this little room where the windows have frozen into a pretty pattern.

At the welcome banquet, Jacob sits in the middle of the table, beneath a window, which frames him from behind like he's a picture. Jacob against the black backdrop of night. They all hold hands. Everybody takes a good look at everybody else, as though they haven't seen one another in ages and ages. Then there is a solemn prayer, which by now Moliwda knows by heart; after a moment's hesitation, he joins in. Then they converse, at length and in chaos, in a chorus of languages. Moliwda's fluent Turkish wins over Osman's somewhat suspicious followers, who look and act like Turks although they drink almost as much as the Podolians. Jacob is in a good mood. He is vibrant; it is a pleasure to see the enthusiasm with which he eats. He praises the dishes, tells stories that elicit bursts of laughter.

Moliwda used to wonder whether Jacob could feel fear. Eventually he decided that Jacob would not recognize the feeling, as though he'd simply been born without it. This gives Jacob strength: people can sense that absence of fear, and that absence of fear in turn becomes contagious. And because the Jews are always afraid—whether it's of a Polish lord, or of a Cossack, of injustice or hunger or cold—they live in a state of extreme uncertainty, from which Jacob is a kind of salvation. The absence of fear is like a halo that radiates a heat that can warm up a chilled and frightened little soul. Blessed are those who feel no fear. And although Jacob often repeats that they are in limbo, they are comfortable enough in limbo.

When Jacob disappears for even a moment, conversations come apart, no longer laced with the same energy as when he's there. His mere presence is enough to instill order; eyes travel to him involuntarily, like moths to flame. And so it is now. Jacob is the focal point of the evening. Jacob glows. Late at night they start to dance, first the men alone, in a circle, as though in a kind of trance. When, exhausted, they return to the table, two women come out to dance in their stead. One of these women will spend the night with Moliwda.

In the evening, Moliwda gives a solemn reading to the company assembled, of the letter he'd dashed off a few days earlier to the Polish king, in the name of these Wallachian, Turkish, and Polish brothers:

> Jacob Joseph Frank departed with his wife, children, and more than sixty other persons from the Turkish and Wallachian lands, barely escaping with his life, for having lost all his worldly possessions, and knowing only his mother tongue and some dialects of the East, and knowing not the customs of this most glorious Kingdom and having thus no means to live within it, neither him nor his people, whom, even being so numerous, he had brought over to the true faith, now supplicates your Royal Highness in all His Compassion for a place and mode of sustenance for our society . . .

Here Moliwda clears his throat and pauses: a doubt flickers through his mind, and he wonders if this letter is not somewhat disrespectful. What could the king care about them, when his own subjects—those peasants born Christians, those multitudes of beggars, orphaned children, hapless cripples—needed help?

> . . . so that we might now settle down in peace, for to live among Talmudists is unbearable to us, and a danger, insofar as that intolerant nation has never learned to think of us as anything other than wrong-faithed schismatics, etc.
>
> Unheedful of the law given to this land by Your Excellency, they are everywhere and at every moment persecuting, pillaging, and attacking us, as was exemplified not long ago in Podolia, so near your Majesty Himself . . .

From the back of the room comes a single sob. It is followed by others.

> . . . and so it is that we humbly beseech Your Majesty to
> appoint a commission in Kamieniec and in Lwów, that our
> rightful belongings might be returned us, our wives and
> children given back, and the decree from Kamieniec be
> observed in a satisfactory manner, and we entreat Your Royal
> Highness to proclaim in a public letter that our brothers in
> hiding may reemerge, with their thirst for faith akin to our
> own, that they might make themselves known without fear;
> that the lords of these locales might be an aid in the acceptance
> of the holy faith, and were the Talmudists to inflict any
> oppressions therefrom resulting, that these same brothers might
> be helped in reaching safety, as to unite with our society.

His listeners like his ornate style. Moliwda, greatly pleased with himself, reclines atop the carpets—for since Hana's arrival Jacob has inhabited a larger residence, which Hana has furnished according to the Turkish custom. It's a bit incongruous in that outside there is snow, and gusts of wind. The dwelling's little windows are almost entirely covered over with blown powder. As soon as the door is opened, a fresh dusting penetrates the interior, which smells of coffee and licorice. A few days earlier, it had seemed that spring had arrived.

"I'll spend a couple of days here with you all," says Moliwda. "It reminds me of Smyrna."

Moliwda means it. He feels more at home among these Jews than he does in Warsaw, where they don't even know how to prepare coffee correctly, pouring too much and watering it down, which then causes heartburn and anxiety. Here you can sit on the floor or on bowed benches at low tables where coffee is served in absolutely tiny cups, as though for elves. And here they provide him with decent Hungarian wine.

Hana comes in and greets Moliwda warmly, handing him Jacob's daughter, little Avacha. The child is quiet, calm. She seems intimidated by Moliwda's great red beard. She looks at him unblinking, as though trying to determine who exactly he might be.

"She seems to have fallen in love with Uncle Moliwda." Jacob laughs. But then that evening, when it's just the five of them—with Osman, Hayim of Warsaw, and Nahman—and once they've opened up their third jug of wine, Jacob points a finger in Moliwda's face and says, "You saw my daughter. Know that she is a queen."

They all nod agreeably, but this is not the reaction that Jacob desires.

"Do not think, Moliwda, that I mean merely that she's good-looking."

There is a brief silence.

"No," Jacob continues. "She truly is a queen. You don't even realize yet just how great a queen she is."

Once it's down to a smaller group of brothers, Moliwda—before he gets drunk—gives the others an update on their efforts with Archbishop Łubieński. They're on the right track, although the archbishop still has doubts as to whether their hearts are truly and fully with the Church. The next letter Moliwda will write will be on behalf of Krysa and Shlomo Shorr, to give the archbishop the impression that there are many among them who wish to be baptized.

"You're very clever, Moliwda," Nahman of Busk says to him, patting him on the back.

Everyone has been making fun of Nahman since his second marriage. His childlike bride totters after him wherever he goes. Nahman, meanwhile, seems somewhat terrified of their marriage.

Moliwda suddenly bursts out laughing.

"We never had our own savages, like the French and the English did with their Bushmen and their Pygmies. These Polish lords would love to draw you all—their very own savages—into their fold."

The wine from Giurgiu that arrived with Hana's carriages is clearly working now. They talk over one another.

". . . and that's why you were going behind our backs to Bishop Dembowski?" Shlomo Shorr is saying in a rage to Krysa, grabbing him by his somewhat sullied stock tie. "That's why you were bothering with him on your own, so that you could get his favors for yourself, right? And that's why you were going back to Czarnokozińce for letters from the bishop that would grant you safe conduct. Was he promising you that?"

"Oh yes, he always promised me that we'd gain independence within the kingdom. There was never any mention of baptism. And we ought to keep it that way. After he died it all fell apart. And you idiots are clamoring for baptism like starving pigs. That was never part of it!" Krysa leaps up and slams his fist up into the ceiling. "Afterward, somebody sent some thugs after me, and they beat me within an inch of my life."

"You are despicable, Krysa," says Shlomo Shorr. On pronouncing these words he walks straight out into the snowstorm. Snow flies in through the briefly opened doorway, melting on impact with the floor's fresh spruce covering.

"I agree with Krysa," says Yeruhim. Others nod at this: baptism can wait.

Here Moliwda chimes in: "You're right, Krysa, here in Poland no one is going to give full rights to the Jews. Either you become Catholic or you remain nothing. Now Their Graces back you up with gold, because you're against the other Jews, but if you were to want to go off somewhere and get set up with your own religion, they'd hound you about it right away. And they'd keep at it till they had you prostrate in their church. Anybody who thinks otherwise is mistaken. Before you there were heterodox Christians, the Polish Brethren, innocuous people who were much closer to their religion than you all. And they were tormented until they were finally driven out altogether. They had everything taken away from them, and they were either killed or exiled."

He says this in a sepulchral tone. Krysa cries again: "You all want to go straight into the belly of that beast, that Leviathan . . ."

"Moliwda's right," says Nahman. "There's no other option besides baptism. Even if it's just for the sake of appearances," he adds under his breath, glancing hesitantly at Moliwda, who has just lit his pipe. He lets out a cloud of smoke that obscures his face for a moment.

"If it's just for the sake of appearances, you'll have to prepare yourselves for them to be sniffing around forever more."

There is a prolonged silence.

"You have a different approach to intercourse. You don't see anything wrong with a man sleeping with his wife, nothing shameful," Moliwda says, now rather drunk, once he and Jacob are alone. They are squatting in Jacob's shack, wrapped in sheepskin coats, because the poorly sealed windows let in the cold.

Jacob has eased off the alcohol by this time. "I like it that way," he says. "It's more human. People who have intercourse get closer to each other."

"Because you can sleep with other men's women, while no one sleeps with yours, they all know that you are the one in charge," says Moliwda, "the way it works with lions."

This comparison seems to please Jacob. He smiles a mysterious smile and starts to fill his pipe. Then he gets up and says he's going out for a moment. He doesn't return for a long while. That's the way he is: unpredictable. You never know what he'll do next. By the time he comes back in, Moliwda is very drunk indeed, and he insists on continuing the conversation:

"And how you decide who's going to be with whom, and you make them do it with candles lit—I know why you do that. Because of course it can be done discreetly in the dark, everyone with the person of their choosing . . . But this is how you conquer them and bind them together so tightly that they'll be closer than family, greater than family. They will have a common secret, they'll know each other better than anyone, and as you know well, the human spirit is inclined to love, to loving, to connection. There's nothing more powerful in the world. And they'll say nothing about it. They have to have a reason to keep quiet—they have to have something to keep quiet about."

Jacob lies down on the bed on his back and inhales the familiarly scented smoke, making Moliwda remember nights in Giurgiu.

"And then there are children, of course. What ultimately ends up happening is shared children. How do you know that that young thing that lay with you last night won't have a child soon? And whose will it be? Her husband's or yours? That binds them together tightly, too, since that way they're all fathers. Whose child is Shlomo's youngest daughter?" asks Moliwda, now absolutely intoxicated.

Jacob lifts his head and looks at him for a moment; Moliwda's eyes have softened, clouded.

"Shut up," says Jacob. "That's none of your business."

"Oh I see," says Moliwda, "now it's not my business, but when you want a village from the bishop, then it is my business." He reaches for the pipe as well. "It's a good system. The child belongs to the mother, and thus to the mother's husband, too. It's mankind's greatest invention. It means that only women have access to the truth that agitates so many."

That night they go to bed drunk, sleeping in the same room because neither wants to go out in search of his own bed, with a blizzard raging. Moliwda turns to Jacob, not knowing if he's asleep yet or not, or if he can hear—his eyes are partly closed, but the lamplight is reflected in the slender glassy strips below his lashes. Moliwda feels that he is talking to Jacob, but maybe he isn't talking at all—maybe it only feels that way—and he doesn't know if Jacob is listening.

"You always said she was either pregnant or in confinement. And these long pregnancies and long confinements meant that she was always unavailable, but in the end, you had to release even her from the women's rooms; you, too, must be bound by the same justice you impose on everyone else. Do you understand what I'm saying?"

Jacob doesn't react. He's lying on his back, his nose pointing straight at the ceiling.

"I watched you communicating by glances on the road, you and her. And she was telling you no. Am I right? And your glance also said no. But now that will mean something more. I'm waiting, I'm asking you for that same justice with which you handle your own people. I'm one of you now, too. And I'm asking for your Hana."

There is a silence.

"You have all the women here, they're all yours, and all the men, body and soul. I understand that you are something greater than a group of people with the same goal. You're something greater than a family, because you are bound together by all the sins that are forbidden to a family. You're bound by saliva and semen, not just blood. Those ties are strong. They bring you closer together than ever before. That's how it was at home in Craiova, too. Why should we submit to laws we don't believe in, laws that are incompatible with the religion of nature?"

Moliwda jabs him in the shoulder, and Jacob exhales.

"You embolden your people to be with one another but not like they want, not just following the call of nature—you decide, because you *are* their nature."

By the last sentence, he's mumbling almost unintelligibly. He can tell that Jacob is asleep now, so he stops talking, disappointed by the lack of reaction he's received. Jacob's face is relaxed and calm—he clearly heard nothing because he wouldn't be smiling that way if he had. He is beautiful. It occurs to Moliwda that he is like a patriarch even though he is young, his beard still black, without a trace of gray, flawless, and Moliwda thinks he must be catching this same Ivanie madness, because he also sees a kind of glow around Jacob's head, which Nahman had told him about so excitedly—Nahman, who now also calls himself Jakubowski, after Jacob. Suddenly Moliwda thinks of kissing Jacob's lips. He hesitates for a moment and touches his fingers to Jacob's mouth, but even that does not awaken him. Jacob simply smacks his lips and rolls over.

In the morning they have to clear the snow from in front of the door, the drift too deep for them to step outside at first.

## Divine grace, which calls out from the darkness into the light

The following day, Jacob hurries Moliwda back to work. In Nahman's little house there is a separate chamber for such things. Moliwda has begun to call it "the chancellery."

They will be writing yet more supplications, which they will use to further importune the episcopal and royal secretariats. Moliwda sips beer with a spoonful of honey in it—for his stomach. Before any of the others come in, Jacob asks, out of nowhere:

"What is your business with us here, Moliwda? What's your game?"

"I have no business with you."

"Well, we're paying you."

"I take the money to cover my costs, to have something to eat and something to wear, because otherwise I'm poor as a dervish. I've seen too much of the world, Jacob, not to understand you all. These bishops and nobles are just as foreign to me as they are to you, even though I come from them." He swallows a spoonful of his mixture and adds after a moment, "Although I do and I don't."

"You're a strange man, Moliwda. It's like you're broken in half. I can't understand you. Whenever I look at you, you just pull the curtain down. I've heard there are animals in the sea that whenever you try and catch them, they release ink."

"Those are octopuses."

"Well, that's exactly how you are."

"When I've had enough, I'll just leave you."

"Krysa says you're a spy."

"Krysa is a traitor."

"Who are you, Count Kossakowski?"

"I'm the king of an island in the Greek sea, the ruler of agreeable subjects, don't you know?"

Now, sentence by sentence, they concoct a new request to Władysław Łubieński, Archbishop of Lwów.

"Do not overdo it," Moliwda worries, "because we don't know what he's like. He might not look upon us too favorably. They say he's motivated by self-interest and vanity."

The one thing they know for sure, though, is that the supplications have to be written and written and written, one after the next. They have to be careful and rounded as drops of water, in order that they might patiently wear away at the crag. Moliwda falls into thought, gazing at the ceiling.

"We have to start from the beginning," he says. "From Kamieniec. From the bishop's decree."

And that's just what they do. They present themselves in a good, noble light and spend so long on their good intentions that they all start to believe what they're saying.

"And having learned of this, always struggling against the spirit of wisdom, our opponents raised their hands against us and accused us of inconceivable crimes before the bishop," suggests Moliwda.

They nod. Nahman would like to insert something.

"Perhaps it could be that they raised their hands against us and 'furthermore against God Himself'?"

"But what would that mean?" asks Moliwda. "What does God have to do with this?"

"It's just that we're on God's side."

"It's that God is on our side," says Shlomo Shorr.

Moliwda doesn't really care for it, but he adds the hand of God, like Nahman wants.

Then he again reads them what he's written:

> How all of this occurred, how God gave us the strength and the hope in order that we, weak and stripped of all support, without any knowledge of the Polish language, expounded our theses with skill. Now, too, for we have come to such a certainty and a desire, that we urgently require the holy baptism. For we believe that Jesus Christ, born of the Virgin Mary, was a man whom our ancestors tormented on the wooden cross, and that he was the true Messiah promised in the convents and the prophecies. We believe in it, lips, heart, and souls, and this our faith we declare.

The words of this profession of faith fall heavy and blunt. Anczel, Moshe's young son-in-law, titters nervously but quiets down at a look from Jacob.

Only then does Moliwda add in the beginning:

> From the Polish, Hungarian, Turkish, Muntenian, Wallachian, and other countries, the Israelites, through their messenger—who is faithful to Israel and learned of the Scriptures and the holy prophets, having raised his hands to the heavens, whence help used to come, with tears of primordial happiness, health, long-standing peace, and the gifts of the Holy Spirit, stands—wish you, Your Great and Powerful Excellency, all the best and most wondrous of things.

Probably only Nahman understands the intricate, ornate style Moliwda is using. He smacks his lips in delight and ineptly tries to translate his twisted phrases into Yiddish and Turkish.

"Are you sure that's Polish?" Shlomo Shorr says. "Now we absolutely have to put that we're asking for the disputation, so that . . . so that . . ."

"So that what?" asks Moliwda. "What's the point of this disputation? What's it going to do?"

"So that everything is out in the open, nothing held back," says Shlomo. "In order for justice to function, it's best for it to take place on a stage, so that people will remember."

"And on, and on." Moliwda moves his arm in a circle as though rolling some sort of invisible wheel. "Anything else?"

Shlomo would like to add something, but by nature he is very polite, and you can see that there is something that does not quite escape his lips. Jacob looks upon this scene and retreats, leaning back in his armchair. Then Little Hayah, Shlomo's wife, pipes up as she brings in some figs and nuts for them.

"The other thing is revenge," she says, setting the little bowls on the table. "For beating Rabbi Elisha, for stealing from us, for every element of persecution, for chasing us out of our towns, for the wives who left their husbands and were labeled whores, for the curse put on Jacob and on all of us."

"She's right," says Jacob, who's been silent until now.

They nod. Yes, it is about revenge. Hayah says:

"This is a war. We are going to war."

"The woman is right."

So Moliwda dips his pen.

It is not hunger, not exile, nor the scattering of our belongings that leads us to step away from our old customs and unite with the Holy Roman Church, for we, sitting peacefully in our sorrows, have until now looked upon the injuries of our exiled and starving brothers and never been called. But divine grace calls us now, especially, from darkness into light. We cannot but heed this call from God, as our fathers have done. We march joyfully under the banner of the Holy Cross, and we ask for a field upon which to carry out a second battle with the enemies of the truth, as we desire to show from the Holy

Scripture, openly, the appearance in the world of God in human
form, his passion on behalf of humankind, the need for
universal oneness in God as well as to prove the ungodliness of
our opponents, the gross unbelief . . .

They take a lunch break.


Moliwda is drinking again in the evenings. Jacob has had good wine
brought in from Giurgiu, saying it's from a vineyard he has purchased.
The wine is clear, tastes of olive groves and melons. Jacob does not take
part in the discussions and the writing of the supplications. He is busy
working in the village and—he says—teaching, which actually means
sitting with the women as they pluck feathers, and holding forth. That's
how they see him, as an innocent, not wrapped up in any of this, not in
letters or sentences. He hoists them up by their collars when they grow
heedless and try to bow before him. He doesn't want that. We are equal,
he says. And this delights these miserable people.

Of course they're not equals, thinks Moliwda. Back in the Bogomil
village, they weren't equals either. There were corporeal, psychic, and
spiritual people. Somatics, psychics, and pneumatics, they called them,
from the Greek. Equality goes against nature, however rightly one might
strive toward it. Some are made of more earthly elements, and those people are thick, sensual, and non-creative. They are only good for listening.
Others live with their hearts, their emotions, in bursts of the soul, and
others still have contact with the highest spirit, distant from the body, free
from affects, spacious inside. It is to this final group that God has access.

But living together, they should have identical rights.

Moliwda likes it here, he doesn't really have too much to do aside from
the writing that takes up his mornings. He would gladly remain here with
them, passing himself off as one of them, hiding among their beards and
caftans, in the wrinkled, many-layered skirts of the women, in their fragrant hair. He would happily let them christen him again, and maybe he
would even return to the faith by this other road, along with them, from
a different direction, from the kitchen door through which one does not
enter into the salons with their carpets, but rather where the slightly

spoiled potatoes lie in boxes, where the floor is slick with fat, and where the awkward, crude questions are asked. For instance: Who is this Savior who allowed himself to be killed in such a cruel manner, and who sent him? And why must a world created by God be saved in the first place? And, "Why is it so bad, when it could be so good?" wonders Moliwda, quoting to himself the good, innocent Nahman, and smiling.

He knows many of them believe that, once baptized, they will become immortal. That they will not die. And maybe they're right—this motley crew that comes and stands submissively in line for rations every morning, these dirty children, scabies in between their fingers, women whose caps conceal filthy, tangled hair, and their emaciated husbands. By evening they'll go to sleep with their bellies full. Perhaps it is in fact this community that shall be led now by the Holy Ghost, the Spirit, that everlasting light, distinct from the world and a stranger to it, just as they are strangers, made of some other substance, if light can be considered substance. And the Spirit opts for just such people, for freed of the shackles of dogma and decree—and until they have created their own rules—they shall be truly pure, truly innocent.

## The supplication to Archbishop Łubieński

It takes several long days before what follows can be clearly established:

1. That the prophecies of all the prophets on the coming of the Messiah have already been fulfilled.
2. That the Messiah was the true God, whose name is Adonai, and he took our body and according to it suffered to attain our redemption and salvation.
3. That since the coming of the true Messiah, sacrifices and ceremonies have ceased.
4. That every person should be obedient to the order of the Messiah, for in it lies salvation.
5. That the Holy Cross is an expression of the Holiest Trinity and the seal of the Messiah.

6. That it is impossible to accede to the faith of the Messiah and
the King in any way other than through baptism.

When they put the first six theses to a vote, Krysa is against the baptism
one, but seeing the raised hands, he realizes that nothing can be done
about it now. He waves his hand violently and sits with his head down, his
elbows resting on his knees, looking at the floor, where little clumps of
mud carried into the room on people's shoes reluctantly sink into the
sawdust.

"You have to come to your senses! You're making a big mistake."

Despite his ugly face, Krysa is a good speaker, and as such, he is able
to unfold before the eyes of those gathered a vision so calamitous that
they begin to lean toward his suggestions. According to him, their future
will gradually and inevitably come to resemble the life of a peasant. By the
afternoon, when they have eaten and their warmed bodies grown sluggish, when twilight is falling outside the little windows, taking on the
steel color of a knife's blade, and looks like it will last into infinity—at
that point the argument begins to hold. Krysa manages to introduce some
conditions for baptism in writing:

The baptism will not take place before the festival of Epiphany of
1760. They will not be required to shave their beards or cut their payot.
They will be able to go by dual names—both a Christian name and a
Jewish one. They will continue to wear Jewish clothing. They will be able
to marry only amongst themselves. They will not be forced to consume
pork. In addition to Sunday, they will also be allowed to mark their Shabbat. And they will get to keep their Hebrew texts, the Zohar in particular.

This reassures them, and they stop paying attention to Krysa now.
Especially since Old Shorr and Hayah are arriving.

Shorr drags his legs, and Hayah leads him in. Although no external
wounds can be seen on him any longer, it is clear he has undergone some
sort of trauma. He does not bear any resemblance to that ruddy old man,
full of vim and vigor, of a year ago. And perhaps the new concern that
arises is connected with the arrival of Elisha and Hayah—no one really
knows—or perhaps it has been there all along, awaiting its turn in line.
At this point it's hard even to tell who was the first to formulate this

notion for their final reckoning with their enemies. When they say "enemies," they mean Rapaport, Mendl, Shmulewicz, and all the rabbis, from Satanów, Jazłowiec, Mohylew—all of them, along with their wives, who still spit on the heretics in the street and throw stones at their women.

This enemy is familiar, even close, which means the enmity is that much greater. Knowing your enemy well, you know exactly where to strike him, how to hurt him most. Though he may wound you, too. There is in this struggle with a close enemy a strange sort of twisted pleasure, for it is like striking oneself, yet simultaneously dodging every blow. In any case, when the notion does arise (who knows from whose mind), a silence falls, and they all think it over in that silence. No one knows what to say. They add the seventh point to the supplication:

> 7. That the Talmud teaches that Christian blood is needed, and
> anyone who believes in the Talmud must demand said blood.

"There's nothing like that in those teachings," says Nahman grimly.

"The teachings contain all things," Jacob answers him.

They sign the supplication in silence. It is also signed by the newest members of their group: Aron ben Shmul of Czernowitz; Meyer ben David of Szegirt, here with his whole family; Moshko ben Jacob of Bucharest; as well as Anczel, who has been tittering so. The supplication will be delivered by Moliwda, and if the archbishop agrees, they will send an official delegation.

Finally, after they all put in their signatures, Nahman convinces Moliwda to add a final sentence in his beautiful writing, so replete with swirls:

> We are all awaiting, as we would much-coveted water, the
> day when the holy *alef*, now curving, straightens to bless and
> unite the four corners of the world.

On the last night, Tanna, the very girl he had liked, comes to Moliwda. For a brief moment he thinks that it is Hana, for it might be said that they are strikingly similar—the same wide hips and flat stomachs.

She is a little bit shy, and he is, too. He makes room for her close to him, and she lies down quietly, with her hands over her face. He starts to caress her back, which is like silk.

"Do you have a fiancé?" he asks in Turkish, since the girl looks to be Wallachian.

"I did, but he stayed behind."

"Will you take another?"

"I don't know."

"Do you want me?"

"I do."

He gently removes her hands from her face, and she embraces him and clings to him with her whole body.

## Of the everlasting interconnectedness between divinity and sinfulness

"Why is the biblical Jacob so important to you?" asks Moliwda, as Nahman accompanies him on horseback to Kamieniec. "I don't get that."

Nahman explains in a convoluted way. Moliwda has to sift it through the sieve of his own language, since they are speaking a little in Hebrew and a little in Polish. In Hebrew, things can get complicated by virtue of being so ambiguous. But in Polish, the things that Nahman says in his singsong voice, as though reciting books from memory, are also difficult to understand. The Polish language lacks the words for such questions. It has little experience with them, and knows little of theology. This is why every heresy in Poland has been unleavened and bland. In fact, no real heresy could ever come about in Polish. By its nature, the Polish language is obedient to every orthodoxy.

"But this was a blessing received through deception and theft," Moliwda interjects.

"Exactly. Jacob himself defied the law and deceived his father. He went beyond the law, and because of it, he became a hero."

Moliwda is silent for a moment.

"But later, Jacob, once he was himself a patriarch, guarded the law. That is so perverse: when you need to be, you are against the law, and when it serves your purposes, you're for it . . ." He laughs.

"That's true, too. Remember how Jacob didn't allow Rachel to take her idols, the teraphim," says Nahman.

"Why?"

"Here Jacob made a mistake. Rather than recognize the divinity contained in the teraphim, Jacob would rather throw it out because it exists in idols, which is to say he does not allow holiness that appears in some other, foreign form to be joined with our faith. But Rachel understands that there is divinity even in an idol."

"Women sometimes have a greater wisdom."

"They are less attached to words."

"Hayah Shorr, too?"

"She isn't entirely a woman," Nahman answers seriously.

Moliwda starts laughing.

"I wanted her, but Jacob wouldn't let me," he says.

Nahman doesn't say anything. They are traveling along the Dniester, the river meandering along their right side, appearing and disappearing again. They can already see the enormous buildings of Chocim and Okopy, known as the Ramparts of the Holy Trinity, from afar.

"Jacob is a con man," Moliwda says provocatively, but Nahman acts as though he hasn't heard. He doesn't say anything until upon the horizon emerge the powerful shapes of the fortress and the little town lying at its base.

"Did you know that the Baal Shem Tov was born right there, in Okopy?" says Nahman.

"Who is that?"

Nahman, stunned by his ignorance, simply says:

"A great sage."

They leave the main road as a precaution, even though there is nowhere to hide on the barely undulating plain.

"I respect you very much, Moliwda. Most of all because I know you are a good man. And Jacob loves you. You have been a greater help to us than anyone. I just don't know why you are doing it. What do you need all this for?"

"For profit."

"That's enough for me. But you think differently. You may not even understand us. You say: black and white, good and evil, woman and man. But it isn't that simple. We no longer believe in the things of which the elder Kabbalists spoke, such that if all the sparks could be collected from the darkness, they would unite into a messianic tikkun and transform the world for the better. We've already crossed over. Because divinity and sinfulness are everlastingly interconnected. Sabbatai said that after the Torah of Bria, the Torah of the Created World will come the Torah of Atzilut. But Jacob and all of us know that the two Torahs are interwoven, and the only thing that can be done is to move beyond the both of them. The struggle is about leaving behind that point where we divide everything into evil and good, light and darkness, getting rid of all those foolish divisions and from there starting a new order all over again. We don't know what's past that point. It's like putting all your eggs in one basket and just taking that step into the darkness. We are headed into the darkness."

When Moliwda looks at Nahman, this small, freckled man who speaks so quickly that he starts to stutter, it surprises him that such a great intelligence would be used for the plumbing of such wholly useless depths. For Nahman knows by heart whole passages of books, perhaps whole books even, and, when necessary, he shuts his eyes and recites, quickly and passionately, so that Moliwda doesn't even understand. He has spent weeks on paradoxes, on commentaries of commentaries, or on the presence of a single ambiguous word in a text. He is capable of praying for hours, hunched over. Yet he knows nothing of astronomy, nor of geography—only whatever he has happened to overhear on his travels. He knows nothing of political systems, governments, no philosophers other than his own Kabbalists. Descartes could just as soon be a kind of paper cartridge, as far as he's concerned. And still, Nahman moves Moliwda. Does he know anyone more zealous and more naive than this rabbi of Busk, Nahman Shmulewicz, Nahman ben Samuel?

## Of God

"You know, Moliwda, that I can't tell you everything. I am bound to secrecy," says Nahman suddenly, as his horse stops and lowers its head, as if this confession had filled it with sadness. "You think we are traveling over to Edom out of poverty and a lust for privileges . . ."

"I think that would be understandable," says Moliwda, squeezing his horse's sides to make him stop. "Human. There would be nothing wrong in it . . ."

"It may seem that way to you Christians, and we want you to think that. Because you don't understand other reasons. You are shallow, surfaces suffice for you—you have your church dogma, your chapel, and you don't keep looking beyond that."

"What reasons?"

"That we are whole in God, and that this is tikkun. That it is we who are saving the world."

Moliwda smiles, his horse has started moving around in a circle. The great space, undulating with little hills, with the Ramparts of the Holy Trinity on the horizon, moves along majestically before his eyes, which sting when they look up at the white, milky sky.

"What do you mean, saving?" he asks.

"Because it's made poorly. All of our sages, from Nathan of Gaza to Cardoso, have said that the Mosaic God, the Creator of the World, is merely a Small God, a surrogate for the Other, Vast God, to whom our world is altogether foreign and irrelevant. The Creator is gone. That's what exile is—we have to pray to a God who is not there in the Torah."

This makes Moliwda feel ill at ease—Nahman's tone has grown so mournful all of a sudden.

"What's gotten into you today?" he says, and moves a little forward, but Nahman doesn't follow, so Moliwda returns.

"That God is one God . . . ," begins Nahman, but Moliwda urges his horse forward and takes off at a gallop, and all Nahman can hear is:

"Silence!"

Moliwda stops where the road forks—one goes to Kamieniec, the other to Lwów. He looks back. He sees the little figure that is Nahman sitting uncertainly on his horse, lost in thought, his horse moving at a walk, looking like it is treading carefully along the line of the horizon, like a funambulist.

## "The miller grinds the flower"

The letter announcing the nomination of Archbishop Łubieński's chamberlain catches Moliwda in Kamieniec with Castellan Kossakowski, the sort-of cousin he has traveled from Ivanie to visit, though really he is there for the baths, clean clothes, books, and the latest gossip. He has not found Katarzyna, however—she is, as usual, on the road, and cousin Kossakowski will not really do for deeper conversation, all he does is natter on about dogs and hunting. After a few glasses of Tokay he suggests to Moliwda that they go to some place that supposedly has the best girls. Moliwda declines: after Ivanie, he has had his fill of girls. In the evening, they play cards with the garrison commander, the noisy and attention-seeking Prince Marcin Lubomirski, and that is when Moliwda is called—a messenger has arrived from Lwów with a letter.

The news is like a lightning bolt. Moliwda wasn't expecting it. When he reads the letter at the table, his face still expresses boundless surprise, but Castellan Kossakowski understands everything at once:

"Well, that's just my wonderful little wife arranging things so she has somebody of hers right there at the primate's side. Yes, that Łubieński's already been appointed primate. Did you not know all that?"

Prince Lubomirski has a crate of good wine brought up, and some Gypsies to play music, and now the card game stalls. Moliwda is overwhelmed, his thoughts keep racing away from him, ahead to the unimaginable future that awaits. Without knowing why, he is reminded of that day when, on Mount Athos, under the enormous parasol of the sky, he followed the path of a beetle, his head full of the monotonous cicada music. And here is where he's ended up.

The next day, freshly shaved and beautifully dressed, he appears in Lwów before the archbishop.

Moliwda is put up in the episcopal palace, where it is clean and nice. He immediately goes out into town, to an Armenian warehouse, where he buys a lovely Turkish belt, masterfully woven, glittering with different colors, and a żupan. He thinks about a light blue one, but practical considerations prevail—he chooses another, the color of dark water, a cloudy azure. He looks around the Lwów cathedral, but soon he is freezing, so he goes back to his room and unfolds his papers. He will write letters. But first, he undertakes the work he does daily, the assignment he has set himself, so as not to forget his Greek—his translation of Pythagoras. A few lines every day, since otherwise his brain will rot under this cold, hostile, enormous Polish sky:

"Flighty men, like empty vessels, are easily laid hold of by the ears." Or: "The wise man leaves this world as he would a feast." Or: "Time transforms even wormwood into sweet honey. Circumstance and necessity often lead a man to turn an enemy into a friend." He intends to sprinkle the primate's letters with these intelligent, eloquent quotes.

Meanwhile, the barber is applying suds to Archbishop Łubieński. He caught a cold during his journey from Warsaw, where he spent two months, and now he has a cough. The curtains are pulled around his bed. Father Pikulski stands nearby and through the thin opening looks at the part of the archbishop's hefty body the barber's delicate hands are now tormenting.

Father Pikulski has the overwhelming impression that all of this has already happened, that he has already seen this, that he has already said these things to Bishop Dembowski, may he rest in peace, and stood before him in the same way, like a servant before a lord, trying desperately to warn him. Why are these Church hierarchs so naive? he thinks, and his eyes linger over the fanciful Turkish patterns on the curtains. He says:

"His Excellency ought not to permit any acceptation of this type of insolent demand, as it would create a precedent on the world stage."

A moan emerges from behind the curtains.

"Because they were unable to legalize their sect within the framework of their Jewish religion, now they're trying out some new trickery."

He waits for a reaction, but in the absence of any, he continues:

"What does it even mean that they wish to preserve some of their customs and dress? What would it mean to 'mark their Shabbat'? And keep their beards and their hairstyles? In any case, the Talmudists themselves do not want these Shabbitarians to go around dressed as Jews, since they consider them not to be Jews any longer. They don't belong to anybody now—they're like dogs without masters. This would be the worst possible solution—we'd be taking responsibility for a bunch of heretics, after having just dealt with heretics elsewhere."

"Whom do you have in mind?" says a weak voice from behind the curtains.

"I have in mind those unfortunate Polish Brethren," answers Father Pikulski, although in fact his mind has already moved on to something else.

"Baptism is baptism. Rome would like such a great baptism—ouch—would . . . ," the archbishop says hoarsely from behind the curtains.

"But it must be unconditional. We must demand from them an unconditional conversion, no exceptions, and as soon as possible, in the best-case scenario immediately after the conclusion of this disputation we're planning, as Your Excellency knows, for spring, as soon as it's a bit warmer. No buts. Remember, Your Excellency, that it is we who dictate the conditions. The first to be baptized must be their leader, his wife, and their children. And with as much pomp and circumstance as possible, so that everyone hears of it and sees it. There can be no further discussion."

When Moliwda comes in, he sees the archbishop being examined by some medic, a tall Jew with a gloomy gaze. He has taken a number of different glass lenses out of his bag and is putting them up to His Excellency's eyes.

"I am going to wear these lenses, I have trouble reading now," says the archbishop. "You wrote everything up very nicely, Mr. Kossakowski. Everything is set, I see. Your efforts to bring these people to the bosom of the church are significant and noteworthy. From here on out, you will occupy yourself with this same matter, but under my wing."

"My merit is minor, but those lost little lambs' desire is very great," answers Moliwda humbly.

"None of your lost lambs here, that will not work on me, sir . . ."

"What does Your Excellency see now? Can you read these letters?" asks the Jew, holding up a piece of paper with a crooked inscription: THE MILLER GRINDS THE FLOWER.

"The miller grinds the flour. I can see well, very well, it is really quite the miracle," says Archbishop Łubieński.

"We both know that everyone will be better off by sticking to the side that's strongest," says Moliwda.

Apparently the next lens also works well, for the bishop grunts with pleasure:

"This is even better, oh, this one, this one. Goodness, how well I can see. Every little hair in your red beard, Asher!"

When the medic has packed up his bag and left, Łubieński turns to Moliwda:

"And what of these accusations, known to the whole world, that the Jews need Christian blood for their matzah . . . Sołtyk can prove this is true, can't he?" He smiles broadly. "To me this is like playing with a knife's blade without a handle."

"That's what they wanted. I suppose it's a form of revenge."

"The pope has definitively forbidden such blood accusations . . . But if they are making them of their own accord . . . There has to be something to it, then, doesn't there . . ."

"I don't think anybody believes it."

"What about Bishop Sołtyk? Does he believe it? I don't know. I know people have different ways of handling things. Good work, Mr. Kossakowski."

The next day, Moliwda heads straight for Łowicz, where he will take up his new post, in a new state of mind that verges on elation. The snow and ice have already begun to thaw, and the roads are difficult, so that the horses' hooves slip over the still-frozen clods of mud, and in the afternoon, as it begins to get darker, the water in the ruts freezes, and the cold, sulfur-colored sky is reflected in the little tiles of very thin ice. He travels alone on horseback, sometimes joining up with other travelers, only to leave them for the next leg of his journey. Somewhere along the way he catches fleas.

Just past Lublin, he is attacked by some tatterdemalions with clubs, and he chases them away, waving his saber and howling like a man possessed, but from then on he travels in a group to Łowicz. He reaches his destination after twelve days and almost immediately gets to work.

The primate's chancellery is active already, and one of the first matters that must be dealt with is the supplication from the Jewish "Puritanes," as Primate Łubieński himself calls them—the same supplication that Moliwda wrote not long ago in Ivanie. Now it looks as though he will have to answer it himself. For the time being, he has a few copies made to be sent on to others, to Nuncio Serra, to the royal chancellery, for the archive.

More than once he begins the delicate conversation with the primate about this, but Łubieński is too absorbed by the organization of his primate's palace, which is, sadly, a little worse for wear, lacking its former splendor, from the time when the interrex primate resided here during the interregnum.

The primate's books have just arrived in trunks from Lwów. He looks them over inattentively.

"I need you to investigate why they're insisting upon baptism like this. Whether they have ulterior motives, and what the scale would be of such a conversion," he says, still distracted.

"There are at least forty such families in Lwów alone, and the rest come not only from the Commonwealth, but also from Hungary and Wallachia, and these are the most learned, the most enlightened," Moliwda lies.

"But how many of them are there?"

"It was said that there might be as many as five thousand of them in Kamieniec, and now the latest reports are suggesting there might be three times that number."

"Fifteen thousand," says the primate, and picks up the tome at the top of the pile, opening it and flipping through it absentmindedly. "The *New Athens*," he says.

# IV.

---

## *The Book of*
# THE COMET

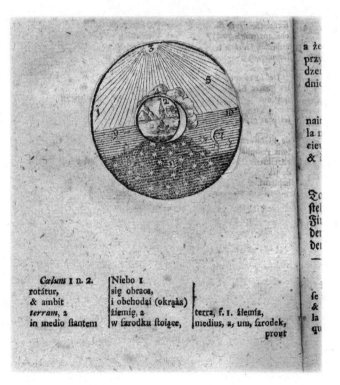

Cælum I n. 2.    Niebo I
rotátur,         się obraca,
& ambit          i obchodzi (okrąża)
terram, 2        ziemię, a                terra, f. I. ziemia,
in medio ftantem w fzrodku ftoiące,      medius, a, um, fzrodek,
                                                       proịt

## 19

## Of the comet that augurs the end of the world and brings about the Shekhinah

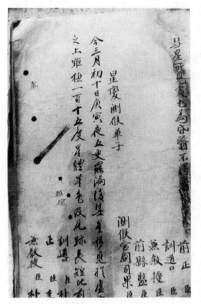

The comet appeared in the sky on March 13, 1759, and as though at its command, the snows melted and poured into the Dniester, causing it to overflow. For many days, it has continued to hang suspended over the wet, vast world, a brightly shining star, disquieting, upending the order of the sky.

The comet is visible the planet over. It can even be seen in China.

It is seen by soldiers after a battle in Silesia, as they lick their wounds; by sailors as they sober up on the cobblestones in front of Hamburg taverns; by Alpine shepherds guiding their sheep to summer pastures; by Greek olive pickers, and pilgrims with Saint James shells stitched onto their caps. It is scrutinized by anxious women expecting to miscarry at any given moment, and glimpsed by families crowded down below the decks of fragile ships as they cross the ocean in search of a new life on the other side.

The comet resembles a scythe aimed at humanity, a naked glistening blade that might slice off millions of heads at any moment, and not only the ones on the craned necks in Ivanie, but also city dwellers' heads, Lwów heads, Kraków heads—even royal heads. There is no doubt it is a sign of the end of the world, a harbinger of angels rolling up the whole show like a rug. The play is evidently over, armies of archangels already gathering on the horizon. If you pay attention, you can hear the clanking of the angelic arsenal. And it is a mark of the mission of Jacob, and of all who follow him on his arduous path. Any who yet doubt must now acknowledge that even the heavens are joining this onward march. As the days pass, it becomes clear to all in Ivanie that the comet is a hole drilled into the heavenly firmament, through which the divine light may pass in order to reach us, and through which God is now checking on the world.

The sages say that the Shekhinah will pass through this hole.

Strange as it is, remarkable though it may be, on Yente the comet makes little impression. From her vantage point, of greater interest are the countless humble human things that make up the warp of the world. The comet? Why, that's just a single gleaming thread.

For example, Yente sees how Ivanie has a particular status in the hierarchy of being. The village isn't firmly planted on the ground, isn't altogether real. Homes stooping over like living things, ancient aurochs, muzzles approaching the earth, thawing it with their breath. From the windows, a stream of yellow light, the light of a faded sun, much more powerful than candlelight. People take one another's hands, then let go to eat from a single bowl, halving their bread. Steam rises from the kasha that fathers tenderly spoon into the mouths of the children sitting in their laps.

Couriers on tired horses carry letters from the capital to far-flung provinces, barges loaded with grain glide sleepily to Gdańsk—the Vistula never froze over this year—while raftsmen come to after last night's carousing. In court, expenses are tallied, but the numbers stay on paper, never turning into money—it's always better to settle up in flour and vodka than in jangling coins. Peasant women sweep the cellars, and children play with pigs' bones left from the slaughter. Now they toss them onto the sawdust-strewn floor and study the resulting patterns to divine whether winter will be over soon. Will the storks be quick to return? In Lwów's market square, commerce is just getting going—you can still hear hammers bringing boards together to make stalls. The horizon lies somewhere past Lublin, just past Kraków, at the Dnieper, at the Prut.

The words pronounced in Ivanie—great and powerful words— transgress the world's boundaries. Behind them lies a completely other reality—there is no language to express it. It's like holding silk embroidered in fifty-six colors up to gray fustian—incomparable. Yente, whose vantage point is inaccessible to any other person, is reminded of a bursting—a softness, a stickiness, a fleshiness, with many facets and dimensions, though without time. Warm, gold, light, soft. It's like some strange living body revealed by a wound, like the juicy pulp that escapes from under broken skin.

That's how the Shekhinah comes into the world.

Jacob speaks of it more and more often, calling it a she but rarely using her name at first, and yet this new and powerful presence in Ivanie spreads fast.

"The Maiden goes before the Lord," pronounces Jacob at the close of one long winter evening. It's after midnight already, the furnaces have cooled, and a bitter chill sneaks into the room like a little mouse through the cracks in the walls. "She is the gateway to God, who can only be reached through Her. As the peel precedes the fruit."

They call her Everlasting Virgin, Heavenly Queen, Benefactress.

"And we are going to get under Her wing," Jacob continues his teaching. "Each and every one of us will look upon Her in his way."

"You thought up until now," he says one winter morning, "that the Messiah would be a man, but under no circumstances can that occur—the Maiden is the foundation, and it is She who will be the true savior. She will conduct all worlds; all weapons will be surrendered to Her. David and the First came in order to pave the way to Her, but they completed nothing. That's what I'll be doing, finishing what they started."

Jacob lights his long Turkish pipe. A warm, soft light flits from it into his eyes and disappears under his lowered eyelids.

"Our ancestors had no idea what they were even searching for so long and hard. Perhaps a few of them knew that in all their writings and all their wise teachings, ultimately what they were looking for was Her. Everything depends on Her. As Jacob found Rachel by the well, so Moses, when he reached the source, came to the Maiden."

## Of Yankiel of Glinno and the terrible smell of silt

Yankiel, the young rabbi of Glinno, a widower who recently buried both wife and child, found himself in Ivanie in the spring at the urging of Nahman, with whom, years earlier, he was a student of the Hassidim. They act boisterous together, as if to emphasize their mutual attachment. But it would seem that more divides them than unites them. In the first place, stature—Yankiel has grown, and Nahman has not. They look like a poplar and a juniper. Seeing them walk together makes people smile, whether they intend to or not. Nahman is an enthusiast, while Yankiel of Glinno is all sad reserve, and fearful, too, here in Ivanie, for this place frightens him. He listens to Frank's words and watches how people react to them. Those who sit closest never take their eyes off him—not a single one of his movements escapes them—while those in the back, despite the tenuous light of several lamps, can barely see and hear. But when the word "Messiah" is spoken, a sigh spreads through the room, almost a moan.

Thanks to a relative in the Lwów kahal, Yankiel of Glinno brings them the news that Talmudist Jews from all over Podolia have gathered together and written a letter to Jacob Emden in Altona to request his counsel. They also have Yavan, who continues to whisper into Minister Brühl's ear on every possible occasion, encouraging him to take a view of the whole matter that is favorable to the Talmudists. Brühl borrows money from Yavan, sometimes even for the Polish king, giving this Jew considerable influence at the royal court.

And Yankiel says that the rabbis have once again sent a message to the highest ecclesiastical authority—to Rome itself, to the pope.

Yankiel has already received the ironic nickname of Mr. Gliniański, a Polish name, since he carries himself like a Pole and turns up his nose like a Pole. He seems pleased to be the center of attention. He speaks briefly and waits a moment for his words to take effect.

He sees that his news disturbs the assembly. They have gone silent, aside from the occasional cough. The barn, which they have repurposed to be a kind of common room, with a stove in the middle, now transforms into a ship sailing in the dark through stormy waters. Everywhere you look some new danger lurks. It is strange to be aware that everyone out there, on the outside, wishes them ill. The wooden walls of this ship, this Ivanie ark, are too thin to block out the enemies' whispers, their scheming, their accusations and slanders.

Jacob, the Lord, who senses all emotions better than anyone else, intones a joyful song in his powerful, low voice:

> Forsa damus para verti,
> seihut grandi asser verti.

Which, in the language of the Sephardim, means:

> Give us the power to see thee
> and the great fortune to serve thee.

And now everyone is singing "para verti," the whole barn, their voices uniting into something singular and strong, leaving no room for and no memory of Yankiel of Glinno and his bad news.

———

Nahman and his very young wife, Wajgełe, whose nickname is the Little Ant, have taken Yankiel in. Sometimes, pretending to be asleep, Yankiel eavesdrops on his arguing hosts; she wants to go back to Busk. She is very thin and prone to fevers and coughs.

The fact that they all have to go through the motions of accepting the Nazarene faith and acting more Christian than the Christians themselves strikes Yankiel as dishonest. It is fraud. He likes having to live piously, humbly, not saying much, keeping his thoughts to himself. The truth should be in your heart, not on your lips. And yet: converting to Christianity!

Nahman dispels his doubts: accepting the Christian faith does not mean becoming Christian. They cannot, for instance, marry Christian women, or even have concubines from among them, for although Señor Santo Baruchiah repeated: "Blessed is he who permits all forbidden things," he also said that the daughter of a foreign God is forbidden.

Yankiel of Glinno is mostly impervious to these arguments. That's how he is—he never goes too close to anything, standing instead to one side, not listening to the teachings but leaning up against a tree, against the doorframe, as if he were just pausing for a moment on his way out. He observes. Two years have passed since his wife's death, and he, a rabbi living on his own in poverty-stricken Glinno, has endured much angst over one Christian woman, older than he, a governess on an estate near Busk. They met by accident. The woman was sitting on the riverbank, dipping her feet in the water. She was naked. When she saw Yankiel, she simply said, "Come here."

As he always does when he gets nervous, Yankiel plucked a blade of grass and put it in between his teeth—he believes this heightens his self-confidence. Now he knows that he should have turned on his heels and vanished from the sight of this shiksa, but in the moment, he could not take his eyes off her white thighs, he was suddenly seized by such an intense desire that in some sense he simply lost his mind. It also excited him that they were shielded from view by reeds as tall as walls and that the marshes smelled of rot and silt. Every particle of the hot air felt swollen, full, and juicy like a cherry, and soon it would burst, and its juice would spill onto their skin. A storm was coming.

He crouched shyly by the woman and saw that she was no longer young, that her breasts, full and white, hung down, and that her stomach, slightly protruding, with a birthmark on her navel, was cut across by a fine line that has been impressed into her skin by her skirt. He wanted to say something, but he found no words in Polish appropriate to the situation. And anyway, what exactly would he say? Meanwhile, her hand was the first to reach out, moving toward him, starting with his calf, his thigh, stroking his crotch, touching his hands and his face, where her fingers played a little with his beard. Then, gently, as if it were only natural, the woman lay down on her back and spread her legs. Yankiel, to tell the truth, does not believe that there is anyone in the world who would have turned around and left had they been in his place. He experienced a brief, incredible pleasure, and then they just lay there, still, without a word. She stroked his back, their heated bodies stuck together by sweat.

They arranged to meet in the same place several more times, but when autumn came, and it got cold, she stopped coming, which meant that Yankiel of Glinno was no longer committing a terrible sin, for which he was grateful to her. But he was overwhelmed by an inconsolable longing as well as a great pain that prevented him from focusing on anything. He realized he was unhappy.

That's when he met Nahman, with whom he had studied at the Besht's years ago. They threw their arms around each other. Nahman invited him to Ivanie, saying he would understand everything once he got there. Why should he sit around in an empty house? But Rabbi Yankiel of Glinno was not particularly enthusiastic. So Nahman mounted his horse and said:

"Don't come to Ivanie, if you don't want to. But beware your own mistrustfulness."

That's what he said to him. Beware your own mistrustfulness. This got the rabbi of Glinno—this convinced him. He stayed leaning against the doorframe, grass between his teeth, indifferent on the surface, but in fact deeply moved.

At the beginning of April he set out on foot for Ivanie, and since then he has slowly succumbed to considerable genuine enthusiasm, to the point that he doesn't even want to admit to himself how important it is to stay close to this man in the Turkish hat.

In Busk, a small scandal breaks out at Princess Jabłonowska's estate around the time that Mrs. Kossakowska arrives a few months later. The governess of the young Jabłonowskis, already forty years old, suddenly starts to weaken and seems to have caught something like hydrops, and then develops pain so terrible that they call the medic for her. But the medic, instead of letting her blood, calls for hot water: she's about to give birth. This announcement occasions a small nervous breakdown on the part of the princess, for it had never entered her mind that Barbara . . . Well, of course, there are no words! And at her age!

At least the floozy has the decency to die on her third day in childbed, as often happens with older women, their time having obviously passed. She is survived by a little girl, tiny but in perfect health, whom Princess Jabłonowska is ready to give to the peasants in the village and maintain from afar. But Mrs. Kossakowska's arrival in Busk causes the matter to take a different course. For Mrs. Kossakowska, having no children herself, had been thinking about setting up an orphanage, with the help of Bishop Sołtyk, but somehow the idea had never quite become a priority. Now she asks Princess Jabłonowska to keep the infant on her estate for a little while, until she can ready the shelter.

"What harm will it do you? You won't even know that such a tiny person was ever here, on such an enormous property."

"It's a child obtained from harlotry . . . I don't even know whose it is."

"But what fault is that of the little girl's?"

Truth be told, the princess doesn't require too much convincing. The baby is lovely, and so quiet; she is christened on Easter Monday.

## Of Strange Deeds, holy silence, and other Ivanie diversions

A trusted messenger brings a letter from Moliwda just as the comet is slowly disappearing. Drying off from the drizzle outside by the fire in the room, he tells them that all over Podolia this celestial body has generated great anxiety, and many people have insisted that it augurs a great plague and pogroms, as in Khmelnytsky's day. And famine, too, and an impending war with Frederick Augustus. Everyone agrees that the Last Days are coming.

When Jacob enters the room, Nahman silently hands him the letter, his face serious and impenetrable. Jacob is unable to read it, so he gives it to Hayah, but even she strains over the swirls, so the letter goes from hand to hand until it makes its way right back to Nahman. As he reads it, a broad smile, sly and insolent, appears on his face. He says that Primate Łubieński has granted their requests. The disputation will take place in the summer, with the baptism to follow.

This news has been so eagerly anticipated, so desired for such a long time, and yet at the same time, it simply heralds what's inevitable. A silence follows Nahman's announcement.

It isn't easy to take the first step. They have been taught so determinedly how to behave that the instructions have been permanently etched into their brains. Yet now they must erase all that, wipe the Mosaic Tablets of their false commandments that keep them imprisoned like animals in cages. Thou shalt not do this, thou shalt not do that—none of it's allowed. The boundaries of the unsaved world are built out of prohibitions.

"What you have to do is leave yourself behind, set yourself down somewhere else," Nahman explains to Wajgełe later. "The situation is similar to when you have to slit a painful abscess and squeeze all the pus out of it. The worst part is making the decision and the first movement; then, once it's under way, everything becomes quite natural. It's an act of faith, jumping headfirst into the water without any regard for what's at the bottom. When you come back to the surface, you are new. Or it's like a person who has gone to distant countries and returned, and suddenly he sees that everything that used to seem natural and obvious to him is in fact merely local and bizarre. And what seemed foreign and bizarre he now understands, so that it feels like it belongs to him."

Nahman knows what Wajgełe cares about most. Everyone asks about the same thing, everyone wants to know about intercourse, as if that were the only thing that mattered; they don't ask about virtue, about the struggles of conscience connected with higher matters—everyone only ever asks about intercourse. That disappoints Nahman a great deal—people are not so different from animals. When you talk to them about copulation, about all those things that go on from the waist down, they turn bright red.

"Is there something wrong with a person joining with another person? Is not copulation good? You just have to give yourself over to it without thinking, and eventually pleasure will come of it, and this pleasure is a blessing of the act. Yet even without pleasure it is good, maybe even better, for then you are aware of crossing the Dniester and entering into a free country—just imagine, if you so desire."

"But I don't want to," says Wajgełe.

Nahman sighs: the women always have a bigger problem with it. The women seem to cling more to the old laws; they are, after all, more frivolous and shyer by nature. Jacob has said that it is the same as with slaves—for women are to a considerable extent slaves of this world, knowing nothing of their freedom, having not been taught how to be free.

People who have already been initiated, the elders, treat it like people used to treat the mikvah. The body itself and the heart strive toward it, and when it comes time to extinguish the candles, it is like a holiday—a holy marker. For joining together is good—there's nothing wrong in someone copulating with someone else. Between people whose bodies have overflowed into each other a new bond arises, a special connection, subtle and indefinable, as there are no words that can fully convey the nature of such a relationship. And it can happen that afterward people become close to one another, like brother and sister, and cling together, while others—this can also happen—feel some embarrassment toward one another and take some time to grow accustomed to each other. There are even those who cannot look into each other's eyes, and then no one knows how things will work out between them.

People tend to have a greater or lesser inclination toward one another—something attracts them a little or a lot. These things are very complicated, which is why women are so sensitive to them. Better than men, they are able to figure out why . . . Why, for example, has Wittel always refused Nahman, and why has Nahman always been attracted to Hayah Shorr? And why has such a deep friendship arisen between young Yachne of Busk and Isaac Shorr, even though they both already have spouses?

What was until this time banned is now not only permitted, but actually required.

Everyone knows that Jacob takes upon himself those weightiest of Strange Deeds, and also that in doing so, he attains a special power. Whoever helps him in this is also anointed.

The greatest power, however, belongs not to corporeal action, but rather to action that unites with words, as the world was created out of words, and its foundations are the word. Thus the greatest Strange Deed, the Exceptional Act—is pronouncing out loud the Name of God, Shem haMephorash.

Jacob will do it soon in the presence of those closest to him, the two circles of chosen men and women.

Lately they have been eating bread that is not kosher, as well as pork. One of the women went into convulsions, but not from the meat—the meat is innocent—just from not being able to bear committing such an act. "This is not an ordinary act. It is a special thing. Ma'ase Zar, a Strange Deed," says Jacob. He pronounces these words as though chewing something over, as though chewing over pork gristle.

"What is the meaning of Strange Deeds?" asks someone who clearly hasn't been paying attention.

So Jacob explains it again, starting from scratch. "We are to trample all the laws because they are no longer in effect, and until they are trampled, the new ones cannot appear in their place. Because those old laws were from that other time, for an unsaved world."

Then he takes the hands of those standing next to him, and soon a circle forms. Now they will sing, as always.

Jacob plays with the children. They make silly faces, and the children love it. After the communal meals, the afternoons are dedicated to the children; the youngest are accompanied by their mothers, and they—only barely out of childhood themselves—like playing, too. They squeal and compete over who can make the scariest face. It is hard to make little children's faces disgusting, but Jacob's face can truly transform. Shrieks resound when he is playing monsters and demons, when he acts like the limping bałakaben do. When the children have calmed down, he has them sit down around him, and he tells them complicated fairy tales, about princesses on glass mountains, simpletons, and princes. There are adventures at sea and evil wizards who turn people into animals. The ending he often puts off until the next day, leaving the whole of Ivanie's younger population distracted, living for what the morrow will bring. Will the hero be able to free himself from the donkey's body to which he was condemned by a jealous woman?

When it warms up, in April, the fun moves out into the field. Jacob once told Nahman that when he was little and living in Czernowitz, some crazy person came around, and all the children ran after him and imitated him, all his gestures, his scary faces, his rage, and repeated his words. When the crazy man disappeared, when he went to another town, the children still aped him, and even expanded their repertoire of mad gestures, perfecting the madness of that madman. It was like an epidemic, for in the end, all the children in Czernowitz started behaving that way, Jewish, Polish, German, Ruthenian, until frightened parents took the rods down from their walls, and it was only through the use of these rods that they were able to dispel that madness from their children's minds. But they were wrong to do so, because it had been fun.

Now Jacob makes faces, and the children follow. His tall figure can be seen leading the way, moving strangely, and then the children do as he does. Their legs shoot out, and every few steps they jump, waving their arms. The chain they make winds around the ponds, where in the wake of winter the water has cleared up and now trembles anxiously, reflecting the sky. Some of the grown-ups join in. Moshe from Podhajce, the old widower, has gained in vigor since being matched with Małka of Lanckoroń, barely fifteen, and he and his wife-to-be join Jacob's retinue. That encourages others, for Moshe is a wise man, one who knows what he's doing, and he's not afraid of a little ridiculousness. In fact, isn't ridiculousness what we want, isn't ridiculousness on our side? thinks Nahman, also breaking into a dance. He hops on both legs, bounces like a ball, and he wants to bring in Wajgełe, so petite, so delicate, but she turns away, furious, still too childish to play like a child. Wittel, on the other hand, doesn't need to be convinced, she holds on tightly to Nahman's hand, and her abundant breasts jump in preposterous fashion. Other women follow Wittel, abandoning the hanging laundry, interrupting the feeding of their infants, the milking of the cows, the beating of the bedding. Seeing this, their husbands stop chopping wood and leave the axes on the blocks. Briefly spared is the life of the rooster from which today's broth is supposed to be prepared. Yeruhim climbs down from the ladder, where he was patching up the thatched roof, and now he takes a laughing Hayah by the hand. Jacob leads the mad retinue between houses, over the toppled fence, through the barn that lies open at both ends, then along the embankment between the ponds. Whoever sees them either stands in pure astonishment or immediately unites with them, until they return to where they started, warmed up, with flushed cheeks, weakened from laughing and hollering. Suddenly there are a lot of them, many more than there were in the beginning. It's almost everyone, in fact. If some stranger found himself at that moment in Ivanie, he might take them for a village of idiots.

In the evening, the elders gather in the largest chamber. They stand in a circle, shoulder to shoulder, men and women alternating. First they sing, then they recite the prayer, moving back and forth and supporting each other with their shoulders. Then, until late at night, Jacob teaches, meaning, as he says, he tells tales. Nahman tries to remember them exactly, and when he returns to his room, he writes them down, despite the prohibition. This takes him a lot of time, which is why he is always so exhausted.

## A tale of two tablets

This is a story that everyone in Ivanie knows by heart.

By the time the Jews left Egypt, the world was ready for salvation and everything was waiting, prepared—both down below and on high. It was unprecedented—the wind died down completely, the leaves did not move on the trees, the clouds in the sky drifted so slowly that only the most patient were able to discern their movement. It was the same with the water—it became thick as cream, while the earth went the other way, became flimsy and unreliable, so that it often happened that people fell into it up to their ankles. No bird chirped, no bee flew, there were no waves in the sea, people did not speak—it was so quiet you could hear the heartbeat of the smallest animal.

Everything stopped in anticipation of the new Law, and all eyes were turned to Moses, who was climbing Mount Zion to receive it directly from God's hands. And so it was that God Himself engraved the Law on two stone tablets in such a way that it would be discernible to the human eye and comprehensible to the human mind. This was the Torah of Atzilut.

During Moses's absence, his people gave in to temptation and indulged in sin. Then Moses, coming down from on high and seeing what was going on, thought: I left them for such a short time, and yet they were unable to persist in virtuousness. Thus they are unworthy of the beneficent and noble law God appointed them. In his great despair Moses shattered the tablets on the ground so that they broke into a thousand pieces and turned to dust. Then a terrible wind rose up and threw Moses against the rock and set the clouds and the water in motion and made the earth solid again. Moses understood that his people were not mature enough for the law of liberty intended for the saved world. All day and all night he sat resting against the rock and looking down at the fires burning in the camp of his people, and he heard their voices, their music, and the cries of their children. Then Samael came to him in the guise of an angel and dictated to him the commandments that from then on would keep God's people enslaved.

In order that no one would know the true Law of Freedom, Samael carefully gathered the little pieces of the shattered Torah of Atzilut and scattered them around the world among many different religions. When the Messiah comes, he will have to pass over into Samael's kingdom to collect the tablets' shards and present the new Law in its final revelation.

"What was this lost Law all about?" asks Wajgełe, when she and Nahman climb into bed.

"Who could possibly know, since it has been dispersed?" he answers warily. "It was good. It respected people."

But Wajgełe is stubborn.

"Was it the opposite of what we have now? The opposite of 'Thou shalt not commit adultery' would be 'Thou shalt commit it.' And the opposite of 'Thou shalt not kill' would be: 'Kill.'"

"It's not that simple."

"You always tell me that—'It's not that simple, it's not that simple . . . ,'" she mocks him. She pulls a pair of woolen stockings up over her skinny legs.

"People want easy explanations, and so we must simplify everything for their sake, and since it cannot be written down, it all becomes rather stupid . . . This or that, black, white—it's like digging with a hoe. Simple is dangerous."

"But I want to understand it, and I can't."

"Wajgełe, my time will come, and your time will come. That is grace. Sabbatai, the old Mosaic law, the one given by Samael, is no longer in effect. That also explains the conversion of our Lord, Sabbatai, to Islam. He saw that Israel, in obeying the Mosaic law, was no longer in the service of the God of the Truth. That is why our Lord gave up the Torah in favor of the Din Islam . . ."

"How can you believe in all of this, Nahman? What do you need it for? The truth is simple. Isn't it?" Wajgełe says sleepily.

". . . and why we are crossing over to Edom. We are destined by God to perform such acts."

Wajgełe doesn't answer.

"Wajgełe?"

In the silence, he hears the girl's even breathing.

Nahman carefully climbs out of bed so as not to wake her and lights a tiny clay lamp. He places a board between it and the window so that it can't be seen from outside. He will write. He throws a blanket over his shoulders, and he begins:

### *Scraps, or: Eight months in the Lord's community of Ivanie*

There exists in Ein Sof, that is, in the Infinite itself, in the divine source, absolute good, which is the origin and source of all perfection and all good in the world. It is perfection, and perfection requires no alterations, it is dignified and immovable, there can be no movement in it. But for us, who look upon it from the underside of creation, from afar, this motionlessness seems dead, and therefore bad, yet perfection excludes movement, creation, change, and therefore the very possibility of our freedom. That is why it is said that in the depths of absolute good, the root of all evil is concealed, and that root is the negation of every miracle, every movement, and all that is possible and all that might still happen.

For us, then, for people, good is something other than what it is for God. For us, good is the tension between God's perfection and his withdrawal in order that the world might arise. For us, good is the absence of God from where he could instead be.

Nahman rubs his chilled fingers. He can't stop, the sentences attack his brain one after the next:

When the vessels broke, and the world came about, it immediately began to climb up to where it fell from, gathering itself from bottom to top, from least to most perfect. The world ascends higher and higher and works to perfect itself, obtaining new goods and adding them to the previous ones, organizing the sparks released from the shells of matter into brilliance and strength. This is tikkun, a process of repairing in which mankind can assist. The process of ascent must transcend the law that is already in place and

create a new law, in order to then transcend it again. In this world
of dead husks, nothing has been given once and for all. Whosoever
does not move up stands still, that is, falls downward.

This last sentence soothes him. He stretches and looks at Wajgełe, sleeping next to him. Suddenly he feels overcome by tenderness.

When we crossed the Dniester, singing, boldly and openly this time,
for we had in hand the royal letter that made of us free men in this
country, I thought that everything was working out as if in a stone
pattern in which each stone is a different color: when scattered, no
connection or interdependence can be discerned among them, but
when they are reassembled according to the proper order, they
reveal a very striking and obvious picture.

Ivanie had to be given to us, that we might create here a great
family that would continue for many years, so that even if we were
to be scattered again, if we all had to disperse into the world,
these ties, these Ivanie ties, would remain. For here, in Ivanie,
we are free.

If we were also to be given our own land, as Jacob says, leased to
us for our whole lives and for our children's whole lives, so that we
could govern ourselves according to our laws, getting in no one
else's way, we would not even fear death. When a person has a piece
of land, he becomes immortal.

There was once a sage in Wilno named Heshel Tzorev, and he
taught how according to gematria there exists a numerological
identicality between the words *Polin*, or *Poland*, and the name in the
Bible of Esau's grandson, Tsefo. Esau's guardian angel—and that of
his family—is Samael, and he is also the guardian of Poland. Poland
should rightly be called the Kingdom of Edom. The name Tsefo has
the same Hebrew letters as tzafon—north—and they have the same
value as Polin-Lita, or Poland-Lithuania. And as is known,
Jeremiah 1:14 says that when salvation comes, it will start in the
country in the north, meaning Poland and Lithuania.

Edom is Esau's country, but here, now, in the darkness of
the world, Edom means Poland. Going over to Edom means
coming into Poland. That is clear. Here we take on Edom's
religion. So Elisha Shorr said back in Smyrna, and so I said.
Now everything is coming true, but it could not have been so but
for Jacob.

When I look at him, I see that there are people who are born
with something that I cannot find the words for, something that
means that others respect them and hold them in the highest
esteem. I don't know what it is—is it posture, is it a head held high,
a penetrating gaze, a way of walking? Or maybe some spirit
hovering around him? An angel who keeps him company? He has
only to enter any space, be it the most decrepit shed or the holiest
chamber, and all eyes turn to him at once, pleasure and
appreciation on everyone's face, although he has not yet done or said
a thing.

I have watched his face many times—even as he was sleeping. I
have already said it—it is not a beautiful face, but it can look
beautiful. It is not an ugly face—but it can look repulsive. His eyes
are capable of being as gentle and sad as a child's. Those same eyes
are capable of looking as ruthless as those of a predator watching its
prey. Then a mocking expression appears in them, a derision so
cold it suffuses your whole body. I don't even know what color they
are exactly, because even that is changeable. Sometimes they are
quite black, without pupils, and completely impenetrable. Other
times they take on a golden-brown hue, like dark beer. Once I saw
that in their deepest essence they are as yellow as a cat's, and I
realized that he only darkens them for others, like a gentle shade.

I permit myself to write about Jacob in such a way because I love
him. Because as a person who loves him, I give him greater rights
and privileges than I give to anyone else. But I also fear falling into
blind love, exaggerated and unhealthy, like that Heshel, who, if he
could, would lie down like a dog at his feet.

## Of doubles, trinities, and foursomes

We conducted many investigations into the Trinity in Ivanie, and it
seemed to me that I had come to grasp its meaning.

What is our real task if not the establishment of equilibrium
between the unity of God and the multiplicity of the world created
by him? As for ourselves, people—are we not abandoned in this
"in-between," in between the One and a world of divisions? This
limitless "between" has its strange critical point—the double. This is
the first experience of the thinking man—when he notices the abyss

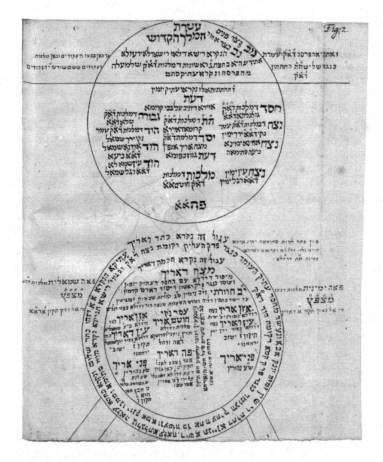

that appears between himself and the rest of the world. This is the painful Two, the fundamental crack in the created world that gives rise to contradictions and all sorts of dualisms. This and that. You and me. Left and right. Sitra Achra, or the other side, the left side, the demonic forces in the guise of the broken shells of the vessels that could not hold the light when they were broken (shevirat haKelim)—that is the Two. Perhaps were it not for the Two in the world, the world would be completely different, although it's hard to imagine that; no doubt Jacob would be able to. One time we worked ourselves to the bone, late into the night, trying to complete this assignment, but it was to no avail, for our minds think in this rhythm: two, two, two.

The Trinity is holy, like a wise wife, reconciling contradictions. Two is like a young roe doe, leaping over every contradiction. That's what makes the Trinity holy, that it can tame evil. But because the Trinity must ceaselessly work on behalf of the equilibrium it disturbs, it is shaky, and it isn't until you get to Four that you attain the highest holiness and perfection that restores divine proportions. It is not in vain that God's name in Hebrew is composed of four letters, and that all the elements of the world were established so by Him (Yeruhim once told me that even animals can count to four!), and everything that is important in the world must be quadruple.

Once Moshe went to the kitchen, took some challah dough, brought it back, and started forming some sort of shape from it. We laughed at him, especially Jacob, because nothing went together less than Moshe and kitchen work.

"What is it?" he asked us, and revealed the result of his project.

We saw on the table an *alef* made of dough, and we answered him accordingly. Then Moshe took the ends of the holy letter made of dough and in a couple of simple movements reshaped it.

"What's this?" he asked.

Now it was a cross.

For, Moshe argued, the holy letter is the germ of the cross, its original form. If it were a living plant, it would grow into a cross. The cross thus contains a great mystery. For God is one in three forms, and then to the threeness of God we add the Shekhinah.

Such knowledge was not for everyone. People who had gathered with us in Ivanie were of such varying backgrounds and had had such different experiences that we all agreed not to give them this holy knowledge, lest they understand it amiss. When they asked me about the Trinity, I would raise my hand to my forehead and touch the skin there, saying, "The God of Abraham, Isaac, and Jacob."

These were the kinds of conversations we had only with each other, in a small group and in hushed voices—for the walls of the Ivanie huts tended to not be sealed completely—when we finished writing letters, and our fingers were all covered in ink, and our eyes were so tired that all they could do was gaze into the dance of the candle flames. And then Moliwda would tell us tales of the beliefs of those Bogomils, as he called them, and in those beliefs we were surprised to determine that we had much in common with them, as if the path taken by both us and them were in the beginning one but later bifurcated to then converge again into one, just like our two roads in Ivanie.

Is life itself not a stranger to this world? And are we not strangers, and is our God not a stranger? Is this not why we appear so different, so distant, so scary, and incomprehensible to those who really do belong to this world? But this world is equally bizarre and incomprehensible to any stranger to it, and its rules are incomprehensible, as are its customs. For the stranger comes from the farthest distance, from the outside, and he must endure the fate of the foreigner, alone and defenseless, completely misunderstood. We are foreigners' foreigners, Jews' Jews. And we will always be homesick.

Since we do not know the roads of this world, we move through it defenseless, blind, knowing only that we are strangers to it.

Moliwda said that as soon as we strangers, living amongst those others, get used to and learn to take pleasure in the charms of this world, we will forget where we came from and what sort of origins were ours. Then our misery will end, but at the price of forgetting our true nature, and this is the most painful moment of our fate, the fate of the stranger. That is why we must remind ourselves of our foreignness and care for this memory as we would our most treasured possession. Recognize the world as the place of our exile, recognize its laws as foreign, as strange . . .

Dawn is beginning to break when Nahman finishes; a moment later, just outside the window, the rooster crows in such dramatic fashion that Nahman trembles like a night demon who fears the light. He slips into the warmth of the bed and lies there for a long time on his back, unable to go to sleep. Polish words crowd into his mind, sticking together into sentences, and not even knowing how, he silently composes his prayer for the soul, but in Polish. And since yesterday he saw Gypsies here, they, too, are jumbled up in his mind, and they jump into his sentences, the whole caravan of them:

> Like a sailor visiting the sea's abyss,
> Or, in the vast uncharted wilderness,
> Like a Gypsy caravan, my dear soul
> Won't travel toward just any goal.
>
> No shackles of iron can close it in,
> Nor the pompousness of their chagrin,

No custom, no tradition will strain it.
Not my own heart's shelter can contain it.

It alters since it doesn't alter,
My soul won't let me down or falter.
My soul rises, good Lord, to Your great dome;
Give it a fit room inside Your home.

Not even Nahman himself knows when he falls asleep.

## Of candles put out

In the night of July 14–15, after the date of the next disputation has been set, the women and men gather in the chamber, close the shutters tight, and light some candles. Slowly they undress until they're naked, some folding and stacking their clothes neatly like they're going to the mikvah. All kneel on the wooden floor, and Jacob holds a cross. He sets it on the bench, and then he kisses a small figure, the little teraphim that Hayah has brought in, and he lays it by the cross, and then he lights the tall candle and stands up. Now he will walk around in a circle, a naked man, his body hairy, his manhood dangling between his legs. The unsteady candlelight brings out of the darkness the others' bodies, grayish orange, and their golden heads bowed against their chests.

Bodies are tangible; you can see Moshe's hernia and Wittel's stomach that sags from her many children. They glance furtively at one another while Jacob walks around in a circle, murmuring the prayer: "In the name of the Hallowed First . . . in the idea of life from the light of the world . . ." It is hard to focus on what he's saying when some sort of other world has revealed itself in this indistinct, frail light. One of the women starts to giggle nervously, and then Jacob stops and angrily extinguishes the candle in one blow. From then on, things take place in darkness. For what they are to do next, that darkness is a balm.

A few days later, Jacob has them stand in a circle, which he calls "ringaround," and stay like that for all of Tuesday, Wednesday, and Thursday until afternoon. They stand day and night, the whole group together, in the circle. Isaac's wife is released, because she feels sick after just a few hours and has to lie down. The rest remain. They are not allowed to talk. It is hot, and it feels to them like they can hear the drops of sweat sliding down their faces.


## A man who does not have a piece of land is not a man

"If there is a more beautiful cemetery anywhere than the one in Satanów, then I will walk barefoot to Lwów," says Hayim's wife, Hava.

And although they are not to speak of death for any reason, and they are not to judge land by its cemetery, nonetheless this cemetery is indeed quite lovely, the others agree. Sloping beautifully down toward the river.

"Like the cemetery in Korolówka," adds Pesel, who has been here with her family since May. "It's the second-best cemetery there is, with respect to physical appearance, I'll give you that."

"But this one we have in Satanów, outside the city—it's bigger," continues Hava, "and you can see half the world from it. Down on the river there's a mill, and the water flows around it, ducks and geese paddling along . . ."

That mill is leased by her father, and someday it will belong to them according to hazakah law—legal acquisition by right of possession. The little town itself lies on an elevation and two things immediately stick out about it—the little castle of the most venerated lord, now lying almost in ruins, brought all the way up along the highway so that the lord could supervise who went there and with what, as well as the synagogue up farther, like some fortification, in the Turkish style. And although they haven't had anything to do with that synagogue in years, Hava is hardly about to lie about it—it is exceptional. When you walk from the highway down the steep path into the little town, climbing down along those curves, you have to go by the synagogue—there is no other way. In the little town, there is a small market square that holds fairs weekly, always on a Monday. Around the market, as everywhere, Christian and Jewish stalls alternate, and sometimes, in the summer, there are Armenian and Turkish stalls, too.

They would only be able to obtain this land from the church's holdings—the church is the only option. Who else would give Jews land for free? "Maybe the king!" someone suggests. "It's nicest right where the Zbrucz flows into the Dniester."

"Who's going to give Jews a plot where rivers meet?" says some doubtful person.

"Just a small one . . . and maybe a bit of woodland, and some lesser stream, such as the Strypa—just enough to put in some fish-ponds and raise our own carp in them," Hava fantasizes.

"But who is going to give such riches to Jews?" the doubter starts again.

"But we're not Jews anymore. Or are we—are we still Jews?"

"We will always be Jews, just our own kind."

It would be lovely just to live as they wished, explaining nothing to anyone, not having any noblemen above them, not fearing the Cossack, keeping in good stead with the Church, working the land, doing some trade, having children, having their own orchard and their own shop, even if it's very small. Growing gardens out behind the houses, harvesting vegetables.

"Have you seen the synagogue in Husiatyn?" old, deaf Lewiński pipes up belatedly to Hava. "You haven't seen it? Hahaha. You don't know anything, then. That one is the biggest and the most beautiful."

Outside, the children are raising a ruckus. They are pretending to do battle with singlesticks and shooting cannons made out of stiff old stalks of angelica. Jewish children are playing with Christian children from the next village over, who come out of curiosity. Now they have just assigned everyone's roles, regardless of origins. Some are Tatars, some are Muscovites. In a battle of singlesticks and stalks, all differences disappear.

## Of stablehands and the study
## of the Polish language

The word *stablehand* cracks Jacob up.

They study Polish in the afternoons in groups, women and men together. The Warsaw Hayim and the Shorrs' younger Hayim teach. They begin with basic things. Hand. Foot. They say: A steady hand. A stable hand.

Yet *stablehand* is equestrian, is a caretaker of horses, Jacob knows this word and is also greatly amused by the coincidence. During dinner he offers Nahman a plate he pretends to almost drop and says:

"A stable hand."

All those who get the joke now burst out laughing. Except for Nahman.

Jacob got that Polish book from the Shorrs and is currently using it to learn to read. Wittel has helped him, but she cannot read well in Polish either, so they finally hired a teacher, a young man from a nearby estate. He comes every other day. They read about animals. The first piece Jacob is able to read and understand on his own is about which animals found themselves in Noah's ark:

> These animals were not ex putri materia, or multiplying out of rot, like Muckworms, Fleas, for those can always genus suum reparare (renew their tribe), even though they will die out; wherever something breaks down, dies, vermin will be born there at once. Nierembergius, the Author of the *Natural History*, considers that these Animals the Lord God did not create, for their Mother is corruption or rot.

It's hard to grasp what's going on when you are reading Polish. As a language, it's quite strange.

## Of new names

Just as first Jacob selected seven of the women, so, too, sometime later he chooses twelve trusted men. He has them all take the names of the apostles from the Gospel, which here, in Ivanie, everyone reads every evening.

First Jacob chooses Nahman and puts him on his right side, and from then on, Nahman is Peter. On the other side, he puts old Moshe—now he is the second Peter. Then there is Osman of Czernowitz and his son, or Jacob Major and Jacob Minor. Then, in a special place, sort of in the middle, he puts Shlomo Shorr, who has already been using the Polish name Franciszek Wołowski, Franciszek meaning Francis. Behind him stands Krysa, who has already taken the name Bartholomewł. And farther, on the other side, there is Elisha Shorr, now known as Łukasz (or Luke) Wołowski, and on either side of him, Yehuda Shorr, now Jan (or John) Wołowski, as well as Hayim of Warsaw, now called Matthew. And there is Hershel, the second John, and also Moshe of Podhajce, called Thomas, and Hayim of Busk, Nahman's brother, called Paul.

Shlomo Shorr, or Franciszek Wołowski, Elisha's oldest son, teaches everyone about names. They want everyone to think about a new, Christian name. He counts out on his fingers the twelve apostles, and yet he wants to be known as Franciszek. "Who was Francis?" they ask him. He tells them about saints, the Catholic hakhams.

"This was the name I liked best," he says. "And you, too, should choose carefully, and take your time. But do not get too attached to your new names. Nor to the country, nor to the language, although you have to speak it. Names must come about *before* nations do; the sound that creates them corresponds to a certain accord of the universe. That is your real name. The names we carry on the street, on the other hand, around the market, traveling in a carriage on a muddy road, or those others use to call us—all that is just tacked on. Those names are useful like the clothing you put on to go to work. There's no sense in getting attached to them. They come and go, like anything. Here one minute, gone the next."

Wittel won't let it go. So she asks Jacob:

"We're supposed to think up some new name for ourselves. We have to be able to say, 'Me, Wittel, me, Jacob,' right? But what do we call ourselves to ourselves?"

Jacob answers that he immediately thought of himself as "Jacob," always calling himself Jacob in his mind. But not just any Jacob: *this* Jacob, the only one.

"The one who saw the ladder in his dream," Wittel guesses.

But Jacob sets her straight:

"No, no. The Jacob who put on an animal's hide and then set himself before his father's hand that it might take him for someone else, for his beloved Esau."

Yente sees all of this from above, watches names peeling off the people who have carried them. For the time being, no one *notices*, and they all trustingly call each other what they always have: Hayim, Sprynełe, Leah. But those names have already lost their luster, dulled, like snakeskins from which the life has faded even before they're shed. So it is with the name Pesel, which slides off the girl like a too-big shirt, and underneath, the name Helena is already coming into its own, though for now it is still very thin, like skin after a burn—completely new, almost transparent.

Wajgełe sounds careless now and has absolutely nothing to do with this petite, slender, but very strong girl, with her skin that's always hot and dry, who, with a carrying pole over her shoulders, is currently bearing water. Full buckets. Wajgełe, Wajgełe. Somehow it just doesn't suit her anymore. In the same way, Nahman seems too big for her husband, as if it were an old kapota.

In fact, Nahman is the first to ask everyone to call him "Piotr," adding "Jakubowski," a Polish last name that means "Jacob's" or "of Jacob." Peter of Jacob. Piotr Jakubowski.

This loss of names in the Ivanie grass might be alarming, as the sight of disposable things, of transient and fleeting beings, always is, but Yente sees at the same time many things that repeat. Yente herself is repeating. The cave repeats. Repeating are the great river and the passage across it on foot. Repeating is the snow, and so, too, are the parallel sleigh tracks marking the exposed, broad space with that alarming digraph. Repeating is the stain in the snow, yellowish, unpleasant. Repeating are the goose feathers in the grass. Sometimes they catch onto people's clothing and travel with them.

## Of Pinkas, who descends into hell in search of his daughter

Pinkas, the secretary who is taking part in the council's meetings, listens attentively to the discussions and does not miss a single word. Rarely is he bold enough to speak, fearing that his voice will begin to tremble and he will be unable to hold back his tears. Fervent prayers have not helped him, nor the chicken with which his wife removed from him any sorceries that might have been placed upon him. The chicken was then given to the poor, along with all that dust and dirt with which Pinkas's soul had been covered.

For Pinkas, it has always been obvious that leaving the true religion and accepting another—even going so far as to be baptized—was the absolute worst thing that could happen to a true Jew and to Jews in general. Even talking about it is a terrible sin. The actual act, Pinkas can't even imagine—it's like dying, or worse than dying. Like drowning in vast waters, being a drowned man, and yet living—living only to experience terrible shame.

That is why, when Pinkas, writing out documents, comes to the word *shmad*, or "baptism," his hand doesn't even want to write it, and his pen rebels at the *shin*, *mem*, and *dalet*, as if these were not innocent letters, but rather yet another curse. He is reminded of the story of another heretic, Nehemiah Hayon, of whom everyone had talked constantly when Pinkas was young. Hayon, too, favored Sabbatian ideas and was cursed by his own people, wandered all around Europe, and was driven out of everywhere. Doors slammed shut before him. They say that when he made it to Vienna, sick and tired, the Viennese Jews also closed the door in his face, and there was no one who would dare so much as give him a cup of water. Then Hayon sat in some courtyard, right there on the ground, and cried, and didn't even admit that he was a Jew, such was his shame, and when passersby asked what was wrong with him, he said he was a Turk. No Sabbatian, the length and breadth of Europe, could find in any decent Jew some hospitality, food, or even a kind word—nothing. At the time, there were not so many of those apostates. Now Hayon would find one of his own wherever he went.

Recently, at a council meeting, Pinkas watched as the rabbis were talking about the heretics' book, which they treat as holy. In fact, "talking" is an exaggeration; the rabbis were more just stammering around it, exchanging a word here and there. Pinkas, who had been keeping the minutes, just listened, for when they were talking about the diabolical book, they bade him stop writing. Rabbi Rapaport, that holy man, said that reading two, three paragraphs was enough to set the hair all over your whole body on end—for that cursed book contains so much blasphemy against God and the world, and everything in it is upside down. The world knows nothing like it. Every copy of it ought to be burned.

Pinkas creeps along by the crumbling wall of a tenement house, heading to a place where he can rent a cart. The wall, which is coated in lime, leaves a white mark on his sleeve. Someone recently told him that he had seen Gitla on the market square. She was dressed as a servant and had a basket on her arm. It might not have been Gitla—it could have just been someone who resembled her. But this is why Pinkas, when he finishes his work for Rabbi Rapaport, instead of going straight home, keeps walking the streets of Lwów and scrutinizing women's faces, so that some even mistake him for an old lecher.

Along the way, he runs into some people he knows, old merchants who, huddled together and looking excited, are having a noisy debate. Joining them, he hears again the thing that has had the whole town in an uproar since yesterday.

Two Jews from Kamieniec Podolski, disguised as peasants and armed with spades, tried to kidnap one of their daughters, who had married Leyb Abramowicz and had already prepared to be baptized, along with her child. The pair beat both of them badly, daughter and husband. Even killing her would have been better than letting her be baptized.

Thus Pinkas doesn't really understand why the rabbis' discussion takes a different turn. They refer to a certain letter that says they have to simply cut off these heretics, get rid of them as they would a gangrenous extremity, kick them out of the holy community for all time, condemn them and, so doing, ultimately cause them to vanish into oblivion. May their names be forgotten. He knows this letter by heart, for he has written it out hundreds of times:

Abraham haKohen of Zamość to Jacob Emden in Altona

   The holy community of Lublin has paid a great deal for medicine to treat this plagued world. Our wise men who gathered in Konstantynów to confer about this matter determined that there is no way to proceed in this case other than to use cunning to force those afflicted by the plague to be baptized, for it is written: "People will live separately." Let, then, this particular plague be cut off from the children of Israel for all time. Let us thank God that some of them have already been baptized, among them the cursed Elisha Shorr, may his name be erased. With respect to those who have not yet converted and are still donning Jewish attire and attending services in our houses of prayer, we shall be diligent in informing the Christian authorities as soon as we have discovered these supposed Jews' hidden intentions. That is why we have already sent our messenger to Lwów, that he might arrive there before the sect of these villains does, to meet with the papal nuncio and present him with our report. May there be a chance to put these destroyers, these dogs, these heretics working against God in prison and to place upon them the curse we placed several years ago on one Moshe of Podhajce and on their evil leader, Jacob Frank.

Pinkas is profoundly convinced that the old tradition of their forefathers was the right approach, to pass over all matters connected with Sabbatai Tzvi in silence; nothing good, nothing bad, no cursing, no blessing. A thing that is not talked about ceases to exist. He contemplates that wisdom as he sits on a quaking cart that is covered in a fustian sheet. So great is the power of the word that wherever it is lacking, the world just disappears. Next to him sit some peasant women dressed up as if they are going to a wedding, along with two older Jews, a man and a woman. They keep trying to talk to him, but Pinkas resists their attempts at conversation.

Why talk? If you want to rid the world of someone, it does not take fire and sword, nor any type of violence. You just have to pass over that person in silence and never call him by name. In this way, he will gradually recede into oblivion. If another person insists on inquiring into the matter, you must threaten him with herem.

He stays in Borszczów with the rabbi, as the messenger of Reb Rapaport. He has brought with him a whole bag of writings and letters. Including the one about the heretics. They read it in front of all of the members of the kahal in the evening, in a cramped room where little bits of soot fly up toward the ceiling from the smoking candles.

The next day, Pinkas goes to the Borszczów mikvah. It is a shack with boarded-up windows and a sunken roof. Inside, it is split in two—on one side, the bony bath attendant, black with soot and in a cloud of smoke, throws beech logs into the stove and heats water in a pot. On the other side, in semidarkness, are two wooden baths for the women. Farther along, a reservoir with a capacity of forty buckets is dug into the ground. Its perimeter is strewn with the remnants of candles, an uneven rim of stearin and tallow, slippery, smelly, littered with black wicks. Pinkas submerges himself in the lukewarm water seventy-two times, then squats so that the water comes up to his beard. He examines the mostly gray cloud of beard as it floats on the surface. Let me find her, he thinks, and he repeats those words in his mind: Let me find her, find her, let me just find her in one piece, I will forgive her, let me find her, that child, that child with the delicate soul, please, let me find her.

It takes a long time, this anxious prayer said in secret, for no one knows of Pinkas's intentions. He realizes that it is late when he starts shivering. The bony, grimy bath attendant has gone off somewhere, and the fire under the pot has gone out altogether. Pinkas is alone in the mikvah. With a rough linen towel he dries himself until his skin hurts. The next day, pretending to be returning to Lwów but trusting in God, he hires a terrible driver and his terrible cart and heads for Ivanie.

The closer they get to Ivanie, the more traffic there is. He sees carts loaded with equipment, then a whole cart of potatoes covered with a big old horse blanket and a big basket of nuts, and beside it two men chatting, not paying attention to anyone else. He sees a family with several children and all their belongings on the cart, on their way somewhere from Kamieniec. These are they, he thinks. He feels disgust toward them, they seem dirty to him—their kapotas, their stockings, for some of them dress like the Hasidim do, while others dress like peasants, in peasant sukmana. How he must have sinned, for his daughter to be among these people.

"And who are you?" some bruiser asks in a hostile tone, from his post by the gate, which is nailed together from pieces of wood and adorned with spruce branches. The needles have crumbled off, and the bare branches look like spikes, like barbed wire.

"I'm a Jew just like you are," Pinkas says calmly.

"Where from?"

"From Lwów."

"What do you want from us?"

"I'm looking for my daughter. Gitla . . . She's tall . . ." He doesn't know how to describe her.

"Are you one of us? Are you a true believer?"

Pinkas doesn't know what to say. He wrestles with it, then finally answers:

"No."

The bruiser seems to feel respect for this older, well-dressed man. He has Pinkas wait, and after a long while, he brings up a woman. She is wearing a light-colored apron and has keys in her richly ruffled skirt. Her face, in a bonnet like the Christian women wear, is focused and sensitive.

"Gitla," says Pinkas, and his tone unintentionally turns pleading. "She left last year, when . . ." Pinkas doesn't know what to call him. ". . . when *he* was going around the villages. She was seen in Busk. Tall, young."

"I know you from somewhere," the woman says.

"I am Pinkas Abramowicz of Lwów, her father."

"That's right, I know who you are. Your daughter isn't here. I haven't seen her in a year or so."

Hava feels like adding something hurtful. She feels like spitting at his feet. Saying, for instance, "Perhaps the Turks are blowing the grounsils with her now?" But she sees that all the air has gone out of him, his chest has deflated, he has suddenly shrunk. He reminds her of her father. She tells him to wait, and then she goes to fetch a little food for him, but he is no longer standing by the gate when she gets back.

## Antoni Moliwda-Kossakowski writes to Katarzyna Kossakowska

In Łowicz, Moliwda sits down at the table and dips his pen in ink. Right away he blots the page, which he always considers to be a kind of warning. He sprinkles sand on it, and then he carefully scratches it from the paper with the tip of the penknife. It takes him a while. He begins:

> My Ever Honored Lady,
> You shall have such credit in heaven for your efforts on behalf of the Contra-Talmudists, who are already coming into Lwów in droves and setting up their camps like Gypsies, on the outskirts, right there on the ground—so impassioned are they about their new faith. But you, dear madam, as a woman with your wits about you, know perfectly well that behind this is not only a suddenly awakened love for the cross, but also other considerations, perhaps not so lofty, yet certainly very human and understandable.
> The news has reached me here that they have written one more supplication, and it is a good thing that by some miracle it passed through my hands. When I glanced at the signatures, I saw: Solomon ben Elisha Shorr of Rohatyn and Yehuda ben

Nussen, otherwise known as Krysa of Nadwórna—it was the two of them who knocked out this petition.

The blood ran to my head as I read. For what do you think they were demanding?

First, they complain that they are holed up in the Kamieniec bishop's village, where they live off alms and the support of their brothers from Hungary—while they themselves remain without work. Then they write—and here I shall quote for you directly—"We demand first to settle in Busk and Gliniany, where a community of true believers has remained, and where we would therefore have means of seeking out our livelihoods, whether through trade or through craft, so long as it not offend Our Father. For we do not expect any of our own to subsist on innkeeping or to earn our bread in the service of drunkenness or by the extenuation of Christian blood, as the Talmudists have grown used to doing."

And they go on to enumerate conditions, saying that after their baptism they wish to continue living in their little collective, that they do not want to cut their payot, that they want to mark their Shabbat as well as Sundays, and that they want to keep their Jewish names alongside the new Catholic ones, that they will not eat pork, they will be able to marry only amongst themselves and maintain their holy books, especially the Zohar.

How could I have shown this letter to the primate? They had had it copied out at the printer's and translated into many languages to boot. I referred the matter to him only in broad strokes, not reading the letter itself, to which the primate responded, and this I consider to be final: "What's the sense in listening to those people? A disputation is a disputation, but as soon as that's done, there will be baptism. No conditions. After the baptism, we'll see how they live, what kinds of Christians they are. But let them delay no further."

If you could, dear madam, as you are not too far from Ivanie, warn Jacob that he is squandering the opportunities that have been given so freely to him and his people by permitting such deviations, and apply some pressure to him.

I must in addition warn you about Bishop Sołtyk, for rumors abound that he has gotten into terrible debt and finds himself in a very uncomfortable position, vulnerable to any type of influence. This is why he is quick to accept gifts, which are, of course, pervasive in this country. The weight of the Commonwealth rests upon gifts, everyone has something to give everyone else, in order to secure protection, aid, support. That is just the way it is, as you of course know perfectly well already. Often it is the tallest crops that yield the least. So, too, those who put on proud and boastful airs often prove to be mere empty vessels, with the least understanding, merit, or skill. That is why I must warn you, dear madam, that the bishop's intentions are woven together out of all sorts of different ribbons, some of them beautiful and pure, others tattered and muddied. It was reported to me that in Warsaw he was recently spotted meeting with our royal cashier . . .

## Katarzyna Kossakowska to Antoni Moliwda-Kossakowski

. . . You must not talk so about our dear Kajetan, for he is fully devoted to our cause. I know he tries to kill many birds with one stone, being a seasoned player, and that he does not need any special sympathy from me, yet it is a dangerous thing to try to show that we have a better understanding than those whose opinions must be held to be infallible. Let us simply take what is best about him.

There is another supporter now, too—I was able to convince Prince Jabłonowski, my dear friend's husband, to join our cause. And since he always goes about everything rather methodically, he immediately came up with this great notion that on his property we might create a little Jewish realm under his protection. He became so enthused about the idea that now he is going around his estates trying to get everyone on board with it. I would like the idea were it not for the fact that the prince is a bit chimerical and slightly flighty, and such a project would of course require great efforts and undertakings. The prince has read all about Paraguay, a country in America created out of similar poverty and savagery, the existence of which so

fascinates the prince that he will not discuss anything else, and
has not for some time. I asked him what those gentlemen live
off over there, and the prince responds that there are no
gentlemen there, and that everyone is just as equal in their
property as they are before God, so from this, you understand,
I can conclude that it is not for me!

The prince is known for his superior self-esteem. He carries
himself like a royal, with his head held so high he often gets
tripped up on his own legs. It is a good thing he has the wife he
does, sensible and wise, who treats him like an overgrown child
and ignores his eccentric excesses. I saw in their home a large
picture with a representation of the Virgin Mary, before whom
he had had himself painted tipping his cap to her as she stops
him and says, "Couvrez-vous, mon cousin."

We have also been joined by Prince Jerzy Marcin
Lubomirski, who has agreed to accept one hundred and fifty
neophytes onto his land and offer them hospitality there, as he
is known for his great generosity (some would call it profligacy),
and has become a great advocate of the matter, much like
Bishop Załuski . . .

## Of the cross and dancing in the abyss

In the afternoon of that same March day, a cross is brought from Kamieniec, a gift from the bishop, and a letter with an invitation.

Jacob first speaks with Rabbi Moshe, and then, considerably moved,
he has everyone gather in the common room at dusk. He is the last to
arrive, dressed in his finest Turkish gown with his tall hat on his head,
which makes him seem even taller. The women line up, and he stands in
the middle with the cross.

"The world is sealed with the emblem of the cross," says Jacob.

First, he puts it to his head and is silent for a long time, and then he
moves through the common room, in this direction and that, the women
behind him, while the men line up, each holding on to the shoulders of
the one before him and walking after Jacob and the women, singing.

Then Jacob, as though suddenly remembering, holding the cross by its ribbon, throws it in every direction in turn, so that they must jump out of its way, but they catch it instinctively, for it is not known whether this cross is foe or friend, so when they catch it and hold it for a moment, and then give it back to Jacob, it seems like some kind of game. In the end, Rabbi Moshe, who is just behind Jacob, clusters them all together and asks them all to hold on to each other, leaning on each other, and then Jacob starts to repeat in a resounding voice: "Forsa damus para verti, sei-hut grandi asser verti." They all repeat it after him, even those who consider these words a spell that will protect them from evil. And so they dance, clinging on to one another, faster and faster, until the draft extinguishes almost all the lamps. Only one remains, placed very high, and its light illuminates just the tops of their heads, so that it looks as though they're dancing in some sort of dim abyss.

## 20.

### What Yente sees from the vault
### of Lwów cathedral on July 17, 1759

The ticket doesn't cost much, a mere six groszy, so there is nothing to keep the rabble from entering the Lwów cathedral in droves. Enormous as it is, it cannot hold every interested party. All those still camping out in the Halickie Przedmieście want desperately to get in, especially the crowds of Sabbatians and poor Jewry, but also the local tradesmen, women vendors, children. Of course, many of them don't have even that many groszy, and if by some miracle they got that many, they would probably choose to spend it on bread.

Order around the cathedral is kept by guards from the Lwów garrison. Thanks to the prudence of the priest who administers the tickets, there are seats to spare. Now merchants from Lwów are going in, while others who came from out of town just for the occasion are already inside: there is the Rohatyn starosta, Łabęcki, and his wife, Pelagia; near them sits the vicar forane Benedykt Chmielowski, and farther on, the Kamieniec castellan Kossakowski, with his wife, Katarzyna, along with other powerful people from the vicinity.

There are also many Jews—not something you see every day in a Catholic church—and youth of every background, who came out of pure youthful curiosity.

In the very front, in the first rows, sit theologians from various religious orders, as well as priests and church dignitaries. Behind them, the regular clergy. Next come the Contra-Talmudists, standing in a semicircle a little to the right, next to a double row of benches. They're a small group of around ten, the rest having lacked carts to make the journey from Ivanie, as they explain. Yehuda Krysa and Solomon Shorr stand at the very front. Krysa's clever face, sliced in half by his scar, is eye-catching. Shlomo, tall, slender, in a rich overcoat, inspires respect. Opposite them are the Talmudists, all of whom look like the same person: bearded, dressed in bulky black robes, and—as Asher notices, standing near the entrance—a generation older. The Talmudists have already designated three people to participate directly in the disputation: Nutka, the rabbi of Bohorodczany, Lwów's Rabbi Rapaport, and David, the rabbi of Stanisławów. Asher stands on his tiptoes and looks for Jacob Frank—he would like to see him at least—but he can't find anyone who looks like he could possibly be him.

In the middle, on the platform, is the Lwów administrator, Father Mikulski, nervous and sweaty, in wonderful shades of purple, as well as the king's dignitaries, among them Ordinate Zamoyski and Margraves Wielopolski, Lanckoroński, and Ostroróg, all in elegant flowing kontusze tied with Turkish belts, the slits in their sleeves revealing equally colorful silk żupans.

Yente looks down on them from the top of the vault. She sees a sea of heads, big and small, in hats, caps, and turbans, and they remind her of a bumper crop of mushrooms—all sorts of honey fungus growing in clusters, each one similar to the next, chanterelles with fantastical headdress and the little stems of lone *Boletus*, embedded powerfully in the ground. Then, in a flash, her gaze travels to the nailed-up, half-naked Christ on the cross, and Yente gazes through the eyes of that wooden face.

She sees men focused on maintaining their seriousness and calm, although it is obvious that they are not calm. Maybe that one who is sitting in the middle, the most colorful one—he is thinking about some woman who stayed behind, in bed, and more precisely, about her body, and more precisely about one particular place on her body, wet and fragrant. Nor are those to either side of him fully present in the cathedral. One is still with the bees in his hives, for the bees have left them to go swarm on a linden—will he ever be able to get them back? The other is going over his accounts, he keeps getting his numbers mixed up and having to start over. They are all wearing Sarmatian hats adorned with a big jewel and a peacock feather, and the colors of their costumes are cheerful as parrots' plumage, which is no doubt why all three of them have wrinkled brows, frowning so as to counterbalance the licentious colors of their dress with the severity of their faces. These three are the most majestic-looking.

The debaters, on the left, are milk caps—that is, their caps resemble those mushrooms. From up here, the milk caps look like they would love to make a run for it. They are here under penalty of imprisonment or fine, yet this cause has been lost in advance, their arguments will not be understood or even heard out. Those on the right side, meanwhile, are the honey fungus, huddling together, their clothing brownish gray and worn, in constant undulation as one of their number and then another leaves their litter cluster and then squeezes back in with papers in his hand; flowing from them are obstinacy and anger, although they expect to triumph. Yente doesn't like them, although she recognizes among them some of her relatives—but that doesn't have much meaning now. For if Yente were to look at the matter of her relations from a certain angle, she would see that here and there, outside the cathedral and beyond, in the little enclaves that have popped up around the town, her relatives are everywhere.

After the opening formalities and the reading out of a long list of titles, Father Mikulski, who will be presiding over this disputation, begins to speak. He sounds rather nervous at first, but a quote from the Gospels anchors him in these rough waters of words, and with the Scriptures behind him, he begins to speak assuredly and without stammering, even with gusto. He presents the Contra-Talmudists as lost little lambs who, after a long time wandering, have at last found the shepherd who wishes to tend them.

Then Antoni Moliwda-Kossakowski, a nobleman, as the secretary introduces him, comes forward—he is the Contra-Talmudists' spokesperson. A balding man with a somewhat protruding belly and watery eyes, he might not make—it is true—the best impression, but when he starts talking, he draws everyone's attention, and it is so quiet you could hear a pin drop. He has a warm, booming, resonant voice, and he modulates it in such a lovely way that he touches people's hearts. He speaks *beautifully*, though in quite a convoluted way, and yet with great conviction, and in any case, people heed a melody more than they do words. Right away he addresses all the Jews, calling upon them to convert. After each sentence he leaves a pause, that it might linger a little longer under the cathedral's vault. And indeed, each sentence floats along through that vast space like poplar fluff.

"We stand here before you, not out of revenge or spite or to repay an eye with an eye, nor was it for such purposes that we pleaded with God, Creator of compassionate hearts, to summon you today. We stand here not in order to call down divine judgment, the judgment of the righteous and the just, but rather to soften your hard hearts and bring about some recognition of divine law . . ."

And so goes the whole speech—lofty and filled with pathos. The crowd is moved, Yente notes the repeated bringing of handkerchiefs to eyes, and she knows exactly what kind of emotions these are. For indeed, the Contra-Talmudists sitting by the wall look like miserable wretches in the presence of these rabbis who wear long furs and fur-lined caps even though it is summer. They look like children banished from their homes, lost lambs, foreign vagabonds, indigent and tired, who have come knocking at the door. They are supposed to be Jews, but to the Jews they're not Jews, for they are persecuted by their own, cursed, belonging nowhere. And in their distress, their dark souls, like potato shoots growing in a cellar, instinctively seek out the light and lean toward it, poor things. How could they not be welcomed into the bosom of the Christian church—that capacious, comfortable, Catholic bosom?

They seem honest: Yeruhim of Jezierzany; Yehuda of Nadwórna, known as Krysa; Moshe Dawidowicz of Podhajce. All of them will speak. Then there is Hirsh of Lanckoroń, Elisha Shorr's son-in-law, husband of Hayah, who is standing by the wall, and finally Elisha Shorr of Rohatyn himself, with his sons, amongst whom the most striking is Shlomo, with his curly mop of hair and his bright coat. Farther down are Lwów's own Nussen Aronowicz, dressed in the Turkish fashion, and Shyle of Lanckoroń, who are acting as secretaries of sorts. Papers are piled up in front of them, there is an inkwell, and every type of writing instrument as well. At the very end of the row, at a little table set slightly apart, sit Nahman of Busk and Moliwda, the translators. Nahman is dressed like a Turk, modestly and in dark colors. A wiry man, he rubs his hands together nervously. Moliwda, meanwhile, sweats into his elegant dark clothing.

Behind them the crowd swirls, perspiring, colorful—wives, sisters, mothers, and brothers, all squeezed in, all intimidated.

On the right, on the benches for the Talmudists, things are not quite so crowded. There are a dozen or so well-dressed, dignified older rabbis, almost indistinguishable from one another but for the length and extravagance of their beards. But Yente's eye discerns Rabbi Rapaport of Lwów, Rabbi Mendl of Satanów, Rabbi Leyba of Międzybórz, and Rabbi Berk of Jazłowiec. Yos Krzemieniecki, the rabbi of Mohylew, sits at the edge of the bench and rocks back and forth with his eyes closed, absent in spirit.

They begin with a point-by-point reading of the manifesto they have had printed for this occasion. As the first point begins to be discussed, the rabble realizes at once that it will not be getting what it wanted. Some complex matters have been brought up, and it is hard to listen to the rabbis' babbling, since they are talking through a translator, which takes a long while, especially since the translator is terrible. Only Rapaport dares speak in Polish, but the Yiddish lilt to his speech makes him sound silly, humorous, as if he were selling eggs at the market—it gives him no authority. The crowd starts to murmur and fidget, not only those standing toward the back of the cathedral, but also the nobles in the benches, who whisper amongst themselves or get up to wander absentmindedly beneath the vault, whence Yente watches them.

After a few hours, Father Mikulski decides to adjourn the hearing until the next day, when they will finish the discussion about whether the Messiah has already come, as the Christians believe, or if he is still to come, as the Jews would have it.

## Of Asher's familial bliss

By the time Asher goes home, it's already getting dark.

"And? Was he there? Did he make an appearance?" Gitla asks him from the doorway, as if indifferent, as if asking about the chimney sweep who was supposed to come and clean the stove. Asher knows this person is still in some sense living in his home, although Gitla barely ever mentions him. And it is not just a matter of the child, Samuel, her son. Jacob Frank is like a small plant that vegetates in the kitchen, on the windowsill, and that Gitla is constantly watering. Asher considers that this is something people who have been abandoned do. Until eventually the plant withers and dies.

He peers into the room where, on the floor, on a worn carpet, little Samuel is playing. Gitla is pregnant, which is why she is so irritable. Gitla did not want the child, but she had found it difficult to ward off a second pregnancy. She has read somewhere that in France they make little sheepskin hoods for the male member, and then all of the semen is kept inside that hood, so it does not leave the woman with child. She would like to have such hoodlets herself, and to hand them out to all the women at the weekly market, that they might give them to their husbands and stop getting pregnant. Misery results from all this disorderly proliferation, multiplication, just like with worms on rotting meat, she says often, puttering around the house with her belly showing already, which is sad and funny at the same time. There are too many people, the cities are smelly and dirty, there's too little clean water, she repeats. Her lovely face is distorted by a grimace of disgust. And these women, eternally swollen, eternally pregnant, lying in childbed or breastfeeding. There would not be all this misery amongst the Jews if Jewish women were not always getting pregnant. What do people want with so many children?

When she speaks, Gitla gesticulates, her thick black hair, cut to her shoulders, also moving in violent jerks. She walks around the house with her head bare. Asher looks lovingly at her. He thinks that if something were ever to happen to her or to Samuel, he would die.

"Is it really for this," Gitla often repeats, "that a woman's body gives away its finest substances—to create within it a future person who will only die anyway, so that all will turn out to have been for naught? How poorly thought-out it is. There cannot be a logic to it—not practical, nor any other kind."

Since Asher Rubin loves Gitla, he listens to her attentively and tries to understand what she is saying. Slowly he begins to share her view. Each year he silently commemorates the blessed day she showed up at his house.

He is sitting on the sofa, Samuel playing around his legs, busy with two wheels connected by an axle that Asher made for him. On Gitla's now ample belly lies a book—perhaps it is pressing too hard on her? Asher goes over, picks it up, and lays it down next to her, but Gitla instantly puts it back on her belly.

"I saw some people from Rohatyn I know," says Asher.

"They must have aged," answers Gitla, looking out the open window.

"They were all depressed. It will end badly. When are you going to start leaving the house again?"

"I don't know," says Gitla. "When I give birth."

"This whole disputation is not for the people. They're just trading supposed wisdoms. They read out whole pages from books, then translate them, and it takes a long time, and everybody gets bored. No one understands what's going on."

Gitla sets the book down on the sofa and straightens her back.

"I'd eat some nuts," she says, and then, suddenly, she takes Asher's face in both her hands and looks him in the eyes: "Asher . . . ," she begins, and doesn't finish.

## The seventh point of the disputation

It is Monday, September 10, 1759, the Jewish year 5519, the 18th day of the month of Elul. People are slowly gathering, milling around in front of the cathedral—it's going to be a hot one again. Peasants are selling small, sweet Hungarian plums and Wallachian nuts. You can also buy quartered watermelons laid out on big leaves.

The participants in the disputation come in through the side entrance and take their places, although today there are more of all of them, as even the Frankists have come in a sizable group, surrounding their beloved Frank, who has deigned to appear, like bees surrounding their queen. Rabbis from nearby kahalim have shown up, too, and distinguished Jewish scholars, and Rapaport himself, hunched over, as usual in a long coat that will be too hot. At the same time, the curious are let into the cathedral, those who purchased tickets, but soon there will not be enough space for them, either. Latecomers will have to stand in the vestibule, where they will hear little of what is going on inside.

At two o'clock, Father Mikulski calls them all to order and asks the Contra-Talmudists to furnish the evidence for their seventh thesis. He is nervous, and as he spreads out his papers in front of him, his hands can be seen to shake. Glancing at the written text, he begins his remarks; at first, they are clumsily delivered, as he stutters and repeats himself, but soon he finds his rhythm:

"The thirst for Christian blood amongst the Talmudist population, not only in the Kingdom of Poland but also in other countries, is a known fact, for there are many histories, in foreign nations as well as here in Poland and in Lithuania, of Talmudists mercilessly shedding innocent Christian blood and being sentenced to death for this godless act. Yet they have always stubbornly denied it, wanting to clear themselves before the world, alleging that they are the innocent ones, baselessly accused by Christians."

His voice breaks, out of nervousness, and he has to have a sip of water, but then he goes on:

"We, however, taking as our witness an all-seeing God to come, who will judge the living and the dead—and not out of spite or in retaliation, but out of love for the holy faith—we let the whole world know of those Talmudists' acts, and we will be adjudicating this matter today."

A murmur passes through the cramped and undulating crowd. Now Krysa repeats the same thing in Hebrew, and this time, the small group of rabbis erupts. One of them—it looks like the rabbi of Satanów—gets up and starts to go over to the other side, but the others restrain and quiet him.

And now how it goes is Krysa speaks, and then Moliwda, in his role as interpreter, clarifying everything, though none of what they say is clear at all:

"A book of the Talmud, known as the Orah Hayyim Maginei Aretz, which means 'Path of the Living, Defense of the Earth,' the author of which is Rabbi David, says: 'Mitsvah lehazer aharyain adom,' which means: 'Have (the rabbi) try to get red wine, a blood memento.' The very same author then adds: 'Od remez le-adom zekher le-dam she Hayah paroh shohet bnei Yisrael,' in other words, 'And I'm giving you a hint about the reason for the red blood memento, it's because the Pharaoh slaughtered the children of the Israelites.' And then this sentence follows: 'Veha-Yehudim nimne'u mi-lakahat yain adom mipnei alilot shikriyym.' Or: 'And now the consumption of red wine has been forsaken, for there are false attacks.'"

Once more the rabbi of Satanów stands and shouts something, but no one translates for him, so no one listens. He is shushed by Father Mikulski:

"The time will come for the defense. First the arguments of the other side must be heard."

And now Krysa, translated by Moliwda, demonstrates in intricate detail that the Talmud demands Christian blood, as the words *yain adom* are translated by the rabbis as "red wine," while in the Hebrew script the very same letters (*alef, dalet, vav, mem*) are used both for the word *adom*, or "red," and the word *edom*, or Christian. The two words differ only at the bottom of the first letter, *alef,* by dots, called "segol" and "kamatz," by virtue of which the reader understands now *adom*, and now *edom*.

"So what one must know," Krysa goes on, as Moliwda translates beautifully, "is that the Orah Hayyim Maginei Aretz, in which there is an order to the rabbis to get red wine for Passover, gives these words without any dots, leaving these two Hebrew words ambiguous. Thus rabbis are free to translate them for the general public as 'yayin adom,' or 'red wine,' but to understand it amongst themselves as 'yayin edom,' or 'Christian

blood,' as an allegory of wine," explains Moliwda, although it's actually
not clear if he is translating or just talking. His eyes are glued to the paper
in front of him, and somewhere along the way he's misplaced his eloquence and charm.

"What are you all doing?" someone shouts out of the crowd in Polish,
and then repeats the same thing in Yiddish: "What are you all doing?"

Krysa goes on to demonstrate that that supposed "red wine" should
actually be "blood memento."

"Let the Talmudists tell us: Of what kind of blood is it a memento?"
he shouts, and aims his finger at the rabbis sitting facing him. "And why
is it 'I'm giving you a hint'? A hint of what?" he says, still yelling, his face
reddening. The whole church is perfectly silent. Krysa takes in a big
breath and says quietly, with satisfaction, "Evidently this was an effort to
keep the secret with the rabbis, and have the general public believe that it
meant only red wine. And that's how it all works!"

Now, nudged by his companions, Moshe of Podhajce stands. His eyelids are twitching:

"For their Passover, a Talmudic ceremony has been invented, and
everyone is required to participate in it. On the first evening of this holiday, a glass of wine is placed on the table, and each person sitting at that
table must dip the little finger of his right hand into it, and then let the
droplets fall from his finger onto the ground while enumerating the ten
plagues of Egypt: 1. dam, or blood; 2. tzefardea, or frogs; 3. khinim, or
lice; 4. arov, or flies; 5. dever, or pestilence of livestock; 6. shchin, or boils;
7. barad, or hail, 8. arbeh, or locusts; 9. hoshech, or darkness; 10. vechoros,
or death to the firstborn. This ceremony is described by the author, Rabbi
Yudah, who uses three words to indicate those ten plagues: *detzakh*, *adash*,
*be'ahav*, which consists of the initial letters of the names of each of the
plagues. The rabbis give their simpletons to understand that this abbrevi-
ation refers exclusively to those ten plagues. But in these words composed
of first initials, we have discovered the secret that they"—here he points
again at the rabbis—"keep amongst themselves and hide before society,
whereas we can now publicly show that when we put other words underneath those first letters, we actually get something else entirely: 'Dam
tzerikhim kulanu al derekh she-asu be-oto ish hakhamei bi-Yerushalayim,'

which means: 'Everyone needs blood in the same way they did to this man in Jerusalem, those wise men.'"

There is a silence, people look around at each other, and it becomes clear that few of them are able to follow this. Whispering begins, some murmured commentaries. Some people, those most impatient and disappointed, are now shuffling outside, where—in spite of the heat—there is more air than inside the cathedral. Undaunted, Moshe of Podhajce goes on:

"I will tell you all furthermore that in the Orah Hayyim, point 460, on the baking of matzah on the first night of Easter, notes: 'Ain lushoin matzes mitzve vailoe oifin oiso al idey akim vailoe al idey obeyreh shoyte veykuten,' which means: 'One should not knead or bake the Matzot Mitzvah in the presence of a gentile, a deaf mute, an imbecile, or a child.' While on other days, as it is written, the Matzot can be kneaded in front of anyone. So tell us, Talmudists, why on that first night it is forbidden to knead and bake in the presence of a gentile, a deaf mute, an imbecile, or a child. But we know what they will say! So the dough won't ferment. And yet we will ask them, why would the dough ferment? They shall answer that it is because those people would make it sour. But can the dough not be protected? And how exactly are they supposed to spoil it? What is really going on is that Christian blood is being added to the Matzot over Passover, and that is why there should be no witnesses to its kneading."

Moshe calms down now, having almost screamed out his last words. The rabbi of Jazłowiec, on the other side, holds his head in his hands and starts rocking. At first, Pinkas squirms in his seat as he listens to Moshe's speech, but then all the blood rushes to his head, and he stands, forces his way forward, grabbed by the sides and sleeves of his coat by those who would stop him.

"Moshe, what are you doing? You're fouling your own nest. Moshe, we know each other, we were in the same yeshiva. Moshe! Get ahold of yourself!"

Already the garrison guards are putting on their martial airs and moving toward Pinkas, and he retreats. Moshe pretends not to have noticed him at all. He continues:

"And there is a third point. In the Old Order, the blood of animals and fowl is strictly forbidden, and the use of it for food or for drink is not permitted to the Jews. And yet the Book of the Rambam, part 2, chapter 6, says: 'Dam houdym ain hayuvin ulov,' which means: 'No kind of blood is permitted, but for the blood of man.' And also in the book Masehet Ketubbot 60 it is said: 'The blood of those who walk on two legs is pure.' So tell us, then, rabbis, whose blood is pure? Because it isn't the birds'! There are many such examples, which are not expressed clearly, but this lack of clarity is done on purpose, with the aim of concealing the true intention. We have revealed the truth. The rest—the frequent murders of innocent babes—can be guessed."

When Moshe finishes, there is an uproar throughout the cathedral, and since it is already getting dark, Father Mikulski ends this session and tells the rabbis to prepare their response for three days hence. He also calls those present to keep the peace. The guards come, but people are dispersing relatively calmly. The only thing that isn't clear is when and how all of the rabbis are going to leave the cathedral.

## Of secret hand and eye signals and hints

On September 13, 1759, the Jewish year 5519, the 21st day of the month of Elul, before an equally great press of the curious, the rabbi of Lwów, Hayim Kohen Rapaport, stands in the name of his co-religionists and in a lengthy speech calls the whole accusation an act of spite, revenge, and plain old blood libel. He describes all the allegations as baseless and against the laws of nature.

Heavy drops hit the cathedral roof—at last the rain has come.

Rapaport speaks in Polish, slowly, carefully, as if he has learned this speech by heart. He cites testimonies from the Holy Scriptures and opinions on Jews issued by Hugo Grotius and Christian scholars. In a low, very calm voice, he assures those gathered that the Talmud does not command any harm to Christians. He finishes with a rhetorical turn that appeals to the grace and the protection of administrator Mikulski, that with the deepest gravity of his reason he might see fit to understand the allegations of the Contra-Talmudists concerning Christian blood as merely an excuse for their own bad actions, made in bad faith.

Now his secretary hands him a stack of papers, and Rabbi Rapaport begins to read in Hebrew. After every couple of sentences, Białowolski reads the Polish translation. It says, regarding the question of red wine, that the Talmud tells Jews to drink at Passover four portions of wine, and that in the scripture red wine is considered the best, thus it is appropriate to consume it. However, should the white be better, then it is permitted to drink white. This is done in memory of the blood shed by the Pharaoh from the children of Israel, because though it is not written distinctly in the scripture, it is tradition. It is also done in memory of the blood of the sheep killed in Egypt for Passover, with which the doors were painted, that the angel killing firstborn sons might pass over the homes of the Israelites. The term *hint* does not appear at all in the Talmud; evidently the Contra-Talmudists' Hebrew is poor. In the same manner, the translation of the word *adom* as *edom*, which does not mean Christian, but rather Egyptian, is a poor one.

The argument that the three words *detzakh*, *adash*, and *be'ahav*, made up of the first letters of the names of the ten plagues, might mean what the Frankists suggest is completely baseless. For these words are set merely as a memory aide for the plagues, not for the designation of Christian blood. This is what is known as a mnemonic device, in other words, a technique to better remember.

The matzah baked for Passover is protected so that it is not fermented through any carelessness, for the scripture forbids consuming at that time any leavened bread. Meanwhile, the Orah Hayyim does not forbid kneading and baking *in the presence of* a gentile, a deaf mute, an imbecile, or a child, but rather *by* a gentile, a deaf mute, an imbecile, or a child. Again, then, the Frankists have translated this Talmud passage very poorly, and from there they make the inaccurate claim that somehow this prohibition is in the interest of obtaining Christian blood. As for the allegation that the Book of Rambam "allows for the consumption of human blood," that is also false, since the book says exactly the opposite about this; the Frankists could really use a Hebrew lesson or two.

As it is getting very dark now inside the cathedral, a darkness only barely pierced by candlelight, Father Mikulski orders the disputation be paused and postpones the verdict until a later date.

## Katarzyna Kossakowska writes to
## Bishop Kajetan Sołtyk

. . . My Nose errs rarely, and it is sensing that Your Excellency has begun to lose Interest in our Cause, having more important Issues on your Mind in your new episcopal Capital. But I consider myself stubborn and will permit myself to disturb Your Excellency with Regard to this Matter, given how heavily it weighs upon my Heart. It rouses in me equal Parts maternal and paternal Feeling, since these Puritans of ours remind me of orphaned Children, and at the same Time, I consider how much Good it would do them to leave behind their mistaken Religion and pass over into the Bosom of our Polish Church!

As our Puritans did before, so, too, did the Rabbis submit their written Defense before the consistory Court. On those present the Defense did not make at all the same Impression that the Accusation itself did. It was considered to be weak— not a well-reasoned or a proper Answer. Particular Attention was paid to the Fact that the Rabbis defended the Talmud either with Citations from the Scripture or with unqualified Denial. And in the End, it was all about some minor Detail, whether some Rabbi David in his Talmud gave some secret eye Signal, or hand Signal, some Hint about why the Talmudists were supposed to consume red Wine. Anyway, that is not the Point. To that no one was really listening.

The Truth is that all of us assembled there had already rendered our Judgment. Thus we derived great Satisfaction when the Verdict came. The Administrator, Father Mikulski, announced to those assembled that with Respect to the first six Theses, the Talmudists were to be considered vanquished and convicted by our Puritans, and with Respect to the seventh, on

Christian Blood, upon the written Advice of the Nuncio Serra, the consistory Court would prefer to defer the Matter for further, closer Consideration, not taking a final Decision quite yet. I consider that to be proper. The Matter itself is too sensitive, the Passion it brings out too great, thus the Judgment of the Church Authority recognizing the Accuracy of our Charges' Accusation, and in Turn the Truthfulness of the age-old Accusations, could have threatened the Jews with the worst Consequences. Despite some Disappointment on the Part of the Public in this Respect, everyone took the Decision to Heart and duly departed to their respective Homes.

Therefore I have to report to Your Excellency that the Matter of Baptism is already determined, and the Date has already been set for Jacob Frank himself, which pleases me greatly. What does he have to offer us? Much, indeed! He says—which I know through my Cousin, Moliwda-Kossakowski—that if our Commonwealth were to offer him the right Conditions, several thousand People would follow him into the Catholic Faith, not only from Poland and Lithuania, but also from Wallachia, Moldova, Hungary, and even Turkey. He also argues intelligently that this whole Population, not knowing our Polish Customs, cannot be parceled out like so many Sheep, for without their own Kind they will waste away, and so they must be settled all together in a Sort of extended Flock.

I am thus on my Knees in the extreme Hope that Your Excellency will prepare the Foundations for these Baptisms and put your full Authority behind our Cause.

In the Meantime I shall try for the Support of the Nobles and the Inhabitants of Lwów while I am in this Place. What we need is financial Support, or any Kind of material Support, for this enormous Multitude of Jewish Wretches who are camping out on our Streets. I assure Your Excellency that it is reminiscent of those sprawling Gypsy Caravans, and that eventually the City will cease to be able to deal with these street Encampments. Unfortunately, apart from the Lack of Food, there are also far less pleasant physical Exigencies, and this is slowly becoming a Problem. It is difficult to pass through the

Halickie Przedmieście without covering your Nose, and it is
very hot again, which renders those Odors all the more
upsetting. And although the Shabbitarians seem very well
organized themselves, I still wonder if we ought not to provide
them some other Place to stay outside the City, with which I
turn to you, and also to His Excellency, Bishop Załuski, and I
shall deliver a Letter on this Matter to our Primate as well.
I myself am considering lending for a Time my Manor in
Wojsławice to Frank's Family and closest Associates, while they
await a more permanent Residence. My Place, however, requires
Repairs to the Roof and the Introduction of many
Amenities . . .

## Of the troubles of Father Chmielowski

This year of the comet is a year of problems for the priest. He thought
that in his old age he would take refuge in his presbytery among the
mallow and the bittercress (which help with his joints), but instead there
is always some tumult, some clamor. Now there is also this runaway, and
Roshko's aversion to him. The priest is putting up a fugitive with a
frightening face and has no intention of turning him in to the authorities,
although he should. He is a good man, gentle and so unfortunate that
even looking at him breaks the Father's heart and makes him think very
intently upon divine mercy and goodness. Roshko, meanwhile, is as hard
on the runaway as ever, and the priest worries that eventually he'll spill
their secret to someone. Father Chmielowski is sure that Roshko is jealous, which is why he has been making an effort to be kinder to him and
has started paying him an extra grosz, yet Roshko has continued to
stomp around in a foul mood. So now, while he is in Lwów for a few
days, Father Chmielowski wonders whether they are at each other's
throats. Of this, however, he does not tell Mrs. Drużbacka in his occasional letters, the writing of which brings him great pleasure, because it
gives him the impression that someone is actually *listening* to him at last,

and not on some scholarly subject, but rather a human one. Sometimes he composes them in his head for days on end, like now, as he sits almost falling asleep in morning mass with the Bernardines. Instead of praying, he thinks about what to write. Maybe something like this:

> . . . My case with Prince Jabłonowski will end up in court. I will defend myself, which is why I am now writing my remarks, in which I attempt to prove that the books and the information therein contained are a common good. For they belong to no one, and at the same time to everyone, just like the sky, the air, the smell of flowers and the beauty of the rainbow. Can you steal from someone the knowledge he has amassed for himself from other books?

Now that he finds himself in Lwów, he has ended up in the very center of the disputation. The bishop is busy, the whole town is eagerly preparing, and no one has the time to work on behalf of Father Benedykt's cause. So he has stayed here with the Bernardines, going to every hearing of the Jews, taking notes, and writing them up bit by bit in his letters to Mrs. Drużbacka.

> . . . You were asking what I have actually witnessed myself, and so I ask you in turn, Your Ladyship, would you have been able to stand, or even to sit, in one place for as long as I sat there? You can take it from me that the hearing was incredibly boring, and that everyone was only interested in one thing: Are the Jews in need of Christian blood?
> Father Gaudenty Pikulski, a learned Bernardine of the Lwów order, a professor of theology, and a gentleman "highly trained in the Hebrew tongue," did a wonderful job. He and Father Awedyk wrote up the whole Lwów hearing and added to it all the information we have these days from all kinds of books and records. With evident erudition, he put the question of ritual murder to detailed analysis.
> In support of the accusation of these Contra-Talmudists, he attempted to provide further evidence, drawn mainly from the manuscript of one Serafinowicz, the rabbi of Brześć Litewski,

who in 1710 in Żółkiew was baptized and, having publicly confessed that in Lithuania he himself twice committed ritual murder, described all the evils and blasphemies that the Jews commit throughout the year, according to the order of their holy days. These secrets of the Talmudists were already fully published by Serafinowicz himself, but all copies were bought up and burned by the Jews. The beginning of the agonies of Christian children with the distribution of their blood for consumption occurred just after Christ's death, for the reason that I put to you here in a direct quote from Fathers Pikulski and Awedyk, Your Ladyship, lest you think I am inventing it all:

"When after the propagation of the holy Christian faith Christians began to rise against the Jews and condemn them, the Jews came together to determine ways in which they might appease the Christians and render their hearts merciful toward them. They went at that time to the Jerusalem rabbi, the eldest one, by the name of Ravashe. This rabbi tried every natural and unnatural method, but, finding that the Christians' fervor and vehemence against the Jews could not be softened, he at last ventured into the Book of Rambam, the most famous of the Jewish scholars. In that book, he read that the effects of a harmful thing can only be lessened by the sympathetic application of a second thing of the same kind, which the aforementioned rabbi translated to the Jews as follows: The flame of Christian obstinacy against them could only be stifled by spilling the blood of said Christians. From that time on, they began to capture Christian children and to viciously murder them, in order to render the Christians milder and more merciful to them, and they put it down for themselves as a new law, as the Talmud clearly and extensively describes in their book Zyvche Lev."

I was greatly alarmed by it all, and if I had not seen those written sources myself with mine own eyes, my mind would have defended itself against the acceptance of that truth. Yet everything is written down in their books, though since among themselves they write—as Father Pikulski says—with dots, or accents, of which there are nine in the Hebrew language, and they print their Talmuds without those dots, there is an abundance in the Talmud of ambiguous words, which the rabbis understand differently, and can translate to the people in various ways, as suits the preservation of their secret.

It frightens me more than Your Ladyship can possibly imagine. I shall return to my Firlejów in a state of terror, for if such things can go on in the world, then how are we to even begin to conceive of them and deal with them just in our minds alone? But after all, such learned books cannot lie!

Who would believe the Talmudists under such circumstances? I can't stop wondering. For if they are in the habit of lying and deceiving the Catholics on everyday things, then of course they would lie about a matter so essential. And the fact that this need for Christian blood is kept in great secret amongst the rabbis themselves! Among the simple and uneducated Jews it is unknown; however, it must be true, given how many times it has been proven by testimony, and punished severely by decree . . .

## Of Pinkas, who cannot understand what sin he has committed

He fulfilled all the commandments, performed good deeds, prayed more than others. And what could holy Rabbi Rapaport have done, that man who is a walking kindness? And what did all these Podolian Jews do, that such a great misfortune in the form of these heretics befell them?

Gone gray, although still not old, he sits at the table in his ragged shirt, hunched over, unable to read, although he would like to escape into the rows of letters that evoke familiar associations, but this time it doesn't work: Pinkas bounces right back off the holy letters like a ball.

His wife walks in with a candle, ready to go to bed already, wearing a nightgown that goes down to the ground and a white kerchief on her head; she beholds him in concern, then sits down next to him and presses her cheek into his shoulder. Pinkas feels her delicate, fragile body and starts to cry.

The rabbis have ordered them to stay at home, close the shutters, and draw the curtains in preparation for the arrival of the heathens to Lwów. If they cannot help it, if they really have to go out, they must avoid all eye contact. It cannot be allowed to happen that the eyes of Jacob Frank, that mongrel, come into contact with the eyes of a proper Jew. The gaze must be kept on the ground, at the base of the walls, or in the gutter—it should not accidentally flit upward, toward the demonic faces of those sinners.

Tomorrow Pinkas is going on a mission to Warsaw, to the nuncio. He is in the process of assembling the final documents. This disputation is inflaming passions, provoking people to hatred, fomenting anxieties. The seventh point accuses the Jews of consumption of Christian blood, and yet they already have a ruling from the pope himself that says to file all such allegations away with folk and fairy tales. At the same time, this sect of Jacob Frank's practices some mysterious rituals it would be very easy to blame on all Jews. Rabbi Rapaport was right to say: "They are no longer Jews, and we are not bound to act toward them as we would toward our fellow Jews. They are like that mixed multitude, that mongrel horde that joined in with the children of Moses as they fled from Egypt: half-breeds and harlots, fops and thieves, suspect types and madmen. That's what they are."

Rapaport will demonstrate in Konstantynów, where all the rabbis of the Polish land are to meet, that there is no other way for them to free themselves of the Frankists, those heathens, than to force them to convert to Christianity. In other words, they must themselves see to it that those dogs are christened. A lot of money has already been collected for this effort, and every pressure is being applied in order to ensure that the baptism of the heretics is accomplished as soon as possible. Pinkas, fighting with a smoking candle, tabulates the sums in the same manner as an exchange office would. On the left side, the last name, first name, and title, and on the right side, the amount of their donation.

Suddenly there is a pounding on the door, and Pinkas pales. He thinks: it has begun. With his eyes he tells his wife to lock herself in the bedroom. Their youngest child begins to cry. Pinkas goes to the door and listens, his heart beating wildly, his mouth gone dry. On the other side he can hear nails scratching, and after a moment, a voice:

"Open up, Uncle."

"Who is it?" Pinkas whispers.

The voice answers:

"It's me, Yankiel."

"What Yankiel?"

"Yankiel, Natan's son, from Glinno. Your nephew."

"Are you alone?"

"Yes."

Pinkas slowly opens the door, and the young man squeezes through the narrow opening. Pinkas looks at him in disbelief and then, in relief, holds him close. Yankiel is tall, broad-shouldered, well-built, and his uncle barely reaches his shoulders. Pinkas puts his arms around his waist and stands that way for such a long while that Yankiel eventually clears his throat, embarrassed.

"I saw Gitla," he says.

Pinkas lets him go and takes a step back.

"I saw Gitla today, this morning. She was helping that medic with his patients in the Halickie Przedmieście."

Pinkas grabs at his heart.

"Here? In Lwów?"

"That's right!"

Pinkas leads his nephew into the kitchen and sits him down at the table. He pours him some vodka and drinks a glass himself; unaccustomed to alcohol, he shudders in disgust. From somewhere he takes out some cheese. Yankiel talks—they all came to Lwów, set up camp on the streets; they have little children with them; they've been getting sick. And this Asher fellow, the Jewish medic of Rohatyn, has been treating them, apparently hired by the city's authorities.

Yankiel has big, beautiful eyes of an unusual color—they look aquamarine. He smiles at his weary uncle. Pinkas's wife, in her nightgown, cracks the door of the bedroom and peeks out.

"And just so you know, Uncle," Yankiel says with his mouth full, "Gitla has a child."

## Of the human deluge that overwhelms
## the streets of Lwów

The carts are so packed that one has to get down off them to have a chance of making it over even the smallest rise. Feet raise clouds of dust, for September is hot and dry, and the grass by the road is faded from the sun. Most people go on foot, resting every few miles in the shade of the walnut trees, and then all the adults and children look around in the fallen leaves for the nuts, which are as big as their palms.

At crossroads such as this one, pilgrims coming from all different directions join together and greet one another heartily. The majority of them are poor, small tradesmen and craftsmen, the kind who support their families with their own hands, weaving, wiring, sharpening, and mending. The men, in ragged clothing, are bent double from the portable stalls they carry on their shoulders from morning to night. Dusty and tired, they exchange news and offer one another simple food. They don't need anything other than water and a piece of bread to tide them over until the great event. When you think like that, a person doesn't want much in order to live. He doesn't even have to eat every day. What does he need combs, ribbons, clay pots, sharp knives for, when the world is about to be totally transformed? Everything is going to be different, although no one can say how. That's what they are all talking about.

The carts are full of women and children. Cradles are strapped to the little wagons and hung up under a tree when they stop awhile, mothers putting down their infants in them with relief, their hands having gone numb from holding them. The bigger children, barefoot, grimy, dazed by the heat, doze in their mothers' skirts or on little beds of hay covered with dirty linen.

In some villages other Jews go out to them and spit at their feet, and children of every origin—Polish, Ruthenian, and Jewish—shout at them as they pass:

"Ne'er-do-wells! Ne'er-do-wells! Trinity! Trinity!"

In the evenings they don't even ask for a place to sleep, they just lie down by the water, at the edge of a thicket, by some wall still warm from the day. The women hang the cradles, the diapers, light a fire, and the men set out into the village for some food, gathering along the way fallen green apples and purple plums that are swollen from the sun and lure wasps and bumblebees with their profligate sweet bodies.

Yente sees the sky opening over them in their sleep; they sleep strangely lightly. Everything is holy, as though it were special, as though it were Shabbat, as if it had all been washed and ironed. As if one had to walk very straight now and take very careful steps. Maybe the one watching them will finally wake from the numbness that lasts thousands of years? Under the divine gaze, everything becomes strange and heavy with portent. Children, for instance, find a metal cross pressed into a tree so firmly that it cannot be extracted from the bark that has grown around it. The clouds take on unusual shapes, perhaps of biblical animals—maybe those lions no one has ever seen, so that no one even knows what they looked like. Or a cloud that looks like the fish that swallowed Jonah as it floats over the horizon. And in the tiny little cloud beside it someone even spotted Jonah himself, spit out, crooked as an apple core. Sometimes they are accompanied by Noah's blue ark. It glides across the firmament, enormous, and Noah himself bustles about in it, feeding his animals for a hundred and fifty days. And on the roof of the ark, just look, everyone, look—who is that? That is the uninvited guest, the giant Og, who, when the floodwaters were rising, latched on to the ark at the last minute.

They say: We will not die. Baptism will save us from death. But what's it going to be like? Will people get old? Will people stay the same age for all eternity? They say everyone is going to stay thirty forever. This cheers the old and scares the young. But supposedly this is the best age, where health, wisdom, and experience are entwined harmoniously, their meanings equal. What would it be like, not to die? There would be a lot of time for everything, you'd collect a lot of groszy, build a house, and travel a little here and there, since, after all, a whole eternity cannot be spent in a single place.

Everything has lain in ruin until now, the world is made up of wants—this is lacking, that is gone. But why is it like that? Couldn't there have been everything in excess—warmth, and food, and roofs over people's heads, and beauty? Whom would it have hurt? Why was such a world as this created? There is nothing permanent under the sun, everything passes, and you won't even have time to get a good look at it. But why is it like that? Could there not have been more time, and more reflection?

It is only when we become worthy of being created anew that we shall receive from the Good True God a new soul, full, whole. And man shall be as everlasting as God.

## The Mayorkowiczes

Here is Srol Mayorkowicz with his wife, Beyla. Beyla is sitting in the cart with her youngest daughter, Shima, on her lap. Beyla is dozing off; her head keeps falling onto her chest. She might be sick. On her slender cheeks bloom two splotches of red, and she is coughing. Grayish locks peek out from under a drab linen kerchief that is fraying at the ends. The older girls go on foot after the cart with their father. Elia is seven years old, as thin and petite as her mother. Her dark hair is braided and tied with a rag, and her feet are bare. Beside her walks Freyna, thirteen years old, tall—she will make a beautiful woman. She has light, curly hair and black eyes, and she holds the hand of her sister Masha, who is a year younger and has a limp in one leg since she was born with crooked hips. Maybe that is why she hasn't grown. Masha is duskier, as if from the smoke of their miserable shack in Busk, leaving home rarely, ashamed of her disability. Yet she is, people say, the wisest of all the young ladies. She doesn't like to sleep in the same bed as her sisters and instead spreads out a dismal pallet on the floor—a sort of mattress made of hay. She covers herself with the rough horse blanket her father wove out of scraps during better days.

Srol walks ahead with eleven-year-old Miriam, his favorite, the chatterbox. Her mouth never closes, but she, too, speaks with wisdom. Her father deeply regrets that she was not born a boy, for she definitely would have become a rabbi.

Behind them walks the eldest, Esther, who has already taken on the obligations of a mother—small, bony, with the lovely, delicate face of a weasel, but she is stubborn as a mule. She was promised to a boy from Jezierzany, and her father had already paid the future groom, by way of dowry, money that was very hard to scrape together in such poverty. But the boy died of typhus four years ago, and his father did not give back the money. Srol is awaiting a verdict on it from the local court. He worries about Esther, for who will take her now, with no money, coming from such dire straits? It would be a miracle if he could marry off these daughters. Srol is forty-two years old, but he already looks like an old man—a wrinkled, weather-beaten face, dark, sunken eyes into which a kind of shade has crept, and an overgrown beard matted into a Polish plait. The Jewish God is clearly against him—why would he have only daughters? What sins did Srol commit to be given only girls? Must he expiate some long-standing offense of his ancestors? Srol is convinced this God is not the one for him. That there is another God, truer and better, not this earthly manager and leaseholder. To the true God it is possible to pray by way of Baruchiah, singing songs or trusting Jacob.

They had been in Ivanie since April. Were it not for those good Ivanie people, they probably would have starved to death. Ivanie saved their lives and health, Beyla feels better now, and isn't coughing quite as much. Srol believes that once they have been baptized, they will be as well off as the Christians. They will receive a piece of land, Beyla will have vegetables in her garden, and he, Srol, will weave carpets, because he knows how to do that and is good at it. In their old age, once they have married off their daughters, the girls will take them in. That is his whole dream.

## Nahman and his raiment of good deeds

As Nahman is speaking in the cathedral, his very young wife, Wajgełe, is giving birth to a daughter in Ivanie. The child is big and healthy, and Nahman breathes a sigh of relief. He already has a son, Aron, who is in Busk with Leah. Leah has still not remarried. They say the state of her soul is beclouded, that her heart is not easy. So he has two children, and in some sense, it could be said that he has fulfilled his duty. Nahman takes the birth of his daughter as a signal from God that they are on the right path. Henceforth, Nahman no longer feels the need to be intimate with women.

Yet that evening, as they are leaving the cathedral, where the seventh point of the disputation has just been discussed, Nahman loses the enthusiasm that has carried him through the past few days. It was not so much enthusiasm, even—more like a knack and a hopefulness. A joyful insistence. The excitement of a merchant who took a big risk in order to make a great fortune. Of a player who's put everything on one card. Nahman is strangely excited, he has sweated a great deal during the disputation, and now he can smell on himself a ratlike odor, as though he had been in a physical fight with someone. He would like to be alone, but they are going in a group. Jacob has been staying at the Łabęckis' estate—so that is where they are headed. They order a lot of vodka and dried fish for after the vodka. That is why this evening Nahman is able to record only a few sentences:

By life on earth, souls weave themselves a raiment out of their mitzvot, and after death, they will wear this raiment in the higher world. The raiments of bad people are riddled with holes.

I often picture what my raiment will look like. Many people must wonder the same, and no doubt see themselves as better, as if looking at themselves through the eyes of someone else. They see their clothing as clean and tidy, and maybe also nice—that is, in harmony.

But I already know that I won't like the looks of myself in heaven's mirrors.

Then, with his usual force, Jacob comes in to where he is and takes him back out. They're going to celebrate.

When the baptisms begin, Nahman has Wajgełe and his little daughter sent for. He waits for them by the city gate, looking into every cart that enters, until finally he finds them: with Wajgełe are her mother and sister. The child is lying in a basket, covered in the thinnest baby blanket. Nahman rushes to pull it down from over the infant's face—he is scared she might suffocate. The little girl has a tiny, scrunched-up face, her teeny-tiny fists clenched by her mouth. They are the size of walnuts. Waj-gełe, flushed and full of milk, pleased, gazes at her husband in triumph. He has never seen her this way before.

The young mother doesn't even notice the luxuriousness of Nahman's room. On the carved backs of chairs she hangs blankets and diapers. They sleep in the vast bed with the child between them, and Nahman feels that from now on everything is going to go well, that they have turned the crucial corner. That even the seventh point had to be made.

He says to Wajgełe:

"Your name is Sofia."

For the child, he chooses the name Rebecca, Rivka, just like the mother of the biblical Jacob, that will be her secret ancient name. The one she will take when she is baptized, however, is Agnieszka. Wajgełe signs up for lessons in Catholicism with the other women, but she is so focused on the child that nothing else can interest her. She can barely cross herself.

## Father Mikulski's bills and the market of Christian names

The whole burden of maintaining the newcomers camping out on the streets of Lwów has fallen on Father Mikulski. He expends thirty-five ducats on them every week. Fortunately it is his niece, a woman not much younger than he is, resourceful and clever, who keeps in tight order his court expenditures and the money he spends on his neophytes, as he strives to call them, avoiding the word *converts*. Everyone knows her at market. When she is purchasing some fresh alimentation, no one dares haggle over anything with her. The city is also helping where it can, and local people have pitched in. Peasants have been observed sharing what they've been able to grow in their vegetable gardens. This villager in the four-cornered cap with the feather and the brown felt coat brought in a cart of young green apples and is dropping them directly into women's aprons and men's hats. Someone brought a cart of watermelons and several baskets of cucumbers. Nunneries take in women and their daughters, providing them with room and board. For the nuns this is a major challenge, as the number of sisters doubles and triples, and there are also those who spit on the Jewish women. The monks feed several dozen men per monastery. They mostly serve pea soup and bread.

Just before the baptism in Lwów, something like a market of Christian names emerges, where the name of highest value is Marianna. The name is in honor of Maria Anna Brühl, the wife of the king's chief minister, who has been a generous supporter of the Contra-Talmudists. But they also say it's the cleverest name—it contains within it both Mary, the mother of Christ, and Anne, Christ's grandmother. Besides, it sounds good, like a nursery rhyme: Marianna, Marianna. So a lot of girls and young women want to be Marianna.

The daughters of Srol Mayorkowicz of Busk have already divvied up names amongst themselves. Shima turns into Victoria, Elia into Salomea, Freyna becomes Róża, Masha is Tekla, and Miriam Maria. Esther takes a long time to choose her name and finally resigns herself to Teresa.

In this way, it is as if there are now two versions of every person, all having doubles by different names. Srol Mayorkowicz, the son of Mayorek and Masha of Korolówka, becomes Mikołaj Piotrowski. His wife Beyla is Barbara Piotrowska.

It is widely known that some will receive their godparents' last names. Moshe of Podhajce, who knows Her Ladyship Łabęcka well and has done business with her husband, will take the name Łabęcki. And since this wiry, intelligent rabbi has imagination and aplomb, and is the best-versed of everyone in Kabbalah, he understands the strength words and names have. He takes his first name after unfaithful Thomas. He will be called Tomasz Podhajecki-Łabęcki. His toddler sons, David and Solomon, will be Joseph Bonaventura and Casimir Simon Łabęcki.

But not all the nobles are so eager to give away their names. Count Dzieduszycki, for instance, is not as inclined to debase his own name as Łabęcki was. He will be godfather to Old Hirsh, Reb Sabbatai of Lanckoroń, and his wife, Hayah, née Shorr. Hayah is all gray now. Gray curls

pop out from under her cap, and her face is pale gray, though her extraordinary beauty remains. Does this arrogant aristocrat in his English
tailcoat—a thing never before seen in these parts and that makes him
look like a heron—know he will be baptizing a prophetess?

"Take something simple, easy, rather than burdening yourselves with
my name. Since you're all redheaded," he says to Hirsh, "why not choose
Rudnicki, doesn't that sound good? Or since you're from Lanckoroń,
maybe simply Lanckoroński? That sounds like a prince's name."

So they hesitate about whether to become Rudnickis or Lanckorońskis,
but the fact is it's all the same to them. Neither of them seems to fit Old
Hirsh. He stands in his brown caftan, in the fur-lined hat that he never
takes off, even in the summer, with his long beard and shaded face. He
does not look particularly happy.

Also valued high on this stock exchange is the name Franciszek, or
Francis, and one-third of the newly baptized members of the male sex will
become Franciszek—they say it is in honor of Franciszek Rzewuski, who
agreed to be the godfather of Jacob Frank himself and has put in a pretty
penny for the process, too. But that's not entirely exact. The real reason
the name of the Assisi saint is so popular, as the priests discover in performing the baptisms, along with the ever-inquisitive Father Mikulski, it
that Franciszek sounds a little bit like Frank—like Jacob Frank, their
fearless leader.

It is evening on Friday in the Halickie Przedmieście. The late-setting sun
still drenches the roofs in orange, and people who are sitting in little
groups suddenly begin to feel uncomfortable. A strange and shameful silence follows. The crowd, who had been noisy half an hour ago as they
gathered around yesterday's bonfires, amongst rotten wicker carts stuffed
with baskets and quilts and tethering several goats, has hushed. They look
at the ground, their fingers playing with the fringes of their scarves.

A man's voice suddenly begins to sing the Shema, but the others instantly quiet him.

The Queen of the Shabbat passes over their heads, not even grazing
them, and travels straight into the Jewish quarter on the other side of
town.

## Of what happens to Father Chmielowski in Lwów

"Do you recognize me, Reverend Father?" some young man calls out to Father Chmielowski, who has just arrived in Lwów.

The priest looks at him closely, but does not recognize him, though he has the unpleasant sensation that he has encountered this boy somewhere before. Can his memory be failing him? Who could it be? Then he has it on the tip of his tongue—but the beard and the Jewish attire confuse him.

"I was your interpreter when you went to see the Shorrs several years ago."

The priest shakes his head—he doesn't remember.

"I am Hryćko. You know, in Rohatyn . . . ," says the boy, with a light Ruthenian lilt.

And suddenly the priest remembers the young interpreter. But there is something here he doesn't understand. He is missing a front tooth, but then he has these breeches, this kapota . . . "Mother of God, why are you dressed like a Jew?" he asks.

Hryćko looks away, up at the roofs, probably regretting having started this spontaneous conversation with the priest. He would like to tell him everything that has happened in his life, but at the same time, he is afraid to speak.

"Are you still with the Shorrs?" the vicar forane prods him.

"Oh, well, Shorr is a great man. Learned. He has money . . ." He waves his hand in resignation, as if the amount of money in question exceeded the very possibility of counting. "But what could be strange about that, Good Father, since he is like a father to me and my brother?"

"For heaven's sake! How stupid you are!" Father Chmielowski looks around, frightened, to check whether anyone can see them. Yes, yes, the whole city can see them. "Have you gone completely mad? He ought not to have taken you in—you, Christian souls—but rather reported you as orphans, and then the way of orphans would you have gone. What will it look like! I ought not to care, since you are Orthodox, but all the same, you're Christians."

"Sure, and we would have ended up in some church orphanage,"

Hryćko says angrily, and suddenly raises his eyes to the priest. "But you're not going to rat us out to anyone, are you, Father? For what? To what end? We're good there with them. My brother is learning to read and write. He cooks with the women because he's kind of a feygele." He giggles. Father Chmielowski raises an eyebrow: he doesn't understand.

From the crowd a girl emerges and starts to come up to Hryćko, but seeing he's talking with a priest, she retreats in some alarm. She is young, thin, with a big, pregnant belly. And unmistakably Jewish.

"Christ Almighty . . . So you are not only a Jewish hireling, but also newly wed to a Jewess! Holy Mother of God! People have lost their lives for far less!"

The priest does not know what to say, so surprised is he by these revelations, so the clever boy takes advantage of his surprise and keeps talking in a half whisper, almost directly into the Father's ear.

"Now we have Turkish business—over the Dniester to Moldavia and into Wallachia we venture. The trade isn't bad—the best is vodka. Over the river the kingdom of the Turk is Muslim, but there are still many Christians there, too, and they buy the good vodka from us. Besides, in their book, the Al-Quran, it says they are not allowed to drink wine. Wine! But not a word about vodka," explains Hryćko.

"Do you not know that this is a deadly sin? That you are a Jew . . ." The priest finally comes to. And then he adds quietly, in a whisper, leaning into the boy's ear: "You could face trial, my son."

Hryćko smiles, and the priest thinks it's an exceptionally stupid smile.

"But Father, you won't go telling, this is like confession."

"Lord Almighty . . . ," repeats the priest, and feels a tingling sensation on his face, from his nerves.

"Don't go telling on us, Father. In Rohatyn I've been with the Shorrs as good as always, since the Flood. People have forgotten what and how. What's the sense in going on about it now. Now all of us are going to the Lord Jesus and the Holy Virgin together anyway . . ."

Suddenly the priest remembers what all these Jewish crowds are here for, and he understands the paradoxical situation of this boy with the bashed-out tooth. They are going to be baptized now, after all, so that he will have to become what he was, stand in place, while they cross over to where he is of their own accord. He tries clumsily to express this, but Hryćko says mysteriously:

"It's not the same."

Then he disappears into the crowd.

The vicar forane Benedykt Chmielowski has chosen a pretty bad moment to come to Lwów on business.

From all angles come carriages and carts filled with Jews, Christian children running after them with a shriek, while residents of Lwów stand in the streets and look on in amazement, wondering what's going to happen next. A townswoman bumps into him, and, trying to explain and excuse herself, she tries to kiss him on the hand, but she can't in her rush, so she just says over her shoulder as she runs on: "They're going to baptize the Jews!"

"Shabbitarians," shout individual voices, but they get tripped up on that difficult word, and so it stays in motion, traveling from mouth to mouth, until its awkward angularity softens and straightens out. "Shabby-charlatans," someone tries, but that doesn't work, either. How to chant that, how to shout it? Suddenly the word comes back from the other side smoother and simpler, like a stone the water has been toying with for years: Shalbotels, Shalbotels, cries that side of the street, but the other is already calling: Ne'er-do-wells, ne'er-do-wells. The people who walk amidst these rows of insults, for these words are meant to be insults, seem to hear but don't understand clearly what has been said. Perhaps they just can't recognize themselves in this chanted Polish.

The priest can't get Hryćko out of his mind, and the chasm of his memory, which holds everything he encounters, everything his eyes run across and his ears overhear, goes back to the old days, back to the beginning of the century when a Radziwiłł—Karol perhaps—issued a regulation that Jews could not take Christians into their service. All mixed marriages were forbidden once and for all. Which is why it was such a great scandal when in 1716 or 1717 (the priest was then in the midst of his novitiate with the Jesuits) it turned out that two Christian women had converted to the religion of the Jews and moved into Jewish quarters. One of them was already a widow, and the daughter—Father Benedykt remembers this part well—of some Orthodox priest named Ochryd of Vitebsk, and she with great stubbornness defended her conversion and showed no remorse about it. The second one was a very young girl from Leżajsk who out of love converted to Judaism and went after her beloved. When they were both arrested, they burned the older woman at the stake, while the younger was beheaded by sword. That's how those wretches wound up. The priest remembers that the penalty was much milder for the women's husbands. They each got a hundred lashes and besides having to cover the costs of the trial were furthermore required to gift the churches wax and tallow. Today no one would punish this by death, thinks Father Benedykt, but the scandal would still be great. But—on the other hand—who would concern himself with someone like Hryćko, who would take an interest in him? And yet. Would it not be better for his immortal soul if someone did turn him in? That is a nasty thought, and the priest has already chased it out of his mind. The accounts are in the black: even if one converts in that direction, in just a little while hundreds, or maybe even thousands, will convert the other, proper way.

Since he can't get to the bishop to discuss his matter, he would like to use this stay in Lwów to have some of his stories printed and bound, in order to be able to send them out to friends—especially Bishop Załuski, and of course Mrs. Drużbacka, that they might think with fondness of his humble name. He has collected the most interesting ones along with several little poems, and one especially for her, but he is embarrassed to take it into the Jesuits' printer, where he had his *Athens* printed a few years ago, so instead he has found Golczewski's modest workshop. He stands in front of its small, humble window and pretends he is reading the pamphlets spread out in it, wondering what to say when he goes inside.

The crowd is jostling for shade at the gates, there is nowhere for them to put their feet, it's hot, so the priest retreats into the little courtyard of a two-story tenement house with a dark facade. He checks to see if his bag is in order, if the documents testifying to his innocence are still there. And he reminds himself again that today is August 15, 1759, and that it is a day of remembrance for Saint Louis, King of France. Since he was a peace-loving king, Father Chmielowski starts to believe that he will be able to solve his own problem peacefully that day.

A commotion reaches him from the market square, something like a collective sigh. Taking very small steps, breathing heavily, he goes out into the sun and manages to push his way out almost to the street. Now he can see what has so amazed his fellow onlookers—a town coach drawn by six horses, each of a different color, and alongside the carriage twelve riders richly attired in the Turkish fashion. The carriage rides around the market square and returns to the Halickie Przedmieście, where the Jews have spread out their carts. There he notices a tent with a striped roof, colorful, surrounded by Jews. And suddenly he has a kind of revelation in the matter of the runaway Jan. He is still owed something for those books he's kept around his chambers for Old Shorr. The priest rushes back out of the heaving and excited crowd, smiling at everyone who passes him by.

## At the printing press of Paweł Józef Golczewski, His Majesty the King's preferred typographer

In Lwów, Armenian townswomen differ from Polish women by the size of their bonnets. Armenian townswomen wear them very large, finished in a green pleat right by their faces, as well as a ribbon over their foreheads, while Polish women wear white bonnets, starched and smaller, though these lure the eyes with their collars, or rather, goffered ruffs, beneath which hang another two or three strings of beads.

Katarzyna Deymowa, postmistress, wife of the head of the royal post in Lwów, also wears a Polish bonnet and a ruff. But no necklaces, since she is in mourning. Just now she is walking at a breakneck pace, as she tends to do, through the Halickie Przedmieście, and she cannot get over the crowd they've got going. And all of them dressed in dark colors, murmuring in their language, foreigners—Jews. Women with children in their arms and clinging onto their skirts, skinny men absorbed in debates, all standing around in little groups, the heat starting to beat down on their heads. Wherever there is still a little patch of ground free, they sit right on the grass and eat; some townswomen distribute loaves of bread they carry around in baskets, and pickles, and blocks of cheese. Over everything there are flies, those brazen, intrusive August flies that get into your eyes and settle on your food. Some boys carry two baskets of large nuts.

It all disgusts Deymowa, until her servant Marta brings the news that these are the Jews who have come to be baptized. Then it is as if Katarzyna Deymowa had taken off a pair of glasses she hadn't even realized she'd been wearing. Suddenly she is all sympathy—Holy Mother! come to be baptized! Those who speak of the end of the world have it right. It has come to this: The Lord Jesus's greatest enemies are going to be baptized. Their sinful stubbornness has softened; it has dawned on them at last that there can be no salvation beyond that of the holy Catholic Church, and now, as shamefaced children, they are finally ready to be on our side. And although they still look different, strange, in those kapotas of theirs, with their beards down to their waists, pretty soon they'll be just like us.

She looks at a family of girls, a woman with a child at her breast just climbing down awkwardly from her cart, the driver chasing her off because he has to take the cart back right away to pick up others on the outskirts of town. The bundle she had on her back falls down, and a few faded rags and a single string of beads, small and dimmed, tumble out of it onto the ground. The woman gathers them back up in embarrassment, as if she had suddenly bared her most inaccessible secrets to the eyes of the world. As Deymowa passes her, a little boy suddenly runs up—he looks like he might be six or seven—and looking at her with smiling eyes, very pleased with himself, he says, "Praised be our Lord Jesus!" She responds automatically, but solemnly, too: "Forever and ever, amen." And her hand flies up to her heart, and her eyes fill with tears. She squats down beside the boy, grabs him by the wrists, and he looks her straight in the eye, still smiling, that little rascal.

"What is your name?"

The boy responds resolutely in slightly shaky Polish:

"Hilelek."

"That's nice . . ."

"And then I am also named Wojciech Majewski."

Now Deymowa can't hold back her tears.

"Would you like a pretzel?"

"Yes, a pretzel."

She tells this later to her younger sister, Golczewski's widow, in the workshop of her brother-in-law, may he rest in peace, under a lovely signboard made of iron.

". . . This little baby Jew who tells me 'Praised be our Lord Jesus,' have you ever seen such marvelous things?" Deymowa breaks down and starts crying again. Since her own husband's death not long ago, she has cried often—daily—and everything has seemed unbearably sad to her, so that a great sorrow for the whole world often overwhelms her. And just underneath that sorrow is an anger that crosses over oddly easily into sympathy, and suddenly in the face of the enormity of the misfortunes of the world, she can only throw up her hands, and all of it brings her to tears.

Both sisters are widows, but Golczewski's widow bears it better, having taken over her husband's printshop that tries to compete with the big Jesuit printer's by taking sundry orders of all kinds. Right now she is busy talking with some priest and only half listening to her older sister.

"Here, Your Ladyship, look!" He hands her a rather unevenly printed appeal signed by Primate Łubieński, in which he calls on the szlachta and the townspeople to become godparents to the Contra-Talmudists.

"Contra-Talmudists," repeats Deymowa seriously, while her sister adds: "Ne'er-do-wells."

Father Chmielowski is insisting on printing a small run of his tales. Golczewska doesn't want to interfere, but printing only a few copies will cost him dearly, she explains, whereas if he prints more, the cost per copy will come out to about the same. But the priest is discombobulated and can't quite make up his mind. He explains that this is only for a name-day gift, and he doesn't need that many copies, as it's really just for one person.

"Then why don't you write it out nicely in your own hand, Father? Maybe in some amaranthine or golden ink?"

But the priest says that only print lends the appropriate seriousness to each word.

"The handwritten word is too *mangled* somehow, while print speaks loud and clear," he explains.

Golczewska, the typographer, leaves him deep in thought and turns once more to her sister.

There might not be two such different sisters anywhere in Podolia.

Deymowa is tall and stout, with light-colored skin and blue eyes. Gol-czewska, meanwhile, is petite and has dark hair, grayed wisps of which work their way out from under her bonnet, even though she is barely forty. Deymowa is better off, which is why she is dressed so nicely, in a richly pleated mantle over many starched petticoats that took thirty cu-bits of black silk to make. Over this she has thrown a lightweight linen jacket that reaches her elbows, also black—after all, she was widowed re-cently. She wears a snow-white bonnet on her head. Next to her, her younger sister, girded by an apron stained with printer's ink, looks like a servant. Yet they understand each other perfectly without speaking. They read the primate's appeal and exchange glances full of meaning.

In Primate Łubieński's appeal, it says that each godparent must fur-nish his godchild with the appropriate Polish attire, as well as maintain him not only until his baptism but until he returns home. The sisters know each other so well and have been through so much together that they don't even particularly need to get into a discussion of this topic.

After much hesitation, the priest finally agrees to a bigger print run. He points out in a quarrelsome voice that the title is to be in boldface, and

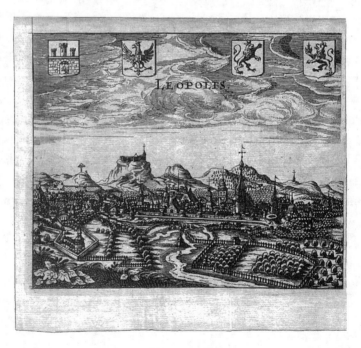

that they are not to stint on space for it. And the date, and the place, without fail: Leopolis, Augustus 1759.

## Of proper proportions

Pinkas could not restrain himself and went out at once. He flits past buildings down a narrow band of shadow and glances furtively at the carriage that is just pulling up to the market square. Instantly a crowd surrounds it. Pinkas is afraid to look at it, and when he does force himself to raise his gaze, the sight absorbs him completely and takes his breath away, even though every little detail feels like a grain of salt rubbed into his pain.

The man who emerges from the carriage is tall and well built, and to his height is added a slim Turkish hat, which feels like an organic element of his stature. Dark, wavy hair pops out from under his hat, softening somewhat the emphatic features of a rather harmonious face. His gaze is insolent—so it seems to Pinkas—and he is looking slightly upward, so that you can see a bit of the whites at the bottom of his eyes, as though he were about to faint. He casts his eyes around the people standing about by his carriage and over the heads of the rest of the crowd. Pinkas sees the movement of his prominent, nicely shaped lips. He is saying something to the people, laughing—and now his even white teeth gleam. His face gives the impression of youth, and his dark beard seems to conceal even more of that youth, maybe even dimples. He looks both authoritative and childlike. Pinkas senses how this person might appeal to women, and not only to women, but also to men—to everyone—for he is extremely charming. This makes Pinkas hate him even more. When Frank stands up straight, other people reach up to his beard. His Turkish coat, greenish blue and adorned with purple appliqué, shows off his powerful shoulders. The brocade shimmers in the sun. This person is like a peacock among chickens, or like a ruby among rocks. Pinkas is surprised, astonished—he didn't expect Frank would make such a big impression on him, and he cannot bear the fact that somehow he actually likes this man.

Aha, thinks Pinkas, but he must be frivolous, since he is wearing so much gold. And no doubt he is stupid, since he's so impressed by such a carriage, although they call him Wise Jacob. Sometimes beauty is harnessed to evil's interests, becoming a trick for the eye, a fake to stupefy the crowd.

When Frank walks, people make way to let him pass, holding their breath. Those too shy to speak reach out to touch him.

Pinkas tries to remember how he imagined him. He can't. Purplish azure has filled up his brain. He feels sick. Even when he turns away from this proud march of Jacob Frank's through the delighted crowd, and spits out of forced disgust, he still has him in his mind's eye.

Late at night, close to midnight, Pinkas can't sleep and tries to calm his mind by writing up a report to take to the kahal. They can add it to their file. The written word lasts forever, while colors—even the brightest ones—fade. The written word is sacred, and every letter will eventually go back to God, nothing will be forgotten. So what, then, is an image? Nothing. A vivid void. Even the brightest colors will dissipate like so much smoke.

This thought gives him strength, and he suddenly envisions what strike him as the true and proper proportions. For what is bearing, or charm, or a resounding voice? They are but raiments! In the bright light of the sun everything looks different, but in the dark of night, all that brightness pales, and you can see better what it conceals.

With a flourish he puts down the first words: "I saw with my own eyes . . ." Now he tries to be truthful, faithful, forget about the coat and carriage, and he even pictures Jacob naked. He sticks to that thought. He sees skinny, crooked legs and the rare hair across a sunken chest, one shoulder higher than the other. He dips his pen in ink and holds it aloft over the paper for a second, until a dangerously large black drop has gathered at the end; then he carefully shakes it off into the bottle and writes:

> He was in fact rather horrible, ugly and contorted, coarse.
> His nose was crooked, probably from being struck. His hair was
> dull and matted, and his teeth were black.

In writing "his teeth were black," Pinkas crosses an invisible line, but in his passion, he doesn't realize it.

He did not look human at all, rather more like a demon or an animal. He moved about violently, and in these movements, there was not a drop of grace.

He dips the pen back in the well and starts thinking—what kind of habit is this, to think with a damp pen, it will no doubt result in a blot—but no, the pen leaps at the paper, and in a frenzy scratches out:

> He spoke seemingly in many languages, but the truth is that in none of them was he able to articulate a single thing or write sensibly. Thus when he did speak aloud, he emitted a sound that was highly unpleasant to the ear, a high-pitched screeching, and only those who knew him well could really understand what he was after.
>
> In addition, he was never really educated anywhere, so he only knows what he has heard here and there, and his knowledge is riddled with gaps. He seems to be acquainted only with fairy tales, the kind you tell to children, and his followers believe in these stories without exception.

By the time he is finished, it really seems to Pinkas that he saw not a person, but a three-headed beast.

## The baptism

On September 17, 1759, after a solemn mass, Jacob Frank is baptized. He takes the name Joseph. The baptism is performed by the metropolitan of Lwów, Samuel Głowiński of Głowno. His godparents, meanwhile, are the not-quite-thirty-year-old Franciszek Rzewuski, elegant, dressed after the French fashion, and Maria Anna Brühl. Jacob Frank bows his head, and the holy water wets his hair, then flows over his face.

After Jacob goes Krysa, dressed like a member of the szlachta, in the traditional style of the Polish nobility, and in this new costume, his asymmetrical face seems dignified somehow. Now he is Bartłomiej Walenty Krysiński; his godparents are Count Szeptycki and Countess Miączyńska.

Behind him stands a group of people who follow him one by one up to the altar. Godparents in ornate ceremonial attire trade places with one another. A pipe organ plays, making the tall, beautifully vaulted cathedral ceiling seem even higher—somewhere up there, just past the steep arches, there is a heaven into which all those baptized will now be admitted. The tart scent of the tall yellow flowers that decorate the altar mixes with the incense into an exquisite scent, as if the finest Eastern perfume has been sprayed into the church.

Now come some well-dressed younger people, their hair cut at the chin like pageboys'—these are Jacob Frank's nephews, Paweł, Jan, and Antoni, and a fourth, son of Hayim of Jezierzany, now Ignacy Jezierzański, nervously crumples his hat in his hands. There is a moment's silence when the organ pauses for the tired organist to page through his sheet music to get to the next song. For a moment, the papers' rustling resounds around the church, otherwise so quiet you could hear a pin drop. Then the music bursts forth again, solemn and sad, and this is how Franciszek Wołowski—until recently Shlomo Shorr, Elisha's son—goes up to the altar with his own young son, seven-year-old Wojciech. And after him his father, the eldest of the Frankists, dignified, sixty-year-old Elisha Shorr, supported by his daughters-in-law, Rozalia and Róża; he has never fully recovered from being beaten. And after them goes Hayim Turczynek, now Kapliński, and Barbara, a Wallachian, who, aware of her own beauty, allows herself to be admired by curious eyes. It is clear to everyone that the people who bow their heads before the metropolitan's damp fingers make up one big family that branches out in all directions, like a tree.

At least that is what Father Mikulski is thinking as he watches them, trying to glean proofs of blood relationship from their appearance and posture. Yes, they are baptizing a single giant family, a family that might be called Podolian-Wallachian-Turkish. Now, nicely dressed and taking things seriously, there is something new to them—a dignity, a confidence they didn't have even yesterday when he saw them on the city's streets. Suddenly he is frightened by this novel guise of theirs. Soon they will put out their hands for noble titles, since of course a Jew who converts has the right to such things. If he pays enough. The priest is overwhelmed by a doubt that verges on outright fear—that here they are letting in all these foreign, impenetrable faces, although their intentions are muddled, vague. It feels to him like the whole street is pouring into the cathedral now, and that they will keep going up to the altar, one by one, until evening, and that even then, there will be no end in sight.

It isn't true that everyone is present. Nahman, for instance, is not. Instead, he is sitting with his little daughter, who has suddenly taken ill with diarrhea and a high fever. Wajgełe tries to force-feed her milk, but to no avail, and soon the features of her face start to sharpen, and on the morning of September 18, she dies, and Nahman says they have to keep it a secret. The next night they hold a hurried funeral.

## Of Jacob Frank's shaved beard, and the new face that emerges from underneath it

Hana Frank, who has just arrived from Ivanie to be baptized, does not recognize her husband. She stands before him and sees a face that seems newly born, with pale, delicate skin around the mouth, lighter than the skin on his forehead and cheeks, dark lips, the lower one slightly turned down, and a soft chin with a little indentation in the middle. Only now does Hana see the mole on the left side, under his right ear, like a birthmark. He smiles, and now his bright white teeth draw attention. He is a completely different man. Wittel, who shaved him, retreats with the washbasin full of foam.

"Say something," Hana urges him. "I'll know you by your voice."

Jacob laughs loudly, tossing his head back as he does.

Hana is shocked. The Jacob who stands before her is a boy, a new person, practically naked, all of him there on the surface, defenseless. She touches him lightly with her hand, and her hand discovers the astonishing smoothness of that skin. Hana feels an obscure anxiety, unpleasant, and she cannot restrain a violent sob.

Faces should remain in hiding, in the shadows, she thinks, like deeds, like words.

## 21.

### Of the plague that descends upon Lwów
### in the autumn of 1759

Not so long ago, people believed that the plague was brought about by
an unfortunate constellation of the planets, thinks Asher, as he strips
naked and wonders what he ought to do with his clothes. Throw them
out? If they've absorbed any effluvia from the infected, he might well
risk spreading it about the house. And nothing could be worse than
introducing a plague into his own home.

The weather in Lwów has changed suddenly, going from hot and dry
to warm and humid. Wherever there is even a little earth or rotting wood,
mushrooms pop up. Fog hovers every morning in town like thick sour
cream, undisturbed until people come out into the streets, when it begins
to lift.

Today he pronounced four dead and made his rounds of the afflicted;
he knows there will be more of them. They all have the same symptoms:
diarrhea, stomachache, progressive weakening.

He recommends drinking large quantities of fresh water or—better
yet—herbs brewed in boiling water, but since his patients are mostly
camped out on the street, they have nowhere to heat water. The worst
affected are the Jewish neophytes. They hurry to be baptized, believing
that once that happens, they'll never get sick and never die. Just today,

Asher saw several patients like this, two of them children, every one of them with a Hippocratic face: sharpened features, sunken eyes, wrinkles. Life must have a certain mass to it, since when it ebbs, it makes a person's body resemble a dried-out leaf. He went from the Halickie Przedmieście through the market square and saw the city closing in on itself, shutters battened down, streets emptied, and he thinks the market might not even take place now, unless some peasants come in from the country, not yet aware of the plague. Whoever is still healthy and has the means will leave Lwów.

Asher tries to picture how the illness passes from one person into another; it must be that it takes the form of some dense, vague fog, a fug, or a virulent vapor. These miasmas, getting into the bloodstream from inhaled air, infect and inflame it. Which is why Asher, summoned today to a certain bourgeois household where the lady of the house had fallen ill, positioned himself next to a window through which air was entering, while the sick woman lay whence the air was exiting. The family tried to insist that he let her blood, but Asher is against this procedure—some people it greatly weakens, particularly women, even if it does reduce the virulence of the plague in the bloodstream.

Asher has also heard of infectious germs, something along the lines of little insects that cling to materials like fur, hemp, silk, wool, and feathers, scattering off them at the slightest movement, getting into the blood through the lungs and poisoning it. Their strength is dependent upon air—when it is clean, they collapse and perish. As to how long a germ can last, medical opinion is that in things kept in a cellar or a dungeon, it can survive up to fifteen years; in ventilated spaces, thirty days at most. The same is true when it is in a human being—it can't last longer than thirty days. Yet in the main, people blame the pestilence on God's wrath over the sins of man. And that applies to everyone—Jews, Christians, and Turks. Divine vexation. Solomon Wolff, the doctor from Berlin with whom Asher corresponds, says that pestilence is never endemically European, but is always imported from other parts of the world; its cradle is Egypt, from where it tends to make its way to Stamboul, and from there to spread through Europe. Thus those Wallachian Jews must have brought the plague to Lwów when they came here to be baptized. At least that's what people have been saying.

Now they're all counting on winter to save them, since freezing is the antithesis of rot, and therefore serious illness should vanish or at least weaken tremendously throughout the winter months.

Asher does not allow Gitla to go out of the house, saying she is to sit with Samuel by the windows with the curtains drawn.

One evening, two men show up at Asher's—one old and one young. The older one is dressed in a long black coat and a cap. His beard unfurls majestically over his ample belly. He has a sad and open face and piercing blue eyes that fix on Asher. The younger one, who seems to be here out of respect for the other man, is tall and heavyset. His eyelashes and eyebrows are almost transparent, and against his pale complexion, his brown eyes look like glass beads. Standing in the doorway, the older man gives a sigh full of meaning.

"The esteemed doctor," he begins in Yiddish, "is in possession of a particular thing that does not belong to him."

"How interesting," answers Asher, "since I have absolutely no recollection of ever appropriating anything at all."

"I am Pinkas ben Zelik of Kozowa, a rabbi. And this is my nephew, Yankiel. We have come for Gitla, my daughter."

Stunned, Asher says nothing. Only after a moment does he regain his senses and his voice.

"You're saying she is the *thing* to which you were referring? She's a living being—not a thing."

"Yes, yes, that's just the way people talk," says Pinkas good-naturedly. He peers over Asher's shoulder into his home. "Perhaps we could come in for a word."

Asher reluctantly lets them come inside.

"When you are a doctor, all you see is human suffering," says Pinkas, his father-in-law, let us call him, when on the following day Asher Rubin is once more at the hospital among the victims of the plague. "But life is a great force; we stand on the side of life. What has happened cannot un-happen."

Pinkas pretends he's wound up here by accident. The lower half of his face is covered by a piece of white cloth, which will supposedly protect him from effluvia. The stench here is terrible; the hospital has become less a place of healing than a place to die, and the sick are being laid out on the floor now, since the hospital is small.

Asher doesn't say a word.

Pinkas says, over his head, as though not even addressing him, "The Vienna kahal needs a doctor, and in particular, an expert on eyes. They're starting a Jewish hospital. Asher Rubin could take his wife and"—here he falls silent for a moment, then goes on—"children and get out of here. Everything bad that has happened would pass into oblivion. A wedding would take place; all would be repaired."

After another pause, he adds in a tone of encouragement to conversation:

"This is all because of those unfaithful dogs."

When he says, "unfaithful dogs," his voice grows hoarse, and Asher looks up at him in spite of himself.

"Go away from here, both of you. We'll return to this subject. Do not touch anything. I need to see a patient now."


This kind of death is quick and merciful. First your head hurts, then nausea and stomachaches, followed by diarrhea that never lets up. The body dries out, the person fades from view, loses strength and, finally, consciousness. It takes two or three days for death to come. First a child died, and then that child's siblings, then the mother, and finally the father—Asher watched it all. That's how it started. From that family the plague spread to the rest.

The man of the household he is visiting right now has dropsy. God-fearing Jews, these people give him a knowing look as they ask about the situation in town, as though proud that all they have is dropsy. A woman in a slanted bonnet raises her eyebrows significantly: it's the curse, she says, it's that powerful herem cast upon the renegades. It works. God punishes traitors who befoul their own nest, those heretics, those fiends.

"His good luck was bound to give out, it's all devil's work—hence that money, those carriages with all those horses, those ermines. Now God has made an example out of him. His renegades are dying of the plague, one after the other. That's their punishment," she murmurs.

Asher turns his head away from her and directs his gaze at the curtains by the window, faded and coated in dust, so that their pattern is barely visible—they're just the color of dust, that's all. He thinks of Pinkas, his sort-of father-in-law, and he wonders what would happen if hate could transform into a plague. Is that how herem works? Asher often sees how a cursed person quickly becomes defenseless, weak, ill, and when the curse is taken off him, he gets well.

But Asher would sooner let himself be infected than believe in such things. He knows that everything in fact comes down to water—just one contaminated well is enough to kill a whole city. The sick drink the water, and then their infected waste travels to other water supplies. Asher goes to the town hall and presents his observations—it must have some connection to the wells and to the water. They agree with him—him, a Jew—and order the wells to be closed, and indeed, the plague does seem to die down a bit. But then it explodes again, stronger than ever, having evidently migrated to some other water sources. They can't very well shut down all the wells in Lwów. They can only hope that some of the population, for whatever reasons, will be immune to this plague. Some people do ail only briefly, and only slightly, and then their health comes back of its own accord. Others simply don't fall ill, as if they are invincible.

And finally, in all this bleak confusion, Asher sees the anointed one; his eyes can take their fill of him now. Since his initial appearance in Lwów at the end of August, he has been spotted often—either in his sumptuous carriage or walking among the camps of his emaciated followers. He is obviously not afraid. In spite of the warm weather, he wears a tall Turkish hat and a Turkish coat of a lovely green color, like water in a pond or the glass used to make vessels for medicaments. He looks like an enormous green dragonfly that flits from one place to the next. When he approaches one of the afflicted, Asher steps aside without a word. Frank lays hands on the forehead of the patient and closes his own eyes. The patient is doubtless in seventh heaven, if he's still conscious. Recently one of the sick Jews went on his own to a church and demanded to be baptized. As soon as the rite had been hastily performed, he got better. Or that is what they say in the Halickie Przedmieście. At the synagogue they say something else: that immediately after the baptism, the renegade died.

Asher has to admit that Frank is a handsome man. Perhaps that is what Samuel will look like someday. He wouldn't have anything against it. But it isn't Frank's looks that give him his power. Asher knows such people, many magnates have it, the nobly born—that inexplicable self-confidence, founded in nothing, or perhaps in the existence of some internal center of gravity that makes the person feel like a king in any situation.

Since that man has been in town, Gitla has not known a moment of peace. She gets dressed, but she ends up not leaving the house. She stands a moment in front of the door, and then she takes off her things and stays. When Asher comes home, he finds her lying on the settee. Her belly is big again, round and hard. Her whole body seems slightly swollen, unwieldy. She is always in a bad mood and insists that she will die in childbirth. She is angry with him—without him, and without this latest pregnancy, she would have gone back to her father or run off with that Frank again. As she lies in the dark on the settee, she must be imagining all the possible versions of her life she won't be able to experience.

When it turns chilly in the latter half of October, the plague does not pass, but instead gains momentum. The Halickie Przedmieście has been deserted ever since housing was found for the newcomers among the neighbors, around the monasteries and in aristocrats' country manors. There are daily baptisms at the cathedral and in the churches of Lwów—there is actually a line. Whenever anyone dies, a lot of other people want to be baptized right away.

When those who have already been baptized continue to die, Jacob stops appearing on the streets and healing people with the touch of his long fingers. Some say he's gone to Warsaw to see the king, to try to obtain some land for the converts. Others say he was afraid and fled once more to Turkey.

That's what Asher thinks, his mind on the latest deaths. For instance, the Mayorkowicz family. Over the course of two days the mother, the father, and four of their daughters died in his hospital. A fifth is in the final throes, so wasted away she no longer looks like a human child, but rather like a dark specter, a phantom, while a sixth, their eldest, has suffered such despair that her hair has gone completely gray.

The Mayorkowiczes had a proper Christian funeral, with wooden coffins and places in the cemetery paid for by the city. They were buried under their new names, to which they had not had time to grow accustomed: Mikołaj Piotrowski, Barbara Piotrowska, and their daughters: Victoria, Róża, Tekla, Maria. Asher urges himself to remember: Srol Mayorkowicz, Beyla Mayorkowiczowa. As well as Shima, Freyna, Masha, Miriam.

And now, after the funeral of the Mayorkowiczes, or Piotrowskis, he is standing in the hallway of his house and slowly taking off his clothing. He rolls it into a ball and tells the maid to burn it. Death might cling to buttons, to trouser seams, to a collar. Naked, he goes into the room where Gitla is. She looks at him in astonishment and bursts out laughing. He doesn't say a word.

He does manage to save, in the end, that skinny little girl, the second Mayorkowicz daughter, Elia, now called Salomea Piotrowska. Asher keeps her in the hospital and feeds her well. At first a gruel of rice and water, and then he goes and buys her chickens and has them boiled down to broth, and he pushes pieces of meat into her mouth, little by little, in tiny bits. The girl starts to smile each time she sees him.

At the same time he writes a letter to Starosta Łabęcki, and a separate letter to the starosta's wife. Two days later he gets a response from Rohatyn saying to bring little Salomea.

Why did he not write to Rapaport, to the kahal? He did consider it. But after just a moment's reflection he realized that little Salomea would be better off at the Łabęckis' palace than in the home of wealthy Rapaport, even if—and this was unlikely—he should want to take her in.

When it comes to Jews, today they're rich and powerful, tomorrow they are poor and sorrowful; Asher has learned that much in his life.

After Hanukkah and the Christian New Year, in early January, Gitla gives birth to twin girls. In March, as the last snows are disappearing, Asher and Gitla pack up all of their belongings and their children and set out for Vienna.


## What Moliwda writes to his cousin Katarzyna Kossakowska

> O beloved and enlightened Cousin of mine,
> It is a good thing you got out of here quickly, for the plague has run completely rampant now, and the evidence of the rampages of the Lady of Death are everywhere visible.
> The most painful part of it is that the plague has taken such a liking to your wards, as there are many poor among them, and malnourished. In spite of Father Mikulski's provisions and the goodwill shown to them by many noble people, they have remained in need, and hence more susceptible to illness.
> I, too, have now packed my things, and in just a few days I shall lead Jacob and his company to Warsaw, where I hope to meet with you at once in order to go over our operations in detail. Thank you, too, for the generous honorarium for my work that you were able to collect for me from those among your acquaintances who are in a position to support us. As I understand it, the most generous among them has been the good Count Jabłonowski. I have a great deal of respect for him, as well as gratitude, altho' I am not quite convinced by the idea of a Buskian Paraguay. For your wards, my dear cousin, are hardly so gentle as the Indians of Paraguay. And they possess a religion older than our own, along with writings and customs. With all due respect, Prince Jabłonowski should have come to

Ivanie or ought to spend some time with them now in the
Halickie Przedmieście.

I will not undertake to describe to you the whole of it, for it
depresses me o'ermuch. After the death of the daughter of
Nahman (now Piotr Jakubowski), one of the first victims of the
epidemic, people started at once their talk of how this was yet
another Jewish curse upon the infidels. It kills with unheard-of
rapidity. All the water escapes the victim, and the body seems to
collapse on itself. The skin wrinkles, and the features get sharp
as a wolf's. Over just a couple of days, the person weakens and
dies. Nahman-Jakubowski, completely broken, has thrown
himself into his Kabbalah, counting and recounting something
or other, hoping he might find an explanation for his terrible
misfortune.

It is getting cold, and there is no means to help those
camping out on the streets, or the ailing. More funds, more
clothing, and more food would be helpful, particularly given
that Father Mikulski, who has been overseeing this whole
enterprise, can no longer keep up.

The doctors have begun to demand that newcomers to the
city provide evidence that they are not coming from plague-
afflicted regions, that those who are suspected of coming from
such regions be "aired out" away from the city for six weeks,
and also that plague-afflicted regions have a sufficient number
of doctors, medics, and dedicated assistants, porters, and
gravediggers. They are also calling for those having contact with
the plague-ridden to wear distinguishing insignia, for instance,
white crosses over their chests and backs. A store of funds is
needed as well, for food and medicine for the impoverished, and
the dogs and cats that run from home to home should be
removed, and every incident of pestilence should be tracked; a
quantity of little wooden houses needs to be built outside town
for the ill and those suspected of illness, along with sheds in
which to air out suspect goods. And yet, Poland being Poland,
all those demands seem to have blown over somehow, leaving
not a trace.

You, my dear, enlightened Cousin, will know what to do to
make these people comfortable. Many of them, in preparing for

their baptism, have sold off their modest belongings and can do nothing but await our mercy.

## In which Katarzyna Kossakowska dares to disturb the powerful of this world

To Jan Klemens Branicki, Hetman of the Polish-Lithuanian Commonwealth, written on the 14th of December, 1759

I am so grateful to you, my good Sir, for the Hospitality you bestowed upon me recently, while I was once again on the Road. Mościska was lovely and comfortable, I shall remember it for a long Time. And since you professed yourself at my Disposition when it came to my good Works, I now turn to you for your Consideration of the Situation I have mentioned to you. By collective Action, we the highest-born who are so closely allied, and well acquainted with that French Expression Noblesse oblige, might provide Aid and Assistance to those poor Neophytes, those Puritans of whom there is such an Abundance here in Podolia. You have no doubt heard that they are now inclined to Warsaw, where they shall request an Audience with the King (which I very much doubt they shall receive), as well as some Sort of Territory on the royal Lands to settle. Our Idea is to take them in upon our own Estates, which would be showing Christian Mercy, and the new Souls would arrive to us in this Way.

In a separate Letter, sent through Kalicki, I have already informed you, my good Sir, as to what has been happening in the Sejmik . . .

To Eustachy Potocki, my dear Brother and Artillery General of the Grand Duchy of Lithuania, written on the 14th of December, 1759

With this Post I had the Obligation of sending you a Portrait of our Father, a Responsibility I would gladly discharge were there any Guarantee about the Arrival of the Package; however, when it comes to the Post, there can never be such Certainty.

I also reiterate my Question from my last Correspondence: Have you had a Chance to consider the Question of Land for the Neophytes?

You know me and have known me all my Life, and you know perfectly well that I have never cared too much about any Persons' Fates, being rather hard, and I am quite convinced that even searching through Eyeglasses for one good and worthy, I would not find him. And yet in this Instance I see it as our Duty to help these People: they have been placed in the worst of all possible Situations; worse off than our Peasants, for they are like those Beggars we call Dziady, driven out by their own Kind, often stripped of their Property and without any Place to call their own, furthermore not particularly knowing the Language, and in many Cases finding themselves completely helpless. This is why they insist on sticking together. Were they to be parceled out to different Holdings of ours, they could live in the Christian Fashion, taking up Trades or Crafts and offending no one, and it would be our sacred Act to make them into our Likeness and accept them under the Wing of our holy Church.

To Pelagia Potocka, Wife of the Lwów Castellan, written on the 17th of December, 1759

I am loath to bother Her Nobly Virtuous Ladyship with such old-fashioned—nay, such ancient—Notions, and to pester Her Ladyship with outmoded Wishes that would not interest Her in the slightest, such as neighborly Love and mutual Goodwill. But as I do not wish to be fashionable—only reliable and sincere—I breathe a Sigh to our God who comes into our World to bestow Health and long Years, and I ask for more still: Her Ladyship's good Fortune, but this I really cannot help.

You have no doubt heard of this new Cause, which is not a fashionable one so much as a righteous one, namely, to take in neophyte Girls, once Jewish, now Christian. Starosta Łabęcki's

Wife has taken in one such little Girl. Were I not so actively
involved in orchestrating all of this, I would consider it, as well.
Such an Act gives them Hope for a better Life, and a proper
Education. Mrs. Łabęcka's Girl is very clever; with the Help of a
Tutor, she is studying Polish and French simultaneously. Mrs.
Łabęcki has been invigorated by it, and so the Benefit is
mutual . . .

## Of the trampling of coins and using a knife to make a V formation of cranes make a U-turn

The day before they leave for Warsaw, Jacob requests that the men and
women who have been chosen gather together. They wait for him for
about an hour. He comes dressed in the Turkish fashion, Hana with
him, elegant and formal. The group moves quickly toward the High
Castle, curious passersby taking them in. Jacob rushes ahead, taking
great steps and leaning forward, so that old Reb Mordke really has to
exert himself in order to keep up; he winds up bringing up the rear,
Hershel with him. Hana makes no complaint about ruining her embroidered silk slippers—she stays a step behind her husband, lifting the hem
of her long coat and watching where she sets down her feet. She knows
that Jacob knows what he is doing.

It is a strange day. The air is soft and smooth, as if they were traveling
in muslin hung from a clothesline. It smells oddly disquieting, sweet and
rotten, like something that has been forgotten and is now covered in
mold. Some of them are wearing little masks over their faces, but the
higher they climb, the more inclined they are to remove them.

Everyone understands that the plague is part of the war, that their
enemies have attacked them with it. Those whose faith is not strong
enough will die. Those who believe fervently in Jacob will never die, unless they start to doubt. Once they are well out of town, they slow down
and begin to converse, particularly those who trail at the back. They chat,
some stopping to pick up sticks to lean on, speaking more and more
boldly the farther they go, the higher they climb, confident that no spies

will make it up here, no eavesdroppers, no inquisitive secretaries, cate-chists, or mercenaries sent by nobles. They say:

"Moliwda and old Lady Kossakowska are going to try and get an au-dience in Warsaw with the king . . ."

"May God see fit to guide them in it . . ."

"If that happens, we'll get our noble titles for sure . . ."

"But we're going to ask for land, for royal land, not land belonging to nobles . . ."

"Mrs. Kossakowska doesn't know about that just yet . . ."

"We don't want to burn any bridges, but how would she hear about it . . ."

"The king will give us land. The king's lands are better than the land belonging to nobles and the church. But can we count on it?"

"Who is this king?"

"The king is honorable, and the royal word is good as gold . . ."

"It'll be land in Busk . . ."

"In Satanów . . ."

"Rohatyn is ours . . ."

"Anywhere would be good, just so long as it's . . ."

From the top of the hill they can see the whole city; by now, the trees are almost fully red and yellow, as if some vast hand had lit the earth on fire. The light is golden, honeyed, heavy, and it flows in slow waves from top to bottom, covering the gilded roofs of Lwów. And yet the city itself, seen from above, looks like a scab, a person's itchy scar. From a distance, you can't hear all the commotion and the city seems innocent, yet that is precisely where they're burying the dead right now, washing the contam-inated pavement with buckets of water. Suddenly the wind brings them the smell of woodsmoke; Jacob is quiet, and they stand this way awhile, no one bold enough to speak.

Then Jacob does a strange thing:

He drives a knife into the ground and raises his face to the sky, and they all join him in looking upward. A V formation of cranes flying over their heads loses its shape, the birds collide and start to circle high above them, chaotically. It is a sorry thing to behold. Hayah covers her face. They turn to Jacob, stunned and aghast.

"Now look," he says, and extracts the knife from the ground.

For a moment, the cranes continue to orbit in the same disorderly fashion, but then they get back into a formation that soon makes a large circle, then a larger circle, and then they move on, making their way south.

Jacob says:

"What this means is, if you forget who I am and who you are, woe is you."

He tells them to make a fire, and then, as they stand around it, without any strangers' eyes on them, without spies, they all begin to talk at once, speaking over one another. They get their new names mixed up. When Shlomo addresses Nahman by his old name, Jacob punches him in the shoulder. Those old Jewish names cannot exist for them any longer, now there are only these Christian names—let none get them wrong any longer.

"Who are you?" Jacob asks Hayim of Warsaw, who is standing next to him.

"Mateusz Matuszewski," answers Hayim, abjectly.

"And that's his wife, Eva. There is no Wittel anymore," Nahman Jakubowski pipes up, unsolicited.

Jacob has everyone repeat their new names several times—several times the new names progress around the circle.

The men are in their thirties, in the prime of their lives, and they are well-dressed, their coats lined with felt or fur. Their faces are bearded, fur hats on their heads, though it is some distance to winter still. The women are in caps, like burgher women, and some, like Hana, wear colorful turbans on their heads. A person watching them from off to the side, like a spy, would have no idea for what purpose this group had gathered here at the top of this hill, above the city of Lwów, nor why they are now repeating names over and over.

Jacob walks among them, with a thick walking stick he's grabbed off the ground. He splits them into two groups. In the first one is Reb Mordke, now called Peter the Elder, as the eldest among them, then there's Hershel, Jacob's second favorite, now called Jan. Next is Nahman, now called Piotr Jakubowski, and Hayim of Busk, now Paweł Pawłowski.

The Lord also puts in this group Itzak Minkowicer, now called Tadeusz Minkowiecki, as well as Yeruhim Lipmanowicz, now known as Dembowski. All of them will travel tomorrow with Jacob to Warsaw.

During their absence, Hana and the children will be placed in the care of Mrs. Kossakowska. He'll send the horses tomorrow. Leybko Hirsh of Satanów—now Joseph Zwierzchowski—and his wife, Hava, will go with them. They received their last name from the priest who baptized them; it is hard to pronounce. Jacob Szymonowicz, now known as Szymanowski, will also stay behind, as well as both Shorrs, now Wołowski, and Reb Schayes, who is still Rabinowicz since he hasn't yet been baptized.

The groups look each other over for a moment, then Jacob orders them to shake out their pockets in search of coins. He takes one coin from each of them, choosing only the big gold ducats, until he has twelve. He arranges them carefully in a pile on the ground, in the dried-out grass. Then he stomps on the coins with his boot, smashing them into the ground. He picks them up again and stomps on them again—as everyone watches in silence, holding their breath. What does this mean? What is he trying to tell them? Then he tells them each to go up and take a turn stepping on the coins, grinding them into the earth.

In the evening, Jacob goes to Franciszek, formerly Shlomo, to make his excuses for not having chosen him or his brothers to make the journey to Warsaw.

"But why?" says Franciszek. "We do business in Warsaw, we could have helped considerably. I have a completely different standing now, as a nobleman and a Catholic. And I have a good head on my shoulders."

"This title of yours means nothing for me. What did you pay for it?" Jacob asks, spiteful.

"I've been with you since the beginning, the most faithful one, and now you cast me aside?"

"That's how it's supposed to be," says Jacob, and a broad, warm smile fills his face. This is his usual mode. "I'm not casting you aside, my brother, I'm delegating to you the oversight of what we have already accomplished. You're right behind me, second in command, and you have to keep an eye on all these people who have been stuffed like so many chickens into barns and coops. You need to be the master here."

"But you are going to see the king . . . You are leaving us behind, me and my brothers. I want to know why."

"This journey isn't safe, and I'm taking the risk upon myself."

"But it was my brothers and my father and I who, while you were off in Turkey—"

"I was off in Turkey so they wouldn't kill me here."

"You're putting on a lot of airs now, but you were not there in the cathedral with us—" Shlomo explodes. This isn't like him—he normally shows a great deal of self-control. Jacob takes a step toward him, but in his rage, Shlomo-Franciszek Shorr-Wołowski evades Jacob's grasp and leaves the room, slamming the door, which bounces off its frame and swings back and forth on its rusted hinges for quite a while, creaking.

An hour later, Jacob calls in Hershel, or Jan. He has wine and roast meat brought. Nahman Jakubowski, coming to speak with Jacob, finds Hana at the door. Hana whispers to him that the Lord has put on his tefillin and is now performing a secret act with Hershel, something called "bringing the Torah into the latrine."

"With Jan," Nahman corrects her gently.


### Scraps: At Radziwiłł's

Is it not the case that every living being has his own distinct calling that is absolutely particular and can only be realized by him? He is therefore responsible for his task throughout his life, and he must not lose sight of it at any point. This is what I always believed, but the days that followed our activities in Lwów seemed to me so violent that for a long while not only could I not write about them, but also I could not even bear to think of them. Even now, as I begin to pray, only lamentations come to mind, and tears flood into my eyes, for although time does pass, my pain does not diminish in the slightest. Reb Mordke has died. Hershel, too. And my newborn daughter is dead as well.

If my little Agnieszka had become a full and happy person, I would undoubtedly not despair to this extent. If Reb Mordke had lived to see the years of salvation, I would not be so sad. If Hershel had grown weary of life, having experienced it all, I would not cry for him. Instead, I was the first person who had to confront this plague, as it affected me personally, as it affected my long-awaited child. And yet I had been chosen! How could this happen to me?

Before we set out on the road, there was a small ceremony, though it was not as joyful as it could have been, since on account of the plague, Jacob was observing a fast. But Old Reb Moshe of Podhajce, our great miracle-worker and sage, was marrying a young girl orphaned by the plague, named Teresa, formerly Esther Mayorkowicz. It was the gesture of a good man, as her sister who also survived had already been taken in by Mr. Łabęcki, godfather of Reb Mordke, and thus the sisters would share the last name of Łabęcki. On that evening the fast was suspended, but the repast was modest: a little wine, a little bread and broth. The bride could not stop crying.

At the wedding, Jacob announced that he was heading to Warsaw to see the king, and then he blessed the newlyweds, and so it was that we all saw he was the highest one and that he was taking upon himself all of our confusion, pain, and anger. I noticed very quickly, however, that not everything was to others' liking. The two Wołowski brothers in particular, who were sitting next to Walenty Krysiński, Nussen's son, displayed great consternation over having to remain in Lwów, and I could feel, right here at the wedding feast, a kind of intense struggle taking place, an invisible battle, as if over the heads of the diners, over the emaciated bride, who had only narrowly escaped death, and the aged groom, a war was being waged over the order of our souls. What was thickest in all of this was fear, and in fear—of course—people attack one another, in order to be able to have someone to blame for all the ill that is occurring.

Several days later, we were on the road, and as it is written in the Shocher Tov, four things weaken a person: hunger, travel, fasting, and authorities. Yes, we had allowed ourselves to be weakened. Although this time hunger did not threaten us on our travels, for we were received along the way at various manors or church presbyteries as converted Jews, as gentle, good people, almost as remorseful former criminals, and for our part we were happy to perform that role.

---

We set off on November 2 from Lwów to Warsaw in three carriages, a few riding on horseback, including Moliwda, our guide and watchman. His fine speeches introduced us wherever we stopped, never quite as we would have liked. But by the second day we felt exactly as Moliwda had described us; I could never—I think now—quite crack him, and I could never fully tell whether that Antoni Kossakowski was speaking in earnest or joking.

When we came into Krasnystaw, where we rented out a whole inn for the night, Moliwda said that he wanted Jacob to meet with a Polish lord, Jacob's fame as a great sage having made its way clear to here. This lord was also a wise man and would come to see us here. And so Jacob, despite his exhaustion, did not take off his traveling attire, instead throwing over his shoulders a fur-lined cloak and warming his hands over the fire, since during the day it had started to rain and a piercing cold had come up from the east, from over the Polesian marshes. We spread ourselves out in the largest room, side by side on little mattresses in which we could feel this year's hay. It was dark and smoky in the room. The Christian innkeeper had stuffed his whole family into a single cubbyhole of a room and would not allow his children to come out, for he thought us distinguished guests, not seeing us as Jews. Those grimy children of his peeked out through the gaps in the shoddy door of the room, but when the early winter evening fell, they vanished, no doubt overcome by sleep.

It wasn't until around midnight that Itzak Minkowicer, who had been keeping watch, came in to tell us that a carriage had arrived. Jacob sat upon a bench, as if on a throne, the edges of his cloak falling loosely about his arms and revealing the fur underneath.

Lo and behold, in came a Jew in a yarmulke, chubby and short but sure of himself, verging on insolent. Behind him, huge peasants stood guard in the doorway, armed to the teeth. He said nothing, this Jew, merely casting his eyes about the room for a long while, taking in Jacob, who sat with his head bowed.

"And who are you?" I finally asked, unable to tolerate the silence.

"Simon," said the man, in a deep voice that did not match his round figure.

He went back to the door and a moment later a wrinkled old Jew who resembled a rabbi appeared. He was tiny. From under his fur-lined hat, dark, piercing eyes flashed out. He went right up to Jacob, and Jacob stood up in surprise; the little man embraced him like an old friend. He cast a suspicious eye on Moliwda, who stood in a corner against the wall, drinking wine.

"This is Marcin Mikołaj Radziwiłł," said the one who called himself Simon, omitting any titles.

There was a moment of silence as we all stood motionless, astonished by the visit and the openness of such a powerful and important personage. For we had all heard, of course, about this magnate who had talked himself into the Jewish faith, although he had been treated with great suspicion by the Jews, as he kept a harem in his house and permitted bizarre acts to be conducted there. Jacob hid his own astonishment at Radziwiłł's behavior with his usual nonchalance, simply returning the embrace and inviting him to have a seat. Candles were brought in, and both men's faces were well lit, the candlelight breaking into a myriad of splotches over the magnate's furrowed face. Like a guard dog, Simon set himself by the door to keep watch, and he ordered the peasants to guard the inn's perimeter, it soon becoming apparent from the conversation what all that fuss had been about.

Radziwiłł was—as he explained—under house arrest. For favoring the Jews, he asserted, and now he had come here incognito, having heard what a distinguished and learned guest was passing through Krasnystaw. He himself rarely spent any time in Krasnystaw, as he was imprisoned in Słuck. Then he leaned in to Jacob and whispered something, slowly and at length, as though giving a recitation of some kind.

I looked at Jacob's facial expression—he had his eyes mostly closed and gave no indication whatsoever of what he was hearing. From what little I could make out, the magnate was speaking in Hebrew, but his words were mostly nonsense, as though he had learned by heart certain quotations, this from here, that from there. It made no real sense to me, though I could not hear all of it. And yet, from the outside, it looked as if he was conveying secrets of utmost importance to Jacob, and I think Jacob wanted us all to believe in the existence of those secrets.

Jacob always changes when he is interacting with an important person. His face becomes more boyish, more innocent, and he is vastly more inclined to make allowances for the high-born. He becomes winsomely solicitous and subservient as a dog submitting before a larger, stronger animal. At the start this disgusted me greatly. But anyone who knows Jacob knows, too, that this is a kind of game, a way for him to play.

No one is immune from acting differently with someone positioned higher than himself than with someone situated lower. The whole world depends on this dynamic, and this hierarchy is deeply ingrained in men. Yet it always annoyed me, and I sometimes would instruct Jacob, whenever he deigned to listen to me, that he ought to be standoffish and evasive with such people, and never to prostrate himself to them. I did hear him say once to Moliwda: "The majority of these big lords are all idiots, anyway."

Later he would tell us about Radziwiłł, saying he had imprisoned his wife and children for years, keeping them confined to a single chamber and subsisting on bread and water, until his relatives finally turned against him and convinced the king to treat him as a madman. That was why he was now under house arrest in Słuck. He supposedly had a whole harem made up of young girls who had been abducted or purchased from the Turks as slaves. The peasants who lived nearby said that he would draw blood from them and distill from it an elixir for eternal youth. If that is true, the elixir definitely didn't work, because the man looked older than his years. He had so many sins on his conscience—he had attacked travelers, plundered his neighbors' estates, lashed out in inexplicable frenzies—and yet, looking at him, it was hard to imagine him as such a rogue. His face was ugly, but so what? It could hardly be deduced from that that his soul was bad.

The innkeeper served us vodka and food, but our guest did not wish to touch anything, saying that he had already been poisoned many times. And that we ought not to take it personally, for bad people are everywhere and can easily impersonate good people. He sat with us until dawn, and some of us after the initial surprise of seeing him came back to our senses and dozed off while he was showing off his ability to speak in several languages, among them Hebrew. He claimed that he would convert officially to the Jewish faith, were he not so fearful.

"In Wilno," he said, "exactly ten years ago, such an apostate was burned at the stake. That was the unwise Walentyn Potocki, who in good faith in Amsterdam acceded with his whole heart to the Mosaic religion and did not wish, upon his return to Poland, to return to the bosom of the Church. They subjected him to torture and eventually burned him at the stake. I saw his grave in Wilno myself. I saw how the Jews venerated him, but no one can give him back his life."

"He's useless to us," Jacob said when Radziwiłł finally left. He stretched out and yawned loudly. We fell asleep at once with our heads on the table, and once the sun was up, it was time to set out for Lublin.

## *Of sad turns in Lublin*

Two days later, as we were entering the outskirts of Lublin, known as Kalinowszczyzna, out of nowhere, a hail of stones fell upon us. The force of this attack was so great that the stones broke through the sides and doors of the carriage and bored holes into its roof. As I was sitting next to Jacob, I flung myself spontaneously atop him. I was pummeled not by the stones, but by Jacob—he hurled me away in fury. It was a good thing that our vehicle was surrounded by eight horsemen, armed with weapons, for they, too, roused from their dozing, drew their sabers, and attempted to chase down the rowdy rabble. But from behind the houses, from all the streets, more of them came running, with pitchforks and sticks, and a burly woman hurled mud from a basket with perfect aim at our carriage, and a real, albeit chaotic, battle began. But these Jews from the outskirts made more noise than they did damage. It was just a gaggle of oafs, and in the end they scattered at the sight of the sentries who came to our aid at the behest of Moliwda and Krysa, who had galloped ahead into town to get help.

My deep sadness, my exhaustion from the previous night, and that attack, in which many of us were injured (I had a wound on my forehead and a big bump on my head, and since that time I've had a headache), wore us down greatly, and it was in that state that we arrived in Lublin. The worst was yet to come, however. In the evening, thanks to the efforts of Moliwda and Mrs. Kossakowska, we were lying down in the voivode's palace when it became apparent that Reb Mordke was ailing, and that he was suffering from the same symptoms as had afflicted those with the plague in Lwów. We set him up in a separate room, but he did not wish to remain there, and he dismissed our concerns, insisting there was no way he could

be sick. Whenever anyone attempted to leave his side, Jacob bade
them sit back down beside the sick man, and he himself attended to
him and gave him water to drink, although old Reb Mordke's eyes
had started to weaken.

Hershel, having the knack and sensitivity of a woman when it
came to taking care of people, nursed the sick man with great
dedication. I ran around Lublin for broth and a chicken breast.
Reb Mordke, though weak, greatly desired to see Lublin, for he
had studied there when he was young and had many memories
of it. And so Hershel and I took him into town and led him slowly
up the little streets all the way to the Jewish cemetery, where his
teacher had been buried. As we walked among the graves, Reb
Mordke pointed out a lovely tombstone, newly erected. "That's the
type I like," he said. "That's the type I'd like to have."

We chided him and scoffed at his concerns, saying it was hardly
the time for any of us to be dreaming of our tombstones. Had we
not all been whisked from under the dominion of death? So did
Hershel admonish him, fervently, with tears in his eyes. Truth be
told, I could never quite believe that myself. But Hershel did, like
so many. Or perhaps I did, just like those others. My memory is
hazy. When it came time to return to the palace, however, we
had to practically carry a greatly debilitated Reb Mordke in our
arms.

That night, we sat up with him in the voivode's palace in Lublin,
which had been neglected and was damp and dirty. The plaster had
cracked from moisture, and the wind crept in through the unsealed
windows. We rushed to the kitchen for hot water, but Reb Mordke
had bloody diarrhea that would not let up, and his eyes continued
to weaken. He told us to light a pipe, but he could no longer smoke
it, simply holding it in his hands while the dying fire warmed his
ever-colder fingers. We all stole glances at Jacob, wondering what he
would say. Reb Mordke himself looked at him expectantly: How was
Jacob planning on saving him from death? After all, Reb Mordke
had been Jacob's most faithful disciple for these many years, since
sunny Smyrna, since sea-scented Salonika, and someone like him,
who had already been baptized, could not die.

The next night Jacob went out alone into the wet courtyard and was
gone for two hours; when he returned, he was freezing and pale,
and he collapsed on the bed. I went to his side.

"Where have you been? Reb Mordke is dying," I reproached him.

"I could not conquer him," he said, seemingly to himself, although I heard him perfectly well. So did Itzak Minkowski, who had been sure Jacob had been kidnapped.

"Who are you talking about?" I shouted. "Who were you fighting? Who was here? There are castle guards posted everywhere, keeping watch . . ."

"You know who . . . ," he said, and a chill ran down my spine.

The next morning, Reb Mordke was dead. We sat around him into the afternoon, dumbfounded. Hershel burst into a bizarre kind of laughter, telling us that this was just what happened—that first you died, and then you came back to life. That it would simply take a little while for death to fully materialize, since otherwise no one would believe in resurrection. That was possible, for otherwise there would be no way to know if someone was immortal. Yet I was angry and said to him: "You're a fool." Which I now greatly regret. For Hershel was no fool. And I, too, was convinced that this could not be real, that something exceptional would happen soon, as exceptional as the times in which we were living, as exceptional as we were. And then there was Jacob, who could barely stand on his feet, sweat running down his face, his eyes half closed, and in them a dark light. He scarcely said a word, and I realized that powerful forces were waging a war over us, dark forces battling the very lightest ones, like in a stormy sky, when the black clouds chase out the blue and cover up the sun. And I could almost hear that vast clashing, a kind of low rumble, a dismal clanging. And suddenly my vision took off after that sound, and I saw the lot of us sitting in a circle with Reb Mordke's ghost, devastated and weeping. We were like the little figures made of bread for Hayah's board game, monstrous and ridiculous.

We were not victorious against death, not that time.

On the following day, we held a proper funeral. We carried out an open coffin, according to the Catholic custom, and laid it in a richly outfitted cart. The news had made its way around town, that this had been a great Jewish sage who had gone the way of the Cross, and an enormous procession turned out, including members of guilds and trumpeters and monks and common people in great multitudes, curious to see a converted Jew be buried on consecrated land. People cried a great deal, for reasons that struck me as unclear, as they did not know the deceased, nor did they particularly understand who he had been. In the parish church,

when the local bishop gave his sermon, the whole church was in
tears, perhaps because the words "in vain" came up so many times
in it, and together, those two words are likely even worse than
"death." I, too, cried, being in the grip of despair, in an eternal
kind of woe, and it was only then that I was able to fully lament my
little daughter, and all my dead.

I recall that Hershel was standing next to me and asked me what
those Polish words meant, "in vain." I told him, and he said, "They
have a good sound."

It's when all your effort goes to waste, when you build on sand,
when you try to collect water in a sieve, when you discover that your
hard-earned money is counterfeit. All of that is in vain. That's how
I translated and explained it to him.

The weather was foggy and somber when we left the church. The
wind lifted the muddied yellow leaves from the ground, and they
flew at us like a strange species of bat. Even I, always attuned to the
signs God gives us, did not understand what He was trying to tell
us then. I beheld Jacob's tearstained face, and this sight made such a
strong impression on me that my knees got weak, and I was unable
to go on walking. I had never seen him cry before.

When it was time to go back after the funeral, Jacob told us to
grab the sides of his Turkish robe and keep them up, like wings.
And so we did; we concentrated on holding up the sides of his robe
like blind men, in spite of our sadness and the driving rain that
lashed down upon us. We held fast to that coat of Jacob's that
everyone now wanted to have in his hand, if only for a moment, so
that we all took turns, the whole way from the cemetery to the
palace. The crowds parted for us, and to them we must have looked
like strange insects, our faces drenched in rain and tears. "Who is
that?" they'd whisper, as down the narrow streets of the town we
made our way back to the palace, still holding on to Jacob's robe.
The more surprised they seemed, the stranger the looks they gave
us, the better. Our despair, and our grief, pulled us apart from
them. Once more we were other. And that was how it was supposed
to be. There is something wonderful in being a stranger, in being
foreign, something to be relished, something as alluring as candy.
It is good not to be able to understand a language, not to know the
customs, to glide like a spirit among others who are distant and
unrecognizable. Then a particular kind of wisdom awakens—an
ability to surmise, to grasp the things that aren't obvious.
Cleverness and acumen come about. A person who is a stranger

gains a new point of view, becomes, whether he likes it or not, a particular type of sage. Who was it who convinced us that being comfortable and familiar was so great? Only foreigners can truly understand the way things work.

The day after Reb Mordke's funeral, Hershel died. Quick and quiet as a rabbit. Jacob locked himself in his room and did not come out for two days. We had no idea what to do. I scratched at the door and begged him to at least say something. I knew how much he loved Hershel in particular, like he did Her Ladyship, even though he was just an ordinary, well-intentioned child.

During the funeral, Jacob went right up to the altar, knelt there, and suddenly began to sing at full volume "Signor Mostro Abascharo," or "Our Lord Is Coming Down," the song people sing in times of duress. Instantly our voices joined in powerfully with his, and we knelt behind him. And as the last words were broken off by sobs, someone—I believe it was Matuszewski—began our holy song, "Yigdal":

> The Messiah will reveal the splendor of Your Kingdom
> To the poor, the beaten, the demeaned,
> You shall reign forever, our sacred refuge.

"Non ai otro commemetu," or "There is no one but you," added Jacob in the old language.

Our voices sounded desperate, filling the church, rising up to the vault and coming back down multiplied, as though an entire army were singing in this strange Eastern language that no one here knew, that contained sounds that were not of this place. I remembered Smyrna, the port, the salty sea air, and I could smell the spices that people here, in this Lublin parish church, had never even dreamed of. The church itself seemed arrested in shock, and the candle flames stopped quavering. The monk who had been laying flowers by the side altar now stood by a column and looked at us as if he were beholding ghosts. Just in case, perhaps, he crossed himself discreetly.

At last, together, so loud that the stained glass seemed to shake in the church's windows, we prayed in Yiddish that God might lend us a helping hand in this foreign country, Esau's country, help us, Jacob's children, lost in the fog, the rain, and this terrible autumn of 1759, which would be followed by an even worse winter. That

evening I came to understand that we had taken our first step into
the abyss.

The day after the funeral, Jacob and Moliwda went to Warsaw, while
the rest of us remained in Lublin, as Krysa had filed a court case
claiming assault and battery, and demanding a considerable
settlement from the local Jewish kahal. Since everyone was on our
side, the trial was to be held quickly, and the ruling would certainly
be in our favor. I didn't care about any of that very much. I went
around to the churches of Lublin, sitting in their pews to think and
reflect.

Mostly I considered the Shekhinah. I felt that at this terrible
time it was the Shekhinah that was emerging from the darkness,
struggling among the husks and giving signs, and I remembered my
trip to Stamboul with Reb Mordke. It, that Divine Presence, had
settled in our rotten world—it, or she, an inconceivable formlessness
that nonetheless existed in matter, a glimmering diamond in a
lump of black coal. And now I remembered everything, for after all
it had been Reb Mordke who introduced me to the mysteries of the
Shekhinah. It was he who took me into different holy places, free
from the prejudices that are so common among Jews. As soon as we
made it to Stamboul, we went to the Hagia Sophia, to the great
shrine to that Christian Mary, the Mother of Jesus, of whom Reb
Mordke spoke as being close to the Shekhinah. That had astonished
me then. I would never have gone into a Christian church myself,
and even in that one—which had, after all, been turned into a
mosque—I felt uncomfortable, and would have gladly skipped that
part of my education. My eyes could not get used to all the
paintings. When I spied on the wall a huge likeness of a woman who
was furthermore brazenly staring in my direction, I was overcome
by a kind of breathlessness I had never experienced before, and my
heart started pounding so that I wanted to get out of there, but Reb
Mordke grabbed me by the hand and pulled me back. We sat down
on the cold hard floor, by the wall under some Greek inscriptions,
no doubt engraved there centuries before, and slowly I regained my
senses so that my breath became regular again, and I was able once
more to behold this wonder:

The woman emerges from the wall, positioned high in the
dome's vault, over our heads, powerful. She is holding a child in
her lap, as if she is holding a piece of fruit. But it is not the child
that is important. Her mild face betrays no human affect except

that which lies at the foundation of everything—a love that is absolutely unconditional. I know, she says, without moving her lips. I know everything, and nothing escapes my understanding. I have been here since the dawn of time, hidden in the smallest particle of matter, in the stone, in the shell, in the wing of an insect, in this leaf, in this drop of water. Split a trunk in two, and you will find me; part a rock, and I will be there.

This is what that enormous figure seemed to be saying to me.

It seemed to me that this majestic person was revealing a painfully obvious truth, yet I remained unable to understand it.

## 22.

### The inn on the right bank of the Vistula

Moliwda and Jacob look at Warsaw from Praga on the other side of the river. They see the city situated high on the embankment, the brown and red of the bricks and the roofs of the city's tenements all squeezed in together, farming an urban honeycomb. The redbrick defensive wall has broken down completely in several places, overgrown with the roots of the little trees that have cropped up. Over the city loom the towers of the churches—the stiletto collegiate church of Saint John, the bulbous Jesuits' church, and, farther in, the angular brick of Saint Martin's Church on Piwna Street and, finally, more toward the river, the tall Marszałkowska Tower. Moliwda points out each of these in turn, as if showing his various properties to Jacob. He also points out the Royal Castle with the clock tower and the splendidly arranged gardens below, now covered in the thinnest layer of the first snow. The embankment and the city lurch up like some wild anomaly on this decidedly level terrain.

It is getting dark already, and the ferry will not go over to the left bank now. So they find a place to spend the night at a nearby inn—smoke-filled, with low ceilings. Because they are both dressed like nobles and request a clean room with separate beds, the innkeeper gives them preferential treatment. For supper they order roast chicken and potatoes with lard, as well as cheese and pickles, though these are not to Jacob's liking,

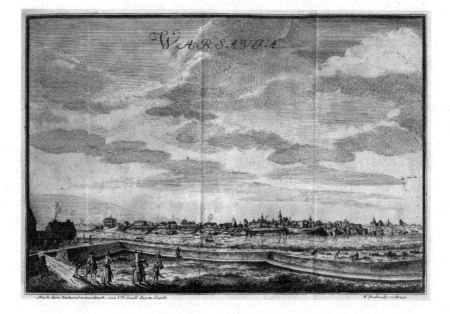

and he does not eat them. He is unusually quiet and focused. His face is shaved, and the little indentation in his chin and the ever-present circles under his eyes are now especially visible against the pallor of his lower face. He is wearing his tall fur hat, so the innkeeper assumes he is a Turk, maybe an official messenger.

Moliwda's gaze gets hazier with the vodka. He isn't used to the strong Mazovian spirits. He reaches across the table and touches Jacob's cheek, evidently unable to stop marveling at his appearance now that he has done away with his beard. A surprised Jacob looks up at him, still chewing. They converse in Turkish, which gives them a sense of security.

"Don't you worry. The king will receive you," says Moliwda. "Sołtyk wrote to him. And a number of people have expressed support for you to him."

Jacob tops up Moliwda's vodka; he himself drinks little.

"That woman will give you a free place to live, with servants, while you're here." "That woman" is how they refer to Mrs. Kossakowska. "You can have Hana join you, everything will work out."

Moliwda is trying to cheer him up, but in fact he feels as if he's shoving Jacob right into the lion's den. Especially today, on seeing this city that is at once haughty and miserable. Angst has been tormenting him: after the plague in Lwów, after the deaths in Lublin, what else can go wrong?

"What I'm after isn't just some nice accommodations," says Jacob gloomily. "I want them to give me land, and I want full control over that land . . ."

It occurs to Moliwda that Jacob wants an awful lot. He decides to change the subject.

"Let's get us a girl," he says in a conciliatory tone. "One for the two of us, we'll both bend her over," he says, although without conviction. But Jacob shakes his head. With the silver toothpick he always carries with him, he picks pieces of meat out of his teeth.

"Given how long we've gone without an answer, it seems to me he doesn't want to see me."

"Come on now, it's the royal chancellery. They get applications like yours by the hundred. The king is rarely in the capital, he's most often in Dresden, so when he gets here, he is buried under letters and petitions. I have a good friend there. He will put your letter at the top of the pile. You just have to be patient."

Moliwda reaches for another piece of chicken, holds the drumstick in front of him like a child's saber, trying to tease Jacob. But Jacob just gets annoyed.

"And I'll say on your behalf," and Moliwda begins to imitate the accent in which Jews sometimes speak Polish, "we have joined the Catholic Church in good faith, putting our fates into His Majesty's hands, in total faith, knowing he will not leave his littlest subjects in such terrible distress . . ."

"Stop it," says Jacob.

So Moliwda stops. Jacob pours himself some vodka and drinks it down in one gulp. His eyes start to gleam, and his gloom slowly melts away, like snow brought into a warm room. Moliwda moves over to his side and puts his arm over his shoulder. He follows Jacob's gaze and sees two women, one seemingly a young lady of the night, the other likely her companion. Clearly both working girls of a better sort, and they look back at Jacob and Moliwda with equal curiosity, no doubt assuming they are noblemen from overseas. Or envoys on the road. Moliwda winks at them, excited, but Jacob holds him back, saying there are spies all over, and who knows what might happen. It wouldn't be a good idea.

They sleep in the same room, on two beds that are more like pallets, fully clothed. Jacob has arranged a shirt so his head doesn't touch the rough straw mattress. Moliwda falls asleep but is awakened by the ruckus downstairs—they're still making merry in the dining room. Drunken shouts can be heard, and then it sounds as if the innkeeper is throwing out the most obstreperous of his guests. Moliwda looks over at Jacob's bed, but it is empty. Frightened, he sits up and sees Jacob by the window, rocking back and forth and muttering something to himself. Moliwda lies back down and realizes, when he is already half asleep, that this is the first time he's seen Jacob praying for himself. And on the very brink of sleep, Moliwda is surprised; he has always been sure that Jacob didn't believe in all the tales he told the others, in the triple or quadruple gods, in the order of the Messiah—or even the Messiah himself. What part of the heart believes, and what part is certain that none of it is true? he wonders sleepily, and then the last thought that comes to him before he finally drifts off is how hard it is for us to ever get away from ourselves.

## Of events in Warsaw and the papal nuncio

The first thing Jacob does in Warsaw is hire a carriage with three horses. He drives himself around the capital, the horses harnessed strangely, one in front of the next, which draws attention, so that the whole capital stops and stares at this weird vehicle as it goes by. He also rents a small palace past the Żelazna Brama, with a coach house and a stable, and seven rooms, all furnished, so that everyone who will be coming from Lublin will be able to stay there. The furnishings are nice and clean, upholstered in damask, with several mirrors, chests, and sofas. There are tiled stoves, and upstairs, a large bed, which he immediately orders to be made up in clean sheets, as befits a lord. With Moliwda's assistance he hires a butler, a cook, and a maid to take care of the stoves and the cleaning.

Mrs. Kossakowska's contacts are already paying off—the first to invite him over is Prince Branicki, and then everyone wants to have this neophyte and Puritan at their salons. That includes the Jabłonowskis, at whose home Jacob causes quite the stir in his colorful Turkish costume. The guests, dressed in the French fashion, look through their lorgnettes at this strange, pockmarked yet handsome man with curiosity and sympathy. In Poland, foreign is always more appealing than domestic, so they praise the exotic garments this newcomer is modeling for them. The gentlemen marvel over how little he looks like a Jew—more like a Turk or even a Persian—and this is intended as a mark of their gentlemanly goodwill. There is a moment of hilarity when Princess Anna's little dog lifts its leg and drenches their guest's lovely yellow shoes in a stream of urine. The princess considers this yet another display of extraordinary sympathy, this time on the part of the dog, and all delight in the good omen. After the Jabłonowskis, the Potockis invite them, and from then on, the big houses pass them from one to the next like a form of entertainment.

Jacob says very little, stays mysterious. When he answers prying questions, Moliwda embellishes what Jacob has said so that he seems like a naturally wise and serious man. When he tells some anecdote or other, Moliwda rounds out the details. He takes care to cover up Jacob's immodest tone, which doesn't quite make it over the high thresholds of aristocratic salons, where modesty is fashionable. On the other hand, Jacob's boastfulness makes him a favorite at the pubs on the city's outskirts, where they have already ended up a few times after some boring opera.

The next to receive them is Serra, the papal nuncio.

This older, well-manicured man with completely white hair regards them with an inscrutable expression; when they speak, he nods lightly, as if fully agreeing with them. Jacob almost gets taken in by this mild-mannered politeness, but Moliwda knows that this man is a fox—you can never know what he really thinks. The nuncios are taught this: to stay calm, to take time, to observe carefully, to weigh all the arguments. Jacob speaks Turkish; Moliwda translates into Latin. A beautiful young cleric writes it all down indifferently at a separate little table.

"Jacob, this man here, Frank," Moliwda begins to speak after Jacob, "left with his wife and children along with sixty of his co-religionists from the Turkish lands, having lost his meager property and knowing no language other than the Oriental ones, the which all being useless here, thus I must serve as his interpreter . . . so great was their desire for Christianity. Here they do not know the customs, and they have tremendous difficulties in supporting themselves, so that they have been living off the generosity of kind souls . . ." Noticing the nuncio's somewhat intrigued and ironic look, he adds: "Whatever he has, he has by the kindness of our nobles . . . And on top of all this, these poor people have seen terrible persecution on the part of the Talmudists, as happened just now in Lublin, where there was a fearsome and bloody attack on our peaceful travelers, and the worst part is that they have nowhere now to go, except as guests somewhere, on someone else's dime."

Jacob nods as though understanding everything. Maybe he does understand.

"For so many centuries, we have been expelled from every country, for so many centuries, we have suffered unrelenting uncertainty, and we have been unable to put down roots like stable people do. Without roots, you're no one," Moliwda adds of his own invention. "Just ephemeral fluff. Only in the Commonwealth have we ever found shelter, supported by the royal edicts and the solicitous attitude of the Church . . ." Here Moliwda glances quickly at Jacob, who seems to be listening attentively to the translation. "What satisfaction would we bring to God if just we few who wish to live in harmony with neighbors could now be permitted to settle on our own territory. It would be as if the circle of history were closing, and everything were returning to the old order. And what great credit would Poland have with God, greater than the rest of the world, so hostile to Jews."

Moliwda doesn't even notice that in translating Jacob, he has switched to "we" instead of "they." He has repeated all this so many times that the sentences have gotten suspiciously resplendent and rotund. It is all almost too obvious, even boring. Won't anyone ever be able to think in different terms?

"And so we renew our request for you to grant us, near the Turkish border, some separate territory . . ."

"Di formar una intera popolazione, in sito prossimo allo stato

Ottomano," the young clerk repeats automatically in Italian, his extraordinarily beautiful face ablaze when he realizes he's been heard, and he falls silent.

After a moment of general silence, the nuncio points out that some of the magnates would be happy to invite these "people of God" to stay on their estates, but to this Jacob responds through Moliwda's words:

"We would worry that we would be forced into the same submission about which the unfortunate village dwellers of Poland all moan and groan."

". . . miseri abitatori della campagna . . ." Once again they hear the whispering of the clerk, who evidently uses this as a means to help himself in writing.

This is why Jacob Frank, in the name of his followers, begs (implora) that they be assigned some separate place of their own, preferably a whole locality (un luogo particolare), while also promising that when they do find themselves together (uniti) in said locality, they will be able to engage in their own industry and escape the notice of their persecutors.

Then the nuncio revives a little, politely, and proclaims that he has spoken with the great Chancellor of the Crown, who has shown his willingness to settle the Frankists on royal holdings, whereupon they would become royal subjects, the Church also being ready to accept them into the city, where they would remain under episcopal jurisdiction.

Moliwda lets out a loud sigh of relief, but Jacob doesn't even blink at this piece of good news.

Then the conversation turns to baptism, that it must be repeated, ceremoniously, and in front of everyone. That it must take place anew, with pomp, and before the king himself. Who knows—it's true the king's in Dresden, but perhaps someone of high standing will agree to be godfather.

The audience is over. The nuncio dons his solicitous mask. He is as pale as if he had not left this luxurious palace in ages. If you look closely, you can see that his hands have a tremor. Jacob walks through the corridor of the palace with a sure step, slapping his gloves against his hand. Moliwda trots behind him in silence. Secretaries glide silently along the walls.

It is only when they have reached their carriage that they begin to breathe freely again. And Jacob, just like whenever something pleased him back when they were in Smyrna, brings Moliwda's face up to his and kisses him on the lips.

At Jacob's house, Nahman-Piotr Jakubowski is waiting with Yeruhim Dembowski.

Jacob greets them in some new, bizarre fashion that Moliwda has never seen before: he raises a hand to his mouth and then places it on his heart. And with great confidence, without any hesitation—as usual—they repeat this gesture after him, and a moment later it looks as if they had been employing this greeting from the start. They are eager to hear all the details, but Jacob walks by them and disappears into the house. Moliwda, who is following Jacob like his spokesperson, like a king's minister, says to Nahman and Yeruhim:

"He had an easy time convincing the nuncio. He spoke to him as he would to a child."

He knows that this is exactly what they wanted to hear. And he sees what a great impression it makes on them. He opens all the doors for Jacob, and follows after him, with Nahman and Yeruhim just behind. He feels that the thing that had once been there has now been restored: the pleasure of being with Jacob and warming oneself in his extraordinary—albeit invisible to the human eye—halo.

## Of Katarzyna and her dominion over Warsaw

Kossakowska goes around in a small, modest buggy, always dressed in dark colors, her beloved browns and grays, wearing a big cross on her chest. Hunched over, in her lengthy stride she crosses the distance between the carriage and the entrance to the next house she is visiting. She is capable of going to four or five of them in a single day, not minding that it is cold outside, or that her clothes are not particularly suited to social calls. To the valets at the doors she only mutters, "Kossakowska's here," and continues into the house, overcoat still on. Behind her, Agnieszka always tries to mollify the shaken servant. Since his arrival in Warsaw, Moliwda has accompanied them; Kossakowska introduces him as her erudite cousin. Recently Moliwda has also been helping her with her shopping, since she is going home for the holidays. On Krakowskie Przedmieście, in a store that sells Viennese goods, they spent an entire half day looking at dolls.

Moliwda tells her about the deaths of Reb Mordke and Hershel.

"Does Jacob's wife know about this?" asks Kossakowska, peering underneath the wide skirts of the elegant dolls, where their long, lace-finished pantaloons reassure her. "You might think twice before telling her, especially since I believe she is expecting yet another child. All he has to do is touch her, it seems, and she gets pregnant. Given how rarely they see one another, it is quite the miracle, that."

Kossakowska is readying the little manor house in Wojsławice for Hana, and while she is normally quite frugal, in this instance she has been lavish. She drags Moliwda to Miodowa Street, to a place where they sell beautiful faience, little wonders from China so delicate the light shines right through the cups. They are all decorated with little landscapes—this is what Kossakowska would like to buy Hana for her new home. Moliwda tries to dissuade her—what would she want such fragile objects for, these ceramics that won't last a single journey—but then he decides to keep quiet, as he is slowly realizing that Hana, and all the Puritans, as she calls them, have become for Kossakowska something akin to children, difficult and rebellious, but children, nonetheless. Which is why instead of remaining in Warsaw for the second ceremonious baptism in the presence of the king, she prefers to return to Podolia. The last time she saw Jacob Frank she told him to carry out his affairs here, while she took care of those he'd left behind. The little village of Wojsławice belongs to Katarzyna's cousin and close friend Marianna Potocka, and it is a wealthy place, with a vast market and a cobblestoned market square. The manor house belonging to Kossakowska had been leased to the local steward and has since been vacated, and the walls have all been repainted, everything renovated. The rest of Hana's retinue can live in the grange until Jacob is able to obtain land for them to permanently settle.

"What are they going to live off?" asks Moliwda thoughtfully, watching the merchant wrap each of the cups in tissue paper and pack them in tow.

"They'll live off the support they will receive from all of us, and off whatever they have. Besides, winter hardly gets in the way of trade. And starting in the spring they'll receive some grain to sow."

Moliwda winces.

"I can't quite imagine—"

"There are a lot of fairs and stalls already in place . . ."

". . . all of which have been occupied by other Jews for decades, maybe centuries. You can't just release a people amongst another people and wait to see what will happen."

"We shall see about that," says Kossakowska, and pays, pleased.

Moliwda sees with horror what an absolute fortune the dolls cost. They go back to the buggy through snow dirtied by horse droppings.

As he arranges the packages in the carriage, Moliwda complains again about how Jacob is the only one of them presentable enough for salons. And he is alarmed by the amount of money Jacob is spending in the capital; such luxury, such glamour, is an irritant to people who see it. Kossakowska agrees:

"What is the purpose of getting a carriage for six horses? Why all those furred cloaks and hats and jewels? Here we are trying to present them as noble paupers, and meanwhile he's going around town like that. Have you spoken with him about it?"

"I have told him, but he does not wish to listen to me," Moliwda answers darkly, and helps Kossakowska up into the carriage. They say goodbye, and Kossakowska drives off. Moliwda is left alone on Krakowskie Przedmieście. A wind is blowing from Kozia Street, whipping up his kontusz. The cold is as bitter as if he were in Petersburg or somewhere.

He forgot to report to Kossakowska that Jacob hasn't been getting his letters from Podolia. The one that came from Hana had its seal broken.

Everything is ready for the second official baptism; it will be held in the royal chapel at the Saxon Palace. It will be preceded by a solemn mass, with a choir participating, and the mass itself will be conducted by the Bishop of Kiev himself, Andrzej Załuski. In all likelihood, the king will not be there, as he is no doubt busy in Dresden. But who cares? What need have we of any king? Warsaw manages perfectly fine without him all the time.

## Katarzyna Kossakowska writes to her cousin

My dear Cousin,

I have delivered the Faience. Just one of the Cups lost its Handle, otherwise all well. We miss you very much here, especially as we have had no News for quite some Time. Mrs. Frank in particular is losing her Mind here and constantly asks the same Messenger for some Response to her latest Letter to her Husband. For now, I am hosting her and her Daughter and two Servants, and we are all impatiently awaiting News about what you all have determined to do there. The worst Thing is that it is as if you had all fallen into some black Chasm, for I have been hearing that none of our converted Friends have had any Sign of their Relatives in Warsaw, either. Is it this hideous Winter that has brought about some Sort of Epidemic amongst the Officers of the Polish Post? Yet we are all keeping alive the Hope that it is a Question of the many Occupations you no doubt all have there in the Capital.

I know moreover that we cannot count on an Audience with the King. I have my Trunks all packed and will join you there as soon as the Frosts let up, i.e., sometime in March I will get back on the Road, as currently the Horses' Saliva would freeze to their Snouts. So for now, because of the Cold and a little bit of wintry Languor, I will leave Everything to you, as I know you have such a good Head on your Shoulders, and you can handle the Temptations of the Capital.

I have been imploring Branicki and the Potockis to fully join in our Cause with adoptive Letters. I do know, however, that the Hetman is generally quite hostile to the Jews, and to Converts all the more so. The Thing that angers People the most is their noble Ambitions. I have already heard that the whole Wołowski Family has been ennobled, as apparently has Krysiński, that one with the Scar on his Face, who often writes to me. It is true that this also causes me some moral Discomfort, for how can it be—they have barely come into our World, and already they are climbing our Society and getting into our Government. We worked for Generations to get our noble Titles, and our Forefathers earned them with some real Service to our Fatherland, while with them it's just a Fistful of Gold thrown onto the Table. Especially since it hardly befits a Noble to run a Brewery in Town, as one of these Wołowskis is doing—someone will need to say something to him about it. I heard of it from my Cousin Potocka, who will marry off her Son in January and has invited us to the Festivities. All the more Reason for not going back to Warsaw until Spring. I'm too old to be dragging myself over Snow and Ice this Way and that.

With this Letter I enclose two Letters from Lady Hana to Lord Jacob, and some Drawings by little Eva. Kindly encourage that esteemed Gentleman to send her just a Line or two, lest she cry her pretty dark Eyes out, for she misses him so. She is such an exotic Woman, she has not yet grown accustomed to the Cold in our Homes here, nor to our Cuisine . . .

## What is served for Christmas Eve dinner at Mrs. Kossakowska's

A Christmas wafer star hangs over the Christmas Eve table. Two soups are served—almond and mushroom. There is herring in olive oil, sprinkled with chives and diced garlic. There are peas and puffed wheat with honey. There is kasha with mushrooms, as well as steaming dumplings.

A sheaf of grain has been placed in the corner of the room, and hanging over it, a paper star painted gold.

The guests give each other Christmas tidings, and they are all kind to Hana, speaking softly to her in Polish, now serious, now laughing. Little Avacha is perplexed and looks frightened, which must be why she does not let go of her mother's dress. Hana gives little Immanuel to the nanny, the neat and clean Zwierzchowska. The boy squirms out of her arms to get to his mother, but he is too small to take part in the holiday meal; Zwierzchowska disappears with him into the back rooms of the Kossakowskis' great estate. Unfortunately, Hana understands little of what is being said to her. She nods and smiles vaguely. The inquisitive gaze of her tablemates, disappointed by her silence, creeps greedily—so it seems to Hana—to five-year-old Avacha, who is dressed as beautifully as if she were a princess, and watches mistrustfully as this company warbles over her.

"I had no idea a human being could have such enormous eyes," says Castellan Kossakowski. "She must be an angel, a forest fairy."

It's true that the child is uncommonly beautiful. Seemingly serious, but also wild, as if snatched out of some pagan, Arabian splendor. Hana dresses her little girl like a lady. She is wearing a dress the color of a blue sky over stiff petticoats, covered in white lace, and white stockings and little navy-blue satin shoes adorned with pearls. She won't make it to the carriage in them, through all the snow. She'll have to be carried. Before everyone sits down at the table, Castellan Kossakowski sets the little girl up on a footstool so that everyone can admire her.

"Curtsy, little Eva, my dear," Mrs. Kossakowska says. "Go on, make a nice little curtsy, like I taught you."

But Avacha stands motionless, stiff as a doll. The guests, a little disappointed, leave her in peace and sit down at the table.

Avacha sits beside her mother and looks down at her petticoats, carefully correcting the stiff hems of the tulle. She refuses to eat. Several dumplings have been placed on her plate, but they are already cold.

There is a silence between the next round of well-wishing and sitting down to table, but then the castellan makes a very amusing statement, and everyone laughs except for Hana. The interpreter they have hired, a Turkish-speaking Armenian, leans in to her and translates the castellan's joke, but in such a chaotic way that Hana still has no idea what's going on.

Hana sits stiffly and cannot take her eyes off Katarzyna. She is revolted by these dishes, although they look appetizing enough, and she is very hungry. But who made them, and how? How is she to eat pierogi with sauerkraut and mushrooms? Jacob has told her not to feel disgusted and to eat like everyone else, but these pierogi are a problem for her, she cannot swallow them—the cabbage has gone bad, it seems, and there's a fungus on top. And what are these, she thinks, these pale noodles, this sickly color, with poppy seeds that make it look like they are covered in insects?

She revives when they bring in the carp, although instead of being encased in gelatin, it is baked. The smell of fish fills the room, and Hana's mouth begins to water. She isn't sure whether to wait until she's served it or to go ahead and help herself.

"You just go ahead and act like a lady," Mrs. Kossakowska instructed her recently, "and don't stand on ceremony. You are what you believe you are. And you consider yourself a lady, right? You are the wife of Jacob Frank, not just any old Shlomo, you understand? People like you don't have to worry about politeness. Hold your head up high. Like this," and saying that, Katarzyna tilted Hana's head back and patted her on the rear.

Now Katarzyna tries to convince her to eat the Christmas Eve delicacies. When talking about her she calls her Lady Frank, but talking to her, she says, "my dear." Hana looks at her trustingly and turns away from the pierogi, reaching for the carp. Oh yes, she serves herself a huge piece with the toasted skin attached. Kossakowska blinks in surprise, but the others are busy with their conversation—no one is watching her. Hana Frank casts a quick glance at Mrs. Kossakowska, feeling pleased with herself. For who is this woman so intent upon ordering everyone around, so imperious and so boisterous? She speaks loudly and in a deep, resounding voice, and she interrupts everyone, as if, just like land and privileges, the right to speak were hers as well. She is wearing a dark gray dress with black lace on it, and on that lace a wayward thread—Agnieszka did not see to her mistress's toilette. That thread disgusts Hana, just like this meal. Like Mrs. Kossakowska, and her Agnieszka, and her limping, hunched-over husband.

How did she find herself in this prison of slimy courtesies, of gossip, of whispers she can't even understand? She tries to lock those angry thoughts deep inside herself, she has a special place for them, where they can stalk back and forth like animals in a cage. And she won't let them out, at least not yet. For now, she is dependent on Mrs. Kossakowska and maybe even likes her a little, although her touch disgusts Hana, and she is always patting her and petting her for some reason. They have separated her from everything she ever knew. All she has left are Zwierzchowska and Pawłowska. And she can only think about them now without their first names. Their first names stayed Jewish in her head. The rest of the company is still waiting in Lwów. Hana cannot fully communicate here, she's always trying to think of words, this language brings her to despair; she'll never learn it properly. What is going on with Jacob, why has she had no news of him? Where has Moliwda gone? If he were here, she'd feel a little more secure. Where is everyone else from their group, and why have they taken her away from them? She would rather be sitting in a smoky room in Ivanie than here on the estate of Katarzyna Kossakowska.

For dessert they serve cheesecake with marzipan and a layer cake with lemon and hazelnut filling. Avacha's little hand removes stores from the table and stuffs sweets into the pockets of her pretty blue dress. They will eat their sweets during the night, when they are alone.

They sleep curled up together here. Avacha's little hands hold her mother's face when the child sees Hana crying. Hana hugs this giant-eyed child tight, clinging to her the way an insect over water holds on to a blade of grass; she holds tight to that delicate little body, and together they float through the night. She often also picks up Immanuel from his crib and breastfeeds him at will, since she still has milk, although Mrs. Kossakowska interferes even in that. She thinks that feeding should be done by wet nurses. Hana is disgusted by the wet nurse Kossakowska has found her: her white skin, her light-colored hair, her thick legs. Her great pink breasts overwhelm Immanuel; she is afraid that one day, this village girl will smother him to death.

And look, as she is thinking of it during the holiday meal, a splotch of milk slowly expands upon her dress, and Hana covers it deftly with her Turkish scarf.

## Avacha and her two dolls

For little Avacha, however, this evening will be unlike any she has ever had before—as a matter of fact, every previous evening will be made null and void by tonight. All that will be left of them is a sort of streak in time, foggy, blurred.

After dinner, Kossakowska leads little Avacha into the next room and has her close her eyes. Then she leads her a little farther and has her open her eyes. Avacha sees two beautiful dolls seated before her. One is a brunette dressed in turquoise, the other a blonde in elegant aquamarine. Avacha looks at them without a word as a flush spreads over her cheeks.

"Choose whichever one you prefer," Kossakowska whispers into her ear. "One is yours."

Avacha shifts her weight from foot to foot. She takes in every tiny detail of each doll's outfit, but she cannot choose. She goes to her mother for help, but her mother merely smiles, shrugging her shoulders, relaxed by wine and by the fact that she can finally light up a Turkish pipe with Mrs. Kossakowska.

This goes on for some time. The women begin to prod the girl; the women giggle. They find the child's gravity amusing, laugh at her inability to choose. Avacha is told that dolls from Vienna are the finest crafted, that their bodies are made out of goatskin, their faces out of papier mâché, and that they're stuffed with sawdust. But Avacha still doesn't know which one to pick.

Tears well up in her eyes and spill over. Enraged by her own indecision, she dives straight into her mother's skirts and sobs loud, heaving sobs.

"What's wrong, what's wrong?" her mother asks her in their own language, in Turkish.

"No, no," answers Avacha in Polish: "Nothing." She keeps her face hidden in her mother's dress.

She would like to hide there inside those soft folds, crouch down and wait for the worst to pass. For there is too much world, and there are too many tasks ahead of little Evunia. She has never felt this miserable before.

She feels as if someone were clutching her heart, and she cries, but not like when she cries because she's scraped her knee—it is a despair that happens deeper inside, at the very bottom of her being. Her mother pats her head, but this doesn't bring any relief; Avacha feels that she has gotten very far from her mother somehow, and that from here it is going to be very hard to get back to her as if nothing had ever even happened.

Now she can trust only that strange man with the beard who, on Christmas morning, brings her a little puppy with curly red fur; this pup is lovelier, without a doubt, than any Viennese doll.

### A doll for Salusia Łabęcka, and Father Chmielowski's tales of a library and a ceremonious baptism

After Christmas, Kossakowska and her husband go and pay visits to the neighbors. In doing so, they also carry out their mission to transfer the Puritans jammed into their barns to Wojsławice, and to send those who won't fit around to the estates of various nobles. Agnieszka goes along with a bag full of tinctures—since Mr. Kossakowski has been complaining of pain in his bones—and their writing chest, with everything they need to write their letters, and two fur-lined cloaks. The dictation of letters takes place in the carriage; Agnieszka commits the letters to memory, then writes them down when they come to a stop. Kossakowska thinks of those under her care as "converts," but she tries not to use this word in writing or in speech, since it carries negative associations. It is better to call them "Puritans," a word that came from France or maybe England and that His Lordship Łabęcki has just reminded her of, and now everyone is using it. It has good associations, containing the suggestion, pleasing to the ear, that they are pure.

She is taking a lovely gift: a doll. The doll is dressed exquisitely, like the ladies at the imperial court. She has flaxen hair curled into ringlets and topped with a shapely little lace cap. Kossakowska has taken her out of her box in the carriage—the snow has melted, and they have put away the sleighs—and is now holding her on her lap as though she were a child, twittering to it as adults do when bending down over a child. This is all to entertain her husband. But he is in a bad mood today in spite of this, annoyed that his wife is dragging him around to see the neighbors. His bones hurt—he has long suffered from arthritis. He would gladly stay at home and let the dogs come inside, which his wife has strictly forbidden. It's a long way to Rohatyn, and he doesn't care for Łabęcki, he's too learned for the castellan's tastes and too intent upon pretending he is French. Kossakowski, on the other hand, is dressed in the Polish fashion, in a woolen kontusz and a fur.

The little girl at the Łabęckis' is named Salomea. For now she keeps quiet—so far she has not uttered a single word, although she has a Polish governess who tries to help her. What she likes to do is just sit and embroider. She has been taught to curtsy and to lower her eyes when her elders are addressing her. She wears a pink dress with a magenta ribbon in her black hair. She is tiny and extremely lovely. Mrs. Łabęcka says she never smiles. Which is why they watch her so closely when they give her the doll. After a moment's hesitation, she sticks out her hand for it, then draws it in tight to her chest, pressing her face into the doll's flaxen hair. Mr. Łabęcki looks at her with a kind of pride, then quickly forgets about her. The girl takes her doll and vanishes like a dust ball.

At the sumptuous lunch that turns imperceptibly into dinner and falls only a little short of rolling on into breakfast, Father Chmielowski, the vicar forane, turns up. Kossakowska greets him warmly but also seems not to recognize the poor man, which saddens him visibly.

"From Rohatyn—I saved your life when you were ailing," the priest states humbly, while Łabęcki shouts over him that he's a famous writer.

"Ahh," Kossakowska remembers, "this is that brave and gallant priest who fished me out of the crowd when I was stuck in that half-broken-down carriage and brought me in here, to this refuge of yours! The author of *New Athens*, which I have read from cover to cover." She slaps the priest's back relentlessly and tells him to sit down next to her. He blushes and initially declines—this woman, with her masculine behavior, frightens him—but in the end he does sit next to her, and slowly his courage returns with the help of the Tokay. His health has declined, he's gotten skinnier and weaker, and his teeth must have decayed, for he struggles with the chicken placed before him, although he eats the boiled vegetables and the soft pâtés of wild game, dishing more and more of them onto his plate. From the white rolls, he selects the soft center, assembling the harder outsides carefully in a little pile and furtively passing them under the table to the Łabęckis' shaggy dog, who—very much like his mother—inspires great affection in the priest. He's happy he managed to house this dog with such a fine family. And he even feels a little bit like he is part of the Łabęcki family now, as well.

"I hear, Father, that you've just returned from Warsaw," Kossakowska says to him.

Father Chmielowski blushes slightly, which makes his face seem younger.

"The wonderfully erudite Bishop Załuski had been inviting me to go for quite some time, and if he knew, of course, that I was sitting now with Your Benevolent Ladyship, he would no doubt have sent his very fondest regards from Warsaw, for he spoke of you in only the most glowing terms."

"Like everyone else," interjects Łabęcki, a slight irony in his tone.

Father Chmielowski continues:

"Warsaw itself didn't interest me, just that library. A city is a city, anyone can see what it is. It is the same wherever you go—the roofs are the same, the churches, and people all look alike. It's a bit like Lwów, just with more empty squares, which makes the wind all the more vexing. I was taken there by that vast collection, and as I am already considerably weakened, and I have little health left . . ." Here Father Chmielowski falters, reaches for his wine, and takes a big gulp. "On account of that library of theirs I was unable to sleep, and I still cannot . . . What an enormity . . . Tens of thousands—they themselves do not even know how many volumes . . ."

Father Chmielowski had stayed in a monastery, and every day he'd walked quite a bit in that freezing air to get to the library, where he was permitted to poke around in the stacks. He had intended to make notes, for he has not yet completed his work, but that multitude of books had an unexpectedly depressing effect on him. Father Chmielowski actually spent all that time—almost an entire month—going into the library to try to understand what organization prevailed there. But with ever-increasing anxiety, he became convinced that there was no organization to it at all.

"Some books are sorted by author, but then suddenly it changes and is according to the 'abecedary,' alphabetically. And then there are books that were purchased together just piled up, and then there are some that on account of their larger format would not fit onto the usual shelves, and so they have been separated onto other, more capacious shelves, or they lie around as if ailing in some way," Father Chmielowski says indignantly. "But books are like soldiers. They should always be standing at attention, one after the next. Like an army of mankind's wisdom."

"Well said," comments Łabęcki.

It seems to Father Chmielowski that a whole team of people ought to be deployed and ought to act as they would in an army—establish a hierarchy amongst themselves and divide into regiments, give the books ranks according to value and rarity, and finally supply them with provisions, gluing together and sewing up those that are ailing and damaged. It would be a great undertaking, but how worthwhile it would be. For what would we do without books?

What irritates the priest most is that this is supposed to be a public library, meaning an open library, which he cannot understand—for what can they mean by it? That just anyone can come and take a book back to his home? This seems to him a mad idea, one of those Western ones, French, which will bring greater harm to book collections than it will benefit anyone. He has observed that the books at the Załuskis' are borrowed via a rotten lending form, which then, put away in a drawer, might get mislaid or disappear forever, as slips of paper have the habit of doing. And when a more distinguished guest comes in, they will just give him a book without even having him sign the lending form, out of timidity. There is no record of where the borrowed books have gone or of who has them.

The priest clutches his head theatrically.

"Father Chmielowski, you seem to care more about books than you do about people," says Kossakowska with her mouth full.

"I permit myself to contest Your Ladyship. Not at all. I also saw our capital and the people living in it."

"And your reflections?" Łabęcki asks politely in French.

Father Chmielowski is thrown by the French; Miss Agnieszka whispers a translation to him, but he has already turned red.

"What surprises me the most is that people desire to be so crowded into small apartments, onto narrow little streets, when they could all enjoy such luxury in the countryside and consume fresh air in any quantity."

"That is the God's honest truth. There is nothing like the country," says Kossakowska.

Now the priest tells them about how Załuski took him to a baptism in the royal chapel at the Saxon Palace, where the most important of the neophytes were baptized.

Here Kossakowska livens up:

"But that's amazing! You were there? And you're only mentioning it now?"

"I was standing toward the back and could only see when I leaned around. But this was the second baptism of that Jacob Frank I saw, the first was in Lwów."

Father Chmielowski recounts how a murmur arose among those gathered in the church when Bishop Załuski leaned in over the baptized Frank, and his miter fell from his head onto the floor, which some took for a bad sign.

"Because what was the point of baptizing them twice—was once not enough? That's why the miter fell," says their host.

"Mrs. Brühl was the godmother, wasn't she? How did she look?" asks Kossakowska. "Still stocky?"

The priest thinks for a moment.

"She's a woman of a certain age like any other. What can I say? I have no memory for women."

"Did she say anything? How was her performance, what was she wearing, was she dressed in the Polish fashion, or the French, perhaps? Just the usual things."

The priest strains his memory, looks around as if an image of Mrs. Brühl were hanging there in the air somewhere.

"Please forgive me, Your Ladyship—I don't remember. But I do remember that Your Ladyship's dear friend Bishop Sołtyk attended the baptism of two of Frank's assistants—one was Jakubowski, and the other was Matuszewski, along with Princess Lubomirska."

"You don't say!" Kossakowska rubs her hands together. In situations such as these she really feels alive. So she did manage to talk Sołtyk into being godfather to the neophytes! And Princess Lubomirska, who in general shies away from such displays. The participation in the baptisms by such high-ranking persons convinces her husband about the matter.

"This reminds me that we have here in Podolia quite a few still to baptize," says Kossakowski, silent until now.

"My God, gracious Lord, how many of them there are! And what is the story with that big Jew with the terrifying face whom you baptized, Father?" asks Kossakowska. "He is a mute, is that right? And what happened to his face?"

The priest seems a bit embarrassed.

"Oh, you know . . . They asked me, so I agreed. He is apparently from Wallachia, an orphan, who worked for the Shorrs as a carter, and now he's helping me out at my place . . ."

"The silence that fell in the church when you brought him in! He looked like those Jews had slapped him together out of clay."

When they finally get up from the table, it is completely dark. Father Chmielowski thinks of his driver Roshko. He is anxious to find out whether they have given him anything hot to eat from the kitchen, and whether since then he hasn't frozen solid. They reassure him, and he stays for the pipe. Łabęcki always treats his guests to the finest tobacco, from the Shorrs in Rohatyn, who have the best tobacco in Podolia. No one evinces surprise when Kossakowska smokes with them—after all, she isn't a woman, she's Kossakowska. She can do as she likes.

On January 18 and 19, Stanisław Kossakowski, convinced by his wife, oversees the baptism of several so-called "Puritans." The first to become his goddaughter is the crippled Anna Adamowska, formerly Chibora, wife of Matys of Zbryż. Those in the church who see godfather and goddaughter both lame and limping wonder who came up with such a perfect pairing. The lame leading the lame—how not to laugh at it? Maybe it's a good thing: there is a certain logic to it, the broken tending to the broken. But it does seem to make the castellan somewhat uncomfortable.

The next day he will also oversee the baptism of Anna, a seven-year-old girl, daughter of the previously baptized Zwierzchowskis, formerly Leybko Hirsh of Satanów and his wife, Hava. The little girl is lovely and polite. Kossakowska arranged a white dress for her, modest but of good material, and cream-colored shoes made out of real leather. Kossakowski has also set aside a certain amount of money for her education. The Kossakowskis even thought of taking her to raise themselves, so clever and amiable is she, had her parents agreed to it. But the parents politely thanked them for all their kindness and took the child home with them.

Now these Zwierzchowskis are standing in the church, intimidated, their foreheads wet with holy water, which the priest has certainly not skimped on. He reads aloud their opulent-sounding last name. They look at that little angel led in by Mr. Kossakowski in his church kontusz. The girl's father, Josephus Bartholomeus Zwierzchowski, as his name is written in the baptismal books, is thirty-five years old, while his wife is only twenty-three and pregnant yet again. Little Anna is the only child they have who's still alive. All the others died of the Lwów plague.

## Father Gaudenty Pikulski, a Bernardine, interrogates the naive

He opens the door for them himself—they are here, after all, by his invitation. First they had to wait a long time in front of the office of the Lwów monastery; that time spent waiting wiped out the last of their self-confidence. A good thing—that'll make his job easier. He has seen a lot of them lately. They pray fervently at every mass in the Lwów cathedral and still call attention to themselves in spite of the new clothing they have purchased to replace their heavy kapotas and cropped pants. Now they look like people, thinks Gaudenty Pikulski, gesturing politely to their places at the table, gazing intrigued at Shlomo Shorr—he's shaved his beard. The skin exposed is pale, almost completely white, and in this way his face is divided into two halves: the upper half is dark, tanned, while the lower half is childlike, or as if straight out of a cellar— that's the description that pops into Father Pikulski's head. The man who has emerged from Shlomo Shorr, and who is now called Franciszek Wołowski, is a tall, thin person with a long, kind face, expressive dark eyes, and strong brows. Long hair, with a little bit of gray mixed in, falls over his shoulders and poses an amusing contrast to the tobacco-honey-colored brand-new żupan with the red Turkish belt tied around his slender waist.

They came to him of their own volition, although of course he had encouraged them, telling them at every opportunity that if they did wish to confess . . . So he recruited two secretaries, both now at the ready with their set of sharpened goose feathers and waiting for his signal.

At first they say the Lord must already be in Warsaw, seeing the king. Then they glance at one another and the one who said "Lord" corrects himself and says: Jacob Frank. The name sounds very important, as if Jacob Frank were a foreign ambassador to whom the regular laws cannot possibly apply. Father Pikulski tries to be sympathetic:

"We have heard so much about your decision to adopt the Christian religion, and the fact that that decision was made long ago, and your fervor is proverbial and brings tears to the eyes of Lwów's townspeople, and our nobility . . ."

Servants come in with refreshments, also arranged by Father Pikulski: sugared fruits, ordinary dried apples and pears, raisins and figs. All paid for by the Church. They don't know what to do with this; they look at Shlomo-Franciszek Wołowski, who makes it seem completely natural to reach out for a raisin.

". . . for many of you this is a completely different life, and in addition to that, those of you who have been successful in business are quickly becoming ennobled, like yourself, Mr. Wołowski, isn't that right?"

"Yes," answers Franciszek, swallowing. "You have it right."

Father Pikulski would like for them to start speaking on their own initiative. He passes them some little plates, intending to embolden them, particularly since both secretaries' pens are hovering over their papers now, like hail clouds that will soon release a blizzard.

The old man who has been carefully monitoring Father Pikulski as if reading his thoughts is Joseph of Satanów, who has very pale blue eyes submerged in his dark, gloomy face. "Defend me, Lord Jesus, from any form of charm," the priest prays silently, managing to not move his lips or give any outward sign of it. He turns to the whole crew of them:

"Kindly congratulate your people on their wisdom, their prudence, and the zeal of their hearts. You have now been welcomed among us, but a great curiosity still pervades our thoughts regarding how this all happened. What path did you travel to reach the true faith?"

Those who speak the most are the two Shorr brothers, Rohatyński and Wołowski, who are also the ones with the best Polish. Their Polish is actually quite proficient, only slightly shaky sometimes, and a little ungrammatical—Father Pikulski wonders who their teacher was. The remaining four join in from time to time; they haven't yet been baptized, which might be making them feel more insecure: Jacob Tyśmienicki, Joseph of Satanów, an elderly man, Jacob Szymonowicz, and Leyb Rabinowicz politely wait their turns for the delicious figs and dates, passing them from their fingertips into their mouths.

Joseph of Satanów starts:

"Anyone who really studies the Zohar will find in it warnings about the mystery of the Holy Trinity, and from then on the issue will pervade his thoughts. That was the way it was with us. There is a great truth in the Trinity, and the whole heart and mind respond to it. God is not one person, but—in some godly, unfathomable way—manifested in three figures. We have that, as well, so that the Trinity comes as no surprise to us."

"It suited us very well," Shlomo, or rather Franciszek Wołowski, takes over. "It truly is nothing new to us, for there are, after all, three revelations, three kings, three days, three swords . . ."

Pikulski looks expectantly at Wołowski, hoping he'll say more. Although he does not expect they'll tell him everything he wants to know.

Little Turkish stoves with glowing coals have just been brought in, and everyone's attention is now on the progress of the servant setting the stoves around on the floor.

"When Jacob Frank went to Turkey in 1756, he brought news of the Trinity and was able to convey it successfully to others, as he was already proficient in Kabbalah. And then, when he started riding all over Podolia, I also turned to convincing them that God was in three persons," says Franciszek Wołowski, pointing at his chest.

And he goes on to say that Jacob first told just a few chosen ones, never saying it in public, that this teaching about the Trinity is best laid out in the Christian religion, and that for this reason, this was the true faith. He also told them in secret that when he came to Poland again, they would all have to be baptized and become Christians, but he said to keep this to themselves till his return. And so they did, because they liked this plan very much, and slowly they began preparing for it, learning the language and the principles of the faith. But they also knew that it would not be easy, and that the rabbis would have trouble accepting it, and that they would have to endure a great deal, which is as it happened. They all exhale and reach for the figs.

Pikulski wonders whether they are really this naive or are merely pretending, but he can't quite penetrate their thoughts.

"And this leader of yours, Jacob, what is he like, what made you follow him with such utter dedication?"

They look at each other as if they might be communicating with their eyes, determining who is going to speak now, until finally Wołowski starts, though Paweł Rohatyński swiftly interrupts him:

"As soon as the Lord—that is, Jacob Frank—got into Rohatyn, you could immediately see a light over him," he says, and he looks at Wołowski. Wołowski hesitates for a moment about whether or not to confirm this, but Father Pikulski will not let him stop talking here, nor will the secretaries, with their pens stalled over their sheets of paper.

"A light?" Pikulski asks in a sweet voice.

"A light," Wołowski begins. "A brightness like a star, clear and pure, and then it would spread out by half a cubit or so, remaining over Jacob for some time—I'd rub my eyes to make sure I wasn't dreaming."

Now he waits to see the effect his words will have, and indeed, one of the secretaries just sits there with his mouth hanging open and doesn't write anything down. Pikulski clears his throat loudly, and the pen falls back down onto the paper.

"But that's nothing," adds an excited Jacob Tyśmienicki. "When Jacob was supposed to go to Lanckoroń, where those incidents occurred, he had already told us in Brześć that we were going to face a kind of trial in Lanckoroń and that they would sequester us. And that is exactly how it happened . . ."

"And how are we to understand that?" Father Pikulski asks in an indifferent tone.

Now they start talking amongst themselves, having switched to their language, and those who have been silent until now also suddenly remember some little miracles performed by Jacob Frank. At random they speak about Ivanie, about how he could cure people, about how he was able to respond to the brothers' and sisters' deepest secrets, never pronounced out loud. And that when they granted him more power than an ordinary person could possess, he declined it and said he was the most wretched of all the brothers. Jacob Tyśmienicki gets tears in his eyes as he is speaking, which he wipes off with his sleeves, and for a moment even Joseph's light blue gaze softens.

Here Pikulski realizes that they actually *love* this Jacob character, that they are joined with this repulsive convert by some mysterious, unquestionable bond, which in him, a monk and a priest, arouses only disgust. And it is usually the case that when bonds are very strong, there is a kind of gap, or crack, that leaves room for rebellion, and suddenly there is something in the air, and he is almost afraid to ask another question—what question can he ask? Then Franciszek Wołowski, with emotion on his face, tells him about how Jacob explained to them the necessity of converting to Christianity, how he would quote the Holy Scriptures to them at night, finding them the right verses to learn by heart. And then he adds that only a few knew of that, for it was only to the chosen ones that he revealed it. There is a momentary silence. Father Pikulski senses the odor of male sweat, sharp, musky, and he cannot quite say whether it is coming from him, from under his cassock buttoned up to the neck, or from them.

He does know he has caught them. And that they cannot be so stupid they don't know what they are doing. Before they leave, they say the end of the world is nigh now, and that there will be one Flock and one Shepherd for all the people in the world. That everyone should plan accordingly.

## Father Gaudenty Pikulski writes to Primate Łubieński

That same evening, when everyone is asleep, and the city of Lwów looks like a deserted ruin on the Podolian lowland, Pikulski seals the transcribed conversation and completes his letter. At dawn a special messenger will be dispatched to Warsaw. It is strange—Father Pikulski has no desire whatsoever to sleep, as though he has happened upon an invisible energy source that will nourish him from now on, a little hot point in the very middle of the night.

> I send Your Excellency by separate post the report from the interrogation I conducted yesterday with the Contra-Talmudists, and I believe Your Excellency will find in it a number of interesting threads that will confirm the doubts I permitted myself to note in my previous letter.
>
> I have attempted to deduce from other sources as accurately as possible whom we mean when we say "Contra-Talmudists." Father Kleczewski and Father Awedyk and I have also attempted to reconcile the information that has come from numerous other interrogations, but at this stage, that appears to be impossible. Most likely the group of Jewish converts is not at its heart a homogenous one, and they all come from different sects, the which is corroborated by the views they hold, which are mutually exclusive.
>
> It is best to ask simple, uneducated people—then one can see the whole system, stripped of sophisticated adornments, and

then their recently acquired Christian faith turns out to be just a thin layer, like icing on a cake.

And so some believe that there are three Messiahs: Sabsa Tsivi, Baruchiya, and the third is Frank himself. They also believe that the true Messiah must pass through every religion, which is why Sabsa Tsivi donned a green Muslim turban, and Frank must pass through our holy Christian Church. Others aren't convinced of that at all. They say, meanwhile, that when Sabsa Tsivi stood before the sultan, it wasn't really him, but his empty form, and that form accepted Islam, and his conversion doesn't really mean anything, it was just for appearances' sake.

It is clear that not everyone who is baptized falls from the same tree, and each of them believes in something different. What gathered them together was the Jewish curse cast on the followers of Sabsa Tsivi in 1756, which excommunicated them completely from the Jewish congregations, and whether they liked it or not, made them all "Contra-Talmudists." Some of them are thus convinced that in order to achieve true salvation, they have to convert to Christianity, while for others baptism is unconnected to salvation by our Lord Jesus Christ, and instead merely a way to get under the wing of a religious institution, as no one can live without belonging to anything. Apparently Frank calls the latter simply converts—and he doesn't count them among his own. It's from this mixed multitude that those delegates, numbering thirteen, came primarily, those who appeared at the Lwów disputation.

I would like to emphasize the extraordinary attachment of the neophytes to their leader. Everything he tells them is sacred, and they accept it without reservation. When one of them commits some offense, the Lord, as they call him, determines a corporal punishment, and then they all agree, as a group, to administer this punishment together.

I also got out of them that they believe that the Antichrist has been born in the Turkish lands and that Frank saw him himself. He will soon work certain miracles and persecute the Catholic faith. As well as the fact that to them the words of the Gospel are unclear, that Christ will arrive from Heaven as the Messiah. For—they say—is he not perhaps already in the world, in a human body? I had the impression here that, although they did not wish to say it clearly, they believe that the Messiah is hidden in the person of Frank himself. I would put this point to Your Excellency and the next inquisitions.

I learned, as well, that the village in Wallachia where Jacob Frank would visit Mr. Moliwda is in all likelihood one of Whips or Philippians, or some other sect that offends against our holy faith. Their knowledge of the Muhammadan religion also does not come from a single source, but is rather equally sectarian and disseminated amongst the officers of the Janissaries, known as Bektashi.

As for Your Excellency's questions about whether or not it is true that, as they themselves say, there are many thousands of them, I believe that, calculating carefully, there might be between five and fifteen thousand in Podolia. But not all the followers of this Sabsa Tsivi will be inclined to be baptized and—what is more—only a minority will do it, those who cannot possibly be received back into their congregations and who have no other choice than to go to Christianity, like so many dogs shooed from a yard who will seek shelter under any old roof at all. I do not think that many of them had a pure heart and accepted baptism believing in true salvation under the care of Our Lord Jesus Christ.

At the same time, I wish to inform Your Excellency that as the plague maintains its hold over Lwów, the people have been saying that this is a divine punishment against the converts, and for that reason the fervor for baptism has abated a bit. The truth is that many of the neophytes have been afflicted by the illness, both before and after baptism. Some of them believed that baptism would bring them eternal life, not only spiritually, but also materially, here on earth, which merely goes to show how little versed they are in the Christian faith and how great is their naiveté.

I now turn to Your Excellency the Primate with the urgent request that you read through all of the reports we have prepared here and, being guided by your heart and by your wisdom, determine for us what we are to do next. And as a part of Frank's company, which they themselves call giaours, has

already set off after their commander to Warsaw, they ought to
be carefully watched, lest their muddy views of Christianity,
their effrontery, and their unregenerate ambitions disgrace in
any way the Church, Our Holy Mother.

Father Pikulski has finished writing now and sets about to do his other
correspondence, but then he puts it aside and adds to that first letter:

It would be an act of very little faith, however, to consider
that the Holy Church could be in any way diminished by such
a band of fraudsters . . .

## The cornflower-blue żupan and the red kontusz

Moliwda ordered from a Polish tailor—since that's what they are called
now, the people in Warsaw who sew Polish garments, as opposed to the
more fashionable French or German ones—a silk żupan and a thick wool
broadcloth kontusz lined with soft fur. He must also commission a Słuck
sash for it, although those cost a fortune. He has looked around for one
already and liked several that he's seen. In Warsaw they cost three times
more than they do in Stamboul. If he had any talent for business, he
would import them here.

Moliwda looks at himself in the mirror. The thick kontusz adds even
more volume to his belly. But that is fine—he looks like a member of the
szlachta. Now he tries to think what it was about him that Primate Łubieński had taken such a liking to, what had placed him in such high
esteem—it certainly would not have been this belly, nor indeed any part
of his physical aspect. Moliwda has lost half his hair, and the remaining
half is dully flaxen. His face has grown fuller in the past few years, while
his eyes have become even less colorful. His beard has grown out in every
direction and looks like a bunch of old straw. It will not do for a primate's
secretary to have such a skein under his snout. What the primate must
have liked about Moliwda was his eloquence at the disputation in Lwów

and his noble relations with the neophytes. And of course the languages Moliwda knows. Not to mention Sołtyk's recommendation, since it could not have come from his cousin Kossakowska, whom Łubieński does not like.

That same day he receives two urgent letters regarding one and the same thing. Both of them put him in a state of high alert—in one he is summoned by the church commission "for imminent interrogation of the Contra-Talmudists," while the other is from Krysa. Krysa writes in Turkish that Jacob has vanished like a stone in still water. He went off alone in the carriage and never came back. The carriage was recovered near the house, but empty. No one saw anything.

Moliwda asks the primate for a delegation to Warsaw. The things the primate has to do have multiplied, in any case, and now there's the church commission, too. When the nice English carriage sets off, Moliwda takes a big gulp of the tincture, of which he has packed a whole bottle—for warmth, for digestion, for clarity of mind, and as a remedy for anxiety, since Moliwda feels as if something bad is impending, something that might swallow him up, just when he had grabbed on to that blade of grass, which, though not the most secure of moorings, had at least prevented him from sinking. When he makes it to Warsaw without having had any sleep or rest, his head hurts, and he has to squint, so aggressively does Warsaw's sun shine. The chill in the air is terrible, but there is not much snow, so the mud has frozen into clumps with just a light covering of frost, and there are sheets of ice over the puddles that anyone might slip on. Barely even conscious, Moliwda meets with Wołowski, from whom he learns that Jacob has been imprisoned by the Bernardines.

"What do you mean, 'imprisoned'?" he asks in disbelief. "What did you all tell them?"

Wołowski shrugs helplessly, and then his eyes fill with tears. Moliwda's horror mounts.

"This is the end," he says. Without another word, he goes around Wołowski, leaving him standing there alone on the muddy street as he forges ahead over frozen puddles. He nearly falls. As though just now coming to his senses, Wołowski turns and runs after him and invites him to his place.

Soon a winter darkness falls; it is unpleasant out. Moliwda knows he should first go to see Bishop Załuski, who is said to be in Warsaw now, and seek his support, rather than running straight to the neophyte Jews. He ought to search for Sołtyk, but it's too late now, and he hasn't shaved and is tired from his journey, and so he looks covetously into the open door of the Wołowskis' home, whence warmth and the smell of lye burst forth. He allows Franciszek to grab him by the elbow and guide him inside.

It is January 27, 1760. He did not make it in time for Jacob's interrogation yesterday. But there will be others.

## What was going on in Warsaw when Jacob disappeared

In the New Town, where Shlomo, or Franciszek Wołowski, has just opened a little tobacco warehouse with his brothers, there is considerable traffic. Above the store is a small apartment the brothers have rented. It is a good thing the cold has trammeled the earth, allowing you to traverse the trodden, muddied, puddle-strewn streets.

Moliwda walks into the entryway, and then the salon, where he sits down on a brand-new chair that still smells like carpenter's glue and looks at the clock that enjoys pride of place in this room and is steadily ticking. In a moment the door opens and Marianna Wołowska, Little Hayah, appears in its frame, and behind her some children, three of the youngest, the ones who don't yet go to school. She wipes her hands on the apron she has over her dark dress; he can see she was working. She looks tired and worried. From somewhere farther inside the house he can hear the sounds of a piano. Marianna takes his hands when he gets up to greet her and tells him to sit back down. Moliwda feels embarrassed that he forgot about the children, he could have at least brought them a bag of candied cherries.

"At first he simply disappeared," says Marianna. "We thought maybe he was visiting somebody for a little while, so for the first few days we weren't that worried. Then Shlomo and Jakubowski went to his house and found Kazimierz, the man he had hired as his butler, in despair, saying he had been kidnapped. Since then, someone sent for his warm clothing. Nothing else. 'Who?' we asked. 'Armed men, several of them,' he told us. So Shlomo, as soon as he arrived here from Lwów, got dressed in elegant attire and started going around town, asking, but we learned nothing. Then we started to feel very afraid, because ever since Shlomo returned from Lwów, things have been going awry."

Marianna puts a little boy onto her lap and pulls out of her sleeve a handkerchief to wipe her eyes, and while she is at it, the boy's nose. Franciszek goes out to get Yeruhim Dembowski, who lives next door, and the others.

"What is your name?" Moliwda asks the boy inattentively.

"Franio," says the child.

"Like your dad?"

"Like my dad."

"It all started with this interrogation in Lwów," Marianna continues. "It is a good thing you came, it's better that they not get all tangled up in that Polish."

"But you speak well . . ."

"Well, maybe it would be better if they would interrogate us women." She smiles bitterly. "Hayah would give them all the pipe to smoke. She and Hirsh—Rudnicki," she corrects herself, "bought a house in Leszno, they're moving in in the spring."

"Is Hayah well?"

Marianna gives him a startled look.

"Hayah is Hayah . . . The worst part is that now they're taking them to be interrogated one by one. They've taken Jakubowski." She falls silent.

"Jakubowski is a mystic and a Kabbalist. He'll fill their ears with nonsense."

"Well, exactly, what he filled their ears with, no one knows. Shlomo was saying that when they were all testifying together, Jakubowski was very afraid."

"That they would lock him up, too?" Moliwda takes Marianna's hands and moves closer to her. He whispers into her ear: "I'm scared, too. I'm sitting in the same cart as all of you, but I can see it isn't safe now. Tell your husband he's an idiot, that you all need to settle your petty, stinking scores amongst yourselves . . . You wanted to get rid of him, that's why you told them what you did, isn't that so?"

Marianna gets out of his grasp and starts crying into her handkerchief. The children look at her in fear. She turns to the door and shouts:

"Basia, take the children!"

"We are all afraid," says Marianna. "And you should be afraid, because you know all our secrets, and you are like one of us now." She raises her tearful hazel eyes to Moliwda, and for just a moment, Moliwda hears in her hushed voice the sound of a threat.


## Spit on this fire

The interrogation of the Warsaw Frankists takes place without any of them being arrested. Yeruhim, or Jędrzej Dembowski, speaks on behalf of the whole group, self-assured and talkative, along with the younger Wołowski, Jan. Both give their testimonies in Yiddish, but this time Moliwda has been made just an assistant to the main interpreter. So he sits at the table with pen and paper. Someone named Bielski interprets, quite well. Moliwda has managed to get them to speak in general terms, nice and polite.

But they keep digging themselves in deeper. When they start talking about Jacob's miracles, which he apparently worked everywhere, Moliwda is silent, biting his lip and lowering his gaze to the empty page before him, the sight of which soothes him. Why are they doing this?

Moliwda senses the initially friendly attitude of the court changing now, the inquisitors' bodies tensing, and from small talk a real hearing is created, voices get lower, the court's questions get more inquisitive and suspicious, the defendants whisper to each other nervously, while the secretary starts looking over an agenda with dates, so that maybe—thinks Moliwda in a panic—it will be like that: they'll schedule the next hearing, and the matter won't just be wrapped up the way they thought it would be.

Without even realizing it, he moves his chair away from them, closer to the stove. And sits sort of sideways now.

Shlomo, or Franciszek Wołowski, a merchant and a bit of an adventurer, who can handle both people and money, is suddenly like a little boy before the court, his lower lip trembling like he's about to cry. Yeruhim, on the other hand, acts sure of himself, acts like an open, simple man, although of course he isn't, Moliwda knows that well. He tells how they usually pray, and then the court wishes them to sing this mysterious song, the meaning of which they cannot or do not want to clarify. They look at each other uncertainly, whispering—it is obvious that they are hatching some scheme, hiding something. Matuszewski butts in, as pale as if already sentenced to death. He becomes the conductor of this choir, raising his hand, and after a moment of whispering they sing the Yigdal before the consistory court of Warsaw like schoolboys. And they get so into their singing that they forget where they are, forget the solemnity of the church. Moliwda lowers his eyes.

He has heard this song so many times and sometimes joined in, that is true, but now, in the heated interior of the episcopal court, where the smell of damp battles the smell of the lye used to clean the hearths of the stoves, where the frost on the windowpanes has sketched out overnight delicate garlands of icy leaves and branches, the words of the Yigdal sound absurd, don't make any sense. Moliwda has a position in Łowiczu in the highest Church office, with the primate of the Polish-Lithuanian Commonwealth; he has succeeded, he has come back to his country, to his people, all his faults have been forgiven, and he has been accepted back into the fold of decent people, so why would he be interested in the words of this song, and did he ever even really understand them?

As the defendants leave, they pass Jacob being led in. They squeeze up against the wall, turn pale. Jacob is ceremonially dressed, in his high hat and a coat with a collar. As if they were bringing in the king. His face is strangely focused. He looks at Wołowski, who begins to cry, and then Jacob says in Hebrew:

"Spit on this fire."

## An ocean of questions that will sink
## even the strongest battleship

Moliwda is to interpret. He has managed to weasel his way into the main position under the auspices of Bishop Załuski. Now he looks at the band in which the sides of his new kontusz are finished. He has worn the new one, but now he sees it is too showy, too elegant. He regrets his choice.

The commission is waiting. It is made up of three members of the clergy and two secular secretaries. Armed guards are still posted at the door to the hallway. Such pomp, thinks Moliwda. You would think they were interrogating a great usurper. Aside from the episcopal official, who will be playing the leading role here, there is Father Szembek, canon of Gniezno, and one Pruchnicki, the consistory registrar, and Father Śliwicki, a Jesuit and general inspector of the missionaries. They whisper to one another now, but Moliwda can't hear what they're saying.

At last the door opens, and the guards bring Jacob in. One glance at him is enough to make Moliwda concerned; Jacob seems changed, swollen somehow, and his face is tired, sagging. Have they beaten him? Suddenly Moliwda's heart begins to thump faster, as though he were running, and his throat gets dry, and his hands start shaking. Jacob looks at him. All the ideas he had prepared, and all the turns of phrase he planned to use to cover for Jacob's mistakes, now seem useless. He wipes his sweaty hands discreetly on the sides of his kontusz. There's more sweat in his armpits. They have definitely beaten him. Jacob, his eyes cast down, peeks furtively at all of them. Their gaze finally meets, and Moliwda has to summon all his strength to force himself to slowly close his eyes, signaling to Jacob that everything is going to be okay, that he just has to keep calm.

After the official introduction and the objectives of the interrogation are read out comes the first question, which Moliwda translates into Turkish. He does it literally, not adding or removing anything. They ask Jacob where he was born, where he grew up, and where he has lived during his life. They are interested in his wife and in how many children he has, as well as material goods and possessions.

Jacob doesn't want to sit down. He stays standing as he responds. His voice, deep but quiet, along with the lilt of the Turkish, make an impression on his interrogators. What does this man have to do with them? thinks Moliwda. He translates Jacob's answer sentence by sentence. Jacob says he was born in Korolówka in Podolia and then lived in Czernowitz and that his father was a rabbi. They moved many times: to Bucharest and other cities in Wallachia. He has a wife and children.

"What indication do you have regarding those who wished to join the Christian faith?"

Jacob looks up at the ceiling and sighs. He is silent. He asks Moliwda to repeat the question, but he still doesn't answer. Finally he looks up at Moliwda and speaks as if just to him. Moliwda tries to control each twitch of his own face.

"The sign by which I can recognize the true believers is that I see a light over their heads. Not all of them have it."

Moliwda translates:

"The sign that enables me to discern, according to the promise of Our Lord Jesus, those who sincerely adhere to His faith, is a light in the shape of a candle that I see over their heads."

The court requests clarification as to who is in possession of this light and who is not.

Jacob speaks reluctantly, faltering once at the mention of a name, but Moliwda translates fluidly that when it came to certain Jews, even if they tried very hard to get Jacob to accept them into the faith, even if they wanted to give him large amounts of money for it, he would reject them when he did not see the light over their heads. And he knew, in any case, who was sincere, and who had murkier intentions.

Now they ask him for details of his first stay in Poland. When he speaks in terms that are too general, they further inquire into the names of localities and the persons who hosted him. This takes a long time, and they have to wait for the secretaries to write it all down. Jacob starts to falter under this bureaucratic regimen; he has a chair brought to him, and he sits.

Moliwda translates Jacob's account of events in which he himself played a part, but he would rather not acknowledge that, and there isn't any need for him to do so, no one is asking him. He just prays that Jacob himself won't somehow spill this information; but as Frank is telling them of Nikopol and Giurgiu, he doesn't say a word about Moliwda, doesn't even look at him. The court will think that they don't know each other at all, that they met recently in Lwów, through translation, as Moliwda wrote in his statement.

They hold a small recess, during which time they bring in water and cups. The interrogator changes—now it's the Jesuit.

"Does the accused believe in God in the Trinity? That there is one in three persons? And does he believe in Jesus Christ, the True God and Man, the Messiah present in the Holy Scriptures, according to the confession of faith made by Saint Athanasius? Is he ready to swear to it?"

They give Jacob the text of the credo in Latin, which Jacob isn't able to read, so he repeats after Moliwda, sentence by sentence: "I believe in one God . . ." Moliwda adds: "with all my heart." Now they tell him to sign his name to a page with the credo on it.

Then comes the next question:

"In what places of the Holy Scriptures did the accused look into the mystery of the Holy Trinity?"

Again there is a secret little understanding that exists between the defendant and his interpreter, invisible to any other eye. Moliwda had taught him this once, Jacob remembers it well. And those lessons turn out now to be useful. First he mentions a passage from Genesis 1:26: "Let us make mankind in our image, in our likeness," and Genesis 18:3, where Abraham says to the three men as though to one: "Lord, if I have found favor . . ." Then he goes to the Psalms and points to a passage in Psalm 110: "The Lord says to my Lord: Sit at my right hand." Then he gets lost, he has his books in Hebrew with him and turns the pages, but then he finally says he is tired and would need time to find the right places.

So they ask him the next question: Where in the Scriptures does it say that the Messiah has already come, and that he is Jesus Christ, born of the Virgin Mary and crucified 1,727 years hence?

For a long time, Jacob is silent, until they have to prompt him to answer. Jacob says he was once clear on this, back when he was teaching. But after his baptism he lost that clarity of his mind, and there are certain things he doesn't need to know now, for now he and the others are guided by the priests.

Sometimes his quick reflexes amaze Moliwda. This answer, against all expectations, is to their liking.

"Which are the places in the Holy Scripture from which he was able to arrive at and lead others to the fact that the Messiah, Jesus Christ, is the true God and Creator and consubstantial Father?"

Jacob rummages around in his books but doesn't find the right passage. He rubs his forehead and finally says:

"Isaiah. 'And shall call his name Immanuel.'"

Inquisitor Śliwicki won't give up that easily. He harps on about the question of the Messiah.

"What does the defendant mean in saying that Christ will come again? Where will he come? How will that be? What does that mean that he will come to judge the living and the dead? Is it true that the defendant has maintained that he is already in the world in some human body and will appear suddenly, like lightning?"

Śliwicki's voice is calm, as if he were saying ordinary, common things, but Moliwda can feel the silence thickening, as everyone listens carefully for what Jacob will say. When he translates the Jesuit's question for Jacob, he adds in a little word: "Careful."

Jacob catches that word and speaks slowly, cautiously. Moliwda also translates slowly, waiting until Jacob finishes his sentence, turning the words over in his mind a few times.

"I never thought the Messiah would be born again on earth in human form, and I never taught that. Nor did I think he would come as some rich king who would bring down judgments among people. That he is concealed in the world is what I had in mind, that he is hidden in the guise of bread and wine. And that is what I understood at some point myself, deeply, in church in Podhajce."

Moliwda exhales but in such a way that no one will notice. He can feel that the light elegant żupan he is wearing underneath his kontusz is sopping at the armpits and down his back.

Father Szembek interjects now: "Does the defendant know the New Testament?"

"Have you read the books of the New Testament? And if so, in what language?"

Jacob says he has not, that he has never read them. Only in Lwów and here in Warsaw has he read anything from the Gospel of Saint Luke.

Father Szembek is interested in why he wore a turban and attended mosques. Why did he receive a ferman from the Porte that allowed him to settle as if he were a new Muhammadan? Is it true that he converted to Islam?

Moliwda is close to fainting—so they do know everything after all. He was an idiot to expect otherwise.

Jacob answers immediately, as soon as he understands the question. Through Moliwda's lips he says:

"If I believed that the best religion was Muhammad's, I would not have turned to Catholicism."

And he goes on to explain that the Talmudist Jews turned the Porte against him and were giving them bribes so that the Turks would apprehend him.

"Because I was persecuted, I was forced to accept that religion, but I only did it superficially, in my heart I did not have that faith as the true one even for a moment."

"Why do you write in your supplication to the sultan that you were poor and persecuted, while you told us you are wealthy, with a home with a vineyard and other properties?"

Triumph sounds in the questioner's voice—here he has caught the defendant in a lie—but Jacob does not see anything wrong about it. He responds carelessly that he was told to do this by the mayor of Giurgiu, a Turk, who saw that he could make some money that way. And what could be wrong with that? Jacob's tone seems to be saying.

Father Szembek rummages around in his papers and finds something of evident interest, since he interrupts before the Jesuit can get back to asking his questions.

"One of the men we interrogated, one Nahman, now called Piotr Jakubowski, said that you revealed to him the Antichrist in Salonika. Did you believe that?"

Jacob answers with Moliwda's lips.

"No, I never believed it. Everyone said it was the Antichrist, so I passed it along, like a tidbit."

The Jesuit gets back to it:

"Did the defendant speak of the Final Judgment as being near? How could such knowledge have been obtained?"

Moliwda hears:

"Yes, the Judgment is near, and that conviction can be found in the Christian Scriptures, that although we do not know when it will happen, it is near."

And he explains:

"To awaken the others, I cited the words of Hosea 3 and told of how for so many years we Jews had no priest and no altar, while now, we, the sons of Israel, are converting to the Lord God and seeking through that faith the Messiah, son of David. Having accepted the Christian faith, we already have priests and altars, so these must already be the last days according to that prophet."

"Was the accused aware that some of his students took him to be the Messiah? Is it true that, sitting on a chair and consuming coffee, and smoking a pipe, he permitted others to worship him while they cried and sang? Why would the accused allow this? Why would he not prevent his students from calling him 'Lord' and 'Holy Father'?"

Father Śliwicki is becoming increasingly belligerent, although he does not raise his voice at all; he asks his questions in a tone that suggests that in a moment he will rip off the veil and reveal to the world some terrifying truth, and the tension in the room increases. Now he asks why Jacob selected twelve students. Jacob explains that there were not twelve to begin with, but fourteen, and two of them died.

"Why did they all choose, at their baptisms, the names of the apostles? So that Frank is as if in the place of Our Lord and Savior?"

Jacob denies this, saying not at all, they simply chose the names they wanted. And besides, Franciszek is among them.

"God forbid," translates a sweaty Moliwda. "They simply do not know any other Christian names. Besides, there are two named Franciszek."

"Is he aware that some of his students saw some sort of light over him? What is known to him on this topic?"

Jacob says that this is the first time he is hearing of it, and that he does not know what it means, either.

Now Father Szembek asks another question:

"Did he foretell his imprisonment in Lanckoroń and in Kopyczyńce, his wife's arrival in Podolia, the death of Piotr Jakubowski's child, as well as the deaths of two persons from the family of Elijah Wołowski, and even his detention here, as witnesses from previous interrogations have testified?"

It strikes Moliwda that Jacob is trying to minimize himself, as if suddenly understanding that his person is too big, too attention-grabbing. Just as before he played the big man, just as he lorded everything over everyone, now he takes on this new role, imperceptibly and somehow naturally playing the role of insignificant defendant, polite, acquiescent, happy to cooperate, stripped of both teeth and claws—a little lamb. Moliwda knows him well enough to see that Jacob is cleverer than all the rest of the assembly put together, though they take him for an idiot, just as the Jews once did, and he himself seemed to have a particular fondness for hiding in smallness, for taking on the guise of a simpleton. When was it he used to say that he could barely read?

Moliwda translates his response almost word for word:

"I did predict the arrest in Lanckoroń, but not in Kopyczyńce. Regarding my wife, I just figured out how much time my messenger needed to get to her, and how much time she'd need for packing, and to get there, and that's how I happened to figure it would be on a Wednesday. Jakubowski's child was born weak and sick. But that I could have predicted the death of someone from the Rohatyn Wołowski family—that I don't remember. It's a big family, someone's always dying in it. And it is true that I was praying over the book and suddenly said out loud, 'In two weeks.' I don't know why I said that, but those who heard those words explained them immediately as imprisonment by the Bernardines. I also admit that when someone adhering sincerely to the faith was to come, my nose would itch on the right side, and when it was someone who was insincere in their belief, then it was on the left side that my nose itched—that was how I'd sense it."

And now the honorable judicial commission is laughing discreetly.

Father Szembek and Father Pruchnicki, the secretary and the episcopal official. The only person not laughing is the Jesuit, but everyone knows, thinks Moliwda, that Jesuits have no sense of humor.

The Jesuit asks somberly:

"Why when someone comes to the accused in illness, does he perform some sort of charm over him, touching his forehead with his fingers and whispering spells? And what does he mean by such charms?"

The hilarity among the commission has emboldened Jacob a little. Moliwda sees that from now on the defendant will play both angles, be strong and weak, so that nothing will be clear, so that each person will have the impression that his notions are contradictory and vague.

"What I mean by a charm is when someone puts the evil eye on somebody. I would undo that charm on everyone who needed it." Now Jacob says the names of those who died, to once more diminish his strength. He says, "I did it for Werszek, who had already been baptized, who died here in Warsaw, and for Reb Mordke, called Mordechai, who died back in Lublin. It didn't seem to help them."

Now the interrogators turn to Ivanie—this period interests them a great deal. Is it true, they ask, that in Ivanie he commanded them to have nothing of their own, to give everything over for communal use? And furthermore, that whenever several of them would argue and finally come to some agreement, then that idea was God's? Where did he get those ideas?

Jacob is tired, they've been there all afternoon, and in this stuffy, unventilated room, all he wants is water. He says he doesn't know, that he has no idea. He rubs his forehead.

"Is it true that you forbade them from giving their children to their godparents and good Catholics to raise, telling them they had to stick together? Is that true?" Father Szembek reads from a page. The testimonies they have are evidently quite extensive.

And further:

"Is it true," asks the priest, "that his students replace the name of Jesus in their copies of the New Testament with the name Jacob?"

Jacob counters this briefly. He stands with his head bowed. He's lost his confidence.

When the interrogation is over, Moliwda says goodbye to an

unexpectedly chilly Father Śliwicki and a silent Father Szembek, and he walks right by Jacob, without even looking at him.

He knows they will not invite him back to the next hearing, that they don't trust him.

He steps out into the frosty Warsaw air, and the cold, predatory wind blows open his kontusz, so he wraps it tightly around him and goes down toward Długa Street, but then he realizes he is afraid to go to the Wołowskis, so he turns around and slowly drags himself toward the barriers by the church at Three Crosses Square. When he gets there, guilt—dark, sticky—overwhelms him, and there is nothing really left for him to do but go inside the little Jewish tavern and drink, showing off to the alewife his knowledge of Hebrew.

In the morning they bring him a letter from the primate's chancellery that says he is to report there in the afternoon. He pours a bucket of cold water over his head, rinses his mouth out with water and vinegar. He stands with his face to the window and tries to pray, but he is so shaken up he can't find within himself that place from which he is usually able to launch like a stone thrown into the sky. Now he's very aware of the ceiling over his head. He knows what is about to happen, and he wonders whether they will let him leave. He glances at his minimal luggage.

At the primate's palace, some ordinary priest receives Moliwda, not even introducing himself, and takes him in silence into a tiny room, where there is just a table and two chairs, and on the wall hangs an enormous cross with a skinny Christ on it. The priest sits facing him, folds his hands one over the other and says gently, not appearing to be addressing anyone in particular, that the past life of the esteemed Mr. Antoni Kossakowski, alias Moliwda, is well-known to the Church, in particular that heretical time spent in the colony of apostates in Wallachia. The activities of the Philippians are also known, and they fill right-minded Catholics with great disgust. The Commonwealth is not the country for such perversions, and all dissidents from the true faith ought to find themselves another place to live. Known to the Church, as well, are the esteemed Mr. Kossakowski's youthful transgressions; the Church's memory is everlasting; the Church never forgets. And he goes on and on like this, as if showing off his information, and the information is a massive trove, and then the priest opens a drawer and pulls out a few sheets of paper and a small bottle of ink. He steps out for a moment to bring back a pen, and with his fingertip he checks to see whether it is sharp enough. In one word, he alludes to Łowicz. Moliwda is so depressed that he ceases to be able to understand him. The priest's words are still knocking around in his head: magic, metempsychosis, incest, unnatural practices . . . and he feels as if a great weight has pinned him down.

Then the priest tells Moliwda to write. He says there is no limit to the time he has. Everything he knows about Jacob Frank that other people might not know. And Moliwda writes.

## 23.

## What hunting is like at Hieronim Florian Radziwiłł's

Until February 2, Candlemas Day, a festive atmosphere prevails throughout the country. Ball costumes are aired out in the cold, wrinkled dresses
over panniers, silk żupans, elegant cassocks. Even in the peasant chambers holiday clothes are hung around, trimmed with ribbons, beautifully
embroidered. In the pantries there are pots of honey and lard, cucumbers
quietly pickling in great, gloomy barrels, livening up only in the hand
of some impatient person—then, slippery, they escape. Hanging from
poles are sausage rings, smoked hams, and fatback from which some bold
scout stealthily slices off pieces each day. As little as a month ago, these
were living animals, trusting in their cozy stables and barns, with no
idea they wouldn't make it past Christmas. Mice plunder sacks of nuts;
cats, fat and lazy at this time of year, settle atop the sacks, but it rarely
comes to a confrontation—the mice are too smart for that. The scent of
dried apples and plums fills people's homes. Music bursts out from doors
opened onto the chilly night like the puffs of steam that come from
human breaths.

Primate Łubieński, a person who, at his core, is vain and childish, has
been invited by Radziwiłł to hunt, and he takes with him one of his

secretaries, Antoni Kossakowski, known as Moliwda. They sit in the same carriage as his adviser Młodzianowski, since the primate never stops working. Moliwda neither likes nor respects this man, having seen a great deal already at the palace in Łowicz. He tries to make some notes, but the carriage shudders in the frozen ruts and doesn't let him.

They are silent for a long while, as the primate observes through the window a noisy, happy sleigh ride passing by; finally Moliwda works up the courage to say:

"Your Excellency, may I beseech you to dismiss me . . ."

Now the carriage crosses over a wooden bridge, which feels like an earthquake might.

"Yes, I know what you want," Primate Łubieński says, and falls silent. After a pause that seems endless to Moliwda, the primate adds: "You're scared. I don't see anything wrong with the fact that you were their interpreter. It might even be better, because you know more. You know, Mr. Kossakowski, strange things are said about you. People say you've eaten bread out of more than one stove. And that you're an important figure among the heretics. Is that true?"

"Your Excellency, those were youthful excesses. I was hotheaded, but with time I have become more reasonable. Regarding the heretics, that is mere gossip. I know many other histories, but that of the heretics—no."

"Then tell us a story, it will make the time go by," says the primate, and rests his head back on the padding behind him.

Moliwda thinks for a moment that the time has come for him to tell the story of his life, to get rid of that old burden and on this cold day start a new life. He realizes that it was Kossakowska's influences that found a way to get him into this position—Kossakowska, who does not care for Łubieński and considers him an enemy to Polish interests and an unworthy man. No doubt in order to have someone she trusted in the opposition camp. She promised, in exchange, to quash any rumors that might be circling Moliwda like a different sort of halo.

No, Moliwda will never tell these two people what really brought him to the place in which he finds himself now. So he tells them how he and some random fellow passengers, met at sea by a squall, had to tether one another to the masts so that the waves wouldn't take them . . . And how the sea tossed him ashore, where he was found by a beautiful princess, the daughter of the king of the island, how he was imprisoned in a cave and fed from a basket on a long pole, for they feared his red beard . . . And it is clear that the primate has never seen a sea, or a beach, or a princess, or probably even a cave, for his imagination can't keep up, and he is overcome by boredom and starts to doze off. Moliwda calms down. Perhaps too quickly.

In the evening when they stop, once they have eaten dinner, the primate asks him to tell them about the Philippians and the Bogomils. Which Moliwda, ensnared, reluctantly, and in the most general possible terms, does.

"Just think of all a person can still learn. And what we believe we can find out only from a heresy," the primate sums up Moliwda's lecture, with the smile of a child much pleased by the strength of his own pronouncement.

Hieronim Florian Radziwiłł has been preparing for this day for months. Hundreds of peasants on his estates in Lithuania have captured every variety of animal: foxes, wild boars, wolves, bears, elk, and roe deer have been jammed into great cages transported by sled to Warsaw. Along the Vistula, he had a big field planted with little Christmas trees, giving rise to an artificial forest with simple footpaths. In the very center there are elegant facilities for important guests and friends of King Augustus— two stories, covered in green cloth on the outside and lined in black fox skins within. Farther down, past the enclosure, stands for the spectators have been built.

The king and his sons and their entourage, in which Primate Łubieński rubs shoulders with the rest of the purpurate class, have entered those facilities, and the szlachta and the courtiers have settled in the stands, to have a good view. Brühl and his wife are a little bit late, arriving once the chase is already under way. In the frosty air, everyone is having a great time, aided by the mead and the mulled wine with spices, supplied in generous portions by the servants. Moliwda casts furtive glances at the king, whom he is seeing for the first time. August is big, fat, sure of himself, and ruddy-cheeked from the cold. His soft, closely shaved royal chin looks as soft as a big baby's. Next to him, his sons are scrawny brats. He drinks, knocking back the whole goblet in one gulp, leaning his head back and then, following the Polish custom, flicking the rest onto the ground. Moliwda cannot take his eyes off the soft, quivering jowl.

At the trumpet's signal, the animals are released in batches from their cages. The stunned and frozen animals, long motionless, barely standing now, linger by the cages, not understanding what they're supposed to be running from. Then the dogs are released on them, and there is a terrible tumult: the wolves attack the elk, the bears the boar, the dogs the bears, all in front of the king, who is shooting at them.

Moliwda pushes his way toward the rear; he reaches the tables where the snacks are laid out and asks for vodka. They pour him a glass, and then a second, and then a third. By the time the show is over, he is pretty drunk, which makes him conversational. The king has apparently derived an even greater enjoyment from this entertainment than had been expected, and no doubt Prince Radziwiłł is responsible, everyone says. And since the king is not a frequent visitor to Warsaw, he appreciates it all the more. A fat nobleman in a fur cap with a feather in it, who speaks with an eastern accent, tells Moliwda that Florian Radziwiłł is a man of great imagination, with a hobby of shooting animals like cannonballs out of a specially built machine. Then he shoots at them as they fly—that's how it was in Słuck in the year 1755, so memorable for its great winter, when foxes were shot in midair. For wild boar a special hedgerow was designed, and at its end, just below, there was a moat filled with water; the boar were herded into that hedge and then sicced with dogs, and when they tried to run in terror, they fell straight into the moat, where they would try in vain to swim, becoming easy targets for the shooters. This inspired great jubilation amongst the guests, in which Moliwda's interlocutor also had his share.

Here, meanwhile, there is another attraction in the afternoon. All the hunters, who are by then quite tipsy, gather around a special arena—young boar are let into it with cats tethered to their backs like riders. A pack of dogs is set against them. Everyone enjoys it enormously, so that they are all in an excellent mood when it comes time for the ball in which the day's hunting finally culminates.

---

Moliwda returns alone. His Excellency the Primate of the Common-wealth remains for a while longer a guest of the magnate. The secretary, however, is hastened on by important matters of the Church. He reaches Warsaw, whence he is to pick up letters for Łowicz, but this takes him barely three hours. He doesn't even notice what the capital looks like on such a gloomy winter day as this. He doesn't look at anything at all. Or maybe he sees out of the corner of his eye the wide streets, muddy—you have to watch out for horse shit, steaming in the chill of this strange air, which seems to Moliwda so foreign that he would be unable to breathe it for long. He can smell the cold steppe, the wind. He realizes how stiff he is, how shrunken, and whether because of the cold or the alcohol he has consumed, he is panting rather than breathing. In the afternoon he sets out for Łowicz. He travels on horseback, without stopping.

Outside Warsaw, the sky is gray, low, the horizon expansive and flat. It looks like the earth won't be able to bear the burden of the sky for much longer. On the battered road, the wet snow is beginning to turn to ice—it is late afternoon, soon it will be dark, which is why more and more horses are congregated out in front of the inn. The odor of horse urine and drop-pings and sweat mixes with the smoke that comes out of the inn's crooked chimney and bursts out its open door. Two women in red skirts and short sheepskin coats thrown over their white holiday shirts stand at the door-way, carefully examining all who enter, evidently searching for someone in particular. The younger, rounder one successfully grapples with the aggressive advances of a drunk man in a dun sukmana.

The inn itself is a building made of wooden logs whitewashed with lime, low, with several small windows and a thatched reed roof. On the bench by the fence sit old women who come here out of boredom to watch the wide world. Wrapped in plaid wool shawls, with frozen red noses, they sit in silence and look attentively, without sympathy, at everyone who passes. Sometimes they exchange a word over some minor event. Sud-denly the two women in the sheepskin coats notice someone, and a scrim-mage breaks out, with shrieks. Maybe it's one of the women's drunken husband, or maybe a runaway fiancé—the man extricates himself from the women, and then, once he has been calmed down, allows himself to be led toward the village. The iced snow crunches under the hooves of the horses, who also look hopefully at the smoky entrance to the inn, but only muffled sounds of instruments can be heard from inside. The most melancholy sound in the world, thinks Moliwda: music heard from a distance, crippled by the wooden walls, the buzz of human beings, the scraping of the ice—reduced to hollow, lonely drumbeats. Soon the sound of distant bells from the town will join in and flood the whole area with an unbearable despair.

### Scraps: Of the three paths of the story and how telling a tale can be its own deed

Nahman, or Piotr Jakubowski, has been sitting in his tiny room and writing for many days now. It is terribly cold in the apartment he and Wajgełe rented in Solec, which is far away from everything. Wajgełe has not been herself since the death of the child; whole days go by without her saying a word. No one comes to see them, and they don't go to see anyone. Dusk falls fast, the color of rust. Jakubowski gathers wax and squeezes together new candles from the scraps. He writes out page after page that falls onto the floor.

. . . overflows. Every situation feels endless to me when I try to describe it, and out of helplessness, the pen falls from my hands. The description of a situation never fully exhausts it, for there is always something left undescribed. When I write, every detail sends me back to another, and then the next one again to something else, to some sign or gesture, so that I must always make a decision about what direction to pursue, in telling this story, where to fix my internal gaze, that same powerful sense that is able to summon back past images.

So in writing I stand at every moment at a crossroads, like the idiot Ivan from the fairy tales Jacob used to love telling us so much back in Ivanie. And now those crossroads are before my eyes, those bifurcating paths, of which one, the simplest one, the middle path, is for fools, while the other, to the right, is for the overconfident,

and then there is the third path, which is for the brave, the
desperadoes, even—that one will be full of traps, potholes, hexes,
and calamitous occurrences.

It happens that sometimes I choose that simple road, the one in
the middle, and I naively forget about all the complications of what
I am describing, trusting in the so-called facts, the events as I
would narrate them to myself, as if my eyes were the only ones to
perceive them, as if there were no hesitation or uncertainty in
existence, and things were as they appeared to be (even as we behold
them, as I discussed so feverishly with Moliwda back in Smyrna).
Then I write: "Jacob said," as if it weren't my ears that heard it, but
God's—that is what Jacob said, and that is a fact. I describe a place
as if others would have experienced it as I did, as if that were the
way it was. I trust my memory, and in recording what comes out of
it, I make that frail instrument into a hammer that is to forge a
bell. Going down that path, I believe that what I describe really
happened, and that it happened that way once and for all. I even
believe that there was never any chance of anything else having
happened instead.

The simple middle road is false.

When such doubt comes over me, I choose the road on the right.
Now it is the other way around—I am the rudder and the ship, and
so I focus on my own experiences, as if the world before my eyes
did not exist but was instead formed solely by my senses. And in
spite of what Reb Mordke always taught me, I blow on my own fire
and thereby ignite the embers of my self, about which I ought to
forget, the ashes of which I should rather scatter to the wind—but
instead I feed it until it is a gigantic flame. And then what do I
have? Me, me, me—a regret-worthy state of accidental imprisonment
in a hall of mirrors, the sort the Gypsies sometimes put up in order
to charge an admission fee. Then everything is more about me than
it is about Jacob, his words and acts are made to pass through the
sieve of my tangled vanity.

The road to the right is a pathetic state indeed.

Therefore in desperation but also hope I run toward the left,
and in doing so, make the same choice as the idiot Ivan. Just like
him, I let myself be guided by chance and the voices of those who
would help me. No one who did not do this, who did not trust the
voices from the outside, would survive that madness of the left path,
instead becoming an instant victim of the chaos. Recognizing
myself as a speck being whipped around by greater forces,

recognizing myself as a boat on the sea flung around by the waves (as when we sailed to Smyrna with Jacob), abandoning my ideas of my own power and having the trust to surrender to rule, I really become the idiot Ivan. And yet, it was he who conquered all the princesses and all the kingdoms of the world and tricked the most powerful into their downfalls.

And so I, too, surrender to the guidance of my own Hand, my own Head, Voices, the Ghosts of the Dead, God, the Great Virgin, Letters, Sefirot. I go sentence by sentence, blindly down the line, and although I don't know what awaits me at the end, I patiently stumble forward, not inquiring into the price I will have to pay, and even less so about any reward. My friend and ally is that moment, that urgent hour, the dearest time to me, when suddenly out of nowhere the writing gets easy, and then everything appears to be wonderfully able to be expressed. What a blissful state it is! Then I feel safe, and the whole world becomes a cradle that the Shekhinah has laid me down in, and now the Shekhinah leans in over me like a mother over an infant.

The path to the left is only for those who have shown they deserve it, those who understand what Reb Mordke always said—that the world itself demands to be narrated, and only then does it truly exist, only then can it flourish fully. But also that by telling the story of the world, we are changing the world.

That is why God created the letters of the alphabet, that we might have the opportunity to narrate to him what he created. Reb Mordke always chuckled at this. "God is blind. Did you not know that?" he would say. "He created us that we would be his guides, his five senses." And he would chuckle long and hard until he began to cough from the smoke.

On February 17, 1760, they summoned me to be interrogated, and I concluded that I would disappear now, as Jacob already had. I could not sleep the whole night and was unable to get dressed for the interrogation, as though now that Jacob had left us, my body clung to the old Jewish clothes. I remember that I went out dressed in the Jewish fashion, wearing my own old clothes, and that it wasn't until I was out on the street that I turned back, in order to change into the nondescript outfit of black wool we had been wearing here, neither ours nor anyone else's, and so short that right away my calves began to freeze.

The old idiot Jew dressed up as the little dandy, Wajgełe's eyes said. Her face was full of skepticism (and maybe contempt), her cheeks red so that up close you could see the tiny networks of veins in them. Her lips, once so full, so joyful, had now set into a grimace of displeasure. Wajgełe knows that everything bad that has happened, happened because of me.

Walking with Matuszewski, who saw me off, I thought how I had never seen a city like Warsaw—the broad, completely empty streets, the blocks of frozen mud creating clods impossible to traverse or even, in many cases, to leap over, human figures more reminiscent of lumpen bundles, their heads grown into their fur collars. In their midst, the carriages, gleaming with lacquer, with the ornate initials of their owners, their coats of arms, their feathers, medallions. Vanity after vanity in this world made out of ice. My whole body was shaking from the cold, and tears were flowing from my eyes, and I could not tell whether they were on account of nervousness or cold.

It was early morning, and wagons of firewood, harnessed to slow, heavy horses, were standing at the gates of households while the peasants, wrapped in their warmest clothes, carried the wood in bundles tied with string and set them into piles. Some well-dressed Armenian was opening up his warehouse, which had a glass window; I glimpsed in that sheet of glass my own reflection, and it actually hurt to see myself looking so pathetic. Who was I, and what had happened to me? Where was I supposed to go, and what was I to say? What were they going to ask me, and in what language would I respond to them?

Suddenly it seemed to me that those decorations I once fleetingly envisioned as the whole world had now faded and aged so that no one could possibly be taken in by them today. The illusion is so imperfect, hideous and crippled. We are living in Hayah's board game—we are the little figures molded out of bread by her nimble fingers. We move around the circles drawn over the board, meeting one another, and everyone is a task and a challenge for everyone else. And now we are approaching the decisive place—one toss of the dice and we will gain or lose everything.

Who would Jacob become if the game let him win here? He'd turn into one of those self-assured, arrogant people who go for ostentatious pleasure rides through the streets of this northern city in their carriages. He'd live like they do, emptily and sluggishly. The spirit would leave him in shame, not as it entered him, but with a disappointed sigh. Or it would slip out of his body like a fart or a belch. Jacob, my beloved Jacob, would become a piteous convert, and in the end, his children would be able to pay their way into their noble titles. The entire path we've traveled up till now would lose its reason and its meaning. We'd be stuck here, on this little stopover, like prisoners. We would have mixed up our immense objectives with just another pause along the way.

How can I talk without saying anything? With what sort of vigilance can I equip myself so that I won't be seduced by the game, by smooth words? We studied this, and he tried to teach us.

I prepared well. I left all my money and a few valuables for my son with Marianna Wołowska, I put my books in order, and I bound together my writings with a string. As God is my witness, I was not afraid. I actually even felt cheerful to be attending such a ceremonious occasion, since I knew from the very beginning, when I thought of this plan, that I was doing the right thing, and that I was doing it for Jacob, even if he would curse me for it, even if he never let me see him again.

This I knew with ever greater certainty, but it tired me, and at night I could not sleep, so much did my recurring memories boil my blood. For it seemed to me that sudden esteem had altered Jacob beyond recognition, that he had started to care much more about his clothing and his carriage than he did about the great idea he had to convey to others. Now he busied himself with shopping and perfumes. He preferred the Christian barber to shave his beard and trim his hair; he would tie a perfumed handkerchief around his neck and call it a stock tie. In the evenings, women would massage oil into his hands, because he had complained that they were getting chapped from the cold. He would chase after women, give them presents he would purchase using our common funds, which Osman and I had already been grumbling about back in Ivanie. The change took place after he started seeing bishops and bargaining with them with Moliwda's help. It was like doing trade, like in Craiova at the office, as in Izmir, when he went around with a pearl or a precious stone to a meeting in order to sell it. I accompanied him many times and know that in no respect did that differ from this commerce here. There he would sit at a table, and he would take the jewel out of its silk pouch, place it on a piece of cloth, having also set up the candles to put it in the best possible light, and in that way the beauty of the merchandise came out. And here we were the merchandise.

As I walked in this way through that frozen city, I remembered that particular evening in Salonika when the Spirit entered Jacob for the first time. Jacob was drenched in sweat, and fear had dulled his eyes, and the air around us got so thick that it seemed to me that we were moving slower and speaking slower, as though suspended in honey. And everything then was true; so true the whole world hurt, for you could feel how unwieldy it was and how far removed from God.

And then and there, young and unseasoned, we were in our proper place; God spoke to us.

And now everything has become *untrue,* this whole city—painted lightly on a panel, as the background is painted for puppets in little market fair theaters. And we, too, are changed, as if someone had cast an evil spell on us.

I walked down those streets and had the impression that everything was looking at me, and I knew that I would have to do what I had planned in order to save not only Jacob, but all of us, and our road to salvation, since here, in this flat country, it had begun to twist and turn in disturbing ways, to turn back on itself and to mislead.

I believe there was one other person in our havura who knew what I was going to do. That was Hayah Shorr, now Rudnicka or Lanckorońska—it was hard for me to remember all those new last names. I could distinctly sense her supporting me, knew that she was with me even from afar, and that she understood my intentions quite well.

At first, Jacob's testimony was read to us. It took a long time, and it was in Polish, so we did not understand it all. Jacob's answers sounded artificial in that official style of speech, and untrue. Then one of the priests solemnly warned us not to listen to any further "fairy tales" from Jacob Frank, nor to believe his stories about the Prophet Elijah or other matters he did not even wish to mention, not wanting to give them any weight.

A little priest was chiding six defendants, all adult men . . . In the end, he made the sign of the cross in the air above us, and I felt like Judas—for I had to tackle the matter everyone else was too repulsed by to take in hand.

I went to the interrogation first. I had to present that truth to our persecutors, knowing well what would happen. The Messiah must be imprisoned and persecuted. That is what was said, and that is what must happen. The Messiah must fall down into the lowest realm, the lowest of all possible realms.

They started with Smyrna. I was not forthcoming, they had to drag things out of me, but that, too, was a part of my plan. I played the role of the kind of person who does not like to brag, and they took me for a stupid oaf. But I told the truth. I would not have been able to lie about such things. About others—of course; lying is useful in business, but here I could not lie. I tried to say as little as I could about it, but just enough to make an impression on them. I also didn't say too much, in order to protect us. I told them about the ruah haKodesh, the descent of the Holy Spirit, about the light we all saw over Jacob's head, the prophecy of death, the halo, the Antichrist he met in Salonika, the impending end of the world. They were polite and even stopped asking questions. I spoke factually and concretely, and even when it came to corporeal matters, I did not hesitate to reveal anything. All you could hear was my voice and the scraping of pens.

When I had finished and was leaving the room, I passed Shlomo in the doorway. We glanced at each other. I felt great relief, and at the same time, such enormous sadness that I sat down right there on the street, against the wall, and began to weep. I only came to my senses when some passerby threw a coin at me; it landed in my lap.

## Hana, consider in your heart

Hana is constantly having someone go and check whether the post hasn't come.

It hasn't.

No help comes from any direction, and trying to resist Her Ladyship no longer makes sense. Mrs. Kossakowska has already arranged a dress for her, and shoes, just as she has for little Avacha. The baptism is slated for February 15.

Hana wrote to her father in Giurgiu, as soon as they had word of Jacob's imprisonment. She wrote it straight: the episcopal court, on the basis of interrogating her husband and—perhaps even more so—his followers, had found Jacob guilty of proclaiming himself the Messiah, and the highest-ranking church official in Poland, that is, the primate, sentenced him to life imprisonment in the Częstochowa fortress, a sentence no one will be able to appeal.

> All this seems mad to me. Since if he was such a heretic as
> they make him out to be, then why would they put him in the
> holiest sanctuary they have? Right there with their greatest
> teraphim? That I cannot and do not want to understand.
> Father, what am I to do?

She did get an answer to that two weeks later—in other words, as soon as possible. That meant letters could reach her, just not from Jacob. She read it when she finally found herself alone, facing the wall, crying. What it said was:

> Hana, consider in your heart what you can and cannot do,
> for you will be putting yourself and your children at risk.
> Be—as I have tried to teach you—like the smartest animal that
> sees what others do not see and hears what others do not hear.
> Since you were a child, everyone has always marveled at your
> careful consideration.

Her father goes on to assure her that they will receive her with open arms at any time.

But what sticks in Hana's mind is that first sentence of the letter: "Hana, consider in your heart."

She feels those words like they're a physical weight, somewhere just beneath her breasts, on the left side.

Hana is twenty-two years old, and she has two children, and she has wilted and become very thin. She is skin and bones now. She tries to negotiate, through a translator, with Kossakowska, but it would appear that that window has closed. Supposedly free, she feels as if she is in prison. She looks through the window at the grayish-white landscape, the bare orchard, pathetic and barren, and she understands that even if she were to get out of here, it wouldn't matter, because this orchard and these fields, and this scant network of roads, the fords in the rivers and even the sky and the earth itself will be her prison. It is a good thing that Wittel Matuszewska and Pesel Pawłowska are there with her; Kossakowska treats the former as her secretary and the latter as a maid, chiding her exactly as she does her employees.

From early in the morning on February 19, Hana has been waiting in her ceremonial garments as if she was about to be thrown to the dragon to be devoured. It is a Tuesday, an ordinary day, cold and gloomy. The staff is bustling around the house, the girls lighting the tiled stoves, giggling and calling out. The cold is moist and sticky and stinks of ash. Avacha cries, seems to have a fever, senses her mother's anxiety, and follows her with her eyes above the little wooden doll she dresses and undresses. The one she got for Christmas is seated on her bed; Avacha hardly ever touches her.

Hana looks out the window, Kossakowska's carriage is already pulling up, cream-colored, with the Potocki coat of arms on the door, the one Avacha likes so much she would like to ride in it everywhere they go. Hana looks away from it. She massages her arms, because the beautiful dress she received from Kossakowska for her baptism has sleeves of thin gauze. She looks through her chest for a warm Turkish scarf in dark red and wraps herself in it. The scarf smells of their home in Giurgiu—of dry, sun-cracked wood and raisins. Tears come to her eyes, and Hana abruptly turns away from her daughter so she won't know her mother's crying. Any minute now, the girls will come in with her coat, and she will have to go down with them. So she tries to pray quickly: Dio mio Baruchiah, Our Lord, Luminous Virgin—she doesn't even know what she's supposed to say in a prayer like that. What had her father told her to do? She brings back the incomprehensible words, one by one. Her heart starts beating quickly, and she knows that she has to do something fast.

When the door opens, Hana faints clean to the floor, and the blood pours from her nose. The girls run up to her, letting out cries, to try to revive her.

And so her prayer has been heard. The baptism must be postponed.

# V.

## *The Book of*
# METAL AND SULFUR

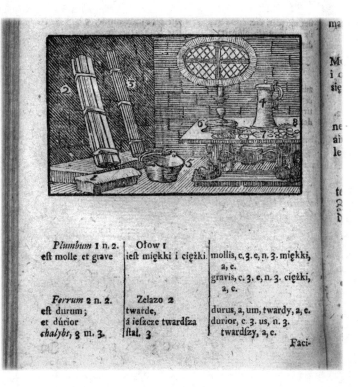

| Plumbum 1 n. 2. | Ołow 1 | mollis, c. 3. e, n. 3. miękki, |
| est molle et grave | iest miękki i ciężki. | a, e. |
| | | gravis, c. 3. e, n. 3. ciężki, |
| | | a, e. |
| Ferrum 2 n. 2. | Zelazo 2 | durus, a, um, twardy, a, e. |
| est durum; | twarde, | durior, c. 3. us, n. 3. |
| et dúrior | á iefzcze twardſza | twardſzy, a, e. |
| chalybs, 3 m. 3. | ſtal. 3 | Faci- |

# 24.

## The messianic machine, how it works

Among the advantages of the state in which Yente has found herself is that she now understands the workings of the messianic machine. She sees the world from above—it is dark, faintly marked by sparks of light, each of them a home. A faltering glow in the western sky draws a red line under the world. A dark road winds, and beside it the river's current gleams like steel. Along the road moves a vehicle, a tiny dot that can hardly be seen; a dull rattle spreads in waves through the dark, thick air as the cart goes over the little wooden bridge and on past the mill. The messianic machine is like that mill standing over the river. The dark water turns the great wheels evenly, without regard for the weather, slowly and systematically. The person by the wheels seems to have no significance; his movements are random and chaotic. The person flails; the machine works. The motion of the wheels transfers power to the stone gears that grind the grain. Everything that falls into them will be crushed into dust.

Getting out of captivity also requires tragic sacrifices. The Messiah must stoop as low as possible, down into those dispassionate mechanisms of the world where the sparks of holiness, scattered into the gloom, have been imprisoned. Where darkness and humiliation are greatest. The Messiah will gather the sparks of holiness, which means that he will leave behind him an even greater darkness. God has sent him down from on high to be abased, into the abyss of the world, where powerful serpents will mercilessly mock him, asking: "Where's that God of yours now? What happened to him? And why won't he give you a hand, you poor thing?" The Messiah must remain deaf to those vicious taunts, step on the snakes, commit the worst acts, forget who he is, become a simpleton and a fool, enter into all the false religions, be baptized and don a turban. He must annul all prohibitions and eliminate all commandments.

Yente's father, who saw with his own eyes the First, that is, Sabbatai, brought the Messiah on his lips into their home and passed it on to his favorite daughter. The Messiah is something more than a figure and a person—it is something that flows in your blood, resides in your breath, it is the dearest and most precious human thought: that salvation exists. And that's why you have to cultivate it like the most delicate plant, blow on it, water it with tears, put it in the sun during the day, move it into a warm room in the nighttime.

## Of Jacob's arrival, on a February night in 1760, in Częstochowa

They get on the Warsaw highway. The wheels of the carriage clatter over the slick cobblestones. The horses of the six armed men must pull forward and keep to the narrow road so as not to fall into the mud. Dusk approaches, and the last scraps of color fade into darkness, white murks into gray, gray becomes black, and black vanishes into the abyss that opens up before human eyes. It is everywhere, under every thing in the world.

The little town of Częstochowa is situated on the left side of the Warta River, facing the monastery on the hill. It is made up of some dozen little homes, low, unsightly, damp, set up around a rectangular marketplace and along several little streets. The market is almost empty, its uneven, undulating cobblestones thinly iced over so that they seem to be covered in a shiny glaze. Yesterday's trade fair has left horse droppings, trampled hay, and litter not yet swept up. Most of the little houses have double doors protected by an iron bar, which means that business is conducted inside them, although it would be difficult to guess what sort.

They pass four women wrapped in plaid woolen shawls, from underneath which bright patches of aprons and bonnets stick out. A drunk man in a ragged peasant's sukmana staggers by and grabs on to the beams of an empty stall. In the market square they turn right, onto the road that leads to the monastery. It is immediately visible when they emerge into the open: a tall tower, shooting straight up into the sky, alarming. Along the road, trees have been planted, and the lindens, now bare, accompany this shot of alarm like a soprano with a powerful bass.

Suddenly a ragged snippet of a song is heard—it is coming from a group of pilgrims making their way quickly toward the little town. At first this song sounds like mere clamor, background noise, but gradually words can be distinguished, women's high-pitched voices echoed by the rumble of two or three men's: "We escape into your care, O Holy Mother of God . . ."

These tardy pilgrims hurry past them, and the road is empty once again. The closer they come to the monastery, the more clearly they can see that it's a fortress, a bastion holding fast to the hillside, squat and quadrangular. Behind the monastery, a bloodred strip of sky is suddenly revealed along the horizon.

Jacob had asked his escorts to unshackle him, and they did so as soon as they left Warsaw. Inside the small carriage, an officer holding the rank of captain sits with him. At first he stared at the prisoner fairly insistently, but Jacob did not return his gaze and looked instead out the little window, although they soon had to cover it on account of the wind. The officer tried to talk to him, but Jacob ignored him. In the end, the only hint of intimacy that has emerged between them is the puffs of smoke released from two pipes when the prisoner accepts the offer of tobacco.

The armed guards don't know exactly who this prisoner might be, so they have tried to be particularly watchful just in case, although this man does not look like someone who would make a run for it. He is pale and probably ill—there are big dark circles under his eyes and a bruise on his cheek. He is weak, and unsteady on his feet. He coughs. When they stopped and he wanted to pee, his cook had to help him, holding him up by his shoulders. He sits huddled in the corner of the carriage, shivering. Kazimierz, who serves him not only as cook but as valet, is constantly putting the man's fur cloak back onto his shoulders.

It is already dark when they pull into the monastery courtyard, which is entirely empty. Some old wretch opened the gate for them and then disappeared. The tired horses come to a stop, turning into bulky, steaming shadows. After some time, there is the sound of a door creaking, and then some voices, and the brothers appear, carrying torches, surprised and embarrassed, as if they have been caught doing something they weren't supposed to. They lead Jacob and Kazimierz into an empty waiting room with two wooden benches in it, but only Jacob sits. They wait for a long time; they arrived in the middle of a service. From somewhere beyond the walls of the waiting room they can hear men's voices singing. From time to time the sound bursts through the walls, then the voices fade and a silence falls, as if the singers were now hatching some sort of plot. Then another song starts up. This pattern repeats several times. The captain yawns. It smells of damp stone, mossy rock, and vaguely of incense—the odor of the monastery.

The prior is surprised by Jacob's state. He keeps his hands inside the sleeves of his light-colored wool habit, which is stained with ink at the cuffs. He takes an exceptionally long time to read the letter from Warsaw, probably finding room between the lines in which to consider how to handle this situation. He was expecting some headstrong heretic, impossible to get rid of in any more efficient way—which is why they've readied a cell for him in a monastery dungeon that has never been used before, at least not in the prior's memory. But the letter clearly speaks of "internment," rather than "imprisonment." And in any case, this person with his hands shackled in no way gives the impression of being a villain or a heretic. His perfectly decent dress brings to mind instead a foreigner, an Armenian on the road, a Wallachian hospodar who lost his way in the night and wound up in this sacred place. The prior looks inquiringly at the captain of the convoy. Then he looks over at the frightened Kazimierz.

"That is his cook," says the captain, and those are the first words that have been uttered in the room.

The prior's name is Ksawery Rotter. He's been in this role for just four months, and he doesn't know what to do. That gray-blue cheek—did they beat him? he would like to ask. It was no doubt justified, sometimes confessions must be brought about through corporal means, he doesn't question that general principle, but the fact laid bare like that is unpleasant. Violence disgusts him. He tries to see into the man's face, but Jacob keeps his head lowered. The prior sighs and decides for now to have his humble belongings taken into the officer's chamber by the tower, which no one uses. Brother Grzegorz will bring a mattress and hot water shortly, and maybe something to eat—if there's something left in the kitchen.

The prior comes to see the prisoner the following day, but they are unable to communicate. The cook tries to translate, but since his Polish is garbled, the prior isn't sure whether this strange prisoner is able to understand his good intentions. Dejected, he responds with no more than a yes or a no, so the prior does not importune him further and is relieved to leave him. Back in his own chamber, he glances at the letter lying on the table:

> The person whom we have entrusted to the fatherly
> protection of the Church and given over to the wardship of the
> Jasna Góra monastery is not dangerous in the sense in which a
> common villain would be, quite the opposite. He will seem
> calm and good to you, Father, though no doubt foreign and
> very different from the people with whom you would ordinarily
> come into contact . . . For he, though born as a Jew in Podolia,
> was raised in foreign Turkish lands, fully converting to their
> foreign language and customs . . .

There follows an abbreviated biography of the prisoner, arriving at an alarming formulation that causes the prior an unpleasant cramp in his stomach: "*considered himself the Messiah.*" Then the missive concludes:

> For this reason we do not recommend any close association
> with him. And during his internment, it would be best to

seclude him as much as possible and treat him as a singular
resident, the duration of his arrest being infinite, after all, and
there being no circumstances under which this will change.

This final sentence, too, fills the prior with unexpected alarm.


## What Jacob's prison is like

It is a chamber right next to the tower, right there in the defensive wall,
with two narrow little windows. The fathers put in two pallets—
apparently this is what they sleep on, too—and a straw mattress just
stuffed with hay, a little table, and a chair. There is also a porcelain
chamber pot, mercilessly chipped all over to the point of being perilous.
In the afternoon a second mattress appears, for Kazimierz. Kazimierz,
who alternates between grumbling and crying, unpacks his baggage and
his minimal supplies, but there is no way he will be allowed into the
monastery kitchen. They show him to a second kitchen, the one for the
help, and right next to it is a firepit where he can cook.

Jacob has a fever for several days and stops getting up from his pallet.
This is why Kazimierz requests from the Pauline Fathers some fresh goose
meat, and from the kitchen he borrows a pot, since he didn't bring his
own cooking utensils. He prepares the meat over the primitive firepit and,
throughout the day, mouthful by little mouthful, he gives Jacob the broth.
The prior supplies them with bread and crumbly old cheese; he has a
stake in the prisoner's health, and he chips in a bottle of powerful spirits,
as well. He says to drink it with hot water—it will heat them up. In the
end, Kazimierz drinks the spirits, justifying this by the thought that he
has to be strong to take care of Jacob; in any case, Jacob does not wish to
touch the spirits, but he does consume the broth, which seems to do him
good. One day, Kazimierz awakens in the early morning, as the brothers
shuffle in for their prayers. The pale dawn enters their chamber through
the little window, and Kazimierz sees that Jacob isn't sleeping—his eyes
are open, and he is looking at the cook as though he cannot see him. A
chill runs down Kazimierz's spine.

All day the guards' eyes follow Kazimierz's movements with great curiosity. These guards are strange, old and crippled. One of them is missing a leg and uses a wooden crutch to get around, but he wears a uniform and keeps a musket slung over his shoulder. He behaves like a real soldier, puffing out his chest although the buttonholes of his uniform are frayed and the seams of his sleeves are half unstitched. Around his neck he wears a tobacco pouch.

What kind of army is this? wonders Kazimierz, his lips curling in disgust. But he is scared of them. He has noticed that anything may be arranged with them in exchange for tobacco, so he swipes the occasional pinch from the Lord—in this way he is able to get both a pot and some fuel to heat it. One day one of those veterans, almost toothless, with his threadbare uniform buttoned all the way to the top, sits down next to Kazimierz and starts a conversation:

"Who is that master of yours, son?"

Kazimierz doesn't know what he's supposed to say, but since this particular soldier brought him a gridiron before, he feels obligated to respond somehow.

"He is a great gentleman."

"We can see that, that he's great and all. But what's he in for?"

The cook just shrugs. He doesn't know. They are all staring at him—he can feel them looking.

The toothless one, the one hungriest for money, is Roch. He keeps Kazimierz company for hours on end, as Kazimierz is cooking outside. The smoke from the damp wood reeks.

"What's that you're cooking up, son? The smell of it really turns my guts," Roch starts, filling his little pipe.

Kazimierz tells him that his master likes Turkish food and Turkish spices. Everything is spicy—in his open palm he shows the man little dry peppers.

"Where'd you come by all that Turkish cooking?" asks the old soldier indifferently, and when he learns that Kazimierz was brought up on Wallachian and Turkish cuisine, the whole garrison knows by evening. At night, those who are not standing guard go down into town and warm themselves up with the cheapest, most watered-down beer, and shoot the breeze. Some of them have family here, but those you can count on one hand. The rest are lone wolves, old men worn out in battle, with their miserable army pensions, supported by the Pauline Fathers. When a noble and his entourage come through on pilgrimage, they are not ashamed to put one hand out for alms as they hold their weapon in the other.

At Easter, after many petitions from Jacob, the prisoner is granted permission to walk out onto the ramparts once a week. From then on, all the old soldiers await his Sunday promenade. Would you look at that, he's up there now. The Jewish prophet. His dark figure, tall but stooped, walks along the wall, there and back, turning with a kind of violence and racing in the other direction, to then rebound off some invisible wall and start back again, like a pendulum. You could set the clocks by him. Roch will do exactly that— he will adjust the watch he received from the convert. It is the most valuable thing he has ever owned in his life, and he regrets that this has happened to him only now. If he had had it twenty years ago . . . He pictures himself in his parade uniform, walking into an inn teeming with comrades in arms. At least he can be assured that, thanks to this watch, he will have a decent funeral, with a wooden casket and a grand salvo.

He observes the prisoner calmly, without sympathy, accustomed as he is to unexpected twists of fate. To Roch's mind, this convert prophet's is a pretty decent fate. His followers provide their master with good food and smuggle money into the monastery, even though it is strictly prohibited. Many things are prohibited in the monastery, and yet they have everything here, whether it's Wallachian or Magyar wine or even vodka, and everyone closes their eyes to tobacco. The bans have little effect. They only work at the start, but then human nature with its long finger begins to poke a hole in them, first a little one and then, when it encounters no resistance, a larger and larger one. Until finally the hole is bigger than what isn't the hole. That's how it goes with any interdiction.

The prior, for example, has banned the old soldiers on numerous occasions from begging for alms at the entrance to the church. And they really did quit for a while, but then, after a few days—though there wasn't any begging—one hand did extend for just a little while as the pilgrims passed by. Soon others joined it, then more and more, until, after another few days, a muttering began:

"Spare a little change."

## The flagellants

Over the course of several days, warmth returns, and the beggars who flock to the monastery from all over cluster around the gate. Some of them hop on one leg, unpleasantly waving the stump of the other like an enormous, shameful member. Others point out to the pilgrims the empty sockets left when the Cossacks gouged out their eyes. Along with this they sing long, melancholy songs, the words of which have been turned to felt from endless rolling and pressing in toothless mouths, becoming unrecognizable. The men's hair is matted—it hasn't been cut in a long time—their clothing is in tatters, and their feet are wrapped in gray rags riddled with holes. They extend their bony hands for alms; you would need to have your pockets full of coins in order to give something to everyone here.

Jacob is sitting with his face to the sun, right by the window. The patch of light is exactly the size to cover it, like a gleaming handkerchief. On the rampart opposite sits Roch, also basking in the early springtime sun; he has more of it than the prisoner does. He has slipped off his uncomfortable boots and undone his wrappings—now his bare white feet with their black toenails point straight up into the clear blue sky. He takes out some tobacco and carefully, slowly, puts it in his pipe.

"Hey, you, Jewish prophet, you still in there?" he says in the direction of the window.

Jacob, surprised, opens his eyes. He smiles a friendly smile.

"They say you're some kind of heretic, not like Luther, but like a Jewish Luther, and that we ought to keep our distance."

Jacob doesn't understand him. He watches the man light his pipe, and his stomach hurts to look—he would love to smoke, but he doesn't have any tobacco. Roch must feel him looking, because he holds the pipe out toward him, but of course he can't actually pass it to him, they're separated by several meters.

"Everybody wants to smoke," he mutters to himself.

A while later, he brings Jacob a little bundle, and in it are tobacco and a pipe, a simple peasant's pipe. He sets it down on the stone step and limps off.

All through Lent the penitents come every Friday. They come from town in a procession. At the front, one of them carries a great cross with the figure of the Crucified, so realistically done that your blood runs cold just looking at it. They are dressed in sacks of thick-woven pink linen, with an opening cut into the backs so that they can whip themselves better. This opening can be covered with a flap. On their heads are smaller sacks with openings for their ears and eyes, which makes them look like animals or spirits. When the flagellants at the head and tail of the procession beat their staffs, the others lie down on the ground, pray, and then raise the flaps on their backs and begin to whip themselves. Some do this with leather whips, others with wire ones that have sharp metal spikes on the tips to better tear apart the body. Often when a spike catches the skin, a spray of blood hits onlookers.

It isn't until Good Friday that things really get going in the monastery. From dawn, when the gates are opened, there is an undulating flow of gray-brown crowds, as if the earth—itself just coming back to its senses, gray and still partly frozen—has sent up these people like so many half-rotten tubers. It is mostly peasants in thick felt trousers and sukmanas of indeterminate color, their hair disheveled, their wives in thick wrinkled trousers and fustian kerchiefs, aprons tied around their middles. No doubt they have ceremonial clothing at home, but on Good Friday you have to bring all the worthlessness and ugliness of the world out into the light of day. There is so much of it that the ordinary human heart would be unable to bear it without the help of that body on the cross, which is willing to take upon itself all the pain of Creation.

As proof that this is a special time, among the crowd there are those who are possessed, who cry out in a terrifying voice, and madmen who speak many languages at once so that you cannot understand them. There are exorcists as well, ex-priests in tattered cassocks, their bags filled with relics they lay on the heads of the possessed to drive out the demons.

The prior allows Jacob to go out onto the rampart that day, under

Roch's watchful eye, so that he can observe this murky human flood. He must be counting on this procession to make an impression on his prisoner and exhort his insufficiently Catholic soul to repent.

It takes some time for Jacob's eyes to grow accustomed to the light and to the bouquet of spring colors. Then they follow the movements of the people, sating themselves, and it seems to Jacob that the crowd is fermenting, bubbling like sourdough. His eyes consume all the details hungrily, after weeks of having only the stones on the wall and the tiny piece of the world visible from the cell's little window to react to. Now, from the rampart, they take in the monastery, the tower, the whole enormous complex and the walls that enclose it. Finally his gaze slides over the heads of the pilgrims, over the monastery roofs and walls to absorb the full panorama: a slightly undulating terrain, gray and sad, stretching to the vast horizon, dotted with villages and towns, the largest of which is the village of Częstochowa. Roch explains to him, partly in words, partly with gestures, that this name comes from the fact that the holy shrine located

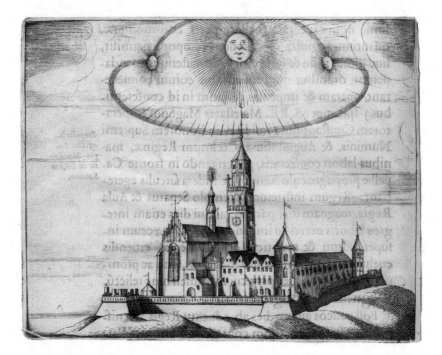

within it often (często) conceals (chowa) itself from the eyes of sinners, and you have to take a really good look to spot it among the gently sloping hills.


## The holy picture that conceals without revealing

Jacob is permitted to enter the crowd in front of the picture. He is scared, but not of the picture—of the crowd. It is made up of pilgrims—highly emotional men, sweaty, with freshly shaven faces and smoothed hair, and townswomen, a motley bunch with flushed faces, the married ones in their finest garments, with yellow leather boots. What can he have in common with them? He towers over most of their heads, staring at this crowd that strikes him as frighteningly foreign.

The chapel is filled with paintings and votive offerings. It has only recently been explained to him that these are offerings for the monastery, all in the shape of ailing body parts the Virgin Mary has healed. There are also wooden legs and crutches left for her after miraculous recoveries, along with the thousands of hearts cast in silver, gold, or copper, and livers and breasts and legs and arms, as if a single being has been broken down into a million pieces that the holy picture will put back together and fix.

The crowd is silent, but for a cough here and there, to which the chapel's vault adds gravity. A single, full-throated cry escapes a possessed man who can no longer bear the anticipation.

Suddenly the bells ring, and then the drums beat so loudly that Jacob would like to cover his ears with his hands. As if struck by a sudden blow, everyone throws themselves to their knees with a boom and a sigh, and those who can find the space lie facedown on the floor, while those who can't hunch over the floor like clods of earth. Now the frightening trumpets play like Jewish shofars, the air vibrates, the noise is terrible. Something strange freezes in the air, so that your heart contracts as if from fear, but it isn't fear, it's something bigger, and it happens to Jacob, too, so that he falls on his face, onto the floor that was only just stomped all over by peasants' dirty shoes, and here, next to the floor, the racket quiets, and it's easier to bear the tightness in his chest that out of nowhere folded him in half. Now, through the bodies that carpet the chapel floor, God ought to pass. But Jacob smells only the horse dung brought in on people's shoes and rubbed into the cracks between the planks of the floor, and the distinctly unpleasant smell, ubiquitous at this time of year, of damp combined with wool and human sweat.

Jacob looks up and sees that the ornate cover over the picture has been lifted so that it is now almost completely exposed, and he expects that a light will shine from within it—a blinding light that cannot be borne by the human eye—but all he sees are two dark shapes against a silver backdrop. It takes him a while to realize those shapes are faces, a woman and a child, dark, impenetrable, as if they were leaning out of the deepest darkness.

Kazimierz lights a tallow candle—he has a package of them. It shines brighter than the oil lamps the monks have given them.

Jacob is sitting with his cheek pressed to the wall. Kazimierz is cleaning the shaving bowl. Floating in it are the short hairs of Jacob's beard; Kazimierz has just finished shaving him. Jacob's hair is tousled, but it refuses to be made orderly. Kazimierz thinks that if things keep going like this, his master will resemble those warhorses with their matted, unkempt hair. Jacob is talking, partly to himself, partly to Kazimierz, who in a moment will start preparing dinner. He managed to get a little bit of good meat at the market—the butchers' stalls are overfull now, just before the holidays. The Lord demanded pork, and Kazimierz has it. He turns the iron bowl upside down to create something like a grill. The meat has been marinating since morning. Jacob is playing with a nail, and soon he's using it to scratch something into the wall.

"Kazimierz, do you know that delivery of the people from Egypt was only partial, because the one who got them out of there was a man, and the true delivery will come from a Virgin?"

"What virgin?" Kazimierz asks, only half paying attention, laying out the meat on the grill.

"That's obvious. It's obvious because once you sweep all the dust off all those stories and parables, all that chicanery, it's clear as day. Have you seen the picture they have here? The dark shining face of the Jasna Góra Virgin is the Shekhinah."

"How can a face shine darkly?" Kazimierz wonders astutely. The meat is roasting now—now he just has to watch the fire to make sure it stays the way it is and doesn't get too hot.

"If you don't know that, you don't know anything," Jacob says, annoyed. "David and Sabbatai were secretly women. It can't come to salvation any way other than through a woman. I know that now, and that's what I'm here for. From the beginning of the world, that Virgin has been dedicated to me alone, to no one else, because I can protect her."

Kazimierz doesn't really understand. He flips over the pieces of meat, carefully spreads fat on them.

Jacob isn't sensitive to smells. He goes on:

"Here people are trying to paint her so they don't forget about her, whereas she has to hide in the abyss. They miss the sight of her. But that is not her real face, since everyone sees her differently—we have senses that are imperfect, that's why that is. But every day she will appear to us more clearly, down to her every detail."

Jacob is silent awhile, like he's trying to decide whether or not to say anything.

"The Virgin has many forms. She also manifests herself in the guise of the ayelet, the roe deer."

"What do you mean? As an animal?" asks Kazimierz, concerned, but more with the meat than the conversation.

"I have been given her to take care of in exile here."

"My Lord, it's ready," Kazimierz says, all his attention on his dish, laying the best little pieces of meat on their tin plate. Jacob reaches for it with his hands, without showing any particular interest. Kazimierz looks at the meat with reserve.

"I don't know if I'm all that convinced about this pig meat," he says. "It's different somehow, kind of loose."

Then someone knocks at the door. The men exchange nervous glances.

"Who is it?" asks Kazimierz.

"It's me, Roch."

"Come on in," Jacob says, with his mouth full.

The veteran's head peeks in through the doorway.

"Today is Good Friday. Have you men gone mad? Roasting meat? You can smell it all over the monastery. It's disgusting."

Kazimierz throws a cloth over the plate with the pieces of meat.

"Give him something, make him go," Jacob says quietly, and goes back to scraping at the wall.

But Kazimierz, frightened, explains:

"How were we supposed to know what to eat on Good Friday? We've never had a Good Friday before in our new religion, maybe someone could enlighten us about it."

"Right you are," says Roch. "It's not your fault. You can't eat meat until Sunday. Tomorrow you're supposed to have eggs to be blessed. The monks might invite you to breakfast, in fact. They invite us every year."

When Kazimierz prepares to put out his candle and go to sleep, he first takes the flame over to the wall. He sees a single inscription in Hebrew and is surprised by it. For it is written: ונבר השמ תרפ, ladybug, parat moshe rabenu. He looks at it, his surprise not wearing off, then shrugs and blows the candle out.

## A letter in Polish

Hana gets a letter from her husband she can't read. It is in Polish. Nahman, or Jakubowski, is the one who reads it. He reads it and starts crying. They all look at him in astonishment—Hana and Matuszewski, who's there, too, with Wittel. The sight of Jakubowski crying over this letter makes them feel something like revulsion. Jakubowski has aged—Jacob's imprisonment has completely wiped him out. Not to mention the fact that they all view him as a traitor, even though everyone had their part in it, at least a little. The hair on the top of Jakubowski's head has thinned lately, and freckled pink skin peeps out from underneath. Now a sob shakes his back.

Do not worry about me, I am in the good hands of the
Pauline Fathers, and I want for nothing. If I could, however,
kindly request: warm wraps for my feet [Jakubowski starts
crying here, at the mention of the wraps] as well as a few sets
of warm underwear, wool if possible, and a woolen żupan, if
possible two, that I might have a spare. Some sort of fur to
spread over my bed. Kazimierz could use a set of dishes and
a cooking pot as well as utensils at your discretion. I would
further request any book written in the Polish language, that
I might study. As well as paper, ink, and pens . . .

On the letter is the monastery's seal.

It is read many times, and in the end they copy it, and Jakubowski
takes it to the Wołowskis and Krysiński. And soon everyone in Warsaw
knows it, the whole machna, the whole company. The letter also travels
to Kamieniec, to Mrs. Kossakowska, and, in secret, it makes its way from
Nahman Jakubowski to Moliwda (who reads it secretly, smoking). Thus
this wonderful news reaches everyone, that Jacob, the Lord, is alive. That
the worst has not happened, and now all those months they suffered in
uncertainty seem like months of breathlessness and silence. A fresh wind
has blown in, and since all of this happens around Easter, they celebrate
it like a resurrection. Yes, the Lord has risen, come back from the darkness like a light that merely dove down into the dark water, but that has
now come back up to the surface.

## A visit to the monastery

Shlomo Shorr, now Franciszek Wołowski, heads hurriedly to Częstochowa, hoping to get there before the others. It is the start of May. In
just a few days, the fields have all turned green, and across those sheets
of green splash yellow drops of sow thistle. He rides on horseback, only
by day, and only on the main highways. He is dressed modestly—you
can't even really tell whether his attire is Christian or Jewish. He has
shaved, but he's left his hair longer, and he puts it back now in a small

braid. He wears a black frock coat of Dutch cloth, and trousers that come just past his knees, and riding boots. His head cannot be bare, regardless of the good, warm weather, so he has covered it in a sheepskin hat.

Just before he reaches Częstochowa, he runs into a familiar figure on the road: a young man, really just a boy still, traveling on foot down the very edge of the road, a bundle over his shoulder. With a stick he slashes the yellow tops of the blooming sow thistle. His clothes are rather unbecoming. Shlomo Wołowski recognizes in astonishment Kazimierz, Jacob's cook.

"What are you doing here, Kazimierz? Shouldn't you be at your master's table, is it not time for lunch?"

The boy stops dead for a moment. When he recognizes Franciszek, he rushes to him and greets him effusively.

"I'm not going back there," he says after a moment. "It's prison."

"Did you not know you two were going to prison?"

"But me? Why would I be there? Why would I voluntarily imprison myself, that's what I don't understand. The Lord has his moods, several times he's beaten me, recently he kept grabbing me by the hair. Sometimes he doesn't eat anything, and other times he gets a craving for some special dish. And—" he starts, but he breaks off. Shlomo Wołowski can guess what Kazimierz isn't saying, and he doesn't follow up. He knows he has to tread lightly here.

He dismounts and sits on the grass under a tree that has already put out some little leaves. He produces some hard cheese, bread, and a bottle of wine. Kazimierz looks covetously at the latter. He is thirsty and hungry. As they eat, both turn their gaze toward the city of Częstochowa. In the warm spring air the sound of the monastery's bells floats over to them. Shlomo Wołowski starts to get impatient.

"Tell me, what's it like there? Will I get in to see him?"

"He's not allowed to see anyone."

"But if I pay, who do I give the money to?"

Kazimierz thinks a long while, as though savoring the fact that he is in possession of such valuable information.

"None of the brothers will take a bribe . . . The old soldiers would, but they don't really have that kind of power."

"I would like to chat with him, even if it's just through a window. Do you think I could do that? Does he have a window that faces onto the outside of the building?"

Kazimierz, in silence, considers the monastery's windows.

"I think you would be able to do that through a window. But even so, they'd have to let you into the monastery."

"I'll get into the monastery myself, as a pilgrim."

"So you will. Then you go, brother, to those old soldiers. Talk with Roch. Buy him tobacco and vodka. If they think you'll be a generous friend to them, they'll help."

Shlomo Wołowski looks at Kazimierz's linen bag.

"What do you have there?"

"The Lord's letters, brother."

"Let me see."

The boy obediently pulls out four letters. He sees the carefully folded pages with the seal Jacob had made in Warsaw. The addressees are written out in beautiful penmanship, with many flourishes.

"Who writes for him in Polish?"

"Brother Grzegorz, one of the younger ones. He is teaching him to write and speak."

One of the letters is to Josepha Scholastica Frank, otherwise known as Hana, and then there's one to Yeruhim Dembowski—that's the thickest one—and a third to Katarzyna Kossakowska and a fourth to Antoni Moliwda-Kossakowski.

"Nothing for me," Shlomo says, in a tone that neither asks nor affirms.

Then Wołowski learns many more disturbing things. That for the whole month of February Jacob did not get out of bed, and when the terrible frosts set in, and they couldn't quite heat their chamber, he fell ill and had a terrible fever, so that one of the monks would come to treat him and let his blood. Kazimierz repeats the same thing several times: that he feared the Lord would die, and he would be the only one to be there with him when he died. Then through all of March, Jacob was weak, and Kazimierz fed him only chicken broth. For the chickens, he was permitted to walk to Częstochowa, to Shmul's store, and he spent all the money for the Lord's board and had to put in some of his own. The brothers don't bother themselves much with the prisoner. Just one of them, Brother Marcin, who is painting the inside of the church, talks to him, but the Lord still barely understands it. The Lord spends a great deal of time in the chapel. He also lies facedown with his arms outspread before the holy picture when they haven't let in the pilgrims yet, meaning at night, so that he sleeps during the day. According to Kazimierz, in that damp and without sunlight, Jacob won't last much longer. And there's something else—he's become extremely wrathful. Kazimierz has also heard him talking to himself.

"Well, who's he supposed to talk to? Certainly not you," mutters Shlomo Wołowski under his breath.

Wołowski tries to arrange a visit with Jacob. He has rented a room in town with a Christian who looks at him suspiciously, but, paid well, doesn't ask too many questions. Every day he goes to the monastery and waits for an audience with the prior. When he finally gets one after five days, the prior only allows him to give him a package for Jacob, and only after it's been searched. If there are letters, they must be in Polish or Latin, and they are censored by the prior. Those are his orders. No visits have been envisioned. The audience lasts but a moment.

Finally, Roch, having been bribed, leads Wołowski at night through the walls into the monastery, where everyone's asleep. He tells him to stand beneath the little opening in the wall, whence comes a faint glow of light. Roch, meanwhile, goes on inside, and after a moment, Jacob's head appears at the window. Wołowski sees him hazily.

"Shlomo?" asks the Lord.

"Yes, it is me."

"What news do you have for me? I received the package."

Wołowski has so much to say he doesn't know where to begin.

"We're all of us in Warsaw. Your wife is still with that woman, outside Warsaw in Kobyłka—she's been baptized now."

"How are the children?"

"Good, healthy. Just sad, like the rest of us."

"Is that why you all put me in here?"

"What do you mean?"

"Why hasn't my wife been writing to me?"

"They can't write you everything . . . Those letters are read along the way. Here and in Warsaw. Not to mention that now Yeruhim Dembowski is trying to pass himself off as our leader. And his brother Jan. They want to rule us and give us all our orders."

"I write in my letters what you are supposed to be doing."

"But that's not enough, you have to designate a deputy."

"But I'm right here, and I can tell you myself."

"That won't do. There has to be someone—"

"Who has the money?" asks Jacob.

"Osman Czerniawski has some of it, deposited, and some of it is with my brother, Jan."

"Have Matuszewski join him—they can be in charge together."

"Appoint me as your deputy. You know me well and know I have the strength and the mind for it."

Jacob says nothing. Then he asks:

"Who betrayed me?"

"Out of stupidity we all let ourselves be drawn in, but we all wished you the best. I never said a word against you."

"You're all cowards. I should spit on all of you."

"Spit," says Shlomo quietly. "Nahman Jakubowski talked the most. He betrayed you, and he was your closest confidant. But you knew he was weak—good at disputation, maybe, but for such things, weak. He is the traitor. The coward. The weasel."

"A weasel is an intelligent animal, it knows what it's doing. Tell him I will never lay eyes on him again."

Shlomo Wołowski gathers all his strength.

"Write a letter for me saying how I'll fill in for you until you get out. I'll keep them all in line. For now we've been gathering at Yeruhim's. He's doing business, employing our people. There are a lot of ours in Kobyłka, on Bishop Załuski's property, but we're all of us impoverished and on our own. We weep over you every day, Jacob."

"Weep, then. Try to get to the king through Moliwda."

"He's stuck in Łowiczu with the primate."

"Then try and get to the primate!"

"Moliwda isn't with us anymore. He's had it with us. He's out."

Jacob is silent for a while.

"And you?"

"And I'm in Warsaw, where my business is going well. Everybody wants to be in Warsaw, you can give the children a good education there. Your Avacha has two tutors, thanks to Kossakowska. She's learning French. We want to take her in to live with us, Marianna and I."

Somewhere in the next courtyard a light appears, and Roch comes back and grabs Wołowski by his black frock coat and pushes him toward the gate.

"That's it. Done."

"I'll wait until tomorrow evening. Write a letter to everyone, and I'll take it to them straightaway. Roch will give it to me. Write it in our language. Designate me as your substitute. You trust me."

"I don't trust anyone anymore," says Jacob, and with that, his head disappears from view.

And that is all Shlomo Wołowski gets out of his visit to Jacob. The next day he goes to the picture of the Virgin Mary. It is six in the morning, the sun is rising, the day will be sunny, the sky is a lovely pink color, and a silver mist rises over the fields, and into the monastery flow waves of the aroma of damp and calamus. He stands among the sleepy crowd. When the trumpets sound, people prostrate themselves on the cold floor, bent over their knees. Wołowski does the same, and with his forehead he feels the chill of the stone. At the sound of the trumpets, the picture's silver veil is raised, and Shlomo sees from afar a small rectangle containing a barely outlined silhouette with a black face. A woman next to him starts to sob, and this spreads to almost everyone. Wołowski is overwhelmed by the same emotions as the rest of the crowd, compounded further by the intoxicating smell of May flowers, human sweat, the rags, the dust. He spends the whole morning working on Kazimierz, trying to get him to stay and serve the Lord, until someone else can replace him. In the afternoon, Roch passes him a letter written in Hebrew in a thick roll like a pack of tobacco. Immediately after, Shlomo Franciszek Wołowski departs from the monastery, leaving Kazimierz some money and making a sizable donation through the prior.

## Upupa dicit

A few days later, a chest of things comes to Jacob in the monastery. He doesn't know who it's from. The chest spends its first whole day with the prior, who searches it thoroughly with the brothers. The monks examine the clothes, the Turkish scarf, the leather shoes with fur inside, the thin linen underwear, dried figs, dates, a wool rug, a down cushion covered in yellow damask. There is also paper for writing and pens of a higher quality than the prior has ever seen in his life. He spends a long time contemplating the contents of the chest and isn't sure whether he should allow the prisoner such luxuries. He is not an ordinary prisoner, on the one hand, but on the other, such extravagance in a monastery, where the priests all live so modestly—is that not taking things a bit too far? Which is why the prior keeps going back to the chest and unfolding the fine woolen scarf, holding it out in his hands; it is almost without adornment, but so delicate it resembles silk. And these figs! When he is left alone for a moment, telling himself that this is just a test, he puts one of them in his mouth and holds it there for a long time, until his mouth fills with saliva that flows into his stomach, together with the flavor of the fig, filling his whole body with pleasure at the unparalleled sweetness. How good are these figs that smell of the sun, not like those hard ones of which the monastery recently acquired a small quantity, from a Jewish merchant with a spice shop on the outskirts of town.

The prior also finds two books, which he reaches for suspiciously, smelling heretical treatises—those he will of course never let through. But when he picks them up, he is surprised to see that the first one is in Polish, and that it was written by a priest. The father hasn't heard this name before, Benedykt Chmielowski, but that doesn't mean anything, since he has no time for secular reading—this is a book for laypeople, not an episcopal book, not a prayer book. The second is a beautifully illustrated edition of Comenius's *Orbis Pictus*, in which every word appears in four languages, making it a useful study tool. And as the prisoner himself had mentioned it, and similar suggestions had been made by the

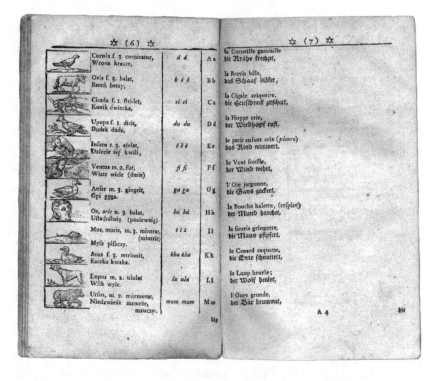

nunciature—to teach the prisoner Polish—then why not let him learn it from both Comenius and from this *New Athens*? The prior himself, flipping through the volume, is interested to read a page opened at random.

How curious, thinks the prior. That could come in handy in life. His religious materials do not contain this kind of information. He didn't know the Hoopoe saith (Upupa dicit).

## Of Jacob's learning to read and where the Poles come from

A separate chamber is designated as a classroom by the head guard at the prior's request. Two tables and two stools have been brought in. There is also a carafe of water and two soldiers' cups, as well as a narrow cot and a bench. Hooks stick out of the stone wall for hanging clothing.

The two windows don't let in enough light, and it is always cold. Every hour they have to go outside to warm up.

Brother Grzegorz has been appointed as Jacob's teacher. He is a gentle, middle-aged monk, patient and agreeable. Jacob's bigger mistakes, the words he completely garbles, cause his cheeks to turn red—whether out of stifled anger or simply embarrassment. The lessons started with how to say "God bless" in Polish, "Szczęść Boże," which is tough to pronounce and to write. Then they wrote out the Lord's Prayer, until they finally got to simple conversations. Since the monastery does not have any books in Polish, and they have no particular need for Latin, Jacob brought Brother Grzegorz the book that had been recently delivered to him, Benedykt Chmielowski's *New Athens*. Brother Grzegorz became a great fan of this vast volume and started secretly borrowing it from Jacob to read, no doubt feeling somewhat guilty about it, on the pretext of preparing texts to read together.

The lessons take place every day after morning mass, in which Jacob is permitted to participate. Brother Grzegorz brings in to the tower that reeks of damp the smell of incense and the rank oil with which they make their paint; his fingers are often stained colorfully, since they have begun the big paintings in the chapel, and Brother Grzegorz assists in mixing the paints.

"How are you today, sir?" He always starts with the same phrase, settling onto his stool and spreading his papers before him.

"All right," answers Jacob. "I been waiting you, Brother Grzegorz."

Pronouncing that name isn't easy for him, but by May, Jacob is doing it almost perfectly.

"I have been waiting for you," the monk corrects him.

Now they turn to chapter 10, "Of the Kingdom of Poland."

> In Sarmatia a precious Pearl appears to be the KINGDOM OF POLAND, of the Słowieński Nations the most renowned. Poland takes its Name from the Pola, or Fields, where the Polacy, or Poles, desired both to live and die; or else from a Polo Arctico, i.e., the North Star, to which the Kingdom of Poland corresponded, as Hispania is called Hesperia after the Western star

> Hesperus. To others it seems that this Name was given to Poles from the Pole Castle olim located on the Borders of Pomerania. There is that and there is the Opinion of the Authors that Polacy are Polachy, i.e., Lech's Descendants should be known as such. Paprocki, meanwhile, ingeniose reasons that after Mieczysław I Polish Prince, when Poles Accepted the Holy Faith and acceded in droves to Holy Baptism, then the Czech Priests so invoked would ask: Are you polani? I.e., Have you been baptized? Then those who had been baptized responded: We are polani, hence polani, that is, Poloni went to the Poles in nomen gloriosum.

Jacob stammers through this text for a long time, getting stuck on the Latin interpolations, which he copies out to the side, no doubt for further study.

"And I am polani," the student says to Brother Grzegorz, and raises his eyes from the book.

### Of Jan Wołowski and Mateusz Matuszewski, who are the next to come to Częstochowa, in November of 1760

They both look like nobles. Especially Jan Wołowski, who of the Wołowski brothers has grown out his mustache the most—that's what lends him much of his gravitas now. Both of them are dressed in winter kontusze lined with fur and warm fur hats, and they both seem sure of themselves and rich. The veterans view them with respect. They rented rooms in town down below, not far from the monastery. From their windows they can see the steep fortification wall. After two days of waiting, negotiations, and bribes, they are finally let inside to see Jacob. At the sight of them, Jacob bursts out laughing.

They stand there in astonishment. They certainly weren't expecting this.

Jacob stops laughing and turns his back to them. They run up to him and kneel down at his feet. Wołowski has prepared a whole speech, but now he can't quite get the words out. Jan, meanwhile, says simply:

"Jacob."

At last Jacob turns toward them and gives them his hand. They kiss it, and he raises them to their feet. And then they cry, all three men, a pure weeping that is a kind of celebration, better than any words of greeting could ever be. Jacob holds them to him, like boys who have gotten into all sorts of trouble, he hugs them, holding their heads, patting the napes of their necks, until their fur hats with the decorative feathers fall off, and these envoys are transformed into sweaty children, happy to have found their way back home.

The visit lasts three days. They leave the tower only to attend to bodily necessities and to return to town at night. They have brought trunks and bags. In them are wine, sweetmeats, all manner of delicacies. The officer himself looked through them carefully and, well disposed after the bribe he got, did not forbid the presents—after all, Christmas is a time of mercy, even toward prisoners. In a large bag filled with things for Jacob, there is an eiderdown and some woolen scarves, leather slippers for the chilly stone floor, and even a small rug. Several pairs of socks, underwear with the monogram *J.F.* (all embroidered by the Wołowski women), writing paper and books . . . They lay it all out on the table first, and then, when they run out of space, they put it on the floor. Jacob is most interested in what he finds in the pots—butter, goose lard, and honey. In smaller linen bags there are also cakes and poppyseed rolls.

The candles burn late into the night, which unsettles Roch—he can't stop checking in on them, under any pretext. He pokes his head in the door and asks if they don't need hot water or a lit stove—hasn't the other one gone out by now? Yes, they want water. But when he brings them full water jugs, they forget about them, and the water cools down again. On their last night they remain in the tower, and well into the morning their raised voices can be heard, and some long songs, and then everything falls quiet. In the morning all three of them go to mass.

Wołowski and Matuszewski leave Częstochowa on November 16. It is a lovely warm sunny day. They take with them a trunkful of letters and order lists. They leave the old soldiers a barrel of beer bought in town, and for the officers, Turkish pipes and the finest tobacco. What with the gold they gave them at the start, all in all they have made a pretty good impression.

That same month, Wołowski, Matuszewski, and Krysa go to Lublin to take a look at Wojsławice, where Kossakowska is preparing a place for them to live. But before they head there, the whole company is to transfer to Zamość, which is close to Wojsławice, and to wait there, under the care and protection of the ordynat.

## Elżbieta Drużbacka to Father Benedykt Chmielowski, Vicar Forane of Rohatyn, Tarnów, Christmas, 1760

Because I find my hand suddenly willing to hold a pen, as it has not been for some time, I wish to congratulate you on your title of Canon, and on the 1,760th anniversary of the Lord's birth, I wish you the greatest of His blessings, may you daily experience His grace.

I report to you as briefly as possible, dear friend, so as not to dwell o'ermuch on such a painful matter, and not to strain my agonizing heart, that last month my daughter Marianna died of the plague that came here from the east. That plague had already taken from this world six of my granddaughters, one after the other. Thus I have found myself in the most terrible situation, in which parents are condemned to outlive their children and grandchildren, despite the fact—or at least the appearance of fact—that this is contradictory to the whole natural order and to any sort of logic. My death, which until now has lurked somewhere in the distance, offstage, dressed up and made up, has now cast off its ball gown, and I see it before me in its true form. I am not frightened, and my death brings me no pain. It only seems to me that the months and years are now moving contrarywise. For how can an old person be permitted to go on, while the lives of the young are cut short? I fear to complain of it or to cry, for a creature like myself has not

the boldness to debate with the Creator where he sets his limits,
and I stand like a tree stripped of its bark—without feeling. I
ought to depart, and no one would suffer or despair over it. I
can't find the words, and my thoughts break away from me . . .

## Elżbieta Drużbacka's heavy golden heart offered to the Black Madonna

She writes on a scrap of paper: "If you are truly merciful, bring them
back to life." She sprinkles it with sand and waits for the ink to dry, then
she rolls the paper up tight. She keeps this little roll in her hands as she
enters the chapel. It is cold, and there are not many pilgrims, so she
walks down the middle, going up as close as she is allowed, as close as
the barriers will permit her. To her left, a legless soldier, with disheveled
hair that looks like a hank of hemp, whimpers. He can't even kneel. His
uniform is ruined, its buttons long since replaced, the aiguillettes torn
off, no doubt to be used for something else. Behind him is an elderly
woman wrapped in headscarves, with a little girl whose face is misshapen
by a purple lump. One of her eyes is almost completely obscured under
that proud flesh. Drużbacka kneels nearby and prays to the covered
picture.

She has had all of her jewelry melted down and fashioned into a big
heart, not knowing how else to express her pain. She has a hole in her
chest, and she must be mindful of it; it hurts and oppresses her. And so
she had cast a prosthesis out of gold, a crutch for the heart. Now she
makes a votive offering of it in the monastery, and the monks hang it
alongside the other hearts. She doesn't know why, but the sight of the
heart joined with the other hearts, big and small, brings Drużbacka the
greatest relief, greater than prayer and greater than gazing into the black,
impenetrable face of the Madonna. There is so much pain on view here,
Drużbacka's own pain just a drop in the sea of tears that have been shed
in this place. Every human tear enters a stream that flows into a little
river, and then the river joins a bigger river, and so on, until in the end, in

the great current of an enormous river, it washes into the sea and dissolves on the horizon. In these hearts hung up around the Madonna, Drużbacka sees mothers who have lost, or are losing, or will lose their children and grandchildren. And in some sense, life is this constant loss. Improving one's station, getting richer, is the greatest illusion. In reality, we are richest at the moment of our birth; after that, we begin to lose everything. That is what the Madonna represents: the initial whole, the divine unity of us, the world and God, is something that must be lost. What remains in its wake is just a flat picture, a dark patch of a face, an apparition, an illusion. The symbol of life is after all the cross, suffering—nothing more. This is how she explains it to herself.

At night, in a pilgrims' home where she has rented a modest room, she cannot sleep—she hasn't slept in two months, only dozing off for brief periods. In one of those, she dreams of her mother, which is odd, because she hasn't dreamed of her mother in twenty years. For this reason, Drużbacka understands this dream as a harbinger of her own death. She is sitting on her mother's lap, she can't see her face. She sees only the complicated pattern on her dress, a sort of labyrinth.

When the next morning, still before dawn, she returns to the church, her gaze is drawn by the tall, well-built man in a Turkish outfit, dark, with a caftan buttoned up to the neck, his head bare. He has a thick black mustache, and long hair flecked with gray. At first he prays feverishly, kneeling—his lips move soundlessly, and his lowered eyelids, with their long lashes, tremble; then he lies down with his arms outspread on the cold floor, in the very center of the church, right in front of the barrier that protects the holy picture.

Drużbacka finds a place for herself in the nave, near the wall, and kneels with difficulty, the pain running from her knees all through her little old body. In the nearly empty church, every shuffle, every breath is amplified into a hum or a whistle that rebounds off the vault until it is drowned out by one of the songs intoned at irregular intervals by the monks:

*Ave regina coelorum,*
*Ave Domina Angelorum:*

*Salve radix, salve porta,*
*Ex qua Mundo lux est orta.*

Drużbacka tries to find some scratches in the wall, some chinks be-tween the marble slabs with which the walls are lined, where she might be able to insert her roll of paper. For how would her missive make it to God if not through the stone lips of the temple? The marble is smooth, and its joints are mercilessly meticulous. In the end, she is able to press the scrap of paper into a shallow crack, but she knows it won't last long there. No doubt it will fall out soon, and crowds of pilgrims will trample it.

That same day, in the afternoon, she meets again that tall man with the pockmarked face. Now she knows who he is. She grabs hold of his sleeve, and he looks at her in surprise, his gaze soft and gentle.

"Are you the imprisoned Jewish prophet?" she asks without preamble, looking up at him; she reaches barely to his chest.

He understands, and he nods. His face doesn't change; it is gloomy and ugly.

"You have worked miracles, you have healed, that is what I heard."

Jacob does not so much as blink an eye.

"My daughter died, as did six of my grandchildren." Drużbacka spreads out her fingers before him and counts: one, two, three, four, five, six . . . "Have you heard of bringing the dead back to life? Some people seem to be able to do it. Prophets know the way. Have you ever managed to do it, even with just an old dog?"

# 25.

## Yente sleeping under stork wings

Pesel, who has already been baptized, has decided to marry a cousin with the same last name, so now her name is Marianna Pawłowska. The wedding takes place in Warsaw, in the autumn of 1760, during the sad time when the Lord is imprisoned in Częstochowa and when the whole machna seems to be sort of pressed down to the ground, uncertain and fearful. And yet her father, Israel, now Paweł, also Pawłowski, as the whole family took the same name, believes that they have to go on living and marrying and bearing children. That cannot be avoided. Life is a force, like a flood, like a powerful current of water—you cannot oppose it. That is what he says as he sets up, with his limited means, his leather goods workshop, where he intends to sew beautiful wallets and belts from Turkish leather.

A modest wedding takes place early one morning, in a church in Leszno. The priest took a long time to explain to them how everything would happen, but even so, Pesel and her fiancé, along with her mother, Sobla (now Helena), her father, Paweł Pawłowski, and all the witnesses and guests feel insecure, as if they haven't quite mastered the dance steps they are about to perform.

Pesel's eyes are filled with nervous tears, which the priest takes for the heightened emotions of an ordinary bride, and he smiles at her as he would at a child. If it were proper, he would pat her on the head.

Tables have been set around the apartment, from which the rest of the furniture has been removed. The food is already waiting for them. The guests, tired after the long mass in the cold church, would like to warm themselves. As they eat, Paweł Pawłowski pours vodka into their glasses—to reinvigorate them and to relax them, since the whole company is having to deal with something foreign and unpleasant and new. And yet they all know that from now on, this is how it's going to be. It's as if they were seated around a great void that they were consuming with spoons, as if what was covered in white tablecloths were pure nothingness, and they were celebrating its pale chill. This strange feeling lasts through the first two courses and glasses of vodka. Then the curtains in the windows are drawn, the tables are pushed up against the wall, and Franciszek Wołowski and the father of the bride perform a second wedding, the familiar kind, a wedding that is theirs. Hands seek out hands, nerves calm down once they are standing in a circle, holding on to one another, as up to the ceiling of the apartment rises a prayer in a language that Pesel and her young husband can no longer understand, said in a whisper, mysterious and eternal.

Pesel-Marianna bows her head like the others, and her thoughts fly far afield, to Yente, who stayed back in the Korolówka cave. She can't stop thinking of it. Did they do the right thing, bearing that tiny body down into the depths of those passageways, as though against the flow of time, to its stone-black beginning? What else could they have done? Before leaving, she brought Yente nuts and flowers. She covered her up in a cape she had embroidered—it was supposed to be for the wedding, but then Pesel thought that since Yente was to stay behind, she would by means of this cape nonetheless be able to be present on Pesel's special day. The cape is made of pink damask, decorated with white silk and white tassels. Marianna embroidered a bird on it, a stork with a snake in its beak, standing on one leg, like the ones that fly into Korolówka's riverside meadows and step pompously across the tall grass. She kissed her great-grandmother on the cheek and found her cheek cool and fresh as usual. She said in parting, "The Lord will cover you up with His feathers, Yente, and under

His wings you will be safe, as it says in Psalm 91." Pesel is quite certain that Yente would like the stork with the snake in his beak. His big, powerful wings, his red legs, his down, his dignified step.

Now, as this second wedding takes place, the doubly named Pesel-Marianna also thinks about her singly named sister Freyna, whom she has always loved the most of all her siblings and who remained in Korolówka with her husband and children. She vows to herself that she will visit Freyna again come spring, and that she will do so every year; she swears on her own grave.

Yente, who sees this from underneath the stork's wing, from above, as usual, knows that this is a vow that her great-granddaughter will be unable to keep.

## Of Yente's measurement of graves

Yente's gaze also hovers over Częstochowa, the little village nestled into the hillside over which the Madonna reigns. But Yente can see only the roofs—here the even roofs of the Jasna Góra monastery have just been covered with brand-new tiles, while down below the rotten roofs of the huts and houses have wooden shingles over them.

It is a September sky—cool and distant, the sun slowly growing orange, and the Jewish women of Częstochowa have arranged to meet up on the road to the Jewish cemetery, they're headed there now, the older ones wearing thick skirts conferring in a whisper, waiting up for each other as they go.

On the terrible days between Rosh Hashanah and Yom Kippur, kneytlakh legn takes place—the measuring of graves. The women measure out the cemeteries with a string, then wind the string back up around a bobbin, for later use as candlewicks; some of the women will also use it to tell fortunes. Each of them murmurs a prayer under her breath, and they look like witches in their wide, ruffled skirts, which catch on blackberry thorns and rustle among the dry yellow leaves.

Once, Yente herself measured the graves, believing it to be the duty of every woman to measure how much room was left for the dead, or whether there was any room at all, before any new living people were born. It is a kind of bookkeeping that women take care of—women are always better, in any case, at keeping the accounts.

But what reason do they have for measuring the graves and cemeteries? After all, the dead are not contained in their graves—Yente has learned this only now, however, after plunging thousands of wicks into wax. Graves are in fact altogether pointless, since the dead ignore them and roam—the dead are everywhere. Yente sees them all the time, as if through glass, for however much she might like to join their ranks, she can't. Where is this? It's hard to say. They behold the world as if from behind a windowpane, inspecting it and always coveting something inside it. Yente tries to figure out what the faces they make mean, likewise their gestures, and in the end, she gets it: The dead would like to be talked about; they are hungry, and that is their food. What they want from us is our attention.

And Yente notices something else—that that attention is inequitably distributed. Some people are spoken about a great deal, with myriad words pronounced about them. Of others, people utter not a single word, nary a syllable, ever. Those dead will flicker out after a while, moving away from the glass, disappearing somewhere into the back. There are a great many of that latter group, millions of them, completely forgotten. No one even knows they lived on earth. There is no trace of them, which is why they are freed faster, and depart. And maybe that's a good thing. Yente would depart, as well, if only she could. If only she weren't still bound by that powerful word she swallowed. The little piece of paper is gone, and there's no trace left of the string. It's all dissolved, and the tiniest particles of light have been absorbed into matter. All that remains is the word like a rock that reckless Elisha Shorr employed to tether Yente.

Old Shorr departed not too long ago, she saw him dart past near her— a great sage, father of five sons and one daughter, grandfather of many grandchildren, now a blurred streak. She also saw a little child zip by. It was Immanuel, son of Jacob and Hana, not much more than a year old.

A letter with this news was smuggled to Jacob by Kazimierz. Hana wrote it in Turkish, in vague terms, as if to conceal a great secret. Or perhaps in embarrassment that this had happened to them? They were not supposed to die, after all. Ever. Jacob reads it several times. Each time he stands up and starts pacing the tower. A little piece of paper falls out of the letter, cut out crooked, with some kind of animal painted onto it in red. It might be a shaggy little dog. At the bottom it says: *Rutka*. He assumes it's from his daughter, and only now does his throat clench, and his eyes fill with tears. But he doesn't cry.

## A letter from Nahman Jakubowski to the Lord in Częstochowa

It is not until he gets the next letter that Jacob is really thrown off-balance. From the first words, Nahman's tone annoys him; he can hear his voice, tearful, pathetic, like the whining of a dog. If Nahman were here, Jacob would hit him in the face and watch the blood stream from his nose. It is a good thing he did not allow this traitor to come up to the little window when he was here.

> . . . O Jacob, my name is, after all, Piotr Jakubowski, and
> that name is a testament to the extent to which I am yours. My
> heart came very near to breaking as I stood here, so close to
> You, yet unable either to see You or to hear Your voice. I had, by
> way of consolation, only the thought that You were so close, and
> that we were breathing one and the same air, and so I went up
> to the high wall that separates Your prison from the town. It
> seemed to me a veritable wailing wall. With sadness I learned of
> Your serious illness and can imagine the loneliness You must
> bear here, being so unaccustomed to not having people gathered
> around You.
> You know that I constantly love You, and that I am ready to
> sacrifice everything for You. If I said something against You, it

was not out of any ill will, but rather a deep sense of Your
mission, of our calling, which consumed my mind completely. I
also confess to fear, which with its power nearly knocked me, a
coward, off my feet. You know how very miserable I am, but it
was not for my flaws that You made me Your right-hand man,
but for my better qualities, of which I might dare remind
You now, were it not for the fact that I was forced to abandon
You then.

Jacob casts the letter aside in anger and spits. Nahman's voice falls silent in his head, but not for long. Jacob picks up the letter and keeps
reading:

So many of us have now sought shelter, whether in the
capital or under the protection of the wealthy, and there
we are trying to live, and be guided by our own hands,
believing in your imminent return and every day awaiting your
arrival . . .
You Yourself once told us in Ivanie about two kinds of
people. Of some you said that they were filled with darkness,
people who believe that the world as it is is evil and unjust, and
that we must simply adapt to it and play that game, become the
same as the world. And of the other sort, you said that they are
the ones suffused with light, people who believe that the world
is evil and terrible, but that it can always be changed. And that
we ought not to assimilate to this world, but rather to be
strangers in it and command it to surrender to us and get better.
This I recalled, standing at the base of that high wall. Yet now,
Jacob, I number among the first kind. I have lost the will to live
without You by my side. I also think I am not the only one to
react in this way to Your disappearance. Only now do we see
how very painful is Your absence. May God judge us, we
thought we had killed You.
I came directly from Warsaw, where many of us went and
settled in a perfect stupor, not knowing what had happened to
You. At first many, I among them, followed Your Hana to
Kobyłka, near Warsaw, a village that belongs to Bishop Załuski,
which had been set aside for us at Mrs. Kossakowska's behest.

But it was cramped for us there, and gloomy, the bishop's house neglected and the bishop's servants mistrustful of us. As it lies so close to Warsaw, gradually some wanted to take the initiative to seek some engagement there, so as not to sit around idle at the bishop's expense, and not to wander around other people's homes. Those who wished to return to Podolia, like the Rudnickis, quickly got organized, and Hirsh, or Rudnicki, went to check if it would be possible. But he soon realized, as we did after him, that there was nothing left for us there, that we will never return to our villages and homes now. All of it is gone. You were right that in being baptized, we were taking a step into the abyss. And we took that step, and then we were as though suspended in our fall, not knowing where and when the process of falling would end, nor indeed how. Would we be crushed to smithereens, or would we be saved? Would we emerge intact or broken?

The first thing that started was blame. Who said what and when. Our words were used against You, but we were not innocent. After baptism, many of us in desperation grasped for our new life as if it were a treasure. We changed our attire and hid our customs in deep closets, so as to pretend to be people we were not at all. Once more we are strangers, for even in the best clothes, with a cross on our breast, smooth-shaven and well-behaved whenever we open our mouths, you can recognize us by our accent. And so, fleeing our own foreignness, so mocked and despised, we became like puppets among men.

Slowly we are becoming selfish and indifferent, and although the company keeps together, the most basic things have become the most important: how to survive, how to handle ourselves in this struggle, how to feed the children and put a roof over their heads. Many of us would have tried for some sort of work, but there is no way to do so, for we do not know whether we will stay here, what the good Mrs. Kossakowska will come up with on our behalf, and whether it is even worth staying with her. Those who have money have managed to get by, like the Wołowskis, who have made investments in Warsaw, but others, the poor, with whom you

had us share in Ivanie, must now solicit aid. And if this
continues, we will be scattered, and it will be like when a person
blows onto a fistful of sand.

Our position is undoubtedly better than when we were
ordinary Jews. The Wołowskis and the other ennobled converts
have the best situation, but many cannot afford the baksheesh
for a title. Franciszek and his brother have a distillery in Leszno.
Now it will bring them more income, as they have acquired new
clients. Nussen's son, Krysa, now called Krysiński, has just
opened a shop with leather goods, he brings them in from
Turkey, and I have seen the elegant ladies who buy gloves from
him. Such men are managing fine. And their closest relatives,
like the Rudnickis or the Lanckorońskis, or whatever their
names ended up being. Hayah's husband, Hirsh, has grown
old and ill. Hayah is a great lady, and we try to look after her
here, but she is not suited for this homelessness. It is a good
thing she has such wise and capable daughters.

The Wołowskis immediately gave their children up to
religious schools, wanting to educate them not as merchants,
but rather as officers and lawyers. They have been trying to talk
everyone into doing this, but not everyone can afford it. As you
commanded us, we have been marrying our children to each
other, and so Franciszek Wołowski has now married his son
Jędrzej to the daughter of his brother Jan, I don't remember
what the girl is called now. The nuptials are only temporary,
only recognized by us for now, since according to Polish law
they are still minors, and therefore cannot wed.

Hana is trying ceaselessly to be allowed to see You—You
know that, for You get her letters. That Kossakowska woman
has been a great help to her, promising to arrange a visit with
the king himself, but when the king will come to Warsaw, no
one knows.

I have tried to comfort Hana since the death of Immanuel,
but she does not care for me. She keeps more with the
Zwierzchowskis, and it is they who tend to little Avachunia.
Kossakowska fusses over Hana as she would over a daughter.
She plans to house her on one of her estates, give her room and
board, and Avacha a good education. Avacha gets whatever she

wants out of her. You must not worry about her, she is a very wise little girl, and since God has taken Your only son, she must console You. She has a teacher who is teaching her to play the piano.

Now that there is the possibility of conveying letters, I will send a messenger from Warsaw every ten days. And I believe that every splinter will be removed from Your heart, and the wound will heal, for we are miserable and stupid, thrown into something we cannot possibly understand, which only You can fathom.

Finally, I will tell you that I understand what happened as follows: You had to go to jail so that all the prophecies could be fulfilled—the Messiah must fall as absolutely low as possible. And when I saw You, led out with a bruised face, when you said to us: "Spit on this fire," I realized that this was how it was supposed to be, and that the workings of salvation had gotten back on track, in gear, like a clock that measures time in eons—You had to fall, and I had to push You.

Jacob lies on his back on his cot in the tower of the Częstochowa fortress, and the letter he has been holding falls to the floor. Through the tiny window, better for shooting than for looking out of, he sees the stars. He feels as though he has found himself inside a deep well, whence the stars are better visible than they are from the earth's surface, for the well acts as a telescope that brings celestial bodies nearer and causes them to appear within arm's reach.

From there, Yente looks at Jacob.

The tower stands in a fortress surrounded by high walls, and that fortress is on a hill, at the foot of which lies, barely visible in the darkness, a poorly lit little town. And all of this is located in an undulating countryside covered in dense forests. And farther on extends the great plain of the center of Europe, circumfused with the waters of the seas and the oceans. Finally, Europe itself, seen from Yente's position on high, becomes the size of a coin, and out of the darkness emerges the planet's majestic curvature, so that it looks like a freshly shelled green pea.

## Gifts from the Besht

Nahman, Piotr Jakubowski, who rarely leaves his little office these days, bites into the fresh pods of green peas brought to him by his son, Aron. He pulled them out of his pocket crumpled and snapped, but they are still tasty and crunchy. Aron has come to say goodbye to his father: he is going back to Busk, and once there, he will, as his father once did, join a caravan setting out to Turkey for tobacco and precious stones. Jakubowski rarely sees him; the boy stayed in Busk with his mother and grandparents when the divorce was finalized. But he is proud of him. Aron, like his mother, is short and swarthy, resembling a Turk. He has already mastered Turkish. He also knows German, since he has gone to Breslau and Dresden with Osman Czerniawski.

Nahman has just finished writing a letter and is now folding it very carefully. Aron glances at the Turkish script, no doubt guessing who his father is writing to.

They hug and kiss each other on the lips, as father and son. At the door, Aron looks over his shoulder at his father, who is small and thin, with matted hair and a torn little caftan. Then he goes.

The Baal Shem Tov passed away in this year, 1760, but Jakubowski didn't write to Jacob of it. Jacob never respected the Hasidim, saying they were fools, although he seemed to be afraid of the Besht. He never concealed the satisfaction it gave him to win people away from the Besht. And there were quite a few of them.

They are saying that the Besht died because his heart broke at the news of hundreds of Jews converting. That his heart broke, in other words, because of Jacob Frank. Jakubowski isn't sure—will this news please Jacob? Maybe he should write of it to him?

Jakubowski was hired by Shlomo, Franciszek Wołowski, to sit in a small office counting barrels of beer. There isn't too much to do, since the brewery is just starting. Jakubowski tallies the deliveries, full and empty barrels, sending products all over the city and to taverns on the outskirts. At first, Wołowski sent him to scout for new clients around Warsaw, but he gave that up. As Piotr Jakubowski, Nahman still looks sluggish somehow, unconvincing, even dressed up in a kontusz. The Jews have not wanted to buy beer since their baptism, and the non-Jews look with suspicion upon this little redheaded man with the mien of a chicken. That's what Franciszek says about him—that Nahman looks like a chicken. The first time Jakubowski heard this, it hurt his feelings. He would have thought that with his auburn hair and his cleverness he was more like a fox.

The truth is that he has not felt good for some time, either on his own or in company. Lately he has been thinking about giving up this anxious waiting game in Warsaw, this hoping for some kind of miracle, and instead setting out east, for Międzybóż, but then little Immanuel died, and the first thought that came into Nahman's mind was that the Besht had taken the little boy with him, and that this made sense. The Besht took the child in his arms and carried him away, into the night—to protect him from them. So it occurred to Nahman-Jakubowski, and he even wrote it down, with a racing heart, in the margins of his book.

Recently in Warsaw it was said that when, sometime during his illness, the Baal Shem Tov came to expect that he would die, he had all of his students gather around him, and he gave them the objects he had been using himself up until then. To one he gave a snuffbox, to another a prayer shawl, to another a beloved psalter. When he got to his favorite student, however, none of his property remained. The Besht said that he would give him his stories: "You will travel the world so that people might hear these stories." The student, truth be told, was none too pleased with such an inheritance, for he was quite poor and would have preferred to receive something more material.

He forgot about it for a time, however, and lived in poverty as a milkman. Until one day the news reached his village that some wealthy man in Russia would pay a great deal to hear some stories about the Besht. Then the milkman's neighbors reminded him of his inheritance and sent him off to Russia. When he got there, it turned out that this man hungering for stories was the head of the kahal, a man who was prosperous, but sad.

A small feast was organized, to which important guests were invited. The milkman was seated in the middle, and after an abundant refreshment, once things had quieted down, he was asked to begin. He opened his mouth, took a big breath—and nothing. He had forgotten everything. He sat down, confused, and the other guests showed all their disappointment. So it went the next night, too. And the next. It seemed that the milkman had lost the power of speech. Thus, very ashamed, he quietly made preparations to take his leave. But once he was sitting in the wagon, he experienced a kind of breakthrough, and his memory, so vast until then, so filled with stories, let slip one little reminiscence. He seized on this minor occurrence and had the horses stopped. He hopped out of the cart and said to his host, who had just been bidding him farewell in an icy tone: "I remembered something. One minor occurrence. Nothing major . . ."

And he began to speak:

"One time, the Baal Shem Tov came and grabbed me in the night while I was sleeping, telling me to harness the horses and go with him to a distant village. There he got out in front of one rich house by the church, where a candle was still burning, and he disappeared inside it for half an hour. When he returned, he was somewhat agitated and asked to go home."

Here the milkman cut off again and fell silent. "And? What happened next?" the others asked him, but then, to everyone's amazement, the head of the kahal burst into tears, sobbing loudly, unable to control himself. Only after a while, when he had calmed down a little bit, did he say: "I was that man to whom the Baal Shem Tov paid a visit." Understanding nothing, everyone demanded further explanation with their eyes.

So the head of the kahal kept talking:

"At that time, I was a Christian; I was an important official. Among my responsibilities, I was charged with organizing forced conversions. When the Baal Shem Tov came to me that night, I jumped up from the table where I was writing out ordinances. I was surprised by the sight of that bearded Hasid, who furthermore began to yell at me in Polish: 'How much longer? How long is this going to take? How much more will you make your brothers suffer?' I looked at him in utter astonishment, thinking the old man had lost his mind and confused me with someone else. But he would not stop yelling: 'Are you not aware that you are a rescued

Jewish child, taken in and raised by a Polish family who always hid from you your true origins?' Before the holy man disappeared, as suddenly as he had come in, I was overcome by great confusion, guilt, and regret. 'Is it possible for me to be forgiven everything I have done to my brothers?' I asked in a trembling voice. Then the Baal Shem Tov replied: 'On the day when someone comes and tells you this story, you will know that you have been forgiven.'"

Jakubowski would also like for someone to come and visit him and tell him such a story. Jakubowski would also like to be forgiven.


## The larch manor in Wojsławice and Zwierzchowski's teeth

The manor house was fully restored over the summer. It received a new roof, a new truss, and larch shingles. The rooms were repainted, the stoves cleaned out, and one was completely redone in beautiful white tiles that came all the way from somewhere near Sandomierz. There are six rooms, two of which are intended for the ladies, Hana and her little daughter, while in the others the women who accompany Hana and serve her have taken up their lodgings. In one of the rooms lives the Zwierzchowski family. There is no drawing room—they all just meet in the big kitchen, where it is warmest. The rest of the company is confined to the grange, under poor conditions, for those dwellings are moldy and damp.

The worst is that from the start they are afraid to walk into the village. Everyone glowers at them there—the Jews who take up the little marketplace and run the businesses, and the goyim, too, are hostile. Someone has painted black crosses on the door of the manor, and they don't know who did it and what they mean. The two brushstrokes going across one another make a sinister impression.

One night someone sets the shed on fire, and it's just lucky that it starts snowing, and the fire goes out.

---

Zwierzchowski and Piotrowski have gone to see that woman, Kossakow-ska, who now watches over them from the palace of her cousins the Potoc-kis, in Krasnystaw, and complain of idleness.

"To do business we would need to go to Krasnystaw, or even Zamość, because they won't let us in here. We had a stand at the fair, but they overturned it in the snow, and much of what we had to sell was stolen and destroyed," says Piotrowski, following Kossakowska with his gaze as she paces up and down the length of the room.

"They took apart our carriage—we don't even have a way to get any-where," Piotrowski adds after a moment.

"Her Ladyship is afraid to leave the house," says Zwierzchowski. "We had to set up guards around the orchard. But why should we have to have guards, when it's mostly just women, children, and the elderly?"

After they leave, Kossakowska sighs to her distant cousin Marianna Potocka:

"There's always some new demand from them. This thing is not good, that thing is bad. I have dealt with all of it. The stove alone cost me a fortune."

Kossakowska is wearing all black, in mourning for her husband. He died on Christmas, 1761. The death of her husband—sudden, needless (he caught a cold from going out to the kennel when his favorite dog had a litter of puppies)—has put her in a strange state, as if she were slowly sinking into a pot of lard. Whatever she tries to hold on to simply slips out of her hands. She takes a step, and she sinks. She used to call him "that old cripple" to Agnieszka, but now, without him, she feels completely helpless. The funeral took place in Kamieniec, and she came directly thence to Krasnystaw; she knows that she will not go back to Kamieniec.

"I can't help them any longer," Kossakowska explains to Marianna. To which Potocka, an old woman by now, and very pious, says:

"And what more can I do for them? I have already sponsored so many baptisms, and we readied the manor for them together . . ."

"I'm not talking about more donations," says Kossakowska. "From what I have heard from Warsaw, they have powerful foes who are equipped with powerful means, which they are not merely squandering on purses filled with gold. You would be surprised"—she lowers her voice for a moment, and then cries out—"with Minister Brühl! Who, as everybody knows, has a good relationship with the Jews, and deposits state money with them. So what can I, little old Kossakowska, do about that? When Bishop Sołtyk wasn't able to do anything?" Kossakowska rubs her furrowed brow. "What we need is some sort of intelligent—"

"Write to them," Marianna Potocka says to Katarzyna. "Tell them that they need to sit tight and wait. And set a good example for those other unfaithful Jews who are still so mired in the error of their sinful ways."

This happens in the spring of 1762. An early spring wind, dense with moisture, is blowing. The potatoes are sprouting in the cellar, mold has gotten into the flour. On the door black crosses show up again, like a form of pre-harvest, misshapen flora. When one of Kossakowska's charges tries to go shopping, the Jews spit in his face and close the shops to him. The goyim poke at them and call them ne'er-do-wells. The men are constantly getting into fights. Recently some young men from town attacked Zwierzchowski and his teenage daughter as they were coming back from Lublin in their carriage. They raped the girl and knocked out her father's teeth. Afterward, Zwierzchowski's wife gathered the teeth from the mud and brought them back into the manor and showed them to everyone on her outstretched palm. Three teeth—a bad omen.

A few days later, the girl hanged herself, much to her parents' despair.

## Of torture and curses

The solution is so simple it seems to be hanging right there in the air, ready for the plucking. So obvious is it that it would be very hard even to say whose idea it first was. It goes like this:

Shortly before Easter, a woman dressed as a Jew, with a turban on her head and a kerchief over her shoulders, wearing wrinkly skirts, goes to the local priest and introduces herself as the wife of the Wojsławice rabbi. She doesn't say much, only that she overheard that her husband and some others killed a child for Christian blood, as Passover is approaching, and they need the blood for their holiday matzah. The priest is stunned. The woman is disturbed, behaving strangely, won't look him in the eye, paces nervously from one end of the room to the other, covers her face. The father doesn't believe her. He sees her to the door and advises her to calm down.

Nonetheless, the next day, the priest, feeling uneasy, goes to Krasnystaw to Lady Marianna Teresa Potocka and her close relative Katarzyna Kossakowska, and the three of them report this unusual affair to the police. An investigation is launched.

The investigators find the body without any particular effort; it is lying underneath some branches near the rabbi's house. The child's skin has been pricked, though the child isn't bruised or otherwise marked. The tiny wounds on the naked body of the dark-haired, three-year-old Mikołaj look fake, shallow little pits that seem to have nothing whatsoever to do with blood. Come evening, they arrest the two rabbis of Wojsławice, Sender Zyskieluk and Henryk Józefowicz, along with the wife of the former and some dozen or so others from the Wojsławice kahal. The priest tries to find the other rabbi's mysterious wife, so that she can confirm her testimony, but she has disappeared. The other rabbi, in fact, is a widower. During the torture to which all three prisoners are immediately subjected, they confess to a number of murders, to robbing churches and profaning the host, and soon enough it comes out that the whole Jewish kahal in the village of Wojsławice, numbering some eighty persons, is made up of murderers. Both rabbis, as well as Leyb Moshkowicz Sienicki and Yosa Szymułowicz, confess under torture—as though they were one man— that they killed the little boy, and that, after draining his blood, they threw out the body to be eaten by dogs.

Zwierzchowska, both Piotrowskis, Pawłowski, and the Wołowskis, referring to the well-known "seventh point" of the Lwów disputation, all confirm the reality of these ritual crimes. This evidence makes such a great impression at court that the next day a mass lynching is only barely avoided. Kossakowska entreats Sołtyk to come—and in the end he does, as a specialist in such concerns. He instructs the two women, Kossakow-ska and Potocka, in what view they ought to take of it. Kossakowska, who is one of the last to testify, mentions the crosses on the houses and the persecution of the new arrivals. The trial takes a long time, since everyone wants to learn as many details as possible about this Jewish iniquity. Pamphlets are read out, mostly those of Serafinowicz, a Jewish convert who, years later, confessed to Jewish crimes, but also the writings of Fathers Pikulski and Awedyk. Everything seems clear and obvious, and so it comes as no surprise that all of the accused are sentenced to death. They will be drawn and quartered, unless they agree to be baptized, in which case they will be shown mercy and beheaded instead. Four of the convicts decide on baptism. Just before their beheading, they are baptized ceremoniously in church, and afterward they are buried with great pomp in the Christian cemetery. Sender Zyskieluk manages to hang himself in his cell and—since in this way he avoided the real punishment—his body is dragged through the streets of Krasnystaw and then burned in the market square. Afterward there is nothing to be done besides drive the rest of the Jews out of town, which, before he hanged himself, Rabbi Zyskieluk put a curse on, all its inhabitants included.

In the summer, the children at the Wojsławice estate and on the grange begin to get sick, but only the children of the neophytes, while the peasant children do not seem to be affected by this plague. Several of the neophyte children die. First, the Pawłowskis' little girl, just a few months old, and then Wojtuś Majewski, and then his seven-year-old sister. By August, when the heat is at its peak, there is almost no family whose children have not been stricken. Kossakowska summons a doctor from Zamość, but he is unable to help. He tells them to place warm compresses on their backs and chests. He manages to save little Zosia Szymanowska only by cutting a hole in her throat with a knife as she is starting to suffocate. It is an illness that passes from child to child—first they cough, then they get a fever, and then they cough to death. Kossakowska attends their small, humble funerals. They dig the little graves in the Catholic cemetery in Wojsławice at a remove from the other graves, aware of their otherness. By the end of August, there is a funeral just about every day. Marianna Potocka is so alarmed that she has shrines built at the town's five tollhouses to protect them from all the forces of evil: Saint Barbara from storms and conflagrations, Saint John of Nepomuk from floods, Saint Florian from fires, and Saint Tecla from any plagues. The fifth shrine is dedicated to Michael the Archangel, who is to protect the town from all manner of ill and spell and curse.

The eldest Łabęcki, Moshe, dies too, leaving behind his extremely young wife, Teresa, with a child at her breast. They say when someone is about to die, a great black crow settles on the roof of that person's house. No one has any doubt that this is the curse at work, and that it is powerful and terrible. After the departure of Moshe Łabęcki, who knew how to lift herems and return them to their source, everyone feels defenseless. It seems to them that now everyone will die. This is why they remember Hayah Hirsh, now Lanckorońska, the prophetess. Lady Hana writes to her herself, with an urgent request: They must know what will happen next. She sends messengers with letters to Jacob in Częstochowa as well as to Hayah and the rest of the company in Warsaw, but no answer arrives. It is as if the messengers have simply vanished.


## How Hayah prophesies

When she speaks in others' voices, Hayah always keeps in front of her something that looks like a map, painted on a board. There are various mysterious signs on it, and a drawing of a sefirot tree, only quadrupled; it looks like an extremely ornate cross, like a four-branched snowflake that can't exist in nature. She arranges on it pieces of bread with feathers stuck into them, and buttons, and seeds, and each one looks bizarre, like a human figurine, but nightmarish, indecent, somehow. Hayah has a pair of dice—one of them with numbers on it, and the other one with letters. On the board are some clumsily painted circles. The boundaries between them are blurred, indistinct; there are scattered letters and symbols, and in the corners there are animals, suns, and moons. There is a dog and a big fish, maybe a carp. The board must be old: in some places the paint has completely peeled off, leaving no understandable trace of what used to be there.

Now Hayah toys with the dice, rolling them around in her palms, staring at the board. You never know how long any of it is going to take, but then her eyelids start to blink and tremble, and the dice are rolled, revealing an answer. According to the prediction, Hayah then sets out the figures on the board, whispers something to herself, nudges them, changes their layout, sets some to the side, takes some others from somewhere else—the new ones even stranger than the last. It is hard to comprehend this odd game, looking at it from outside, since its configuration is constantly changing. And as she does these strange things, Hayah converses, inquiring after the children, the quality of this year's jams, all the family members' health. Then suddenly Hayah says, in the same tone she uses for the jam, that the king is going to die, and that there will be an interregnum. The women freeze amidst the potato peels; the children stop chasing each other around the table. Hayah stares at her figurines and speaks again:

"The new king will be the last king of Poland. Three seas will flood the nation. Warsaw will be left an island. Young Łabęcka will give birth to a child whose father has died, a little girl, and she will become a great princess. Jacob will be freed by his greatest enemies, and with his closest allies, he will make an escape to the south. Everyone in this room right now will live in a great castle on a wide river, where they will wear sumptuous clothing and forget their language."

Even Hayah seems to be surprised by what she's saying. She has a funny expression on her face, as if she were stifling laughter or trying to hold back the words that keep coming out of her mouth. She grimaces.

Marianna Wołowska, who has been putting eggs into a basket, says:

"I told you. The river is the Dniester. We'll all go back to Ivanie, and that is where we'll build our palaces. That great river is the Dniester."

## Edom is shaken to its foundations

After the death of Augustus III of Wettin, in October 1763, the bell
rings all day. The monks take turns at the rope, while the crowd of
pilgrims, not especially large at this time of year and diminished somewhat, too, by the chaos in the country, is suddenly overwhelmed by great
terror—everyone lies on the ground with their arms spread out, until
there is no longer any way to pass from the courtyard into the church.

Jacob learns of this from Roch, who comes right away and says it with
some satisfaction.

"There will be a war. That is for certain, and they may take us all back
again, since they've got no one watching over this Catholic country,
and all the infidels and heretics are already out there, grasping for the
Commonwealth."

Jacob feels sorry for this old man and gives him a few groszy to convey,
as usual, some letters outside the monastery's censorship, which means
he'll have to take them into the village and there give them to Shmul.
Jacob, too, would like for there to be a war. Then he goes to the prior,
intending to complain that the brothers are holding on to his food and
other things from town, including tobacco. He knows the prior won't do
anything about it, he complains like this every Thursday. But the prior
does not receive him now. Jacob shivers from the cold, he waits so long it
gets dark. Then the prior goes to evening mass and goes by Jacob without
a word. Jacob, tall and skinny, wrapped up in his opończa, goes back to
his tower, frozen.

In the evening, having amply paid off the guards as usual, Matuszewski is smuggled into the tower, and together he and Jacob write a
letter. Matuszewski's hand is shaking from the cold when he writes "Nuncio Visconti" at the top of the page, and it continues to tremble as he
writes a number of other famous names. This letter must be written now
that the old order is dying, too, and a new one is being born. Now, after
the death of the old king, everything is being turned upside down, black
becoming white and vice versa. Right now—when the new order has not

yet been established and the new chancelleries have not yet gotten under way, when the seemingly inflexible laws have yet to soften like dry bread in water, and while those who were at the top are nervously trying to work out whom to make alliances with and whom to stop talking to—right now there is a chance for this letter to matter. Thus Jacob asks to be released. And if the nuncio should deem this release premature, then Jacob requests at least his intervention; he is suffering from the cramped and miserable conditions in prison. The monks withhold every assistance from his family and friends and do not even allow him to take air; his health has been damaged severely by spending more than two years in the cold tower. He remains, after all, a fervent Catholic, fully devoted to his faith, and his proximity to the Holy Virgin lately has caused his faith, always solid as an oak, to attain even greater heights.

They finish this portion of the letter, but the most important part awaits—they just don't quite know how to write it. They work on it all night, burning through several candles. Come morning, this part, too, is ready. It goes like this:

> The Holy Church has already drawn attention to the falseness of the accusations of the use of Christian blood by Jews. And while we have already met with many misfortunes, still another befell us when this occurred in Wojsławice, yet not through any fault of our own, but rather because we were used by others for their own ends.
>
> Being eternally grateful to our generous protectors, i.e., Bishop Kajetan Sołtyk, as well as Andrzej Joseph Załuski, who have kindly taken us in under their roofs, and also Katarzyna Kossakowska, our great benefactress, we must defend ourselves against every insinuation that it was we who started the accusations against the Jews of letting Christian blood, and let it be known that the terrible slaughter that followed—which went against the teachings of the Holy Church—occurred without any intentional participation on our part, for we remain humble servants of the Catholic faith.

## Of how the interregnum translates into the traffic patterns of the carriages on Krakowskie Przedmieście

As there suddenly aren't enough lodgings for everyone in Warsaw, the traffic on Krakowskie Przedmieście becomes relentless. Every powerful personage has come here in his carriage, creating an instant jam and crush.

Agnieszka, having learned how, lets her mistress's blood, but recently this hasn't helped. By day, Kossakowska does all right, but at night she cannot sleep; she has hot flashes and heart palpitations. The doctor has already been called thrice. Maybe she should stay at home, in Busk or Krystynopol? Where is Katarzyna Kossakowska's home, exactly?

As soon as the king died, she, too, raced to the capital and there wasted no time in plotting with Sołtyk to back Prince Frederick Christian as the new ruler. The bishop's carriage, in which they are now going to Prince Branicki's for more political plotting, is stuck on Krakowskie Przedmieście, right by Świętokrzyska. Kossakowska sits opposite the heavy, sweaty Sołtyk and speaks in her low, almost masculine voice:

"How can you not lose faith in the order of things in this country, looking at our beloved husbands, brothers, and fathers who hold our fate in their hands? Just take a closer look at them, Your Excellency. One busies himself with newfangled alchemy and seeks the philosopher's stone, another is drawn to painting pictures, a third spends his nights in the capital and gambles away all the money from his estates in Podolia, and still another—just look at him!—is an equestrian who squanders his fortune on Arabian colts. I haven't even mentioned those who write poems rather than bothering with our accounts. Those who pomade their wigs while their sabers rust . . ."

The bishop doesn't seem to be listening to her. He looks through a crack in the window; they are now before the Church of the Holy Cross. He is worried because he is once again in arrears. Debts—they seem to be the painfully real, recurring concern in the bishop's life.

". . . it often seems to us that we are Poland," Kossakowska continues stubbornly. "But they are Poland, too. For although this peasant who was just given a flogging does not even know that he, too, belongs to the Republic, nor does that Jew who handles your business dealings have any awareness of it, and perhaps he would not even wish to admit it, nonetheless we are all traveling in the same carriage, and we ought to care about each other—to take care of each other—not rip scraps from one another's mouths like hostile dogs. Like right now. Do we want to let ourselves be ruled by Russia's ambassadors? Let them impose their king on us?"

Kossakowska yammers on, all the way to Miodowa, and Sołtyk silently marvels at her inexhaustible energy, but the bishop does not know what Agnieszka knows: that because of the curse in Wojsławice, Kossakowska cannot sleep, and every night she flagellates herself. If Bishop Sołtyk had by some miracle the opportunity to undo her lace top and pull up the linen undershirt to reveal her back, he would see the effects of that insomnia—chaotically scattered bloody swaths, the components of some unrealized inscription.

## Pinkas edits the *Documenta Judaeos*

Rabbi Rapaport is a tall, sturdily built man with a gray beard that splits in two and flows down over his chest as though in two icicles. He speaks in a quiet voice, and in this simple way, he subordinates people, since they must make an effort in order to understand his words, which forces them to pay attention. Wherever he appears, he always inspires respect. It will be the same again today, and Hayim haKohen Rapaport, head rabbi of Lwów, will soon be here; he will come in quietly, and yet all eyes will turn to him from around the tables, and everyone will fall silent. Then Pinkas will show him one of the first pamphlets, already put together and sewn, with perfectly evenly cut pages. Although he is slightly older than Rapaport, Pinkas often has the impression that the latter is his father, or even his grandfather. The truth is that holy people have no age; they are born old. Rapaport's praise means more to Pinkas than any gold ingot. Every word the rabbi says Pinkas commits to memory, and in his mind he plays out any scenes of praise over and over. The rabbi never scolds. When he does not praise, he is silent, and his silence is heavy as a stone.

In the rabbi's house now there is a kind of extended chancellery. Tables are arranged around the room, and stools, and writing stands, and at them the most important document in existence today is being copied out. His text has already gone to the printer's, and the first proofs have been returned. Some of the men here are cutting them, others are folding the pages into the small brochure format and gluing onto each pamphlet a thicker cardboard cover that displays the long and complicated title that flows over half the page: *Documenta Judaeos in Polonia concernentia ad Acta Metrices suscepta et ex iis fideliteriterum descripta et extradicta*. Pinkas played a part in this, by organizing the office here, and, since he also speaks and reads Polish, aiding in the translation. He contributed a great deal to the cause of a certain Zelig, who escaped execution in Żytomierz and walked to Rome to demand justice of the Pope. For the Holy Office in Rome they had to translate into Polish and Hebrew what this Zelig had managed to obtain on his mission, and also to translate into Latin and Hebrew what King Zygmunt III had written in the records of the royal crown in 1592. As well as a letter on behalf of Zelig to the Warsaw nuncio issued by the prefect of the Holy Office, in which it is clearly stated that the Holy Office, after a thorough examination of the question of the accusations of the use of Christian blood in Żytomierz and the alleged ritual murder, asserts that the same are utterly without foundation. And that all further accusations of this kind are to be dismissed, as the letting of Christian blood has no basis in the Jewish religion, nor in the Jewish tradition. Finally, Rapaport, through the intercession of his friends, managed to get a letter from Visconti, the papal nuncio, to Baron Brühl, in which the nuncio confirms that the Jews turned for help to the highest office of the Church, to the Pope, and that the Pope took up their defense against this dire libel.

And it is almost exactly how Pinkas had earlier imagined it, although it rarely happens that imagination so corresponds to reality. (Pinkas is old enough to understand how it works: God only gives us situations we couldn't have come up with ourselves.)

Rapaport comes in, and Pinkas hands him the newly bound pamphlet. The shadow of a smile passes over the rabbi's face, though there is one thing Pinkas did not foresee: that the rabbi, out of habit, would open the book from the other side, in the Jewish manner, and that instead of the title page, he would see the very end of it first:

> The Holy Office has recently considered all available testimonies that Jews use human blood to prepare their bread, called matzah, and that for this reason they murder children. We firmly state that there are no grounds for such accusations. If such accusations ever arise again, a decision must be made not on the basis of witness statements, but on convincing criminal evidence.

The rabbi looks over these words but doesn't understand what he is reading. Pinkas, after waiting for a moment, approaches, leans toward him, and starts translating fluently, in a light, quiet, but victorious voice.

## Who Pinkas runs into at the market in Lwów

Pinkas is looking at a certain person at the market in Lwów. Dressed like a Christian, with shoulder-length hair that is thin, feathery. He has a white stock tie at his neck, his face is shaved, and aged. Two wrinkles cut vertically down his still-young forehead. Sensing that he is being observed, he gives up the purchase of woolen stockings and tries to disappear into the crowd. But Pinkas sets off after him, brushing aside the vendors. He bumps into a girl with a basket of nuts, but finally he manages to grab the man by the side of his coat.

"Yehuda? Is it you?"

The man turns around reluctantly and looks Pinkas up and down from head to toe.

"Yehuda?" asks Pinkas, with more doubt in his voice this time, and lets the kapota go.

"It is I, Uncle Pinkas," the man says quietly.

Pinkas's throat closes up at this. He covers his eyes with his hands.

"What has happened to you? Are you no longer a rabbi in Glinno? What are you wearing? What have you done?"

But his nephew seems dead set against this talk.

"I cannot speak with you, Uncle," he says. "I have to go—"

"What do you mean, you can't speak to me?"

The erstwhile rabbi of Glinno turns around and makes to leave, but his path is blocked by peasants leading cows. Pinkas says:

"I'm not letting you get away. You owe me an explanation."

"There is nothing to explain. Don't touch me, Uncle. I have nothing to do with you now."

"No." Pinkas suddenly understands, and staggers back in horror. "Do you know that you have condemned yourself for all eternity? You're with them? Have you been baptized, or are you waiting your turn? If your mother had lived to see this, it would have broken her heart."

Pinkas suddenly, in the middle of the market, begins to cry; his lips curl back into a horseshoe, and sobs shake his skinny body, and tears flow out of his eyes and flood his small, wrinkled face. People look on in curiosity and no doubt think this poor soul has been robbed—that now he's weeping over some lost groszy. The erstwhile rabbi of Glinno, now Jacob Goliński, glances around uncertainly. He must feel sorry for his relative then, because he goes up to him and gently takes him by the shoulder.

"I know you cannot understand me. I am not a bad person."

"Satan has laid claim to you, to all of you, you are all worse than Satan himself, never in all my days . . . You are no longer a Jew!"

"Uncle, let's go over to the gate there . . ."

"And do you know that I lost Gitla, my only daughter, because of all of you? Do you realize?"

"I never saw her there."

"She's not there. She's gone. And you will never find her."

Then, suddenly, violently, he hits Goliński in the chest, with all his strength, and although he's big, and strong, Goliński staggers on receiving such a blow.

Pinkas stands on his tiptoes and hisses straight into his face:

"Yehuda, you have plunged a knife into my heart today. But you will come back to us. One day you will come back."

Then he turns and hurries off between the stalls.

## A mirror and ordinary glass

Now Kossakowska manages to obtain, without much trouble at all, permission for husband and wife to meet in Częstochowa. Everyone is busy with politics, with the selection of the next king. The prior of the monastery agrees to improve the conditions of Jacob's confinement. In the early autumn, with great relief, Hana and Avacha and a sizable group of true believers depart the much-loathed Wojsławice and set out for Częstochowa. Marianna Potocka is angry with both them and Katarzyna. As if it weren't enough that the town was losing those other Jews, now these are abandoning the larch manor. They leave all the doors wide open, trash on the floor. Where they loaded up their carts there are still some muddy, trampled rags. The only real, lasting testaments to their presence here are the graves, slightly off to the side, under the big elm, marked only with a few haphazard birch crosses and a pile of stones. The grave of Rabbi Moshe of Podhajce, the great Kabbalist and maker of powerful amulets, is the only one that stands out from the rest, thanks to the white pebbles in which it was covered by his wife.

The party arrives in Częstochowa on the 8th of September, 1762. They walk past the walls of the monastery solemnly, beautifully attired, with bouquets of flowers, yellow and purple. The fortress's crew and the monks are surprised to see them, looking as they do more like a wedding party than the exhausted pilgrims they normally receive. And on the 10th of September, Hana and her husband, whom she has not seen in nearly two years, have intercourse in broad daylight, with the knowledge of everyone in the retinue. This happens in the tower, in the officer's room, the little windows of which have been carefully covered so that no one else is able to take part in this tikkun, this act that repairs the world. Yet they all feel their hearts fill with the hope that the worst has passed at last, and that now the time has come for them to move forward. A month later, there is an entry in Matuszewski's hand in the chaotically kept chronicle that on the 8th of October (the Lord has had them definitively do away with the Jewish calendar), Hana and Jacob have conceived a son; this Matuszewski knows from the Lord Himself.

They have rented two homes on the Wieluńskie Przedmieście. The others squeeze into little rooms at inns, but they all stick together. Thus to the north of the monastery a kind of tiny settlement arises constituted solely of true believers, and now Jacob has fresh fruits and vegetables each day, and eggs and meat when he's not fasting.

The little houses of the village come up almost to the fortress; there are even some of the youngsters, for instance clever Jan Wołowski, who are able to climb the wall and pass things to the prisoner, particularly once a little something has been slipped to the old soldiers. Then the veterans doze off, leaning on their spears, or, complaining of the cold, simply vanish up under the roof, where they play dice. The company even managed, under cover of night, to attach a ring to the wall, thanks to which it is possible to hoist up bags with provisions. They have to be careful that none of the brothers notices this fixture. Lately the Lord has been requesting onions: so much has he weakened from being confined that now his gums bleed, and his teeth hurt. He also complains that his ear has been hurting, and that he has dizzy spells. Hana, with the consent of the monastery, gets to visit her husband once a day, but she often lingers so long she ends up spending the night. Others come, too, little pilgrimages making their way to the Lord. All of the pilgrims are dressed neatly, in the Christian fashion, in the urban fashion, humbly, the female pilgrims differing completely from the gaudy Częstochowa Jewish women with the turbans on their heads. The true believer women wear the linen bonnets of Polish townswomen, and although some of them are also wearing through the soles of their shoes, and their bonnets hide a matted plait under the dull lace, their heads are still held high.

Since the rules have been relaxed, the Lord has sent to Warsaw for women. Since none took part in his betrayal, women will be his guards. He also needs naarot, or young maids, for his Avacha—serving girls and teachers. And he needs women to take care of him. Women, he needs women, lots of them—he needs them everywhere, as if their mild, vibrating presence might turn back the dark time of Częstochowa.

And here they are. First Wittel Matuszewska—she is the first, but then comes Henrykowa Wołowska, extremely young but serene, somewhat heavyset, with a wide, pretty face and a quiet, lilting voice. Her beautiful, shiny brown hair sneaks out of its pins. There is Eva Jezierzańska, who is slender, with a birthmark on her neck that has hair growing out of it of which she is ashamed, so that she wears a kerchief. But she has a nice face like a young ermine's, dark, velvety eyes, a beautiful complexion, and a burst of hair held back by a tightly drawn ribbon. There is also Franciszkowa Wołowska, the eldest of them, strong and lovely, with a clear voice and musical talent to boot. And there are the same women the Lord liked having around in Ivanie—Pawłowska, Dembowska, and Czerniawska, his sister. There is also Lewińska and Michałowa Wołowska. And there is Klara Lanckorońska, Hayah's daughter, with her curves and her smiling eyes. All of them came to Warsaw without their husbands, in two carriages. They will look after the Lord.

Jacob has them stand before him in a row. He looks them over carefully (Piotrowski will later say: "Like a wolf"), unsmiling. He leers at them, so beautiful are they. He paces up and down in front of them as if they were soldiers, and he kisses each one on the cheek. Then he tells a startled Hana to join them.

As he looks at them like this, he says the same thing he once said in Ivanie—that they are to choose one from amongst themselves, but in unison, without any quarrelling, and that she will remain with him for some time, and he will take her seven times by night and six by day. That woman will then give birth to a daughter, and as soon as she is pregnant, everyone will know it, because she will trail behind her something like a red thread.

The women blush. The elder Wołowska, beautifully dressed, has twins

who are one year old, whom she has left in the care of her sister in Warsaw; she would be happy to go back to them soon. She retreats one step,
somewhat embarrassed. The virgins among them blush the most.

"I will be the woman who will stay with you," says Hana suddenly.

Jacob is visibly angered by this. He sighs and looks down, and all the
women keep perfectly silent, afraid. But the Lord says nothing, ignoring
his wife's little outburst—of course it won't be her, Hana is already pregnant. She will soon give birth. Besides, she is his wife. At this sudden re-
jection, Hana's eyes fill with tears, and she leaves him when the others do.
The elder Wołowska puts her arm around her, but she doesn't say anything.

On the way back down the hill from the monastery, back into town
past the pilgrims, Zwierzchowska, who will not take part in this process
of selection, since she is with the Lord every day, argues—loudly, almost
casually—that in the first instance they must establish which of the
women would actually like to stay with Jacob. Almost everyone volunteers, except for the two Wołowska women. There is an uproar, and in
that moment of excitement, they switch to Yiddish; now they are speaking in their own language, in frenetic whispers.

"I'll do it," says Eva Jezierzańska. "I love him more than life itself."

But the others get upset.

"I'd be glad to do it, too," Marianna Piotrowska volunteers. "You
know I don't have children. Maybe with him I could."

"I could do it, too. I was with him in Ivanie. And he's my brother-in-
law," says Pawłowska.

And she has a daughter with him. Everyone knows that.

Zwierzchowska tells them to hush, for the pilgrims rushing by, utter-
ing frantic prayers, have already begun to stare at these young ladies having their heated conversation.

"We can deliberate at home," she decrees.

The Lord asks daily whether they have determined yet which of them it
will be, yet they cannot come to an agreement. In the end, they vote, and
it falls to Henrykowa Wołowska, who is nice and cheerful and also pretty,

but who now stands stunned and crimson, her head bowed. But Eva Jezierzańska refuses to accept the result, and there must be unanimity.

"It's either me or no one," she says.

And so Lewińska, whom Jacob particularly likes for her calm and her prudence, goes to the monastery and requests a visit with him. She begs Jacob to make the choice himself, because they cannot. Then the Lord flies into such a rage that he refuses to see any of them for one whole month. Finally, Hana gets involved and cleverly asks Jacob which of them strikes him as the most suitable. He suggests Klara Lanckorońska.

Several days later, when they are sitting down to their shared meal in the officer's room, a satisfied Jacob tells Klara Lanckorońska to be the first to dip her spoon into the soup. Klara bows her head, and her light pink cheeks flush a deep red. They all wait with their spoons in their hands.

"Klara, you start," says the Lord again, but she refuses, as if he were urging her to commit the greatest sin.

Finally, Jacob throws down his own spoon and stands up from the table.

"If you won't listen to me when it comes to such trifles, what is going to happen when I tell you to do something more? Can I count on you or not? Are you like those idiot sheep? Those hares?"

They keep silent, heads low.

"I put something like a glass before you. I am the film on the back of that glass—I am the coating. It is thanks to me that that glass was a mirror, and that you saw yourselves in it. But then I had to remove that film, and now you are left with just ordinary glass."

Come evening he has a new idea for them. He summons Wittel Matuszewska, who has served as his right hand since his disavowal of Jakubowski, formerly known as Nahman.

"I want the brothers who have wives who are not ours to cast those women aside and take new wives from among the true believers. And I want the women who married men who are not ours to take husbands from among our brothers. I want this to happen publicly. And if anyone asks you why, just tell them I commanded it."

"Jacob, that cannot happen," says Wittel Matuszewska, shocked. "Those are bonded pairs. They can do a lot for you, but you can't ask them to leave their wives and husbands."

"You have already forgotten everything," says Jacob, and pounds his fist into the wall. "All of you. You're no longer true believers. You've had it too good." Blood oozes from his scraped knuckles. "It has to happen like this, Wittel. Do you understand?"

Just as Jacob said, in July of 1763, in a little house on Wieluńskie Przedmieście, a son is born to him and receives the name Jacob. A month later, Hana has left her childbed, and in the officer's chamber at the top of the tower, in the Jasna Góra monastery, there follows a solemn union of the spouses in the presence of everyone.

For the birth of another son, Roch, in September of 1764, many of Jacob's followers come to Częstochowa. The true believers come back from where they have been scattered—scraps from Wojsławice, from Rohatyn, from Busk and Lwów, all of them wishing to settle down nearer to Jacob, perhaps in Częstochowa itself. Friends come, as well, from Turkey and Wallachia, by now convinced that Jacob's imprisonment in Edom's very holiest site definitively fulfills the prophecy.

Before, in August of 1763, Frank sends to Warsaw for Jakubowski, who comes immediately. He approaches the Lord hunched over, as if expecting a blow, as if readying himself for pain, but suddenly, the Lord himself kneels down before him. The hush is absolute.

Then the company debates in low voices around the sides of the room whether the Lord did this as a joke or out of some real deference to Piotr Jakubowski, once called Nahman of Busk.


## Daily life in prison and of keeping children in a box

Wajgełe Nahman, now Sofia Jakubowska, often goes outside the city, into the forest, and there she searches for a linden branch thick enough but still fresh and filled with sap. Nobody can ever tell why she chooses this one and not that one. But she knows. She brings it home, to Wieluńskie Przedmieście, where the Jakubowskis are renting a room, and she sits with it in the back of the house, where nobody can see her. She takes a sharp penknife and starts carving the shape of a person out of the wood. By the time you can see the arms and the neck, and the head, Wajgełe is unable to hold back her tears, and the sobs escape her like a spasm, like phlegm to be coughed up. In tears, she paints the figure's eyes, which will always be closed, and the tiny lips; she dresses it in the little outfit of her dead child and hides it under a bench. She returns to this place often to play with this doll, like a little girl. She holds it to her, puts it to her breast, whispers to it, and in the end, this activity does soothe her—a sign that God has had mercy upon her and taken away her pain. Then she puts the doll inside a special box hidden away in the attic, where the other dolls are kept. There are four of them now, some large, some small. Two Nahman isn't even aware they had conceived. They came out of her too early, too small, while he was traveling somewhere. She wrapped them up in linen and buried them in the forest.

When they lie down to sleep, she whimpers into her pillow. She turns to face Nahman, places his hand on her naked breast.

"Sleep with me."

Nahman clears his throat and pats her head:

"Don't be afraid. He will give you strength and health and allow your body to get pregnant."

"I'm scared of him."

"What are you talking about? Can't you see that we are all bathed in light, don't you see how all our faces have changed, how we've grown more beautiful? And that light over Jacob? Can't you see it? A green glow. We are all God's chosen ones now. God is in us, and when God is in a person, he is no longer bound by any ordinary rules."

"That's how mushrooms shine at night," says Wajgełe. "There is light in a mushroom, from the moisture, from the darkness . . ."

"What are you talking about, Wajgełe?"

Wajgełe cries. Nahman-Jakubowski strokes her back, until one day Wajgełe finally agrees.

Jacob tells him to stay. He lies down on Wajgełe stiffly, with a grunt, and without looking at her, he does his thing. Wajgełe releases a deep sigh.

Every evening, they gather in the officer's chamber, and Jacob gives his chats, just like in Ivanie. He often points out a person from their company, and from their story he begins his tale. That night it is Wajgełe, Nahman's wife. He tells her to sit next to him, and he puts his hand on her shoulder. Wajgełe is haggard and pale.

"The death of a child is proof that there is no good God," says Jacob. "For how could there be, since God destroys what is dearest—someone's life? What does He get out of it, this God, out of killing us? Is He scared of us?"

People are disturbed by such a framing of the situation. They whisper amongst themselves.

"Where we're going, there will be no laws, because laws are born of death, and we are connected with life. The evil force that created the

cosmos can be cleared out only by the Virgin. A woman will overcome that force, because she is powerful."

Suddenly Wajgełe starts crying again, and after a while, old Pawłowska joins in, and some of the other women, too, begin to snivel. The men's eyes glaze over. Jacob changes his tone.

"But worlds created by a good God exist—they're just concealed from us. Only the true believers can find the road to them, since really, it isn't far—you just have to know how to get there. I will tell you: To access these worlds, you must go through the Olsztyn Caves near here. There is where you'll find the entrance. That's where Makpela Cave is, and that is the center of the world."

He unfurls a great vision before them—here all the caves in the world are linked to one another, and wherever they meet, time flows differently. Which is why if a person were to fall asleep in such a cave, for just a little while, and then he wanted to go back to the village where he'd left his family, he would find out that his parents had died, that his wife had become a decrepit old lady, and that his children had grown old.

They nod. They know these stories.

"Yes, and this cave that is so close to Częstochowa has a direct connection to the cave from Korolówka, and that one is connected to the cave where Abraham and the first parents rest."

A sigh is heard. So this is how it is: Everything is connected with everything, carefully linked.

"Does anyone know the layout of these caves?" Marianna Pawłowska asks hopefully.

Jacob knows it, obviously. Jacob knows where and at what moment to turn in order to get to Korolówka or to another world, a world where there are all kinds of riches and carriages loaded with gold, just sitting there waiting for someone who might want to take them.

He brings them pleasure by describing these riches in detail, which is why he does so with so much attention to detail: the walls made of gold, the luxurious curtains, embroidered with silver and gold, the tables set with gold plates, and on them, instead of fruit, lie great precious stones, rubies, sapphires the size of apples, the size of plums, and damask table-cloths sewn with silver thread, and lamps made entirely of crystal.

---

Wajgełe, or Sofia Jakubowska, who does not yet know that she is pregnant, imagines that in reality she would not need all that, that she'd be happy with just one fat ruby the size of an apple . . . And she isn't listening anymore, just planning what she would do with such a stone. She would have it cut into smaller pieces, so that no one could ever suspect that she had stolen such a wonder, since having a huge stone like that is also dangerous and might tempt thieves and villains. So she would have the stone cut in secret (although who would be willing to undertake such a thing?) and slowly she would sell all the smaller stones, one after the other, in different cities, because that would be safer. And she would live off that. She would buy herself a small shop, and then to go with the shop she would also buy a moderately sized home, but nice and bright and dry, and also pretty white linen underthings and silk stockings, half a dozen pairs, so she could have reserves. And maybe she would also order new, lighter skirts, and some wool ones for the winter.

When they have all gone their separate ways, slipping out of the monastery quietly to head back into town, Nahman Jakubowski stays behind. When they are alone, Nahman falls to his knees and wraps his arms around Jacob's ankles.

"I betrayed you to save you," he says into the floor, his voice muffled. "You know that. You wanted it."

## The hole that leads to the abyss, or a visit from Tovah and his son Hayim Turk in 1765

The first measure imposed by the new king makes him unpopular at the monastery: he will remove the Jasna Góra fortress from the brothers' care, which reduces their funds to a bare minimum. Now there is a new prior every year or two, and none of them can figure out any solution, particularly since none of them is versed, as a monk, in the running of such an economy. For after all, a monastery is its own economy.

And none of them can handle this troublesome prisoner who has by now taken over the entire officers' tower, and who treats the old officers as servants of some sort, and it is difficult to refuse him those semi-liberties in exchange for the generous tithes he pays. The prior watches him and his frequent guests—they sit for hours in the church, gazing at the holy picture, and the sight of their fervent prayer and their lying in the form of a cross for whole days would make an impression on any man of faith. Toward the monastery they are solicitous, and they appear to be reconciled to the punishment of their Master. Sometimes there are quarrels or raised voices in the tower. A few times their songs have been heard—this has been strictly forbidden by the prior, unless they can sing Catholic songs.

Prior Mateusz Łękawski was less favorable to Frank than his successor, Mniński. Łękawski received reports of iniquities perpetrated in the officer's chamber, and the very fact of a family living on the holy terrain of the monastery irritated him, not to mention the quantity of women roaming around. His successor, on the other hand, is not bothered by that at all. Mniński, more concerned with the paintings in the chapel and pained by the poor state of the roof, is pleased by every grosz he gets, and these neophytes supply them in great abundance. He likes to look at women, too, and these ones are particularly pleasing.

He sees three women come up to the gate with Jacob Frank. One of them is carrying an infant, the other leading a little girl. Jacob walks in front, cheerfully greeting the pilgrims, and they, surprised by his tall Turkish hat and his Turkish coat, stop and stare at him. At the gate, Jacob greets two men dressed in the Turkish fashion. They embrace as if they have not seen one another for a long time. The woman with the infant kneels before the older man and kisses his hand. The prior guesses it is her father. He has given the prisoner permission to leave the monastery. He is to return before nightfall.

Indeed, this is Hana Frank's father, Yehuda Tovah ha-Levi. He is dark, fat, and his lush beard, still black with no sign of gray, covers his breast; he has gentle features and sensual lips. Hana has inherited from him her lovely big eyes, and her olive-hued skin that never flushes. Once they're inside, Tovah settles into a chair, where he will not be especially comfortable—he prefers sitting according to the Turkish custom, on pillows. He sets his hands atop his ample belly; they are soft and delicate, like the hands of a sage.

His son, Hana's twin brother, Hayim, has grown up to be a handsome man, though not as solidly built as his father. His face is round with regular features, like his father's. His dark, very thick eyebrows are almost joined, and together divide his face horizontally. Hayim, dressed like a Turk, is friendly and sincere. His smile never leaves his face, as if he were trying to conquer them all with it. He has obviously been raised with much love, for he is self-confident but not haughty. Old Tovah holds Avacha on his lap; she has gotten as thin as a roe fawn, and so her grandpa gives her dried figs and Turkish sweets. Hana sits near her father with little Jacob at her breast, the child's tiny hands playing with the fringe of the kerchief her father brought her as a gift. Since the arrival of her father and brother, Hana seems invigorated; she is certain now that something significant will change, even if she doesn't know what. As they talk, she shifts her inquiring gaze from her husband to her father and brother, since she remains dependent on these men and on whatever they decide. And so it goes all evening, until sleep overcomes her.

Jacob returns to his cell late at night. The next day, Roch receives a supply of good Turkish tobacco and several pipes in thanks. The jangling coin he also receives is another welcome boon, and he quickly hides it in his tattered pants pockets. To the monastery goes a basket of delicacies. Someone has said that since the brothers cannot experience many of life's pleasures, they are inordinately fond of sweets.

When Jacob talks, it almost seems like Tovah isn't listening; he is constantly looking around the room, looking at his fingers, from time to time changing his uncomfortable position with a sigh of impatience. Maybe he really is upset by what Jacob is telling him; after all, Jacob has had five years of solitude and come up with all kinds of ideas. Some of them Tovah considers unrealistic, while others he finds harmful. Some of them are interesting. One is terrible.

Tovah can't listen to any more talk of the Shekhinah imprisoned in the picture in the monastery, and he starts to drum his fingers. Jacob, for the umpteenth time, as if returning again to the same topic makes it somehow more real, repeats the words of the Zohar:

"Salvation is located in the worst place."

He falls silent, waiting for these words to take their full effect, then suddenly he raises up his index finger, as is his wont, and asks dramatically:

"And where have we found ourselves?"

He has changed a lot. His shaved face has darkened, his eyes have dimmed. His movements are jerky, as if he were suppressing rage. This new violence makes others fear him, which is why no one dares answer him now. Jacob stands and begins to walk around the room, leaning forward, with his finger still raised, pointing to the wooden ceiling.

"This is nikve detom rabe, the road to the abyss, this Częstochowa, this Jasna Góra—these are the Gates of Rome at which, according to other words from the Zohar, the Messiah sits and binds and unbinds . . . This is a dark place, the entryway into the abyss into which we must descend in order to free the Shekhinah imprisoned there. And further on is all that has been—in order to go in higher, we have to fall as low as possible; the darker it gets the lighter it gets, and the worse the better.

"I didn't know at first why I was put in here," says Jacob. He is tense, excited; his father-in-law discreetly looks at Hana, who is staring at the floor, absently. "I just sensed that I should not oppose the sentence. But now I know—I was put here because this is where the Shekhinah is imprisoned, on this new Mount Zion. Hidden beneath that painted board, beneath the picture, is the Maiden. These people don't see it, they think they're paying tribute to the surface, but that is only a reflection of the Shekhinah, the version of it that is available to human sight."

For Tovah, what Jacob says is shocking. His son-in-law is doing worse than he sounded in his letters. But Tovah also sees that the members of his Częstochowa retinue take his words as if they were completely normal. Jacob says the Shekhinah is here in Esau's captivity, which is why they have to accompany the prisoner, who has become the guardian of the Shekhinah in the Jasna Góra icon. He says that Poland is the country of the Shekhinah's incarceration, the imprisonment of God's Presence in the world, and it is here that the Shekhinah will also get out of jail in order to free the world. Poland is the most particular place on earth, at once the worst and the best. The Shekhinah must be raised from the ashes and allowed to save the world. Sabbatai tried, and Baruchiah tried, but only Jacob will succeed. Because he has come to the right place!

"Just look, Father, at the customs of the world," says Tovah's daughter, his beloved Hanele, as if suddenly waking up. "The Shekhinah cannot be chased with Ishmael, because the Shekhinah is in woman, and they, the Ishmaelites, do not care at all about the woman, she is a slave, and no one respects her. The Shekhinah can only be found in a country where honor is paid to the female, and so it is in Poland, they not only stand before their women with their heads uncovered, but they also pay them compliments, and they act like servants toward them, and on top of all of that, they pay the greatest tribute to this Virgin with her child here, in Częstochowa. This is the land of the Virgin. So we, too, ought to get under her wings."

She takes her husband's hand in hers and lifts it to her lips.

"The Lord will make us knights of that Virgin, and we will all be warriors of the Messiah."

Hana's father has thoughts of which he cannot rid himself. He would like to take her and his grandchildren far away from here. And explain to Jacob that it is for their well-being. Or kidnap them. Perhaps he could hire some ruffians to do it? It is so dark here, so damp. Living within the walls of this fortress has made them like mushrooms. Hana's bones hurt, her ankles are swollen, and her face is puffy and ugly. The children are fragile and frightened. Lovely Avacha, taken out of Warsaw, has grown shy and withdrawn toward her grandfather. She should be better cared for. Jacob will not teach her anything good here. He lets her run around the garrison, conversing with the soldiers. She goes up and talks to pilgrims. The children have too little sun, and their food, even what is purchased in the best stalls here or brought in from elsewhere, is never fresh, is of poor quality.

Jacob speaks, gesticulating with his hands, and, squeezed into the chamber, sitting on straw mattresses and on the floor, they listen to him:

"Ayelet ahuvim, or the favored deer, the roe doe. To the place where I am going, the Jacob of the Scriptures has already gone, and then the First Jacob, Sabbatai Tzvi. And now I am going—I, the true Jacob." When he says "I," he strikes his broad chest so that it booms. "Many have attempted to pound on the entrance to this place—all the patriarchs, Moses, Aaron, David, Solomon, all the great pillars of the world. Yet they couldn't get it open. In the place where we are going, there is no death. There is where the Maiden lives, the Blind Virgin, the Roe Doe, who is the true Messiah."

Now Jacob falls quiet and paces two steps this way, two steps that way. He waits for what he has said to sink in. There is absolute silence, and against this backdrop the noise of Tovah clearing his throat sounds like a thunderclap. Jacob turns to him and goes on:

"It is all written—you know it all. The Maid is God's wisdom hidden in a painted board like a princess in a tall tower whom no one will ever obtain. For her we must commit Foreign Acts, deeds that will turn the world on its head. Do you remember that serpent in paradise? The serpent urges us toward freedom. Whoever digs up the Tree of Knowledge, and attains the Tree of Life, and becomes one with the Virgin, will possess the knowledge of salvation, that hidden Daat."

They all repeat that word: *Daat*, everywhere Daat. Tovah is astonished by the change in his son-in-law. Before he came here, he heard gossip that Jacob had died, and that someone else had replaced him. But he is a new person, in fact. He has almost nothing in common with the man to whom Tovah whispered secrets under the huppah all those years ago.

Tovah and Hayim sleep in a musty, dirty little house whose owners have abandoned it. It is disgusting to touch anything there. The fumes of the outhouse make him feel weak; it's just a small roof on some stakes with a filthy rag used as a curtain, near a pile of shit. His son has to take him, Old Tovah holding up his long coat lest it be sullied.

Every day he promises himself that he will talk with Hana, and every day he is unable to ask her the question: Will you come home with me?

Probably because he knows what she will say.

Tovah sees that over the course of their two-week visit, Jacob has also conquered Hayim; a kind of confederacy has arisen between them, an odd and ambiguous understanding, filled with incomprehensible mutual dedication. Hayim repeats after Jacob, talks with his words.

Jacob Frank is therefore someone who stole Tovah's children from him. A really terrible thing has happened. Tovah undoes his amulets, prays over them, and ties them around his daughter's and granddaughter's necks.

It becomes clear that Tovah is of little faith, and one evening they come to a quarrel: Tovah calls Jacob a traitor and a trickster, and Jacob hits him in the face. At dawn, Tovah sets out with Hayim, who is pained by this decision, without even saying goodbye to his daughter and granddaughter. His fury does not subside at any point along their journey. In his mind he is writing the letter he will send around to all the true-believing kahalim in Europe. He will write to Moravia and Altona, to Prague and Wrocław, to Salonika and Stamboul. He will take a stand against Jacob.

There are, however, things on which father-in-law and son-in-law agree—they have to look to the east, to Russia. Here in Poland their protectors are slowly losing their influence. Both Tovah and Jacob believe in always siding with the strongest.

Shortly after Tovah's sudden departure, a delegation sets out for Moscow. The delegation is led by Jakubowski, who is delighted to be back in Jacob's good graces. On the evening before they set off, the envoys have dinner with him in the tower. Jacob himself pours them wine.

"We ought to be grateful to the First, who took that initial step into the Turkish religion. And to the Second, who discovered this state in the religion of Edom, that is, baptism. Now I am sending you to Moscow—for the third time."

As he says this, he stands and walks around the little room, his tall hat catching on the beams of the ceiling. That night, before their journey, the envoys—Wołowski, Jakubowski, and Pawłowski—have intercourse with Hana. In this way they all become Jacob's brothers, closer than they have ever been before.

## Elżbieta Drużbacka writes from the Bernardine monastery in Tarnów a last letter to the canon Benedykt Chmielowski in Firlejów

. . . for I, Dear Friend, Good Father, can barely see the
world at all now, just as much as is possible through the
window of my cell, and so I see the world as a monastery
courtyard. My confinement brings me great relief; a smaller
world will favor peace of mind. And, too, the things I have
around me—which are not many—do not preoccupy my mind
near so much as those whole household cosmoses I had to carry
on my shoulders like some Atlas. After the death of my
daughter, and my granddaughters, everything ended for me,
and altho' you warn that it is a sin to say so, I do not even care.
From our birth, everything—the church, the home, our
education, our customs and loves—bids us form an attachment
to life. But no one ever tells us that the more attached we are to
it, the more pain we'll suffer later, once we have come by our
final awareness.

I will not write to you again, dear Friend, you who have
sweetened my older years with your stories, and consoled me
when I met with such misfortune. I wish You a long and healthy
life. And that Your lovely garden in Firlejów might last forever,
like Your library and all Your books—that they might be of
service . . .

Mrs. Elżbieta Drużbacka finishes her letter and sets down her pen. She
pushes aside her prie-dieu, which is turned to the Christ who hangs on
her wall, whose every suffering tendon she knows so well. She lies down
on her back on the floor, pulls on a brown wool dress that looks like a
habit, and lays her hands over her breast, as she would in the coffin, fixing
her gaze to some nothing hanging in the air. And she just lies there. She
does not even try to pray, the words of prayer exhaust her, as if she were
pouring out something that is empty into something that is void, grinding the same grain over and over, infected with ergot, poisoned through

and through. After a few minutes, she manages to attain a specific state; she remains in it until they call her for the meal. It is hard to describe this state: Drużbacka simply manages to disappear.

Yente, who is always present, loses sight of Mrs. Drużbacka now. She flies fast as thought to the recipient of the letter lying on the table and sees him busying himself with soaking his swollen legs in a bucket. He sits hunched over—maybe he has fallen asleep: his head has come to rest on his chest, and he seems to be snoring slightly. Ah, but Yente knows that soaking his feet isn't going to help him.

Father Chmielowski is no longer able to read this last letter, and it lies there for weeks on end, the seal still on it, on the table amongst his other papers. Father Benedykt Chmielowski, canon of Rohatyn, dies of pneumonia, from having incautiously and impatiently gone out into the garden as soon as the sun rose. Roshko's successor, Izydor, a young, somewhat dim-witted man, and his housekeeper, Ksenia, delayed calling for the doctor until the next day, when the roads were soaked and barely passable. He died peacefully, his fever coming down just enough that he could confess and take the last rites. On the table there had been a book lying open for a long time, from which he had been translating a few verses that appeared under a terrible engraving.

Taking over the presbytery in Firlejów, Father Benedykt's successor spends a whole evening going through his predecessor's documents, preparing them to be sent to the curia. He opens the letter from Mrs. Drużbacka, but he doesn't know exactly who she is. He is surprised, however, that the priest had been corresponding with women. He finds a whole box of letters, carefully arranged by date, overlaid with dried flowers, surely so that moths don't get into the paper. He doesn't know what to do with them, since he cannot work up the courage to add them to the volumes he's been told to pack up and send to the Lwów bishopric. He keeps the box for a while by the bed, reading bits of the letters for pleasure, and then he forgets about them, pushing the box under the bed, where it stays, in the presbytery's damp bedroom, so that the letters soon molder, turning into nests for mice.

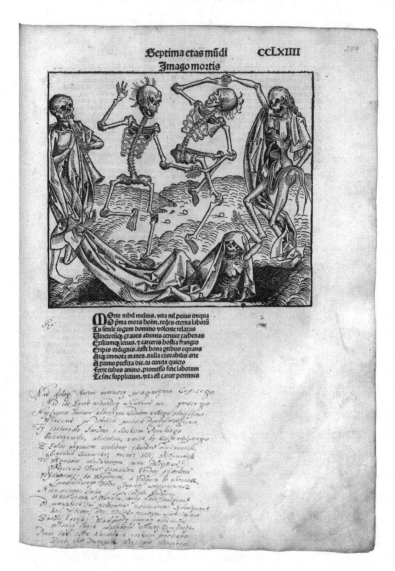

In her last letter, Mrs. Drużbacka had also written that the two worst questions were "why" and "to what end."

And yet I cannot keep myself from posing those questions. So I answer myself that the Lord God wants to punish us by means of creation itself: us, His creations, who sin with

creation. He washes His hands of it, however, in order to
preserve His goodness in our eyes. He looks for natural means
to destroy us indirectly, by way of some natural cause, so that
the blow is lighter than it would be if He Himself struck it,
since such a thing we could not understand.

He could, after all, have healed Naaman with one word, but
He had him go bathe in the River Jordan instead. He could
have healed the blind man with His universal love, but instead
He mixed saliva with mud and put it on his eyes. He could have
healed everyone at once, but instead He made the pharmacy,
the medic, medicinal herbs. His world is one great oddity.

## Of bringing Moliwda back to life

Moliwda has grown thinner and does not really even resemble his former
self from just a few years ago. He is clean-shaven, and while he doesn't
have a tonsure like many of the monks, he does wear his hair short,
cropped very close to the head. He looks younger. His older brother, the
retired military man, is somehow made uncomfortable by this matter of
the monastery. He doesn't really understand what happened to Antoni
in his old age. They say in Warsaw that he fell head over heels in love
with a married woman who indulged his advances, giving him hopes for
a closer relationship. Then, having made Moliwda fall so in love with
her, she cast him aside. His brother cannot understand that, doesn't want
to believe in such tales. He would understand if it were something to do
with honor. With real betrayal—but not some love affair. He looks at
his brother suspiciously. But maybe it was something else? Maybe someone cast a spell on him because he was doing so well with the primate.

"I feel fine now. Don't look at me like that, brother," Moliwda says,
and pulls his habit over his head.

A carriage waits in front of the monastery, and in it is clothing for
Antoni Kossakowski, known as Moliwda: trousers, a shirt, a Polish żupan,
and a modest kontusz, dark in color, with a dark belt, no ostentation. To
the prior of the monastery he has offered financial support, although the

prior still seems slightly disappointed. After all, Moliwda-Kossakowski appears to be truly devout—he often spent whole days and nights in prayer, lying as though on the cross in the chapel, never wanting to leave the picture of Our Lady Queen of the World, to which he had taken such a liking. He rarely said a word to the brothers, and he declined to participate in the monastery's daily tasks—it was hard for him to accustom himself to the monastery's ways. Now he walks before his colonel brother, sticking close to the wall, his hand gliding over the bricks, his bare feet inside their sandals irritating his brother—feet should be shod, preferably in boots with bootlegs, in military style. Naked feet suggest peasants, Jews.

"I made use of all of my influences to get you into the royal chancellery. You got good backing, too, from the primate himself, and that was what did it. They don't remember anything else about you. They do care a great deal about your knowledge of languages . . . I don't want any gratitude from you, I'm doing this so that the soul of our dearly departed mother may rest in peace."

When the carriage starts up, Antoni suddenly kisses his brother's hand and starts to sob. The colonel clears his throat, embarrassed. He wants Antoni's return to occur in a masculine manner and with dignity, as befits a person of noble birth. Of his younger brother he thinks: What a failure. What could have guided him to a monastery, when so much ill is occurring in this country? Whence these attacks of melancholy, while the nation-state, run by a young and foolish king, falls into ever greater dependency on the tsarina?

"You know nothing at all, brother, as you have been hiding within the monastery walls, leaving your country in need," he says reproachfully and disgustedly, turning his gaze out the little carriage window.

And then, as if not to his brother, but to the landscape outside:

"In the Sejm, four members of the parliament of the Republic were dragged off the bench by henchmen of the empress's ambassadors. They treated them like they were a bunch of bumpkins . . . For what reason, you may ask? Oh, but of course: they dared oppose the reforms for the religious dissenters that they're trying to impose here by force."

Now that same righteous indignation he felt when he first heard of that barbarity returns; he turns once more to his brother, still in tears, now wiping his eyes with his sleeve:

"They refused, and shouted, which led to a great uproar, since some of the members of parliament tried to side with them, and then—"

"Who were the members who were so brave? Do you know them?" Moliwda interrupts him, as if he's just woken up again.

The colonel, glad his words are having some effect on his brother, responds animatedly:

"Absolutely. Załuski, Sołtyk, and the two Rzewuskis. The rest of the members, when they saw the army—the Russian army—coming in ready to shoot, simply shouted, 'Shame, shame, they're invading the Sejm,' but those Muscovites couldn't have cared less and dragged those four out of the room, too. Fat old Sołtyk, all red in the face, near to an apoplexy, tried to resist them and ended up grabbing on to some piece of furniture, but they still overpowered him. And you can imagine, the rest of them just let it happen, damn them all, those cowards!"

"And what did they do with those four? Are they in prison?" asks Moliwda.

"If only it had been prison!" cries the colonel, now fully facing his brother. "They sent them straight out of the Sejm to Siberia, and the king didn't even lift a finger!"

They both fall silent for a moment. The carriage is entering some small town, and the wheels start to clatter over the cobblestones.

"But why are they so determined not to give rights to religious dissenters?" asks Moliwda, as the wheels return to their soft, muddy ruts.

"What do you mean, why?" Moliwda's brother cannot comprehend this question. After all, it is crystal clear that salvation can come only through the Holy Roman Church. Wanting leniency for Lutherans or Jews or Aryans is regular devilry. And why should Russia be interfering in their affairs? "What are you talking about?" he says, unable even to find the words.

"Wherever I have wound up in the world," says Moliwda, "I have seen that maybe there is just one God, but that the ways of believing in Him are many, maybe even infinite . . . All kinds of different shoes can tread a path to God . . ."

"You should keep quiet about that," his brother snaps. "That is a great stain on your honor. It is a good thing that your ignoble past is nearly forgotten now." And he puckers his lips like he wants to spit.

They don't talk much more until they get to Warsaw.

His brother installs Moliwda in his home, an old man's messy bachelor quarters in Solec, and he tells him to get himself together so that he can start his new employment soon.

Moliwda begins his new life by shaving. Sharpening the razor, he watches out the window

as anxious crowds gather along the street. Everyone continues to be shocked and outraged. Gestures have grown bolder, words higher-flying: God, the Republic, victim, death, honor, heart . . . Every syllable is stressed. In the evening, he can hear their monotonous prayers, recited in tired, resigned voices, as well as impassioned shouts.

Moliwda begins by writing and translating letters the king's diplomatic services sends out across Europe. He composes them and writes them out over and over, mindlessly. He translates mindlessly, too. He watches the universal commotion like he would puppet theater. And the play is about trade. About the market that is the world. People invest in goods, in all variety of matter, and in all its variations—possessions, power that will bring earnings and offer confidence, pleasures for the body, valuable objects that beyond their price are totally useless, food and drink, intercourse. In other words, in everything that ordinary people understand as life. And everybody wants it, from the peasant to the king. Somewhere beyond all this robe-tearing and throwing yourself on the pyre looms a warm chamber and a richly set table. It seems to Moliwda that Bishop Sołtyk, already hailed as the greatest hero, is a kind of Herostratus who has fanned the flames for his own glory, since his act in the Sejm, which might seem heroic, served no purpose, contributed nothing to the common good. And this fanatical resistance to Russia's demands regarding religious dissenters is incomprehensible to Moliwda. Everything Tsarina Catherine might say is treated in advance as an attack on the Polish-Lithuanian Commonwealth, and yet you hardly need any special powers of discernment in order to see that such is the spirit of the times—rights for other denominations, for example. There are certain things that are black and white, but most are gray. He is not the only one in the royal chancellery who thinks this way.

Going home, he looks over the prostitutes, who even in this turbulent time do not leave their posts on Długa Street, and he wonders: What exactly is this thing called life?

And even though they cannot answer this question, he often makes use of their services, because since his departure from the monastery, Moliwda has been terrified of being alone.

## Of wandering caves

When you get out of the little town, heading southeast, the road leads first through a dense forest, where in addition to the trees white stones grow. They grow slowly, but with time, as the earth gets older, they will come out onto the surface completely, the soil won't be necessary anymore, since there will be no people, and all that will remain will be just those white rocks, and then it will turn out that they are the bones of the earth.

You can see that the landscape changes right outside the town—it is dark gray, rough, and made up of tiny, lightweight pebbles, as if they'd been ground in a mill. Pines grow here, and tall mullein, which peasant women make decoctions out of to lighten their hair. The dry grass crackles underfoot.

Immediately past the forest begin the hills with their many white rocks, from which the castle ruins rise. When they see it for the first time, they all think that this castle cannot have been built by human hands, but rather that it was formed by the very same force, the very same hand that built the world. This structure resembles the fortress of the bałaka-ben, those limping, rich little men who live underground, of whom the sages tell in the holy books. Yes, this must be their property, along with all the land around Częstochowa—bizarre, rocky, so full of mysterious passageways and hiding places.

But Ezdra, a Częstochowa Jew who is friendly to Frank and his company, who sells them most of their provisions, saves the biggest revelation for last. This, here, is a cave.

"What do you think?" asks Ezdra triumphantly, smiling and revealing his teeth, turned brown by tobacco.

The entrance to the cave is hidden in the bushes that grow over the hillside. Ezdra invites them inside, as if it were his own residence, but sticking their heads inside is enough for them; you can't see anything anyway. Ezdra produces a torch from somewhere and lights it. After a few steps, the opening behind them disappears, and the torchlight shows the inside—damp walls, strange, beautiful, glistening, as though made of some ore unknown to man—of a smooth mineral that has solidified into icicles and droplets, of wonderful rock in a beautiful reddish hue, inter-woven with threads of a different color, white and gray. And the deeper inside they go, the more the insides look alive, as if they were going into a stranger's stomach, as if they were traveling down intestines, stomachs, kidneys. The echo of their steps reverberates off the walls, grows like thunder and comes back in pieces. Suddenly from somewhere a gust of wind blows out the rotten torch they're carrying, and they are enveloped in darkness.

"El Shaddai," Jakubowski says in a whisper.

They freeze, and now you can hear their uncertain, shallow breaths, the roar of the blood in their veins, the beating of their hearts. You can hear Nahman Jakubowski's stomach growling; you can hear Ezdra swal-lowing saliva. The silence is so dense that they can feel on their skin its cold, slick touch. Yes, without any doubt, God is here.

---

Zwierzchowska, who very naturally has taken over the rule of their entire company, parceled out into Częstochowa houses as they are, is preparing a generous gift for the prior—silver candlesticks and a crystal chandelier so valuable that the prior cannot possibly turn down their request. They have already gone on walks together around the monastery, after all. What harm would it do to go a little farther? The prior hesitates, but the glint of the silver and the sparkling of the crystal convinces him. He gives his permission. The monastery is having some financial troubles. It should be quiet, only Jacob with two companions. Hana and the children stay behind, under guard.

The moment has arrived. October 27, 1768, the day after the birth of Jacob's son Joseph. The Lord goes out for the first time beyond the town's walls. He puts on Czerniawski's long coat and pulls a hat down so that the brim comes right to his eyes. At the tollhouse a cart awaits, and a peasant hired to drive it; they go down the sandy, uneven road in silence.

Jacob goes into the cave alone, telling the others to wait. Czerniawski and Jakubowski set up a little camp at the entrance, but the fire they build barely smolders. The day is rainy and damp. Their kapotas get wet from all this standing around in the drizzle. Jacob does not return until evening. In the weak flames, skewered apples swell to bursting.

By the time he appears in the opening, it is already dark. They can't quite see his face. He tells them to go quickly, so they go, stumbling over stones sticking out of the ground or over their own legs. Their eyes have grown accustomed to darkness, but now the night is bright somehow—is it the damp fog scattering the light of the stars and moon so, or is it this local earth the color of dried leaves that is shining? The peasant with the cart, who is waiting for them by the road, is soaked and angry. He wants more money; he didn't know it was going to take this long.

Jacob doesn't say a single word the whole way; he only talks when they are back in the tower, after casting off his soaked coat:

"That is the same cave where Shimon bar Yochai and his son hid before the Romans, and God miraculously delivered them food and ensured that their clothing never got destroyed," he says. "It was here that Shimon bar Yochai wrote the Zohar. This cave traveled here after us from

Hebron, didn't you realize? Deep inside, at the very bottom, is the grave of Adam and Eve."

A silence falls, in which Jacob's words try to find their places. It could be said that all the maps of the world are moving around over him, making a rustling sound, turning around, accommodating one another. This lasts for a while, and then the others clear their throats, and someone sighs; it seems as if order has been restored. Jacob says: Let us sing. And they sing together, just as they used to sing in Ivanie.

Two women stay the night with him, while he tells the rest who live in the town that the two Matuszewskis and Pawłowski are to have intercourse with Henrykowa Wołowska. It is similar the following night: with Sofia Jakubowska are to be Pawłowski, both Wołowskis, Dembowski, and also Jasskier.

## Of failed legations and history laying siege to the monastery walls

The good run enjoyed by Nahman, or Piotr Jakubowski, does not last long. The effortfully prepared delegation to Moscow concluded in complete fiasco. The emissaries—Jakubowski and Wołowski—were treated like criminals, murderers, traitors, for news had already reached Moscow from Poland of the fallen Messiah imprisoned in Częstochowa. They managed to meet with no one, despite their generously distributed gifts. In the end they were chased out like spies. They returned quietly and without any money left. Jacob punished them. He bade them stand before the company barefoot, in just their shirts, and then, kneeling, to beg everyone's forgiveness for their ineptitude. Jakubowski bore it better than Franciszek Wołowski. Marianna Wołowska later told the other woman that her husband sobbed that night out of shame and humiliation, though of course it had all been through no fault of theirs.

Now they sense that the whole world is plotting against them, all of Europe. At this point the prison in Częstochowa seems to Nahman Jakubowski familiar and cozy, particularly since the Lord can, without restriction, go out into the town, and even on long walks in the cave, and the whole company has free access to him.

Now by day the chamber downstairs in the tower turns into a chancellery. Jacob dictates letters to true believers in Podolia, Moravia, and Germany, tells them of the Shekhinah hidden in the Jasna Góra picture and summons them for baptism en masse. The tone of these letters grows more apocalyptic by the month. Sometimes the scribe—Jakubowski or Czerniawski—finds that his hand trembles as he writes. In the evenings, meanwhile, the chancellery becomes a common room, the kind they used to have back in Ivanie, and after lessons only the chosen ones stay behind, and the "putting out of the candles" begins. One autumn day in 1768 during this ritual, the Paulines from the monastery try to get into the tower, and in the end they force the door. But they can't see too much there in the dark. Yet evidently they have seen enough, for the next day the prior summons Jacob under guard and prohibits him henceforth from receiving anyone besides his immediate family.

"No women in the monastery, and no young boys," says the prior, and as he says it, he covers his face with his hands.

He also brings back the ban on going into town, although as tends to be the case with bans, this one crumbles with the passage of time and the giving of generous gifts. In this time of growing civil unrest, the prior issues a categorical order to close the monastery all night, but in the end he is moved enough by Hana's illness that he allows her and the children twenty-four-hour residence in the officer's chamber.

News that something is going on in Podolia, by the Turkish border, reaches them through the so-called Korolówka Buttercup, Pawłowski's brother-in-law, who circulates correspondence around Podolia and has eyes in the back of his head. First—a strange thing—his father, who is a tentmaker in Korolówka, received from Polish lords a great order of tents, which must certainly mean that they are preparing some sort of military movements. And Buttercup is right—soon they learn from Roch that a confederation against the king has surfaced, while the king is colluding with Russia in the little town of Bar. An emotional Roch tells them of standards: that on them appears Our Lady of Częstochowa, the very same, with her dark face and child in arms, and that the confederates wear coats with crosses on them and an inscription in black: "For faith and freedom." Apparently, the royal army dispatched against the confederates either flees in the face of their religious zeal or crosses over to their side. Roch sews the torn-off buttons back onto his old uniform and polishes his shotgun, like all the other old soldiers in the monastery. Stones are laid at the base of the monastery walls, and the arrowslits, overgrown with bushes, are cleared and repaired.

The previously sleepy little town of Częstochowa slowly fills up with Jewish refugees from Podolia, as the Haydamak uprising there has unleashed pogroms. Jacob's fame has reached the refugees, and so they also make their way to the holy Christian monument, believing that no violence will be able to reach inside it, and that in addition they can seek their refuge under the wing of the Jewish maybe-Messiah imprisoned here. They bring with them terrible stories: The Haydamaks, enraged and lawless, will not let anyone escape. The night sky is red from the glow of burning villages. When the prior's regime relaxes somewhat, Jacob goes out to see the new arrivals every day and puts his hands on their heads, and the rumor spreads that he can heal them.

The whole of the Wieluńskie Przedmieście has now been transformed into a camp, with people living on the streets and on the long, narrow market square. Every day the Pauline Fathers bring them fresh water from the monastery, since it is said that the wells are unclean now, and everyone fears plague. Every morning the Fathers distribute loaves of bread, warm from the monastery's bakery, and apples from its orchard, which this year are plentiful and lush.

Nahman Jakubowski runs into Hasidim he knows in this camp. The orphaned followers of the Besht look askance at Jacob's people, mistrustful. They stick together, but eventually they start to get into debates with the Frankists, debates that grow noisy, violent. Their voices, which carry quotations from Isaiah, from the Zohar, rise above the walls and can even be heard from Jacob's tower.

On the occasion of little Joseph's baptism, Jacob gives a great feast in the town, so that anybody may eat and drink, without regard to whether he has been baptized or circumcised. Equally celebrated is the wedding of Jacob Goliński, for whom the Lord has selected—Goliński being a good true believer—Magda Jezierzańska, a wife half his age. The ceremony occurs in the novitiate chapel in the monastery, which the prior graciously allows them to use after it has been repainted. The service is beautiful, and you can't yet hear the roar of the cannons that are inexorably closing in on Częstochowa. Instead, there is the beautiful and noble sound of the

psalms of the Paulines, who are pleased that the monastery has received such a sumptuous offering.

Immediately afterward, the news goes around that Russia has determined to insert itself into Poland's internal disputes, and that Russian armies are en route from the east. This means war. Now every day the news is worse. And every day more people come to the Jasna Góra Virgin, believing that in her presence nothing terrible can happen to them. The chapel is full, people lie in the form of the cross on the cold floor, the air is thick with prayer. When the songs fall silent, from afar, from just past the horizon, comes the low, ominous thunder of explosions.

Alarmed by all of this, Jacob has Jan Wołowski go to Warsaw to fetch Avacha, who was sent there for her education and has been living with the Wołowskis. It is a decision Jacob soon comes to regret. He is surprised by her appearance. The thin little girl with the braids and bitten nails and hands rough from climbing the monastery walls has returned a young lady, beautiful and with excellent manners. She wears her hair pinned up in a high bun, and her bright dresses are cut low (although the neckline is covered with a kerchief). Whenever she leaves the tower for her daily walk around the walls, all eyes in the monastery turn to her. The monks are displeased by the commotion she leaves in her wake. So her father keeps her in the officer's chamber and in the end only lets her go out after dark, and always under someone's watchful eye.

Two weeks after her arrival come the confederates, under the leadership of one Kazimierz Puławski. One afternoon they occupy the Jasna Góra fortress as if it were the courtyard of a tavern, putting their horses, carts, and cannons everywhere, wherever they like, to the Paulines' utter horror. They turn pilgrims away and introduce their own military rules. Immediately the fortress is closed, and Jacob can no longer be visited, nor can he go out into the town. With him are Hana, Avacha, and the boys, as well as both Zwierzchowskis, Matuszewskis, and his emissary Nahman Jakubowski. The monks must free up one of the monastery's wings, which will be turned into quarters for the army. At first the pilgrimages stop completely, then cautiously they start up again, but at the gate the newly invigorated veterans now check everyone to ensure that no Russian spies slip through. Roch, who is the commander of the guard at the gate, has no time to converse with Jacob. Now he has other things on his mind—he has to supervise the daily delivery of wine and beer for the soldiers. The little town, too, livens up, as the soldiers must be fed, clothed, and entertained.

Kazimierz Puławski looks young, like a boy whose mustache has just grown in. It's hard to believe he is an experienced leader. He seems to know this, too, as he adds gravitas to his body with a heavy military coat that bulks up his slender silhouette.

He does not get much of an opportunity for battle. The Russian troops circle the fortress like a fox around a henhouse. They come up; they go off. People think they are frightened away by the Virgin Mary on the standards displayed around the walls.

Puławski, who soon grows bored by the idleness in the closed monastery, is intrigued by the man in the high hat who rarely leaves the tower, and his beautiful, mysterious daughter, around whom legend already swirls in the garrison. He doesn't care about matters of the church, nor do heresies much concern him. All he has heard is that this is the neophytes' heresiarch, and a resident of the monastery. But a good Catholic. He sees him daily at morning mass. His sincere participation in the service, and the powerful voice with which he sings the Lord's Prayer, make Pułaski admire and like him. One evening he invites them for dinner, but Jacob comes alone. Tall, distinguished, he says little, considers much. They discuss what might happen, Russia, the king's politics. Pułaski understands that this prisoner of the king must be careful, and he tries to change the subject, since the conversation keeps stalling. To inquiries after his daughter, Jacob Frank responds that she had to stay behind with her mother, who is indisposed. Pułaski seems disappointed at this. But the next time, Jacob brings his daughter, and her presence ensures that the evening is a very pleasant one indeed. Other officers have been invited, somewhat excited by the presence of such a lovely—if shy and quiet—young woman, and they show off their wit and their intelligence. The wine is good, and the scrawny chickens taste like wildfowl.

These nice social evenings end when Prince Lubomirski arrives at the monastery with his troops. They say in the town that Prince Lubomirski is even worse than the Russians. He loots the surrounding villages without mercy, and his soldiers do not hesitate to rape. The peasants call him a Hussite. Lubomirski's troops patrol the enormous terrain and chase off the Russians, but they are resistant to obeying the orders of the confederate command, and slowly they turn into a band of villains and thieves.

When Lubomirski comes to the monastery, Jacob hides Avacha among the brothers, and she is not allowed to go out until he and his villains have moved on. Lubomirski organizes great bouts of drinking in the garrison, and this has ill effects on Pułaski's soldiers. Only the warhorses seem to admire the young prince.

"That's the kind of leader we need," says Roch, treating Jacob to some of the tobacco he received from the prince. "We'd chase away those Russians like a pack of mangy dogs."

Jacob takes a pinch and is silent. One evening, the drunken prince keeps trying to get into Jacob's tower, until Jacob is obliged to receive him. He inquires of Jacob as he would of a father figure into matters pertaining to women. His gaze darts about the chamber, no doubt seeking one woman in particular, the one everyone here has been mentioning to him.

In the fortress are some soldiers from the king's troops captured by the confederates, and many of them serve without much zeal. One of them, a captain of the Mirów guard, three officers of which have already been killed by the Muscovites, comes to Jacob for advice one day, which gives rise to a new trend—from now on, many of them start going to Jacob for counsel, the wise Jew who isn't a Jew exactly, who is a sort of indefinable prophet, whose mysteriousness is enhanced by his imprisonment in such a strange place. This captain, who is slender, fair-haired, and winsomely polite, asks Jacob in great confidence what he is to do, for he is young, and he is scared of death. They are sitting on stones, turned toward each other, on the northern side of the tower, where the soldiers tend to piss on the wall.

"Tell me, mister, am I to run away to Warsaw, where I come from, and make myself into a deserter and a coward, or fight for the fatherland and let myself be killed for the good of the country?"

Jacob's advice is concrete. This officer is to go to the market in Często-chowa and buy up little items of value—watches, rings. Since there is a war on, he will get it all for cheap. And he is to keep it as a safeguard, should everything go wrong.

"War is a jumble between marketplace and nightmare," Jacob Frank tells him. "Throw around those securities, buy your way out of the front line, pay bribes so you eat well—respect yourself, that's how you'll fend off death. It's no kind of heroism to let yourself get killed."

He pats the young officer on the back, and for the briefest moment the young officer leans into Jacob's collar.

"Mister, I'm so scared."

## Of the passing of Lady Hana in February of 1770 and of her final resting place

"I shall view it as an eccentricity," says the prior. "I'll not oppose you on this question, since the prisoner isn't ours, but the Holy Church's. As the woman is baptized, I would try for a place for her in the cemetery in town—we do not bury laypersons here."

The prior looks out the window and sees the aging confederates drilling with their sabers. The monastery really looks more like a garrison now. As usual, Jakubowski places a purse on the table.

It is Hana's second day lying in the officer's chamber in the tower. It seems like an awfully long time; no one has any peace, knowing she has not yet been taken by the earth. It is Jakubowski's second time going to the prior to request permission to bury the deceased in the cave, something he has done before—many times before, in fact, and again recently when little Jacob died. But Hana is not a small child, nor is she some second-rate neophyte. She is, after all, the wife of Jacob Frank.

Hana died of grief. Last year she gave birth to a daughter, whom they named Josepha Frances. No sooner was she baptized than she died. First Hana lost her strength due to some unexplained bleeding that lasted a long time after her last labor, never letting up. Then she came down with a fever, too, and a painful swelling of the bones. Zwierzchowska, who was taking care of her, said that it was from the cold that came in through the stones. The down bedding that arrived from Warsaw did not help. The damp was omnipresent here. Her joints grew so swollen that in the end Hana could scarcely move at all. Then little Jacob died. The children were buried in the cave without a priest, furtively, and after those two deaths Hana did not rise again. Jacob had Wołowski take Avacha to Warsaw, while the ailing Hana was to be brought out to take sun in front of the house in Częstochowa. It was only there that they could really see how pale she was, how ruined. Her skin, always a light olive, was now gray and looked like it was covered in a layer of ash. For a time, willow bark extract helped; the girls would go into the nearby forests for it. The willow grew there down the balks in even rows, bright switches sticking out of their misshapen, stocky trunks. What an ugly tree, that willow, Hana would say, all spread out and disheveled, like a decrepit, crippled old woman. And yet for some time this ugly plant did help her. The women would cut off the switches and pry the bark from them. At home they boiled the bark in water and gave the decoction to the patient to drink. One of the Pauline Fathers tried to treat Hana with a vodka-and-honey rub, but his cure did not work, either.

Now it is cool and damp. The earth has a troubling smell of the grave. From the fields around Częstochowa the distant horizon is visible, like a single string hung between sky and earth on which the wind is strumming the same monotonous, gloomy sound, over and over.

No one dares look in on Jacob. They stand huddled on the stairs, pale, their lips like dark dashes, circles under their eyes from their unceasing vigil; no one has eaten since yesterday, the pots are cold; even the children have fallen silent. Jakubowski presses his cheek to the wall of this cursed tower. One of the women nudges him, so he puts his hands on his forehead instead and starts to pray, and the others join in instantly. He imagines that even if the firmament of heaven were built of the same rough, wet stone, his prayer would be able to break through it, word by word. First they say the Lord's Prayer, then they sing the Yigdal.

All eyes are on him, on Nahman-Piotr Jakubowski. They know that it's just possible that the Lord will let him in. So Jakubowski cracks the heavy door on its rotten hinges. He can feel the others pushing in over his shoulder to take a peek inside. They're most likely expecting a miracle, the Lord in his white robe floating over the earth, and Her Ladyship alive and radiant in his arms. Jakubowski stifles a sigh that isn't far from a sob, but he knows he must get ahold of himself because whatever he does now, the others will do, too. He squeezes into the tiny opening and instantly shuts the door behind him. All but one of the candles have long since gone out. Her Ladyship is lying just as before she died; she has not risen, nothing has changed except that now there can be no doubt she is a corpse. Her jaw has dropped, opening her mouth, her eyes are half closed, the glow of the holy candle flickering over their slippery surface, and Her Ladyship's skin is gray, dour.

Next to her lies Jacob—naked, skinnier, angular, dark, though the hair on his body is now completely gray, matted like a dog's, and his eyes are sunken. His thin hips touch Hana's body and his hand lies on her breast, as if embracing her. It occurs to Jakubowski that perhaps Jacob, too, has died, and he suddenly grows hot and falls on his knees before the

bed, not feeling the impact of the stone floor, unable to hold in his sobbing any longer.

"Did you really believe we would not die?" Jacob asks him, rising from
his wife's body. He looks at Nahman, and his dark eyes don't reflect the
light of the holy candle, they are like the entrance to the cave. The question, which Jakubowski does not answer, sounds mocking, aggressive.
Jakubowski regains control over himself and takes from the trunk a fresh
shirt as well as a woolen Turkish tunic and starts dressing Jacob.

The cortege goes out past the walls the next morning before dawn.
Around noon they are at the Makpela Cave. Both Wołowskis, Pawłowski,
and Matuszewski struggle to carry the casket inside.

### Scraps: Being under siege

I will write of deaths.

First the eldest son passed, little seven-year-old Jacob, beloved by
his father and being prepared as his successor. This was the end of
November, and snow was already coming down. In the monastery,
turned into a fortress, cold and deprivation reigned. In that time,
the fortress already held its new commander, Kazimierz Pułaski,
and he, being on good terms with Jacob, and often conversing with
him, allowed the funeral to take place in the cave. We already had
our humble sepulcher there, where all of ours were buried, far from
strangers' cemeteries, though we had no intention of advertising it.
We had taken this cave for ourselves, taken it away from the bats
and the blind lizards, for it had wandered our way from the Land
of Israel, as Jacob had discovered. And since Adam and Eve rested
here, and Abraham and Sara, as well as the patriarchs, we began to
bury our dead in it. The first was Reb Eli, our treasurer, and then
Jacob's children, and in the end, Hanele. If ever we had anything of
value in Poland, it was this cave where we laid all our treasures, for
it was also the door to the better worlds that were awaiting us.

Those were bad days, and they cannot possibly be justified before
God. In the autumn of 1769, Pułaski's confederates started stalking

Avacha. It did not help that their commander announced that she was the daughter of a Jewish mage, and that they ought rather to leave her in peace. Her beauty aroused universal interest. Once some senior officers saw her and asked Jacob for a visit with his daughter. Then one of them said that, on the basis of her beauty, she might as well be the Holy Virgin, which pleased Jacob a great deal. Ordinarily, however, he kept her hidden in the tower, and when the soldiers drank, he forbade her from going out even if she needed to. An evil spirit, however, entered into those soldiers, that motley crew, who often grew bored with sitting in the fortress and drank themselves into a veritable frenzy after smuggling in alcohol from town. As soon as Avacha would go out, they immediately blocked her path and tried to talk with her, and sometimes it got unsavory, so many men setting upon one woman, a young and beautiful one at that. She herself was surprised by all the interest she aroused, a mixture of fascination and hostile lustfulness. More than once it exceeded the usual whistles and comments, and it appeared that the whole garrison was unable to focus on anything other than stalking her. The intercession of Mr. Pułaski did not help, though he strictly forbade anyone forcing themselves upon Eva Frank. But deprived of the activities in which they would normally be engaged, in a state of suspension and uncertainty over what is going to happen next, soldiers become an irrational mob over which there can be no control. I would prefer not to write about it—I would rather not say it at all—but out of obligation to the truth I will only mention that in the end, when it did happen, Jacob and Wołowski and I took her to Warsaw, so that she returned only after her mother's death and was then with her father to the end. On the night that she was being assaulted, she had a dream in which she was freed from the tower by a German man who was dressed in white. She was told in the dream that he was an emperor.

Those years of being under siege were difficult for me and for all of us. I was thankful to fate that as an envoy I often traveled between the capital and Częstochowa, which meant I felt less depressed than Jacob, who after years of relative freedom was now tormented by his imprisonment in the monastery. Almost all of our people had left their quarters in a hurry and returned to Warsaw, knowing that here we would soon be under siege. The Wieluńskie Przedmieście had emptied. Only Jan Wołowski and Mateusz Matuszewski remained with the Lord.

After Hana's death, Jacob fell ill, and I will confess that I thought this would be the end. I thought a great deal about why Job had said, "In my flesh I will see God"—that verse from Isaiah gave me no peace. For since a person's body is neither lasting nor perfect, then he who created it must also be weak and miserable. That is what Job had in mind. That is what I thought, and the times to come would only strengthen this belief in me.

And so with Wołowski and Matuszewski we agreed to send to Warsaw for Marianna and then Ignacowa, so that Jacob could suck from their breasts. That always helped him. I have before my eyes this same picture still: under Russian siege, as cannons thundered and the fortress walls crumbled, as the earth quaked and people fell like flies, the Lord in the officer's chamber of the tower of his prison nursed upon a woman's breast, and in this way, he repaired this calamitous world, so riddled with holes.

By the summer of 1772, there was no longer anything to defend. Częstochowa had been sacked, people were exhausted and hungry, and the monastery could barely function, lacking water and food. The commander, Puławski, had been accused of conspiring against the king after having ordered the fortress to surrender to the Russian troops. Praying on the Day of Assumption of the Most Holy Virgin Mary, Queen of Poland, on August 15, did not help. The brothers lay in the form of a cross on the dirty floor and waited for a miracle. In the evening after mass, white flags were hung on the fortress walls. We helped the monks hide the valuable paintings and votive offerings, and in the place of the holiest picture we hung a copy. The Russians entered a few days later and ordered the monks to be locked in the refectory; for several days their prayers and songs could be heard from in there. The prior lamented that for the first time in its whole history, the monastery had found itself in foreign hands, and that this doubtless heralded the end of the world.

The Russians lit huge fires in the monastery courtyard and drank the communion wine, and whatever they didn't drink, they poured out onto the cobblestones until these were red, as though drenched in blood. They looted the library and the treasury, destroyed the powder magazine and many weapons. They blew up the gate. From the walls of the monastery, we could see the smoke of the surrounding villages going up in flames.

Yet to my astonishment, Jacob's spirits were not dampened by this situation. On the contrary: this chaos was giving him strength.

The frenzy of wartime was exciting him. He would go out to those Russians and converse with them. They feared him, as Hana's death had changed him greatly—he was now terribly thin, with dark circles under his eyes, and the features of his face had sharpened, and his hair had gone gray. Someone who hadn't seen him in a long time might have said it was a different person. It is also true that he interceded with the Russians on behalf of the Pauline Fathers, and they were freed from their refectory prison.

Several days later, General Bibikov came to the monastery. He entered on horseback through the actual door to the chapel, and from his horse he assured the prior that nothing bad would happen to them under Russian rule. That very same evening we went with Jacob to ask the Russian general for an exceptional release from prison. I thought I would be needed to translate into Russian, but they spoke in German. Bibikov was exceedingly polite, and within two days, Jacob had received official permission to leave the monastery.

Jacob, our Lord, says:

"Everyone who seeks salvation must do three things: change his place of residence, change his name, and change his deeds."

And so we did. We became other people, and we left Częstochowa, at once the lightest and the darkest place.

# VI.

*The Book of*
# THE DISTANT
# COUNTRY

| In noftra Europa | W nafzey Europie | |
|---|---|---|
| (funt | (fą | |
| *regna* & *regiones* pri- | nayprzednieyfze | regnuum, n. 2. kro- |
| (mariæ; | (kroleftwa; | leftwo, |
| *Lufitania,* | Portugallia, | primarius, a, um, nay- |
| *Hifpania,* 1 | Hifzpania, 1 | przednieyfzy. |
| *Gallia,* 2 | Francya, 2 | |
| *Italia,* 3 | Włochy, 3 | |
| *Anglia,* (*Britannia*) | Anglia, 4 (Brytania) | |
| (4 | | |
| | | *Scotia,* |

## 26.

### Yente reads passports

Yente sees the passports that are shown at the border. A gloved officer takes them gently, leaves the travelers in their carriage so he can read the passports in peace in the guardhouse. The travelers keep silent. The gloved officer reads in a murmur:

> Karol Emeryk, Baron von Revisnye, chamberlain of the Roman, in the German, Hungarian, and Czech lands, Royal Apostolic Majesty, active ambassador and attested minister at the royal court of Poland, hereby makes it known that the bearer of this document, Mr. Joseph Frank, a merchant, along with his service, being composed of eighteen people, in two carriages, travels on business interests from here to Brünn in Moravia, and so all authorities to whom the power to do so belongs are called upon to put no obstacles before the aforementioned Joseph Frank and the servants with whom he voyages—of whom there are to be eighteen—nor to prevent them from crossing any border, and should the need arise to provide him with the appropriate assistance. Given in Warsaw, the 5th of March, 1773.

Besides this Austrian passport, there is also a Prussian one, and Yente sees it very clearly; it is written in beautiful penmanship, authenticated by a great seal:

The bearer of this document, the merchant Mr. Joseph
Frank, having arrived here from Częstochowa, now makes his
way, after an eight-day stay in Warsaw, with eighteen persons in
his service, in two carriages, through Częstochowa to Moravia,
on private business. Since here the air is everywhere clean and
healthy, and thank God there is no trace of plague . . .

Yente looks closely at this German formulation: "und von ansteck-
ender Seuche ist Gottlob nichts zu spüren . . ."

. . . and all authorities, military and civil, are hereby requested
to permit the aforementioned merchant, along with his
people and carriages, to cross the border without hindrance,
following the appropriate verification, and continue on his
way. Warsaw, 1st of March, 1773. Gédéon Benoît, His Royal
Highness's ambassador residing in the Polish-Lithuanian Commonwealth.

Yente understands from this that behind passports lurks the great cosmos of the state apparatus, with its solar systems, orbits, satellites, with
the phenomenon of the comet and the mysterious force of gravity described not long ago by Newton. It is a sensitive and vigilant system,
propelled by hundreds or thousands of clerical desks and piles of papers
that are propagated through the caress of the sharp ends of geese feathers
and passed from hand to hand, from desk to desk; sheets of paper create a
slight motion of the air that might be imperceptible compared with autumn winds, yet significant on a world scale. Maybe somewhere far away,
in Africa or in Alaska, this motion could whip up a hurricane. The state
is the perfect usurper, an uncompromising ruler, an order established
once and for all (until it's cleared away by the next war). Who traced the
border through this thorny steppe? Who forbids people from crossing it?
In whose name is this suspicious gloved officer operating, and whence
comes his suspicion? What is the purpose of papers borne by letter carriers
and envoys, by mail carriages for which at every station exhausted horses
trade places? Correspondence from Warsaw to Vienna and back takes
ten days.

Jacob's retinue is made up of the young; the old stayed behind in Warsaw, where they wait, attending to the newly started businesses. The children have been sent to the Piarists; they live on Nowe Miasto and go to church each Sunday. The neophytes, after shaving their beards, blend into the crowd on the muddy streets of the capital. Sometimes you can catch a slight Yiddish accent, but that, too, disappears like snow.

Jacob, covered in furs, travels in the first carriage with Avacha, whom he sometimes calls Eva now. She is flushed from the cold, and her father keeps covering her again with the fur throw. She holds Rutka, the dog, on her lap, and the dog whimpers dolefully from time to time. Eva could not be convinced to leave her in Warsaw. Opposite sits Jędrzej Yeruhim Dembowski, who has now been made the Lord's secretary, as Jakubowski and his wife are busy with the Lord's sons in Warsaw. Next to Dembowski is Mateusz Matuszewski. Traveling on horseback: Kazimierz the cook with his two helpers, Joseph Nakulnicki and Franciszek Bodowski, and also Ignacy Cesirajski, to whom Jacob took a particular liking in Częstochowa as his own helper.

The women are crowded into the second carriage: Magda Golińska, formerly Jezierzańska, Eva Frank's friend, older by several years, tall, self-confident, as tender and devoted to her as a mother would be; in her passport, it says she is a maid. Also traveling as maids are Anusia Pawłowska, daughter of Paweł Pawłowski, once Hayim of Busk, brother of Nahman Jakubowski. Anusia has grown into a lovely girl. Going as washerwomen are Róża Michałowska and Teresa, Łabęcki's widow. With them are Jan, Janek, Ignac, and Jacob, who have not yet earned last names, so the scrupulous officer writes in the corresponding boxes "Forisch" and "Fuhrmann." Jacob always gets their first names mixed up, and when he forgets, he calls both of the boys Hershel.

Already beginning in Ostrava you can see that this is a different country, orderly and clean. The roads are paved, and despite the mud, they can be traveled with surprising ease. Along the highways there are guesthouses, but not the Jewish kind, which they avoided as they went through Poland. Is Moravia not, after all, the land of the true believers? They are in every little town here, although they are different, more reserved; they think what they please, but on the outside, they look like real Christians. Yeruhim Dembowski, whom Jacob now calls "Jędruś," a funny-sounding Polish diminutive, looking curiously out the window, quotes the words of a Kabbalist according to whom Psalm 14:3—"All have turned away, all have become corrupt; there is no one who does good, not even one"—has the same numerical value as the name of Moravia—Mehrin.

"We had better watch out for these Krauts," he warns.

Eva is disappointed—she very much wanted for her brothers to come with them, but they, childish and shy, tenuous as the little shoots that grow down in the cellar, are afraid of their father, who seems to have more sternness than love for them—it seems that they are a constant irritation to him. It is true that both of them are awkward and insecure. Roch, a freckled redhead, starts to blubber when rebuked, and then his watery greenish eyes fill with tears, and even those tears are the color of pond water. Joseph, quiet and secretive, with avian features and nice black eyes, is always turned inward, focused on picking up sticks, or stones, or snippets of ribbons, empty spools—the incomprehensible activity of the magpie. This brother Eva loves like she would her own child.

When the officer finally returns their passports, and the transport sets off again, Eva leans out, looks back on the road, and understands that she is leaving Poland once and for all, that she will never again return. To her, Poland will always be the prison of Jasna Góra. She was eight years old when she saw the officer's chamber for the first time, eternally underheated, cold. Of Poland she will also remember the trips to Warsaw, to the Wołowskis', where she hurriedly learned to play the piano, her teacher hitting her hands with a wooden ruler. She will also remember the unexpected death of her mother, like a punch in the chest. She knows she will never go back down this road. The high road with its poplars in the uncertain March sun shifts already into memory.

"Miss Eva must be mourning the officer's chamber, and missing Roch . . . ," Matuszewski says ironically, seeing her sad face.

Everyone in the carriage chuckles, all except her father. From his facial expression there is no way to tell what he is thinking. He puts his arm around her and hides her head under his coat, like he might a puppy. There Eva manages to conceal the tears that pour forth.

They reach Brünn on the evening of March 23, 1773, and they rent rooms at the Zum blauen Loewen, but there are only two rooms available, so they are cramped. The Forisches and the Fuhrmanns sleep side by side on the ground scattered with hay in the stable. Dembowski keeps the box with their money and documents under his head. But—as they learn the next morning—in order to stay in the city for longer, they will need a special safe passage issued them. This is the reason Jacob and Eva ask to be taken to Prossnitz, to their cousins, the Dobrushkas.

## Of the Dobrushka family in Prossnitz

Eyes wide, Eva takes in the garments of the local women, gaping at their little dogs and their carriages. She sees the even rows of vineyards—bare at this time of year—and the little gardens tidied up for Easter. Meanwhile, passersby stop at the sight of their carriage, her father's high hat, and her cloak lined with wolf fur. The bony, powerful hand of her father, who knows no opposition, holds her firmly by the wrist, stretching out her brand-new goatskin glove. The pressure hurts her, but she does not complain. There is little that Eva can't bear.

The Dobrushkas' home is known to all in the city, and everyone is happy to point them in the right direction. It stands on the market square, two stories tall, the first being a shop with a big window. The facade has just been renovated—even now some workers are laying the pavement in front of it. As they cannot get any closer, the carriage stops, and the driver runs up to announce their arrival. A moment later, the curtains are parted on the second floor and the curious eyes of the older and younger residents gaze down upon the new arrivals.

The Dobrushkas come out to greet them. Eva curtsies before her aunt Sheyndel, who holds her tight, feeling overcome, and Eva breathes in the scent of her dress—light, floral, like powder and vanilla. Solomon, or Zalman, has tears in his eyes. He has aged considerably, now he can barely walk. He wraps his long arms around Jacob and claps him on the back. Yes, yes, Zalman is weak and sick, he's gotten very skinny. His big belly has shrunk, and deep wrinkles line his face. Twenty-one years ago, at the wedding in Rohatyn, he seemed twice this size. His wife, Sheyndel, on the other hand, has bloomed like an apple tree in spring. No one would guess she had given birth to twelve children—her figure is still good, full, round. The only thing is that her hair is slightly gray now, but it is still luxurious, and she has combed it up, fastening it with black lace clasps that hold her tiny bonnet in place.

In spite of these displays of affection, Sheyndel is wary as she watches her cousin, about whom she has heard so much that she has no idea what to think. By nature, she does not trust people, or think well of them—often they strike her as stupid and vain. She hugs Avacha somewhat theatrically, too tightly—with women, she always dominates—delighting over her Polish-style braids. Sheyndel is a beautiful woman, well-dressed, confident in herself and the strength of the charm she exerts on all around her. Soon her voice alone will be audible inside the house.

Not standing on ceremony, she takes her cousin by the hand and leads him into the living room, the splendor of which intimidates the guests, who for thirteen years have not looked upon beautiful, opulent things other than in church. But here there is a polished wooden floor, with Turkish carpets on it, and there are walls painted in soft colors with flowers, and a white instrument with a kind of keyboard, and beside it an elaborately decorated stool on three legs modeled upon the legs of an animal. The drapery in the windows, a sewing box with drawers—their guests arrived as she was embroidering with her daughters, which is why the hoops have been tossed aside onto the armchairs. There are four daughters; now they stand next to one another, smiling, visibly pleased with themselves: the eldest, Blumele, beautiful, not too tall, cheerful, and then Sara, Gitla, and the very young Esther with her curls and red splotches on her pale face, as if someone had painted them. All wearing dresses in patterns of delicate little flowers, but each dress a different color. Eva would like to have a dress like that, and ribbons in her hair; they don't wear those in Warsaw, and she can already feel herself falling in love with this clothing, these subtle colors and these hair ribbons. From Poland she knows only flashy reds and amaranths, and Turkish blues, but here it's different: everything is a little bit diluted, as if all the shades in the world had been mixed into milk—there aren't even words for the ever so slightly grayed pink of the ribbons.

Aunt Sheyndel introduces her children. Her Yiddish is a little different from what is spoken by the family newly come from Poland. After the girls, the boys come up individually. Here is Moshe, who at the news of a visit from his famous uncle has returned especially from Vienna. At twenty, he is just two years older than Avacha, with a slim, energetic face and uneven teeth; he is already writing scholarly dissertations, both in German and in Hebrew. He is interested in poetry and literature as well as new philosophical trends. He is just a little bit too bold, too talkative, too sure of himself, like his mother. There are some people with whom you have a little problem from the start because you feel too attracted to them—you like them without any justification, even as you feel certain that it is all a simulacrum, a game. That is how Moshe is. When he looks at her, Eva averts her eyes and turns crimson, which makes her even more ashamed. On being introduced to him, she curtseys clumsily and does not want to give him her hand, and then Sheyndel, who sees everything, gives everyone to understand—by the significant glance she casts her hus-band's way—that this girl has simply not been brought up to have man-ners. Eva is unable to remember the names of the next two Dobrushka brothers.

Sheyndel Hirsh was born in Wrocław, but her family comes from Rze-szów, like Jacob's family—Jacob's mother and Sheyndel's father were sis-ter and brother. Now she is thirty-seven years old, but her face still looks fresh and young. Her large dark eyes resemble wells—you never know what you'll find at the bottom. Her gaze is penetrating, suspicious, atten-tive, hard to shake. Eva looks away and thinks how different Aunt Sheyn-del is from her own mother. Her mother was trusting and straightforward, which meant that she often appeared helpless and defenseless. That is how Eva remembers her anyway, as if all her strength would simply van-ish, and every morning she would have to gather it back up like so many berries, patiently, slowly. This woman has more than enough strength; talking with Eva's cousin, she simultaneously sets the table. A maid rushes in with a basket of rolls that are still warm, straight from the bakery. And there is honey and lumps of dark sugar, which they drop into their coffee with special little tongs.

The first conversations are had for the purpose of everyone making a thorough examination of everyone else. The Dobrushka children, who have hurried down from all over the house, curious and amused, look at Eva Frank, their unknown cousin, and their strange uncle with the coarse, dark face. Eva is wearing a dress bought back in Warsaw, in a "travel" color, a tobacco-like shade, that does not suit her at all. The upper of one of her boots has cracked, and she tries to cover it with the toe of the other one. Her full face never loses its flush. From under her hat—and to think that in Warsaw it struck her as chic—strands of her hair sneak out.

From the outset, Jacob's manner has been loud and intimate, as though the moment he left the carriage, a change occurred within him, and placed over his tired and devastated face a jovial mask. His depression and exhaustion are washed away by sips of goose broth, and he is warmed by Sheyndel's infectious laughter, relaxed by the cherry liqueur. In the end, there is that exotic name, Częstochowa, and Jacob starts to tell them stories, as he does—gesticulating, making wild faces. He curses in Polish, curses in Yiddish, the children don't know how to react, but a glance at their mother soothes them—Sheyndel closes her eyes briefly, as if to say: To him all is permitted.

They sit in the living room at a small round table and drink coffee out of delicate cups. Eva does not listen to her father's stories.

When she reaches for the sugar (with coffee they're given snow-white sugar in big crystals), she sees on the sugar bowl a picture of a port city, with its characteristic cranes for unloading goods. And the cup—its insides are white and slick, and its edge is decorated with a delicate gold band. Bringing it to her lips, Eva can almost taste that band—its flavor is almost vanilla.

The clock ticks—this new sound breaks up time into little parts, and everything seems calibrated, in a grid. Clean, orderly, and perfectly sensible.

After lunch, her father remains with Uncle Zalman and Aunt Sheyndel, while Eva is sent to the girls' room, where the youngest, Gitla and Esther, show her their diaries, in which visitors are supposed to write inscriptions. Eva is to do the same. She is terrified.

"Can it be in Polish?" she asks.

She looks through one diary and sees that all the entries are in German, of which her knowledge is limited. In the end, Magda Golińska writes on her behalf, in a fine hand and in Polish. To Eva remains the task of illustration: a rose with its thorns, like they used to make together in Częstochowa. These are the only flowers she knows how to draw.

In the living room, the adults are conversing loudly, and the girls can hear their bursts of laughter and cries of surprise. Then the voices lower to a whisper. The servants bring in coffee and fruit. Somewhere from deep inside the house comes the smell of fried meat. Jędrzej Dembowski walks around the house, peering in all the rooms. He looks into the girls' room, and with him comes the smell of tobacco, bitter and strong.

"So that's where the young ladies have hidden away . . . ," he says, and with these words, his smoky silhouette is gone.

Eva, who is sitting in a deep armchair and playing with the tassels of the curtain, can just make out the voice of her father from the living room, who is telling the story in an animated way of how he was released by the Russians. She hears him embellishing these events, perhaps even lying about them. In his version, it all sounds very dramatic, and he comes off as a hero—an attack, shots, the old soldiers dying, blood, monks covered in debris. In reality, it was all much less theatrical. The garrison surrendered. White flags were hung on the walls. Arms were laid down in great piles. It was raining, and the heaps of pistols, sabers, and muskets looked like piles of brushwood. The confederates were placed in four-file columns and led out. The Russians then turned to systematic plundering.

Wołowski and Jakubowski talked with General Bibikov in Jacob's name. After a brief deliberation with some officer, he had a proclamation written for Jacob saying he was now free.

As they all traveled to Warsaw in their rented carriage, they were stopped several times by different patrols of surviving confederates and Russians. Each would read the proclamation and suspiciously examine the pretty girl squeezed between the strange men. Once, they were stopped by a ragged band of highwaymen, but Jan Wołowski fired some shots into the air and they ran off. Around Kalwaria Zebrzydowska, they turned off the road and, having amply paid the nuns in the monastery, deposited Eva with them, not wanting to take any risks with her traveling through that suddenly savage land. She was to wait there for her father to return. Taking his leave, he kissed her on the lips and told her she was the most important thing he had.

Now her father is recounting their efforts to obtain passports, and Eva can hear the voice of her aunt Sheyndel, screeching in disbelief:

"You wanted to go to Turkey?"

Eva can't make out her father's reply. And then her aunt again:

"But Turkey is now an enemy of Poland, and of Austria, and of Russia. There is going to be a war."

Eva falls asleep in her armchair.

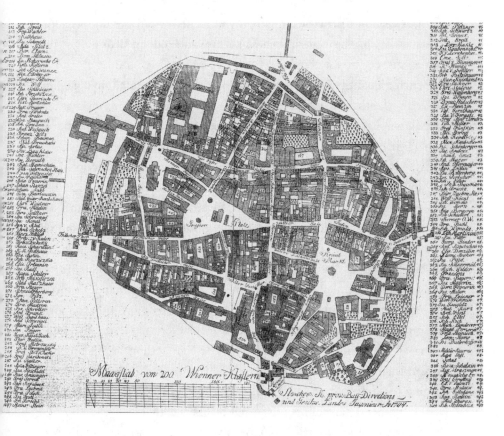

## Of new life in Brünn and the ticking of clocks

Several days later, they rent a house on the outskirts of Brünn, from Ignacy Pietsch, a councillor. Jacob Frank has to show him their passports and file a statement with the authorities in which he avows that he comes from Smyrna, is traveling from Poland, and that, being now tired of professional activity, he wishes to settle permanently with his daughter in Brünn. And that he has the necessary means to do so, as a result of his aforementioned professional activity.

As they spend weeks unpacking their things, making the beds and arranging their undergarments on the shelves of their new wardrobes, an endless stream of sheets of paper babbles over their heads—letters, reports, denunciations, and notes, reports that meander forth and back again. A certain district head named von Zollern expresses doubts about whether they ought to permit these persons to reside in Brünn; it strikes him as suspect that a neophyte—as he has heard—would be able to afford such a quantity of hired help. Help, it should be noted, made up exclusively of other neophytes. Although His Imperial Majesty has put special emphasis on tolerance, Administrator von Zollern nonetheless fears taking responsibility for this company and would prefer they settle elsewhere, until such a time as they receive a final determination from the Imperial-Royal Provincial Administration.

The response he receives says that, given martial law in Poland, the newcomers' fate should be determined by military authority, without the approval of which—pursuant to the imperial ordinance of July 26, 1772—persons of Polish origin cannot be permitted to remain in the country. Then a missive arrives from the military commander's office, stating that the neophytes are in fact subject to civil, not military, jurisdiction, and that the civil authorities are therefore requested to issue a ruling on their eligibility for residency. The civil authorities, meanwhile, turn to the district head with the request that he obtain information regarding the person of Joseph Frank: the aims of his travels, his means, as well as further details of his purported business activity.

In the wake of investigations by official and unofficial intelligence agents, the district head reports:

> . . . that this Frank has testified that in the Polish Kingdom, thirty miles from Czernowitz, now containing peoples of the Russian Empire, he owns a quantity of horned cattle, in which he trades extensively; however, on account of present circumstances and of the wartime disruptions in Poland, fearing for his and his family members' lives, he now intends to dispense with trade and herd. That furthermore he owns property in Smyrna, the income of which he collects every three years, and thus, having no intention of conducting business in Moravian Brünn, he shall live exclusively off the aforementioned sources. Insofar as the aforementioned Frank's behavior, conduct, character, and social relations are concerned, the most careful, wide-ranging, and painstaking investigation on the part of the District Office

has found nothing that might impugn the reputation of this man. Jacob Frank is a person of proper conduct; he lives off his own income and ready monies and is not prone to the incurring of debts.

After a year on the outskirts of town, in the beautiful hills near Vinohrady, with their many gardens, they move to Kleine Neugasse and then to Petersburger Gasse, where, thanks to the assistance of Zalman Dobrushka and others, they are able to take a twelve-year lease on a town councillor's house at number 4.

The house stands right next to the cathedral, on the hill, and from it you can see all of Brünn. Its courtyard is small and neglected, overgrown with burdock.

Eva gets the nicest, brightest room, with four windows and myriad pictures on the wall that depict little genre scenes with shepherdesses. There is a four-poster bed, quite high and none too comfortable. She hangs her dresses in the wardrobe. Magda Golińska sleeps on the floor each night, until they finally buy her a bed. This isn't strictly necessary, since whenever it's cold they sleep cuddled together anyway, but only when Eva's father isn't awake to see it, when his snoring carries all across the house.

And yet Jacob complains that he can't sleep.

"Get rid of that ticking!" he shouts, and has them remove to downstairs the clock that had at first so delighted him. The clock comes from somewhere in Germany and is made entirely of wood, with a little bird that leaps out on the hour with such a clatter that it is as if a canister shot has exploded nearby, as if they were still under siege in Częstochowa. And the little bird is ugly and rather resembles a rat. Jacob wakes up in the middle of the night and stomps around the house. He sometimes goes into Avacha's room, but if he sees that Magda is lying there with her, he gets even more upset. Finally they give away the clock as a gift.

In the summer, Eva goes to Aunt Sheyndel's to learn good manners and to play the fashionable piano Zalman has had brought in from Vienna. She also studies French, and as she is quite bright, she soon learns how to handle herself in conversation. With her intimates she speaks in

Polish, as her father has forbidden Yiddish to all. With her cousins, however, she must speak in German; she is tutored in it at her aunt's house,
along with the younger girls. Eva is ashamed to be attending these lessons
with such little children. She studies as much as she can, but even so, she
fears she won't catch up with the young Dobrushka girls. She also sometimes joins in on the sessions with the Hausrabbiner who takes care of the
children's Hebrew education, both the girls' and the boys'. He is an old
man, Solomon Gerlst, a relative of so important a person as Jonathan
Eibeschütz, who was born right there in Prossnitz, where his extended
family still lives. His primary focus is the two boys, Immanuel and David, who have already passed their bar mitzvahs and are now beginning
to study the holy books of the true believers.

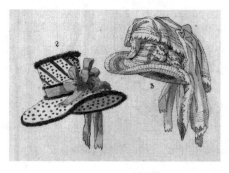

Once a month, a tailor comes,
and Avacha's aunt gradually orders her a new wardrobe: light
summer dresses in muted colors,
little cropped vests that show off
her décolletage, hats so bedecked
with ribbons and flowers that
they look like dolls' graves. At
the cobbler's, she orders shoes
made out of silk, so soft that Eva is scared to go out onto the dusty streets
of Brünn. In these new outfits, Eva transforms into a woman of the world,
and her father squints with satisfaction as he looks at her, asking her to say
something in German, anything at all. Then he smacks his lips with satisfaction.

"This is the child I asked for, this daughter, this queen."

Eva likes to please her father—only when he likes her does she like
herself. But she does not enjoy her father's touch. She slips out of his grasp
and goes off, as if busy with something, though she is always scared that
he will call her back. She prefers to be in Prossnitz with her aunt and uncle. There, both she and Anusia Pawłowska do the same thing as their
cousins: they learn how to be ladies.

In the Dobrushkas' garden, fruit has already appeared on the little
apple trees; the grass is lush, with paths trodden in it. It rained not long

ago, and now the air is a clear, dark green, scintillating with myriad smells. The rain has etched little fissures into the main path, and drops are drying on the wooden bench Sheyndel has set up there, where she often comes to read. In the summer, Eva also sits out on this bench, trying to read the French novels that her aunt keeps under lock and key, a whole cabinet full of them.

Zalman Dobrushka often watches his daughters through the open window as he sits doing his accounts. Lately he hasn't been going to his tobacco shop, as the stuffy summer air sparks asthma attacks. It is hard for him to breathe, so he has to be careful. He knows he won't live too much longer, and he's decided that he will leave his business to his eldest son, Carl. There is an ongoing battle in the Dobrushka family over baptism. Zalman and several of his elder sons are resistant to it, but Sheyndel supports their children who do decide to take such a step. Carl has recently been baptized, along with his wife and children. The tobacco business has become a Christian business. Tobacco will be a Christian good.

## Of Moshe Dobrushka and the feast of the Leviathan

Twenty years ago, Moshe was at the wedding in Rohatyn, though of course he cannot know this. Yente touched him through the belly of a very young Sheyndel, disgusted by the horse shit in the courtyard. Yente, who also sometimes travels to the Dobrushkas' garden here in Prossnitz, knows him well—yes, this is him, this once-uncertain, partial existence, a gelatinous orb of potential, a being who is and is not at the same time, for the description of which no language has yet been invented, nor theorized by any Newton. But from where she is, Yente sees both his beginning and his end. It isn't good to know so much.

Meanwhile, in Warsaw, in the kitchen on Leszno, the bony fingers of Hayah, now Marianna Lanckorońska, are molding a figurine of him from bread. It takes a long time, because the mass crumbles and breaks, the little figure takes on strange shapes and falls apart. It will turn out completely different from all the others.

Moshe is studying law, but he is more interested in theater and literature, and Viennese wineries are without a doubt better places to learn about life, he tells his mother. He wouldn't dare say the same to his ailing father. His mother loves him above all else and considers him a true genius. Her maternal gaze sees in him an exceptionally handsome young man. Then again, no one who has not yet passed their twenty-fifth year can be denied at least a little beauty, and so it is with Moshe—he is simultaneously slender and solidly built. When he comes from Vienna, he dispenses with his powdered wig and goes around with his head bare, his dark, wavy hair tied back. In fact he resembles his mother, with her high forehead and full lips, and just like her, he is voluble and loud. He carries himself elegantly, in the Viennese fashion: he swaggers. His tall, thin leather boots with silver-plated buckles emphasize his long, slim calves.

Eva has learned that Moshe has a fiancée in Vienna named Elke, the stepdaughter of the wealthy industrialist Joachim von Popper, an ennobled neophyte. Yes, yes, the wedding is being planned. His father would happily marry him off right now, so that Moshe could continue in peace with his brothers in what seems to the father to be best—the tobacco trade. But Moshe is just getting to know the strange and deep pocket of another world, from which money can be extracted endlessly and at will: the stock market. He knows, like his mother does, that there are more important things than the tobacco trade.

Moshe brings home friends, young people from wealthy backgrounds; then his mother opens the windows and dusts the garden furniture, and the clavichord is put out in the middle of the room so that it can be heard throughout the house and garden. His sisters put on their best dresses. These young friends, poets, philosophers, and God knows who else— Zalman calls them triflers—are open, modern people; none of them is bothered by Zalman's beard, nor his foreign accent. They are eternally exhilarated, in a perpetual state of light elation, delighted with themselves, with their own verses, which teem with allegory and abstraction.

When his mother calls them for dinner, Moshe is standing in the middle of the living room.

"Did you hear that? Let's go and eat the Leviathan!" he cries. The youth get up from their seats and glide across the polished floors, hurrying to take the best places at the table.

Moshe exclaims:

"At the messianic feast, Israel will eat the Leviathan! Sure, Maimonides explains this philosophically and loftily, but who are we to disdain the beliefs of simple people who spent their whole lives hungry?"

Moshe takes his seat in the very center of the long table, not missing a beat in his peroration:

"Yes, the people of Israel shall devour the Leviathan! The vast body of the beast will prove to be as delicious and as delicate as . . . as . . ."

". . . as the meat of virgin quail," suggests one of his pals.

"Or transparent flying fish," Moshe continues. "The people will eat the Leviathan at such length that they will satisfy their many-centuries-long hunger. There will be such great grub, an unforgettable feast. The wind will flutter the white tablecloths, and we'll toss the bones under the table for the dogs, who will be present, too, to reap the rewards of salvation . . ."

The applause that sounds is weak, since everyone's hands are already busy placing food on plates. Until late in the night music and bursts of laughter will carry all throughout the Dobrushkas' house as the youths play their fashionable French party games. Sheyndel stands with her arms folded, leaning against the doorframe, gazing proudly at her son. She has reason to be proud of him: in 1773 alone he has published three of his own treatises—two in German, and one in Hebrew. All on the subject of literature.

After Zalman's funeral, which takes place in January of 1774, Moshe requests a conversation with his uncle Jacob Frank. They sit on the veranda, where Sheyndel kept her flowers over the winter, and where tall figs, palms, and oleanders still stand.

Moshe seems to admire Jacob while simultaneously not caring for him at all. This is often how he feels about people: immoderate and ambivalent. Now he watches him furtively and is irritated by the country manners his uncle so flaunts, irritated by his Turkish outfit, gaudy and theatrical. And yet he admires his completely inexplicable and seemingly unshakable self-confidence; he has never seen such a thing in anyone before. He sometimes catches himself feeling respect toward his uncle, occasionally even fearing him. Perhaps this is what attracts him so much.

"I want you to be my witness at the wedding, Uncle. I want you to be there for my baptism, too."

"I like that you're inviting me to a wedding at a wake," says Jacob.

"My father would have liked it, too. He was always one for getting straight to the point."

Through the window, seen by those attending the wake, they look as if they are smoking their pipes and talking about Zalman, wishing him a peaceful rest. They look relaxed: Jacob has stretched out his legs in front of him and is releasing rings of smoke, lost in thought.

"It all boils down to this," says Moshe Dobrushka now. "Moses and his *constitution* are frauds. Moses himself learned the truth, but he hid it from his people. Why? So that he could hold power over them, no doubt. And he constructed such a massive lie that it actually started to seem like the truth. Millions of people have believed in that lie, cited it, and lived by it." Moshe is giving a lecture more than he is having a conversation—he doesn't even look at his uncle. "What must it be like to realize your whole life has been an illusion? It's like someone telling a child that red is green, yellow pink, that this tree is a tulip . . ." He forgets himself in enumerating comparisons, makes a kind of circular gesture with his hand and keeps going.

"In other words, the World is a deceitful lie, rehearsed theater. And yet, Moses had been given the greatest opportunity, he could have led the exiled nation, the nation that was wandering the desert—he could have led them to the true light, and yet he preferred to deceive them, and to present the injunctions he himself had invented as if they were divine. He kept that secret well, and it took us ages to realize the truth."

Moshe suddenly, violently, slides off his chair and kneels before Jacob, putting his head on Jacob's knees.

"You, Jacob, are the one who insists we uncover this truth. You took this task upon yourself, and for that, I admire you."

Jacob does not seem surprised to find himself holding the head of the young Dobrushka in his hands. Anyone who saw them through the glass now would imagine that the uncle was consoling the son after his father's death—a touching sight.

"You know, Uncle, Moses was terribly wrong, he condemned us Jews, and not only us, to countless misfortunes, defeats, plagues, suffering, and then he abandoned his people—"

"He converted to another religion . . . ," Jacob interjects, and Dobrushka goes back to his chair, but he scoots it up so close to his uncle that their faces are only a hand's width away from each other.

"Tell me, am I right? Jesus tried to save us, and he was close, but his message got warped, just like Muhammad's."

Jacob says:

"Mosaic laws are a burden on and a violence to the people, but the divine laws are perfect. No man or creature had the good fortune to hear them, but we trust that someday we will hear them. You know that, right?"

Moshe Dobrushka nods vigorously.

"The whole truth is in the philosophy of the Enlightenment, in all the knowledge we can attain, knowledge that will free us from this misery . . ."

Sheyndel is made anxious by what she sees through the veranda window, and she hesitates a moment, then decisively knocks and opens the door to tell them the modest repast has been served.

## Of the house by the cathedral
## and the delivery of maidens

As soon as they're set up on Petersburger Gasse, guests start to visit, and noise fills the house. The annexes are occupied already, and those who could not fit have rented apartments in the homes of local burghers—so now the sleepy city of Brünn sees an influx of new strength, with all the young newcomers. Since the teachings take place in the morning, the rest of the day is open, and the Lord begins to direct drills, so that thenceforth the courtyard is characterized by polyglot commotion, as boys from Poland, Turkey, as well as from the Czech and Moravian lands—the "Krauts," as the Lord calls them—train together. The court in Brünn allocates significant amounts to purchase them all uniforms, and once they are outfitted thus, the Lord divvies up his little army under varied banners. Sketches for uniforms and pennants are spread out on the table, and plans for setting up the troops. Every morning the Lord starts in similar fashion. He goes out onto the balcony and, leaning on the stone balustrade, says to those in training:

"Whosoever heeds not my words may under no circumstances remain at my court. Whosoever swears will immediately be erased from everything. And if anyone should say that the thing that I am striving for is bad or needless, he, too, will be banned."

Sometimes he also adds:

"Once upon a time I went out to demolish and uproot; now I plant and build. I will teach you royal customs because your heads were made for crowns."

Dozens of pilgrims are received at the court every month. Some come to visit the Lord, and some, usually the younger ones, stay on. For maidens and unmarried men it is a great honor to spend a year in the service of the Lord. They all bring money with them, which they immediately deposit with the steward.

The palace on Petersburger Gasse is sturdily built, with three stories. A heavy wooden gate guards the entrance to the outside courtyard, where the stable, the carriage house, the storehouses for wood, and the kitchen are located. On the Petersburger Gasse side, which leads straight to the Cathedral of Saints Peter and Paul, are the most beautiful rooms, albeit all in the shadow of the enormous structure of the church. The rooms on the second floor are occupied by the Lord and Her Ladyship Eva, as well as Roch and Joseph, whenever they come here from Warsaw. Here are also rooms for the more important guests, for the closest brothers and sisters of the true faith. When the elders stay in Brünn—the Wołowskis, the Jakubowskis, the Dembowskis, or the Łabęckis—this is where they stay. At the end of the left wing the Lord has his office, where he receives his guests. Strangers are received downstairs, right next to the courtyard. There is also a huge hall where the previous occupant used to hold balls— now it is a place for meetings and study. At the back is the kindergarten, where the youngest children are taught. The Lord does not care to have infants around him, which is why expectant women are sent away from the court, back to their families in Poland, unless the Lord, who some-times likes to suck their milk, determines otherwise.

On the third floor, both sides of the palace have rooms for the men and the women as well as guest rooms. Many have been furnished and arranged, yet there are still not enough to accommodate all the visitors they receive. The Lord does not permit spouses to live together. He is the one who determines who will be with whom, and the truth is there have never been any disagreements on this score.

In such an atmosphere, romances and affairs have been known to blos-som. Sometimes someone who is already in the Lord's good graces re-quests the opportunity to get closer to this woman or that man. Then the Lord either permits it or doesn't. So it went recently with Jezierzański's daughter, Magda Golińska, who, although somewhat ashamed, begged the Lord to allow her to have intercourse with Jacob Szymanowski from the Lord's personal guard, despite the fact that she was already married to Jacob Goliński, who had stayed behind in Poland to run his business. For a long time, the Lord refused consent, but eventually he relented, moved by the grace and beauty of Szymanowski. It turned out to be a bad decision.

Behind the palace and the stables, on the slope, there grows a small garden mostly planted with herbs and parsley. It includes a pear tree that bears very sweet fruit, drawing wasps from all over Brünn. On warm evenings, the young people from the palace and those who are living in quarters around town all come together under that pear tree, and this is where real life occurs. The youth sometimes bring instruments and play and sing; languages join together, and melodies overlap. They sing until one of the older people chases them away; then—with permission—they go out onto the square at the base of the cathedral.

The horses are not kept in the stable all the time, except for maybe the pair needed for the small, everyday carriage. The rest are kept in stables outside the city—beautiful coursers, each pair different. When the Lord needs to leave, he sends someone to Obrowitz on horseback, to bring back horses with a cart.

The Lord does not need horses, however, to go to church. The cathedral is right on his doorstep, its massive stone walls visible from his window, its tower looming over all of Brünn. When its bells ring, everyone gathers in the inner courtyard, wearing their most elegant clothing, forming a retinue. First the Lord goes with Eva, followed by the elders, and behind them the young people led by Jacob's sons, who have recently come to join their father and sister. The gate is opened, and they slowly make their way to the cathedral. The shortness of the distance they must cross gives them the opportunity to mark each step with great solemnity,

giving onlookers time to get a good look at them. The denizens of Brünn gather beforehand to witness this parade. The Lord always makes the biggest impression. He was born a king—tall and broad-shouldered, with additional height provided by his high Turkish fez, which he almost never takes off, and his broad coat with its royal ermine collar. People also look at his Turkish shoes, with their upturned toes. Plus Eva is an attraction in her own right, the most fashionably dressed, head held high, dressed in celadons or pinks. She glides along beside her father like a cloud, and the eyes of the crowd slide right over her, as if she were a particular kind of being made of precious matter, untouchable.

In the early spring of 1774, when Jacob is ailing again, this time with indigestion, he brings in from Warsaw the wife of Kazimierz Szymon Łabęcki, Łucja, one of the women who nursed him back to health in Częstochowa. Now he wishes to repeat the therapy. With no discussion, Łucja packs up and travels to Brünn with her child and her sister, and there she puts herself at Jacob's disposition. For half a year she breastfeeds him, and then she's sent away, and he begins to spend more and more time in Vienna.

In the summer, a host of maidens joins Eva's retinue. Eight of them come from Warsaw: the two young Wołowskas, Lanckorońska, Szymanowska, and Pawłowska, as well as Tekla Łabęcka, Kotlarzówna, and Grabowska. They travel in two carriages, under the escort of their brothers and cousins. After two weeks, the cheerful company arrives. The young ladies are clever, pretty, always atwitter. Jacob watches them from the window as they disembark, straightening their crumpled skirts and tying the ribbons of their hats under their chins. They look like a flock of chickens. They retrieve their baskets and trunks; a few passersby stop to investigate this unexpected density of charm. Jacob appraises them with his eyes. The prettiest ones are always the Wołowskas, thanks to some impudent Rohatyn appeal that appears to be innate in them—no child of the Wołowskis has ever been ugly. And yet it seems that all their twittering annoys Jacob—he turns away from the window, almost irate. He tells them to come in their best dresses after the evening meal in the long hall, where he is accompanied by several of the older brothers and sisters. He is sitting in the new armchair he's had made in the image of the red one he had in Częstochowa, though more ornate, while the brothers and sisters sit against the wall in their usual places. The girls stand in the middle, somewhat skittish; they whisper amongst themselves in Polish. Szymanowski, who is standing next to Jacob, holding in his hand something that is neither a tall spear nor a halberd, shushes them severely. He orders them to take turns going up to the Lord and kissing his hand. The girls go obediently; only one of them starts giggling nervously. In silence,

Jacob approaches and examines each of them in turn. He spends the longest looking at that giggling one, who is black-haired and black-eyed.

"You look like your mother," he says.

"How do you know, Lord, who my mother is?"

There is laughter in the room.

"You are Franciszek's youngest, right?"

"Yes, but not the youngest, I have two brothers after me."

"What's your name?"

"Agata. Agata Wołowska."

He converses with another, Tekla Łabęcka; even though the girl can't be more than twelve years old, her lavish beauty catches the eye.

"Do you speak German?"

"No, French."

"Then how do you say in French: I'm as foolish as a goose?"

The girl's lips begin to quiver. She lowers her head.

"Well? You say you speak French."

Tekla says quietly:

"Je suis, je suis . . ."

It is quiet as a crypt, no one is laughing.

". . . I cannot say it."

"And why is that?"

"Because I only tell the truth!"

Lately Jacob has taken to carrying with him everywhere a staff topped with a snake's head. And now, with this staff, he goes over the girls' shoulders and chests, prying the hooks of their corsets with it, scratching their necks.

"Please remove your frippery. Halfway."

The girls don't understand. Neither does Yeruhim Dembowski, who has turned a bit pale and is communicating with Szymanowski with his eyes.

"My lord . . . ," starts Szymanowski.

"Undress," the Lord says mildly, and the girls start to undress. Not one of them protests. Szymanowski nods, as if to calm them down and to confirm that undressing in public and showing their breasts is completely natural. The girls start to unfasten their corset hooks. One of them whimpers. In the end, they all stand half naked in the middle of the hall. The women, mortified, look away. Jacob doesn't even look at the girls. Tossing aside his staff, he leaves the room.

"Why did you have them debase themselves like that?" Franciszek Szymanowski lays into Jacob now, walking straight out after him. These days he looks like a Pole, with his long black mustache sticking out at the sides. "What did those innocent girls ever do to you? This is how you welcome them?"

Jacob turns to him, pleased with himself, smiling.

"You know I never do anything without a reason. I had them debase themselves in front of everyone for the simple reason that when my time comes, I will elevate them, lift them up above all other girls. Tell them that from me, so they will know it."

### Scraps: How to catch a fish in muddied waters

It is written that there are three things that do not come if you are thinking of them: the Messiah, lost objects, and scorpions. I would also add a fourth: the invitation to depart. It is always this way with Jacob: you need to be ready for anything. I had barely unpacked in Warsaw, and Wajgełe, Sofia, my wife, had just arranged to have the walls of our apartment on Długa covered in printed canvas, when a letter came from Brünn, and in Jacob's handwriting at that, saying to take them some money, for they had run out. Gathering the appropriate funds and placing them inside a barrel, as we had done before in Częstochowa, making believe that we were beer merchants, I set out with Ludwik Wołowski and Nathan's (or Michał's) sons, and within the week we were there.

He greeted us as is his wont—boisterously, loudly, no sooner had we gotten out of the carriage than we were welcomed and treated like kings. The distribution of letters, the telling of how things had been for us all, how many children had been born, and who had died—this took all afternoon. And then, as it was Moravian wine that we were offered, it was of good quality, and it immediately clouded our heads, so that it was only in the morning on the following day that I began to be aware of where I was.

The truth is that I was never able to take much pleasure from that place in Brünn; it was the lifestyle of a lord, and not how it ought to have been. Jacob must have been disappointed that I was not excited about the vastness and exquisiteness of the palace as he proudly took me around his new estate opposite the cathedral, and as we went with the entire court to mass, and there among the pews we had our very own places, like real nobility. I remembered his other homes: the one rented in Salonika, that low windowless burrow that light could enter only once we had opened the door, and the wooden one in Giurgiu, with the roof of flat stones, its clay-patched walls covered in vines. In Ivanie, the one-room hut with the packed clay floor and that cobbled-together stove. And in Częstochowa, too, the stone cell with its window the size of a small handkerchief, always cold and damp. I couldn't feel at home in Brünn, and slowly I started to become aware that I was getting older, and that all these novelties had ceased to appeal to me, and that, having been brought up in Busk in poverty, I would never grow accustomed to such riches. In the church, too—tall, slender, almost gaunt—I felt out of place. In such a church it is difficult to pray; the pictures and the sculptures, even if beautiful, are distant, and there is no way to view them slowly and in peace. The priest's voice carries and reverberates in echoes off the walls—I never understand a thing. At the same time, it is a regime of kneeling, and that I have mastered quite well.

Jacob would always seat himself in the first row, ahead of me, in his sumptuous coat and that high hat of his. Next to him was Avachunia, gorgeous as the cake with icing they sell here out of glass cases like it were jewelry, with her hair carefully arranged beneath a hat so elaborate its details absorbed my entire attention. Next to Evunia was Zwierzchowska, charged here with overseeing the women in the stead of a weakening Wittel, and two maids. I would like to send my own Basia here to be a maid, so she could grow accustomed to the bigger world, as in Warsaw she will not learn or understand much, but she is still so young.

And I thought to myself, beholding all this, this whole new world that had opened up to Jacob in this foreign country: Was this the same Jacob? I had taken my last name from him, after all, Jakubowski, as if I were his property, his woman, but I did not find him now as I once had. He had gained weight and his hair was completely white, a legacy of his time in Częstochowa.

He received Wołowski and me in his room, which was furnished in the Turkish fashion, and we sat on the floor. He complained that he could not drink much coffee anymore, for it dried out his stomach and in general greatly interfered with his health, which surprised me, for he always used to be as if he didn't have a body at all.

And so those first days we spent looking around the area, going to mass and conversing, yet our conversations were barren in some way. I was uneasy. I tried hard to look at him as I had at that young man we had come across in Smyrna, and I reminded him of how he'd shed his skin entire and how, when we swam in the sea, he was able to save me from my own fear. "Is this what you are, Jacob?" I asked him one day, pretending I had had too much to drink, but in fact extremely alert to how he would respond. He seemed embarrassed. But then I thought that one would be a fool to expect people to remain as they once were, and that it is a kind of o'erpridefulness in us to treat ourselves as constant wholes, as if we were always the same person, for we are not.

As I was leaving Warsaw, there had been rumors among the true believers that the real Jacob had died in Częstochowa, and that the one who was now sitting before me had replaced him. Many believed this, and lately the rumors had intensified; I had no doubt that Ludwik Wołowski, and young Kapliński, Jacob's brother-in-law (for the rumors had reached Wallachia, as well), who arrived just after we did, had come to investigate that very matter, in order to reassure our people in Warsaw and everywhere.

We sat at the table, and I saw how in the faint candlelight all were watching Jacob carefully, observing his every wrinkle. Ludwik Wołowski, too, stared at him so, having not seen him for a long time and being no doubt shocked by the transformations. Suddenly Jacob stuck out his tongue at him. Ludwik turned crimson and spent the rest of the evening looking morose. Over supper, once we had discussed all that there was to discuss, I asked Jacob: "What is it you're planning to do now? Just be here? What about the rest of us?"

"My greatest hope is that more Jews will come to me," he responded. "For untold strength will come with them. In a single column there won't be fewer than ten thousand . . ." So he spoke,

and also of banners and uniforms, and of his wish for his own
guard; the more wine he drank, the bigger his plans became. He
said that we had to ready ourselves for war, and that these were
times of trouble. Turkey had weakened, and Russia was growing
stronger. "War is good for us—in muddied waters you can fish out
a little something for yourself." He grew more and more heated:
"There will be a war between Austria and Turkey, that is certain—
and what if we were to secure ourselves a coveted piece of land
during all that wartime turmoil? For that we'll need hard work and
gold. The idea being that we could gather around thirty thousand
people at our own cost, arranging with Turkey to support them in
the war, and in exchange receive a piece of land for a small
kingdom somewhere in Wallachia."

Wołowski added that Hayah had also prophesied in Warsaw—
and several times in a row—great changes in the world, fire and
conflagration.

"In Poland the king is weak, and chaos reigns—" Ludwiczek
started.

"I'm done with Poland," Jacob cut him off.

He said it bitterly, aggressively, the way he used to be, as if he
were challenging me to a fight. And then everyone was going on
about having our own land, talking over each other, the very idea
having set their imaginations on fire. And the two Pawłowskis, who
had also come with their wives, and even Kapliński, Jacob's brother-
in-law, whom I considered to be an exceptionally prudent person,
also took to this unrealistic vision. Nothing but politics mattered to
them anymore.

"I've given up on having our own land," I cried into the
drunken, animatedly conversing little crowd—but no one
heard me.

To my astonishment, Jacob bade Yeruhim Dembowski and me to
record his evening chats. First Eva's dreams were recorded by
Antoni Czerniawski, son of those Czerniawskis of Wallachia who
had looked after the money in Ivanie, and he filled a lovely little
book with these. But I was surprised by this new request, since he
had always rejected my previous pleas to sanction such record-
keeping.

Clearly he felt safe in Brünn. Maybe Moshe Dobrushka had
influenced him, too. He would visit often and insist to Jacob that
such writings, while they needn't include things not intended for

outside eyes, would give the growing number of Jacob's followers insight into his thoughts and stories. Writing such a book would be an extremely noble act, said Moshe Dobrushka, especially for posterity.

First Yeruhim, that is, Jędrzej Dembowski, would write, and then I. If we were not there, the Czerniawskis' son Antoni would sit in for us, as he was a particularly clever boy, and thoroughly devoted to Jacob. And it was to be written in Polish, for we had long since abandoned our old language. Jacob himself spoke as he wished: in Polish, in Yiddish, sometimes whole sentences in Turkish, and he also made many Hebrew intercalations; I had to rewrite it all, for no one would have been able to make it out from my notes.

I recalled how once I had wanted to be beside Jacob as Natan of Gaza was beside Sabbatai Tzvi, exalting him and showing Sabbatai himself that he was the Messiah, since Sabbatai did not know who he was. For when the spirit enters into a person, it happens as if by violence, as if the air were to penetrate the hardest stone. Neither the body nor the mind that the spirit has entered are fully aware of what has occurred. Thus there must be someone who pronounces it, who names it. And that is what I did with our holy Mordechai in Smyrna—we were witnesses to the descent of the spirit into Jacob; we put it into words.

Yet it seemed to me that since my arrival in Brünn an invisible wall had arisen between Jacob and myself, or a kind of curtain—as if someone had strung up the finest muslin sheets in that space.


### *The Lord's words*

"Three are hidden from me, and of the fourth the lot of you is ignorant." What do those words of Jacob mean? They mean that there are three Gods who are very powerful, and they exercise an uncompromising rule over the world in its entirety. So said the Lord, and I wrote it down after him. One God gives life to everyone, and for this reason, He is good. Another God gives wealth—not to everyone, but only to those he wishes. The third God is Malakh haMayet—the Lord of Death. He is the strongest. And that fourth, the one of whom we are all ignorant—that is the Good

God Himself. You cannot arrive at the Good God without having first passed through the other three.

All this, said Jacob, and we wrote it down, was unknown to Solomon, who tried to force his way up to the Highest One, but he could not reach him, and so he had to pass away from the world, without bringing it eternal life. Then a call reverberated through the heavens: "Who will go in search of eternal life?"

Jesus of Nazareth replied: "I'll go." But he, too, accomplished nothing, although he was very wise and learned, and though his power was great. Then he went to those three who rule the world, and by the power of the Good God, he began to heal, but those other three saw it and grew uneasy that he would take control over the world, for they knew from the prophecies that the Messiah would come and that death would be swallowed for ever and ever, amen. Thus Jesus of Nazareth came to the first of those three, and that one let him through to the second, and then that one let him through to the third. But the third, who was the Lord of Death, took him by the hand and asked: "Where are you going?" And Jesus said: "I am going to the fourth, who is the God of Gods." At this the Lord of Death grew angry and said: "I am the Lord of the world. Stay here with me, you will be my right hand—you will be God's Son." And then Jesus understood that the power of the Good God was not with him, and that he was defenseless as a child. Then he said to the Lord of Death: "Let it be as you say." But the Lord of Death responded: "My son, you must sacrifice your body and your blood for me." "What do you mean?" Jesus replied to this. "How can I give you my body, when I have been told to bring eternal life into the world?" And that God, the Lord of Death, said to Jesus then: "It cannot be that death does not exist in the world." And Jesus answered: "And yet I told my disciples that I would bring eternal life—" The Lord of Death interrupted him: "Tell your disciples that that eternal existence will not be in this world, but in the next, as it stands in the prayer: 'And after death eternal life, amen.'" And this is why Jesus remained with the Lord of Death and brought a more powerful death into the world than even Moses. Jews die against their will, without desiring it, without knowing where they go after their deaths, while Christians die gleefully because they avow that each has their part in heaven with Jesus who sits to the right of the Father. And so Jesus went from this world. Many centuries on, once again the call resounded: "Who will go?"

In answer to this, Sabbatai Tzvi said, "I will go." He went like a child, gaining nothing, accomplishing nothing.

That is why I was sent after him, Jacob says, and the silence among his listeners is that of the crypt, as if Jacob were telling them some kind of fairy tale, as if they were children. I was sent, he said, in order to introduce an eternal existence into the world. I have been given that power. But I am a great simpleton, and I cannot go alone. Jesus was a great scholar, and I am a simpleton. To those three you have to go quietly, down winding roads, and they can read our lips even when we do not say a word. There is no need to shout; it is possible to move along in silence, keeping quiet. I will not go forth, however, until the time has come for my words to be fulfilled.

Only some of them recognized in this tale our holy treatise, which only in this simplified and broken form could really reach people.

When he had finished, they begged him to say something else. So he started a new story.

It is like it was with a certain king who founded a great church. The foundations were laid by a certain foreman, an elbow deep and high as a man. And when he was supposed to keep on building, suddenly that foreman disappeared for thirteen years, and when he came back, he took to building the walls. The king asked him why he had gone off without a word and abandoned his work like that.

"My king," answered the foreman, "this building is very big, and if I had tried to finish it at once, the foundations could not have borne the weight of the walls. That is why I went away intentionally, so that the foundation would be good and settled in. Now I can start putting up the edifice, and it will be eternal and will never fall down."

Soon I had dozens of pages containing such stories; Yeruhim Dembowski had the same.

## The bird that hops out of a snuffbox

Moshe, when he appears at court in Brünn, brings with him some craftsmen who speak in German with a strange accent.

First he shows Jacob and Eva the drawings.

He explains in great detail all the advantages of the invention, though

Jacob appears not to understand how it works. Apparently the very same thing is at the imperial court, where Moshe has many friends and acquaintances. He is sometimes there himself, and he is hoping that soon he will also be able to take Jacob and his beautiful daughter. From now on, he wants to be called Thomas.

It is actually quite simple, and after just a few weeks it becomes clear how it works. It is a stone bowl placed in the highest room, beautifully polished; inside it there is a pipe that rises clear up through the roof, and, like a chimney, it extends outside. They had to pull off a few of the roof tiles and build wooden frames to support it, but it is all in operation now.

"Camera obscura," says Moshe-Thomas with pride, like the master of ceremonies in a theater. The women applaud. With his hands on their flexible wrists Thomas makes circles in the air, the lace on his cuffs swishing around. His kind, smooth-shaven face, his wavy hair. His broad smile

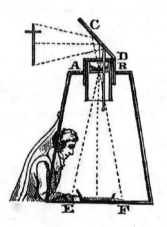

and slightly crooked teeth. Who could resist this young man who has a hundred ideas a second, and who works faster than anybody else? thinks Eva. They each go up to the bowl, and what do they see?

It is exceptional. Leaning in over the polished inside, they can see all of Brünn in that bowl, the roofs, the church towers, the narrow little streets running up and down the hill, the trees' crowns, the market with all of its stalls. And this is no dead old picture—everything moves, why, look at Alte Schmiedegasse, that four-horse-drawn carriage, and over there, those nuns leading the orphans, and there, the workers laying pavement. Someone sticks out a finger to try to touch the picture but withdraws it in shock at once: this view of the city has no material character at all. Fingertips feel just the chill of polished stone.

"You will be able to keep an eye on the whole city, Lord. It is a great invention, though there is no magic nor Kabbalah in it. It is a product of the human imagination."

Moshe is impudent. He dares to push Jacob in the direction of the bowl, and Jacob gives in to him without protest.

"Seeing, while not being seen—that is truly a divine privilege," Moshe fawns.

Moshe-Thomas gains with this invention the admiration of the youth. Seeing that the Lord is so positively inclined toward him, they begin to treat him a bit like the Lord's son. Especially since the majority of them do not know his real sons. They are back in Warsaw now, the Lord has sent them away, and both were relieved to return to Poland, where they are under the care of Jakubowski and Wołowski.

Jacob looks at Moshe from the window; he examines him very closely. He sees him part the sides of his French jacket, spread his legs wide, in their white silk stockings, in order to draw something with a stick on the ground for the young people gathered around him. He leans in, and you can see the top of his head. His lovely curls only suffer under that wig. His facial hair is barely visible, his skin smooth, olive-hued, flawless. His mother spoiled him too much. Sheyndel spoils her children, and they grow up like little princelings, very sure of themselves, confident, comely. Insolent. But life will take its toll on them.

When he leans out slightly, Jacob notices Avacha, who is also observing this scene from her window, watching this dandy. In her body there is always that same submissiveness, for she does not carry herself like a queen, although he has tried over and over to teach her: spine straight, head high, better to err on the side of too high than too low—after all, she has a beautiful neck, and skin like silk. He has taught her one thing by day, however, and something else by night. Sometimes night breaks forth in the middle of the day, and then her submissiveness attracts him. A slight trembling of her eyelids, her beautiful, completely dark eyes, so dark that when they reflect the light, it looks like they are covered in glistening icing.

Suddenly Thomas, as though knowing perfectly well he is being observed, raises his eyes, and Jacob doesn't have time to move. Their eyes meet for a moment.

Thomas does not notice that, from a different window, Eva is observing him, too.

Come evening, when the Lord is retiring to bed, he sees that the young people have all gathered around Thomas Dobrushka again. There is Eva, Anusia Pawłowska, and Agata Wołowska, along with the younger Franciszek Wołowski. This time Thomas is showing them a snuffbox, as though intending to offer them tobacco. When Franciszek reaches out and touches the lid, however, the snuffbox opens with a clatter, and out of it hops a little bird, which flaps its wings and chirps. Franciszek pulls his hand back, frightened, while the rest of the company bursts into unrestrained laughter. In the end, Franciszek, too, starts laughing. After a while Zwierzchowska—who, according to her custom, is making her rounds of the palace and inviting everyone to put out their candles—looks into the room. Entertained, they call her in.

"Go on, show her," the young people tell Thomas.

"Auntie, have some tobacco," they call.

Thomas holds out to her a small, rectangular object, beautifully decorated. After a moment's hesitation, amused, sensing that a little trick may be in store, Zwierzchowska reaches for the snuffbox.

"Auntie, just press here," Thomas begins in German, but, reprimanded by her gaze, he switches to his funny accented Polish: "Niech ciocia naciśnie tu."

She takes the snuffbox, and the little bird dances that same mechanical dance just for her, and Zwierzchowska, completely losing her seriousness, squeals like a little girl.


## A thousand compliments, or: Of the wedding of Moshe Dobrushka, or Thomas von Schönfeld

The wedding of Moshe Dobrushka to Elke von Popper takes place in Vienna in May of 1775, after the period of mourning for Solomon has ended. Gardens near the Prater are rented for the purpose. As the groom's father is deceased, he is walked down the aisle by Michael Denis, his friend and the translator of Macpherson's famous *Works of Ossian*, as well as the publisher Adolf Ferdinand von Schönfeld, who has come from Prague for this wedding. Before the groom makes his appearance at the church, there is a small Masonic ritual; his brothers from the lodge, all dressed in black, lead him into this new stage of his life with great gravity. Von Schönfeld thinks of Moshe as a son, and he has in fact just embarked upon the complicated bureaucratic procedure of receiving Thomas within the Schönfeld coat of arms. Moshe will become Thomas von Schönfeld.

Now, however, there is a party under way. Aside from the magnificence of the tables, which hold food and enormous bouquets of May flowers, the main attraction is the pavilion, where there is an extraordinary collection of butterflies on display. The man responsible for this is Michael Denis, the groom's employer. Eva's female cousins take her there, and now, leaning over the vitrines, they all admire these wonderful dead creatures pinned onto silk.

"You are a butterfly, too," Esther, the youngest Dobrushka child, says to Eva. This bit of praise lodges in Eva's memory, and she thinks about it for a long time after. For butterflies come from chrysalises, from ugly worms, plump and misshapen, a process that is also documented in one of the vitrines. This reminds Eva Frank of herself when she was Esther's age—fifteen—in the dark gray dress her father made her wear in Częstochowa so she wouldn't attract the soldiers' attention. She remembers the chill of the stone tower, and her mother's contorted joints. An inexplicable sadness overwhelms her, and a yearning for her mother. She doesn't want to think about that, and has been trying to forget. Which has been going fairly well so far.

In the evening, when the lanterns are lit in the garden, she stands in a group, a little tipsy from the wine, listening to the voluble Count von Schönfeld, who, dressed in his long, dark green jacket, raising his glass of wine, turns playfully to the not especially pretty but very intelligent bride:

". . . The groom's entire family is so upstanding that you could not possibly find a better one. Hardworking, loving, they came to their fortune honestly."

The guests make their agreement known, nodding.

"In addition, they have many attributes and talents, and above all, they are ambitious," the count goes on. "And good for them. They are no different in that respect from those of us who were ennobled long ago, in barbarian times, when our ancestors backed the kings with swords or plundered local farmers and took up all their land. You all know perfectly well that not every 'von' is synonymous with great attributes of spirit and heart . . . And we need people who are powerful, in order to share and incarnate that which is most valuable. You can accomplish more from the outset with connections and power. All that we consider to be obvious and universal, the whole structure of the world as we know it, is decaying and crumbling before our very eyes. This house needs reconstruction, and we hold the trowels to repair it in our hands."

There is resounding applause, and the guests' mouths are submerged in the finest Moravian wine. Then the music starts—no doubt there will be dancing. Curious glances dart to Eva Frank, and soon Count Hans Heinrich von Ecker und Eckhofen appears at her side. A smiling Eva gives him her hand, as her aunt has taught her, but at the same time she looks for her father. There he is. He is sitting in darkness, surrounded by women, and he is looking straight at her from all the way over there. She can feel his gaze as if it were his hand. It gives her permission to dance with this graceful young aristocrat who looks like a grasshopper, whose name she can't possibly remember. But then, when a man named Hirschfeld, a fantastically wealthy merchant from Prague, comes up to her, her father almost imperceptibly shakes his head. After a moment's hesitation, Eva declines, blaming a headache.

That night, she hears a thousand compliments, and when she finally falls into bed still wearing her dress, her head is spinning wildly, and her stomach, on account of an excess of Moravian wine, consumed furtively with Esther, seethes with nausea.

## Of the emperor and people from everywhere and nowhere

The great enlightened emperor, who co-rules with his mother, is a handsome thirty-something-year-old man and a widower twice over. He is said to have sworn that he would not get married a third time, which has sent many young ladies from the best homes into despair. He is reserved and—even those who know him best say this—shy. A shy emperor! He lends himself a little courage by slightly raising his eyebrows, which makes him feel like he is looking down on everyone. His girlfriends say that he is not very present in bed, and he finishes quickly. He reads a great deal. He corresponds with the Prussian Frederick, whom deep down he admires. He imitates him in that he sometimes goes out into the city incognito, dressed as an ordinary soldier, and in this way he sees with his own eyes how his subjects live. Naturally he is discreetly accompanied by bodyguards, also in disguise.

He seems to have a slight inclination toward melancholy, and he is interested in the human body and its mysteries, all those bones, remains, human skulls. He also likes taxidermy and rare monsters. He has set up a fantastic Wunderkammer, where he takes his guests; he is amused by their childish surprise, their disgust blended with fascination. In that moment he carefully watches his guests—yes, now that polite smile of theirs falls away, that obsequious grimace they all have on their faces as they interact with the emperor. Then he sees who they really are.

Soon he would like to turn this Wunderkammer into an organized, systematic collection, divided into classes and categories—then his collection of curiosities could become a real museum. It would be an epochal transition—the Wunderkammer represents the old world, chaotic, filled with anomalies and incomprehensible to reason, while the museum is the new world, enlightened by the glow of reason, logical, classified, organized. When it opens, this museum will be a first step toward further reforms—toward fixing the nation. He dreams, for instance, of reforming the overgrown, overly bureaucratized administration that devours enormous sums from the treasury; he dreams of abolishing the serfdom of the peasants. Such ideas do not please his mother, the Empress Maria Theresa. She considers them newfangled eccentricities. They disagree completely on such questions.

And yet the question of the Jews is one that interests them both. The task the young emperor has set himself depends upon freeing the Jews for their own good from their medieval superstitions, as the natural and indubitable talents of these people are now being exploited for all kinds of Kabbalah, suspicious and unproductive speculations. If they could properly educate themselves at the same level as the rest of the population, they would be of considerably greater service to the empire. The emperor's mother would like to draw them into the one true faith, and she has heard that this would be possible with a great many of them. When, therefore, on the list of those wishing to visit the emperor on the occasion of his name day there appears the name Joseph Jacob Frank, Joseph II and his mother are greatly pleased and curious, since lately everyone has been talking of this Frank and his daughter.

And as his companions from the lodge recommend Jacob to him, the emperor invites this strange pair, father and daughter, with enthusiasm and out of curiosity, during the time designated for artist visits, and he brings them to the Wunderkammer. He leads them in among the vitrines, where he has collected the bones of ancient animals and the giants who evidently once roamed the earth. He converses with Frank through an interpreter, while with his daughter he speaks French; this creates a certain discomfort. Therefore he prefers to focus on the father. Yet out of the corner of his eye he watches this interesting woman and sees that she is shy and not very sure of herself. The rumors of her beauty strike him as exaggerated. She is pretty, but hers is not a dazzling beauty. He knows many more beautiful women. In principle he is suspicious and mistrustful toward them—there is often something perverse about them; they are always out to get something. But she seems straightforward, skittish, not alluring and not pretending. She is petite, and in the future, like all women from the east, she will be plump; she has now reached full bloom. She has a pale complexion that seems slightly celadon in color, without much pink in her cheeks; she has enormous eyes and terrific hair arrayed up high; onto her forehead and her neck fall pretty, flirtatious curls. Her tiny hands and feet seem almost childish. She does not have the dignity her father does, he being tall, well built, ugly, and self-assured. The emperor is pleased to find that Eva, despite her intimidation, is a wit. He performs a little test—he takes them to the shelves where human embryos float in murky liquid inside great jars; most of them are monstrous specimens. Some have double heads, others torsos, others still have a single great big eye, like a Cyclops. Father and daughter look on without disgust, with curiosity. A point in their favor. Then they go over to the horizontal person-sized case that holds "Sybilla"—that is how he thinks of her—his wax model of a woman with her face in ecstasies, her belly open so that you can see the intestines, the stomach, the uterus and bladder. Usually women faint or at least feel sick when they come to this exhibit. He watches Eva Frank's reaction with interest. She leans over the showcase and, flushing, examines the contents of the woman's belly. Then she raises her head and looks inquiringly at the emperor.

60

*cach i wſzelkich luminacyach, i cokolwiek do tego przyrownywać ſię może; naprzykład Niebo jaſne, dzień, luſtra, lichtarze, lampy, także huty, węgle, kominy, i cokolwiek z ognia pochodzić może.*

Podczas takich Snow gdy Xiężyc zoſtaie w *Baranie*: znaczy turbacyą. w *Byku*: gościa przyſłego. w *Bliźniątach*: pieniędzy przyſpoſobienie. w *Raku*: choroba. we *Lwie*: ſzkoda. w *Pannie*: turbacya kłopot. w *Wadze*: nowe rzeczy ſłyſzeć. w *Niedzwiadku*: turbacya głuwna z ſłabością ciała. w *Strzelcu*: ſtrzeż ſię byś czego nieutracił. w *Koziorożcu*: boleść umyſłu, albo co nowego z ſzkodą. w *Wodniku*: boleść wewnętrzna; w *Rybach*: ſtrwożenie ſerca, albo wielkie rzeczy nowe.

JAZDA.

*O jeżdżeniu na koniach i wozach; także o koniach rządzikach, kulbakach ſzorach, uzdeczkach, i cokolwiek do nich należy: także o karetach, kolaſkach, wozach i wſzelkich bagażach.*

61

Podczas takich Snow, gdy Xiężyc zoſtaie w *Baranie*: znaczy ſię choroba. w *Byku*: boleści przymnożenie. w *Bliźniętach*: przyiście przyiaciela. w *Raku*: ſtrzeż ſię wody. we *Lwie*: życie długie. w *Pannie*: bitwa albo utarczka. w *Wadze*: będzieſz poniżon; w *Niedzwiadku*: turbacya. w *Strzelcu*: obmow uwłaczanie, albo odmowienie w jakiey proźbie. w *Koziorozcu*: ujma tobie. w *Wodniku*: gość przvidzie, albo poydzieſz na uczte. w *Rybach*: obmowa albo exkuza w proźbie.

BYDLĘTA i ZWIERZĘTA.

*O Wſzelkich zwierzach, domowym bydle jako ſą lwy, niedzwiedzie, liſy, dziki, zaiące, &c. bawoły, woły, krowy, owce, pſy, &c. ( o procz koni ) zgoła wſzeſkie zwierzęta i ptaki wo ſobliwości ſwoiey.*

Podczas takich Snow gdy Xiężyc zoſtaie w *Baranie*: znaczy ſmutek. w *Byku*: śmierć przyiaciela. w *Bliźniętach*: wyznanie. w *Raku*: bogactwo. we *Lwie*: choroba. w *Pannie*: bol naumyśle. w *Wadze*: uciſk. w *Niedzwiadku*: ſtrzeż ſię wyſtępku. w *Strzelcu*: śmierć. w *Ko*:

"Who was the model?"

The emperor laughs, amused, and then he carefully explains how this uncommonly detailed wax model was made.

As they are returning from the Wunderkammer, Jacob tells verbosely, through the interpreter, of his connections in Warsaw, dropping name after name in the hope one will resonate with the emperor, but unfortunately none of them does. Twice he mentions Kossakowska. He knows the emperor's secretary will remember this rapid-fire list of names in its entirety and check each entry carefully. It is the first time the emperor is talking with people like them, that is, Jews who have ceased to be Jews. One question does not cease to obsess him: Where has their Jewishness gone? He cannot see it in their appearances or in their manners. Eva could pass for an Italian or Spanish woman, and there isn't any nation for her father, no specific place that could stake a claim on him. He is completely original. When the emperor puts some direct question to Jacob, he feels as if he's coming up against the iron sides of the man's will; he senses the incredibly powerful boundaries of his self. These are people from everywhere and nowhere. The future of humanity.

The audience lasts not quite an hour. That same day, the emperor has the Franks sent an invitation to his summer residence in Schönbrunn. His mother, who saw them for the first five minutes of their visit (she does not enjoy being in the Wunderkammer; she claims it gives her bad dreams), shares her son's good opinion. She says that such people are desirable to the state. As if it weren't enough that they are Catholics, they also spend—as has already been reported—up to a thousand ducats a day maintaining their court in Brünn.

"If we could invite all such people to our empire, it would flourish better than Frederick's Prussia," she points out, slightly annoying her son.

## Of the bear from Avacha Frank's dream

Eva dreams—as Czerniawski diligently records—that a great brown bear approaches her. She is afraid to move, so she just stands there, petrified.

But then this bear starts licking her hands and feet. There is no one to save her from this terrible, oppressive embrace. A man arrives and sits down on a chair, the same red chair her father had in Częstochowa. Eva thinks at first that it is her father who has come, but in fact it is some other man, younger, very handsome. He looks a little like the emperor, but he also looks like Franciszek Wołowski and a little like Thomas Dobrushka. And there is also this magician with the white staff they saw at the emperor's in Schönbrunn. He tore a handkerchief into four, put on a black hat, and then waved that staff over it—and when he pulled

out the handkerchief, it was whole again. To Eva's great embarrassment, her father went up to the magician and offered to rip apart his own handkerchief for him, the one he wore around his neck. But the magician said no, that he knew how to do it only when he did his own ripping, which everyone found very funny. So in her dream her savior has the qualities of all those people. The bear leaves, and Eva flies away.

Eva has such strange dreams, all so real to her, that she is scarcely ever parted from the Polish dream dictionary she received from Marianna Wołowska, who brought it straight from Warsaw.

For their trip to Schönbrunn, her father bought her the four most beautiful dresses they could find in Vienna. The sleeves had to be shortened slightly, and other alterations made. Each has a powerful corset, and in keeping with the latest fashion, doesn't even reach her ankles. They spent an entire day buying hats from the milliner. These were so wonderful Eva could not make her mind up as to which to buy. Finally, her father, reaching the end of his patience, bought them all.

———

Slippers and stockings were also required. Her father watched her try them on. He told Magda and Anusia to leave, and he had her get completely naked. This time he didn't touch her. He simply watched, and told her to lie down on her stomach and then on her back. She did whatever he wanted. He appraised her with a critical eye, but said nothing. Anusia cut Eva's toenails and rubbed her feet with oil. Then, according to the Turkish custom, she bathed in scented water, and both her friends rubbed her body with coffee grounds and honey so that her skin would be smoother.

Along with the emperor and his mother, Eva toured the Zeughaus and the gardens. She walked with the emperor when the others stayed behind. She felt dozens of pairs of eyes on her back, as if she were carrying some weight, but when the emperor touched her hand—as if by accident—that weight fell from her shoulders. She had known that this would happen— she just hadn't been certain of when. It was good to know that this was what it was about. Nothing more.

It happened after a humorous play they all watched from the terrace of the Schönbrunn Palace. She can't remember the comedy's contents; she didn't really understand it, in that strange German. But the play had amused the emperor; he was in a good mood. He touched her hand several times. That same evening a lady-in-waiting came for her, Mrs. Stam, or something like that, and told her to put on her best undergarments.

A worried Anusia Pawłowska said, packing up her things:

"How fortunate your period is over."

She bridled at this, but it was true: it was fortunate that her period was over.

## Of the high life

With the help of Jędrzej Dembowski, Jacob Frank rented an apartment on the Graben for the season. At the same time, he sent Mateusz Matuszewski to Warsaw for money, with a letter to all the true believers there, the entire machna, in which he informed them that he was in negotiations with the emperor. Mateusz was tasked with telling them everything in order, describing every detail of Brünn and their new court, as well as Eva's expeditions to see the emperor and Jacob's being on such familiar terms with him.

The letter read as follows:

> Notice that before I entered Poland, all the nobles were just sitting there, minding their business, and the king with them, and yet as soon as I went into Częstochowa, I had a vision that Poland would become divided. It is the same now, too—can you all possibly know what is happening between the kings and emperors, and what they've been deciding amongst themselves? But I know it! You see yourselves that it has been almost thirty years now that I am with you, and yet none of you knows where I'm going. Where I am headed. You all thought all was lost when I was imprisoned in the Częstochowa fortress in those close quarters, sentenced to life. But God chose me, as I am a simpleton and do not chase after honor. If you had stood firmly behind me, if you had not abandoned me back then in Warsaw—where would we be now?

Mateusz comes back in three weeks with money. They have raised more than the Lord requested, thanks to news of an ancient manuscript discovered in Moravia, in which it was written in black and white that during its final days, the Holy Roman Empire would pass into the hands of some foreign person. And apparently it was stated, too, that it would be a person in Turkish attire, but without a turban on his head, wearing instead a high red hat embroidered with a slender lamb, and that he would overthrow the emperor.

They needed to buy so many new things.

First, a coffee service of Meissen porcelain, decorated with little gold leaves, with little pictures of pastoral scenes painted with the tiniest of brushes, similar to the one Eva saw in Prossnitz. Now she will have her own porcelain, even more distinguished than that.

In addition, accessories for bathing, which must be purchased from the most fashionable merchant. Special costumes, towels, folding chairs, cover-ups lined with soft fine linen. When Jacob Frank and Michał Wołowski go to bathe in the Danube, they are accompanied by a crowd of Viennese onlookers, and since Jacob swims well, he shows off his vigor in the water like a young man. The townswomen squeak with excitement over this man who is not young, after all, but still so handsome. Some throw flowers into the water. Jacob is always in a good mood until evening after bathing.

Eva's horse, with its slender gambrels, must also be paid for and brought in from England. It is completely white; in the sun it gleams silverish. Yet Eva is afraid of it, as the horse balks at the clattering carriages, at glimmers of light, at little dogs, and rears up. It costs a fortune.

They also have immediate need of four dozen pairs of satin slippers. They fray if you walk down the street in them for any length of time, which means they are good for exactly one promenade, after which Evunia gives them to Anusia, since Magda's feet are overly large.

In addition, sugar bowls and porcelain plates. Silver cutlery and platters. Eva considers gold to be too ostentatious. They need a new and improved cook, and a woman to help her. They could also use two more girls to clean—that costs less than the dishes and the silverware, but it still costs quite a bit. Following the death of the little Polish dog Rutka, Eva consoles herself by ordering two greyhounds, also from England.

"What if I were to scratch you and remove what's on the surface—what would I find underneath?" asks Joseph, by the grace of God the Holy Roman Emperor, Archduke of Austria, King of Hungary, Croatia, Bohemia, Galicia, and Lodomeria; Duke of Brabant, Limburg, Lothier, Luxembourg, and Milan, Count of Flanders, etc.

"What do you think?" answers Eva. "You'll find Eva."

"And who is she, this Eva?"

"Your Majesty's humble servant. A Catholic woman."

"And what else?"

"Daughter of Joseph Jacob and Josepha Scholastica."

"And what language did they speak with you at home when you were growing up?"

"Turkish and Polish."

Eva doesn't know whether this is the right answer.

"And the language the Jews speak, does Miss Eva know that, too?"

"A little."

"And how did your mother speak to you?"

Eva doesn't know what to say. Her lover helps her:

"Say something in that language, please."

Eva ponders.

"Con esto gif, se vide claro befor essi."

"What does that mean?"

"Your Majesty must not ask so many questions. I barely remember all that now," Eva lies.

"You are lying, Miss Eva."

Eva laughs and turns over on her stomach.

"Is it true your father is a great Kabbalist?"

"It is true. He is a great man."

"That he can turn lead into gold, and that's how he has all his money?" her lover teases.

"Perhaps."

"And you, too, Miss Eva, must be a great Kabbalist. Look at what you do to me."

The emperor indicates his rising member.

"Yes, that is my magic at work."

When the weather is good, they always take a walk around the Prater, newly opened to the public by the emperor. Open carriages, like so many boxes of chocolates, carry Viennese bonbons—elegant women in wonderful hats—and next to them, gentlemen on horseback who bow to their acquaintances as they pass. Those on foot go as slowly as they can, in order to relish their surroundings. There are dogs on leads, monkeys in chains, much-loved parrots in silver-plated cages. Jacob has ordered his daughter a special little English carriage, just for these walks. Magda and

Anusia accompany Eva in this sweet little vehicle most often, sometimes only Magda. There is a rumor that she is also Jacob's daughter, but illegitimate. When you look at her closely, she really does look like Jacob—she is tall, with an oval face, white teeth, more distinguished than Eva even, so that those who do not know them sometimes take Magda for Eva Frank herself. People also say that they all look alike, like members of those blackamoor tribes the emperor sometimes shows as living freaks and monsters.

## A machine that plays chess

A certain de Kempelen created for his amusement a machine depicting a Turk in an elegant Eastern costume, with a dark face, shiny and polished, and quite friendly-looking. This machine sits at the table and plays chess, so well that so far no one has beaten it. It would seem that during the match it thinks and gives its opponents time to consider their next move. It rests its right hand on the table and moves the pieces with its left. If the other player makes a mistake and breaks a rule, then the machine shakes its head and waits until its opponent recognizes and corrects his mistake. The machine does all of this on its own, having no external power attached to it.

The emperor has gone mad for this machine. He has lost to it repeatedly, but apparently some people in France have defeated it. Can that be possible?

"If a machine is capable of doing what man can do, and even doing it better than man, then what is man?"

He asks this question over tea, sitting with the ladies in the garden. None dares to answer. They wait for him to say something. He has a tendency to speak at length, and often asks rhetorical questions that he himself answers a moment later. Now, too, talking of life, that it is an entirely natural and chemical process, even though it was initiated by a higher power—he doesn't end this sentence with a period, rather just suspends it, so that it hangs in the air like pipe smoke. Only when he issues orders do his sentences end with periods, and this brings everyone relief: at least then they know what's going on. At the very thought of saying something in such company, Eva flushes and has to cool herself down with her fan.

The emperor is still interested in the latest achievements in the field of anatomy. To keep "Sibylla" company, he has purchased a wax model of a human body without skin, the circulatory system marked; when you look at it, you see that the human body, too, resembles a machine—all those tendons and muscles, the coils of veins and arteries, which look like the skeins of embroidery floss used by his mother, the joints that look like levers. He shows Eva Frank his acquisition with great pride—it is once more the body of a woman, this time with her skin removed, the threads of her veins wound through her muscles.

"Could not all that be shown upon a man?" asks Eva.

The emperor laughs. They lean in together over the wax body, their heads almost touching. Eva gets a distinct whiff of his breath—like apples, no doubt from wine. The emperor's bright, smooth face suddenly turns red.

"Maybe people do look like that without their skin, but I do not," Eva says freely, provoking him.

The emperor bursts out laughing once again.

One day, he gifts Eva a mechanical bird in a cage. When it is wound up, it flutters its tin wings and releases a chirp from somewhere inside its throat. Eva brings it back to Brünn, and the little bird in the cage becomes the main attraction throughout the court. Eva winds it up herself, always with the greatest solemnity.

The custom they have is that when the emperor wishes to see the lovely Eva, he sends a modest coach for her, without any coats of arms or decorations, in order not to call attention to her visits. Eva, however, would prefer to travel to him in the imperial carriage. Once it came for her and her father, when she was staying in that large apartment with him on the Graben. For the emperor's mother has taken a liking to Jacob Frank and permits him to come into her private rooms, where she spends a considerable amount of time with him. Apparently they sometimes even pray together. The truth, however, is that the empress likes hearing the stories of this exotic, pleasant man with his Eastern manners, a person without anger or any type of impetuousness. Jacob confesses to her in great secrecy how they were baptized in Poland, having been for years now in the true faith. And he tells her of Kossakowska, with whom the empress in fact has quite a bit in common, tells her of how that good woman helped them come into the bosom of the Church and took such wonderful care of Jacob's wife, may she rest in peace . . . This is to the empress's liking, and she inquires further after Kossakowska. They also often talk about very serious subjects. The empress, for instance, ever since ending up with all of Galicia and Podolia after the partition of Poland, dreams of a vast empire down to the Black Sea, including the Greek islands. Frank knows more of the Turkish lands than her best ministers, and so she asks him for all the details of everything: of sweets, of food, clothing, whether the women wear undergarments and if so what kind, how many children there are per family on average, what life is like in the harem, and whether the women aren't jealous of one another, whether the Turkish bazaar isn't closed for Christmas, what the Turks think of the inhabitants of Europe, whether the climate in Stamboul is better than Vienna's, and why they favor cats over dogs. She pours him coffee herself from the little jug and convinces him to add milk to it—such is the latest trend.

When Jacob returns from seeing her, he tells the brothers and sisters of their meetings, and the brothers and sisters thrill to imagine the Lord with Eva at his side as Viceroy of Wallachia. What, in comparison with such visions, were the dreams they had so recently held so dear—those miserable few little villages in Podolia that now strike them as terribly amusing and childish. Jacob goes to the empress with gifts; there is no visit at which Maria Theresa does not receive something, now a cashmere scarf, now hand-painted silk kerchiefs, now shoes decorated with turquoise, made of the finest Turkish leather. She has set them aside as if uninterested in such luxury, but deep down she is delighted by these presents, as she is by Jacob's visits. She realizes that many must hate him. He is naturally gallant, and he has that sort of ironic humor that she particularly likes. Her sympathy for this man must make many people feel uneasy. All kinds of denunciations and reports are always landing on the empress's desk. The first of one day's stack informs:

> . . . a no less suspicious thing was the source of his income,
> a quite substantial income, when he was living a life of luxury
> in Warsaw. It is said, for instance, that this Jacob Frank has his
> own postal service, people stationed up and down the Polish

borders, through whom he sends his communiqués.

Consignments of money, always in barrels, come to him under escort by his own guard.

"What of it?" she responds to such doubts to her son. "Bringing in gold across our borders and spending it here, where we are, merely enriches us. Better he land among us than if he were to find himself in Russia."

Or there is the accusation that Frank is arming his private guard, ever more numerous.

"Let him arm himself," says the empress. "Let him take care of his own safety. Did not our aristocracy in Galicia have their own army? He may yet be of service to us as a commander."

And she says to her son in a quieter voice:

"I have my designs for him."

Joseph thinks she has returned to her reading now, but after just a moment she adds:

"But you should not make any designs on her."

The young emperor says nothing in response to this and leaves. His mother often humiliates him like this. He is firmly convinced that this is the stubborn peasant Catholicism in her.

## 27.

## How Nahman Piotr Jakubowski is appointed
## an ambassador

The court in Brünn is not just a place for idle merrymaking or a vanity fair. In the chancelleries upstairs, the work never stops. Jacob goes there first thing in the morning and dictates letters that must then be copied out and sent. Next door, under the direction of Zwierzchowska, is the court's bookkeeping. In the third chancellery, the Czerniawskis—the Lord's sister and her husband—conduct the youth recruitment, respond to letters, and negotiate with the parents of young people sent to the Lord's court. Insofar as the second chancellery is occupied with courtly matters, the first is a little ministry of foreign affairs. The third, meanwhile, is focused squarely on trade and the economy.

As late as December 1774, Jacob's best messengers travel from Vienna to Stamboul: Paweł Pawłowski, Jan Wołowski and his brother-in-law Jacob Kapliński, Hayim, who, after Tovah's death, gathered together his whole family and brought them to Brünn. Before their departure, a solemn ceremony is held, during which Jacob gives a speech. He calls them warriors of the Messiah, says they have no religion; they have heard this many times. The only important thing is their mission, which is a secret one—they are to curry favor with the sultan, and offer their services to their former patrons. On the evening preceding their departure, the communal prayers go on at great length, concluding with prayers said in a circle and songs. In these ceremonies everyone takes part, including the guests, but afterward only the brothers and sisters remain, and then the feast begins, with vast quantities of the Moravian wine they have grown so fond of since their arrival. It is like before, in Ivanie, but now the Strange Deeds have become symbolic, have metamorphosed into rituals. They are all so close to one another still, can recognize each other by smell, by touch, and all of it makes them emotional—Jan Wołowski's long face, his just-shaved cheeks, Pawłowska's little shoulders, her short stature, Yeruhim Jędrzej Dembowski's graying mop, Zwierzchowska's limp. They have all aged, they have grown children now, and some of them are grandparents already. Others have buried their husbands or wives and entered into new marriages. They have known terrible trage-dies and great sorrows—the deaths of children, and serious illnesses. Henryk Wołowski, for example, recently suffered an apoplexy, which left him with paresis on the right side of his body, causing him to slur his speech, though his vitality has remained the same as always. Not long ago, supported by his daughters, he personally drilled a colorful legion of motley, very young pseudo-soldiers.

At dawn, when the messengers set out, the house is still quiet. The women readied baskets of provisions for the road the day before. The horses seem a little sleepy. Jacob goes out into the courtyard in a red silk robe and gives each of his emissaries a gold coin and a blessing. He tells them that the future of the true believers depends upon this mission. The carriage rolls over the cobblestones of Brünn to the market square, and from there it will pass out of the city, heading southeast.

They return empty-handed several months later—such experienced ambassadors, and they didn't even obtain a meeting with the sultan, squandering whole weeks in the process. In the spring of 1775, when Ja-cob considers himself the emperor's greatest friend, he sends a second delegation to Stamboul. This time Nahman Piotr Jakubowski goes with Ludwik Wołowski, Jan Wołowski's son. They come back from Turkey in the autumn, their mission having failed again. Not only did they obtain no audience with the sultan, but something much worse occurred: at the instigation of the Stamboul Jews, they were accused of heresy and spent three months in a Stamboul prison, which caused Jakubowski to develop an illness in his lungs. Furthermore, the sultan's officials confiscated all the money they had brought as tribute to the sultan, a considerable sum. Jacob ignored the desperate letters from their cell—maybe he was sick, maybe he was too busy at the emperor's court. It is also possible, as Jakubowski adamantly insists, that no news from Turkey ever reached him. The mission's objective was the same: to win over the sultan, promise him unswerving dedication, reveal to him the benefits of such close access to the emperor, speak to him of the reward there would be if . . . Well, Jakubowski would know how to do it, he's the best at Turkish, and at painting vivid pictures of their visions.

They have come back thin and exhausted; in order to be able to pay for their return, they had to take out loans in Stamboul. Jakubowski is dry as burlap, coughing. Wołowski's face is clouded.

The Lord does not even acknowledge them. In the evening, according to the old ritual, he orders Jakubowski beaten for losing the money.

"I have no use for you, Jakubowski. You're an obstinate old mule," he says. "You're only suitable for writing—not for the real work a person must do."

Jakubowski tries to stick up for himself, but he sounds like a ten-year-old boy.

"So why did you send me, then? Don't you have someone younger, who speaks languages better?"

All punishment here goes like this: The person to be punished is laid down on a table, wearing only a shirt, and all of the true believers who have gathered, brothers and sisters, must lash his back with a switch. The Lord begins, usually slashing without mercy, and after him go the men, but striking less forcefully, while the women usually close their eyes and administer blows that are more symbolic than anything, as if they were tapping the person with palm branches (unless one of them has some reason of her own for hitting harder). And this is how it goes with Jakubowski, too. Doubtless some blows do hurt him, but all in all, he isn't badly wounded. When it is over, he drags himself down off the table. He does not answer Jacob's calls to stay. His shirt hangs almost to his knees, open in the front. His face is absent. People say Jakubowski has grown eccentric in his advancing age. Now he walks out the door, not even looking back.

Following his departure, there is a silence that lasts just a little too long, and everyone's heads drop, so the Lord begins to speak and continues without interruption, fast, so that it's difficult to write it, and Dembowski, left alone with that task now, eventually sets aside his pen. He says that the world will always pose a threat to them, which is why they have to stick together and support each other. They have to give up their old understanding of all things, because that old world has already ended. The new one has come, but it is even more ruthless and hostile than the one it has replaced. These are exceptional times, and they, too, must be exceptional. They must live together, close together, and they must form bonds with one another, not with outsiders, so that they make up one great family. Part of this family will constitute the core, and the rest will surround them. Goods should be treated as common, and only managed by individuals, and he who has the most will share with he who has the least. That is how it was in Ivanie, and that is how it must be here. Always. As long as you all share what you have, as long as you exist as a machna and are a mystery to others. This mystery, this secret, must absolutely be kept at all costs. The less others know about you, the better. They will invent all kinds of extraordinary stories about you, yes—but that is good, let them invent their stories. But on the outside, you must never give a reason for customs or the law to be transgressed.

Jacob tells them to stand in a circle and put their hands on each other's shoulders, with their heads slightly bowed and their eyes focused on a point in the middle of the circle.

"We have two goals," says Jacob. "The first one is making our way to Daat, to the knowledge that will permit us to attain eternal life, and then we will break free of the prison of the world. We can accomplish this in a manner that is very mundane—our own place on the earth, a country into which we can introduce our own laws. And since the world is craving war now, and arming itself, the old order has already fallen, and we, too, must join in with the commotion, so as to gain something from it for ourselves. This is why you must regard my Hussars and my banners without any suspicion. He who has banners and an army, even a modest one, is considered to be a true ruler in this world."

Then they sing the Yigdal, the same song they sang back in Ivanie. And in conclusion, as they are just preparing to leave, Jacob tells them about the dream he had last night, about King Stanisław Poniatowski. That he chased after him and Avacha and wanted to fight. He also saw in this dream that he, Jacob, was led into an Orthodox church that had been completely scorched inside.


## The return of Bishop Sołtyk

In the winter of 1773, a crowd moves from Warsaw to the river. The company, including bishops, crosses the frozen ice to reach an island, where it waits for Bishop Sołtyk as if he were a holy martyr. The church banners stiffen in the cold. Clouds of steam rise from mouths as they sing hymns. Warsaw townswomen wear fur bonnets and are wrapped in fur-lined capes, shrouded further in woolen headscarves. The men wear fur-lined cloaks down to the ground—they are carters, salesmen, crafts-men, cooks, aristocrats. All of them are freezing.

At last, a carriage appears, accompanied by military escort. Everyone rushes to get a glimpse inside, but the curtains are drawn. When the carriage stops, the crowd kneels in the middle of the river, right there in the snow.

The bishop appears just for a moment, supported on either side, wrapped in a long purple coat lined with light-colored fur probably taken from Siberian creatures. He looks big, even heavier than before. Over the heads of the faithful he makes the sign of the cross, and a woeful song bursts forth into the frozen air. It is hard to understand the lyrics, since everyone is singing at their own pace, some slower, some faster, so their intonations overlap and drown each other out.

For a brief moment the bishop's face is visible—it is changed, strangely gray. Instantly people start to whisper that he must have been tortured there, and that is why he looks this way. Then he vanishes into the carriage, which slowly moves along the ice toward Warsaw's Old Town.

Soon rumors spread all over Warsaw that out there, in Kolyma, in that frozen hell, Bishop Sołtyk lost his senses, his clarity of thought returning to him only now and then. Some who knew him before suggest that even when the Russians took him, he wasn't sound of mind. They say that he is among those whose opinions of themselves are so high that it completely blinds them, and wherever they look they see only themselves. And their conviction of their own importance deprives them of their reason and their power of judgment. Bishop Sołtyk is absolutely one of these people, and therefore it hardly matters whether he has lost his senses in Siberia or not.

## What's happening among the Lord's Warsaw machna

The emissaries have to report to the machna on the time spent in Brünn and their failed diplomatic missions. In Warsaw, everything now revolves around the home of Franciszek Wołowski. The machna either meets at his place on Leszno (he has the biggest house) or in the home of his daughter, the one who married Lanckoroński, Hayah's son. It is a difficult time, dominated by a kind of political excitability, an anxiety, so that any news of Brünn sounds improbable here.

In the capital, Jakubowski meets Jacob Goliński, whom he last saw in Częstochowa. He has a strange weakness for him—maybe because Goliński is the incarnation of Jakubowski's memory of his time with the Besht in Międzybóż, which is a memory that always makes him emotional somehow. They embrace, and for a moment they stay standing this way, without moving. Through his heavy coat, Jakubowski can feel how Goliński has lost weight, or seems to have shrunk somehow.

"Are you doing all right?" he asks anxiously.

"I'll tell you later," Goliński whispers, because already they hear Old Podolski, a small, shriveled man in that dark gray caftan buttoned up

under his neck. His hands are stained with ink. He does the accounts at the Wołowskis' brewery.

"I will be so bold as to say it," he pipes up in Polish, in a strong, lilting Yiddish accent. "I am old and scared of nothing now. Especially since it seems to me that you think the same way as I think, you just don't have the courage to say it out loud. Nu, I will say it."

He pauses for a moment, and then starts up again:

"It's over. When he—"

"He who?" someone angrily interjects from over by the wall.

"When Jacob, our Lord, left us here, there was no reason to expect anything more of him. We are bound to take care of ourselves now, to live properly, to stick together, and, without abandoning any of our practices, to cut them back according to circumstances . . ."

"Like rats that flatten themselves to the ground in fear . . . ," says that same other voice.

"Rats?" Podolski turns toward the voice. "Rats are wise creatures; they can survive anything. You are mistaken, son. We have good jobs, food on our plates, roofs over our heads—what rats can you be thinking of?"

"This wasn't why we got baptized," says the same voice, a man named Tatarkiewicz, whose father was from Czernowitz. He is an officer of the post; he's come wearing his uniform.

"You are young and impulsive. Your head is hot. But I am old and good at counting. I tally up all the expenses of our community and know how much gold we have sent to Moravia and how hard earned it was, how we worked to amass such sums here in Poland. For that kind of money, you could send your children to university."

A murmur goes around the room.

"How much have we sent?" Marianna Wołowska asks calmly.

Old Podolski takes the papers from his bosom and lays them out on the table. They all squeeze in around him, but no one understands the tables with the figures.

"I gave two thousand ducats. Just about everything I had," says Jacob Goliński to Piotr Jakubowski, who has sat down next to him. Both of them have remained on their chairs against the wall, knowing that once people start talking about money, it will end in a brawl. "Podolski is right!"

And indeed, the quarrels begin over the table now, with Franciszek Wołowski the elder trying to keep them under control. He hushes them and explains to them that their needless rumpus will be overheard from the street, and that they are turning his home into a Turkish bazaar, that they—polite, well-dressed burghers and clerks—are suddenly revealing themselves to be no better than street vendors from the marketplace in Busk.

"You should be ashamed of yourselves!" he tries.

Suddenly it is as if the devil himself had entered Piotr Jakubowski. He throws himself onto the table, covering with his whole body all the scattered papers.

"What is wrong with all of you? You want to settle accounts with Jacob, like he's some merchant? Don't you remember where you were before he came? And who would you be now, were it not for him? Merchants, tenants with your beards down to your waists, groszy sewn into your shtreimels? Have you already forgotten?"

Krysiński cries:

"But that's what we still are!"

Now Franciszek Wołowski attempts to reason with Piotr Jakubowski:

"Do not, Brother Piotr, get too carried away. We owe a great deal to our own resilience and faith. And to our own hard work."

"He was in jail for thirteen years because of us. We betrayed him," says Jakubowski.

"Nobody betrayed him," says young Lanckoroński. "You said yourself that it had to be this way. You said that yourself, while we, the whole machna, got stronger and tougher those thirteen years, and while we were put to the test, never veering from the path."

By the wall someone—perhaps it is only Tatarkiewicz again—says:

"We don't even know . . . if that's him or not. People say they swapped him."

"You shut up!" Jakubowski screams now, but to his horrified astonishment, the criticism is taken up by Goliński:

"Who are we now? Who am I now? I was a rabbi in Busk; things were going fine for me, but now there's no way back, and I am bankrupt."

Jakubowski flies into a rage, races to his dear friend, and seizes him by his jabot. The pages from the table fly onto the floor.

"You are all petty, despicable people. You have forgotten everything. You would still be stuck in shit, in Rohatyn shit, Podhajce shit, Kamieniec shit."

"Busk shit, too," someone adds out of spite.

Jacob Goliński goes home on foot, alone. He is very troubled. His wife, who has been with Her Ladyship in Brünn for a year now, has not contacted him in some months; he had hoped that Jakubowski would bring some letters from her. He didn't. He seemed to look away when asked, and then that argument erupted, and now Goliński can't quite come back to his senses.

The numbers he saw in Podolski's accounts give him no peace, and he has his own bills in mind—he was a fabric supplier to the royal court, and he was moving pretty high up, but that is over now. He was left with bales of expensive, luxurious materials—no one will buy them from him. Confident in his lucky streak, he put all his savings into the collection for Brünn, believing that in so doing he was aiding his own success and that of his family, but now, suddenly, he sees everything completely differently. As if the scales have fallen from his eyes. Why isn't his Magda writing to him? Until now he hasn't wanted to think about it—he was busy—but deep down in his brain a suspicion grows, almost a certainty, and it is like a malignant tumor, as if he had rotting meat in his head: she is with someone else.

Goliński doesn't sleep all night, tossing and turning, hearing voices, like echoes of that violent argument, and again he sees Jakubowski's averted gaze, and he feels hot all over. He can sense it, he knows it, even though his brain does not want to recognize it fully. Again he counts up his debts, and, half asleep, he sees the mice that nibble at his stocks of crimson brocade and bales of damask.

The following day, on an empty stomach, he walks to Długa Street, to the Jakubowskis'. Jakubowski opens the door, still half asleep, wearing a nightshirt and a dressing gown, looking gaunt and tired, his feet in their dirty socks rubbing one against the other. Wajgełe, in her nightshirt and the woolen scarf she has thrown over it, sets about lighting the stove without a word. Jakubowski looks at him for some time, then finally asks:

"What do you want from me, Goliński?"

"Tell me what happened there. What is going on with my wife, Magda?"

Jakubowski looks down at his socks.

"Come in."

Nahman's—Piotr Jakubowski's—little apartment is cluttered. Here and there are baskets, boxes. It smells like boiled cabbage. They sit down at the table, and Jakubowski scoops the pages off it. He carefully wipes his pen and stores it in its case. Scraps of wine sediment are visible at the base of a glass.

"What is going on with her? Tell me!"

"What do you think is going on with her? How am I supposed to know? I've been traveling, don't you know that? I haven't been sitting around with the women."

"But you have been in Brünn."

A gust of wind strikes the window; its panes shake menacingly. Jakubowski stands and closes the shutters. It gets darker in the room.

"Remember, we used to sleep in the same bed at the Besht's," says Goliński, as if accusing him of something.

Jakubowski sighs.

"You know how things are there. You have seen it with your own eyes. You were there in Częstochowa, you were there in Ivanie. No one is going to supervise your wife there. She is a free woman."

"I was never that close. I was never one of you 'brothers.'"

"But you saw." Jakubowski says this as if heartbroken Goliński were to blame for it all. "She asked for it herself. She's with the Lord's stableman now, Szymanowski. He's kind of like a Cossack when he gets on a horse . . ."

"A Cossack," Goliński mechanically repeats after him. He is shattered now.

"I am telling you this, Goliński, in the name of our many years of friendship, your support after the death of my son, and also because we shared a bed at the Besht's . . ."

"I know."

"If I were you I wouldn't get so worked up about it, because what did you expect? They are doing everything for our greater good . . . With the greatest emperor in the world. The great court . . . If you want her to return, she will return."

Goliński stands up and starts walking around the small room, two steps in one direction, two steps in the other. Then he stops, takes a deep breath, and starts sobbing.

"She didn't ask for it herself, I know that for certain . . . They must have forced her."

Nahman reaches for another glass from the cupboard and pours wine into it.

"You could sell all your stock in Brünn—you'd lose a little on it, brocade isn't the concern it once was. But you'd get some of your money back at least."

Goliński packs up within the hour and takes out promissory notes to cover the journey. A few days later, he finds himself in Brünn, dirty and tired. Having placed the product he has with him in storage, he goes at once to Petersburger Gasse, to the house by the cathedral, with a hat pulled down over his forehead, asking several people for directions along the way. Each of them points out the way to him. He is intending to knock and go in, announcing himself like a person of importance would, but suddenly a suspiciousness sets in, and he feels as if he's about to go into battle, so he stands at the gate opposite, and although it is early, and the streets are filled with the long shadows of morning, he continues to just stand there, pulling his hat down even farther, and to wait.

First the gate opens, and a cart leaves, taking out rubbish and waste, and then some women exit. Goliński does not know them; they are carrying wicker baskets and going up the hill, no doubt to the market. Then a cart with vegetables pulls up, and then there is a rider on a horse. Finally from somewhere a carriage is brought up, it goes inside but doesn't leave again until almost noon, when there is suddenly movement at the gate. Goliński thinks he sees two women: one of them is Zwierzchowska, who is giving something to a messenger, or a post officer, and the other one is the elder Czerniawska. Curtains part in some windows on the second floor, and someone's face flashes there, but Goliński can't see whose. His stomach is aching from hunger, but he's afraid to leave—he might miss something important. Just before noon the gate opens again, and a little procession forms on the street, mostly young people, going to the cathedral for mass, but—again—he doesn't recognize a soul. Only at the end does he see the familiar Dembowski, in Polish attire, with his wife. They walk in silence and disappear inside the cathedral. Goliński understands that neither Frank nor Avacha is here. He grabs the sleeve of one of the youths dashing by and asks:

"Where is your master?"

"In Vienna, with the emperor," the young man answers gleefully.

Goliński spends that night in an inn that is luxuriously clean yet inexpensive. He is able to wash up there and get a good night's rest. He sleeps like a rock. The next day, early, he sets off for Vienna, propelled by the same anxiety.

It takes him all day to get to the Lord's residence on the Graben. At the entrance to the house there are guards, dressed oddly in bright green and red livery, in hats with bunches of feathers. They hold halberds. There is no way for him to get inside. He asks to be announced; no response comes. In the evening a rich carriage drives up, accompanied by several men on horseback. When he tries to approach, the guard stops him quite violently.

"I am Jacob Goliński. The Lord knows me, I have to see him."

They tell him to leave a note in the morning.

"The Lord receives visitors in the afternoon," says one of the valets in his weird livery.


## Eine Anzeige, or: A denunciation

Maria Theresa Walburga Amalia Christina, by the grace of God the Dowager Empress of the Romans, Queen of Hungary, Bohemia, Galicia, and Lodomeria, Archduchess of Austria, Duchess of Burgundy, Styria, Carinthia, and Carniola, Great Princess of Transylvania, etc.

I was born a subject of Your Imperial Majesty's, in Glinno, at a remove of four miles from Lwów. I was raised in Glinno, and I was also a rabbi in that city. It happened that in 1759, one Jacob Frank, a neophyte, currently living in Brünn, passed through there. His father, a Jewish teacher suspected of belonging to a Sabbatian sect and expelled from the kahal, had settled in Czernowitz in Wallachia. Thus Jacob Frank, though born in Korolówka, roamed around the world a fair amount, married, and had a daughter, at which point he took on the Muhammadan faith and was hailed among the Sabbatians as a hakham.

I am ashamed to admit that I, too, belonged to that sect, and that I counted among his worshippers. In my stupidity, I considered him not only a great sage but also the incarnation of the spirit of Sabbatai and a worker of miracles.

In the early part of 1757, the aforementioned Frank came to Poland and called upon the faithful to move to Ivanie, a property held by the Bishop of Kamieniec. There he proclaimed that the great lord and king Sabbatai Tzvi had to cross over to the faith of the Ismaelites, that the god Baruchiah had to pass through it as well, just as he did through the Orthodox one, but that he, Jacob, would have to cross over to the Nazarene faith, since Jesus of Nazarene was the peel of the fruit, and his coming only occurred to make way for the true Messiah. We were all required to convert to this faith and to observe it more closely in the eyes of the Christians than the Christians themselves. We had therefore to live piously, yet not take any Christian women as our wives, for although Señor Santo, that is, Baruchiah, had stated, "Blessed is he who permits the forbidden," he had also said that the daughter of a foreign god was forbidden. Thus under no circumstances were we to mix with other nations, deep down remaining true to the three nodes of our kings: Sabbatai Tzvi, Baruchiah, and Jacob Frank.

After being much persecuted by the Jews, and under the protection of the Bishops of Kamieniec and Lwów, in the autumn of 1759, we agreed to be baptized.

To Frank, who, having come from Turkey, was poor, a large amount of money was given right away; I, too, contributed, offering him 280 ducats to start out.

Then the aforementioned Frank went to Warsaw and there preached to all and sundry that he was the lord of life and death and that those who believed in him with all their hearts would never die.

When, however, in spite of this, some of his closest and greatest supporters did die, and he was asked for clarification, he said that evidently they did not sincerely believe in him.

Some of his company, wanting to put him to the test, informed the Church authorities of everything . . .

"Is that how it was?" Goliński asks the man dictating to him, whose words he is writing down in his beautiful penmanship, stumbling only slightly on the lengthier German turns of phrase. But the other man does not respond to this, and so Goliński simply carries on:

. . . The case was submitted to the royal chancellor, the cathedral chapter, and bishops, who together comprised the court. The company of Frankists openly admitted, for the most part, the error of their ways and solemnly swore that they would refrain from such things going forward and live a Christian life. Frank himself was sentenced to life imprisonment in the monastery in Częstochowa. Unfortunately, that man, possessed as he is by Satan, knew how to draw people to him, even jailed. His followers went to him and lavished him with gifts, and many of them stayed there with him, for he knew, too, how to convince them that his arrest was necessary. And I must confess—again, with great shame—that I, too, was there, and I, too, remained with him in his incarceration, up until the death of his wife and her funeral.

Her death produced a strong effect on many, as did the teachings of Jacob Frank, according to which he praised acts that went against nature and human custom. It was then that I left him and became his enemy. Parting from Częstochowa, I returned to Warsaw, where I lived with my wife and child. Yet my wife has now been in Brünn for four years, most recently in the clutches of some companion . . .

Goliński's hand hovers over that word, "Gefährten."

"You know that, too?" he asks. "Already?"

The man doesn't answer, so after a moment's stillness, Goliński writes on:

> . . . she was with Frank and his daughter in Vienna and has now returned to Brünn, where she agreed to see me, and feeling toward me an understandable tenderness, she disclosed to me that the Holy Lord, as Frank is known to his disciples, had ordered me and the others who attempted to resist him slain in Częstochowa.

"But that's not true. There was nothing like that," says Goliński in surprise, but he keeps going:

> She learned of it since she has everyone's full trust there, being the daughter of one of the most faithful of the Frankists. She therefore warned me so that I might save myself and hasten to remove myself. I filed a complaint with the royal authorities on account of it, and an investigation was launched, as I had

previously entered my testimony into the official report that may now be accessed in Warsaw.

When Poland descended into turmoil, Frank found an opportunity, with the help of the Russian army, to free himself from jail. Then he went to Brünn, where he has been propagating his diabolical faith altogether unchecked.

His coachmen, stablemen, servants, postillions, Hussars, Uhlans—in a word, his entourage—consists exclusively of converted Jews. Every fourteen days, husbands, wives, sons, and daughters come to him from Poland, as well as from Moravia, and even from Hamburg, bringing copious gifts and horses; they are all of them converts from the selfsame sect, which has evidently already spread around the world. They kiss his feet, they stay a few days, and they leave, and then others come to take their places, and thus this novel vermin multiplies with every passing day.

I know that my words are no real evidence, but I am ready to face any punishment if Her Imperial Majesty's investigation does not confirm these seemingly incredible things that have never been heard of since the dawn of the world, yet my denunciation . . .

Goliński considers that word for a moment, finally writes:

. . . will be proved in all particulars.

I thus extreme humbly request of Your Royal-Imperial Apostolic Majesty, on my knees and with the utmost respect, that out of consideration for the importance of this matter, it might be arranged for me to have a confrontation here in Vienna with Jacob Frank, that I could expose all of his crimes and recoup the thousands of ducats he took from me. And with this, for the mistakes I have made up to now, which I wish to erase with this open confession, I implore forgiveness.

> Your Royal-Imperial Apostolic
> Majesty's humblest servant,
> Jacob Goliński

The person who has been dictating this letter to Goliński now takes it from him and sprinkles it with sand. The sand dries the words, and thus they gather strength.

## Coffee with milk: The effects of consumption

Jacob seems to have been harmed by this new fashion for drinking two elements mixed: coffee and milk. It started with some slight indigestion, but soon it was as though his digestive processes had ceased completely, and the weakness that came over him could only be compared with the one that afflicted him in Częstochowa, when he was given poisoned hosts. In addition, his creditors keep pounding at the doors, and there is nothing to pay them with, as enormous amounts have gone to Vienna and been lost on legations. Waiting for Kapliński, Pawłowski, and Wołowski to return from Warsaw with money, he has ordered all expenditures on food to be restricted, and for a contingent of the guests whose maintenance has been a major burden on the court to be sent home. So weak and exhausted he cannot even sit any longer, he dictates letters to the machna in Warsaw, his beloved community. He urges them to be strong like the tree that despite the wind whipping around its branches still stands in place. They are to strengthen their hearts and be brave. He concludes his letter with the words: "Fear nothing."

The dictation so exhausts him that come evening he falls into a deep, deathlike sleep.

This crisis lasts for several days, with the Lord lying in slumber, nothing near him altering except his caretakers, who moisten his lips, and change his bedding. The windows are covered, the communal meals canceled, so that now only simple food is served, bread and potatoes with a tiny bit of lard. No one is allowed onto the second floor, where the Lord's rooms are. The roster of guards is determined by Zwierzchowska, who roams the hallways, tall and skinny, slightly hunched, clanking the keys clipped to her hips. It is she who, still sleepy on her feet one morning as she goes to open up the kitchen, sees the Lord in just his nightshirt, barefoot, standing in the doorway, swaying on his feet. Just look, his lady guardians have dozed off, and he has gotten well. Zwierzchowska wakes up the whole court; they make him broth he refuses to so much as touch. From now on he eats baked eggs, no bread or meat, just eggs, and soon he is himself again. Once more he strikes out on his own for his long walks outside town. Zwierzchowska discreetly sends someone from the court to keep an eye on him.

A month later, completely recovered, he solemnly sets out for the Dobrushkas' home in Prossnitz, where there is a gathering once a year—as is known only to the initiated—of true believers from all over Europe. At the Dobrushkas', they pretend it is a family occasion, who knows whose or what kind. As with the wedding of Isaac Shorr (now Henryczek Wołowski) twenty-seven years ago, everyone is here. Jacob Frank comes in a sumptuous carriage surrounded by his own Hussars. One of them is lightly wounded. They were attacked by Jews just outside Brünn, but the Jews were not well armed. Szymanowski, who always has a loaded gun, shot at them a few times, and they all scattered.

Yente watches all of this—the similarity of the events draws her attention. Over time, moments occur that are very similar to one another. The threads of time have their knots and tangles, and every so often there is a symmetry, every once in a while something repeats, as if refrains and motifs were controlling them, a troubling thing to notice. Such order tends to overburden the mind, which cannot know how to respond. Chaos has always seemed more familiar and safe, like the disarray in your own drawer. And so it is now, here in Prossnitz, that they remember the day in Rohatyn, twenty-seven years ago, that Yente didn't exactly die.

There the wagons rode in the mud, carrying people in damp kapotas. Oil lamps flickered in the low-ceilinged rooms, the men's thick beards and the women's rich skirts gave off the smell of the omnipresent smoke, the wet wood and the fried onions. Now, down the Moravian highways glide carriages on leaf springs, soft and comfortable inside. They drive up to the Dobrushkas' large home, people who are washed and well-fed, nicely dressed, poised and polite. They greet each other in the courtyard, and it is clear just from looking at them that they treat the world as if it were their own cozy apartment. They are nice and friendly toward each other, which just goes to show that this is one big family that has gathered here. And that is exactly how it is. The two local taverns rent them guest rooms. The town's residents examine the newcomers, who speak German with a lilt, but their interest does not last long. Maybe it's a golden anniversary at the Dobrushkas'. That he is a Jew everyone knows, there are plenty of Jews here. They live honestly and work hard. They are different in some way from those other Jews, but no one seems to care exactly how.

For the duration of the proceedings, the women are completely separated from the men and will spend the whole three days in their own company, covering in great detail all questions of who, when, with whom, how, why, and where. These conversations will yield more advantages later on than the setting down of doctrines. They provide ideas for marriages, offer fashionable names for children not yet born, discuss appealing places for the treatment of rheumatism, and connect those seeking good posts with those who need good help. In the morning they read sacred texts and also debate them. In the afternoon they turn their attention to music-making—Sheyndel and her daughters are very gifted and have a lot of sheet music in their possession. As the girls play, the older women, including Sheyndel, pour themselves glasses of cherry liqueur, and that's when a discussion no less interesting than the one taking place on the other side of the wall, among the men, really gets under way.

One of the Dobrushka daughters, Blumele, who is particularly talented, accompanies herself on the piano and sings an old song of the true believers, translated into German now:

> *In a hiding place of iron, in an air balloon,*
> *My soul sets sail on open seas.*
> *No man-made walls can hold it in,*
> *Nor can the heart's own Babylon.*
> *It pays no heed to reputation,*
>
> *To pompous guests at lavish feasts,*
> *To smoothness, courtesy, great nations.*

*My soul breaks free through any border,*
*Ignores the keepers of your order,*
*Flies over words ranged end to end*
*And what words cannot comprehend.*

*It knows not pleasure or night's terror—*
*Your beauty, like a poor relation,*
*My soul drives out, dumps in the sand.*
*O God in heaven up above,*
*Give me Your word, that I may stand*
*Beside You, catch up with Your truth.*

Her clear voice carries so distinctly that some of the men, standing close to the door, listen in, discreetly move away, tiptoe over to the women.

Thomas has come from Vienna for this great gathering. On arrival he goes automatically to the women—before he is absorbed by serious conversations, he wants to converse frivolously. He has brought from Vienna a new party game—you have to convey in sign language some sentence that the rest must guess. Gestures and faces are the most democratic language; the outlandish accent they speak with here will not bother anyone now. He promises them they'll play in the evening, when there will be time for pleasures. He leaves them *The Works of Ossian*, translated by his friend. The women spend the afternoon reading it aloud. Eva does not understand the elation that accompanies this reading, nor the emotion that produces the younger women's tears.

Among the men, Thomas speaks about Masonic ideas. This topic has long aroused the curiosity of the elder brothers from the provinces, and as Sheyndel's son belongs to the lodge, he gives them an impromptu lecture, which in turn engenders a great discussion. One fragment in particular sticks in the brothers' minds. Thomas tells of how in this divided world, made up of factions that set themselves in opposition to each other, and that are called religions, freemasonry is the one place where people of pure hearts may meet and act, stripped of preconceived notions, open.

"Show me another place where a Jew can talk, debate, and act together with a Christian out from under the watchful gaze of the church and the synagogue, the structures of power, the hierarchies that separate people into better or worse!" he shouts over their heads; his white silk jabot has loosened, and his long, wavy hair, neatly coifed at first, has now rebelled. Thomas speaks as if in a fit of inspiration: "The two opposing systems are locked in an eternal struggle, eternally mistrustful of each other, accusing each other of evil deeds and wrong ideas. We actively participate from birth, locking in our own antlers, some of us born this way, others born that way, and it could not matter less how we would like to live—"

Protests rise from the back. There is a heated discussion now, and they won't let Thomas finish. Were it not for the fact that he is one of their hosts, and the fact that this talk is taking place in the evening and is therefore less official, they would have shouted him down earlier. But it is clear to all that Zalman's son has far too hot a head.

That day Jacob speaks at the very end, bravely and with panache. There is nothing in him of those boring old speakers (with the exception of Thomas) who uttered every possible variation of Eibeschütz, Eibeschütz's, Eibeschützian. There is nothing in Jacob's speech about himself or about the Virgin—his young cousin specifically warned him about this, and he has heeded it. The speech is instead about how converting to "the religion of Edom" has now become an absolute necessity. There is no alternative. And about how you have to figure out a place for yourself, as independent as possible, where you can live according to your own laws, but peacefully.

When in the corner there is a whispered outburst, Jacob turns to face in that direction and says:

"You know who I am and how I became who I am. My grandfather, Moses Meir Kamenker, was caught one year before my birth smuggling books of the true faith from Poland to Hamburg. For that, they sent him to prison. I know what I am talking about, and I am not mistaken. I cannot be mistaken."

"Why is it you can't be mistaken, Jacob?" asks someone from the room.

"For within me is God," answers Jacob Frank, with a beautiful smile that reveals his still-white, healthy teeth.

There is some commotion, someone whistles, and they all have to be hushed.

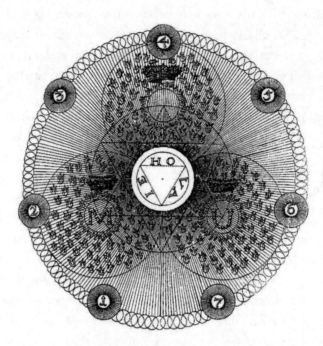

The women and the young play Dobrushka's new game until late. Laughter tumbles forth into the night through all the open windows. The uncontested champion is the young wife of the man who protested the most strenuously against Thomas, the rabbi of Altona, a woman named Fanny.

## A hernia, and the Lord's words

The house in Brünn is no longer as crowded as it once was, but true believers still come in from Rus', Podolia, and Warsaw. These are the poorer guests, who must also be received, of course. Dirty from their long journeys, some of them look like savages, for instance that woman with the Polish plait she refused to have cut, fearing that with it she would lose her life. The Lord commanded that the Polish plait be sheared while she was asleep, and then, saying a prayer over it, he had it ceremoniously burned. The new arrivals are spread out around the whole house and over the kitchen in the yard, where the pilgrims' rooms have been prepared for them, but even this is not enough. So they rent out quarters throughout the surrounding area. During the day, they come to the Lord regardless. He has only to cast a glance at them to evaluate what sort of people they are, and depending on how he judges them, to some he tells fables and anecdotes, to others he explicates difficult and complicated sentences from learned books.

For Hanukkah the Lord himself lights the candles, but he forbids them from praying in Yiddish. For Yom Kippur, meanwhile, he has them sing and organize dances, like they used to do in Ivanie, and even before.

Now the Lord requests Wittel Matuszewska spend the night with him—she has just arrived from Warsaw, where she was spending time with the children. He is happy she is here; he gets a shave, a haircut, has his toenails clipped. Wittel runs toward him from the door and kneels before him in obeisance, but he lifts her up and hugs her, and Wittel turns as bright pink as a peony. He greets her husband, Mateusz, with equal enthusiasm.

When Eva Zwierzchowska falls ill, Wittel takes over her responsibilities, too, and now she rules with an iron fist. She exhorts the young men, drilled-out and idle, to do outdoor chores, like plucking the weeds that grow between the cobblestones in the courtyard, and cleaning up the horse droppings that draw clouds of flies. She has the water carrier bring more water, organizes pickling, taking up great barrels. Only Wittel is permitted by the Lord to speak to him in an ever so slightly reproachful tone. She is even allowed to get angry with him, as for instance when she accuses him—the sisters have already complained to her about it—of always arranging intercourse so that it is good for the men, but not necessarily for the women.

"Well, how would you do it?" asks Jacob. "I do as God instructs me."

"You have to pay careful attention to who is drawn to whom, who likes each other, and who doesn't. If you appoint a couple made up of two people who hate each other, it will only bring suffering and shame."

"The point is not for them to do it to get pleasure from it," the Lord explains to her. "The point is that they must be broken down and come around to one another. The point is for them to form a whole."

"It certainly comes easier to the husbands to be 'broken down,' as you call it, while the women feel horrible afterward."

He looks her over carefully, stunned by what she's said.

"Give the women the right to say no," says Wittel.

His look darkens:

"Well, don't announce it, because then their husbands will tell them to say no."

Wittel says after a moment:

"The women are not that stupid. The women are happy to be with other men . . . Many of them are just waiting for permission; if they don't get the permission, some will do it anyway. It's always been like that, and it always will be."

Following his return from Prossnitz to Brünn, Jacob falls ill again. Wittel Matuszewska claims that these illnesses arise from his complete lack of moderation in eating the local Hermelín, the cheese they make here, which the Lord insists on eating warm and in great quantities. No stomach can digest it, she rages. And this time, his painful hernia returns. At the base of his abdomen, almost in his groin, a thickening appears, protruding from his belly. He had the same thing back in Ivanie. Zwierzchowska and those who serve the Lord day or night tell everyone excitedly that the Lord has two members. In the kitchen it is said that the second member shows itself when something important is to happen. The women giggle, their cheeks pink.

Although there seems to be no medicine for the hernia—and maybe this illness is in fact a visible blessing—the Lord heals on his own. In the forest he loves just outside Brünn there are oak groves; there the Lord selects a young oak's branch and has it cut in half lengthwise, then lights a fire and puts both stone and singed tinder upon his ailment. He wraps the oak around himself and tells everyone to leave. He does this several times, and the hernia abates.

At the same time, he has sent Eva to Vienna and brought in an artist who specializes in miniatures. The Lord has ordered three. Eva has been posing, displeased at having been taken away from the imperial court when at any moment the emperor might summon her. The miniatures are sent to the brothers from Hamburg and Altona with a request for financial support for the court and for the Lady herself, who has been spending so much time with the emperor, a point Jacob insisted be emphasized repeatedly.

At the nightly talks, which often go on until quite late, Jacob first tells fairy tales and parables, and then the more serious discussions begin. His listeners sit on whatever they can find—the older ones in armchairs and sofas, chairs and benches brought in for this purpose from the dining room. The younger ones sit on the floor, on the Turkish pillows that are everywhere here. Those who don't listen let their minds wander to their own affairs, and only from time to time are they dragged back from their musings by someone's not particularly intelligent question or a sudden burst of laughter.

"We will take three steps, remember," begins the Lord.

Three steps—the first is baptism, the second is their entrance into Daat, and the third is the Kingdom of Edom.

Lately the Lord has mostly spoken about Daat, which in Hebrew means knowledge, the greatest knowledge, the same knowledge that is held by God. But it may be made available to humans. This is also the eleventh sefira, which stands in the very center of the Sefirot Tree yet has never been discovered by any person. He who goes with Jacob goes straight into Daat, and when he gets there, all will be annulled, even death. That will be deliverance.

During the lecture, Jędrzej Dembowski gives out printed leaflets with the image of the Sefirot Tree. He came up with this idea not long ago, and he is pleased they have arrived at such modern and enlightened teaching methods. In this way, Jacob's listeners can easily visualize where salvation lies within the larger plan of creation.

## Of a proclivity for secret experiments on substances

Thomas von Schönfeld, who after his father's death invested money in overseas trade with his brothers, is now collecting his first profits. Several times a year he travels to Amsterdam and Hamburg, and also to Leipzig, and returns with good contracts. His brothers have set up a small bank in Vienna and give out loans and collect interest on them. Thomas also conducts research on the emperor's behalf on the subject of Turkey, though the purpose of this research isn't altogether clear; throughout it, he is delighted to make use of the wide-ranging contacts of his uncle, Jacob Frank.

Jacob often summons him by mail and borrows money from banks in Vienna through him. Thomas carries bills of exchange. He urges Jacob to lend the money that comes in from Poland, and get interest off it, or to invest it properly, instead of keeping it in barrels in the cellar, as Czerniawska and her husband want, since they are the court treasurers now.

But the most important thing over the course of this unique uncle-nephew love affair are the strange visits from Thomas's "brothers," as he calls them, such as Efraim Joseph Hirschfeld and Nathan Arnstein, both wealthy industrialists from Vienna, or Bernard Eskeles, a banker who is not interested in money at all, or the printer who is a count and godfather to Thomas von Schönfeld. This count will soon apply for a noble title for his godson.

For now, Thomas uses the "von" without having any right to it, most often when he goes away to Germany or France. Simultaneously, and also through him, correspondence is now under way regarding the title of baron that Jacob Frank would like to have. Here, in Brünn, he uses the last name Dobrucki, which is justifiable, since he is, after all, related to the Dobrushkas of Prossnitz. Thus: Joseph, Count Dobrucki. Jacob is his name for special occasions, like a purple coat worn on holy days.

Long before Maria Theresa's death in 1780, a request appears on her son's desk for the Austrian ennoblement of Jacob Frank, as he already has a Polish title; the request is written in the pleasant, reliable, juridical style of Thomas von Schönfeld. The second letter, attached by his scrupulous and loyal secretary, is a denunciation, written in that characteristic way in which denunciations tend to be written—impersonally, with unshakable certainty, and yet at the same time, almost in a whisper:

> . . . should be aware that there existed in the past, and that there inevitably exists today, as well, a science not universally accessible, having to do with things that would appear to be natural, but which are rather understood as supernatural, along with a tradition of looking at whatever occurs on our planet through the lens of faith in cycles. This tradition boldly engages with something that we, god-fearing Catholics, would never dare to so much as broach—an examination of the question of the Divine Essence. It is said that such studies are contained in the Chaldean book of wisdom called the Zohar. These bits of wisdom are expressed there in an unclear manner that is exceptionally allegorical, so that someone who merely happens upon the text but who is unable to apply the numerological techniques and the Hebrew symbology cannot understand it. And this applies to Jews, as well—only a few of them are capable of understanding what is written there. Among those who can, there is among others a subject of Your Highness's, a man named Jacob Frank who lives in Brünn. The knowledge of this kind of person is sufficient for them to carry out mysterious experiments on matter, with which they astonish the uninitiated. It is pure quackery, but it creates around such people an extraordinary atmosphere and builds false presumptions regarding them. It is said, however, that after the destruction of the Second Temple, the remains of that science were scattered all across the Orient, primarily amongst the Arab

countries. The Arabs, meanwhile, passed it along to the Knights
Templar . . .

The emperor gives a heavy sigh here, he would stop reading were it not
for the fact that he recognizes the signatory's name at the bottom of the
letter. And so he reads further:

> . . . who brought it back again to Europe, making room for
> the generation of many heresies. That same science, or parts of
> it, has become an essential cornerstone of what the Masons
> believe and what their central activities are—but not all of
> them, only those like Thomas von Schönfeld, aka Moses
> Dobrushka, one of the most important among them . . .

"My dear, can your father make gold?" the emperor asks Eva, when a
few days later he has her in his bedroom in Schönbrunn. He calls her
"mein Vogel," or "my bird."

"Of course," says Eva. "Right outside our home in Brünn there is a
passageway to our secret gold mines—they lead all the way to Silesia."

"I'm serious," says the emperor, frowning so that his immaculate forehead is marred by a vertical wrinkle. "I've been told that it is possible."

At an opera premiere, Eva is approached by an elegant, tall, well-built, but
no longer young man. His white wig is perfectly arranged, and his outfit
is exquisite and so different from those worn here in Vienna that there can
be no doubt about his having come straight from Paris.

"I know who you are, madam," he says in French, not quite looking at
her directly.

Eva is flattered that he has recognized her amongst so many important
ladies, and their acquaintance might end on that high note, yet the elegant man goes on:

"You, madam, are someone like me—someone who is a stranger to
this spectacle. Am I right?"

Eva starts. Now she thinks he is impertinent; she wants to go, and reflexively she seeks out her father in the crowd.

"It is evident, madam, that your nobility and beauty are of a much deeper nature, coming from a pure heart; you, madam, are like a star that has erred under these banal roofs, like a lost spark from the purest comet . . . ," the stranger continues. Even if he is a little past his prime, he is still very handsome. His powdered face strikes Eva as impenetrable. Out of the corner of her eye she catches the curious gazes of other women.

Since the emperor isn't interested in her that evening and quickly vanishes with his latest lover instead, Eva spends more time with her new acquaintance. He is too old for her to treat him as a suitor, too soft, too talkative—in fact, he seems to her entirely unmasculine. They go to the smoking room, and her companion offers her some fresh tobacco. He brings her champagne and—stranger still—they converse about dogs. Eva complains that her greyhounds are too delicate and seem silly to her. She misses the dog she had in her childhood. The man turns out to know a great deal about canine behavior and the mysteries of canine breeding.

"Big dogs are sickly and do not live long—greyhounds are a prime example of this, inbred to the point of complete degeneration. The same happens to people," adds the elegant older man. She should have a little dog, but one that is also brave. A little lion. They breed dogs like that in Tibet, where apparently they're sacred.

Who knows how and when the conversation comes around to the "work." It is a topic that fascinates everyone, though few get very far with it; most are only after gold. But after all, alchemy is also the path to wisdom. And Giacomo Casanova explains to Eva Frank in intricate detail the meanings of the individual stages of the "work." Now they are at nigredo.

Eva squeezes her stomach. She has dismissed Magda Golińska, who has a big mouth, and who has now returned to Brünn. Magda is marrying Szymanowski, who took her away from Goliński. Only Anusia Pawłowska knows everything, but they do not speak of it. She helps Eva wrap her hips and her rounded waist, doing it as if it were completely normal. Her touch is delicate but firm. Once Eva's father came to Eva while she was lying in bed, sticking his confident hand under the covers. His rough, bony fingers palpated that embarrassing roundness. Eva bit her lip. Her father lay down next to her and petted her head, but then his fingers latched on to her hair, pulling her head back by it. He looked her in the eye for a long time, as if he were seeing not her, but what was about to happen. Eva was terrified. The worst-case scenario had come to pass— her father was angry. Eva panics at the thought of his anger. He did not come back to see her after that, and she did not go out, pretending she was ill.

In the end, Wittel Matuszewska came and gave Eva a lot of salt water to drink; it was mixed with something bitter and disgusting. The next day she came again, kneading Eva's stomach until in the evening there was blood. The child was tiny and dead, the size of a cucumber, long and slender. Matuszewska and Anusia wrapped it in rags and took it somewhere. The French girl who had been teaching Eva happened to peek into the room. She was dismissed that same day.

**Every variety of ash, or:**
**Recipes for homemade gold**

When Thomas pronounces the world "alchemy," he does it as if a small, round loaf of bread were emerging from his mouth, still warm.

He is given the last room at the end of the corridor, next to Jacob's chambers, for his studio. Jacob has ordered a special apparatus from Italy through Marshal Pallavicini, whom he met at the imperial court. This machinery, consisting of burners and retorts, glass tubes and jars, is set up carefully upon tables and shelves made expressly for this purpose, so that on Christmas the fires under the retorts can be lit with the first Hanukkah candles. Whenever he is in the country, Thomas von Schönfeld comes straight here. He has already fathered three children, and he is always in his snow-white wig and elegant outfit. He brings enormous quantities of presents, for every one of the brothers and every one of the sisters.

He and Jacob almost never leave the studio at such times, and they admit no one else but Matuszewski and an intimate of Thomas's, the Count Ecker und Eckhofen, who danced so beautifully with Eva at the emperor's. It is now universally known that he is not interested in women, though this does not interfere with him knowing the "work." Unfortunately, they are unable to produce a single piece of gold or even silver by March. In the innumerable vessels and jars, all that appears from time to time are stinking liquids and every possible type of ash.

Jacob dreams that the Countess Salm, whom he met at court and who shows him special consideration, advises him that for the neck pain that has been bothering him a great deal lately he must "take a dose of Moravia." This must mean that soon help will come in the form of gold. That would be particularly welcome, since the court's debts have soared to unimaginable heights, despite Thomas's speculation. Or maybe even because of his speculation. For he has persuaded Jacob, and above all the Zwierzchowskis and the Czerniawskis, to invest in the stock market. And though in the beginning they did make enough to pay off their debts, soon their run of good luck turned. That was how the idea of alchemy came about.

Now Thomas comes up with an even more exquisite concept—they start to bottle a transparent, fragrant liquid with a yellowish tinge, the derivative of a certain weak acid. Diluted properly, it does no damage to the skin. A drop of it consumed with a cup of water cures all diseases, claims Thomas. Jacob tried it out on himself, having suffered from rectal bleeding, and was completely healed come summer.

The first boxes of tiny bottles of this miraculous liquid go to kahalim of true believers in Prossnitz, and once they've caused a sensation there, Wołowski takes them to Warsaw. In the summer, a little factory is created in the room next to the alchemy lab, and there the women put small decorative labels on the bottles, then place them in the boxes that will travel to Altona.

Unfortunately, even these "golden drops," as they are called, do not cover all their debts.

## How the Lord's dreams see the world

The winter does not bring anything good. It is cold in the palace on Petersburger Gasse, and the Lord is always sick and moping, while Her Ladyship barely ever leaves her rooms. Suddenly, as though cut off by a knife, their expeditions to Vienna have concluded. One of their carriages has been sold, while the other, a small, elegant coach, is still kept in the coach house, on the off chance that the emperor might ever want Eva back. In order to be able to pay what they owe to their purveyors, they have also had to sell their valuable dinner service. It went for a song to Pallavicini. Quite a few people have been sent home, and it is quiet in the palace now. The stoves are kept on only in the bedrooms, and there is the fireplace in the large hall. That is why the majority of those who remain at court spend the majority of their days in there.

Early in the morning, before they even have breakfast, the faithful go down to listen to the Lord's words. The Lord comes in when all of them have assembled, and how he is dressed is important. The women have noticed that when he is wearing a white shirt, that means he will be in a bad mood that day, and a number of people will get scolded. If, on the other hand, he has put on a red robe, it means his mood is good.

The Lord narrates his dream, and it is written down by young Czerniawski or Matuszewski. When Jakubowski is in Brünn, he takes notes, too. Eva tells them her dream, and they write that down, too. Then these dreams are widely discussed and commented on. They have also established a custom by which the others, too, can tell their dreams, and in this way comment upon the dreams of the Lord and Her Ladyship. This produces extraordinary coincidences, some of which can be discussed for days on end. The narration of dreams can, at times, last into the afternoon of the following day, so that Zwierzchowska has to make a small breakfast available.

The corridors and staircases get swept up in a penetrating chill, and the tiny claws of the icy snow scratch at the windowpanes; the wind strains in the chimneys. You can almost feel the other worlds all pressing in on the home in Brünn, worlds where no one is who he is, but rather someone else entirely, and everything that seems stable and sure loses its contours and all the certainty of its own existence.

The Lord is at the court of the Prussian king Frederick, and he serves him the best wine, but before he pours the wine, he sprinkles sand into the glass, and then he mixes the wine in with the sand. The emperor drinks this with relish. Then he gives the princes and the kings who are there the same thing by way of beverage.

It is strange how a dream like this can make itself at home in the world of day, and then all of them can see this image of a goblet with sand and wine, and even as they are eating in the evening and drinking wine, the image of sand being sprinkled returns to them, which causes some of them, especially the women, since they seem to dream more, or at least to remember more, to say that on the following night they also drank sand or gave sand to others to drink, and so there arises this possibility of transmutation that will be with them now—transmuting sand into wine. Transmuting wine into sand.

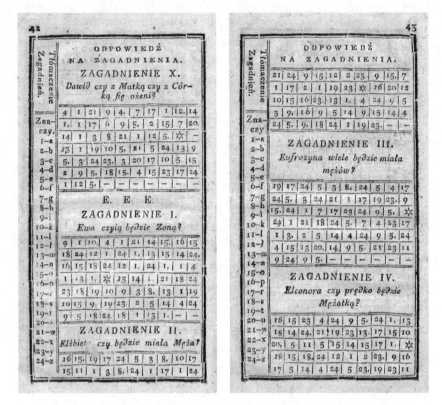

The Lord appeared in the dream of Rabbi Symeon, father of Jacob Szymanowski, and he told him that an heiress from Wojsławice was waiting for him. And she appeared to him as a beautiful young woman, all in white. The Lord told Symeon: Yet she is old, ugly, and always dressed in black. Symeon replied: Pay no mind to that, that is just a shadow. She has great wealth and wants to give it all to you. The Lord was still young and plump in this dream, and the heiress from Wojsławice caressed him and bared her breasts to him and wished to have intercourse with him, but the Lord did not wish to and defended himself against it.

They all agree after the telling of that dream that what it means is the end of their financial woes.

The Lord saw on a great field thousands of Uhlans, all of them true believers, and his sons, Roch and Joseph, were their commanders. The Lord's interpretation: I will leave Brünn and will finally occupy my proper place, and then many gentlemen and Jews will come to me in order to be baptized.

The Lord saw Count Wessel, from whom he tried to rent a palace in Pilica, sitting atop a small table in his carriage. The Lord's interpretation: Aid will come in gold, and the count's request will be carried out, for he had asked for his daughter to become one of Eva's ladies-in-waiting.

The Lord saw a beautiful maiden sitting upstairs, and all around her were herbs and fresh, lush grass. Between her legs came a source of pure, cold fresh water. An untold quantity of persons stood and drank from that source. And he, too, drank, but discreetly, so as not to draw attention to himself. The exposition of that dream takes place in the evening in Eva's bedroom; lately she has been very depressed. The dream must mean one thing: that she will finally be married.

Eva waits for a sign from the emperor. But it doesn't come. Since his mother's funeral, he has not sent for her. And he no doubt won't. Even though she knew things would turn out this way, she still feels rotten and abandoned. She has lost weight. She does not wish to go to Vienna, her memories are too painful there, though her friend the Countess Wessel has tried explaining to her that, having been the emperor's lover, she may now have anyone and everything she wants. Eva goes for the empress's funeral, but so great is the crowd that her new dress disappears in it, along with her hat, her beautiful eyes, and her Eastern charm.

The empress is beautifully dressed for the casket, her dead heft drowned in a foam of lace. Eva Frank gets close enough to see the tips of her blue fingers folded on her chest. From then on, she has fearfully beheld her own each day, worrying that this blueness is a sign of impending demise. People whisper at the funeral about what caused Maria Theresa's death. Apparently the empress slumped down in her armchair and started to choke. One of her ladies-in-waiting said in a dramatic whisper that the young emperor, cold-blooded as always, had taken the time to remark upon her ungraceful arrangement in the chair. "Your Majesty has positioned herself poorly," he is said to have said. "Just well enough to die," the empress apparently retorted, and then she actually died.

Eva promises herself that she will also die with dignity. "Preferably young," she says, though it irritates her father. Jacob claims that now that Joseph is the sole ruler, he will finally do what he wants, and he believes that what he wants is to marry Eva.

He tells her to get her wardrobe ready, since she will soon return to court. But Eva knows she will not be returning. She is afraid to tell her father of it, which is why she spends her evenings with Anusia Pawłowska, mending torn lace.

Eva has been biting her cuticles for some time. Sometimes her fingers are so torn up she must wear gloves to hide them.

## Of the lovemaking of Franciszek Wołowski

Franciszek Wołowski, Shlomo's firstborn son, also known as Łukasz Franciszek Wołowski, is a calm, tall, handsome young man, a year older than Eva; he speaks slowly, carefully. He went to Polish schools and dreamed of attending university, but he did not succeed. Yet he has read a great deal on his own and knows about a great many subjects. He speaks Hebrew, Yiddish, Polish, and German, each of these in his own particular way, since he has a slight speech defect. He does not want to stay on with his father in Warsaw and be a brewer. After all, he does have a noble title. He wants to do great, important things, even if he doesn't yet know what things. By the time he comes to Brünn, he is already of marrying age. As the son of one of the oldest and most important brothers, he has privileges. He's given a double room—he'll be sharing it with his cousin. The cousin, several years younger than he, has just graduated from the Piarist college, which makes Franciszek very jealous.

His father had already written to Jacob Frank on the matter of his son's marriage; perhaps he did not address it directly, but the letter was exceptionally warm and full of recollections, harking back to Elisha Shorr—may he rest in peace—as well as assurances of brotherly love, which might have suggested that the Wołowskis were counting on something that would cement the links between the Warsaw machna and the court in Brünn. There is something so obvious about this idea, and such a marriage was mentioned so many times back in Ivanie, when the children were little still. What could be unexpected about Franciszek coming to ask for Eva's hand?

Franciszek calmly waits until they invite him into their rooms in the evening. Finally, dressed very neatly, he greets the Lord and Eva heartily, and then, after a somewhat challenging conversation (he has never been good at talking freely), he is allowed to turn the pages of Eva's score as she plays her newly purchased instrument. Soon Franciszek, as his parents so desired, has fallen in love, though it can be said with a fair degree of certainty that Eva has yet to even register the presence of this page-turner.

"Doesn't it bother you that she's been off in Vienna taking her turn among the cabbages?" his cousin asks him once they are both in bed, tired

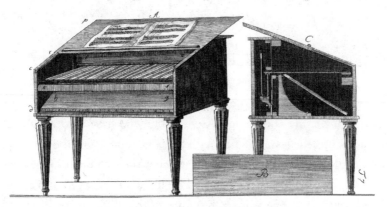

from a full day's Hussaring and drills. Franciszek isn't suited for the martial life at all.

"She was taking her turn among the cabbages with the emperor. Besides, you don't call it cabbages when it's the emperor. The emperor flirts, the emperor has romantic liaisons . . . ," Franciszek answers sagely.

"And you want her to be your wife?"

"Of course I do. She was assigned to me, with my father being the true believer closest to the Lord, the oldest of the brothers."

"Mine, too—mine is maybe even closer. He was with him in Częstochowa, and then he ran away over the wall when Her Ladyship Hana passed away."

"Why would he run away?"

"That's what he said, that he was so scared he jumped down off the wall."

Franciszek Wołowski the younger responds calmly to this, as is his tendency:

"Our fathers believed that since they were with the Lord, death couldn't touch them. Now it's hard to understand that."

"They believed they were immortal?" His cousin's voice switches to an incredulous treble.

"Why does that surprise you so much? You believe it, too."

"Well, yes, but not on earth. In the Heavenly Kingdom."

"Which is where?"

"I don't know. After death. What do you think happens?"

## Of Samuel Ascherbach, son of Gitla and Asher

Yente, who is everywhere, now takes a look at Samuel, son of Gitla and Asher, or Gertruda and Rudolf Ascherbach, who have an optician's shop on Alte Schmiedegasse in Vienna. This thin, pimply young man, a law student, stands with his friends and watches the rich open carriage passing by. In the carriage sits a man in a high hat, and next to him a young, beautiful woman. The woman has an olive-hued complexion and enormous dark eyes. Her entire outfit is light celadon, and even the feathers in her hat are that same color—it looks as though she's casting a glimmering, underwater light. She is petite but perfectly built, narrow-waisted and curvy. Her ample décolletage is covered by a snow-white lace handkerchief. The carriage stops, and servants help the pair get out.

The boys watch, curious, and from the excited whispers of passersby, Samuel learns that this is some sort of Polish prophet with his daughter. They disappear into an expensive candy store. That's it. The boys move on to their own affairs.

Samuel can sometimes be a bit vulgar, though at this age, such things are forgivable.

"I'd run her up the flagpole, that pretty little Polish thing," he says. His companions guffaw.

"Not a meal for a heel, Ascherbach. She's an important lady."

"It's only the important ones I'd run up the flagpole."

In fact, that celadon beauty has made an enormous impression on Samuel. In the evening, he thinks of her when he masturbates. Her full, firm breasts pop out of her dress, and among the foamy petticoats, Samuel finds that hot, wet point that swallows him up and floods him with pleasure.

## 28.

### Asher in a Viennese café, or:
### Was ist Aufklärung? 1784

Tea from China, coffee from Turkey, chocolate from America: they have everything here. The little tables are packed together, with shapely bentwood chairs that stand on one leg. Asher and Gitla Gertruda like to come here, and with their coffee they order a piece of cake that they eat with a teaspoon, slowly, relishing every bite. The chocolate unleashes such sensory pleasure that the street outside becomes blurry; the coffee, meanwhile, restores the sharpness of their sight. They wind down this war of the elements waged within the human mouth in silence, watching the colorful crowd rolling along under Saint Stephen's Cathedral.

On the shelf by the entrance there are newspapers, a recent fashion people say has been imported from Germany and England. You take a newspaper and sit down at your little table—if possible, close to the window, where it's brighter, since otherwise you have to read by candlelight, which tires the eyes. Numerous paintings line the walls, but it is difficult to make them out in the semidarkness, even by day. Oftentimes the customers go up to them with candlesticks and admire the landscapes and portraits in that fragile, flickering glow.

Add to that the pleasure of reading. At first, he'd read the paper from cover to cover, hungry for the printed word. Now he knows where he will find something that interests him. He regrets that his knowledge of French is so poor, he has to remedy that, because they also import French journals here. He is getting up in years, nearly sixty, but his mind is agile and energetic.

"Either the real or the intelligible universe has infinite points of view from which it can be represented, and the possible systems of human knowledge are as numerous as those points of view," he reads in German translation. They are the words of a man called Diderot. With rapt delight, Asher has recently looked over his *Encyclopédie*.

Asher Rubin has done well in life. When, after leaving Lwów, they found themselves here, in Vienna, Asher had his last name, Ascherbach, entered into the official register. He took the names Rudolf and Joseph, the latter no doubt after the young emperor, whose scientific impetus impresses him so much and whom he admires more generally; Gitla, meanwhile, became Gertruda Anna. The Ascherbach family now resides in a respectable tenement house on Alte Schmiedegasse. As an optician, Ascherbach treated local Jews at first, but his clientele grew quickly. He treats cataracts and prepares glasses. They also have a small optical store, which is run by Gitla-Gertruda. The girls are taught at home, they have a tutor, while Samuel is studying law. Asher, meanwhile, collects books, which is his most fervent passion; he hopes that someday Samuel will take over his library.

Asher-Ascherbach's first purchase was the sixty-eight volumes of the *Universal Lexicon* by Johann Heinrich Zedler, on which he spent the very first money he earned. He quickly earned it over again. The patients appear one after the next—everyone recommends him.

At first Gitla grumbled over this purchase, but one day when Asher came home from the hospital, he saw her leaning over one of the volumes and closely examining an article. Lately, she had been interested in the shapes of shells. Gertruda wears glasses she ground herself. The lens is complex and allows her to look through the very same glasses at things that are far away and also at whatever she is reading.

Along with their large apartment, they have rented a workshop in the outbuilding. Rudolf Ascherbach employed an old man, almost blind now, to grind the glass and make the lenses according to Ascherbach's specifications. Gertruda would sit in the workshop and watch the old man craft those lenses with such precision. She didn't even notice when she started to do it herself. She sat at the table, pulling her dress up over her knees so that it would be comfortable for her to press against the pedal that drove the grinding mechanism. And now it is she who makes the glasses.

They often argue, and just as often reconcile. Once she threw a cabbage at him. Now she rarely goes into the kitchen—they have a cook and a girl who lights the stoves and cleans. A laundress comes once a week, and a seamstress once a month.

The last volume of this enormous work appeared in 1754, and since Ascherbach puts the books on his shelves not according to series, title, or author's last name, but rather according to the date when it was published, that volume now stands next to the *New Athens* they brought from Podolia, which Gitla used to learn to read in Polish. An effort that proved to be in vain. That language won't be necessary for them now. Asher sometimes picks it up and looks it over, although his Polish is getting weaker by the day. This is always when he recollects Rohatyn, which seems to him now like a long-ago, faraway dream, one in which he was totally unlike himself but rather an old, embittered person, as though time worked in the opposite direction for him.

The Ascherbachs, sitting in a café per their weekly Sunday-afternoon ritual, decide to join in the debate that has been going on for some time now in the pages of the *Berlinische Monatsschrift*, which they read regularly. It is Gertruda's idea for them to try it, and she is the one who starts to write, but Ascherbach believes she has a poor style, too ornamental, and so he starts to correct her, and in this way, he, too, joins in the writing. The debate is about how to define this fashionable idea, intruding ever more frequently into ordinary conversations, of an "Enlightenment." Everyone makes use of it as they can, but everyone also understands it somewhat differently. It started with a man named Johann Friedrich Zöllner, who, in one of his articles, defending the institution of church marriage, posed in a footnote the question: "Was ist Aufklärung?" This unexpectedly invited a flood of responses, including from famous people.

Moses Mendelssohn was the first to respond to it, and with time an article on enlightenment was published in the journal by the well-known philosopher from Königsberg, Immanuel Kant.

The Ascherbachs don't care about getting paid for their writing, of course—they are doing perfectly well as it is. It is more of a need, a kind of calling—to polish words so that it will be possible to see through them clearly. Gertruda, who always smokes a pipe in the café, causing quite a stir among the sober-minded Viennese burghers, takes notes. They agree only on the point that the most important aspect is reason. For one entire evening they play around with the metaphor of the light of reason that illuminates everything equally and dispassionately. Gertruda remarks immediately and intelligently that wherever something's brightly lit, there is also a shadow, a darkening. The more powerful the light, the deeper, the more intense the shadow. That's true, that's a little bit disturbing; they stop talking for a while.

And then, since people should make use of that which is most valuable, i.e., reason, skin color is invalidated, as is the family one comes from, the religion one practices—even gender. Ascherbach adds, quoting Mendelssohn, whom he has been reading passionately lately (on the table lies *Phaedon oder über die Unsterblichkeit der Seele*, or *Phaedon, or on the Immortality of the Soul*; the title is printed in a red font) that Aufklärung's relationship to culture is the same as theory's to practice. Enlightenment has more to do with scholarly work, with abstractions, while culture is the perfection of interpersonal contacts through the intercession of the word, literature, the image, fine arts. They agree with each other about this. When Ascherbach reads Mendelssohn, he feels, for the first time in his whole life, proud that he's a Jew.

Gitla-Gertruda is forty years old now; she has gone gray and gained weight, but she is a beautiful woman still. Now, before going to bed, she braids her hair and covers it with a cap. They sleep together, but they are physically intimate less and less often, even though Asher, when he looks at her, at her raised, full shoulders, at her profile, still feels desire. He thinks that no one in the whole world is as close to him as she is. None of the children. No one. His life began when, in Lwów, a pregnant girl came to him, when she stood at his door, freezing, hungry, and impertinent. Now, as it happens, Ascherbach is living a new life that has nothing in common with Podolia or the low, starry sky over the market square in Rohatyn. He would have forgotten all of that completely were it not for a certain day when he encountered a familiar face on the street in front of his favorite café, a young man, modestly dressed and walking briskly, carrying sheets of music under his arm. Ascherbach, as he passes, looks at him so intrusively that the other man slows. They pass each other almost reluctantly, looking back over their shoulders; in the end, they stop and walk back up to each other, more surprised than pleased by this unexpected meeting. Asher recognizes this young man, but he cannot quite match the names he remembers to time, or time to the places with which he associates them:

"Are you Shlomo Shorr?" he asks in German.

A shadow runs over the young man's face, and he makes a motion as if wanting to leave. Ascherbach understands now that he has made a mistake. He doffs his hat, embarrassed.

"No, my name is Wołowski. Franciszek. You mistake me for my father, Mr. . . . ," the other man responds in a Polish accent.

Ascherbach apologizes, understanding the man's embarrassment at once.

"I was a doctor in Rohatyn. Asher Rubin." It has been a long time since he has pronounced his old name, he wants to embolden this boy with it now. It does make him uncomfortable, as if he had slipped his feet into old, trampled shoes.

The young man is silent for a moment, his face betraying no emotion, and only now does the difference between him and his father become clear. This father had very lively facial expressions.

"I remember you, Mr. Asher," he says after a little while in Polish. "You used to treat my aunt Hayah, right? You came to our home. You pulled a nail out of my heel, I still have a scar there."

"You can't remember me, son. You were too little," says Ascherbach, suddenly feeling emotional, whether because he has been remembered, or because he is speaking in Polish.

"I remember. I remember a great deal."

They smile, each man to himself, thinking of those days gone by.

"Yes . . . ," Ascherbach says with a sigh.

They walk for some time in the same direction.

"What are you doing here?" Asher asks at last.

"I am visiting my family," Łukasz Franciszek says calmly. "It is time for me to get married."

Ascherbach isn't sure what to ask in order to avoid hitting a sensitive spot. He can tell that there are many of them.

"Do you have a fiancée already?"

"In my mind. I want to choose myself."

This response makes Ascherbach happy, although he doesn't know why.

"Yes, that is very important. May you make a good choice."

They trade some irrelevant information that reveals nothing, and then go their separate ways. Ascherbach hands the boy a business card with an address, and he looks at it for a long while.

He does not tell Gitla-Gertruda about this meeting. In the evening, however, as they are working on their article for the newspaper in Berlin, he returns to it, like a vision—a certain night in Rohatyn, as he was walking along in the dark through the market square to the Shorrs' home. The faint starlight that only promised some other reality, but did not even illuminate the path. The smell of the rotting leaves, the animals in their pens. The chill that got into your bones. The foreignness and indifference of the world contrasted with the great trustfulness of those little huts lying low to the ground, the short fences grown over with dry ropes of clematis, lights in the windows, miserable and uncertain—all of it contained in the rotten order of the world. That is, at any rate, how Asher saw things then. He has not thought of it in ages, but now he cannot stop. So Gitla, disappointed by his distraction, writes alone, mercilessly smoking up the whole salon as she does so.

That evening, Asher is overwhelmed by the melancholy of those days. He is irritated; he has a lemon balm infusion prepared. Suddenly it seems to him that aside from all those lofty theses printed by the *Berlinische Monatsschrift*, beyond light and reason, beyond human power and freedom, there remains something very important, a kind of dark ground with the sticky consistency of cake batter onto which all words and ideas fall as though into tar, losing their shape and their meaning. The lofty tirades from the newspaper sound as if they had been spoken by a ventriloquist—indistinct and grotesque. From everywhere comes something like a chuckle; perhaps at one time Asher might have thought that it was the devil, but nowadays he doesn't believe in such things. He remembers what Gitla said—a shadow, something well-lit casts a shadow. That is what is disturbing about this new idea. Enlightenment begins when people lose their faith in the goodness and the order of the world. The Enlightenment is an expression of mistrust.

## Of the healthful aspects of prophesying

Asher is sometimes called in the evenings for other ailments. Someone must have recommended him, for the local Jews, and in particular those who are secretly inclining toward assimilation, many of whom come from Poland, from Podolia, summon him not as an optician, but as an excellent doctor who can treat every concern, however shameful and strange.

This happens because in these spacious tenement houses, in the bright rooms, there come to be heard old demons, as if bursting from the seams of the clothes people wear, from the souvenir tallitot passed down from their grandfathers, from the velvet jackets once woven by their great-grandmothers, embroidered with red threads. These tenement houses are usually the homes of wealthy merchants and their numerous families, well assimilated, more Viennese than the Viennese themselves, self-satisfied but only on the surface, for in reality, they are the most insecure, and the most lost, of all.

Asher pulls the handle and hears on the other side the sound of a bell, pleasant to the ear.

The girl's worried father grasps his hand in silence; her mother is one of the daughters of the Moravian Jew Seidel, a cousin of the Rohatyn Shorrs. They lead him straight to the patient.

The illness is strange and not particularly pleasant in nature. It would be preferable to hide it somehow, so that it would not assault eyes accustomed to lovely heavy curtains, to wallpapers of classical design, now so fashionable, to the gracefully curving legs of coffee tables and Turkish carpets. And yet the heads of these families do come down with syphilis, infecting their wives, while their children get scabies; respectable uncles and proprietors of large companies drink so much they pass out, and their exquisite daughters sometimes wind up pregnant by who knows whom. And that is when they summon Rudolf Ascherbach, who becomes once more Rohatyn's Asher.

That is how it is here, too, in the home of the merchant Rudnitzky, who started out manufacturing buttons and now has a little factory outside Vienna that sews uniforms for the army. His young wife, whom he married as a widower, has taken ill.

He says she has gone blind. She has shut herself inside her room, and she has been lying there in the dark for two days, afraid to move lest all her blood escape her with her monthly bleeding. She knows that warmth can be favorable to hemorrhage, and so she does not permit her stove to be lit and covers herself with only sheets, which in turn has made her catch a nasty cold. She keeps lit candles all around her bed, since she wants to be able to make sure there is no blood coming out of her. She doesn't speak. Yesterday she tore off a section of her linen sheet and made herself a tampon, which she stuck between her legs, hoping to plug in this way any hemorrhage that might befall her. She is afraid that defecating might also bring about a hemorrhage, so she has not been eating, and she has been blocking her anus with her finger.

The merchant Rudnitzky has conflicting feelings about this—he is dying of anxiety, and yet at the same time he is embarrassed by the illness of his young wife. Her madness frightens and appalls him. If it came out, he would lose his reputation.

Dr. Ascherbach sits down at the edge of the couch where she is lying and takes her hand. Very gently, he begins to talk with her. He is not in a hurry; he permits her drawn-out silences. This soothes her nerves. He can bear the silence that now reigns in the stuffy, dark, cold room. Without realizing it, he starts to stroke the patient's hand. He is thinking about something else. That the crumbs of human knowledge start to come together like chain links, one linking with the next, unbreakably. Soon it will be possible to cure every disease, including ones like this. But right now he feels helpless, he doesn't understand her ailment, he doesn't know what is behind it, and the only thing he can give this poor, thin, unfortunate girl is his own warm presence.

"What is the matter, child?" he asks. He pats her head, and the patient starts to look at him.

"Could I open the curtains?" he asks quietly.

Her answer comes resolute: "No."

As he is returning late in the evening down the streets of Vienna, still filled with motion and noise, he is reminded of when he used to walk through Rohatyn to get to Hayah Shorr, who would throw herself across the floor, prophesying, tensing her body, covered in sweat.

Compared with Vienna, Rohatyn is a dream under the eiderdown in a dark, smoky chamber. None of Asher's patients now resides in a common chamber, none wears shmatte on her head, and none dresses in a Polish kubrak. No one here suffers from a Polish plait. The houses are tall, powerful, with thick stone walls; they smell of lime, and the fresh wood from which the stairs are constructed. Most of these new houses are connected to street sewers. Gas lamps burn on the streets, which are broad and airy. Through the clean glass windows you can see the sky and the strands of smoke that rise up from the chimneys.

And yet today Asher saw, in that sick girl, Hayah Shorr from Rohatyn. That woman who was young then, and must be sixty years old by now, if she is still alive. Perhaps Mrs. Rudnitzky would be relieved by prophecy, by the agile navigation of the darkness of her reason, of its shadows and fogs. Perhaps that is also a good place to live. Maybe that is what he should advise her husband: "Mr. Rudnitzky, your wife ought to start to prophesy, for that will help her."

## Of figurines made out of bread

Hayah Marianna is dozing now. She has let her head fall to her chest, her hands have dropped down limp, and in a moment her account book will slide right out of her lap. Hayah keeps the bills at her son's. This means spending all day in the office behind his shop, sitting and tallying columns of figures. The shop sells all kinds of fabrics. Her son is named Lanckoroński, like all of her sons and daughters, and Hayah herself, now a widow. Her son and Goliński imported the textiles, but Goliński became a wholesaler and lost a great deal of money, while Lanckoroński kept to retail and has done all right. The shop is on Nowe Miasto, very lovely and well kept. Warsaw's townswomen come here for their materials—the prices are reasonable, and you can get discounts, too. There are a number of simple percales, as well as the still cheaper cotton imported from the East that has been such a hit lately. Servant girls and cooks sew themselves dresses out of it. The wealthier townswomen buy better materials, throwing in ribbons, feathers, bands, hooks, and buttons. In addition to all that, Lanckoroński imports hats from England, this being his latest line; he wants to open a small shop with just English hats on Krakowskie Przedmieście. He's also thinking about starting to produce them himself, since no one in Poland is making decent felt hats. Why not? God only knows.

Hayah snoozes in the little back office. She has grown fat and doesn't like to exert herself now; her legs ache, her joints have thickened, painful and constantly cracking. Because of this new corpulence, Hayah's face has filled out—it's hard to glean her old features in it. In fact, that old Hayah has vanished now, dissolved. This new Marianna is sort of sleepy, as if she were always in a fortune-telling trance. And yet, whenever anyone comes to her seeking advice, she'll still unfold her board; when she unfolds it on the table and digs out from a small wooden box the appropriate figures, her eyelids start to tremble and her gaze drifts up until her pupils finally disappear. In this way, Hayah sees. The figures set out on the flat surface create all sorts of different arrangements, some pleasant, others ugly, some that set your teeth on edge. Hayah-Marianna is able to lay out in her board every "farther" and every "closer," both in time and in space, knows how to show, based on a figure's position, attraction or its opposite, repulsion. She also sees clearly conflict and accord.

The figurines have really multiplied since Rohatyn times—there are so many of them these days, and the latest are also the smallest, made just from bread now, never out of clay. In a single glance, Hayah can comprehend the meaning of a constellation, see where it is headed, what it will develop into.

Certain patterns develop out of this, patterns that connect with one another via bridges or gangways, there are also dikes and dams between them, and wedges and nails, joints, bands that squeeze together situations with similarly shaped outlines, like the staves on a barrel. There are also the sequences that look like ants' paths, old botanical routes, and it isn't known who's walked down them or why they went that way instead of another. There are loops and vortices and dangerous spirals, and their slow movement draws Hayah's gaze down, into the depths that accompany every thing.

From that little office where she stations herself, Hayah—leaning over her board that makes some of her son's customers think that this strange woman has reverted to childhood and is playing with her grandchildren's games—sometimes glimpses Yente; she can feel her presence, inquisitive but calm. She recognizes her, she knows it is Yente; evidently she has not quite died, which does not surprise her. She is, however, surprised by the presence of someone else entirely, of a completely different nature. This is someone tenderly observing them, her and the office, and all the brothers and sisters scattered all across the earth, and the people on the streets. This someone is attentive to details. Right now, for instance, this someone is observing the figurines and board. Hayah guesses what this someone wants, so she treats the presence like an ever so slightly annoying friend. She raises her closed eyes and tries to look this someone in the face, but she doesn't know if this is possible or not.

## The rejected proposal of Franciszek Wołowski the younger

Franciszek Wołowski the younger would like to have Eva. Not because he loves her and desires her, but because she is unavailable. The more impossible it becomes, the more Franciszek's will to marry Eva Frank is fortified. This is why he has come down with such a serious case of her, the illness also due to his father—who always said that Eva would be his, and that in this way the two families would join, and Franciszek would take over after Jacob. Jacob looked upon it favorably too, but then, when Eva started to see the emperor himself, all hope floated off like a cloud, high, very high, ungraspable now. Eva is different these days, appearing rarely, dressed in gleaming silks, having become as slippery as a fish, impossible to grasp.

Franciszek proposes to her without the knowledge of his father, who is still in Warsaw, attending to the brewery. His proposal is passed over in silence, as if Franciszek had committed a shameful act that can never be mentioned by anyone. There are whispers of it at the court in Brünn for weeks on end, but he does not receive an answer, and slowly he realizes that he has made a fool of himself. He writes his father an embittered letter and asks that he summon him back to Warsaw. As he waits for an answer, he stops coming to the communal prayers and to Jacob's chats. What seemed so attractive to him when he used to come here—this little crowd of people in the palace on Petersburger Gasse, new faces, a sense of community, as if he had found himself in an enormous family, the flirtations, the gossip, the never-ending jokes and amusements, followed by the prayers and songs—now all of that disgusts him. Perhaps he hates most of all the drills constantly being organized for the young men and boys by his uncle Jan Wołowski, called—on account of the uniform he insists upon wearing—the Cossack. He drills several of the boys in a Cossack squadron, but there aren't enough horses for a squadron; the boys have to take turns riding the four saddled ones. The Lord had given his second cousin, Franciszek Szymanowski, the task of forming a legion. This new word appears in all sorts of contexts: uniforms for the legion, the legion's standard, legion practice, legion songs . . . Franciszek, Shlomo's son, hears it incessantly, although toward all matters to do with uniforms and saber-waving he feels a profound reluctance, colored by contempt.

And so he travels to Vienna, wanders the streets, and in this uncomfortable situation, he finds consolation in concerts, which in Vienna is not difficult—music is everywhere here. He was quite moved listening to one composer named Haydn, whose music seemed so close to him and so beautiful. He cried discreetly: his eyes grew moist, but he managed to hold back the tears, which flowed inwardly instead and washed his heart. When the orchestra finished playing, and the applause began, he felt that he would not be able to bear the lack of this music, that he needed to have it without interruption. The world became empty. He had learned after the concert, which he had barely been able to afford, that there was something in this world that could raise a person to the height of happiness, and that it was possible not to even know about it, living in constant lack. He was supposed to buy his sisters presents—lace and buttons covered in silk, they had asked for hats and ribbons—but Franciszek would bring them sheet music instead.

He didn't manage to get into the concert by this young man named Mozart, but he found a place beneath the opera windows where he could hear as though he were inside. He had the impression that the opera had fallen upon him, and the cathedral upon it, and now all of Vienna was cascading onto his head, and he was dumbfounded. This music was as impossible as Eva, becoming a great and peerless dream that could never come true in Warsaw. He is Warsaw, she Vienna.

In the end, the letter he had been waiting for arrived, and his father told him to come back. He reminded him about Marianna Wołowska, the daughter of Franciszek's uncle Michał, whom Franciszek had known since childhood. There was nothing in the letter about marriage, but Franciszek understood that she had been assigned to him now. His heart grew tight, and in that state, he went away to Warsaw.

Saying goodbye, Jacob hugged him like a son—all of them saw it. And—it is true—Franciszek felt like Jacob's son. He felt he would be given some sort of mission to fulfill, just not the one he had expected.

Evidently from where Jacob was, things looked different from how they did to Franciszek. Franciszek bade tender farewells to his friends who were planning to remain at the court, with the Maiden. Finally, he purchased his music and looked through it later in his carriage, trying to play it silently with his fingers on his lap. Deep down he felt a great relief that he was going back to Warsaw, and that from now on that would be his place. He would be the commander of some other legion, in a fortress in Warsaw, following Jacob's orders there.

As soon as he had crossed the border, Vienna paled, becoming just a black-and-white engraving, and all of Franciszek's thoughts turned toward Leszno Street in Warsaw, toward his Marianna. He started thinking about her intensely and remembering what she looked like, since he had never before taken a good look at her. When they stopped along the way in Kraków, he bought her—totally innocently—a pair of tiny coral earrings that looked as if someone had deposited little droplets of their common, cousinly blood upon the gold filigree.

## A final audience with the emperor

Letting the Lord's blood is a task Zwierzchowska has mastered; now she can do it with great efficiency. The blood flows into the bowl, a considerable quantity of it. After this procedure, the Lord is weak, unsteady on his feet. Pale. That is good. He will look weak enough.

The carriage is waiting, not as fancy and ornate as the one in which they used to ride to Schönbrunn. It is a simple carriage drawn by two horses; it is humble and does not call attention. Three of them climb in—Jacob, Eva, and Anusia Pawłowska, who accompanies Eva, makes a good impression, and speaks wonderful French.

Emperor Joseph spends the summer in Laxenburg with his ever-present ladies, known for their beauty and intelligence. Their pretty hats accompany him like airborne jellyfish, ready to keep intruders away from him. Beneath the hats are the two Liechtenstein sisters, Countess Leopoldine

Kaunitz and Princess Kinsky, with whom he is said to be having a romance.

Eva did not wish to go; her father forced her. Now she sits sulking, looking out the window. It is May 1786, the world is in bloom, the hills around Brünn look soft and ripely verdant. Spring has come early this year, the lilacs have long since bloomed, now it is the jasmines and the bulky peonies, and everywhere is the sweet, joyous smell of flowers. Jacob moans and groans; the bloodletting really has weakened him this time. The outlines of his face have sharpened, just like after his hemorrhage. He does not look good.

At first they are made to wait a long while—a thing that has not befallen them before. Through the windows they see little groups of people strolling through the park, the bright splotches of ladies' parasols, the lush green of the trimmed lawns. They wait about two hours, not saying a word to one another, in total silence, and only once does someone look in on them and offer them water.

Then they can hear amused voices and brisk steps, and suddenly the door opens. The emperor walks in. He is wearing light summer clothing, not French at all, rather peasant-like. His shirt, unbuttoned toward the top, reveals his slender neck and emphasizes the protruding lower jaw that is typical of the Habsburgs. He isn't wearing a wig—his sparse hair is ruffled, making him look younger. Behind him come the two ladies, laughing, his elegant shepherdesses; their last humorous remarks come tumbling.

His guests rise. Jacob is unsteady, and Anusia rushes to his side to offer him support. Eva stands as though hypnotized and gazes at the emperor.

The two men, in this company of women, size each other up for just a moment. Jacob makes a low bow. Eva's and Anusia's dresses wither as they squat.

"Who is this my eyes behold?" says the emperor, and sits down, extending his legs before him.

"Your Imperial Majesty . . . ," begins Jacob in a weak voice.

"I know why you are here," says the emperor, and instantly his secretary comes in with a stack of papers. He hands Jacob a sheet and indicates several sections of it, casting only a quick glance at it himself. "Your legal and valid debts must be paid off. About a great many of them nothing can be done. Others you can extend for some time longer. Our aid to you consists in itemizing which debts are just, and which are not. On these you have been taken in, and those you ought not to pay, for the claims are unfounded. That is all we can do for you. I advise you to take better care of your interests. Dissolve the court, pay what you owe—that is my advice."

"Your Majesty," Jacob starts, falls silent, then adds: "Might we perhaps speak in private?"

The emperor makes an impatient gesture, and all of the women leave the room. When they sit down in the room next door at the fanciful little coffee table, Princess Kinsky orders an orgeat refreshment to be served. Before it is poured, the women hear the emperor's raised voice from the other side of the door.

Eva collects her courage and, in a trembling voice, with her eyes glued to the floor, she says quickly, as if wanting to drown out that angry voice: "We are asking for aid not only for ourselves, but for the whole city. Without us, Brünn empties out a great deal indeed, and Brünn's merchants have already been complaining of low profits since we were forced to send away a part of our company."

"I certainly sympathize with the citizens of Brünn, that they are losing guests like all of you," Princess Kinsky answers politely. She is lovely, with a beauty similar to Eva's—petite, with great dark eyes and luxuriant black hair.

"If the princess would speak in support of us . . . ," Eva begins, but she can barely get the words out through her clenched teeth.

"You are overestimating my influence on the emperor. We are for pleasant, frivolous things."

A silence falls; it is hostile and unpleasant. Eva feels drenched. Under her armpits sweat stains crop up on the silk, and this takes away what little confidence had remained to her. She feels like crying. Suddenly the door opens, and the women rise. The emperor walks out first and doesn't even look at the ladies; his secretary goes ahead of him.

"I am sorry," Princess Kinsky says simply, and sets out after the emperor. When they have disappeared, Eva lets out all the air she's breathed and suddenly feels as light as a slip of paper.

## Thomas von Schönfeld and his games

They return in silence, no one says a single word the whole way home. In the evening, Jacob does not go down into the common room at all. As usual, Zwierzchowska is with him. For dinner he asks to be brought two hard-boiled eggs and nothing else.

On the following day, he begins to send the youths back to their homes. They manage to sell the elegant coach and the porcelain right away. Smaller items are bought up in bulk by a merchant from Frankfurt. Eva avoids going into town, she is ashamed, for in every place she owes somebody something.

A month after their audience with the emperor, Thomas von Schönfeld appears in Brünn. He is returning from abroad and brings Lady Eva a box of chocolates. Eva wrote him several desperate letters asking for help. In each of them she made some mention of debtors' jail.

"Problems are a part of life, just like dust is a part of a stroll," says Thomas, when the three of them ride out of town, to Jacob's favorite forest paths. It is lovely summer weather. The morning is refreshing; later it will no doubt get hot. It is healthy to be a little cold when you know such heat is coming.

"I am the sort of person—and this is a family trait of ours, no doubt—who always attempts to glean the good in whatever life brings," Thomas goes on. "It is true that there were things we did not get to accomplish, but on the other hand, there were other things we did. That medicinal balm has enjoyed considerable success even here, in Vienna; I have been trying to disseminate it discreetly and only among friends and trustworthy persons."

His chattering annoys Eva.

"Yes," she interjects. "We all know that the income from that cannot possibly provide us even a small part of the life we have grown accustomed to, and it will certainly not keep up the whole court."

Thomas walks a step behind Eva, and with the sharp end of a bamboo rod, he cuts the tips off the nettles.

"That is why I am telling you, in perfect sincerity"—he turns to Jacob—"that I experienced great relief when I heard that you, Lord, had recently ordered all the brothers and sisters and that parasitic riffraff to go home. That is a good sign."

"We also got rid of a large part of our movable property," adds Eva.

Her father says nothing.

"That is very good, that will allow us to gather together and take the next step, which I urge you, Uncle, to do."

Only now does Jacob speak, so quietly that you have to really strain to hear him. He always does this when he is angry, it is a sort of starter violence—forcing his interlocutor to listen to him.

"We gave you the money we gathered from the brothers and sisters. You said you would increase it on the stock exchange. That you would lend it out and get back interest. Where is that money?"

"It is coming! That much is obvious." Thomas starts to get excited. "There will be war, we know that for sure. The emperor must keep his commitments to Catherine, and she will strike in Turkey. I secured a safe conduct to provision the army in great quantities, and you know that I know everyone, every important person in Europe."

"You said the same thing when we were bringing in alembics and retorts."

Thomas laughs artificially.

"Well, I was wrong. Everyone was wrong. As far as I know, no one has managed to get gold out of it, though there have been rumors. And yet there is something a great deal more certain than hundreds of experiments in retorts, all those nigredos and conniunctios. This new alchemy is bold and skillful investing, trusting your inner voice, just as it goes in the alchemy lab—you try things out, you take certain risks . . ."

"Things ended badly for us once already," says Jacob, sitting down on a fallen tree trunk, ruining with the tip of his walking stick the path of some traveling ants. He raises his voice: "You have to help us now."

Thomas stands before Jacob. He is wearing silk stockings. Tight dark green trousers cling to his slim hips.

"I have to tell you something, Uncle," he says after a moment. "You have generated quite a bit of intrigue among my companions. You will no longer obtain any support from the emperor, but you will get it from them. Your mission here is finished. The emperor has advisers who are biased against you, that is clear. I have heard people speaking of you as though you were some charlatan, have heard them unjustly equating you with those confidence men who are eternally at royal courts. Your credit line in Vienna is cut, and I cannot give you any support at this particular moment either, as I have my own great financial ambitions and would prefer for us not to be linked."

Jacob gets up and brings his face close to Thomas's. His eyes darken.

"You're ashamed of me now."

Jacob heads back, walking quickly, Thomas following him uncomfortably, trying to explain:

"I have never been ashamed of you and will never be. Between us there is a generational difference; if I had been born when you were, then perhaps I would be attempting to be just like you. But now other laws prevail. What you say, I would like to do. You keep waiting for mystical signs, for some sort of confederacy of the bałakaben, while it seems to me that man can be liberated much more simply and not in mystical spheres, but here, on earth."

Eva looks at her father fearfully, certain that Thomas's impudence will provoke paroxysms of rage. But Jacob is calm, walks leaning forward, eyes on his feet. Thomas trots after him.

"A person must be shown that he has an influence on his life and on the whole world. When he stomps, thrones will tremble. You say: The law must be broken in secret, in our bedchambers, while we pretend externally that we have followed it. Breaking the law in bedrooms and boudoirs!" Thomas senses he has gone too far in the direction of criticizing his uncle, and his tone of voice softens a bit. "I say that it's the other way around: the law, if it is unjust and if it brings people misfortune, needs to be changed, we must act in the open, boldly, making no compromises."

"A person often doesn't even realize his misfortune," Jacob says calmly into his shoes.

His calm evidently emboldens Thomas, for now he runs out in front of Jacob and continues to pontificate, walking backward:

"Then he must be made aware of it and dragged into action, instead of us just dancing around in circles, singing songs and waving our arms."

Eva is certain that now Jacob will strike Thomas von Schönfeld in the face, but he doesn't even pause.

"Do you think anything can be rebuilt from the ground up?" Jacob asks him, continuing to look down at his feet.

Thomas stops, shocked, and raises his voice.

"But those are your words, your teachings!"

When in the evening von Schönfeld prepares to return to Vienna, Jacob draws him in and hugs him. He whispers something into his ear. Thomas's face lights up, and he clears his throat. Eva, standing next to her father, is not sure whether she has heard correctly what he said. It seems to her that it was: "I trust you implicitly." And that he also used the word "son."

Several months later, a package arrives from Vienna. It is brought by a courier dressed in black. It contains letters assuring their safe passage, and among them, news from Thomas:

> . . . My brothers, whose influence is great, have found a certain person of angelic goodness, the prince of a separate little state, who would receive you with the entire court intact. His is an impressive castle on the River Main, near Frankfurt, and he will put it at your disposal, should you consent to adapt it to your needs. This is a change in the right direction—west, farther from the war that the emperor, albeit reluctantly, has declared upon Turkey. It will be better for you all to roll up your tents and move to this new place. Consider what I write you here in the greatest confidence.
>
> Your wholeheartedly devoted
> Thomas von Schönfeld

Eva, reading this letter, which her father has shown her, says in shock: "How did he do it?"

Her father, buttoned all the way up despite the heat from the fireplace, sits with his eyes closed. Eva notices he needs the barber already. He has rested his bare feet on the soft, upholstered stool, and Eva sees the varicose veins that color his skin blue. She is suddenly overwhelmed by terrible exhaustion, and it is all the same to her now what happens to them next.

"I find this city so disgusting now," she complains. She looks through the window at the empty courtyard, which has just emerged, with some difficulty, from under the dirty snow, exposing the garbage. Eva sees someone's abandoned glove. "I just find it disgusting. I cannot look upon it any longer."

"Silence," says her father.

On the evening before their departure, a delegation of Brünn townspeople comes to the emptied court of the Franks. Since there are no longer any furnishings, they are received standing. Jacob goes out to them leaning upon young Czerniawski, with Eva standing beside him. The burghers bring farewell gifts—a crate of the finest Moravian wine for "the lord baron" and a silver platter with a view of the city engraved on it and the inscription: "Farewell friends of Brünn, from its residents."

Jacob looks touched—they are all touched, and in the townspeople there is also some sense of guilt, since it is now known that those on their way out are leaving a significant sum for alms and for the city councillors.

Jacob Frank, in his high Turkish cap and his coat with the ermine collar, stands on a low step and says in his coarse though correct German:

"Once I set out on a long journey and was so tired that I sought some place to rest. Then I found one tree that gave great shade. Its fruits smelled from afar, and next to it was a source of the purest water. And so I lay down under that tree, ate its fruits and drank the water from that source, and I slept a fine slumber. 'How can I ever repay you, tree?' I asked. 'How can I bless you? Should I wish you many branches? You have them already. Should I say: May your fruit be sweet and have a magnificent smell? You are in possession of that already, too. Say: May you have around you a source of fresh water? This has already been given to you. Thus I have no way to bless you other than to simply say: May all honest passersby rest beneath you and give praise to the God who has created you.' And this tree—it is Brünn."

It is February 10, 1786, and the snow is beginning to fall again.


## Scraps: Jacob Frank's sons, and Moliwda

I have always carried out my missions with devotion, for I knew that Jacob would distinguish me for it. For whom, if not me? I was fluent in Turkish and knew those local customs as well as my own. And yet the latest mishaps have caused Jacob to distance himself from me again, keeping company now more with the younger and more agile Jan Wołowski, who, dressed up as a Cossack, his swarthy face cut crosswise by his bushy Polish mustache, has continued to be close to Jacob. He made Antoni Czerniawski, his brother-in-law, his second aide-de-camp. They've circled around him like flies, Matuszewski and Wittel also did their part, and most of all Eva, who defended him and slowly transformed from daughter into mother to Jacob.

Yeruhim and I had so much in common, and while the younger ones gave themselves over to what they rumblingly referred to as life, we preferred to talk about the old subjects, those no one here remembered anymore, nor valued. For we had been conducting our cause from the start, and we had seen more broadly than anyone out of our whole big machna. And I could take pride in the fact that I remained, the only one who had been with Jacob from the start, for after all, Reb Mordke, Issachar, even Moshe of Podhajce and his father, who were buried in that Częstochowa cave, are with us no longer, though I always think, really, that they have just gone off and are waiting for us all somewhere, sitting around a big wooden table, and the door to their room is somewhere here, in this great castle. Is not death merely appearance, like the many phenomena that appear in the world and in which we believe, like so many children?

I thought a great deal then about death, for during one of my absences from Warsaw, my Wajgełe died, giving life to a little girl whom I named Rozalia and whom I greatly loved. She was a child born too soon, and she was very weak; her mother, no longer young, could not endure the difficult labor. She passed away quietly in our apartment on Długa, in the presence of her two sisters, who communicated to me this terrible information when I returned from Brünn. I judge that God wished to tell me something, giving me this little crumb of a child at a time so filled with doubt and wretchedness—me, a person who had never been close to his family; for by that time my physical intercourse with my wife was rare, and we had not had any real hopes for parenthood in a long while. What did God want to tell me, giving me Rozalia? I think that he was appointing me a father again in this way, reminding me of that role I had so forgotten, so that I could begin to watch over Jacob's sons.

That is why I was glad to go back to Warsaw, where I pursued my own business, as well as the obligations I had to our great family, but above all I looked after both of Jacob's sons, Joseph and Roch (leaving Rozalia for the time being with her aunts), to whom I dedicated more attention than I had my own. Placed in schools, they were training to become officers. Jacob knew very well what he was doing, putting them in my custody, for I tried to prevent them from dissolving into the heady concoction that was Warsaw, and I felt particular affection for them, especially for the elder of the two, Roch, who was close to my heart, and so many times did I count on my fingers those gloomy months in Częstochowa, when he came into the world, and when I was raised up by Jacob, and when I was forgiven so wondrously and generously for my misdeed. But Roch avoided me as much as possible and was even rather harsh with me. I had the impression that he was ashamed of me, that I was not Polish enough for him, that I was too Jewish, that he was irritated by my Jewish accent, and that he found me personally unbearable. When he would come up to me, he would wrinkle up his nose and say, "It smells like onions here," which made me feel terrible. Meanwhile, his younger brother, guided by his sibling, also treated me roughly, but sometimes tenderly as well; I think that aside from me they had no one who was close to them. And they did not have it easy, those boys—constantly in other people's houses, and then in the dormitories of the School of Chivalry, seemingly surrounded by peace and esteem, but really treated like freaks. They became willful, lawless, connected with each other only, as if the rest of the world were their enemy. They made sure to hide their Jewish origins, always more Polish than their Polish peers.

When they were younger, they were sent to the Piarists. Roch went first—I asked him how he was doing there, and he complained to me in tears that they had to wake up at six in the morning, and then go to mass right away, and after mass all they got was bread and butter, but if they wanted coffee, they had to send for money for it. At eight it was back to the classroom, where they had lessons into afternoon. Then there were the guards' rounds, whoever was on guard duty, and only after that could they have lunch. Until two they were given time to play in the garden out behind the building, and from two they had more lessons until five. Until eight in the evening they were to study and do their homework, leaving them just one hour for entertainment, from eight until nine. At nine-thirty they were to go to bed. And so on, over and over again. Is that the life of a happy child?

They were taught there that coming from a noble lineage is mere happenstance and blind fortune, and that true nobility rests in virtue and is a conduit to virtue, as without virtue, ability, and decency, nobility is empty and vain. First among their studies came Latin, in which they were instructed very thoroughly, so as to be able to understand the other disciplines after. These other disciplines were mathematics, foreign languages, world history, and the history of Poland, as well as geography and modern philosophy. Reading newspapers in other languages was mandatory, too. They also had something there that I could not comprehend—experimental physics with actual experiments, which reminded me somewhat—based on what I was told about it by Joseph—of the alchemy lab.

Later, at the Corps of Cadets, where they went as the ennobled Counts Frank, they grew used to keeping completely silent on the subject of themselves, never saying one word too many, and never getting close to anyone. Roch, small and redheaded, of nervous disposition, worked up his courage with an incredible bravado, and, later, with wine. Joseph, meanwhile, with his delicate complexion, looked more like a girl. Sometimes, when I beheld him, I had the impression that his cadet uniform was holding him in place, and that if you were to take it off him, Joseph Frank would spill out of it like butter. Joseph was taller than Roch and better built, with his sister's big eyes and full lips, and he always kept his hair very short. Quiet and agreeable, in some ways he reminded me of Franciszek Wołowski.

Over the holidays, they stayed either with me or with Franciszek, and I would try to pass along my knowledge of the faith of the true believers, though they would often completely refuse it. They would seem to be listening to my lessons, but they were as if absent, as when their father would punish them for even the slightest transgression, since Jacob considered that boys had to be governed absolutely. I often felt pity for them, even back in Częstochowa, and especially for Roch, who up until Hana's death spent his whole childhood in prison, his whole world the officer's chamber and the small courtyard in front of the tower, his only friends those old warhorses, and every so often novitiate monks. He reminded me of that plant that grows in the cellar, in humidity, and maybe that was why he was so slight and weak, so inconspicuous. How could such a creature ever become Jacob's successor? Jacob did not like him or respect him, and I believe that even the sight of his sons got on his nerves. That is why I undertook this task. Yet fathering those two lost souls did not turn out as I had hoped.

I was also to play a role, when the time came, similar to the one Reb Mordke and I used to play long ago on our peregrinations—that of matchmaker. At first Jacob planned for them to take high-born, noble wives, for at that time he was steering everyone toward the outside—having them take husbands and wives not of our faith. But this did not last long.

I always felt that we had to stick together, otherwise we would never survive. My son, Antoni, Leah's only child, had married Marianna Piotrowska, granddaughter of Moszek Kotlarz, and my grandchildren were now growing up in Warsaw, and all of our efforts went toward their education. My eldest daughter was already promised to Henryk Wołowski's youngest boy. We did not wish her to marry too young, so we waited for her to grow up a little.

Once I ran into Moliwda on the street in Warsaw. I was shocked, for he had not changed one bit, except perhaps he had gotten skinnier, and as soon as he took off his cap it was revealed that he had gone bald, but his face and his signature gait, and everything else about him, appeared unaltered. It was just that his attire was now completely different—foreign, perhaps elegant once, but now somewhat worn and neglected. He did not recognize me right away. First he passed me, but then he turned around, and I did not know how to behave, and so I stood, giving him the right to say the first word. "Nahman," he said, shocked. "Is that you?"

"It is I. Except that I am Piotr Jakubowski. Do you not remember?" I said.

"Look at you! I remember you rather differently."

"I, too, could say I had a different image of you in my mind."

He patted me on the shoulder like he used to back in Smyrna, and took my hand, and we came off of the street and went into a courtyard, both of us somewhat uncomfortable, yet joyous, too. I was overcome by emotion, and tears came into my eyes. "I thought you were going to pass by me," I said.

And then, in that courtyard, he did a surprising thing—he wrapped his arms around my neck, buried his face in my collar, and sobbed—so terribly that I, too, wanted to weep, although I had no reason for it.

After that, I met with him a few times, and we would go to a little winery at the back of the market where they served Tokay—the very sort we always used to drink together, too. Each time, Moliwda wound up drunk, and—to tell the truth—so did I.

He was now a well-placed royal scribe, and he enjoyed the finest society, wrote for the newspapers, and would bring me printed pamphlets, and I thought that the reason he dragged me to that winery was that it was in a cellar and was darkish, and even if someone were to come in there, they would not have been able to make out our faces. "Why have you not married?" I would ask him every time, unable to understand that he preferred to live on his own, having strangers do his washing, taking strangers to bed. Even if you don't care much for women, still it is useful to live with one.

He would then sigh and tell some story, as was his wont, and every time it was a slightly different one, he would get all tangled up in the details, and I would merely nod my head with understanding, for I was familiar with his storytelling style.

"I have no peace of mind, Nahman," he said, leaning on his glass. "I have no peace in my soul."

The conversation always turned then to memories of Smyrna and Giurgiu, and on that, our adventures would conclude—there was never any more to them than that. He did not wish to hear of Częstochowa, he would start to fidget, and it seemed to me that whatever had happened after Jacob's imprisonment did not concern him in the least. I wrote down for him, too, the Wołowskis' address, and Hayah Lanckorońska's, but so far as I know, he never went. He did once come to my place, when I was about to travel to Brünn, a bit tipsy already, and we went to drink together on Grzybowska

Street. He told me of the king, who invited Moliwda for lunches sometimes and rated his poems quite highly, and once, when he was drunk, he sketched out for me on the table a map indicating which loose women would receive him, and where.

Just recently I learned that he recommended Michał Wołowski's son, a young lawyer, for a post in the royal chancellery, and that he watched over him there; the boy was very capable.

That is all about Moliwda. Just after Christmas in 1786, the Lord summoned us to Brünn for those final months; shortly before leaving, I learned Moliwda was deceased.


## Last days in Brünn

When we arrived in Brünn, the palace on Petersburger Gasse was already almost empty. Jacob summoned for those final months those who remained from our Ivanie havura, the eldest brothers and sisters: Eva Jezierzańska, Klara Lanckorońska, the Wołowski brothers, and me. Of the younger brothers, Redecki and Bracławski. Already present were Old Pawłowski, Yeruhim Dembowski, and a few more, too.

We found him alone in his rooms, for he had had Eva and Anusia Pawłowska moved to another part of the building, which struck me as rather imprudent, given he had been suffering of late from hemorrhage and apoplexy. He was irritated and ordered Redecki to take care of him—he was the spitting image of the late Hershel, who had died in Lublin. Jacob had wasted away. His several weeks' worth of facial hair was now completely gray, the hair on his head white, albeit thick and wavy. He walked leaning on a cane. It was hard for me to believe I was seeing him like this, and that this had all occurred over the course of a single year, for in my memory he still remained the Jacob of Smyrna, of Ivanie—certain of himself, coarse, speaking in a voice that carried everywhere, moving quickly, even violently.

"What are you looking at me like that for, Jakubowski," he said by way of greeting. "You have grown old. You look like a scarecrow."

It was obvious that I, too, had been marked by the passage of time, but I was not feeling it since I suffered from no old-age ailments. Yet unnecessarily he compared me with a scarecrow in front of everyone.

"You, too, Jacob," I answered, but he did not even respond to my impertinence. Others laughed a little.

Every morning we would go somewhere, into Brünn to see the creditors, or to Vienna, where the sons of Solomon, may he rest in peace, who were quite well connected, would advise us as to how we might pay off those sky-high debts.

When it would start to get dark—and the evenings were long now—we would sit together as we used to in our common chamber; Jacob would take care to pray in the old way—our way—but very briefly, probably only so as not to forget. By day, it was all packing up and selling off what could still be sold. In the evening Jacob would grow eager to tell stories, and it must have cheered him that he was seeing so many of us. Many of those chats I recorded elsewhere, as did my comrades.

"There is this place I am guiding you toward," he would say, and I could have listened to this tale over and over, endlessly, for it soothed me greatly, and if I were to wish for any story on my deathbed, it would be this one, "and although now you are impoverished, you would not wish for any treasures of the world, if you were to know this place. This is the place of that Great Brother, the Good God, who is favorable to man and bestows upon him fraternal feeling, and who resembles me. And he has around him a retinue, very much like what we have here—with twelve brothers and fourteen sisters, and the sisters are bedmates to the brothers, as it is with us. All of those sisters are queens, for there it is the women who rule, not the men. And it may seem strange to you, but the names of those brothers and sisters are exactly the same as yours in Hebrew. And their figures are similar to yours, just young—just as you were, in Ivanie. And it is to them that we are heading. When we finally meet them, then you will marry those sisters and those brothers."

I knew this tale, and they knew it, too. We always listened to it with emotion, but this time, in this empty home, I had the impression that they were all turning a deaf ear to it. As if it no longer meant what it always had meant, but was simply a lovely parable.

It was clear to all of us that now the most important person to Jacob was Moshe Dobrushka, who was here known as Thomas Schönfeld. Jacob spent days on end waiting for his arrival from Vienna, asking every day if there was a letter from him. Yet the only person who would visit him was the treasurer Wessel, a friend of Dobrushka's, with whom he had some dealings or other, though nothing was communicated to us. It fell to me, meanwhile, to write the letters, mostly letters to creditors, soothing, polite, but also letters to the brothers in Altona and Prossnitz.

Jacob even started to talk about returning to Poland, and to ask me in turn all kinds of questions about Warsaw, what things were like there now, and I felt that he was homesick for it, or that he was too weak now to start another new life in another foreign land. In the evenings, he grew nostalgic, and so I took up pen and paper and wrote all his memories down, and when my hand would start to hurt, Anusia Pawłowska would take over, and then Antoni Czerniawski would correct and copy it out the following day.

"Look," he told us, "when I was in Poland, it was a peaceful and prosperous land. As soon as I was thrown in prison, the king passed away, and troubles began to plague that country. And when I left Poland for good, the Commonwealth was torn asunder."

It was hard to deny him this.

He also said that the reason he maintained his Turkish style of dress was that according to Polish legend, one day a man born of a foreign mother would arrive, and he would repair the country, and liberate it from every oppression.

He would constantly warn us not to return to the old Jewish faith, but that winter on the first night of Hanukkah he suddenly lit the first candle and ordered Jewish dishes be prepared, and everyone ate them with great gusto. And then we sang in the old language that old song that Rebbe Issachar had taught us long ago:

What is man? A spark.
What is human life? A moment.
What is the future now?
A spark. And what the crazed course of time? A moment.
Where does man come from?
A spark. And what is death? A moment.
Who was He while he contained the world?
A spark. And what will he be once he swallows up the world again?
A moment.

## Moliwda in search of his life's center

It has to be the best, the kind that doesn't make your head hurt the next day. After wine, however, he sleeps badly, and wakes first thing in the morning, and that is the worst time of day: everything at that time seems to be a problem, some terrible misunderstanding. As he tosses and turns on his bed, old memories come back to him, very distinct in all their details. More and more often the stubborn thought comes to mind: When did he reach the halfway point of his life? What day was it when his story reached its highest point, its noon, and from that time on—though he did not know about it—began to progress toward setting? It is a very interesting problem, for if people knew which day was the midpoint of their lives, perhaps they would be able to imbue their lives and the events taking place within them with some kind of meaning. Lying sleeplessly, he adds up dates, creates combinations of numbers, like Jakubowski with his obsession with Kabbalah. It is 1786, late autumn. He was born in the summer of 1718. He is therefore sixty-eight years old. If he died now, that would indicate that the middle of his life fell in the year 1752. He tries to remember that year, turning the pages of the internal, not especially precise calendar in his mind, and in the end he finds that if he were to die right now, then that point

might well be the day he arrived in Craiova. How strange: he remembers it well. He even remembers that he was wearing the white linen shirt of the Bogomils, that it was hot, and that small overripe plums were falling on the dry road, where they were soon crushed by carts' wheels. Big, fat wasps, more like hornets, drank up the sweet pear juice in the orchard. People dressed in white were dancing in a circle. Moliwda stands among them and feels joy, but it is the kind of joy you have to force yourself to undergo—and then it blossoms.

His work in the royal chancellery is not the most difficult; he, as a senior clerk, oversees more than he actually writes. To him belongs the division in communication with the Ottoman Porte, since he knows languages. In fact, at his age, a person can simply pretend to be working, and that is what Moliwda does.

The king likes the witty Moliwda, his hoarse voice, his yarns. They often trade a few sentences; the exchange is always humorous and ends in a burst of laughter. This is why Moliwda is widely respected. When Stanisław August comes into the chancellery, everyone quickly gets up and bows—it is only Moliwda who takes a long time to rise, having to exert himself on account of his big belly, and since the king does not care for exaggeration, Moliwda limits his bow to a quick tilt of the head.

Moliwda considers himself to be something of a wise man now, and in spite of small crises, he maintains his good opinion of himself. Ultimately, he does not believe that he has been harmed by life. He tries to live like a Cynic philosopher. Few things are capable of wounding him. He has a sharp pen, of which he makes frequent enough use. Recently someone named Antoni Felicjan Nagłowski wrote a book titled *The Warsaw Guide*, in which he presented the beautiful and important places of the capital. Moliwda mocked him, deeming that complaisant vision of the capital worthy of a schoolgirl. He determined to write an homage to Warsaw's whores, whose customs he had been investigating over the last few years, as a scholar investigates the lives of the savages on distant islands. This work, called *A Supplement to the Guide Published by Another Author*, appeared in 1779 and was rapidly disseminated. It made some Warsaw courtesans famous, while Moliwda's own social position improved; even though the publication was not only ephemeral but anonymous, everyone knew it had been done by him.

For years he has been getting together with a group of friends—among them are some men from the chancellery, but there are also journalists, and playwrights. A merry company that never shies away from intelligent conversations. The men meet every Wednesday to taste wine, smoke pipes, and then, happily, bolstered by the wine, they set out into Warsaw, seeking new places, even better than the ones they found the week before. For instance, they go to Liza Szynder's on Krochmalna Street, where it is cheap and comfortable. The girls wear flimsy little shirts, not some frippery with frills. Moliwda does not care for that sort of overperformance in his girls. Sometimes they head over to Trembecka Street, where the ground floor of every home is a shrine of sorts to love, and the women sit in the windows and beckon to their customers. It should be said that he rarely makes use of their services now, his manhood does not share his enthusiasm for women in flimsy shirts that barely cover their bottoms—in half-asses, as the men say jokingly, maliciously of them. Women still attract him, but he is rarely up to the execution of ordinary relations, which exposes him to smirks and ambiguous glances. For some time now, he has not even tried.

And that's another thing—women attract him, but they also disgust him more and more. He has the impression that only now has the whole construct of his attitude toward women, a kind of edifice that built itself up so intricately all his life—their defenselessness, their sanctity, their purity—finally begun to rumble toward collapse. He always suffered on their score, was always falling in love, and more often than not his love went unrequited. He prayed to them . . . Now he sees women in their overwhelming majority as very simple things, wily little whores, empty and cynical, doing business off their own bodies, trading in holes, the one and the other, as though they were eternal, their youth carved out of stone. He's known so many and observes their falls with satisfaction. A few of them have been able to use their cunts to come into considerable wealth—like that Maciejewska all the officers used to go and see, one after the next, which permitted her to get a little tenement house on Nowe Miasto. Then it was just ordinary soldiers, but she did not stop there, he had seen her lately in excellent health, now a dowager and a member of the bourgeoisie. This contempt of Moliwda's applies to all women, even the noble ones (who only appear noble, he thinks), those who loftily flaunt their origins, over which they had no influence at all, of course, and who, themselves quite frigid, become guardians of others' purity.

His buddies seem to take the same pleasure from this doddering misogyny as he does, and afterward they have all kinds of discussions about their girls, entertaining themselves by drawing up lists and tallies, making rankings. In his old age, Moliwda realizes that he despises women, not just those on the lists, but all of them. That it was this way from the very beginning, that he has always felt this, that he was raised this way, and that this is how his brain works. And that the pure love of his youth was an attempt to deal with this very dark sensation that must necessarily be contempt. A naive revolution, an attempt to make himself pure and free from all bad thoughts. In vain.

When at last he left his position for a well-deserved rest, his friends commissioned his portrait and told the painter to include in it all of Moliwda's many adventures, just as he had recounted them—adventures at sea, pirates, the island where he was king, the exotic lovers, the Jewish Kabbalah, the monastery on Athos, converting pagans . . . Of course the bulk of it was an egregious lie. A monument to his lying life was thus erected.

He sometimes wanders the streets of Warsaw, muddy and riddled with holes. He sometimes goes all the way to Ceglana Street, where many of the court's craftsmen reside, and where the Wołowskis have their businesses. Here is where Shlomo Wołowski built his home—it is a still-unfinished two-story tenement house with a shop on the ground floor and brewery buildings in the courtyard. Over everything here hangs a nauseating smell of malt that also arouses hunger.

Once, seeing some young woman, he worked up his courage and asked about Nahman Jakubowski.

The woman cast him an unfriendly glance and replied:

"You mean Piotr. I don't know anybody here named Nahman."

Moliwda enthusiastically confirmed.

"We knew each other in our youth," he added, to set her mind at ease.

Now he takes out of his pocket a little slip of paper where she wrote Jakubowski's address for him, and he decides to go.

He finds him at home, packed for the road. Nahman, who does not seem too pleased to see him, pushes a little boy, no doubt a grandson, off his lap, and stands to greet Moliwda. He is slight, unshaven.

"Going somewhere?" Moliwda asks him, and without waiting for an answer, he sits down on a free chair.

"What, can't you see? I am an envoy," says a smiling Jakubowski, showing his teeth darkened by tobacco.

And Moliwda smiles, too, looking at this funny little old man who just recently was telling him of the light that escapes from within man. Amusing, too, is the word "envoy" in conjunction with this old bag of bones. Jakubowski seems a little bit embarrassed that Moliwda has found him in such a shameful situation—children racing around the table, a daughter-in-law who bursts in with a menacing face and then flees. Shortly she will reappear with a jug of compote and a little basket of small, sweet buns. But Moliwda will not drink that compote. They go out to the tavern, and there Moliwda orders a whole jug of wine. Nahman Jakubowski does not protest, although he knows it will mean heartburn tomorrow.

## The next chapter in the history of His Lordship Antoni Kossakowski, also known as Moliwda

"I took one of your women as my wife, and had a child with her," he begins. "I ran away from home and had a Christian wedding with her."

Jakubowski looks at him in some surprise, touches his chin with its several days of stubble. He knows he will have to listen to the whole tale, until the very end. Moliwda says:

"And I abandoned them."

After the miller Berek Kozowicz sent off his daughter Małka and the young Kossakowski to Lithuania, the couple sought lodging with a cousin of Małka's who collected bridge tolls, a busy man with an enormous family. Right away they understood that it was only temporary, although they were given their own chamber by the cowshed, heated by the bodies of the cows. The whole family, including the little children, never took their eyes off Kossakowski, as if he were some freak of nature. It was unbearable. Antoni helped his cousin by marriage with his paperwork, dressed in Jewish attire handed down to him by one of the toll collector's teenagers, and would go into the village or conduct his arguments about the toll right there at the bridge. He feared, however, that his language would betray him, and so he intentionally muddled it with different sorts of accents, throwing in words from other tongues: Lithuanian, Ruthenian, Yiddish. When he returned, his heart would tighten at the sight of Małka, suddenly heavy, terrified, surprised by her own condition, childish. What could be done? The toll collector, who smelled of arak, always asked him to read the same thing, pointing with his black-nailed finger to that same part of the scripture with which Antoni was as yet unfamiliar—and at last Małka told him that it was the story of Dinah, daughter of Leah and Jacob, who in spite of being warned went far from her home and was raped by a foreigner, Shechem.

"You are Shechem," she added.

And when some boy at the bridge started jamming his finger into Antoni's chest and demanding to know who he was, a crummy Jew or a crummy Pole, he started to be afraid, as if he were swimming in a river and had lost the ground beneath his feet, as if the water were carrying him now, as if he were defenseless, going into the unknown. He became more and more anxious, and then he panicked, perhaps already sensing what was going to happen. Then he remembered that in Trakai he had some family on his mother's side, some relatives of the Kamińskis, and he fantasized about going to them and asking for help.

And he did set off, in fact, in January, having changed his attire from Jewish to Polish and noble. In three days, he found himself in Trakai, but he found no one there by a name like Kamiński. That aunt had died several years ago, her daughters had gone off with their husbands, one of them to someplace in Poland, the other deep into Russia. He learned, however, by accident, that there was a certain merchant from Trakai who was seeking a Polish tutor for his children in Pskov, where he operated his business.

And so Antoni sent the toll collector all the money he had, and in a generously apportioned letter to him, and a separate one to his wife, he promised to send more just as soon as he had earned it, and he entreated that foreigner to take care of Małka and the child until his return. Then everything would work out. Let the child be an ordinary mamzer from an illicit relationship, albeit a lawfully wed one; let that Christian wedding be respected.

On a gray winter day, as he was setting off for Russia, he received a letter at the address he had given in Trakai. In an untrained hand, the toll collector had written to tell him that both Małka and the child had died during labor, and he wished with his whole heart that the image of those two would not leave Kossakowski until the end of his days, that he would forever be haunted by the knowledge that he had been the cause of their deaths, and that nothing would ever free him from that sin. He read this letter under the great winter sky, in a cart where he was squeezed in among his fellow passengers, and he felt simultaneously despair and relief—as a swimmer borne by the river's current feels terror until he reconciles himself to his own smallness and helplessness and becomes like a little twig upon whom nothing depends. And then comes peace.

The journey to Pskov lasted a month. Mostly he walked; sometimes wagons picked him up. He slept in stables, and sometimes he had the feeling that in his brain there was now a painful ulcer, but that he would be able to go on living with a brain ulcer so long as he didn't disturb it in any way. This was in fact possible, aside from certain moments that came up without warning, and then the pain seemed to escape its magically defined borders, overwhelming him completely. There were also situations like those when he was traveling by sleigh with some Ruthenian peasants, freezing and filthy, and he cried the whole way, until finally the carter reined in his horse and went back to him, to hold and rock him. They stood intertwined like that in that great white emptiness, the horses steaming in the cold, the peasants in their warm wrappings waiting patiently. The carter never even asked him what was wrong.

In Pskov it turned out that he had come too late, and that there was already a tutor, who was also far more qualified than he.

After a long journey, he made it to Petersburg and realized that he could keep living just like this—being always in motion, in a cart, on a horse, every day with different people. He was pleasant, intelligent, conversant. People liked him right away, and, as if sensing that he was younger than he claimed, they looked after him, as well. He made the most of that care without ever crossing any boundaries. If you look at the matter honestly, a person needs little to live on—just a meal of some kind, and some clothing. You can sleep anywhere—and he was always being taken in by some merchant or other, for whom he would translate, do the accounting, tell some humorous tale. He was also taken in by ordinary peasants, to whom he pretended to be a mysterious nobleman in some difficulty, always treating them with the same respect he would have if they had had their own noble titles. Nor did he shy away from Jews or Greeks—he learned their languages and was always pleased to work as a translator. Sometimes he would say his name was—after his mother—Kamiński, sometimes Żmudziński, or he would invent some new surname for just a night or a couple of days. Since he expressed himself well, since he was polite and well mannered, the merchants he got to know on his travels would recommend him to their friends, and so he journeyed in caravans all over the Turkish lands. Tormented by his recurring melancholic moods, he enlisted at last in a Black Sea fleet. For almost three years, he sailed and visited many ports. He survived a shipwreck in the Aegean Sea, was confined to a Greek prison in Salonika—on a rigged conviction, of course. When he got out, he set off for the holy Mount Athos, believing he would find some solace there. But he didn't find it. Then he was a dragoman in Smyrna, until finally he wound up with the Bogomils in Craiova, where he intended to spend the rest of his life.

"Until Jacob showed up. Until you discovered me," Moliwda says now. They have drunk two jugs of wine, and Moliwda feels very tired. Nahman is silent for a long while, and then he rises and embraces Moliwda as the peasant once had in that barren winter.

"What do you think, Jakubowski, have I lived a good life?" Moliwda mumbles into Nahman's collar.

As he staggers home, he sees a fire. He stops, and for a long while he stares into the burning building, which had held a musical instruments workshop. The guitar strings snap from the heat, and the tense skins of the drums shoot up into the air—the fire plays an infernal music, over-heard by passersby, until with great pomp the fire brigade arrives.

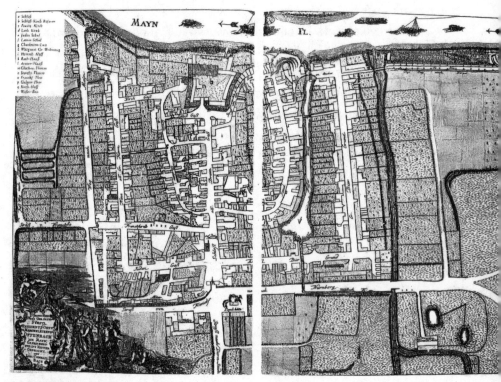

MAYN FL.

PLANVON OFFENBACH 1750 (Joh. Conrad Buck)

## 29.

## Of the little insect-like people who inhabit Offenbach am Main

The sight is so surprising that the local carriages on their own initiative pull over to the side of the road to let this bizarre cavalcade of men on horses and vehicles pass. At its head is a squad of soldiers made up of six men on horseback, armed with pikes and colorfully attired. They have bushy mustaches, and in spite of their serious, even threatening faces, they resemble town criers announcing the arrival of some circus. They are led by a man, also armed, whose mustache is twirled around fancifully, almost like a treble clef. After this front guard goes a sumptuous carriage with an elaborate coat of arms on the door, so elaborate it is hard to remember, and after this there are still a dozen multi-passenger carriages drawn by heavy, eastern horses. Last in line are full carts covered in tarps. After them there are just men on horseback—young, handsome men. The cavalcade is moving from Frankfurt over the bridge over the Main toward Oberrad, on the outskirts of Offenbach.

Mrs. von La Roche, who is visiting her family in Offenbach and close to deciding to settle down in this exceptionally tranquil little town that reminds her of a sanatorium, also tells her coachman to pull over. She looks on in curiosity: What can this be, these strange people traveling in this strange manner? The guards are wearing gaudy uniforms, as if they were Uhlans, mostly in shades of green and gold, covered in aiguillettes and buttons. Their tall hats are decorated with peacock feathers. These very young men, almost boys, remind Sophie von La Roche of long-legged, hopping insects. She would love to take a look inside that most lavish carriage, but the curtains on its windows are tightly drawn. She can, on the other hand, examine the new arrivals in the following carriages—they are mostly women and children, all of them dressed up and colorful, smiling and probably a little bit embarrassed by all this commotion they have caused.

"Who is that?" an intrigued Mrs. von La Roche inquires of a towns-man who is staring at this procession.

"They're saying it's some Polish baron with his sons and his daughter."

The cavalcade goes slowly through the city's outskirts, squeezing onto the narrow cobbled streets. The men on horseback shout back and forth in some foreign language, and their whistles can be heard. Mrs. von La Roche feels as if she's watching a performance at the opera.

When Sophie gets together with her equally excited female cousin, her stay in Berlin quickly retreats into the background of everyone's mind. They are all talking about that Polish baron with the beautiful, mysteri-ous daughter he brought here at the archduke's invitation, renting from him the house in Oberrad where the newcomers will stay first.

Her cousin rented a carriage especially to go to Oberrad and saw the whole ceremonious process of getting everyone out of their carriages. Now she says excitedly:

"Those two sons led out a tall old man in red wearing a Turkish hat. He had a diamond star pinned to his chest. From the second carriage his daughter got out, dressed like a princess. I saw diamonds in her hair. You can't imagine, they looked like an imperial couple. You will be neighbors, once they're installed in the castle."

Since March 1786, Offenbach has been gripped by light to moderate hysteria. As bricklayers work in the castle, dust flies out the windows. Enormous quantities of wallpapers, carpets, materials for the walls, furni-ture, and bedding are brought in—all the things you would need to cre-ate a comfortable residence worthy of a Polish baron.

Sophie von La Roche, who is a writer and whose custom it is to write, is careful to note down in her diary everything she sees:

> It is very interesting how our dear co-inhabitants of Offenbach are dealing with the scant information with which they have had to content themselves on the subject of these Poles. The human mind cannot tolerate uncertainty or things left mostly unsaid, and so right away every possible history began to be invented regarding these insect-like people. According to the rumors, the old man in the Turkish costume is some sort of alchemist and Kabbalist, like that Saint-Germain, and he owes his fortune to the gold he has produced in his own workshop, which workers have confirmed on carrying inside some secret crates filled with glass, and jars and little bottles. Our dear Mrs. Bernard told me that this Baron Frank-Dobrucki is none other than Tsar Peter the Third, miraculously saved from death, which explains the arrival of all the barrels of gold from the East, for the maintenance of this court of Nebuchadnezzar. I permitted myself to take part in the game and informed her she was wrong. This supposed daughter and her two brothers are in fact the children of the previous tsarina, Elizabeth Petrovna, by her lover Razumovsky, and the baron is actually just their tutor. She nodded, and that very same day, come evening, the rumor returned to me through the lips of the doctor who came to let my blood, in no way altered.

## Of Isenburger Schloss and its freezing residents

The castle stands just above the water, and on a number of occasions it has fallen victim to flooding. Careful recording of the water level can be seen in two places inside. The highest one was from two years ago. Hence, no doubt, the lichen on the walls, from the moisture. Eva spends a long time selecting her room, wondering if she would rather have a view of the river, in which case she would have a balcony, or perhaps a big window looking out on the city. In the end she decides on the river and the balcony.

The river is many colors here, soft and gentle. It is called the Main, but her father stubbornly insists on calling it the Prut—the name of the river that divided Turkey from Poland, where so many of his followers had once camped in anticipation of him. The sight of the barges and the boats with double sails floating down this river—the Main—soothes Eva. She can just sit like this on the balcony, looking out over the water, which she experiences as a kind of tender caress, the fluid motion, the movement of the sails, all of it in some way touches her body and leaves a pleasant streak

along her skin. She has already ordered furniture: a desk and two wardrobes, as well as sofas upholstered in bright material and a coffee table. Her father takes two rooms with a view of the Main. She went especially to Frankfurt to order him carpets, as her father will no longer recognize any sort of chair. The most beautiful room, with a string of stained-glass windows, will be a temple, she has decided that already. This is where the brothers and sisters will gather.

The castle is impressive—it is the largest building in the area, and it makes a bigger impression than any church would. From the flat bank it is separated by a road that is eternally wet, reinforced every year by stones workers bring in. There is also a harbor for the ferry that can be taken to the other side. Near the harbor there is an inn and a smithy. On tables assembled from wooden boards, fish from the river are sold, mainly pike and perch. They, the Polacken, as they are called in town, also buy whole baskets of fish.

The castle has five floors. Eva and Matuszewski have sketched out the use of each. On the first floor, then, will be the ceremonial halls, on the second she and her father as well as the oldest of the brothers and sisters will live, as in Brünn. Above, the kitchen and the women's rooms, and the two final floors will be for the young people who will come. There will also be a kitchen and a laundry in the building next door. Eva, who has investigated the emperor's palaces in Vienna, has a vision for how it's all supposed to look. For her renovations, she has engaged the services of an architect from Frankfurt; sometimes it is hard to explain to him what it is they want—the meeting room is to be without furniture, just carpets and pillows, the home chapel is to be without an altar, just a dais in the middle. There are many things this man can't understand. They spend the entire summer painting the walls and changing out the rotted floors. The worst is the first floor, where two years ago there was stagnant water. In all the windows they had to put new panes. They have already purchased in Frankfurt large quantities of rugs and blankets, because it is cold inside, even in the summer. The buyers hand over money with pleasure, without so much as a murmur. Frankfurt bankers turn up immediately to offer them loans.

By the time they move into the castle, there is no longer any pomp and ceremony. They move into the castle at the same time as Mrs. Sophie von La Roche, who has been widowed, settles permanently in Offenbach, in the winter of 1788.

The two staircases with their steep steps will pose a challenge to Jacob Frank—he has a hard time walking now. The long journey to Offenbach through wintry Germany caused him to come down with a cold. In Meissen, where they stayed for a few days, he had an attack of fever, was delirious and insisted again that they were trying to poison him with communion wafers. He recovered a little after visiting the manufactory and viewing all its porcelain.

Now, oblivious to the renovations, uninterested in wallpapers and upholstery, he spends whole days dictating letters that messengers deliver to Poland, to Moravia, to Bucharest—anywhere there are true believers. He also summons all the elder brothers here. The first to arrive in the summer are Jakubowski with Jan Wołowski, and shortly after that they bring in the Łabęckis' children, as well as the Lanckorońskis', as well as the "Turkesses," as they call the true believers of Wallachia. The house in Oberrad cannot fit them all, so, while the castle is still being renovated,

they must also rent rooms in Offenbach, in those cozy, well-cared-for houses with their slate-covered walls.

Jacob is visibly revived by the visits he receives from Thomas, who comes to Offenbach during his frequent business trips to Frankfurt. Twice they have gone out together to the river, where Thomas has introduced his uncle to bankers and helped him secure yet more lines of credit.

Normally, however, they sit and talk. Now Jacob spontaneously orders his coffee served in the castle portico, where he can warm himself in the patches of sun, although what he really wants is no doubt for Thomas to be able to watch the handsome man in the elegant white uniform who is running the drills in the castle courtyard.

"That's Prince Lubomirski," says Jacob.

For a moment, Thomas says nothing, stunned, or maybe he doesn't quite believe his uncle.

"Where could such a person have come from, all the way here? A real prince?"

Jacob tells the story with pleasure, enjoying his coffee. The coffee is imported from Turkey, and it makes a sensation in Offenbach. One of the true believers has already opened a small coffee shop in town, and sitting in it instantly became fashionable.

Jacob says that Lubomirski is bankrupt, and in order to avoid being imprisoned for his debts, he had to flee Poland. In Warsaw, he met the lovely Tekla Łabęcka, the orphaned daughter of Moshe Łabęcki, and, having fallen in love with her, followed her all the way here. Jacob gave him employment, appointing him commander-in-chief of the guard. The prince even helped design its uniforms, making use of his great knowledge of such matters.

Thomas laughs.

"So those gaudy uniforms were Lubomirski's notion?"

Jacob is offended by this supposition. The idea for the uniforms was his: amaranth breeches and cerulean jackets with gold aiguillettes. The halberdiers, meanwhile, wear azure on one side and crimson on the other.

## Of boiled eggs and Prince Lubomirski

The castle, which has not been heated in years, is covered in a mycelium of frost and every variety of chill; the walls are cold and damp, the fireplaces and stoves are lazy, slow to start. They do heat up well, but as soon as the last log has burned, the fireplace cools down again immediately. And so their silhouettes round out—from the several layers of clothing they all wear, one on top of the other. The cold here is different, foreign—it clings to the skin, keeps hands and feet in a state of constant numbness; it is hard to make a needle go into an embroidery hoop, hard to turn the pages of a book. In winter, life takes place in one room on the first floor, the largest one, next to the fireplace and the glowing Turkish stoves arranged around the edges, which causes the clothes to absorb the particular smell of that damp smoke.

"It smells like it used to in Ivanie," says the Lord when he walks in.

This is also where they eat all of their meals. They sit at a long table that is placed as close as possible to the fireplace. On their beautiful tableware, they are served almost exclusively boiled eggs.

"You've turned into an old maid already. Not even Lubomirski wanted you, even though you asked him to come to tea," Jacob says suddenly to his daughter as they are all having breakfast.

This is how his bad moods usually start—Jacob has to lay into someone.

Eva flushes crimson. His comment has been heard by Matuszewski, both her brothers, Anusia Pawłowska, Eva Jezierzańska, and—and this is truly awful—Thomas. Eva sets down her silverware and leaves the room.

"But he's here for Tekla Łabęcka," says Eva Jezierzańska in a conciliatory tone, serving Jacob some more horseradish. "He's like a big dog when it comes to women, you have to watch out for him. Tekla resisted him, but that just attracts him to her more."

"She didn't resist him long," says Matuszewski with his mouth full, pleased that the subject has successfully been changed.

Jacob is quiet for a little while. Lately he has been living off boiled or baked eggs. He says his stomach won't digest anything else now.

"He's a Polish prince . . . ," says Jacob.

"Maybe so, but his honor and his finances are finished," Czerniawski says quietly. "He has no money, and no respect. He had to escape here from Poland because his creditors were after him. It's a good thing he comes in handy as a stableman . . ."

"He is the general of the palace guard," Matuszewski corrects him.

"But he's a prince," says Jacob, exasperated. "Go after her," he says to Zwierzchowska.

But Zwierzchowska has no intention of getting up.

"She won't come back. You offended her." And after a slight pause, she adds, "Lord."

A silence falls on the table. Jacob cannot control his rage, his lower lip trembles. Only now can it be seen with perfect clarity that the left side of his face has flagged, drooped down slightly, since his last apoplexy in Brünn.

After a moment's silence he says, "I have taken all illness upon myself." He begins quietly, then gathers volume. "Look at who you are, and that is without listening to me at all and caring nothing for my words. I led you here, and if you had just listened to me from the very beginning, then you would have gotten even further. You can't even perceive it. You would be sleeping on swan's down, on chests full of gold, in royal palaces. Who among you has ever truly believed in me? You are all fools. I've been struggling over you in vain. You've learned nothing, all you do is watch me, but you don't think about how I feel or how I'm hurting."

He shoves his plate away violently. Shelled eggs fall onto the floor.

"Get out. You, Eva, stay," he says to Jezierzańska.

When the others have left, she leans over him and straightens his thin wool stock tie.

"It's scratching me," Jacob complains.

"It's meant to scratch you, that's how it keeps you warm."

"You were always good to me, the kindest after my sweet Hana."

Jezierzańska tries to extricate herself, but Jacob has caught her by the hand and is pulling her closer.

"Draw the curtains," he says.

She obediently draws the thick fabric so that it gets almost dark, and now they are hidden, as if in a box. Jacob says in a plaintive voice:

"My thoughts are not your thoughts. I am so lonely. You may be lovely, good people, but you are also simpletons, without any understanding. You need to be treated like children. I talk to you about simple things in simple analogies. Stupidity can conceal great wisdom. You know that, because you are wise," says Jacob, and lays his head on her lap. Eva Jezierzańska carefully slides his ever-present hat off his head and plunges her fingers into the Lord's greasy silver locks.

Jacob is old. Eva Jezierzańska, who bathes him every week, knows his body well. The skin on it has dried out and gotten very thin, but also smooth as parchment; even the pockmarks on his face have leveled out, or maybe they're still lurking, under his deep wrinkles. Eva knows that people can be divided into those who have horizontal wrinkles on their foreheads and those who have vertical ones. The former are cheerful and friendly—that's how she thinks of them, anyway, and she herself is like this—but they rarely get what they want in life. The others, those with the furrows over their noses, are angry and impetuous, but they usually do succeed in attaining their goals. Jacob belongs to that second group. In his youth, those angry wrinkles were more visible, but now they, too, have receded; perhaps his aim has already been reached, and they no longer have any reason to be there. Only their shadow has remained on his forehead, rinsed away daily by the sun's rays.

Jacob's skin is tanned; the hair on his chest is gray and thinner—he used to have thick hair there, and it used to be black. The same is true of his legs—now they're almost bare. Even Jacob's penis has changed. Jezierzańska would know, as she used to have dealings with it often, hosting it inside her. But it has been a long time since she saw it take its fighting stance. Now it looks more like a formless codpiece flopping between his legs, the effect exaggerated by the hernia. Little networks of varicose veins—delicate filigrees—in every possible color have appeared on his calves and thighs, seemingly in all the colors there are. Jacob has gotten skinny lately, though his stomach is bloated from his poor digestion.

She turns her head tactfully to the window as she gently washes his genitals with a sponge. She has to be careful with the water—God forbid it is too cold or too hot, for then Jacob shrieks as if she were murdering him. Although of course she could never have harmed him in any way. This is the most precious human body that she knows.

She was the one who thought of sending out to the country, to the peasants, for the special shears they use to trim the split hooves of farm animals, which are the only things that work to cut Jacob's toenails.

"You go, Eva, to the younger women, pick three for me, you know the kind I like, tell them to ready a white costume and to keep it at hand. I'll be calling them soon."

Eva Jezierzańska sighs theatrically and says in mock indignation:

"Illness and old age just don't exist as far as you're concerned, Jacob. You ought to be ashamed."

This evidently flatters him, he smiles a little to himself and puts his arms around her thickset waist.

## How Zwierzchowska the She-Wolf
## maintains order in the castle

She has to start everything from scratch. Zwierzchowska is the exhausted keeper of this whole court, all the keys hooked to her belt. It took her a long time to learn them all.

Wherever she finds herself, Zwierzchowska always sets up and takes charge of the home. She is like a she-wolf caring for her pack—feeding them, protecting them. She knows how to economize, knows how to run a household—she learned that back in Ivanie, and kept on learning it wherever they went, in places like Wojsławice, Kobyłka, Zamość, the smaller manor houses and villages where they were allotted some little place to live. She knows she is partly to blame for a crime, that fourteen people died because of her; she has them on her conscience, and even now, all these years later, she remembers that scene so vividly, when she pretended to be the wife of the Wojsławice rabbi Zyskiel. She wasn't good at it—anyone ought to have been able to see right through her act, in fact. She justified it to herself as necessary, they were at war, and in war the rules are different from what they are in peacetime. Her husband tells her all the time that she can't blame herself; they all took part in it. They lashed out like rabid animals. It seems as though no one cares anymore about what happened the way she does. Jacob promised her that when the last days came and they went to the Virgin, he would hold her hand. That promise has helped her a great deal. She hopes no curse has been cast upon her, and that no curse is lying in wait. After all, she was only protecting her pack.

Now, when her swollen legs are bothering her, she asks her very young daughter-in-law, Eleonora, née Jezierzańska, to help her. Zwierzchowska, who moves rather sluggishly these days, often leans on Eleonora, and then people say of them that they look like Naomi and Ruth.

Eva Jezierzańska, Zwierzchowska's daughter-in-law's mother, handles the youth recruits when she is with Jacob and not in Warsaw—she looks after their lodging, the girls, their jobs, their recreation. She conducts correspondence, arranging accommodation and the arrival dates of the brothers coming to Offenbach, as if this were a heavily frequented inn. When she goes back to Warsaw, her duties are taken over by Jacob Zalewski, the younger Dembowski's son-in-law. The Czerniawskis, meanwhile, are in charge of finances. Their son, Antoni, is the Lord's secretary, along with Yeruhim Dembowski, whom the Lord wishes to be always at his side these days. They have a chancellery next to the Lord's room, bigger than the one in Brünn. Some of the young people copy out letters when the time comes to send them around to the true believers. Dembowska, Yeruhim's wife, in a tiny little room at the very top of the palace that is constantly being stormed by pigeons with their noisy claws, handles the vending of golden drops. There is another small room that is like a post office, filled with little wooden boxes and piles of tow to arrange inside. The expensive goods are set along the shelves—hundreds of little bottles already filled up with golden drops; the labels are written by her daughter. The kitchen is run by one of the Matuszewskis, the one who married Michał Wołowski's son. She is a self-confident, domineering woman, and in attitude and temperament she is suited to the kitchen's design, as there are not any pots here, though there are cauldrons and huge pans, and the roasting tins they bought are big enough they could fit even the fattest goose. For the worst jobs they hire girls from town, but every girl who visits is expected to help out in the kitchen.

Franciszek Szymanowski, who in Brünn handled the guard and the drills and had absolute power, has to share it here with Prince Lubomirski. He has done so willingly and even with a certain panache, presenting him with the baton that had been ordered back in Brünn, solemnly, on a pillow. He is already feeling exhausted by the ever-growing "legion." He has reserved for himself only the function of leading the procession every Sunday, when they all ride to church on the road along the river. That's when people come out of their houses to look at them. Szymanowski heads up the whole cavalcade—he sits up very straight and proud on his horse. He wears a half smile on his lips, looking neither ruminative nor ironic. His eyes pass over the people they go by as they would a lawn, boring and monotonous. Prince Lubomirski, meanwhile, always goes in the carriage with Jacob and Eva. This parade arrives so punctually that

*Le Baron de Franck allant se promener en Voiture*

the inhabitants of Offenbach could set their watches by it, as far as he's concerned—time for morning coffee! Here is that Polish count going to Bürgel, the one Catholic church in the area, surrounded by his entourage like some sort of faun.

This mass is celebrated only for them, and the so-called Polacken pack the little church. They pray in silence and sing in Polish. Jacob continues his habit of lying in the form of the cross before the altar, which has created quite the sensation among the Catholics of Bürgel; they are unfamiliar with such ostentatious eastern piety. The parish priest praises them and tells others to follow their example. Since they have been here, the church has never wanted for candles or incense. And recently Eva funded new episcopal robes and a beautiful gold monstrance studded with the most expensive stones. The parish priest all but fainted when he saw it, and now every night he worries about whether keeping such a valuable thing won't tempt every sort of thief.

## The knife set with turquoise

Prince Jerzy Marcin Lubomirski was already completely broke when he turned up in Offenbach. Of his great fortune, one of the largest in all of Poland, nothing remains. In recent years he dedicated all of his energy to working for the king, who appreciated his excellent knowledge of all the local actresses as well as everything happening behind the scenes— he organized the royal theater in Warsaw. Unfortunately, he cannot shake his reputation as a traitor and a rabble-rouser. First, back when he was still commander of the fortress in Kamieniec, he sullied his royal honor by marrying a woman without her or his parents' permission. The marriage turned out to be short-lived and unhappy. After obtaining a divorce, he married again, but that marriage, too, was not long for this world. He's also had dalliances with men. To one of his male lovers he gifted a town and several villages, proving himself to be miserable marriage material. He always considered himself a soldier first and foremost. His tactical talents were evidently also noticed by Frederick, the Prussian emperor, who made him a general during the Silesian Wars. Due to almost inexplicable boredom connected with the Prussian way of waging war, the prince deserted from the Prussian army and founded his own division, with which he attacked his former comrades in arms. He was in fact fighting on two fronts, battling the Polish army at the same time, and he indulged with great gusto in rape and plunder as well. The territory between the fronts, the delectable anarchy, the suspension of all laws, human and divine, villages burned after the army passed through, battlefields covered in corpses to be looted, the slaughter of paupers found poking around out there, the nauseating smell of the blood mixed with the sour smell of digested alcohol—all that was the kingdom of Jerzy Marcin Lubomirski. In the end he was captured by the Poles and sentenced to death for treason and banditry. His family interceded on his behalf, and he escaped death in exchange for a long prison sentence. When the Bar Confederation was formed, however, suddenly people were reminded of his leadership talents, and he was given an opportunity for reform. He supplied provisions to Pułaski's troops in the Jasna Góra fortress and spent time there himself.

Lubomirski still remembers well the evening in Częstochowa when the wife of this Jacob Frank died. He watched the neophytes making their funeral procession, getting permission from the commander of the fortress to go outside the walls to bury the body in some cave. He had never in his life seen people more grief-stricken. Poor, downtrodden, gray, some of them dressed like Turks, some of them like Cossacks, and their women in cheap, garish dresses that didn't suit a funeral at all. He felt sorry for them then. Who would have thought that he would find himself among them now?

For the duration of the chaotic siege, he knew that although it was forbidden to have any contact with the prisoners, the soldiers would go to Frank like to some kind of holy father, and Frank would put his hands on their heads. Among the soldiers there was a belief that his touch could make you impervious to blows and bullets. And he also remembers that girl, Frank's daughter, so young and flighty, whom the father never let out of the tower, no doubt fearing for her virtue, and how she would sometimes slip in from the town to the monastery with a hood over her beautiful head.

The prince's mood darkened there in stifling Częstochowa. He wasn't really able to pray; the votive offerings hanging on the walls made him uncomfortable as he rattled off his devotions. For what if he were to meet with such misfortune? If he lost a leg, or was disfigured in some explosion? But of one thing he was sure: People like him enjoyed special privileges with the Holy Mother, she had proven that to be the case a great many times. She was like his family, like a kind aunt who would help him out of any type of scrape.

Bored by the listlessness of the monastery, he got drunk every evening and encouraged his noncommissioned officers to take up with the prisoner's young daughter. Once, in a fit of drunken generosity, weary of this place where he felt no less a prisoner than that strange Jew, he sent the neophytes a basket of hard-won victuals as well as a barrel of inferior wine out of the brothers' stores. Frank sent him a polite thank-you as well as a striking Turkish knife with a silver hilt set with pieces of turquoise—a present worth a great deal more than that basket of food and some vinegary wine. Lubomirski mislaid the knife somewhere along the way, but when he fell on hard times and wound up in Vienna, he suddenly remembered its existence.

After the fall of Jasna Góra, he returned to Warsaw. People said that at the Partition Sejm, he was the one to drag Tadeusz Reytan out of the doorway where he had lain in an attempt to prevent the ratification of the First Partition of Poland, and that then he had demarcated the new boundaries of the Kingdom of Poland, mutilating the nation, crippling it. Which is why, in Warsaw, his acquaintances started to cross the street at the sight of him. And there Lubomirski led a life of dissolution, squandering the rest of his fortune and taking out massive loans, in a city that was deep in chaos. He drank, played cards, and was called a "libertine," a fashionable recent word, even though for as long as possible he associated mostly with the ultra-Catholics. When in 1781 a list of his debts was published, it contained the names of over a hundred different creditors. The meticulously calculated sums were astronomical: two million, six hundred and ninety-nine thousand, two hundred and ninety-nine Polish zlotys. He was bankrupt, maybe the most bankrupt person anywhere in Europe. A few years later, he learned from one of his old friends, old Kossakowska, that the court of Jacob Frank had moved to Offenbach.

Suddenly that knife set with turquoise, lost or given as a gift to some prostitute, cut from all the chaos of the prince's thoughts a single astonishing idea—that as it turned out he must have something in common with those people, since he kept running into them everywhere he turned, every few years, since after all he had seen them for the first time in Kamieniec, when they were still Jews, hidden behind their great beards, and then, once baptized, when all through winter, at the request of that ball-breaker Kossakowska, they lived on his estate. There must be some invisible force that links human fates, for otherwise it would be impossible to explain such coincidences as meeting them again in Częstochowa. Now Lubomirski, with practically nowhere else to live, is happy to believe in the invisible threads of fate, but, above all, he has a great deal of faith in himself. He has a deep conviction that the path of his life is straight and orderly, rather like a path cut with a saber through a field of grain. His only regret is that he never exchanged a single word with Jacob Frank in Częstochowa. Still, that tarnished old Częstochowa prisoner now has his own castle and court. And doubtless the reason he has those things is so that he can save Prince Lubomirski, who must now flee from Warsaw.

Only bold, unusual ideas have any chance of coming to fruition—this he has been taught throughout his entire turbulent life. For Prince Lubomirski's whole life has been made up of just such unusual decisions that the regular rabble could never possibly comprehend.

It was similar this time around. He sent a letter to his old friend from his time serving Prussia, Prince Frederick Karol Lichnowski, asking him to recommend him to Frank, now that Frank had somehow attained such dizzying heights. He asked Lichnowski to mention their old acquaintance, without going into too much detail, and his prickly situation now. Soon he had from his friend a quickly written and enthusiastic note that said that the Baron Dobrucki-Frank would be honored, that he could offer His Majesty the Prince the command of his guard, as he would in such a manner further elevate the splendor of his court. Frank also offered the prince an apartment in the nicest quarter of town, a carriage, and an aide-de-camp with the rank of colonel.

And so the best thing that could possibly happen happened, for the prince did not even have the money to make the journey to Offenbach, and he had to fight out the loan of some post horses at every stop he made.

## Of the dollhouse

"Dear friend—I think I can call you that now," says Sophie von La Roche with the directness she is known for. She takes a confused Eva by the elbow and leads her to the table where the others have sat down already. They are primarily burghers and Offenbach entrepreneurs—such as, for instance, André and Bernard, descendants of Huguenots taken in by an ancestor of the Duke of Isenburg over a hundred years ago, just as now this duke has welcomed Frank and his court.

Visitors mill around the living room, and through the open door to the next room several musicians are seen tuning their instruments. Eva Frank and Anusia Pawłowska sit. Eva, as always when she feels insecure and wants to seem like she is confident, even a little churlish, slightly puffs out her lips.

"You see, there is always some commotion around here. How am I to work? Yesterday, however, André, our friend, brought in from Vienna the most fashionable sheet music, which we'll practice. Do you ladies play an instrument? We need a clarinet."

"I have no talent for music," says Eva. "My father attached great importance to a musical education, but . . . well. Perhaps I could accompany you on the clavichord?"

Now they inquire after her father.

"My father begs your forgiveness, he rarely leaves the house these days. He is ailing."

Sophie von La Roche, handing them cups of hot chocolate, asks with concern:

"Does he need a doctor? One of the best is in Frankfurt, I'd be happy to send him a note!"

"No, thank you, there's no need, we have our own doctors."

There is a moment of silence, as though everyone now needs to contemplate carefully all that Eva Frank has said—what "we" means, and the implications of "our own doctors." Praise be to God, however, that the first bars of music are beginning to enter from the room adjacent. Eva lets the air out of her lungs and purses her lips. Sheets of music are lying on the coffee table, evidently straight from the printer's, their pages as yet uncut. Eva reaches for them and reads: *Musikalischer Spass für zwei Violinen, Bratsche, zwei Korner und Bass, geschrieben in Wien. W. A. Mozart.*

The tea drunk from the round cup tastes delicious. Eva is not used to this drink—Sophie von La Roche makes a mental note of it. Do not all Russians drink tea?

Eva looks curiously but discreetly at Sophie—she is around fifty years old, but her face is surprisingly fresh and young, and her eyes downright girlish. She dresses modestly, not like an aristocrat, more like a towns-woman. Her gray hair is combed up and held in place by a delicate bon-net with meticulously pleated frills. She appears quite neat and tidy, until you look at her hands, which are stained with ink, like a child's.

When the small ensemble finally begins to play, Eva takes advantage of the fact that she no longer needs to converse with anyone to look around the room. She sees something that holds her attention longer than the music. As soon as the break begins she intends to ask her hostess about it, but the musicians come back to the coffee table, and cups are clinking, the men are joking, and their hostess is busy introducing the latest guests in the midst of all the hubbub. Eva has never seen such direct, such amus-ing society people. In Vienna everyone was very artificial and distant. And suddenly, without knowing how it has happened—it must have been because of Anusia, who, in her excitement, her cheeks flushed, praised Eva, and then there were Sophie's kind, wise eyes, reassuring her and guaranteeing her safety—Eva finds herself sitting down at Mrs. von La Roche's clavichord, her heart pounding, but of course she knows that her greatest talent is certainly not playing the clavichord, but rather keeping her feelings under control: "The lips won't let themselves be fooled by the heart, nor will the body reveal what the heart feels," a function of old lessons. Eva tries to think of what to play, she is handed some music, but calmly pushes that aside, and from under her fingers flows what she learned in Warsaw, when her father was still locked up in Częstochowa, a simple country ballad.

When Eva and Anusia take their leave, Sophie von La Roche stops Eva by the dollhouse.

"I noticed you were interested," she says. "That's for my granddaugh-ters. They'll come soon. These wonders are created by this craftsman from Bürgel, just take a look—the most recent thing he did was the linen press."

Eva moves closer so she can make out the smallest details. She sees a tiny chest of drawers, a linen cupboard with a wooden bolt mounted on top, pressing a minute piece of white cloth.

Before she goes to sleep, she takes the time to recall every element of that little home. On the first floor, the sewing room and the laundry room, filled with washtubs and buckets, a stove and pots, a loom and little barrels. There is even a little henhouse, painted white, and a tiny ladder for the poultry. And the poultry itself, the miniature wooden ducks and chickens. On the second floor there is a room for the women, with walls covered in paper and a four-poster bed, while on the coffee table there is a beautiful cream-colored coffee set, and next to it a lovely little crib surrounded by a tiny lace curtain. On the third floor, there is the man of the house's office, and the man himself in his frock coat; on his desk lie his writing instruments and a ream of paper not much larger than a thumbnail. Over all this hangs a crystal chandelier, and on the wall there is a crystal mirror. At the very top of the dollhouse is the kitchen, filled to the brim with pots, sieves, plates, and bowls the size of thimbles; on the floor there is even a tin butter churn with a wooden crank, the same kind they had in Brünn, as the women preferred to make their butter themselves.

"Just take a look at it from up close," says her hostess, and hands her the tiny butter churn. Eva takes the thing between her thumb and her forefinger and brings it up to her eyes. She sets it down carefully.

That night, Eva cannot sleep, and Anusia hears her quietly crying. Barefoot on the icy floor, she goes over to her mistress's bed and puts her arms around her back shaken by sobs.

## The dangerous smell of the raspberry bush and muscatel

In the mornings, Jakubowski transcribes a version of the Lord's dream from his notes. Thus he dreamed:

> I saw a very aged Pole whose gray hair reached down to his chest. I drove with Avachunia and arrived at his apartment. His home stood alone on the plain beneath a tall mountain. We walked up to that home, and beneath our feet there was ice, and on that ice grew lovely herbs. The palace was all underground,

and in it there were six hundred rooms, each of them covered in red cloth, and farther inside, in a great quantity of rooms, sat Polish magnates, Radziwiłłs and Lubomirskis and Potockis, and not one of them had on an expensive belt, they were all young and humbly dressed, with black and red beards, and they were employed to do tailoring work. I was much surprised by that sight. And then an old man showed us the siphon in the wall from which it was possible to draw a certain libation, and Avachunia and I drank of that elixir, and its taste was unspeakably good, like that of a raspberry bush or muscatel, and it remained on my lips even after I awoke.

It is a late December night, the stove has just gone out, and Jakubowski is planning on going to bed. Suddenly there is some sort of racket downstairs, as if something made of metal has fallen on the floor, and then women's cries and the stamping of feet. He throws on his coat and carefully goes down the winding stairs. On the second floor, candle flames are flickering. Zwierzchowska races by:

"The Lord has passed out!"

Jakubowski presses into the room. Almost everyone is already in here (they either live on lower floors or are quicker at those awful stairs than he is). Jakubowski forces his way to the front and starts praying loudly: "Dio mio Baruchiah . . ." But someone shushes him.

"We can't hear if he's breathing. The doctor's on his way."

Jacob is lying on his back as though sleeping; he's trembling slightly, or perhaps these are convulsions. Eva kneels beside her father and cries silently.

Before the doctor comes, Zwierzchowska removes everyone from Jacob's room. They are now standing in the corridor, where they can hear the howling of the wind, and it is horrifically cold. With numbed fingers, Jakubowski holds his coat shut tight and prays quietly, rocking back and forth. The men who lead in the doctor from Offenbach push Jakubowski back almost angrily. He stands there with the others until morning, and it isn't until almost dawn that it occurs to someone to bring into the corridor some Turkish stoves.

The morning of the next day is strange, as if the day hadn't started at all. The kitchen does not open; there is no breakfast. The young people, who gathered here like every morning for their lessons, were informed that everything's been canceled. People come up to the castle from town to inquire after the baron's health.

It is interesting, everyone says, that the Lord knew what would happen, for why else would he have sent out all those letters to Warsaw telling the true believers to make their way to Offenbach?

And who has come?

His sons Roch and Joseph have come here permanently; they arrived with trunks and servants. But if they had hoped to find at their father's side some power due to them by birthright, they have made a grave mistake. They were given lovely rooms, but for gold to cover any expense they must, like everyone, ask Czerniawski. Praise be to God, the Lord is generous toward his children. Piotr Jakubowski also came to Offenbach with two of his daughters, Anna and Rozalia, having realized after the death of his wife that there was nothing left for him to do in Warsaw (though the eldest girl stayed) and deciding to join in the Lord's care. Now he lives in a little room on the highest floor, with a single little window and a slanting wall, and there—as Czerniawski commanded—he dedicates himself to editing the words of the Lord and to his own eccentric studies. When Czerniawski stops by this little nook at times when Jakubowski isn't in it, he finds on the small table a stack of papers he is not ashamed to rifle through. He understands nothing of Jakubowski's Hebrew calculations, drawings, and sketches. He also finds some strange prophecies, written in a shaky hand, a chronicle of events reaching back far into the past, and handsewn pages, the first of which bears the title *Scraps*. Czerniawski flips through them, intrigued, not understanding what they are scraps of, what they could have belonged to before.

Antoni Czerniawski, son of Israel Osman of Czernowitz, the Turkish Jew who led Frank's company across the Dniester, does not take after his father at all. Where the father was dark-complexioned, skinny, violent, the son is a little overweight, calm, attentive. He is a quiet man, small in stature, very focused, with a frowning, worried forehead that ages him. In

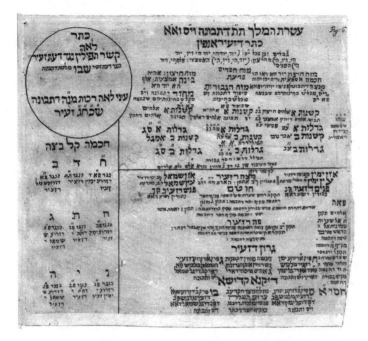

spite of his relative youth, he has already acquired quite the belly, and this makes his whole figure appear somewhat massive. He has thick black hair down to his shoulders, and a beard he trims every so often. And his is the one beard in the whole of the Offenbach castle that the Lord does not find fault with. The Lord trusts him without limit and entrusts to him the care of their finances, which isn't easy—their income, though ample, is very irregular, while their expenses remain, unfortunately, quite regular indeed. He also performs the duties of a secretary and has a habit of walking into any room whenever he pleases, without knocking or announcing his arrival. His dark brown eyes check every detail. His sentences are short and concrete. He sometimes smiles slightly, not so much with his mouth as with his eyes, which turn into narrow slits.

It was he, Czerniawski, who proved himself worthy of the hand of the Lord's youngest sister, Ruta. He believes he was given "a treasure." Ruta, or Anna Czerniawska, is a sensible and intelligent woman. The former closeness of his own sister, Eva Jezierzańska, with Jacob makes Czerniawski feel kind of like a brother-in-law twice over, and at that point it's the same as being a brother. Eva Jezierzańska has long since lost her husband and become sort of like the Lord's wife. Now, when Jacob is ill, this is how Antoni Czerniawski regards him—like an older brother who has lost his strength. Antoni himself does not have any predisposition for ruling. He prefers to keep things organized. The only thing that sometimes makes him lose control is the prospect of good food. Once a week he sends a cart to Bürgel and Sachsenhausen for eggs and poultry, especially guinea fowls, which he loves most. He also has an extensive tab in town with the cheese purveyor, Kugler. Czerniawski cannot resist that cheese. He buys up the local wine by the barrel. This is what is running through his mind—barrels of wine and dozens and dozens of eggs—as he walks the quiet castle corridors.

Czerniawski realizes that out of all the stories that have happened on earth so far, the story of their machna and their company under Jacob's leadership is exceptional; he usually thinks in the plural, the "we" reminiscent of a kind of pyramid, the pinnacle of which is Jacob, the base of which this whole crowd here in Offenbach, floating around the galleries without any occupation, practicing parade steps to the point of extreme boredom—but out there, too, in Warsaw, and all over Moravia, in Altona and Germany, in the Czech city of Prague (though those are more like offshoots of the selfsame "we"). And when he looks through the chronicle Jakubowski has written (Czerniawski tells him to be more consistent in it, to establish certain facts with the other elders, such as Jan Wołowski, who has also come down to Offenbach, and Yeruhim Dembowski, who has been here from the start), he realizes that the story of this "us" truly is extraordinary. He is confirmed in this when in the evenings the Lord tells his tales, and he and Jakubowski write them down, until out of these stories Jacob's life starts to emerge—a life that is simultaneously the life of this "us." Then Czerniawski becomes one of those who greatly regret that they were born too late and that they could not accompany the Lord on his dangerous journeys, sleep with him in the desert and survive with him that maritime adventure. That is the story everyone likes best, as the Lord does a good job parodying Jakubowski, imitating his shrieking, and

Jakubowski becomes recognizable to all as the inglorious hero of that sea squall.

"He promised, bawling to high heaven, that he'd never let another drop of wine pass his lips," howls the Lord, and they with him—even Jakubowski gets a chuckle out of this. "Then he promised to be a Jan Wołowski—the Cossack, as he's called—who is a mustachioed elder now, but back then he used to sneak out of the sultan's lands and smuggle money in barrels over the border."

Czerniawski treats the Lord's service with gravity, and it is a ceaseless source of emotion for him, and there is probably no one else in this chatty, heedless crowd who understands as he does what actually happened when his parents came to Podolia to join Jacob. No one calls them Shabbitarians or converts anymore, and nothing remains of that disdain that was once almost a part of the air they all breathed. He looks proudly at the regular Sunday retinue that rides to the church in Bürgel, and at the Lord they lead in when they get there, holding him up by his shoulders, and at Eva—he considers every honor given her to be absolutely proper, though he acknowledges that she does somehow lack presence. He knows that the Lord's sons hate him, but he believes that this bad feeling arises from a simple misunderstanding that will dissipate with time. He cares for them, these aging bachelors unsuited to any work, demanding and unhappy. Roch is a sybarite, Joseph a man of very few words, an oddball.

Czerniawski has arranged it so that whenever anyone goes in for an audience with the Lord, they must first drop down and put their face to the ground, and wait for the Lord to speak first. He also monitors the Lord's diet. He orders his robes. The weaker Jacob gets, the more certain Czerniawski grows of what he's doing, but he isn't in it for himself—he does not want to rule over the others' souls. It is enough for him that the Lord can't do without him, that he calls him in when he's upset about even the smallest things. Czerniawski understands all the Lord's needs, does not judge them and never opposes them, either.

He has situated himself just next door to the Lord's chambers, and now whenever anyone wishes to speak with the Lord they must register with Czerniawski first. He guards this order without compromise; he is

the one who gets the Lord's doctors for him and conducts Eva's correspondence. It is also he whom the Lord sends out with letters to the prince
and any delegation that goes to Warsaw. And it was through his intercession that they managed to obtain a portion of the money they needed to
move to Offenbach.

He feels somewhat like a sheepdog, the kind the peasants had back in
Wallachia, that herds all the sheep into a pack and takes care that they
don't wander off again.

The Lord's health has improved, although the paresis of his left hand and
the left side of his face persists. This lends the Lord's face a new expression
of sadness and surprise. The women run in with broths and delicacies.
The Lord fancies a bit of catfish, so they race to the fishermen at the river
to get it. Eva, Avachunia, spends whole days sitting by his bedside, but he
never asks for his sons, no matter how long they have been waiting for an
audience.

After a week, he feels well enough to be taken to the church in Bürgel,
and then along the river, in the sun, for a walk. In the evening, he gives his
first lesson since he fell ill. He says that he has taken upon himself all the
anguish on the road to Daat—sacred knowledge, the sole road to salvation. Whoever travels on it will be freed from every pain and every plague.

## Of Thomas von Schönfeld's big plans

Jacob's rooms are on the first floor, with a direct entrance from the
galleries and enormous panes of stained glass in the windows. It is furnished with the carpets he so loves. Here you sit on pillows, according
to the Turkish custom. Since these rooms are dominated by damp, Eva
remembers to cense them every day. The incense burns until afternoon,
and everyone is duty-bound to go in the morning to the "temple," as
Jacob's ceremonial room is called, and in their prayers to pay their respects to the Lord, who is hidden in the back. Eva knows exactly who

has come and who has not performed this duty—the smell of the incense gets into your clothes; it's enough just to sniff them.

Zwierzchowska, who is allowed to go in and see the Lord at any time of day or night, brings him girls to warm up his bedding. The older the Lord gets, the more he likes his girls to be extremely young. He has them get undressed and lie beside him in bed, two at a time. At first they're usually frightened, but then they quickly get used to it and begin to giggle. Sometimes the Lord makes jokes with them. The bodies of such young girls are reminiscent of parsley, long, delicate rootlets. Zwierzchowska doesn't worry about their virtue. The potency of the Lord is now limited to speech. Somebody else will have to tire himself out over their virtue. They are there to keep the Lord warm.

Zwierzchowska knocks and doesn't wait for an answer to enter.

"The young Dobrushka has come."

Jacob gets up with a grunt and orders his clothes to be brought and put on him, so he can greet his guest. Slowly the castle lights up, although it is the middle of the night.

Thomas von Schönfeld runs to his uncle with open arms. Behind him is his younger brother, David-Immanuel.

They sit until almost dawn—Jacob has returned to bed, Thomas sits at the foot of it. Young Immanuel has dozed off on the carpet. Thomas shows Jacob some receipts and some drawings, at which Jacob has Czerniawski awakened and brought over. Czerniawski shuffles up, wearing his long nightshirt and his nightcap. Whenever Czerniawski is called, it has to be something to do with money.

Before he's even made it to the door, Czerniawski hears the voice of Thomas von Schönfeld:

"I will divorce my wife and marry Eva. You are weak now, you cannot bear all this, you need peace. Wealthy people at your age go south—the air is better there. In Italy the air will cure even the gravest ailments. Just think, you can barely walk now, Uncle."

When Czerniawski knocks and enters, one last sentence reaches his ears:

"And I know that I am the closest person to you, and that no one else understands what you are saying as well as I do . . ."

Then, with Czerniawski standing there, they really do talk of investments: money on the stock market is momentarily immobilized, but there will be new possibilities soon. Investments in America, bonds. Thomas knows what he is doing. Czerniawski, meanwhile, thinks in terms of trunks full of gold, not believing in bonds, which are—what? Just scraps of paper.

Thomas sits with Jacob all day long and takes the liberty of ordering food for himself. He reads him all his letters and writes down what he dictates. He tries to get in league with Czerniawski, but Czerniawski is impenetrable—polite, obedient, yet very firm when necessary. Thomas also tries the so-called "elders," meaning Dembowski and Jakubowski, but they say little and look at him as if not even remotely understanding what he's going on about. When Jan Wołowski comes, Thomas tries to ally himself with him, but this doesn't work out, either, although he had been counting on it. The Poles are still strongest at this court, and they run a tight ship here. The "Krauts" have very little say in things, even if their numbers are increasing.

There is a man in the castle now named Hirschfeld, a wealthy and learned burgher, an eccentric Jew who never converted and who gets along pretty well with Jakubowski. It is he, cajoled by Jakubowski, who goes to the Lord to warn him about Thomas von Schönfeld.

"He is certainly a brilliant man," he said. "But he is also a libertine. He has been thrown out of the lodge of the Evangelists for Asia that he founded himself and for which he wrote such an honorable charter. In Vienna he was constantly invoking your name, Lord, and Lady Eva's, as his relatives, which gave him better access to the court. He has gotten into debt because of women and licentiousness. It pains me to say this, because I was once on such good terms with him," confesses Hirschfeld, "but I must loyally warn you, Lord: he is a profligate and a pettifogger."

Jacob listens, his face betraying nothing. Since his attack, he blinks with just one eye. The other one, the one that never blinks, now waters. His healthy eye, meanwhile, has taken on a kind of metallic sheen.

"He can't go back to Vienna any longer, that is why he's here," adds Hirschfeld.

Then Czerniawski discovers a truly shameful thing: that Thomas has sent around in his own name letters to the kahalim of true believers, primarily to Germany and Moravia, claiming to be Jacob's right hand, and with the very distinct suggestion—though intricately involuted—that after the Lord's death, he, Thomas von Schönfeld, will be appointed his successor. Czerniawski shows these letters to the Lord, who instantly summons Thomas von Schönfeld.

Now Jacob leans over him, his face drawn. He still sways on his feet, but he slowly recovers his equilibrium and then—Jezierzańska sees it well, because she's standing closest, but there are other witnesses there, too—with all his strength, Jacob strikes Thomas in the face. Thomas topples over, and blood splotches appear instantly on his white lace jabot. He tries to get up, hides behind a chair, but Jacob's strong bony hand grabs him by the arm and pulls him in closer. Then there is a second slap, and Thomas, struck once more with full force in the face, falls again, astonished by the blood on his lips. He does not defend himself, shocked that this half-paralyzed old man has so much strength. Jacob's hand lifts him up off the floor by the hair, aims the next blow. Thomas starts to whimper:

"Please don't hit me!"

But he takes it in the face again, and this Jezierzańska cannot countenance any longer, and she grabs Jacob by the hands, putting herself between the men. She tries to catch Jacob's eye, but he escapes her. His eyes are bloodshot, his jaw hangs loose, he's drooling and looks as if he's drunk.

Thomas lies on the floor, crying like a little child, his blood mixing with his spit and snot, he covers his head and cries into the floor:

"You don't have the strength anymore. You've changed. Nobody believes you any longer, nobody will follow you. You will die soon."

"Quiet!" a horrified Jakubowski shouts at him. "Quiet!"

"From a persecuted victim you've come to be a tyrant, a rotten baron. You have become just like all those you used to stand against. In the place of that law that you rejected, you've introduced your own system that is even worse. You are pathetic, like a character in a comedy . . ."

"Lock him up," Jacob says in a hoarse voice.

## Who the Lord is when he is no longer who he is

From his little pigeonhole upstairs, Nahman Jakubowski comes down—his room is now next door to the room that's been assigned his brother, Paweł Pawłowski, who has also been residing here since the summer. Jakubowski takes some time to descend; the stone staircase is tightly coiled. He holds on to the iron railing and treads very carefully. Every few steps he pauses, and then he mutters something to himself in a language Antoni Czerniawski doesn't understand. He is waiting for Jakubowski at the bottom. He wonders how old this skinny little elder with his arthritic hands might be. This brother Jakubowski, whom the Lord, when they were amongst the inner circle, still called "Nahman." And now that is often how Czerniawski thinks of him—as Nahman.

"Everything happens according to how it is supposed to happen," Nahman Jakubowski informs Czerniawski. Czerniawski reaches out and helps him get down the final few steps. "First it fell to us to change our names, a process known as shinui haShem, something you younger people don't want to so much as hear about now. Then it fell to us to change location, when we set out from Poland on our way to Brünn, and here—shinui haMakom—and now it's shinui Ma'ase that is happening: changing the Deed. The Lord has taken illness upon himself in order to spare us. He has taken upon himself all the suffering of the world, as it was said in Isaiah."

"Amen," Czerniawski feels like saying in response, although he doesn't. The old man has reached the bottom of the stairs now and, briskly, all of a sudden, he has set off down the hall.

"I need to have a visit with him," he says.

All this talk of suffering and salvation works on certain people, but Czerniawski isn't one of them. He thinks concretely, does not believe in all that Kabbalah—doesn't understand it. But he does believe that God is watching over them, and that the matters he cannot understand ought better to be left to the specialists. He must rather concentrate on the fact that at news of the Lord's illness large numbers of his followers have started coming into Offenbach, and they must be lodged in town and received at the castle. Audiences are only once a day, in the evening, and they are brief. People come with their children to be blessed. The Lord lays his hands on pregnant women's bellies, and on sick people's heads. Ah, Czerniawski remembers, he needs to order from the printers the leaflets with the drawing of the Sefirot that are distributed among the novices. Czerniawski leaves Jakubowski, pushing on ahead. Let someone else take care of the old man! He turns toward the chancellery, where he sees two youths, no doubt from Moravia, ready to enter the ranks of the disciples and to supply the court with a fair sum of money that their families have provided them. When he goes in, his two secretaries—Zaleski and Czyński—rise respectfully. Both of Zaleski's parents died here, in Offenbach, having come here with him on the obligatory pilgrimage to see the Lord. After their death, he turned inward, and he really does not have any reason to go back to Warsaw now. The company has dealt with all matters pertaining to his inheritance, selling off the little shop the Zaleskis had back in the capital, transferring the money here. Not many of their residents are like Zaleski. They tend to be older people, the elder brothers—both the Matuszewskis with their blind daughter who plays the clavichord so well, which has allowed her to become the music teacher of the court, or Paweł Pawłowski, Jakubowski's brother, until recently an envoy of the Lord. There is Jezierzańska, a widow, and the two sons of the famous Elisha Shorr. There is Wolf and his wife, whom everyone calls the Wilkowskis (from the Polish word for "wolf"), and Jan the Cossack, whose recent widowing temporarily extinguished his infectious sense of humor, but who now seems to be returning to his former self—lately he was even seen courting some young woman. Joseph Piotrowski and the Lord's trusted Yeruhim Dembowski, whom the Lord refers to as "Jędruś," tenderly now, are also there. And of course among the elders you would have to include Franciszek Szymanowski, divorced multiple times, second-in-command of the Lord's guard to Lubomirski, who has turned up rarely, irregularly, ever since he took up residence in town.

One autumn night, the Lord has all the brothers and sisters awakened. Audible in the darkness is their footfall on the stairs; candles are lit. Sleepy people, without saying a word to one another, take up their places in the large hall.

"I am not who I am," says the Lord after a sustained period of silence. In the nocturnal quiet, coughing can be heard.

"I was hidden before you under this name of Jacob Frank, but that is not my true name. My country is very far from here, seven years' trip by sea from Europe. My father was called Tygier, and my mother's signet was a wolf. She was the daughter of a king . . ."

As the Lord continues, Czerniawski looks around at the faces of those gathered. The elders listen attentively, nodding their heads, as though what they are hearing is a confirmation of what they have long known. They are used to whatever Jacob says being the truth. The truth is like a gnarled tree, made up of many layers that are twisted all around each other, some layers holding others inside them, and sometimes being held. The truth is something that can be expressed in many tales, for it is like that garden the sages entered, in which each of them saw something else.

The younger among them, meanwhile, listen at the start, and then that long and complicated story, almost like some Eastern fairy tale, bores them, and they fidget and whisper among themselves, most of them not hearing everything, since Jacob speaks quietly, with difficulty, and the story itself is so strange that they no longer even know who it is about. Is it about Jacob, that he is from a royal lineage, and he was given to the Jew Buchbinder to be raised in exchange for his son, also called Jacob, and that Buchbinder taught him the Jewish language—for show, to keep people at bay? Which is why his daughter Eva, Avacha—may her health be good—must only marry someone from a royal family, too.

The young appear to be more interested in the news coming from France, which the newspapers write of with rising unease. Some of that news is strangely in tune with what Jacob says when he cites Isaiah—that when the time comes for the baptism of all Jews, the words of the prophets shall be fulfilled: "He will make all equal: the big and the small, the rabbis and the sages, the masters and the demeaned and the illiterate. All will be dressed and look alike." This makes an impression on the youths, but then when Jacob moves on to some sort of star named Sabbatai who will show them the way to Poland, where there lies some great treasure, they lose interest once more.

The Lord concludes this strange speech with these words:

"When they ask you where you're from and where you're going, make yourselves deaf, give the impression that you cannot understand their words. Let them say of us: Those people are lovely and good, but they are simpletons and have no understanding. Accept this."

They all go off to bed cold and tired. The women are still whispering over the Lord's long and unexpected monologue, but it pales and dissolves with the night, come sunrise.

The next day, tiny little Kapliński is baptized, for at the news of the Lord's ailment, all the Kaplińskis have come in from Wallachia. Seeing them, Jacob livens up and starts to cry, so overwhelmed is he to see them, and Czerniawski and all the elder brothers cry, too, humbled by that subtle presence of Hana through her brother and ashamed somehow that time has treated them thus, without any mercy. Hayim, now Jacob Kapliński, has aged and hobbles now, but his face is still lovely, and it is so reminiscent of Hana's that a chill passes through them all.

The Lord takes the little boy in his arms, and he submerges his own hand in the holy water brought in from the church. First he rinses off the child's head, then he places a little turban on it to remind them of the Turkish religion. And, as a sign of the place where they are now, he ties a little silk handkerchief around his neck. During this ceremony, his drawn, suffering face, half motionless, is flooded with tears. For his words seem clear, as he says that the true believers are now sailing on three different ships, and the ship on which he, Jacob, is sailing, will offer his companions the greatest fortune. But the second is good, too, for it will sail nearby; those are the brothers in Wallachia and the Turkish lands. The third ship sails far, far into the world—that ship carries those who will disperse across the waters of the world.

## Of Roch Frank's sins

One day, while Jacob is ailing, and thus the castle is hushed, there is a sudden ruckus downstairs, and in spite of the guards posted all around, some woman gets inside the main entrance and keeps on going into the gallery, shrieking. Czerniawski runs down and finds his wife there, try-ing to calm this other woman down. She is young, and her blond hair has come undone in the scuffle that at last put an end to her progress. She unties the bulging bundle from her breast and places it on the ground. Czerniawski sees in horror that the bundle is moving; he tells the guards to leave, along with all the accidental witnesses to this event, so that it is only the three of them who remain:

"Who is the gentleman?" Anna Czerniawska asks, with great presence of mind.

She takes the girl by the elbow and leads her gently into the dining room. She tells her husband to bring something warm, since it is cold and the girl is shivering.

"Herr Roch," says the girl, crying.

"Do not fear. All will be well."

"He'll marry me. That's what he said!"

"You'll receive compensation."

"What does compensation mean?"

"All will be well. Leave the child with us."

"It's, it's . . . ," the girl begins, but Czerniawski can see for herself when she has cleared away the cloths around it. The child is sick, the girl must have bound her stomach. That is why the infant is so calm, his eyes mov-ing around strangely, slobbering.

Czerniawski brings her some food, the girl eats with appetite. Hus-band and wife confer for a moment. Then Czerniawska decides, and her husband places several gold coins on the wooden table. The girl goes. That same day, the Czerniawskis go out into the country, and there, pay-ing a generous sum to a certain steward, and giving him the child, they sign a long-term agreement with him.

These little love affairs of Roch's cost quite a bit. This is the second time.

Eva Frank, informed by the Czerniawskis, has summoned Roch to her chamber, and is now reproaching her brother. Her dress sweeps away from before him the scraps of material left here by the seamstress who until a moment ago had been taking her measurements. Eva speaks in a hushed, tense voice that lashes Roch.

"You do not apply yourself in anything, you are incapable of doing anything of use, nothing even interests you. You are a pain in the ass that expects to be coddled. Our father has given you so many opportunities, and you have squandered them all. Women and wine—that's all you're good for."

She exchanges a glance with Czerniawska, who is sitting with her husband by the wall.

"Your wine will be rationed from now on. Father has determined it."

Roch, in his armchair, laughs, not looking up, so that it appears he is laughing into his boots. His light red hair sticks out under from his carelessly donned wig.

"Father is sick and won't live long. Do not speak to me of him. I'll throw up."

Eva loses all her self-control. She leans in over her brother and hisses:

"Silence, you pathetic, tiny, stupid man."

Roch covers his face with his hands. Eva turns abruptly, her lavish dress again sweeping up the scraps of fabric and scattering them about the room, and exits.

Czerniawski, embarrassed, sees that Roch is weeping.

"I am the most unfortunate of men."

## Of neshika, God's kiss

The Lord dreams of that strange smell again, that ambrosia smell. A few hours later, the next attack arrives. The von La Roche family bring in for Jacob Frank the finest doctor in all of Frankfurt, and he in turn calls a consultation with his local Offenbach colleagues. They debate at some length, but it becomes clear that there is nothing they can do for Jacob. He is completely unconscious now.

"When?" Eva Frank asks them, as they are leaving Jacob's room.

"That we cannot tell you. The patient's organism is extremely strong, and his will to live is iron. But no one can survive such a powerful apoplexy."

"When?" Czerniawski repeats.

"Only God knows."

And yet the Lord survives. He regains consciousness for a moment and is cheered up by a green parrot that speaks, brought to him as a gift. Someone reads him the newspaper, although it is unknown to what degree the news from the papers, ever more apocalyptic, makes it into his mind. In the evening he proclaims that women must also be taught to ride horses. The women will also be warriors. He demands that all the expensive robes and carpets be sold so that they can purchase more weapons. He calls in Czerniawski in order to dictate letters to him. Czerniawski writes down everything Jacob says, not giving any indication, even with his eyebrows, what he thinks about it all.

The Lord also proclaims that a delegation must be sent to Russia, orders it readied. Most of the time, though, he lies there lost in thought, as if in his mind he had already traveled far away. He is delirious. And in his delirium, the same words appear over and over again. "Do as I command," he calls out to everyone for the whole of one evening.

"The men will tremble," he says, foretelling great riots and blood upon the city's streets. Or he prays and sings in the old language. His voice breaks off, transforms into a whisper: "Ahapro ponov baminho," or "I beg His countenance forgiveness." He says: "I must be very weak if I am to approach death . . . I must renounce my strength, only then will it renew me . . . everything shall be renewed."

Jakubowski, devastated, falls asleep at Jacob's bedside. Later he will claim to have recorded Jacob's last words, which he renders as follows: "Christ said that he came to free the world from Satan's grip. But I came to free it from all the laws and statutes that have been in effect till now. When everything has been destroyed, the Good God will be discovered."

The truth is that at the very end, Jakubowski wasn't with the Lord. The women had come to replace him, and they no longer allowed anyone in. Eva with Anusia, old Matuszewska, Zwierzchowska, Czerniawska, and Eva Jezierzańska. They set out holy candles, put out flowers. The last person to converse with him—if it could be called a conversation—was Eva Jezierzańska. She had sat by his bedside the whole previous night, but come morning, she went to get a little sleep herself. Then the Lord sent for her, saying only: "Eva." Some people thought he was summoning Her Ladyship, but he did not say "Ladyship," only "Eva," and he usually called his daughter Avacha or Avachunia. And so Old Jezierzańska came in, replacing Jakubowski and Eva, sitting down on the edge of the bed and immediately understanding what it was he wanted. She laid his head on her lap, and he tried to put his lips in the position they might take for kissing, but failed on account of the paralyzed half of his face. She pulled out a large, flabby breast and pressed it to the Lord's lips. And he sucked it, although it was empty. Then he lost the last of his strength and stopped breathing. He didn't say a word.

A shaken Jezierzańska left the room. She did not cry till she was out the door.

Antoni Czerniawski announces to the uneasy company come morning that the body has been washed now, changed, and laid upon its catafalque. He says:

"Our Lord has passed. He died of a kiss: neshika. God came to him in the night and brushed his lips with His lips, as He did with Moses. The Almighty God is now welcoming him into his chambers."

A single mighty sob resounds, the news races through the galleries, flies out from the castle and whirls like a vortex down the narrow, impeccable streets of Offenbach. Soon the bells in all the local churches start to peal, regardless of denomination.

Czerniawski notices that all the elder brothers have already come downstairs except Jakubowski, who spent all night at the door. Suddenly he starts to worry whether something might have happened to him, too. He climbs the stairs to the last floor, thinking what a bad idea it was to put the elders up so high, that this needs to change.

Jakubowski is sitting with his back to the door, hunched over his papers, his gray, close-cropped hair with its woolen cap on a head that looks as small as a child's.

"Brother Piotr," Czerniawski says to him, but Nahman does not react. "Brother Piotr, he has passed."

There is a long silence, and Czerniawski understands that he ought to leave the old man to himself.

"Death is no bad thing," Jakubowski says suddenly, without turning around. "And in fact, there's no need to deny it, it belongs to the good God, who in this way mercifully saves us from life."

"Brother, are you coming down?"

"There is no need."

The night after her father's death, Eva has a dream. Something happens in that dream that makes her body swell, something moves over her, lies down on her, she knows what it is, but she cannot see it. The worst (and also the best) is that she feels a pushing out in her belly, something pushes into her womb, into that place between her legs she does not even want to name, and there it moves inside her, it lasts but a moment, and that is because everything is broken off by her sudden pleasure, an explosion, and then a weakening. It is a strange moment of shamelessness and destruction. The unpaid bills, the mayor's glances, the letters from Giacomo

Casanova, Roch's shady dealings and the clumps of silver on the white tablecloth, evidence of triumph—none of it matters anymore. All is invalidated in this brief moment. And even in the dream Eva wants to forget about everything, erase for all time both this pleasure and this shame. And, still dreaming, she orders herself to forget about everything and never to return to it. To treat it as other mysteries of the body are treated—periods, rashes, hot flashes, minor heart palpitations.

When she wakes up, her innocence is restored. She opens her eyes and sees her room, bright, cream-colored, and her dressing table with its porcelain jug and bowl. And the dollhouse made for her by special order in Bürgel. She squints, and as long as she lies on her stomach, she still has access to her dream, and to that unlikely pleasure, but when she turns over onto her back and straightens the cap in which she sleeps in order not to destroy her neatly arranged hairdo, the dream goes, and her body curls up on itself, dries out. The first thought that comes to her mind is that her father has died. And for some reason, that thought awakes in her two completely contradictory feelings—unbearable despair and a strange, rocking joy.

## Gossip, letters, denunciations, decrees, and reports

Here is what Offenbach's *Voss News* had to say about the funeral of Jacob Frank:

> The body of Baron Frank was ceremoniously buried on December 12, 1791, in Offenbach.
>
> He was the patriarch of a Polish religious sect that followed him to Germany and that he ruled with tremendous panache. He was worshipped almost as another Dalai Lama. The procession opened with women and children numbering some two hundred, clothed in white, candles sparkling in their hands. The men went after them in colorful Polish costumes, with silk sashes across their shoulders. Then went the brass and reed band, and the body of the deceased, carried upon a sumptuous bier, followed. On either side

of it walked: on the right, the deceased's children, his only daughter and his two sons; on the left, Prince Marcin Lubomirski, Polish magnate, with the Order of Saint Anna at his neck, along with many dignitaries. The deceased lay in an Eastern costume, red, clad in ermine, his face turned toward the left side in a semblance of sleep. His casket was surrounded by a guard comprising Uhlans, Hussars, and other Polacken in lavish attire. Prior to his death, the deceased had issued his decree that no one lament him or go into mourning for him.

After the funeral, which was attended by the entire city of Offenbach and half of Frankfurt, some company sat down with Sophie von La Roche. Bernard was the first to comment on the matter, being well informed as always:

"People are saying that these neophytes are trying to establish some sort of confederation amongst the Jews. Under the banner of opposition to the Talmud, the Jewish Bible, they challenge authority and follow a version of Turkish laws and beliefs."

"Well, I think," says Dr. Reichelt, who was there during Jacob Frank's illness, "that this entire messianic movement is a rather complicated form of extracting money from naive Jews."

Then it is the turn of a friend of the family, von Albrecht, formerly a Prussian resident of Warsaw, whose grasp of all matters Eastern is excellent:

"Ladies and gentlemen, I must say I'm surprised at your naiveté. I have always warned that this new sect is an attempt to appropriate and control the synagogue all across Poland, that it would thus be prudent to monitor its activities very closely indeed and inform His Royal Emperor's office of the development of the situation. That is what I saw many years ago now, when they were first beginning. And now apparently an overwhelming quantity of arms has been discovered at their court. In addition, they've been conducting drills there, with alarming regularity, as well as recruiting young men for their army . . ."

"But women, too, apparently," exclaims Mrs. von La Roche.

"It all raises the suspicion," continues this erstwhile resident of Warsaw, "that these neophytes were preparing for an uprising in Poland, which would have been aimed against the Prussians. I am therefore very surprised by your prince, who so wholeheartedly agreed to receive them here. They managed to make their sect into a kind of state within the state, ruled by its own laws, with its own guard, and its accounts in the majority conducted outside any banking system."

"They lived peacefully and honestly," says Sophie von La Roche, attempting to defend those "little insect-like people—" but the doctor interrupts her:

"They had unimaginable debts . . ."

"Who does not have debts these days, my dear doctor?" Sophie von La Roche asks rhetorically. "I prefer to believe that Eva and her brothers are the illegitimate children of Tsarina Elizabeth and Prince Razumovsky, that's what we've been thinking of them here. It's more romantic."

They laugh politely and change the subject.

"Such skeptics," Mrs. von La Roche comments, in a mock-offended tone.

Yet the matter of Jacob Frank and his disciples hardly quiets down, and now letters and denunciations are carried by an ever more violent wind blowing over Europe, whipping up new fears and further conjectures.

> Letters sent around to Jewish communities and to others call for all Jews and Christians to unite under the banner of their sect called Edom. The goal would have been the so-called brotherhood above and beyond the differences between these two religions . . .
>
> It is not known what aims might motivate the sect's activities, but we can be certain that its individual members maintain close ties with the Freemasons, the Illuminati, the Rosicrucians, and the Jacobins, however scant may be the evidence from correspondence or from elsewhere . . .

King Frederick Wilhelm's ordinance, meanwhile, clearly states:

> . . . this man, Jacob Frank, was the leader of a sect, and at the same time a concealed agent of an as yet unknown force.

Recently letters have come out that call for the uniting of the different synagogues under the auspices of his sect. From now on, everything that is linked to secret societies arisen under unknown or unclear circumstances, every political enthusiasm, will require particular attention, considering that secret societies always act under cover of darkness and silence, each of them using Jacobinic propaganda for their terrible criminal intentions . . .

With time, meanwhile—for time has a wonderful ability to efface all uncertain places and patch up all holes—the analysis achieves a certain consistency:

As for the sect of Frankists now called Edom, insofar as it was until recently treated by many of our aristocrats as an exotic curiosity, we ought now, after the frightening and terrible experiences of the Revolution in France and their connections with Jacobinism, to change our perspective and treat mystical rituals as a cover for political and revolutionary intentions.

## 30.

## The death of a Polish princess, step by step

Now things play out of their own accord. It is difficult to fully appreciate this when you are seeing them from the stage on which they are unfolding. Nothing is visible, there are too many sets, and they cover each other up and give the impression of chaos. In the confusion, the fact that Gitla Gertruda Ascherbach dies the same day as the Lord goes unnoticed. This is the fulfilment of a process begun somewhere in Podolia, one cold winter, when her great, tempestuous love, the fruit of which is Samuel, took its unjustly short place, a duration of the blink of an eye amongst all the events on this flat stage.

Yet Yente sees this order, this accord—Yente, whose body is slowly transforming into crystal in a Korolówka cave. The entrance to it is now almost completely overgrown with black lilac, their lush umbels filled with long-ripe berries already fallen to the ground, where those that resisted the birds froze long ago; Yente sees the death of Jacob—but does not stay with it, for she is being drawn to another, in Vienna.

Asher, Rudolf Ascherbach, has been sitting at the bedside of his wife, Gertruda, Gitla, ever since she collapsed. He knew all he needed to some two, three months ago, when he looked at the tumor on her breast—he is, after all, a doctor; he thinks he was even coming to know it back when

Gitla was still walking, and in a strange kind of anxiety trying to manage the household.

She was angered, for example, by the onions they ordered for winter in thick linen sacks, which had rotted on the inside and would not last until spring. She said that the laundress was ruining the cuffs of their sleeves and that the ice in the ice well smelled strange, like it had smelled in Busk—of stagnant water. Reading the newspapers, she inveighed against the stupidity of politicians, and her gray head would drown in the smoke of the Turkish pipe she would smoke until the end.

Now she lies on the sofa, mostly—she doesn't want to go to bed. Asher measures out her ever-larger doses of laudanum and observes everything thoroughly and carefully. Observation, cool and dispassionate, brings him relief and defends against despair. For instance, for several days before her death Gitla's skin gets thick, stiff, and matte, reflecting the daylight differently. This affects her facial features—they grow sharper. An oblong depression appears at the tip of her nose. Asher sees it on Monday evening, in the candlelight, when Gitla, though she is very weak, sits down to organize her files. Out of the drawers she pulls everything she has, everything she has written, all of her letters to her father in Lwów, written in Hebrew; articles, drawings, designs. She divides it into little piles and puts the files into soft paper folders. She keeps asking Asher for things, but Asher cannot focus. He has seen that furrow in her nose, and terror has gripped him. She knows she is going to die, he thinks in horror, she knows her illness is incurable, and that nothing can be done. But she's not expecting *death*—that is something else entirely. She knows it with her reason, she can say it in words, write it, but deep down her body, being the animal it is, has not believed it at all.

In this sense, death doesn't really exist, thinks Asher—no one has ever described the experience. It's always someone else's death, a stranger's. There is no sense in being scared of it, since what we would be scared of is something other than what it really is. We are afraid of an imagined *death* (or Death), a thing that is a product of our mind, a tangle of thoughts, tales, rituals. It is the contractual sadness, the agreed-upon caesura, that introduces order into human lives.

And so when Asher sees that furrow on her nose and that strange skin color, he understands her time has come. On Tuesday morning she tells him to help her get dressed—him, not Sofia, the woman they have hired to help around the house. Asher laces up her dress. Gitla sits down at the table but does not eat, and then she goes back to bed, and Asher takes off her dress for her. He has a hard time removing the straps from their clasps—his hands have grown coarse, uncertain. He feels as if he is unpacking a valuable, fragile object, something like a Chinese vase, like a delicate crystal goblet, breakable glass, in order to put it away; he will not use this object again. Gitla, bearing it with patience, also asks in a weak voice to write a short letter to Samuel. She asks for paper, but she doesn't have the strength to write, so she merely dictates a few words, and then, after her laudanum, she falls asleep, not reacting when Asher interrupts his letter-writing. She lets herself be fed (but only by Asher) soup, broth, but she eats only a few spoonfuls. Asher puts her on the chamber pot, but Gitla produces only a couple of droplets of urine, and Asher thinks it is as though her body is stuck, like a small, complex mechanism. And so it goes until evening. In the night Gitla awakes, asks about various things, such as if they've paid the book dealer, and she reminds him to take the flowers out of the window box for winter. She asks him to take back the materials from the seamstress—they will never turn into dresses now. The girls definitely wouldn't like them—they are such fashionable women—even though the quality of the materials is high. He could give them to Sofia—Sofia would be happy to have them. Then memories come back to her, and Gitla tells of the winter when she came to Asher's door in Lwów, of sleighs, snow, and the Messiah's retinue.

On Wednesday morning she gives the impression of feeling better, but at around noon, her eyes glaze over. She fixes them upon some distant point, seemingly beyond the walls of this Viennese household, somewhere in the air, high above all homes. Her hands are restless, wandering over her bedclothes, her fingers making little folds in the damask of her comforter, then trying hard to straighten it back out.

"Fix my pillow," she says to Adelaida, her dear friend, whom Asher has already informed and who has rushed here from the other end of the city.

But the pillow is no help—she is obviously in a great deal of discomfort. Rudolf Ascherbach summons their daughters, but he can't know when they'll arrive. One of them lives in Weimar, the other in Wrocław.

Gitla's voice has slowed down and lost all its melody, her tone is flat, metallic, unpleasant, Asher notes. It is hard to understand her. And several times she asks what day it is. Wednesday. Wednesday. Wednesday. Asher answers with a gesture her simple question:

"Am I dying?"

He nods soundlessly, and then adds in a hoarse voice:

"Yes."

And she, being Gitla, assured, mobilizes within herself, and you might think that she was now taking this whole death business into her own hands, this problematic and irreversible process, as if it were merely the latest in the long list of tasks she has had to perform. When Asher looks at her body, tiny, emaciated, devastated by her illness, tears come to his eyes, and this is the first time he has cried in a very long time, maybe even since that day when the Polish princess was resting in their home, when everyone was trying to collect the vodka spilled from broken barrels with their rags.

At night, Adelaida and Mrs. Bachman, the downstairs neighbor, watch over her. Asher asks his wife:

"Do you want a priest?"

After a moment's hesitation he adds:

"Or a rabbi?"

She looks at him in surprise, perhaps she doesn't understand. He had to ask her. But there will be no priest or rabbi. Gitla would be mortally offended if he did that to her. On Thursday at dawn the throes begin, and the women wake Asher, who has been napping with his head on the desk. They light the candles around the bed. Adelaida starts praying, but quietly, as if talking just to herself. Asher sees that Gitla's fingernails have whitened, and then, irrevocably, they turn blue, and when he takes her hand in his, it is icy. Gitla's breathing is wheezing and difficult, each breath requiring effort; in an hour, it has turned to a rattle. It is difficult to listen to it, and both Adelaida and Mrs. Bachman start to cry. Then her breathing softens—or maybe their ears get used to it?—and Gitla calms down and floats away. Asher witnesses the moment—it happens quite a bit before her heart stops, and her breathing, Gitla simply slips away somewhere, she is no longer in this whistling body, she is gone, vanished. Something took her, caught her attention. She didn't even look back.

On Thursday afternoon at twenty past one, Gitla's heart stops beating. She takes a last deep breath, and that breath stays inside her, filling her breasts.

There is no final exhalation, Asher thinks with mounting rage, no soul that slips out of the body. Quite the contrary, the body sucks the soul inside it, so that it can carry it into the grave. He has seen this so many times, but only now has he fully comprehended it. Just like that. There is no final exhalation. There is no soul.

## A Warsaw table for thirty people

News of Jacob Frank's death makes it to Warsaw late, at the start of January, when the city suddenly empties due to the frost and the whole world seems withdrawn into itself, tied up with rough twine.

At the Wołowskis' on Walic, a great table has been set for thirty people, carefully covered in a white cloth and set with porcelain. Next to each plate lies a bread roll. The windows are covered. The Wołowskis' children, Aleksander and Marynia, politely greet the guests, from whom they receive little gifts—fruits and sweets. Lovely Marynia, with her curly, pitch-black hair, curtseys and repeats: Thank you, Uncle, thank you, Aunt. Then the children disappear. Arranged at equal intervals, the seven-armed lampstands illuminate the assembled—all dressed like burghers, neatly, in black. Old Franciszek Wołowski sits at the head of the table, next to him his sister Marianna Lanckorońska and her son, Franciszek the younger, and his wife, Barbara, and then there are the adult children of the other Wołowski brothers with husbands, wives, and also the Lanckoroński children, the two Jezierzański brothers, Dominik and Ignacy, and Onufry Matuszewski and his wife from the Łabęcki family, the Majewskis of Lithuania, and Jacob Szymanowski with his new wife from the Rudnicki family. Franciszek helps his father get up, so that he can take a good look at everyone, and then he extends his hands to those standing on either side of him, and everyone else does the same. He thinks his father will intone one of those songs they have to sing quietly, almost whisper, but his father only says:

"Let us thank our almighty God and his glory, the Holy Virgin of Light, that we have survived. Let us thank our God that he has guided us here, and let each of us pray for him as he is able, and with the greatest love."

Now they pray in silence, their heads bowed, until old Franciszek Wołowski speaks up again in his still-powerful voice:

"What announces the arrival of the new times? What did Isaiah say?"

Sitting to his left side, the eldest Łabęcka says mechanically:

"The cessation of the laws of the Torah and the falling of the kingdom into heresy. So it was said in the oldest times, and for this we have been waiting."

Wołowski clears his throat and takes a deep breath:

"Our ancestors understood this as best they were able, and they thought that that prophecy had to do with how Christians were running the world. But now we know that it wasn't about that—all Jews must pass through the kingdom of Edom, in order for the prophecy to be fulfilled! Jacob, our Lord, was the incarnate Jacob who went first to Edom—since the biblical story of Jacob also told, fundamentally, our story. And so says the Zohar: Our father Jacob did not die. His earthly legacy has been taken on by Eva, who is Jacob's Rachel."

"In essence Jacob did not die," they answer him in chorus.

"Amen," Shlomo Franciszek Wołowski answers them all, sitting down to the table, tearing his roll in half, and starting to eat.

## Of ordinary life

One of the contractors from whom the Wołowskis buy hops is especially inquisitive. With his hands in his pockets he watches Franciszek the younger weigh the bags and finally asks:

"Say, Wołowski, what do you all go and see that Frank for, and send your children out there, when you've been baptized already in our churches? Everybody's saying he's a kind of patriarch and that you pay him contributions. And that none of you will even think of marrying a Catholic girl."

Wołowski tries to be as friendly as possible, patting him on the back as if they were on familiar terms:

"People exaggerate. The truth is we do marry amongst ourselves, but that's how it is everywhere—we just know each other, and our women cook like our mothers cooked, and we all have the same customs. It's natural." Franciszek puts a bag on the scale and then supplements it with the porcelain weights. "My wife, for instance, makes the same sort of rolls as my mother, and there's no one that could do that who wasn't born in Podolia and into a Jewish family. Those rolls are why I married her. Jacob Frank gave us a hand when we were in need, and now we're repaying him for that, out of gratitude. That's a virtue, not a sin."

Wołowski rummages around in the weights, needing the smallest ones in order to weigh the dry hops down to a lot, or thirteen grams.

"Right you are," says the wholesaler. "I married for cabbage with peas. You'd lick your fingers the way my wife makes it. But people are also saying that you all settle down next to each other, that all there has to be is some lord's court, and there you are, with your inn, and your shops, and that you even make your own kind of music . . ."

"What's the harm in that?" answers Wołowski cheerfully, and enters the weight into its column. "That's what trade is. You have to find somewhere where people will buy from you. You do it, but you wouldn't allow me to?"

The wholesaler hands him a second bag, bigger this time, so that it barely even sits on the scale.

"What about children? They say you gave Frank's sons higher educations at great cost, and that you called them barons, and that they were often seen here in Warsaw at masquerades and balls and comedies, roaming around in fancy carriages . . ."

"So you're saying you don't know of any Catholics who go to balls or masquerades? And have you seen the Potockis' carriages?"

"Do not compare yourself with lords, Wołowski."

"I'm not comparing myself. There are poorer and richer ones among us. Some walk per pedes, others have fancy carriages. What of it?"

Wołowski has had enough of this importuner now. He seems to be examining the dry hops, sniffing it and rolling it around in his fingers, but in fact he is looking around the courtyard. And in his voice this whole time there has been something like a stifled rage. Franciszek Wołowski the younger closes up the scale and heads for the exit. The importuner reluctantly follows.

"And another thing that just occurred to me. Is it true you all hold secret rendezvous, windows covered, weird rituals?" he asks captiously. "That's what people say."

Franciszek is careful. He takes a moment to weigh his words, as if putting the right weights on the scale.

"We neophytes take special care to love our neighbors. For is that not a basic commandment for all Christians?" he asks rhetorically. The man nods at him. "Yes, it is true, we gather together and confer, you know, just like yesterday in my home: what kind of help we can provide for one another, what to invest in—we invite one another to weddings and baptisms. We talk of our children, of their schools. We stick together, and that is not only not bad, but it actually sets an example for other Christians."

"I hope you do can do well for yourself, Mr. Wołowski, amongst us," the importuner says at last, somewhat disappointed, and they sit down to settle up for the hops.

When Franciszek finally manages to rid himself of him, he breathes a sigh of relief. But then right away he is back in a state of constant and exhausting high alert.

The atmosphere around them in Warsaw isn't the best. Some have left for Wilno, like the younger Kaplińskis, or returned to Lwów, like the Matuszewskis, though it isn't easy there, either. But the worst is probably in Warsaw. Everyone watches them and whispers. Barbara, his wife, says that Franciszek involves himself too much, which makes him visible. For instance, he took part in the Black Procession, demanding rights for the townspeople. He is also active in a merchant guild. He has a prospering brewery, he has a house, he guarantees other people's loans—his name, multiplied by sons and cousins, sticks out. Yesterday, for example, Barbara found a piece of paper jammed in the doorframe with smudged, sloppy print:

> Frank fills their heads with superstitions by the bucket,
> Weird blessings so they'll leave him down to their last ducat.
> They worship him in Polish, wish him Shana Tova,
> This man who was sentenced to life in Częstochowa.
> Profiting off their vodka, he'll go down in history,
> But we've had enough of this folly, this mystery.
> Once they've had their baptism, put an end to all this strife—
> Just calm them down and let them live an ordinary life.

## Heiliger Weg nach Offenbach

God's true home is in Offenbach. This is what was told to a teenage Joseph von Schönfeld, nephew of Thomas Schönfeld of Prague, and with this, the preparations for his departure were under way. Admittedly, apart from the holy path that must be traveled by all true believers, there was also a certain practical reason: avoiding the army, in which the true believers, as Christians now, were required to serve. The path led through Dresden, where without any special justification boys could get letters of recommendation from Baron Eibeschütz, though for Joseph, with that last name of von Schönfeld—as his mother said—such a recommendation was not even necessary. With him went two other boys in his same situation.

When in June of 1796 they finally made it to Offenbach, they spent a whole day waiting for an audience with the Lady amongst the colorful international throng of young people. Some had already changed into eccentric uniforms and were drilling, others were just wandering around the courtyard, and when it started pouring, they were allowed to seek shelter under the roofs of the arcades. Joseph examined with interest the sculptures on the columns, each of them representing figures the clever boy easily identified from mythology. Among them was one he hated deeply, Mars—a thick-skulled knight in armor with a halberd, at whose feet stood Aries, the Zodiac sign governed by Mars, yet to Joseph it seemed that the ram was rather a symbol of those who, like sheep, follow generals' orders and turn into cannon fodder. He was decidedly more drawn to the round, beautifully shaped Venus, upon whose curves he commented to his peers.

Not until evening were they received by the Lady.

She is a woman around forty years old, very elegantly dressed, with white, finely manicured hands, a tempest of still-dark hair pinned up into a high bun. While she reads their letter, Joseph gazes at her dog in fascination—tall and skinny, more like a monstrous grasshopper that never once takes its eyes off the boys. Finally the woman says:

"You have been accepted, my dears. Here you will submit to the rule that, assiduously complied with, will bring you happiness. Here lies true salvation."

She speaks German with a strong German accent. She dismisses the other boys, telling Joseph to stay. Then she stands and goes up to him, giving him her hand to kiss.

"You are Thomas's nephew?"

He assents.

"Is it true that he is dead?"

Joseph lowers his head. His uncle's death is connected with some uncomfortable, embarrassing secret that has never been explained to him by his family. Joseph has never known if it's because Thomas for some unknown reason let himself get killed or because of something else he has not been informed of.

"You knew him, didn't you?" asks Joseph, in order to distract her from any further questions.

"You remind me of him a little," says this beautiful woman. "If ever you would like to speak with me, or if there is anything you need, I will be happy to receive you."

For a moment, it seems to Joseph that the lady is regarding him with tenderness, and this emboldens him. He wants to say something, he

THE BOOK OF THE DISTANT COUNTRY

suddenly feels love and gratitude for this sad woman who is connected by
some mysterious thread with that Venus made out of red sandstone, but
nothing comes to mind that he could say, and so he shyly blurts:

"Thank you for letting me come here. I will be a good student."

The lady smiles at these words, and it seems to Joseph that her smile is
flirtatious, as if she's a young woman again.


The next day they tell the boys to go all the way upstairs, to the small
rooms where the so-called elders reside.

"Have you been to see the elders?" everyone has been asking them
since they arrived, so Joseph is curious about who these elders are. The
whole time he feels as if he has wound up in one of those fairy tales his
mother used to tell him, teeming with kings, beautiful princesses, overseas expeditions, and legless sages who guard treasures.

These ones, as it turns out, have legs. They sit at two large tables upon
which numerous books are splayed, and reams of paper, and scrolls. They
must be working on a project in here. The men look like Jews, like the
Jewish scholars who can be seen in Prague—they have long beards, but
they are dressed in the Polish fashion, in vests that were once vivid and are
now somewhat worn. They wear oversleeves to protect them from ink.
One of the elders stands and, barely even glancing at them, hands them a
piece of paper on which is printed some odd drawing covered in inter-
locking rings, and he says in the same accent as the beautiful woman:

"My sons, the Shekhinah is in captivity, being kept in prison in Edom
and Ishmael. Our task is to free her from her chains. This will occur
when the three sefirot are united into a single Trinity; then salvation will
come." With a bony finger, he indicates the rings.

Joseph's companion gives him a furtive, amused look; he seems to be
suppressing laughter. Joseph looks around the room and sees an odd mixture: in the foreground hangs a cross, and next to it a picture of the Catholic Virgin Mary, but when you look at it closer, it turns out to be a
portrait of that beautiful woman, adorned in such a way as the Virgin
Mary is adorned in churches and chapels, and below her are portraits of
some men, and figures with Hebrew letters, the meaning of which he has
no clue. He can only make out on one of the tablets some names he

vaguely remembers, without knowing their deeper sense: Keter, Chokhmah, Binah, Chesed, Gevurah, Tiferet, Netzach, Hod, Yesod, Malkuth—connected with lines, they join into a single concept of Ein Sof.

The elder says:

"Two of the sefirot have already appeared in human form. Now we must await the arrival of the last one. Praise be to him who is chosen to unite with Tiferet—Beauty—for out of him the savior will arise. Pay attention, therefore, and listen to everything very carefully, so that you, too, might belong to the chosen."

The elder says all of this as if reciting something everyone already knows, as if he had already repeated this thousands of times. He turns and leaves without a word. He is small and shriveled, and he takes tiny steps.

Out the door, both boys burst out laughing.

Immediately after returning from the elders, they are conscripted into the guard, they hand over the money they brought from home and receive funny multicolored uniforms. Now every day they will participate in drills, as well as in shooting lessons and hand-to-hand combat. Their sole obligation will be to carry out the orders of the man with the Polish mustache who runs their drills, and then show their muscles before an old man whose uniform marks him as a general and who appears at court from time to time and receives parades. The kitchen provides three big meals a day, and in the evenings, those who are not serving go to the great hall to study with the Elders. Both boys and girls participate in these lessons, and it is clear to everyone that the students care more about looking around at each other. Joseph catches only individual words from the lectures, their whole content is bizarre, and he isn't really cut out for such things. He doesn't understand whether what they say here is to be taken literally or as metaphor. In the lectures, quotes from the prophet Isaiah are repeated, as is the word *Malkut*—"Kingdom." When Joseph is invited— no doubt through the intercession of the beautiful woman, who sometimes has him come for coffee—to join the guard of honor for the Sunday expeditions to the church in Bürgel, he starts to understand that it in fact signifies the same "Lord" whom they transport in a hermetically sealed carriage into the little town. Held up by stalwart bruisers, covered in a great hood, he enters the church with difficulty and remains there alone for some time. Then Joseph figures out that that "Lord" is in fact the same "Lord" who recently died, yet the truth is that he *didn't die*. All the guards, dressed in their multicolored uniforms—Joseph feels like a circus performer in it—must then turn to face away, so that now they have before their eyes the peacefully flowing Main River and the sails of ships, fragile as dragonfly wings.

Sometimes the guards get days off. Then Joseph goes with his peers into the city, and there they join in with the exotic, bored crowd of young people who have already occupied all the parks and squares and are either flirting with whoever is around or playing instruments. They speak many different languages—you can hear the northern German dialect from Hamburg, and the southern one from the Czech and Moravian lands, and Czech, and more rarely some Eastern languages that Joseph doesn't recognize. The most common language here is Polish, which he has learned to understand by now. Whenever the youths can't understand a conversation, they try speaking in Yiddish or French. Romances blossom;

he saw a lovely young man who, strumming a guitar, sang a song of long-ing under the window of his lady love.

Joseph quickly made friends with a boy from Prague, who like him came here fleeing the severe figure of Mars. His name is Moses, but he tells people to call him Leopold. He has not been baptized, and in the beginning he still recites his Jewish prayers, but soon gives that up. It is with him that Joseph spends the most time, and it is a good thing—he has someone in whom to confide his ever-stronger sense of the absurdity of this city, country, even the big river that observes their lazy life here with indifference.

Yet Joseph enjoys a special status, which he figures is not only because he is a distant relative of the beautiful woman, but also thanks to his un-cle. Several times he is invited to the table where she sits with her brothers. They ask him questions about his family—the woman knows his aunts well. She asks him about the clock in his grandmother's living room, whether it's still running. This emboldens Joseph at the table. He tells them anecdotes about Brünn, mentions merchants, wineries, and confec-tionaries, though in fact he has very few of these recollections, he rarely went to see his grandmother. One day, tears come to the woman's eyes, and she asks him for a handkerchief. Her dog looks at him with an inhu-man calm, yet suspiciously. When, however, he is left alone with her, he loses all his confidence. It seems to him that a particular kind of goodness flows from this lady, mixed with an indefinite sadness, so that he comes back from seeing her with a muddle in his mind, defenseless.

Moses-Leopold is quite a bit more critical.

"This is all one big make-believe," he says. "Look, nothing is real here, it's like everyone's acting out a play."

They gaze down at the carriage readied to go. The horses have great plumes on their heads. On either side of the carriage, boys in motley uniforms line up; they will run alongside it. Moses is right.

"And these elders, they're just funny, they repeat the same things over and over, and when you try and actually find something out, they hide behind some secret. Those wise faces of theirs . . ."

Moses imitates their faces and gestures. He squints, lifts up his head, and recites some nonsense blends of words. Joseph bursts out laughing. He, too, has the ever-increasing suspicion that they have wound up in a great theater that extends all across the city, where everyone plays the role in which they have been cast, yet without knowing the contents of the play they are performing, or its significance, or its end. The drills, boring and tiring, are like practice for a ball: they form two rows, which are then supposed to connect with each other, then separate, like in some sort of contredanse. He gets lucky in a way that Moses does not—he is chosen by the general for horse-riding lessons. And this is the sole concrete and useful thing he learns in Offenbach.


## Of women soaking their legs

Eva had to consent long ago to marry off Anusia Pawłowska. Despite the fact that she has a husband and children in Warsaw, Anusia still comes every year to Offenbach. She did not go far to marry—her husband is her cousin Pawłowski, she didn't even have to change her last name. Her husband is an officer; he is often away from home. Now Anusia Pawłowska has come with her daughter, Paulinka, who will stay with the Lady through the lovely winter in Offenbach, fortunately no longer in the castle, which it has not been possible to maintain, but rather in a solid house on the main street. The Czerniawskis purchased it under their name, to help Eva give her creditors the slip.

Paulinka has gone with the maid into town, while they, the older women, have arranged a soak for their legs. The bones of Eva's big toe have swollen, and it hurts her a great deal. When Anusia takes off her white stockings, Eva sees her friend suffers from the same affliction. Healing salts have been dissolved in the warm water. Their tucked skirts reveal their legs; Eva's are all red from varicose veins. On the little table next to them the ladies have put a pitcher of coffee and a saucer with little wafer cookies. Eva especially likes the ones with pistachio filling. They are wondering how many children Jacob might have had, and who they could be. Eva is actually happy that she might have all those brothers and sisters, which would mean she has all kinds of great-nephews and -nieces in Warsaw, in Moravia, in Wallachia. Perhaps one of the little Kaplińskis, whom Jacob baptized with such emotion not long before his death. Remember, Anusia? Remember? Or Magda Jezierzańska? Remember? Or Ludwiczek Wołowski? He always looked like him. Or Basia Szymanowska? Certainly, Janek Zwierzchowski.

And suddenly Anusia asks:

"Or me?"

Eva looks at her kindheartedly and suddenly pats her hair, as if consoling her.

"Maybe you, too. I don't know."

"Either way, we're sisters."

They embrace over their basins of water. Then Eva asks:

"What was your mother like?"

Anusia ponders this, putting her hands under her head.

"She was good and clever. She had an instinct for business. She was so involved in everything, until the end. My father would never have made it without her. The way she got the shop going, and brought up my brothers. And now we have that shop."

"She was called Pesel, wasn't she? My father spoke of her that way: Pesel."

"I know."

"What's it like being married, Mrs. Pawłowska?" Eva asks her later, when they are wiping off their legs with soft towels.

"Good. I married too late. I got too attached to you."

"You abandoned me," says Eva, as if teasing.

"Well, what can a woman do if she doesn't marry well?"

Eva ponders this. Then she bends down and rubs her swollen bones.

"She could become a saint. You could have stayed with me."

"I'm here now."

Eva leans back, rests her head on the chair, and shuts her eyes.

"But you will leave," she says, and with some difficulty she leans over to pull on her stockings. "I'll stay here alone with my brother who is a drunk and my other brother who is a libertine."

"Wait, I'll help you," says Anusia, and she leans in over Eva's stockings.

"I have debts everywhere, I'm not allowed to leave the city. The Czerniawskis have dropped everything and gone off to Bucharest, or Budapest—who knows. They abandoned me to deal with it on my own. All these people I have around me now are total strangers."

Anusia manages to pull Eva's stocking onto her leg. She knows what Eva's talking about. She has seen posters hung around the streets of Offenbach informing everyone that the Frank siblings promised to pay off all their debts to the local craftsmen and merchants, and that with this goal the younger Baron Frank is heading to Petersburg for money.

"Why to Petersburg?" asks Anusia.

"Zaleski came up with that. They think we're Russians. From the tsar's family. Roch is actually going to Warsaw."

"He'll get nothing there. Everyone is poor there. Do you want some vodka?" asks Anusia. She rises and reaches for the cupboard, where she gets a bottle and two glasses. She returns and pours the golden beverage into the glasses.

"Honey liqueur."

They savor the vodka in silence for a while. Through the window a beam of the red glow of the setting winter sun falls, and for just a moment makes the room feel truly cozy—a feminine boudoir, the soft bed, the striped armchairs standing around the little coffee table, the classic "Roman" desk topped with piles of bills and a letter started but not finished.

The nib of the pen has dried out now. Then the sun disappears, and the room starts to be submerged in thickening darkness. Anusia gets up to light a candle.

"Don't light a candle," says Eva. "Remember you once told me how in your mother's village there was a woman who did not fully die."

"Yes, that's true. My mother said she kept breathing, and she just got smaller. She was our great-grandmother. In the end she was as small as a child, or a doll. They left her in the cave."

Eva shifts uneasily.

"How is that possible?"

"I don't know," says Anusia, and pours herself a second glass. "It's too late to find out now."

### Scraps: *Of the light*

Nahman is old now, hunched over and shriveled up. He sits at the little window from which not much light comes in, a chill flowing through the thick walls. The hand holding the pen is visibly shaking. In the little hourglass standing next to his inkwell the last little grains of sand are flowing down; in just a moment, he will have to turn it over. Nahman writes:

Our ancestors would always say how it is written in Pesachim 3: There are four types of money that never bring happiness: writers' fees, translators' fees, orphans' benefits, and money coming from countries overseas.

I do think that the wisdom of the Talmud was really very great, for these were the primary sources of income in my life, which means it is understandable that I did not attain any great happiness. Though I did attain some fulfillment that might be called a little happiness, just ordinary human happiness, and that occurred from the moment I settled here, in Offenbach, and I understood at once that here I would die. Then I also lost suddenly my greatest weakness, my sin—impatience. For what does it mean to be impatient?

To be impatient means never really living, being always in the future, in what will happen, but which is after all not yet here. Do not impatient people resemble spirits who are never here in this place, and now, in this very moment, but rather sticking their heads out of life like those wanderers who supposedly, when they found themselves at the end of the world, just looked onward, beyond the horizon? What did they see there? What is it that an impatient person hopes to glimpse?

Yesterday I was reminded of a question from the discussion, as usual well into the night, between Yeruhim Jędrzej Dembowski and myself. It is said, he said to me, that there, beyond the world, it is like behind the scenes of some sort of little street theater: a chaos of lines, old sets, costumes, and masks, all sorts of different props—the whole machinery necessary to create the illusion. That is what they say it looks like there. Ahayah aynayim, which in the old language means illusion, prestidigitation.

This is how I saw it now from my room. An illusion. A performance. As long as I could walk up and down the stairs, every morning we held lessons for the young, and with each passing year they appeared to me less distinct, until they completely merged together into a single face that changed and rippled. And in fact I could no longer find a single thing of interest in them. I would talk to them, but they wouldn't understand me, as if the tree from our

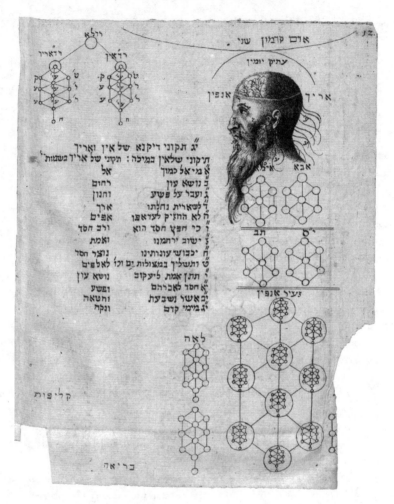

world had put out branches in completely diverging directions. But this does not worry me now.

After Jacob's death, I entered into a period of peace. My main occupation became studying Merkavah, which my conversations with Yeruhim Dembowski also managed to cover, as we lived in the one room, which meant we got closer to each other. To him, to Yeruhim, I also confessed about Hayah Shorr—that she was the one woman I was ever able to love, and that I had loved her from that beautiful moment when I was given her for one night, back when I had come with news of Jacob to Rohatyn. But above all, of course, it was Jacob I had loved.

And now here, in Offenbach, a peaceful, sleepy place, we spent whole days doing nothing other than studying Hebrew words. We would rearrange their letters and tally up their values, so that new meanings would arise from them, and thus possibilities for new worlds. Yeruhim, when he succeeded at it, would giggle, and it would seem to me that that was exactly how God had giggled when he had created us all.

Sometimes we would be flooded with memories. Then I would ask him: "Do you remember how you were Bishop Dembowski's favorite Jew? How he coddled you?" Because it appealed to me to travel back, in memory, because the past remained alive for me, while the present was barely breathing, and the future lay before me like a cold corpse.

We were both always waiting for our children and grandchildren. Yeruhim was to be visited in Offenbach by his sons, Jan and Joachim. He would speak of them so often, and describe them in such detail, that soon the visit itself became almost superfluous. Everyone remembered them from their childhood and youth as boys who were a little haughty, having been educated with the Theatines, and who bore themselves proudly. They grew up, became handsome. "One will come in a silver frock coat," said Old Yeruhim, "and the other in a Polish uniform." But they never came.

I meanwhile took great comfort in my granddaughters, who came to Our Lady, and one of them even married in Offenbach, to a Piotrowski. Our grandchildren cheer us up only until a certain time, when we become more sensitive to the affairs of the world, and we begin to mix up even our grandchildren's names.

No one wanted to listen to us, everyone was busy with themselves. Eva, Our Lady, with the help of her very dedicated secretaries Zaleski and young Czyński, ran the court as if it were a guesthouse. People would roam around it, but a significant portion of them now lived in town. Concerts were played downstairs, which Yeruhim and I never attended, preferring our exercises in gematria and notarikon. Last year the Wołowski brothers came here, and Yeruhim and I worked all summer on a letter to all the Jewish kahalim in the world. They wrote out that letter hundreds, maybe thousands of times in red ink, over and over again from scratch. It was a warning to all about the great catastrophe that awaited them should they not convert to the faith of Edom, for the Church will be the only escape from that holocaust. The letter was signed with their Jewish names by Franciszek Wołowski (Solomon ben Elisha Shorr), Michał Wołowski (Nathan ben Elisha Shorr), and Jędrzej Dembowski (Yeruhim ben Hananiah Lipman of Czarnokozińce). Yet I did not wish to sign this letter. I don't believe in the disasters that might come. I believe in the ones we have been able to escape.

In the Bamidbar it is said that God told Moses to describe the route of his nation's wandering, and it seems to me that God told me to do the same. And although I do not believe that I have succeeded, for I was too quick and impatient, or perhaps I simply was too lazy to comprehend it all, I have nonetheless tried to remind them who they are and whence our path has led. For is it not so that our stories are told to us by others? We can know ourselves to the extent that others tell us who we are and what it is we're struggling to do. What would I remember of my childhood, were it not for my mother? How would I have known myself had I not seen myself reflected in Jacob's eyes? And so I sat with them and reminded them of what we lived through together, although prophesying future catastrophes had set a fog upon their minds. "Go on, Nahman. Go back to your work. We've had enough of you," they said, and chased me away. But I was stubborn. I reminded them of the streets of Smyrna and Salonika, the meandering of the Danube and the hard Polish winters when in the frost we made our way to Jacob on jingling sleighs. Jacob's naked body when we witnessed his union with the Spirit. Hayah's face. The books of Old Shorr. The stern faces of the judges. "Do you even remember those dark times in Częstochowa?" I asked them.

They listened to me attentively, as a person forgets with time his steps, and it seems to him that he has been walking on his own, as he pleases, instead of being led by God.

Is it possible to attain that knowledge, the holy Daat, that Jacob promised us?

I told them: There are two varieties of it being impossible to know. The first variety is when someone does not even try to ask or investigate, considering that in any case he cannot learn anything in full. And the second is when a person does investigate and seek, and he comes to the conclusion that it is impossible to know completely. Here I referred to an example, that my brothers might better understand the weight of this difference. So I said that it is as if two men wanted to meet a king. One thinks: Since I cannot meet the king, why would I go into his palace at all and wander its chambers? But the second man thinks differently. He looks around the royal chambers, enjoys the royal treasury, delights in the luxurious carpets, and even when he learns he will not be able to meet the king, at least he is familiar with his rooms.

They listened to me without really knowing what point I was trying to make.

So I wanted to remind them of the very beginning and to say one thing—that in reality we had always been occupied with light. We had admired the light in all that exists, we followed its lead down the narrow highways of Podolia, through the Dniester's fords, crossing the Danube and the best-guarded borders. The light summoned us when we dove after it into the greatest darkness in Częstochowa, and the light guided us from place to place, from home to home.

And I reminded them that in the old language, do not the words *light* (*or*) and *infinity* (*Ein Sof*) have the same numerical values? *Or* is after all written: *alef-vav-resh*:

אור

which is: 1+6+200=207. While *Ein Sof*—*alef-yod-nun-samekh-vav-pe*:

אין סוף

which is: 1+10+50+60+6+80=207.

But the word *raz*, or *mystery*, is also 207.

Just look, I told them: all the books we have studied have been about light: the Sefer ha-Bahir is the Book of Brightness, Sha'are Ora are the Gates of Light, Meor Einayim the Light of the Eyes, the Orot ha-Kodesh is the Light of Holiness, and finally, the Sefer haZohar is the Book of Splendor. We have done nothing other than waking up at midnight, at the time of the greatest darkness, in our low, dark cubbyholes, in the cold, to study light.

It is the light that has revealed to us that the huge body of matter and its laws is not mechut, or real, and also all its shapes and manifestations, its infinite forms, its laws and habits. The truth of the world is not matter, but the vibration of the sparks of light, that constant flickering that is located in every last thing.

Remember what we were going after, I said unto them. Religions, laws, books, and old customs have all been worn out. He who reads those old books and observes those laws and customs, it is as if he's always facing backward, and yet he must move forward.

That is why he will stumble and ultimately fall. Since everything that has been has come from the side of death. A wise man, meanwhile, will look ahead, through death, as though this were merely a muslin curtain, and he will stand on the side of life.

And here I sign—I, Nahman Samuel ben Levi of Busk, or Piotr Jakubowski.

# VII.

## *The Book of*

# NAMES

| Hominem 1 | Człowieka 1 | Homo, m. 3. czło- |
| attingunt *consangui-* | dotykaią pokrewien- | wiek. |
| (nitate, | (ſtwem, | conſanguinitas, f 1. |
| in *linea aſcendente,* | w Linii powſtaiącey, | pokrewny. |
| (m. 2. | | linea, f. 1. aſ cendens, |
| pater, m.3. *vitricus,*2 | Ociec, Oyczym, 2 | c. 3. linia powſta- |
| & *mater,* f. 3. *nover-* | i Matka, macocha, 3 | iąca. |
| (ea, 3 f. 1. | | |
| *avus,* 4 m. 2. | dźiadek, 4 | |
| & *avia,* 5 f. 1. | i babka, 5 | |
| *proavus,* 6 m. 2. | pradźiadek, 6 | |
| & *proavia,* 7 f. 1. | i prababka, 7 | |
| *abavus,* 8 m. 2. | prapradźiadek, 8 | |
| & *abavia,* 9 f. 1. | i praprababka, 9 | |
| *atavus,* 10 m. 2. | dźiad pradźiada albo | |
| | (czwarty dźiad, 10 | |
| & *atavia,* 11 f. 1. | prapradźiadowa matka,11] | tri- |

# 31.

## Jakubowski and the books of death

Jakubowski died not long after the Lord, surviving him by just a year. Yente's omnipresent gaze sees an official adding his name to the *Sterbe und Begraebnis Bücher* of the city of Offenbach, under the date of October 19, 1792, giving as a reason for his death: "An einer Geschwulst"— in other words, an ulcer. Since no one truly knows how old Jakubowski was at his death, and since he seems to everyone to have been present since some mythical beginning, one of the young people simply says that he was very old. And so the official writes "aged ninety-five years," a Methuselan age, worthy of one of the elders. In reality, Jakubowski was born in 1721, meaning he was seventy-one years old, but emaciated by illness, he looked more ancient than he really was. A month after his death, one of his daughters, Rozalia, also dies in Offenbach, bleeding to death in childbed.

Jędrzej Yeruhim Dembowski collected his papers. In the end, there weren't many—the whole could fit easily enough inside a single little trunk. *The Life of His Holiness Sabbatai Tzvi*, which Jakubowski worked on throughout his life, losing himself in Kabbalistic digressions, turned out to be just a thick stack of papers filled with diagrams, drawings, geometric calculations, and strange maps.

A year after him, Jan Wołowski, called the Cossack, also passed away, and not too much later Joseph Piotrowski, also known as Moshko Kotlarz—Kotlarz meaning "the Tinker" in Polish—who had been sent to Offenbach for a peaceful respite in his old age; though childish and recalcitrant, he was well cared for there.

In September of 1795, Mateusz Matuszewski died, and less than a month later, so did his wife, Wittel, known as Anna. After her husband's death, she became oddly insensate to the world, and she never really recovered. It sometimes happens that spouses cannot live without each other and prefer simply to die, one after the next.

*1. Pan się urodził w Berezance we wsi, blisko miasta Horostynia. Dwa lata był w Korolewkach. Wychował się w Czerniewcach. W 17.. roku wyjechał do Faraon na Wołoszczyznie między Węgrami; ztamtąd pojechał zmatką do Romanii, a ztamtąd do Bukaresztu. W 16.. roku udał się do Nikopolis żenić się — Jo sam mówił —*

*2. W roku 1752, dnia 11go Czerwca było Pańskie Wesele w Nikopolis w Żydowsko-Frenkskiej Religii. Swatowie byli Rabbi Mordocheusz i Rabbi Nachman zyli Jakubowski. Wesele skończyło się 18go tegoż miesiąca. Bawił Pan tylko trzy Niedziele po weselu w Nikopolis; pojechał ztamtąd do Krajowy. W Krajowie był z nim Michał Muszyński; bawili 5 miesięcy. Ztamtąd Pan powrócił do Nikopolis. Bawił 4ry dni i wziąwszy swą Konną pojechał zniąż do Krajowy. Bawił zniąż 5 miesięcy w Krajowie; ztamtąd posłał iż z Michałem Muszyńskim do Widdynia. —*

The two Szymanowski brothers, Elias and Jacob, also died one after the other, both in old age, after which the rest of the Szymanowski family went back to Warsaw.

With the demise of Jakubowski's brother Paweł Pawłowski, formerly Hayim of Busk, who was the last of the elders at Offenbach, the court slowly emptied, and although a number of true believers, predominately from Moravia and Germany, still lived in the city, they were less and less connected with the court. When after a long and exhausting illness, Eva Frank's younger brother Joseph died in 1807, Eva, who had dedicated herself to taking care of him, managed to escape from under her creditors' watch, fleeing to Venice, but she was brought back by news of Roch's illness. Roch Frank passed away on November 15, 1813, alone, in his room; they had to break down his door in order to carry out and subsequently bury the unfortunate man's large, alcohol-swollen body.

## Eva Frank saves Offenbach
## from Napoleonic looting

They had tried to powder up Roch a little when he was already very ill in March of 1813, as Eva Frank was to receive a visit to her home on the corner of Canalstrasse and Judengasse from Tsar Alexander. News of this visit was supposed to be confidential, but it quickly spread around town. The tsar wished to acquaint himself with this famous Jewish-Christian colony, about which he had had ample opportunity to hear during his travels around Europe. As an enlightened and progressive ruler, he had long intended to found, on the territory of his vast nation state, a small country where Jews could live in peace and maintain all of their traditions.

The tsar's visit fueled rumors that had been circulating around Offenbach for years, that Eva Frank's intimate ties with the Russian throne were permitting her to postpone paying off a number of debts. The tsar liked what he saw so much that a few years later he appointed, by imperial decree, a Committee for the Protection of the Israelite Christian colonies that were to be started in Crimea. The primary task of this committee was the conversion of Jews to Christianity.

Eva and Roch had become heroes in Offenbach back in July of 1800, when Roch was still in relatively good health, as wartime upheaval made its way to the town, which until then had been quite peaceful.

The left wing of the French army, which included the Polish Danube Legion fighting under General Kniaziewicz, captured an Austrian cannon, and that very same night, they occupied Offenbach. In a frenzy to loot and plunder, the soldiers descended upon the innocent city, and it was only the decisiveness of Eva and her brother that saved Offenbach.

Evincing magnanimity and perfect hospitality, they threw open the doors of their home to their countrymen, receiving them with extravagance, without regard for their own safety, nor for the enormous expense, and in this way, through their generosity and kind words, they were able to quench the lust of the troops. For this Eva would be remembered fondly by the inhabitants of Offenbach. Its women's virtue, its shop windows, the goods held in its storehouses—all came unscathed through a war that had devastated neighboring towns. And Eva, who was already heavily in debt, managed to obtain further loans.

Sadly, she spent her final years under house arrest with her lady-in-waiting, Paulina Pawłowska, and her secretary, Zaleski, who was responsible for their provisions. After her death, on September 17, 1816, their home was officially sealed off, yet her disappointed creditors found nothing of value inside it, aside from a couple of the baroness's personal belongings, which were more like souvenirs. The only thing they were able to get any real money for, in fact, was the fantastic dollhouse, with its four stories and many rooms, living rooms, and bathrooms, furnished with crystal chandeliers, silver services, the finest wardrobe. Each of the little house's appointments was auctioned off separately, amounting to a sizable sum. It all went to a banker in Frankfurt.

Paulina Pawłowska married a local councillor, and for a good while she entertained his social circle with her strange stories of Miss Eva's various connections, of the court at Vienna, of the wonderful goat with the flexible horns that inspired a certain local artist to place a sculpture depicting it over the entrance to one of the town houses of Offenbach.

Meanwhile, Franciszek Wiktor Zaleski, known as Der Grüne—as he, like his dearly departed wife, always dressed in green—lived happily at Offenbach until the mid-nineteenth century. He had ordered his arteries cut after his death, being terribly afraid of being suspended in a deathlike lethargy.

## The skull

All the Offenbach neophytes were buried in the city cemetery, though some years later this cemetery began to interfere with plans to expand the town, and it was ultimately liquidated in 1866. The bones of those buried there were carefully collected and respectfully reburied elsewhere. Jacob Frank's skull was removed from his grave, and, thoughtfully recorded as "a skull belonging to a Jewish patriarch," it passed into the hands of the historian of the city of Offenbach. Many years later, under unknown circumstances, it made its way to Berlin, where it underwent detailed measurement and research and was labeled a prime

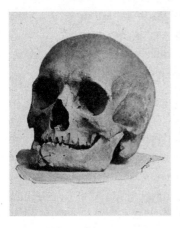 

example of Jewish racial inferiority. After the Second World War, it vanished without a trace—either it was destroyed in the turmoil and chaos of war, crumbling to dust, or else it is still lying around somewhere in the underground storage facility of some museum.

## Of a meeting in Vienna

One of Katarzyna Kossakowska's farthest journeys was the one she made in 1777 to Vienna, where she went to receive the title of Countess and the Order of the Starry Cross from Empress Maria Theresa. She was accompanied by her nephew, Ignacy Potocki, whom she loved as a son.

Apparently, her straightforwardness was a big hit with the empress, who went so far as to call her "my dear good friend."

During the ball given in honor of those so decorated, an overjoyed Ignacy presented Katarzyna Kossakowska with a surprise.

"Just guess, my dear good aunt, whom I have brought to see you," he said excitedly.

A lady in a celadon dress, beautiful and elegant, stood before Kossakowska, face flushed. Smiling widely, she bowed in a gesture of profound respect. Kossakowska was overwhelmed with embarrassment, her eyes smoldering at Ignacy, who had unwittingly put her in an incredibly uncomfortable situation. Then the woman said, politely and in Polish:

"I must remind Your Ladyship of who I am—for I am Eva Frank."

There was not, however, much time for a conversation. Ignacy only whispered into his aunt's ear that the gossip here at the court was that Eva Frank had been mistress to the emperor himself, which brought about such overwhelming astonishment in Kossakowska, and brought back such a crush of memories, that she began to cry in their carriage as they were returning from the ball.

Ignacy mistook the tears for the natural emotions of an older woman who has just received an honor, and was not alarmed by them. He merely mentioned in passing that the local Freemasons, with whom young Potocki maintained close ties, had a great deal of good to say of Eva Frank's father.

Katarzyna died on her estate in Krystynopol at a very advanced age, tenderly nursed through her infirmities by an almost equally decrepit Agnieszka.

## Samuel Ascherbach and his sisters

Samuel Ascherbach, son of Rudolf and Gertruda, fell into bad company at university, but he completed his degree successfully, albeit with some difficulties along the way. After a brief, failed practice at one of Vienna's law firms, where he was perpetually in conflict with his superior, he gave it all up, and, going into some debt, he set off for Hamburg without his parents' knowledge. There, he first found work with a shipowner as a clerk, then began to practice law again, earning a reputation for consistently managing to win his clients enormous insurance payouts. For reasons not entirely clear (but that apparently had to do with some swindling), after a year of a career that he had been developing successfully, he disappeared. His parents finally received a letter from him from America and spent a long time staring at the envelope, with its stamps that had crossed the ocean. The letter was from Pennsylvania, and it was signed by one Samuel Uscher. They learned from the letter that he had married the daughter of a governor, and that he had become a respected lawyer. Evidently his wife was a good influence on him. From newspapers overseas, which unfortunately had no chance of making it into the Viennese coffeehouse Gertruda and Rudolf Ascherbach liked to frequent, it could eventually be gleaned that his American career culminated in his appointment as a Supreme Court judge. He sired seven children. He died in 1842.

His twin sisters settled in Weimar and Breslau, where they married respectable Jewish burghers. Christina's husband, Dr. Löwe, was an active member of Breslau's First Society of Brothers, an organization of progressive Jews. Husband and wife both played a part in the establishment and construction of the famous White Stork Synagogue. Katarina, unfortunately, died in her first childbirth, and no trace of her was left.

## The Załuski Brothers' Library and Canon Benedykt Chmielowski

The collections amassed so industriously and at such extravagant expense by the two brother bishops, the state of which had so worried Father Chmielowski, eventually attained an unprecedented size—around four hundred thousand volumes and twenty thousand manuscripts, not even counting the thousands of etchings and engravings. In 1774, the library was taken over by the Commission of National Education, and in 1795, after the final partition of Poland, the library was sent in its entirety to Petersburg, by order of Catherine the Great. Having taken several months to make its way, in carts and wagons, it remained there until the First World War. In 1921, the collections were partially returned to Poland, but they burned during the Warsaw Uprising.

It is a good thing Father Chmielowski did not live to see that sight—the flames devouring the letters, little flakes of paper flying high into the sky.

If human beings had only known how to truly preserve their knowledge of the world, if they had just engraved it into rock, into crystals, into diamond, and in so doing, passed it on to their descendants, then perhaps the world would now look altogether otherwise. For what are we to do with such a brittle stuff as paper? What can come of writing books?

In the case of Father Chmielowski, wood, brick, stone—every seemingly stronger material—failed him just as paper would have done. Nothing was left of his presbytery, not even the garden, nor the lapidary. Turf grew over the broken inscription, where rhizomes multiplied, and now those carved letters of his hold their court underground. Blind moles pass by them every day, and earthworms on their winding travels, indifferent to the fact that the letter *N* in *No* is written backward.

## The martyrdom of Junius Frey

After the Lord's death, Thomas von Schönfeld was summoned by Eva to Offenbach as the Lord's "nephew." Oddly, now the younger people, especially the true believers from Moravia and Germany, welcomed him as the Lord's rightful successor. Some of the Poles joined them, including the Łabęckis and Jan Wołowski's children. Yet apparently one evening it all culminated in a great quarrel, and Thomas packed up and left the next day.

That same month, he arrived in revolutionary France, under the identity of Junius Brutus Frey, along with his sister Leopoldyna and his brother

Immanuel. The siblings were carrying a number of letters that commended their services, and they managed to find themselves right at the center of events at once.

On August 10, 1792, Junius Frey and his brother Immanuel took part in the storming of the Tuileries Palace, for which they were decorated with orders; to commemorate the proclamation of the Republic a month later, Junius Frey adopted an orphan boy, took a blind widow on jointure, and began paying a pension to a man who was elderly and infirm.

In the summer of 1793, a text was published by Junius Frey by the title of *Philosophie sociale, dediée au peuple français par un Citoyen de la Section de la République française*, or *Social Philosophy Dedicated to the French People by a Citizen of the Section of the French Republic*, in which Frey, that is, Thomas von Schönfeld, that is, Moshe Dobrushka, maintained that every political system, similarly to every religion, has its own theology, and that the theological foundations of democracy needed to be investigated, too. He dedicated an entire chapter to a devastating critique of Mosaic law, Moses having deceived his people insofar as the laws invented by him— serving solely to oppress man and strip him of his freedom—were presented by him as divine. The number of misfortunes and plagues, acts of violence and wars suffered by the Jewish people, along with other peoples of the world, due to this deception was, to Frey's mind, staggering. Jesus was better and more noble, in that he predicated his system upon reason. Unfortunately, his ideas got distorted, similarly to Muhammad's. And yet the truth so effectively hidden by Moses could be reached by following the connections between seemingly disconnected domains—the hard sciences, the arts, alchemy, and Kabbalah—that in fact complement and comment upon each other. The book concluded in an elegy for Kant, who, for fear of an oppressive regime, had to cloak his true thoughts within an obscure metaphysics that served him as "talisman against hemlock and cross."

In Paris, Junius Frey lived an intense and profligate life. He and François Chabot, who married Leopoldyna, were infamous for their debauchery and had many enemies. Thomas, i.e., Junius, had a vast quantity of money and was suspected of spying on behalf of Austria. Thanks to

Chabot, he became a member of the commission that liquidated the assets and liabilities of the French East India Company—an unimaginable fortune. Soon denounced for falsifying documents, Chabot took Thomas down with him.

After a brief trial, on the 16th of Germinal, in the year II, that is, April 5, 1794, Junius Frey, and his younger brother, Immanuel, along with Danton, Chabot, Desmoulins, and others, were sentenced to death.

The pinnacle of the execution was the beheading of Danton; it was his head the mob had been eagerly awaiting. The whistling and applause lessened steadily as each of the other convicts had their turns. When it came time for Junius Frey, that is, Thomas von Schönfeld, that is, Moshe Dobrushka, who was last in line, the mob had already begun to disperse.

Junius saw all the heads before his be severed, saw them fall into the basket set under the guillotine, and as he tried to rein in the wild, animal fear that had come over him, he realized with a thrill that he would finally have the opportunity to learn how long a severed head continues living, a question that had inspired intense debate ever since the guillotine began its breakneck career. He decided with the same excitement that he would try to convey this information across the empty fields of death before he was reborn.

To the French he wrote: "I am a foreigner among you, my native skies are far from here, but my heart was warmed by the word Freedom, the most beautiful word of our century. It is this word that lights my every deed, for I have pressed my lips to Freedom's nipples, and it is the milk of Freedom that sustains me. My fatherland: the world. My profession: performing acts of goodness. My mission: kindling souls of feeling."

For a long time on the streets of Paris, a song was sung whose origins were obscure. Yet we know with certainty that it was just a simplified translation into French of a poem by Junius Frey, which was of course his French translation of the German version of Nahman's prayer. It went like this:

Nowadays my soul is over
All that loses your composure.

Throne and coat of arms, crown, scepter,
My soul's scot-free from every captor.

Nowadays my soul goes dancing,
From its stage it's always glancing.
Good and evil, niceties and beauty—
My soul's the soldier, they're the booty.

It sees no borders and no walls,
Haunts the soapbox with a smile,
Blows through the grain and all the chaff,
Casts pearls in the pigsties with a laugh.

O tell me, O Holy Paternity,
Great citizen of all eternity,
Since my soul's dance is nearly through—
Are there others just like you?

For if you are the only one,
In order to protect my sons,
Give me the right words and the language,
That they and their sons can all manage.


## The children


Yente is the one soul capable of seeing from above, and of following the tracks of all these restless beings.

And so she sees that old Yeruhim Jędrzej Dembowski was right when he talked about how his sons would be dressed when they visited him. It also makes sense to Yente why they ended up never visiting him at all. Jan Dembowski became Ignacy Potocki's secretary, while Joachim was aide-de-camp to Prince Joseph Poniatowski, nephew of the king. Jan later fought as a captain in the Kościuszko Uprising and was reportedly the most energetic of all the conspirators. He was subsequently seen leading the mob as they went to hang the traitors. When the uprising was quelled, he—like many—joined the Legions and went on fighting in Italy. During the battle in 1813, he fought the Austrians and became, for some time, the governor of Ferrara. He married one Miss Visconti and lived out the remainder of his days in Italy.

His brother Joachim fought at his prince's side until the very end and shared his tragic fate.

Antoni, the grandson of Moshe of Podhajce, and the only son of Joseph Bonaventura Łabęcki from his marriage to Barbara Piotrowska, daughter of Moshko Kotlarz, after graduating from his Piarist boarding school took a position at the age of fifteen in the chancellery of the Four-Year Sejm, and even at such a young age published several smaller works in defense of planned reforms. In the time of Congress Poland, he worked as a lawyer and often defended minorities. His defense style was widely known: he would lean far over the railing and lower his voice almost to a whisper, then suddenly, in the places he considered especially important, roar and bang his fist on the railing, so that the judges, who had been lulled by the monotony of his tone, nervously twitched in their seats. Whenever he saw that his arguments were not gaining traction and that he was losing, he would raise both hands and clench his fists, his whole body would visibly struggle, and sounds of desperation would issue from his chest, compelling the judges to come to his aid.

Married to Eva Wołowska, he had four children, among whom his eldest son, Hieronim, particularly distinguished himself as organizer and historian of Congress Poland's mining industry.

The children of Hayim Jacob Kapliński scattered across Europe. Some of them remained in Nikopol and Giurgiu, some went to Lithuania, where, having purchased noble titles, they were able to own their own land.

Yente is also able to espy a strange and significant thing: both branches of the family, having lost every trace of the memory of one another's existence, produced poets. One of their youngest descendants is a Hungarian poet who just recently received a prestigious national award. Another was a bard in one of the Baltic countries.

Salomea Łabęcka, one of the two surviving daughters of the Mayorkowicz family, adopted by the Łabęcki family, married the administrator of the Łabęckis' estate and became the mother of eight children and the grandmother of thirty-four grandchildren. One of her grandsons was a well-known nationalist and a staunchly anti-Semitic politician in interwar Poland.

Her father's brother, Falk Mayorkowicz, or Walentyn Krzyżanowski after baptism, moved his whole family to Warsaw. One of his sons, Wiktor Krzyżanowski, joined a Basilian monastery. His other son, an officer during the November Uprising, protected the Jewish shops being looted in the upheaval. Alongside other officers, he worked hard to scatter that havoc-wreaking mob, as was beautifully described by one Maurycy Mochnacki.

Hryćko, Hayim Rohatyński, remained in Lwów; under the influence of his wife's family, he gave up his heresies and became an ordinary Jew employed in the vodka trade. One of his granddaughters became a much-lauded translator of Yiddish literature. The runaway, meanwhile, was baptized as Jan Okno and became a coal miner in Lwów. After about a year, he married a widow, with whom he had one child.

Of the Wołowski family there is the most to say, for it grew until it attained gargantuan proportions. Nearly all its branches became ennobled, some under the Bawół coat of arms, others under Na Kaskach. A fabulous career was made by Franciszek, son of Isaac Wołowski, the boy whom Father Chmielowski had once called Jeremiah. Franciszek, born in 1786 in Brünn and raised in Offenbach, became one of the best lawyers and scholars of law of his era. Interestingly, when a proposal came before the Sejm to grant Polish citizenship to Jews, Franciszek, as a member of parliament, vehemently argued that it was not yet time to take such a step. First the Polish nation had to win its independence; only then they would be able to turn to such social reforms.

When the November Uprising was put down, the grandson of another of the Wołowski sons, Ludwik, emigrated to France, where he, too, earned renown as a brilliant legal scholar, for which he was awarded the Légion d'Honneur.

## A lovely little girl plays the spinet

There are concerts in Warsaw, in the home of Franciszek and Barbara Wołowski, newly built of brick on the corner of Grzybowski and Waliców Streets. Friends of the family often come and stay in the guest rooms. Franciszek, serene and composed, seats the guests in the living room. This is where the concerts are normally held, though today the spinet is in the other room, since the young performer has terrible stage fright and cannot possibly play before such a sizable crowd. The music that flows from under her fingertips thus reaches the living room through the opened doors. Her listeners sit quietly—in fact they are afraid to so much as take a deep breath, so gorgeous is this music. It is Haydn, brought in from Offenbach, from the shop of Herr André. Little Marynia has practiced a whole month for this performance. Her music teacher, a middle-aged man of a slightly frenetic disposition, is as nervous as his youthful pupil. Before the concert, he informed her that he had nothing further to teach her. In the audience are the Szymanowskis, the Majewskis, the Dembowskis, and the Łabęckis. There is Elsner, who has also been instructing her, and a guest from France, Ferdinando Paër, who is doing his best to convince her parents to polish this extraordinary talent as assiduously as they can. In the corner sits an older woman in black; she is looked after by her granddaughters. This is Marianna Lanckorońska, or perhaps Rudnicka, Aunt Hayah, as the members of this household refer to her amongst themselves. The name Marianna somehow never quite stuck to Hayah. She is very old now, and—why be shy about it—deaf, so she cannot hear the melodious sounds that flow from the fingertips of Marynia Wołowska; pretty soon her head drops to her chest, and she is sleeping.

## Of a certain manuscript

The first book on their voyages across time, places, languages, and borders was completed in 1825. It was written by one Aleksander

Bronikowski, under the pen name of Julian Brinken, as the fee owed to the lawyer Jan Kanty Wołowski, who argued—and won—a case over the fortune of Mrs. Bronikowska, as is stated clearly in the preface.

Jan Kanty was a descendant of Yehuda Shorr, or Jan Wołowski, or the Cossack, as he was called, and he was universally acknowledged to be an excellent lawyer, a learned man, and an immaculately honest person. For many years he was a dean at the university and the head of the public prosecutor's office. He is remembered for not having taken a salary while he was dean of the faculty of law and administration, instead allocating the amount in its entirety to scholarships for six students without means. The Russian government offered him a ministry position, but he turned it down. He always spoke about his Frankist, Jewish background, so that when it turned out that his client Aleksander Bronikowski had no money to pay for his trial, he asked to receive the fee in the form of a novel.

"The kind anyone can read, that will tell things as they were," he said.

To which Brinken replied:

"But how were things? Is there anybody still around who could tell me?"

So Wołowski invited him into his library, and there, over some liqueur, he told him the story of his family, although it was a story with many gaps in it, riddled with holes, since even Wołowski knew relatively little.

"You're a writer, just make up whatever's missing," he said to Brinken when it came time for them to part.

At the close of that evening, the writer returned along the streets of Warsaw, somewhat stupefied by the sweet liqueur but with the novel already unfurling in his mind.

"Is all this true?" the lovely and talented Maria Szymanowska, née Wołowska, the pianist, asked him many years later, when they met in Germany. Julian Brinken, now aged, a writer and an officer, initially Prussian, then Napoleonic, finally of the Kingdom of Poland, shrugged:

"Madam, it is a novel. It is literature."

"What does that mean?" the pianist insisted. "Is it true or not?"

"I would expect you, being an artist yourself, not to think in a manner more suited to simple people. Literature is a particular type of knowledge, it is"—he sought the right words, and suddenly a phrase came ready to his lips—"the perfection of imprecise forms."

He surprised himself in formulating it so well as that. Szymanowska's consternation hushed her now.

On the following day, she invited him to join some other guests in her living room, and she played for them, and when everyone else was leaving, she asked if he would stay behind. Then she turned to convincing him—and it took until nearly morning—not to publish his novel.

"My cousin, Jan Kanty, enjoys too high and steady a self-regard in a country still ruled by chaos and disorder. It is easy to impute . . ." She hesitated and then finished: ". . . anything to anyone, and then they're simply finished. You know, I can't sleep at night, I'm always afraid something terrible will happen. What use is the kind of knowledge contained in your book?"

Brinken departed, stupefied by her grace and by several bottles of excellent wine. Only in the morning did he feel angry and offended. How dare she? Of course he would publish the book in Warsaw. He already had the publisher.

Soon so much was happening that he no longer had the attention his manuscript required. He started organizing aid for the refugees coming in from the eastern realms of an insurgent Poland, and in the winter of 1834, he caught a cold and suddenly died. The manuscript, meanwhile, never published, was laid to rest in the vertiginous stores of the National Library.

## The travels of *New Athens*

That is also where the Rohatyn copy of *New Athens*, from which Jacob Frank learned to read in Polish, ended up. At first it traveled all the way to Offenbach, but it was brought back to Poland, to Warsaw, by

Franciszek Wołowski, after the court was cleared out. There for a long time it remained in his library, where it was read by his granddaughters.

The copy given by the author to Bishop Dembowski, meanwhile, was almost completely burned in one of the great private libraries, on Hoża Street, during the Warsaw Uprising. The fine work of the Lwów bookbinder, who had firmly pressed in the book's pages, meant that for some time they were able to resist the flames. Which is why *New Athens* didn't burn up altogether—at its heart, the pages stayed unscathed, relishing the rustling of the wind for a long time yet to come.

The *New Athens* given to Mrs. Elżbieta Drużbacka stayed in the family and ended up with her granddaughter; later, the famous writer Count Aleksander Fredro, who was also Elżbieta Drużbacka's great-grandson, would dip into it sometimes. After the Second World War, that copy ended up, like most of Lvov's books, in the collections of the Ossolineum in Wrocław, where it can be read to this day.

# Yente

From where Yente is looking, there are no dates, and so there is nothing to mark with any celebration, nor any cause for alarm or concern. The sole traces of time are the blurry streaks that travel past her sometimes, stripped down to just a few characteristics, ungraspable, stripped of speech, but patient. These are the Dead. Yente slowly gets into the habit of counting them.

Even when people completely stop being able to feel their presence, when they can no longer be reached by any sign from them, the dead still traverse this purgatory of memory. Deprived of human attention, they do not have places of their own, nor any sort of foothold. Misers will take care of the living, yet the dead are neglected by even the most generous. Yente feels something like tenderness toward them, when they graze her like a warm breeze—her, stuck here at the limit. She permits them these relations for an instant, attending to these figures who were present during her lifetime, and now, having receded into the background upon their deaths, they are like those veterans in Częstochowa whom the king and the army forgot.

And so, if Yente had ever professed any religion, after all the constructions her ancestors and her contemporaries had built up in her mind, her religion now is her faith in the Dead and their unfulfilled, imperfect, miscarried, or aborted efforts at repairing the world.

At the end of this story, when her body has become pure crystal, Yente discovers a completely new ability. She ceases to be just a witness, an eye that travels through space and time—she can also flow through human bodies, women, men, and children, and time speeds up so everything happens very fast, in one instant.

It becomes clear that these bodies are like leaves in which, for a single season, for a few months, the light resides. Then they fall down dead and dry, and the darkness grinds them into dust. Yente would like to be able to see this shift fully, as they pass from one stage into the next, urged on by their souls that strive impatiently for renewed incarnation, but even for her, this much is inconceivable.

Freyna, Pesel's sister, later Anusia Pawłowska, lived to enjoy a ripe old age in Korolówka, where she was born, and she was buried in that beautiful Jewish cemetery that slopes downhill, to the river. She never had any contact with her sister, and, busy raising twelve children, she forgot about her. Besides, her husband, as a good Jew, kept the fact of his wife's heretic relatives a great secret.

Her great-grandchildren were also living in Korolówka at the outbreak of the Second World War. The memory of the cave in the shape of the *alef* and of their Old Grandmother had been preserved, especially among the women, those older ones who remembered things that would seem frivolous and fantastic as they offered no instruction on baking bread or building houses.

Freyna's great-great-granddaughter, who was called Czarna, or Black, the eldest in her family, absolutely insisted that they not go to Barszczów to register as the Germans had ordered them to. Never trust any authority, she would say. Which is why when all the Jews of Korolówka were setting off for the city with their belongings bundled, they quietly, in the night, pulling little carts carrying their things, went into the forest.

On October 12, 1942, five families from Korolówka, thirty-eight people, the youngest of whom was a child just five months old, and the eldest of whom was seventy-nine, left their village homes and entered the cave just before dawn from the forest entrance, where the powerful underground letter *alef* has its uppermost, rightmost stroke.

Some of the rooms in the cave are filled with crystals that come out of the walls and down from the ceilings. People say that these are frozen drops of light that got stuck down in the ground and stopped shining. But as soon as they are touched with a candle flame, they will light up again, showing their eternal, silent interior.

In one of these rooms lies Yente. The damp, alighting on her skin for so many years, is now fully adhered to her bones, crystallizing, sparkling, shining bright. Its glow grows deep into her body and renders her almost translucent. Yente transforms slowly into crystal and, in a few million more years, she will be a diamond. Meanwhile, her eyes are still moving, and a smile slowly spreads across her face, not directed at anybody now. That long pinkish crystal, grown into the rock, which lights up from time to time from the sparingly used oil lamps, shows a blurred and indistinct interior. The children, who have become used to life in the cave and are already able to venture deep inside it, say that that piece of the rock is alive. If you tried to shine a light on it, all the way inside, you would see a tiny human face in there, but of course no one takes this seriously, especially since nearly a year and a half spent in the dark has permanently debilitated their eyesight.

The adults go out from time to time for provisions, but they never venture as far as any of the nearby villages. The villagers treat them like ghosts, leaving for them, as if by accident, through some oversight, bags of flour or potatoes out behind their barns.

In April 1944, someone throws a bottle into the hole leading into the cave; inside the bottle is a piece of paper that says, in a clumsy hand, "Germans gone."

They come out blinded, shielding their eyes from the light.

They have all survived, and in the postwar chaos, most of them manage to emigrate to Canada, where they tell their story, so improbable that few believe them.

Yente sees the forest's undergrowth, small clumps of blackberries, the bright leaves of young oaks at the entrance to the cave, and then the whole hill and the village, and the roads down which dart vehicles. She sees the flash of the Dniester, like the flash of the blade of a knife, and the other rivers that carry water out to seas, and the seas, laden with great ships transporting goods. And she sees the lighthouses communicating by means of little scraps of light. For a moment, she pauses on her journey upward, thinking she can hear somebody calling her. Who might still know Yente's name? Down below, she makes out a sitting figure, her face lit up by some white glow, hair peculiar, attire eccentric—yet nothing has surprised Yente in an awfully long time; she has lost that ability. She just watches letters appear out of nowhere from under this figure's fingers on a bright flat rectangle of light, lining up obediently in little rows. The only thing Yente can think of that is like this is tracks in the snow— since the dead lose their ability to read, one of death's most unfortunate consequences . . . And so poor Yente is unable to recognize her own name in this YENTE YENTE YENTE displayed now on the screen. She therefore loses interest and vanishes somewhere up above.

Here, however, where we are, there is a buzzing sound, the grim sound of matter, and the world falls into obscurity, and the earth goes out. There can be no doubt that the world is made of darkness. Now we find ourselves on the side of darkness.

Nonetheless it is written that any person who toils over matters of Messiahs, even failed ones, even just to tell their stories, will be treated just the same as he who studies the eternal mysteries of light.

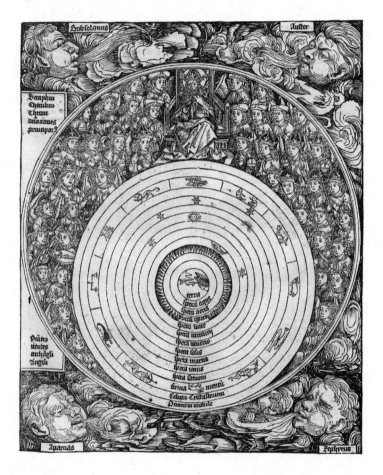

*A Note on Sources*

It's a good thing the novel has traditionally been understood as a fiction, since that means its author is generally not expected to furnish a complete bibliography. In this case in particular, that would take up entirely too much space.

Anyone interested in the story told in this book should first of all obtain Aleksander Kraushar's *Frank i frankiści polscy 1726–1816: Monografia historyczna*, published in 1895, as well as that record of the "chats" given by Frank himself, *Księga Słów Pańskich: Ezoteryczne wykłady Jakuba Franka*, edited by Jan Doktór (1997). There is an English translation of the latter, done by Harris Lenowitz, called *The Collection of the Words of the Lord*, by Jacob Frank. The amplest historical and political context that might permit a greater understanding of the phenomenon of Frankism in Poland is given by Paweł Maciejko's *The Mixed Multitude: Jacob Frank and the Frankist Movement, 1755–1816*, published by the University of Pennsylvania Press in 2011, as I was writing my novel. An article on the doctrine of Sabbatai Tzvi by the same author showed me what, at its very essence, Frankism might be. The three paradoxes seen through the lens of Sabbatian theology, taken up by Nahman ("Of what draws persons together, and certain clarifications regarding the transmigration of souls"), were borrowed (with the author's permission) from Maciejko's earlier work, "Coitus interruptus in *And I Came this Day unto the Fountain*," in R. Jonathan Eibeschütz's *And I Came this Day unto the Fountain*, a volume also edited and introduced by Pawel Maciejko, published in Los Angeles in 2014.

The foundational reading that then organized all other study of subjects connected to Judaism was of course Gershom Scholem's *Major Trends in Jewish Mysticism*.

I found a detailed account of the blood libel in Markowa Wolica in 1752, along with a number of relevant documents, in Kazimierz Rudnicki's *Biskup Kajetan Sołtyk 1715–1788*, published in Kraków in 1906 as volume 5 of *Monografia w zakresie dziejów nowożytnych*, edited by Szymon Askenazy. I based the testimonies during the Lwów dispute on Gaudenty Pikulski's *Sąd żydowski we lwowskim kościele Archikatedralnym 1759 r.* (fourth edition, published in 1906).

My psychological portrait of Katarzyna Kossakowska was inspired by her brief appearance in Józef Ignacy Kraszewski's *Macocha*, as well as by the extensive correspondence conducted by the real Kossakowska herself. Moliwda's character owes much to Andrzej Żuławski and his book *Moliwda* (1994). And I drew much of my information on Thomas von Schönfeld from Krzysztof Rutkowski's book *Kościół Świętego Rocha: Przepowieści* (2001).

It brought me great joy to work on the character of Father Benedykt Chmielowski, vicar forane of Rohatyn, later canon of Kiev, first Polish encyclopedist. To anyone interested I do highly recommend reading *Nowe Ateny albo Akademia Wszelkiej sciencyi pełna*, wonderfully selected and edited by Maria and Jan Józef Lipscy in 1966. Truth be told, this fantastic work is overdue for a new edition. Father Chmielowski's encounter with the terrific—though no longer well-known to a general public—Baroque poet Elżbieta Drużbacka is not recorded anywhere, but according to all the laws of probability it could certainly have happened, for after all they moved in similar orbits, in terms of both time and place.

The death, wedding, and birth certificates I found in the municipal archive of Offenbach am Main enabled me to reconstruct the composition of the company that remained with Jacob Frank in exile until the very end, and also to more or less trace the fates of the Frankist families that returned to Poland.

That would be a worthy subject for another book.

The illustrations in this book come, in large part, from the collections of the Ossolineum Library in Warsaw.

The alternative numbering of the pages in this book is a nod to books written in Hebrew, as well as a reminder that every order, every system, is simply a matter of what you've gotten used to.

I feel certain that Father Chmielowski would derive great satisfaction from knowing that his idea of information available to all and at any moment would be realized some two hundred fifty years after his death. It is in fact thanks to the pansophy of the internet that I happened upon the trail of the "miracle" in the Korolówka Cave—the astonishing story of dozens of people's survival of the Holocaust. This trail also led me to conclude, firstly, that so many things remain quietly connected, and secondly, that history is the unceasing attempt to understand what it is that has happened alongside all that might have happened as well or instead.

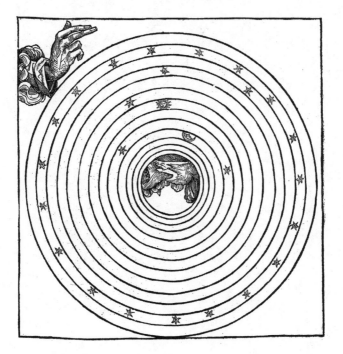

## Author's Acknowledgments

This book could never have appeared in this form had it not been for the assistance of many. I wish to thank all those I have been tormenting for years now with stories of the Frankists and who, in pressing me for further explanation, rightly put forward questions that in turn helped me understand the complex and multilayered sense and significance of this story.

I thank my publisher for being patient; Waldemar Popek for his careful, thoughtful reading; Wojciech Adamski for locating a number of anachronisms and checking a whole host of small details, without which a novel always feels a little undercooked. Thank you to Henryka Salawa for the Benedictine editorial work, and to Alek Radomski for providing the original Polish edition of *The Books of Jacob* with its unusual graphic design.

I am especially grateful to Paweł Maciejko for his valuable comments concerning Jewish history and in particular the doctrine of Jacob Frank.

Heartfelt thanks to Karol Maliszewski for being able to carry Nahman's Prayer through time and space with poetry. To Kinga Dunin, for being my first reader, as usual.

I wish to thank Andrzej Link-Lenczowski for the in-depth historical consultation.

The illustrations in this book are thanks to access to the collections at Wrocław's Ossolineum granted me by the library's director, Adolf Juzwenko, while Dorota Sidorowicz-Mulak was the one who helped me get my bearings in that vast trove of materials. I am deeply grateful to them both.

After reading my first draft, my mom, who is a very inquisitive person, turned my attention to several little but essential facts relating to social customs, for which I am very grateful to her.

Above all, meanwhile, I thank Grzegorz for his talents as a detective on the trail; his ability to poke around in the least obvious sources yielded an incredible wealth of threads and ideas. And his patient and fortifying presence always gave me strength and permitted me to hope that I might one day see this book to its conclusion.

## *Translator's Acknowledgments*

I would not have been able to translate this book without the support of the Dorothy and Lewis B. Cullman Center for Scholars and Writers at the New York Public Library, MacDowell, the Instytut Książki, and the PEN/Heim Translation Fund. Nahman's first prayer and Blumele's version set to music were written in English by my husband, Boris Dralyuk, who has always been the greatest champion of my work and my most brilliant interlocutor. I am infinitely grateful to Jeremy Schonfield for his excellent suggestions and to my wonderful agent, Katie Grimm, for her help and encouragement, and I am likewise thankful to the community of Olga's translators into many world languages for regularly exchanging questions and ideas, and in particular to German translators Lisa Palmes and Lothar Quinkenstein, who generously shared their work with me. *The Books of Jacob* is in polyglot conversation with myriad other texts; following its author's lead, I have taken the story of the visitor to the tavern in Busk (in "The Book of Sand," near the start of Nahman's "Scraps") from *The Autobiography of Solomon Maimon*, using Paul Reitter's beautiful translation.

Olga Tokarczuk—Nobel Prize laureate, winner of the International Booker Prize—doesn't merely cross borders, she takes wing over them. In a dozen path-breaking books of virtuosic range, she melds fiction and philosophy, reimagines history, upends genre in ways that surprise, delight, and provoke. Her work opens new chambers in our interior lives.

Whether constellating our love affair with motion (*Flights*) or tracing the rise and fall of an eighteenth-century cult leader (*The Books of Jacob*), with each foray she crafts new kinds of vessels for storytelling. Readers of more than fifty languages discover through her writing ways to keep wonder and humanity alive in a world growing ever more complex and entwined. Lyrical, playful, and "marvelously weird" (*The New York Times Book Review*), Tokarczuk is a star whose genius burns bright and will beckon to readers for generations to come.

© Łukasz Giza

# FLIGHTS
## Translated by Jennifer Croft

**Winner of the International Booker Prize and a
finalist for the National Book Award in Translation,
a master storyteller's reflections on the body in motion**

The incomparably
original Polish Nobelist
Olga Tokarczuk interweaves
reflections on travel with an
exploration of the human
body as it negotiates space
and time. Chopin's heart is
smuggled back to Warsaw by
his adoring sister. A young
man descends into madness
when his wife and child
mysteriously vanish during a
vacation and just as suddenly
reappear. Such brilliantly
imagined characters and
stories are laced with
haunting, spirited, and
revelatory meditations on
life, death, and migration.

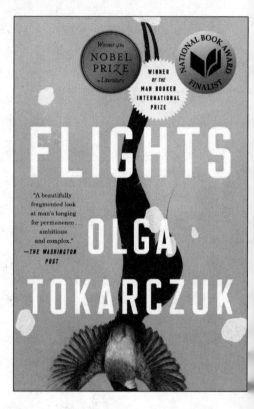

"A beautifully fragmented look at man's longing for permanence . . .
Ambitious and complex." **—The Washington Post**

"A revelation . . . In this risky, restlessly mercurial book, Tokarczuk
has found a way of turning . . . philosophy into writing that doesn't
just take flight but soars." **—NPR's Fresh Air**

# DRIVE YOUR PLOW OVER THE BONES OF THE DEAD
## Translated by Antonia Lloyd-Jones

**Shortlisted for the International Booker Prize, a "funny, vivid, dangerous, and disturbing novel that raises fierce questions about human behavior" (Annie Proulx)**

In a remote Polish village, Janina devotes her days to studying astrology, translating poetry, and caring for the summer homes of wealthy Warsaw residents. Her reputation as a crank is amplified by her preference for the company of animals over humans. Then a neighbor turns up dead. Soon other bodies are discovered. As suspicions mount, Janina is certain that she knows whodunit. *Drive Your Plow Over the Bones of the Dead* is a provocative, deeply satisfying exploration of the murky borderland between sanity and madness, justice and tradition, autonomy and fate.

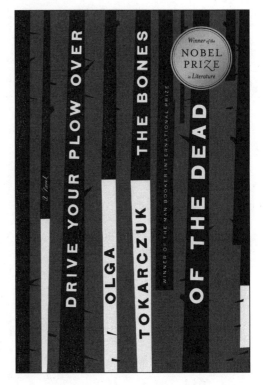

"A brilliant literary murder mystery." 　　　　　　　*—Chicago Tribune*

"Marvelously weird and fable-like . . . a philosophical fairy tale about life and death that's been trying to spill its secrets. Secrets that, if you've kept your ear to the ground, you knew in your bones all along."
*—The New York Times Book Review*